The
PSI Corps
Trilogy

The PSI Corps Trilogy

*Based on the
original outline by
J. Michael Straczynski*

DARK GENESIS
DEADLY RELATIONS
FINAL RECKONING

J. GREGORY KEYES

SFBC
SCIENCE
FICTION

CONTENTS

CONTENTS

Dark Genesis

The Birth of the PSI Corps

For Tim, Steve, Jim, and Hud

ACKNOWLEDGMENTS

Many thanks to Fiona Avery and her tireless efforts to answer my constant questions.

PROLOGUE

Alice Kimbrell pushed back from the screen angrily.

"Ridiculous!" she snapped, to no one.

It was a word she would repeat, often. A word that would haunt her when the killing began.

She went to the kitchen to make coffee, which she always needed midafternoon. She stopped, reaching for a cup. There sat Albert's old mug, asking to be filled.

Ridiculous. She should throw it away.

The coffee steaming, she stepped out to her balcony and tried to take a moment to contemplate the sea. But the paper's title glowed in her mind, and all the coffee did was brighten the glare.

Investigations into Biochemical Sensory Transmission by Duffy and Philen, June 2115.

Ridiculous.

She stared hard at the lavender sea, as if concentrating could make her appreciate it. "I love this view. It reminds me of Denmark," Albert had once remarked. It had seemed a soulful thing to say at the time. As if Albert had more than the parody of a soul.

She wished she had an office. People who had offices could escape their homes.

She stalked back to her workstation and looked at the abstract again. It hadn't changed.

A sample population of 1,000 volunteers was screened for metasensory abilities using standard set Zener cards, Black Box Randomizer, and blind curtain tests. Two individuals demonstrated consistently accurate results for each test, and ten demonstrated statistically improbable accuracy. HCI and Dao imaging demonstrated collateral brain cortex activity between senders and receivers in accurate tests. The sample population was increased to 5,000 individuals. Two members of the larger sample conclusively demonstrated

metasensory abilities, with thirteen sets of statistically improbable results. Cortex imaging was consistent with the findings of the preliminary study.

Okay, she thought. *Prove it to me.*

Unfortunately, they did. She read it again, summoning even more skepticism.

Of course, data could be faked, but as per usual, they had included a complete data set with verifying codes. Most damning of all, there was the cover letter signed by Drs. Jacqueline Wilson and John Yazhi. The authors might be graduate students, but two of the most prestigious neuropsychologists at the Harvard School of Medicine backed them up. That was probably what got the paper past her screeners to start with.

Worse and worse. As editor of the *New England Journal of Medicine,* she could think of no good reason not to publish. Which was a shame, because then her career would join her personal life on the slag heap.

She reached for the phone. By God, she would *find* a reason not to publish it.

"It's not a joke," Dr. Yazhi said, swaying his long physique up from behind his desk to shake her hand.

"Dr. Yazhi, you must understand—"

"Look, it started out that way. Ms. Duffy and Mr. Philen were writing a paper for the *New Drinkland Journal of Medicine.* You know it? It's a sort of hazing ritual. The first year students are required to write at least two hundred pages of garbage on some nontopic, but they have to research it, give it all the good form of a journal article. It's a student competition to see who can treat the most absurd subject in the most clinical fashion, using the most jargon and academic doublespeak. It's a bonus if they can make it recognizably similar to something that has actually been published.

"Philen and Duffy chose to research telepathy. They set up a study and—and, well, they began to get results. When they were sure they brought it to me, and I came on board as their adviser."

"Yes, but Zener card readings—"

"Can be faked, yes. But we went on from there. In the end—you read the paper, I assume? In the end we did simultaneous pattern scans on the brains of the subjects, first with an HCI and then a Dao imager. The results were what you saw in your data sets. Spontaneous—and I might add, impossible—cortex pattern similarities at the moment of 'transmission.' "

He paused, stroking his lean, dark face. "I've read your work, Dr.

Kimbrell, and I think you've been a credit to the journal since you began editing it. I understand your reluctance, but I think the data behind this paper is quite solid. I'm certainly willing to say so."

"It's just that—" She paused, marshaling arguments. "All through the twentieth century they did these same tests, and nothing. Why?"

He shrugged. "Maybe when they got results they didn't like, they ignored them—that was pretty common in the nineteens. They didn't have HCIs then, just EEGs and the like, nothing that could holistically image microneural activity. That's what convinced us, of course." He pursed his lips. "Just ask yourself—if this paper were on any accepted subject, or even a marginal one, would you publish it? Is it well written? Is it evidenced? Is the data set verifiable? Are the experiments replicable?"

She met his eyes, wanting to challenge him further, finding she could not. She sighed. "Thank you, Doctor."

"My pleasure."

She put it off. Albert called and she hung up on him. Her father called, and she pretended not to be home. Her stockbroker called, wanting to buy a thousand shares of something-or-other and she told him to buy Antarctica if he wanted, but to leave her alone.

She went to a salon, had her hair cut into a short, blond bob. She picked away at her own research, wrote letters to some colleagues, went running and swimming, lost three pounds. In the end she returned, saw the submissions piling up, and sighed.

She remembered how proud she had been—the youngest editor in chief of the oldest continuously published medical journal in history. Quite the coup. As she sat down at her workstation, she wondered if she would be able to get a teaching position somewhere, perhaps at a community college. In the Yukon maybe. At least it would be easier to dodge Albert there.

Senator Lee Crawford sighed as he strode into the sunlight and saw the reporter. Was that all he rated these days, a single reporter from a minor newspaper? It seemed so.

He put on his most genial smile.

"Senator Crawford," the young woman began—in a rush, as if she feared he might brush past her—"I'm with the *Union Discoverer*—"

He shoved his hands into his pockets and cocked his head slightly. "Couldn't find anyone more important to talk to, Ms. Hoijer?" He said it without accusation—just a gentle self-deprecation. He let a little drawl through. They liked that.

It got her. The *Discoverer* was far from the most prestigious reporting syndicate around, and she must have had her own share of snubs. And he had remembered her name from, what, three months ago. Her eyes softened a bit. She was a pretty thing, dark skin, green eyes, slim, perhaps thirty.

"I" She paused and cleared her throat, and he revised her age downward to twenty-five. "Would you care to comment on the defeat of your latest bill?"

"Only that it's a shame, a shortsighted shame," he said, without heat. "In time, people'll come to see that." He relaxed his shoulders. "Tell me, what do *you* think?"

"Excuse me?"

"You asked what I think. What do you think?"

"Senator, that's my job, asking you what you think."

He shrugged. "And what's mine? I represent people, Ms. Hoijer. Aren't you a person?"

"But I am not American, Senator—I don't vote for you."

"Details. C'mon, what do you think? Phrase it as a question, if you must, but tell me."

"If you insist," she said, "I have to say I agree with your opponents. Our taxes have funded the DeepProbe project for twenty years, with no results. I don't see why we should fund yet another—and more expensive—search for extraterrestrial life."

"Intelligence," he corrected gently. "Life we have found, and yet at one point it was far from clear that we would. And you answer your own question. The DeepProbe project uses technology twenty years out of date. It's time to upgrade."

"But why? The search for extraterrestrial intelligence began more than a hundred years ago. Don't you think that if there were anything to find, we would have found it by now?"

He chuckled his patented chuckle and nodded as if in agreement. "Do you know why the people at home voted for me? Do you know why I ran?"

"You ran on a Globalist platform. And you were the hero of Grissom colony—"

"There's that—that's how I got on the ticket, not why I ran, not why people voted for me. For almost two hundred years, change in science and technology has been the most important fact of life on this planet, and for two hundred years politicians have lagged so far behind the leading edge—well, it would be funny if it were a joke. People who don't understand the first law of motion make decisions regardin' the funding and disposition of space platforms. Doesn't that strike you as even faintly

ridiculous? I ran because I think at least one politician should have some conception of more than how to schmooze.

"And to answer your question directly, no. With the technology available in the last hundred years, we couldn't even find one of our own space probes without knowing exactly where it is, much less intelligent life among a trillion trillion worlds."

"Be that as it may, Senator, the polls would seem to indicate an erosion of your popular support. How do you respond to that?"

He shrugged. "My opponents are very good at politics—I've never denied that. But politics—as you must know, being a reporter—is a world unto itself, and unfortunately has little to do with the world we live on. It's too bad my opponents are more concerned with that than the welfare of our race. I trust the voters, Ms. Hoijer. They have common sense. Never tell me what the polls say."

"You accuse your opponents of playing politics, and yet there are some who charge that your entire posture on extraterrestrial intelligence was a calculated response to the panic of '10. That you latched onto a popular sentiment, which has now begun to flag."

He chuckled again. "Well, I can hardly blame you for saying that— after all, who can trust a politician to be sincere about anything? But the people who voted for me know better. I'm dead serious. Look at history. Robert Goddard invented the liquid-fueled rocket in North America, and yet there was no funding for rocket research there until after Nazi V1s and V2s had shown their usefulness by blowin' things up. Underfunding the near-Earth asteroid search nearly got us all dinosaured in 2011—it was a miracle that got us through that, pure and simple. The political machine registers nothin' till it's already too late.

"I'm still determined to change that, uphill battle though it may be. And, frankly, I hope to do it before it *is* too late. There's more than enough hints that there's somebody out there. They might be angels; they might be devils. Frankly, I think they'll be most dangerous if they're just folks like us. But this I know—we'll be a lot better off all around if we notice them before they notice us."

"Then you will continue to bring your bill before the Senate?"

"Damn right. And you can quote me on that."

"Even without the support of your party?"

"Ms. Hoijer, I'm only doing what I promised. That might be a shock to my colleagues—it might even be a shock to my party—but it's no shock to the voters. You'll see that come the election. Now it's been a real pleasure, and I thank you for your time, but I have an engagement across town."

* * *

He found Tom Nguyen waiting for him in his office.

"The party has withdrawn their support," Tom said, youthful face twitching with agitation.

Reaching for the bottle of oude jenever, Lee froze momentarily. Then he finished his motion. "Why, thanks, Tom, I'm doin' fine. Nice day to you, too. How about a drink?"

"No, no, Lord, that would *kill* my stomach right now."

"You have t' build up an immunity," Lee said, pouring the shot and resting a bit of the potent stuff on his tongue. "They really did it, huh?"

"Lee, you had to know it was coming. That bill was dead when you wrote it. Face it. The science thing got you elected, but people have forgotten it now. In their eyes, Senator Tokash made you look foolish. U.S. voters don't like the U.S. to look foolish, and the party doesn't like its golden boy to look foolish."

"Pinheads. People are such idiots."

"That may well be, but they pay your salary. Lee, this is serious."

"No shit." He downed the shot. "Anything else?"

"I think we should discuss strategy. You were offered the chair of the Committee on Technology and Privacy—"

"It's just a bone they're throwin' me, Tom. A tired old bone. Pity won't get me any votes. I can just see Hirosho's campaign ads now. Me, on the do-nothing committee, with my head down and great big *Z*s comin' up. What happened? Last year we were on top of the world!"

"Well, that was last year. Forty is too young to be living in the past, Lee."

"Thirty-nine, damn your eyes." He leaned back in his chair and blew out, found a grin. "Just hang in there, Tom, and let me know if you have any ideas. We aren't licked yet. Now, go on, I want to look at my news."

"Ignoring it won't make it go away."

"I'm not ignoring it. Take the day off. Go see your kids."

Tom hesitated. "You're okay?" he asked.

"Watch it, Tom, you're lettin' that all-business face slip off again. You might learn something from me yet, and that'd be a shame. Sure you won't have that drink?"

Tom managed a little smile. "Maybe just one," he said.

He talked Tom into two, before it was over, and told a few jokes that even got him to laugh.

When the door was closed, he went to the window and looked out at the city of Geneva. The smile fell away, and he felt that old familiar hole opening under his feet. "You've bitten off more than you can chew, this time, haven't you, Lee?" He grunted. He could see his reflection against the glass. Close-cropped brown hair, fast going grey, the angular face

that had been likened variously to Andrew Jackson, David Bowie, and Luis Espinosa. "Enough," he said, this time to the universe at large. "I'll beat you, you bastard."

He went to his desk, sat down, and tapped his terminal on.

"Index," he said. "Journal abstracts."

He began a slow scroll though the lists his computer had assembled. Four new planets that might be Earth-like, some interesting speculations about the self-replicating goo beneath Europa's icy crust, a better fusion reactor, a new theory of language origins. All interesting, but useless.

But then, toward the end, he came to the *New England Journal of Medicine.* A headline caught his eye, so he scanned the story. He stopped, read it again. And again. He printed the whole article and read that, too.

"Nguyen, Tom," he said, keying the phone link on the terminal.

After a pause, the screen flickered and his aide appeared, leaning into his car. Behind him, the snowcapped Alps were etched against a very blue sky.

"Lee?"

"Sorry, Tom, I know I gave you the day off, but I need you on something right away. I've highlighted a journal article for you. I want to know who else in the Senate has read it, and I want to know who has it selected to read. Their aides, too."

"Lee, I'm not sure if the disclosure rule covers—"

"Then be discreet. But find out. I want to know in an hour. Just do it there and drop it back here. And Tom—I want on the Technology and Privacy Committee after all. Posthaste."

He returned to his terminal, looking for other things, smiling grimly as they accumulated. Forty-five minutes later, the transfax beeped for his attention, and he stopped to watch a list of names appear. There were only five, and it took just an instant to choose.

Lee found Senator Ledepa Koya standing outside of the Senate chamber, conferring with a handful of aides in rapid-fire Indonesian. When he noticed Lee, he waved them off and approached.

"Senator Crawford," Koya said.

"Ledepa. How are you today?"

"Very well, thanks. I'd like to congratulate you."

"On the failure of my bill?"

"No, no. And I really hope you understand my position in that matter. I, personally, think you are right, but what am I to do?"

"It's the name of the game, Ledepa. We all have to respond to our constituency. Now what can I do for you?"

"I understand you've just been appointed head of the Committee on Technology and Privacy."

"News travels fast."

"I have a particular interest in that committee. I would like to be on it."

"It's goin' to be a yawner, Ledepa. I can't think of any issue that hasn't been addressed to death. It's just nit-picking now."

"Maybe not."

"What do you mean?"

Koya lowered his voice. "Have you seen the *New England Journal of Medicine*?"

"As a matter of fact, I have. Some mumbo jumbo about telepathy."

"I don't think it's mumbo jumbo. Some in my government have had suspicions about this for years. And the study looks very solid to those whose opinions I trust."

"I'd like to see it replicated," Lee replied, allowing curiosity to creep into his voice. "But I'm starting to see your interest in this. You think this will be a privacy and technology issue?"

"Yes, of course. Haven't you gotten any letters?"

"Since yesterday? I haven't had time to check."

"I have received many. The news of this is already spreading."

"Really? Surprising. A journal article." But inwardly he smiled. He had spent all night anonymously bringing the article to the attention of various Indonesians. Companies with much to hide. Reactionary but popular religious leaders. Anyone from whom he thought he could elicit a panicked response.

He pretended to consider. "Okay, Ledepa, you're on the committee. I need some opposition members anyway, and it seems like we're of a mind about this—even if I'm a little slow on the uptake, today. The first order of business is to get copies—"

His pocket tel-phone burred. "Wups. If you'll excuse me, Ledepa?"

He pulled the featherlight tel-phone from his jacket and thumbed the channel open, then said, "Lee Crawford here."

He listened for a moment, nodded. "That sounds great. We'll see you there." He closed the link and turned to Koya. "Well, I'm a popular man today," he said. "That was Ramira Alejandro's assistant. She wants me and someone from my committee to come on her show to discuss the telepath article." He shook his head. "Let's you and I meet for lunch, see if we can come to some agreement about what we'll say."

Koya nodded enthusiastically.

* * *

"It's nonsense," Crispin Dover said, "pure and simple. I find it unbelievable that Ms. Kimbrell published this tripe." Dover looked, Lee thought, like a bulldog, but somehow his clipped, educated British enunciation worked against that to lend him a sort of credibility.

"And yet, our oldest legends speak of these powers," commented Ramira Alejandro, a striking woman in late middle age, with classical Brahman features and a streak of pure silver through her otherwise midnight hair. She radiated a quiet smugness born of knowing she had a guaranteed audience of upward of two billion people.

"Yes, well, our oldest legends also speak of magical beanstalks, talking bears, and the birth of various gods from the armpits of other gods, and I quite agree, it's among such peers that these so-called extrasensory powers belong. In the past two centuries, the scientific method has been repeatedly brought to bear on the myth of telepathy—and shown it to be just that. A myth. I don't think I go too far in suggesting that Ms. Kimbrell should consider editing another journal altogether."

Kimbrell, a professional-looking woman with closely cropped blond hair, pursed her lips angrily.

"What about it, Dr. Ortiz?" Ramira asked. "We've heard what a neurochemist has to say about it, but what does psychology have to offer as an opinion on this matter?"

Ortiz clasped his seamed fingers together. At eighty, his skin rather resembled leather. Lee found himself a bit impressed, despite himself. Ortiz had been a prominent vid commentator since before he was born, a real celebrity.

"Well, Ms. Alejandro, I have read the paper, which I can't tell for certain that our friend Dr. Dover has—"

Dover sputtered, "I read the abstract. That was quite enough. I—"

Ramira silenced him with a small, cool smile. "You'll have another say, Dr. Dover."

"Nevertheless," Ortiz went on, "I must to some extent agree with him. The methodology looks fine, and the results seem conclusive. And yet, how do we explain the lack of similar results in every prior study—some of which, I might add, used the same methodology? And so I must doubt these conclusions as some kind of statistical fluke, until we see them replicated."

"What do you think, Mr. Philen? Will they be replicated?"

Philen, a pale, nervous fellow who couldn't be more than twenty-four, raised his hands defensively. "Look, we didn't expect these results. It started out as a lark, a joke really—"

"And yet you published it."

"Well—yes, because the hypothesis was supported. Look, I was

there, I saw it. It was uncanny. I have the greatest respect for Dr. Ortiz, of course. Who wouldn't? But this was no statistical fluke. There were people in our test groups who were telepaths. No doubt about that at all."

There certainly wasn't any doubt in his young, earnest, and distinctly untrained voice. In contrast, Dover suddenly sounded like what he was— a pompous ass. "Well, then, you would seem to have been duped by a stage magician. Why not have one of these subjects come on this show, under controlled conditions, so that we can see this ability demonstrated?"

"I—of course I can't disclose their names," Philen said.

"Of course," Dover replied sarcastically.

Ramira turned her attention to the editor. "Ms. Kimbrell, you've borne the brunt of much criticism for publishing this article."

Kimbrell frowned thoughtfully. "It's right to be skeptical. It should be hard to prove something new—it should require rigor. I checked the facts and sources very carefully before publishing. Dr. Ortiz may be right—this may represent some impossible statistical fluke. But the research is not fraudulent, and it is not sloppy, as Dr. Dover implies. I am perfectly aware that I have staked my reputation on this, and I feel secure doing so."

Funny, Lee thought. *You don't* look *secure.*

"Well," Ramira continued, turning toward the camera, "we also have with us Senator Lee B. Crawford of the United States, and Senator Ledepa Koya of the Indonesian Consortium. Senator Crawford is well known as the hero of Grissom, and as an advocate for good science in government—that was your campaign slogan, I believe?"

"I'm guilty of that one," Lee drawled. "My campaign manager wanted 'no new taxes,' but I overrode him."

Ramira smiled. "Senator Crawford also comes to us with a degree in astrophysics. Senator Koya has a master's degree in sociosemiotics. Both of these gentleman serve on the Committee on Technology and Privacy. Tell me, gentlemen. Let us assume for a moment that this report is true—that there are among us those who can 'read minds.' What are the social—and political—implications of this? Senator Crawford?"

"I'm still digesting this a bit, Ramira. And although I'm now the head of the committee, Dr. Koya has seniority in the Senate. My daddy always told me to let my elders speak first anyhow." He sent Koya a conspiratorial wink.

Ramira turned toward Koya. "Senator?"

Koya cleared his throat. "Well, obviously, if this study is valid, it reveals a serious situation. Our daily lives, our respective cultures, our

political systems, our legal systems—all are intrinsically dependent on privacy to ensure their very existence. The Earth Alliance mandates rights of privacy at the level of the nation-state, and at the individual level. This has been worked out in great detail, over the years, particularly as technology has made intrusions into privacy potentially deeper and easier.

"I'm afraid if there are, in fact, telepaths, that we're right back to square one. What technology can protect us against them? How can we detect them? How can we stop them? For that matter, how long have they been around? Imagine, each of you, the damage to your private lives if someone were to read your every thought, wish, notion. Now imagine governments and corporations hiring telepaths as spies. Or criminals who can easily stay one step ahead of the authorities. It could undermine the entire fabric of our global society. Yes, I think the Senate has many important questions to ask, if these findings are true."

"Senator Crawford? Comment? Or are you still digesting?"

Lee scratched his chin. "Tryin' to avoid heartburn. I think my colleague is being a bit alarmist. Ledepa, it almost sounds like you're suggestin' witch-hunts." From the corner of his eye, he caught the flash of betrayal on Koya's face.

"First of all," he continued, "their special abilities aside, telepaths are just going to be people. Your schoolteacher, your boss, your mother"—he smiled—"maybe even your senator. Just people like you and me. Not monsters. And they have the same rights and freedoms as everybody else. That said, they don't have special rights either—like the right to poke around in our heads. Still, let's all just take a deep breath. I intend to start hearings on this as early as next week, beginning with a select panel of scientists whom we will recruit to see if these results can be replicated. I would be honored if Dr. Dover and Dr. Ortiz would agree to be a part of that panel, and to act as advisers to this committee, along with Mr. Philen and his research associate, Ms. Duffy, who could not be with us today."

Lee loosened his collar and sprawled his lanky frame on the couch. Tom Nguyen took a seat, and they both watched the vidscreen as it ran through channels, following the search menu.

"How did you know he would fall that way? Koya?" Tom asked.

"Simple. We all know Indonesia has a lot to hide after the transcom affair. Some don't think they should be allowed membership in the Alliance, and it wouldn't take much to get them out. So as a nation, they can't like the idea of telepaths who might ferret out where the bodies are

buried. But it's more basic than that—I checked Koya out. He's a believer."

"Believer?"

"Yup. Ever read much anthropology? As late as the twenty-first century, people were still massacred over witchcraft scares. At one time or the other, belief in malicious sorcery existed among every people on Earth. There've been lots of studies of it—anthropological, psychological—but in the end, it all boils down to one thing. People don't like to think bad things happen to them for no reason. Somebody has to be responsible. God. The devil. A witch. Hell, in my home state, Mississippi, there was still talk about juju and such in some places.

"I checked out Ledepa's hometown—only ten years ago, somebody was arrested for beatin' up a man he thought had hexed him. So I figured the belief is still hangin' around there, and that Ledepa might have grown up with it. It's hard for the intellect to entirely reject something it learned when it was young." He poured a tumbler of scotch. "That, and I played him. Made it seem I felt the same way, and would back him up all the way."

He lifted his drink as the screen settled on a scene.

"It's startin'," Lee said. He turned up the sound.

". . . shot in Jakarta today. The suspect claimed that the victim was a telepath who had cheated him at poker. Several unsubstantiated reports of similar attacks have surfaced in the last hour."

The view switched. He recognized a street in Paris.

". . . only hours after a vidcast on the new report in the *New England Journal of Medicine*. He claimed his lover was a telepath who drove him insane . . ."

And from a town in Mexico:

". . . apparently in response to the alarmist reaction of Senator Ledepa Koya to a recent journal article alleging proof of extrasensory perception. No deaths are reported, though one man was critically wounded . . ."

The screen began splitting, then recording what it couldn't show. The reports increased, ten, thirty—in less than an hour it was over a hundred.

"Oh, my God," Tom whispered.

"Yep. Now people have a whole new thing to blame their problems on, something real, something tangible."

"But you—"

"Me? Listen to the 'casts. It's Koya that's gettin' the credit for this. This is going to get worse, and he's gonna be the guy who started it. Couldn't have happened to a nicer guy, the little two-faced sumovabitch.

One of Tokash's toadies." He smiled. "So Koya gets credit for starting the killings, and the worse stuff that'll come later. Me—people will remember I was cautious, tried to talk sense. They'll see me as the one to pick up the pieces, and the guy who'll protect them from the big bad telepaths, all at the same time."

"But Lee, those people are dying."

"Tom, this was going to break, and they were going to die. That's life. Hell, this is nothin'. These are the lunatics, the ones who were already closest to the edge. Most of these murders and what have you would have happened anyway, but under a variety of justifications. The real mess is coming if the results are replicated and even the skeptics give the whole thing the nod. When the sane people believe it, the implications will really sink in. It's our job to handle the damage, and we've got a jump on it. We can make it better. Now, are you gonna mope, or are we gonna get to work?"

Tom nodded, though his face was still troubled. "Work," he said.

PART 1

Holocaust

1

Earth & Moon Today, **3 October 2115**

A team at Johns Hopkins University Medical School today joined the ranks of those who confirm the findings of the Philen-Duffy study. Dr. Richard Stepp, chair of the Experimental Psychology Department, announced the conclusions today at a press conference. "I was as skeptical as anyone," Dr. Stepp told the audience, "but I really don't see any room for doubt now. Extrasensory perception is no longer a fantasy or a possibility—it is a fact."

The Miami Herald, **English edition, 5 December 2115**

Pope Pius XV disclosed today that a number of as-yet-unnamed priests have voluntarily come forward to be tested as telepaths. "It should be clear to us all," the Pope said at his address in Caracas, "that the sudden appearance of these people among us constitutes a miracle—the scientific community has no explanation for them. God has given us men and women who can see into our souls, and this is a blessing we must embrace. They are God's gifts to us, a reminder of His love, a way to true confession and salvation." His Holiness went on to decry the violence and suspicion surrounding the discovery of telepaths, and called for the world to join in "peacefully embracing our new brethren."

The snow wasn't pretty anymore, it was just *cold.* His pants were frozen and they chafed hard against his legs.

"It hurts, Mama. I want to stop."

She squeezed his hand tighter. *Not yet,* she said, in their secret voice. *We have to finish our game.*

I don't want to finish it. I want to go home.

Things tumbled out of Mama, then, a whole lot of things he didn't

understand. Some were shiny and made him want to cry, others just scared him. Gripping her hand, he felt tall and sick, an itchy wetness in his side, sharp pain when he took a breath.

It started snowing harder, so hard he could barely see the red cliffs all around them.

And he heard something else. Little voices that talked only of hunger and need, bigger ones that were angry and hard. Too far away to hear words, but he didn't like them.

Don't like what? his mother asked.

The men and the dogs. He sulked. *I don't like this game.*

A feeling from Mama, like when he woke up dreaming of falling. Her heart was beating hard, like someone was pounding on her chest.

She stopped and hugged him to her. Her clothes were cold and stiff like his, but her cheek turned warm after only a second. Then she led him over to one of the cliffs.

"Let's climb up here," she said aloud.

The rock was smooth and hard to climb, even though it wasn't very steep. In the steeper parts, Mama pushed him from behind and showed him the handholds.

Someone made those handholds a very long time ago, she told him. *Your great-great-many-greats-grandfather, maybe. Did you know that?*

Why? Were they playing hide-and-seek, too?

He thought she laughed inside, the laugh that didn't really mean she was happy or that she thought something was funny. *Yes,* she said.

Did they win?

No.

The last part was the steepest, but then they were inside the cave. It was pretty big, but not too high. Mama could only stand up in a few places. There was some kind of old house in the cave, made out of lots of flat rocks. Mama took him behind one of the walls and sat down there.

"Come here," she said, in sound words, very softly. Her lips had little spots of red on them.

He came up under her arm.

"Now we have to be very quiet," she said. "And when they come, you have to play your very best. You have to think about this cave being very empty—think about you and me just being rocks. Can you do that? Like when you play this with the other kids?"

Yes.

"Use sound words," she gasped. "And remember, only use your quiet words with me. No one else. Ever. Do you understand?"

"Yes, Mama."

"Good."

They sat that way for a long time, and Mama fell asleep. Outside, he knew the men and dogs were getting closer. He felt them looking hard at the cave, but he did as he was told, and pretended that he and Mama were just rocks, just part of the old house. After a while, they went on.

He noticed Mama's voice was getting smaller. He held both her hands—that usually helped—but it just kept getting smaller. He shouted at her, in the quiet way, but nothing she said made much sense, and so he listened as hard as he could, harder, straining.

Goodbye. I love you, he finally heard.

And then something else, something like rushing water, not just a sound but something sucking all around him. Someone singing, and maybe a drum beating, like at the Shalako dances. And then it was like a hole under his feet, and he was falling, falling through a thunderstorm, lightning and black clouds all around him, down and down, and something seemed to tear out of his chest, and he heard his mother's voice, but not saying anything he understood, and then nothing, nothing.

Except he was still falling, and he saw himself from inside out, like a sock turned inside out, except it was everything he thought and felt and knew, and there was a Shalako there, shining brighter than the Sun, telling him something. And Mama was with the Shalako, and they were all going down, down into the dance hall of the dead, and he was getting cold, and he didn't care anymore.

Then Mama gave him something. The Shalako gave him something. And it hurt.

He screamed and he pushed, like he was swimming, and he swam and beat and pulled at something. Or maybe he found handholds like his mother had shown him, but not rock, and he climbed, and then he was out of the cloud, out of the water, the thunder and lighting getting smaller behind him, and a different kind of darkness came, one that wasn't as scary.

He woke up in his mother's arms. She was holding him tight, and he couldn't make her let go. He finally had to wriggle away, and she kept her arms there, like he was still in them. He wanted to cry, but there was nothing to cry. He had left his tears back in the storm, with his mother.

Slowly Marvin raised his head and spit out a tooth. Liang—that giant son of a bitch—reached down for another piece of him. The most horrible thing was, he could feel nothing from Liang—not anger, not fear, nothing. Liang was stone cold.

Not so the others. Even from across the room he could sense their disgust.

"Liang, man, what'd I do?"

Liang shrugged. "The boss knows, man. He knows what you are. He's been watchin' you at the poker tables."

"So I'm good at poker. What's the beef?"

Liang smiled indulgently, picked him up, and hit him again.

"Yer one a them mind readers, ain'tcha?"

"What the hell are you—" This time he felt ribs crack.

"Ain'tcha?" Liang repeated, pulling a pistol.

"Okay, okay, yeah. Maybe a little bit."

"Good enough to cheat at poker. Good enough to cheat the *boss*."

"Yeah."

"And what happens to them that cheats the boss?"

"Oh, God, Liang, come on—"

Liang pumped a round into the chamber and placed the cold muzzle of the weapon under Marvin's chin.

"C'mon, man—"

He waited.

Liang tousled his hair. "Here's the deal, Marvin. The boss is a good Catholic, so yer gonna live, if that's what you want. But you're his bitch from now on, *deng*? We're gonna fit you out with a 'sponder, and yer gonna work for him."

"Yeah, yeah, I can do that. Help him out. Find feds—anything. Just don't kill me, man."

Liang smiled toothily. "Well, I'll tell the boss we have an agreement, then. But Marvin—"

"Yeah?"

"I *ain't* a good Catholic. You shine the boss, and you'll wish I'd shot you."

They threw her in a pit, and she landed on a bed of corpses. She couldn't even see the ground.

Others fell all around her. Up above, she heard the trilling of birds, the chug of a bulldozer. It began to rain.

"Marta?"

"Boselee!" They found each other and clung together, as if the familiar touch and smell of each other could take them away somewhere else, somewhere safe.

Don't look, don't look, he told her, told her in words that sank through her skin and bones, soaked in like the monsoon rain.

But some were shouting angrily, now, and she did look. Joe, the old man, fixed each soldier with his gaze.

"Your heart will rot in you!" he shouted. "We will live on, but you will rot. Repent of this. These people have done nothing."

A man with reddish hair and a lieutenant's uniform peered into the pit and frowned. He pulled an evil-looking pistol and shot Joe in the head. The old man gurgled and pitched back. "You are all cursed by the devil," the lieutenant replied. "I merely send you home to hell."

He motioned to the soldiers, and the rain changed to hail.

The Night, the Wind, the Sorcerer, our Lord.

Blood's thoughts drifted in the halls of the temple and brought them all running. She had brief fragments of herself from each of them—her hair was black in each, her eyes almond. But her height varied—Smoke looked down on her, Mercy was almost level. Herself in a kaleidoscope, refracted by love, jealousy, lust, fear.

"They're here." She spoke aloud for Mercy's benefit. Mercy wasn't strong enough to follow their conversations unless their hands were touching.

"How far?" Teal asked, fingering his milk-white beard.

"On the bridge, six miles up where we put the alarm. Looks like a couple of truckloads. Heavily armed."

Images of men with guns, of men with comically thick limbs dragging the ground. That last had to be from Monkey.

"Monkey, can you try to be serious?" Blood sighed. "At best, these men are coming to kill us. At worst—"

"They'll have to cut through our loving followers, first," Monkey said, grinning his narrow grin, tossing his long copper hair nonchalantly over his shoulder.

Blood returned a crooked smile.

"How could this happen?" Teal murmured. "Why do they want to kill us?"

Monkey hooted at that, sounding not unlike his chosen namesake. "They've wanted to kill us ever since we got here. You don't plop a bunch of mindless zombies and a Mayan temple out in the middle of bumpkin-land without creatin' a few hard feelings."

"We shouldn't have used our powers so freely," Teal complained. "We shouldn't—"

"Come on. How could we have known science was going to all of a sudden discover us? Hell, we thought we were the only ones. We ran across one another in the space of two years, and then nothing, no matter how we looked. Up until now, the believers thought we got our powers from the ancestors and everybody else assumed we were frauds. Fair enough, and it got us some good times. Now the rules have changed, and our kind are takin' it in the butt. The sooner we learn to live with that, the better."

Smoke, who had been customarily silent, unknotted his massive jaw long enough to say, "We go."

"Yeah, big fellah, we go. Do you think the followers need to be pumped up a little bit more, Blood?"

She nodded. "Sound the drums. It's show time."

Her pain spattered out into the congregation like her blood onto the paper, as the others picked it up and threw it out as far as they could. She pulled the string of thorns through her tongue, grateful that it was the last time. It was fine being the dark goddess, waited on hand and foot, sucking the last dime out of the fools in their congregation, watching their herd of normals grow, but maybe it wasn't worth this. Of course, it was moot now.

She felt a little dizzy as Monkey lit the paper and started his speech. She looked out over the glazed eyes of two hundred people and wanted to laugh at them. Pitiful sheep.

"The time has come, the Katun-ending draws nigh, the cycle begins again," he intoned. "The maggots of the world are coming to eat its meat. As they came to the prairies to slay the buffalo, as they came to the Amazon to strip our mother bare, now they come here. But though the wheel of time turns, it is yet never the same. It can be changed. The buffalo can come back. The redwoods can return. The Amazon can be green as once it was. The ancestors are watching, who fought and died for you. You can see their eyes, in the night sky. Will you shame them, when the enemy comes? Will you do less for them?"

The sound of the crowd was inarticulate, but all of their minds screamed *No*.

"We go inside to gird ourselves. We will emerge at the last, when you have proven yourselves."

You okay, Blood?

Dizzy. I'm okay.

It was Monkey, naturally, who had insisted on the escape tunnel. Once again he was proved right.

Well, you got your wish, Monkey told her, as they moved down the tunnel. *For a while, anyway. The Man Who Would Be King was always your favorite book.*

Uh-huh. I'm just remembering how that ended.

Not this time, Monkey promised.

After ten or fifteen minutes they came up in the deep Alaskan woods, cautiously. In the distance, Blood heard the familiar tearing sound of automatic gunfire, something she hadn't heard since they had

been mercenaries in Kamchatka. She found she almost welcomed it. It was a somehow honest sound.

Mercy was pale, though. She had not been one of them, back then, and probably had never heard gunfire.

She took Mercy's hand. *Don't worry,* she told her. *We'll be okay. But we have to run silent now.*

Mercy nodded, and took hold of Smoke's hand. Blood raised her pistol, checked to make certain it was loaded.

She knew the men were ahead, waiting for them, and when she could see them through the trees, she tasted them. The bloodletting sometimes made her like this, as if she were evaporating, thin but large, a mist hearing and feeling all within her. Spreading over them she felt their angry, stupid, piggy little minds. That one was mean because he had nothing else to be; that one wasn't mean but did what he was told.

She suddenly felt a cold, hard anger. Normals. She had watched the news reports, those smug bastards on the news shows, the yapping pundits. Look what they had done. People were dying all over the world because normals were stupid and afraid.

She would give them something to be afraid of.

The anger gave her strength, so when she stepped into the clearing, they saw more than a slightly built woman. They were standing around a Cortez four-wheel drive, drinking beer. Three of them. As if they were hunting deer.

Their faces changed as they saw her, Kali, Gabriel, the skull and the sickle, the wings of the stooping hawk. They fumbled at their rifles as she calmly shot each of them in the head, delighting in feeling their dirty little minds wink out, vanish down the rabbit hole. Only the last one managed to fire, but he missed and she spattered him against the truck.

Then it all sucked back in, blew the fire out, and she was hollow, without even enough muscle or tendon in her legs to stand. But she felt the ground shake as she collapsed to it.

"Nice shootin'," Monkey allowed.

"What was the explosion?" Mercy asked.

"That would be our temple," Monkey said. "Sixty kilos of plastique."

"Oh, my God," Mercy said. "Our followers . . ." She started to cry, and for once she was strong, her tears washing over them all.

"Not anymore," Monkey said, putting his arm under Blood's and lifting her up. "That game's over. It's time to move on."

2

Lee cheered along with everyone else when the actinic glare of a small, new star appeared above the Lunar horizon.

The probe had actually been launched half an hour before, of course, from the ugly snout of the mass driver he could barely see poking up from the Von Braun Shipyard a kilometer away. While cost-efficient, a mass-driver launch offered no sound and fury, no glare of rockets. By long tradition, it was the first flash of the engines that signaled a successful launch.

Still clapping and grinning, he turned to face the reporters.

"I'd just like to say how gratified I am to be here," he began, as the ruckus calmed to a general murmur. "I feel greatly privileged and enormously excited. There were those who said that this moment would never come—that the curiosity that carried humanity from continent to continent and from world to world had begun to dwindle. Here is proof that they were wrong."

Hands shot up everywhere as he paused. "Well," he said, "I had a longer speech planned, but you folks seem pretty eager." He selected Robert Tanaka, one of the front row of reporters. "Bob? What can I do for you?"

"I'd just like to know how it feels, Senator, to be vindicated. And what do you think the aliens will be like?"

"Well, Bob, in keeping with the dignity being a senator of the Earth Alliance carries—ah, hell, it feels damn good."

He waited for the chuckles to float around. "But let's keep this all in perspective. Our experience with tachyon emissions is mighty limited, and for all we know that signal the DeepProbe detected could have come from a natural source. But still, this is what I—and many others—have wanted for a long time. The DeepProbe network was put in place four years after tachyons were proven to exist. The Heimdal probe will upgrade the system at a bargain price, and I think one day—maybe sooner than you think—she'll answer your second question."

"Thank you, Senator."

"Very welcome. What about you—Ms. Bochs, isn't it?"

"Yes sir, with *Izvestia International.* I was wondering how you respond to Senator Tokash's recent statement that you have mishandled the telepath problem."

He felt the smile freeze on his face. "Well, I was hoping we could chat a bit more about the hope and future of humanity before we retreated back to the Neanderthal cave of politics. But if we have to go there, let's carry at least some of what we've seen today with us—some hope and faith in ourselves as a race. Senator Tokash has his own point of view, to be sure. He and I have differed about many things—the Heimdal project itself, for instance, which many of you may remember he opposed not long ago. As for the telepath 'problem'—we're dealing with the issue as sensitively as we can."

"Some charge that you would make telepaths second-class citizens."

"Yes, on the one hand—and on the other I'm criticized for not rounding them all up and throwing them into death camps. It's easy to make sweeping and extreme statements. It's harder to deal with complex reality. The truth is that we have to regulate telepaths, and at the same time we must respect their rights as citizens. I wish we could have avoided the regrettable incidents of the past few months, and I pray we've seen the end of them."

"Senator, regarding your proposal for a specific committee on telepaths—"

"Yes. The Privacy and Technology Committee was a good stopgap, but telepathy is not technology. This is a special problem that needs special attention. I've proposed a Committee on Metasensory Regulation."

"Can you respond to the rumors that Senator Tokash has been appointed head of that committee instead of you?"

Lee was proud of himself—he kept his smile in place. "I'm sure that the president will appoint whoever she feels will do the best job. If that's Tokash, then I trust her judgment."

Alone, he wasn't so cool, as the shards of an empty decanter settled to the floor of his room with the patience of snowflakes. Breaking things on the Moon lacked a certain satisfaction, but the moment of rupture, when even the smallest fragments ballooned outward like a dust cloud, made up for the lack of calamity. He had to retreat into the small washroom until the air filters took care of the danger the fragments posed to his lungs.

It had been too long since he had been off planet, way too long. His instincts were betraying him like those of a rookie.

When he reemerged and finished cleaning up the room, he felt calmer. He checked his messages and found among them a discouraging note from Tom Nguyen. Tokash would almost certainly get the committee.

That wasn't right—it was his hearings that had begun it all, his voice the world had clung to. Now Tokash wanted to take that away from him. But what could he do?

Nothing, not on the Moon, and he was stuck here for several more days, at least. By the time he returned to Earth, the decision would be made.

He put on his weights and began calisthenics, working his muscles savagely. Whether people knew it or not, they responded better to a man who looked capable than one who did not. Sweat was just beginning to collect in improbably large droplets when the room link warbled.

"Sound only," he told it. "Yes? Senator Lee Crawford here."

There was a small pause, and then, "Senator Crawford? This is Alice Kimbrell."

"Dr. Kimbrell, how nice to hear from you. To what do I owe the pleasure?"

"I'd like to talk to you, as soon as is convenient."

That raised his brows. No three-second delay—Alice Kimbrell was on the Moon.

"What does this regard?"

"Something very important."

"Very well. How about the Ix Chel, in one hour?"

"I would prefer somewhere less public."

"Indulge me, if you don't mind. It's almost lunchtime anyway."

The Ix Chel was, like everything on the Moon, small, but made up for that in elegance. Dug into a hillside, it featured a thick dome that filtered gentle blue Earthlight into the room. The light was picked up by the water rushing from behind one curved wall. Water on the Moon was a precious thing, mined from brittle, powdery seas—the corpses of long-dead comets. The colony had tons of it, but to see more than a cupful at a time was rare. To be all but surrounded by it was a miracle, and he silently toasted the owner's enterprise in having the restaurant butted up against one of the nodes of the colony's cooling/water-processing torus.

The place was packed to capacity when Alice Kimbrell walked in, but she had no trouble spotting him when he stood. He admired her as she

approached. He liked something about her eyes, and the crisp wear of her modest grey suit, almost like a uniform.

"Dr. Kimbrell," he said, extending his hand. She took it, stiffly.

"Senator."

"Please, have a seat." Once she had done so, he flashed her a smile. "Quite a coincidence, both of us bein' on the Moon right now. Did you come to see Heimdal launched? I could've gotten you front-row seats."

"I came to see you."

He raised an eyebrow. "I'm flattered. That's an expensive jaunt for a private citizen."

She acknowledged that with a curt nod. "I heard you were here."

"I'll be in Geneva in six days. Or you could have called me."

"It's too important to wait—or to trust to the comlinks."

"Really."

"Yes. And I still wish we had gone somewhere more—private."

He broadened his smile. "My papa used to say you ought not to bend to tie your shoe in the neighbor's pumpkin patch."

"What does that mean?"

"Well, a pumpkin is a sort of big—"

"I know what a pumpkin is. I mean, what are you implying?"

He idly tapped one of his chopsticks. "How many reporters do you see right now?"

She looked around. "None."

"There are two, at least. If I'm to meet with the woman who turned the world upside down, I want to do it where everyone can see. If you came to my room, they might wonder what secret we were exchangin'. Worse, they might think we were joining the Exsex club. You want to see that in the papers?"

The waitress, a small, white-haired woman with a heavy Austrian accent, chose that moment to arrive.

"Drink with dinner?"

"Scotch. Laphraoig," Alice said.

"Make mine an Evan Williams."

Alice raised an eyebrow.

"They keep a bottle just for me. I am the hero of this colony, you know."

"Yes, but—correct me if I'm wrong—isn't Evan Williams fairly cheap, awful stuff?"

"Cheap, yes, awful, yes. But it's the oldest distillery in North America, which has to count for somethin'. More to the point—it reminds me of where I'm from and who I am. Now Laphraoig, that's good, expensive stuff."

"It reminds me of who *I* am," Alice replied.

The drinks arrived. "Here's to knowin' where you're from," Lee said, and they clinked glasses, and both took a drink.

"Healthy stuff," he observed. "It'll grow moss on Lunar soil." He cocked his head quizzically. "So what *are* we here to talk about, Doctor?"

"Can they hear us? The reporters?"

He shrugged. "It's against the law to eavesdrop. I ought to know, I'm on the Technology and Privacy Committee." He leaned forward. "You must feel very pleased. The last of your critics have pretty much shut up, haven't they? Now that so many studies have replicated the findings you published."

She stared at him. "Vindicated? How can I feel vindicated by the deaths of more than ten thousand people? The massacre Wednesday in Shanxi? The bombing in Utah? The rioting in Chicago—the spacings in Armstrong?"

"All right," he soothed. "I get your point. Dr. Kimbrell, as you must know, every new discovery has its price. These findings would have been published, with or without you."

"I realize that, Senator. But the very simple fact is that it *was* me." Her sipping escalated to a moderate gulp.

"And you were dragged through the heap for it. And now that that's done, you're draggin' *yourself* through the heap."

"No. Just taking responsibility."

"Which brings you to me? Because I can't imagine that you flew all the way to the Moon to take advantage of my credentials as a psychotherapist."

That got a small smile from her. "No. I came to see you because I want to be involved. Involved in the solution."

"And you think I'm the solution? That's very flattering, Doctor. But you didn't think so when I initially invited you to advise me. What's changed?"

"I've followed the hearings closely, as you might expect."

"Get you another scotch?"

She hesitated a moment, staring blankly at her empty tumbler. "Yes."

"I'm sorry, you were saying?"

"I think you have conducted the hearings in as sane a manner as possible, but they've made things worse."

He frowned. "Surely you see that they're necessary, Dr. Kimbrell? It's unfortunate, but telepathy is too powerful a tool—and a weapon— not to be regulated. What do you think the killings are all about? People

are afraid, afraid that the person next to them might be reading their minds."

"They're jealous."

"That, too. Human society is structured around secrets, around limited disclosure. Success has always meant being able to navigate in that world, guess the unspoken, erect a facade. And now we find that there are people who have the inborn ability to simply cut through all that. Would you like to play poker with a telepath? Or trade stocks against someone who could secure inside information simply by being in the room with the right person? It's not so much a matter of specifically regulating telepaths as it is of making certain that existing laws regarding privacy and disclosure aren't violated by them."

"And yet you *are* specifically regulating telepaths—telepaths can't be lawyers, or stockbrokers, or Olympic fencers—"

"Plenty of precedent for that. Specific exclusions were spelled out for the use of the radar tap, too, when it was invented."

"These are people, not listening devices."

"They are both, I'm afraid, which makes regulation all the more necessary. People won't stop killing telepaths—and people they suspect of being telepaths—until they stop feeling threatened by them. That won't happen without regulation."

She nodded. "I know. But you agree, as matters stand, that the hearings are only making things worse—you daily present potential abuses that most people haven't even thought of. The fact that you regulate these abuses is meaningless—"

"—because we still have no way of knowing who the telepaths are. Exactly. And so we worry people more and more without giving them any tangible hope. But what else is there to do?"

She was silent for a moment, taking a significant drink of her new scotch.

He leaned forward and said, very softly, "You know what we can do, don't you?"

She stared hard at the table. "I'm going to lose my job," she said very simply. "I'll never work in academia again if I do this. I need some guarantees."

"You'll have them. You want a job, you've got it. Money."

She suddenly seemed very young, very vulnerable. "I have money, Senator—how do you think I got to the Moon? That's not my concern. I want to know that this will be handled *right.* I don't want to place *another* loaded gun in the wrong hands. I"

"You came to me because you thought I would do the right thing."

She nodded. "A paper just came across my desk. It involves gene sequencing—"

"The telepathy gene?"

"It's not so simple as that. No one has found any gene that seems to control for telepathy. It appears to be like intelligence, an emergent property found in many different genes. But the author of this paper did find a marker."

"Really? What do you mean?"

"Most of us are now postulating that telepathic ability is either a recent mutation or the result of an isolated one that has only recently entered the global gene pool. For instance, one of the Highland New Guinea groups may have had telepaths for a thousand years, but since they were isolated from the rest of the world until relatively recently, the genes didn't get around."

"I follow you. That would explain a lot."

"Yes, it would. Unfortunately, as it turns out, it isn't true. The mitochondrial DNA of fifty demonstrated telepaths was analyzed and correlated with their family histories and other genetic tests of relatedness. As I'm sure you know, mitochondrial DNA is passed only through the mother's line—it isn't affected by the father's at all, but only by very gradual random mutation—the rate of which is known. A brother and sister have virtually identical MDNA, cousins slightly divergent sequences, and so on. Initially, there were some problems with mutation rates, but that was all corrected for by the Vasquer calibration—"

"Yes, I'm aware of all of this. So this analysis did not indicate that these telepaths have a common heritage?"

"On the contrary. More than half of them had MDNA that were near perfect matches. Too perfect. Other genetic data—and records—indicate that the individuals have no ancestors in common in recorded history."

He shrugged. "Good records on most of humanity weren't available until a hundred years ago. I don't see the point."

"The point is, this mutation they all share seems to be less than a hundred years old."

He stared at her for perhaps ten heartbeats as that sank in. "Holy shit," he said. He looked around. "Okay, you were right, I was wrong. Press be damned, let's get out of here."

"I thought you said the reporters aren't listening?"

"I doubt they are. I doubt anyone is—I come to this place because they keep a randomly modulated interference wave going that jams most peepers. But there is an old art called 'lip-reading'—come on. We'll finish this in my room, which I *know* is safe."

* * *

The train arrived with a faint vibration, but no sound—the tube it traveled in was at the Moon's surface pressure. As the car doors kissed their gaskets against the entry ports, Lee gave one of the private cars his personal code that let them in. Once they were inside, he confirmed it for billing via a retinal scan.

"That's better," he said, as the train glided into motion. "Now. Who else knows this?"

"I'm not sure. The authors of the paper, of course, and anyone they've told. I haven't told anyone else. I gather from your reaction you understand the implications."

"Yep. Our telepath friends were engineered. The question now is— by whom? The old United States? That's where most of them have turned up."

"Only because that's where the original testing was done. We've got a good worldwide distribution, now."

"That might be meaningless—they might form some elaborate spy network, or something. Or it could be corporate. Or—frik." He felt the hairs on the back of his neck pricking up. "I need time to think about this."

"Where are we going?"

"Hmm? My room is near Malibu Station. Maybe ten minutes from here."

"I would have thought things would be closer together."

"Never been to the Moon before? Grissom is a mining colony, so buildings tend to sprawl a bit, mostly along this line, toward the water mines at Malibu. Ever since the depressurization of the old dome, nobody wants to be in the basket with all of the rest of the eggs."

"I should think you would be particularly wary," she said.

He shook his head in grim agreement. "I've seen enough people die of explosive decompression in one lifetime, thank you. And been too close, myself."

"Is that why you left the colony?"

"That's part of it," he said.

"Your wife died in the accident."

"No offense, Dr. Kimbrell, but this is a little personal for me."

"None taken. And I'm sorry."

They continued in silence for a moment.

"I'm glad you brought this to me," he said at last, reaching to grip her hand. "You did the right thing."

"I hope so." She did not move his hand.

The train sighed to a stop, and unexpectedly, their door slid open.

"Excuse me," Lee told the man who stood framed in the entry. "This is a private car, and as you can see—"

Then it hit him. The door shouldn't even have opened. He was bolting up from his seat when the man stepped quickly in, a nine-millimeter pistol trained on his heart.

"Sit back down, Senator," the man said, softly.

3

"Don't point that at me, son," Lee said. "In fact, don't point it at any-thing. Do you understand what will happen if you rupture the coach wall?"

The young man nodded solemnly. He had a softly rounded face and a thin mustache, very black hair. A faint accent—Eastern European? "Yes," he said, "the train will stop and emergency membranes will close the tube so they can pump air in. That will make things tricky for me, but I can deal with it. Did you expect I thought the car would explode, or something?"

"What do you want with me, son?"

"It's not really important that you know that, Senator, only that you do what I say. Right now, we're going to change our destination, but you have to do it. If you don't, I will shoot Dr. Kimbrell, and if you still refuse, I will shoot you, too."

"Why can't you do it yourself? You faked my personal code, so—" Then he understood. He leaned up to the retinal scanner. "Fine. Train, personal code Crawford—"

"Stop," the man snapped, stepping quickly to Lee and placing the muzzle of the weapon against his head. "Don't do that."

"I was doing what you said."

"No you weren't, you were going to order an emergency stop. If you do that, I'll shoot you."

"You're going to kill us anyway!" Lee retorted. "That's why you want me to make the destination change, so it'll go on record." He paused a moment, and then said, "Why me, son? I'm only trying to help your kind."

The man smiled indulgently. "Yes, of course you are. Change the destination."

"To where?"

"Not far different. Malibu Station. And now that you know what I am, you know not to try and trick me."

Lee changed the destination, and eyed the man speculatively. "What's it like?" he asked. "Can you hear all of my thoughts? Can you feel my emotions? How will it feel to you when you kill us?"

The young man's face changed, then, quite without his consent.

"Shut up," he demanded.

"You see, you *do* intend to kill us, but you want to make it look like an accident, am I right? So you aren't a terrorist."

"He was in the restaurant," Alice said. "Across the room."

Lee nodded. "He's been following me for months. I thought he was a reporter."

"So you 'overheard' us," Alice said. "You know about the genetic marker."

"Yes."

"Then surely you know this information can't be suppressed for long."

"Oh, but it can, Dr. Kimbrell. The people I work for can do it, and they will. I already know from you who the authors were. They will be dealt with, and the paper will quietly vanish."

"Nonsense. Even if you succeed, someone else will come up with the same results any day now."

"Yes," Lee said, nodding thoughtfully, "And I think I know who. Am I right?"

"Sorry, Senator. Go fish."

"Sure, son. Sure I'm wrong. You can read my mind, so you know how much you've convinced me."

"I know you're bluffing." But his face was pinched in irritation. He sat back against the wall, the gun quite level. "I know you still hope to escape by upsetting me. But here we are."

The doors slid open. "Get out."

Lee looked around hopefully as they exited the car, but the man and woman waiting for them did not look like ice miners—they looked like Vikings. Lee mentally dubbed them Hans and Greta.

Their captor—one of the newcomers called him Piotr—spoke to the two in a language Lee did not know, then motioned them down the corridor toward one of the industrial-sized air locks.

"You're gonna space us?" Lee asked. "Heck, that won't look suspicious at all, will it? 'Senator and noted doctor take stroll on Moon without pressure suits.' That'll make a plausible headline. Grissom is a small place. We'll be missed fast, and you'll be found fast."

"Give me a little credit," Piotr said. "That's why the two of you are going hiking. Regrettable accident, of course, but then you were never known for your caution, Senator. And the record will say you reserved

both of these early this morning." He motioned at the two bright yellow sport-hiking pressure suits Hans was pulling from a nearby locker.

"If you would now be so kind as to put them on . . ."

Lee pursed his lips angrily, and then began unbuttoning his shirt. Blushing, Alice did the same. When she was down to her underwear, Hans gave an appreciative whistle.

She slapped him, hard. He never saw it coming, but only reddened and frowned. Lee tensed, but Piotr's gun never wavered from him.

"Enough," Piotr said, quietly.

Grumbling, Hans began donning his own suit—heavy mining armor, much heavier than their lightweight climbing suits. As Alice Kimbrell put on her helmet, she shot Lee a small triumphant smile. He smiled back, to let her know he understood.

"Put on your helmet, Senator," Piotr said.

"What's the matter?" Lee asked. "Aren't you comin' along? Can't stomach 'hearing' us die? Or will you hear it anyway?" He stepped toward the gun muzzle. "Look at me, boy. Look me in the eye."

Piotr had some difficulty doing that. "You tell me why I have to die, why Dr. Kimbrell has to die. We deserve that. And while you're at it, why don't you tell us what lab you were made in? Who created you? Just to satisfy my curiosity."

The young man's dark eyes flashed with some anger, then. "I was born of man and woman just like you, Senator. I have no more idea why I can do this than you do, nor did I ask for it. And as for the rest—I don't feel compelled to explain anything to you. Good day." And then, to Hans, "We'll wait for you here."

The big man nodded, and once they were suited and pressurized, motioned them into the lock.

They cycled through it into a bowlful of night. The sky was ink sprinkled with powdered sugar, and the sickle Earth stuck up in the south like a blue horn. But of the Sun, there was no sign, nor would there ever be, day or night. Over a billion years, a lot of water had fallen on the Moon, ephemeral oceans of ice, but it only stayed where the Sun never came to lick it up.

It was here, beneath his feet, the stuff of life—water, oxygen, hydrogen for fusion engines. A thin powder in the regolith at the Moon's north pole.

Hans flipped on his lamp and gestured toward the crater rim, maybe a mile away, visible thanks to light generated by Grissom colony.

And they trudged in silence. The links had been disabled, of course. Hans stayed behind them, armed.

And so the Earth pulled across the near horizon like God's own

plow, and after a while they began to climb, higher and higher. They would, Lee supposed, have a fall of some sort.

The rim was nearly sheer toward the top—perhaps having shattered in some geologically recent moonquake. A trail had been worked up a talus slope, though, and they went up that.

Hans' light shone occasionally through Alice's helmet and Lee saw her face. Not frightened, but determined, and he felt a hard knot of admiration form.

They reached the ridge of the crater, which rose and fell in an irregular line around the mines. South, the jagged silhouettes of mountains rose, as if cut from the star field by a deranged god with a razor. North, more shadowed ranges, except that the summit of a single, high peak blazed in the light of the unseen Sun, giving the eerie impression of an island in low orbit. On the Moon, the line between light and dark was never blurred. Where would Hans do it? Would he shatter their faceplates with something first, or simply march them up the ridge until the drop was enough to kill them?

He looked down at a straight drop of perhaps two hundred feet.

Don't think about it.

He didn't. He jumped.

On the way down he worked on the math. On Earth, one fell about thirty-two feet per second squared. Multiply that by mass, and that told you how much force you hit the ground with. He was falling with maybe a sixth that acceleration, so it was as if he had jumped only fifty feet. With the recreational suit he probably massed two hundred pounds. He weighed less here, but the mass was all still there . . .

He hit, flexed his legs, and rolled, just like a parachute drop. It felt just like a parachute drop, too, except with a skeleton almost twenty years older than when he had last done that. His helmet cracked against a rock, sounding a sharp note in his ear—as if someone had thumped a champagne glass.

But it did not break.

A light fell from above, hit the ground, bounced, creating a crazy cone in the dust his fall had kicked up, now this long, now that long, and finally it stopped, spotlighting a boulder as if it were some piece of found art or geological specimen.

Cursing, he went for it.

And got it. Holding it well out to one side, he turned it around, sweeping it over the ground. Light didn't bleed on the Moon, of course, so he could see only just where the spotlight shone. He broadened the beam.

There was Alice, slowly standing up, looking unsure. There was

Hans, crumpled on the ground, one leg obviously sporting several more joints then it had had when last Lee saw him.

Something in Hans' hand made a little red spark, and Alice sprawled comically backward. Then the hand sparked at him.

Hans was maybe ten feet away. Lee turned off the light, waited for the next silent spark of gunfire and leapt. The fall and the broken leg had made Hans as weak as a kitten. Lee got the gun away and shot him.

Dumb bastard. In his mining suit, he probably massed four hundred pounds, and he had jumped after Lee. People always thought they were supermen in low-g.

Alice was thrashing, trying to get a patch over the hole in her suit. Hans had hit her in the arm. As Lee approached, her movements grew more feeble. In the light, he could see her face clearly—she couldn't see his at all. She might not even know it was him.

He considered. Her nose was starting to bleed. She looked desperate, angry, young.

And she knew something she shouldn't know. He hesitated an instant longer, as her eyes rolled back.

Sighing, he bent, finished patching her suit, and then went to Hans to get his air supply. To his surprise, he found that Hans was still alive, big finger jammed into the bullet wound, blood frozen around it like a gasket. He looked up wildly at the light, lips moving, either cursing or begging.

Lee detached the cylinders and opened the suit to space. He turned away rather than watch the rather messy thing that happened to Hans then.

After that, he moved as if in a dream—just like before, when the dome cracked.

He walked until he found one of the big mining tractors, drove it to the pod where he thought Piotr and Greta were, and using the vehicle's plasma torch, blew a hole in the pod's side. A gale came rushing out, and when it had slowed enough, he went in, found Greta struggling toward a pressure suit, and shot her.

Piotr was bleeding from his eyes and mouth, but Lee dragged him into the air lock and pressurized it. The telepath sat, blinking away sanguine tears, shivering uncontrollably.

"Now," Lee said, using the suit PA. "You and I are gonna have a little chat. If you give me an answer I don't like, the air lock door goes open. *Capische?*"

The telepath nodded, and they spoke. After a time, Lee got an answer he didn't like.

* * *

"Thank you for saving my life," Alice Kimbrell said. Her face was bruised from shattered capillaries, but she managed a weak smile.

"Joint effort," he said. "Once you proved to me that the big fellow wasn't a telepath—or at most was a very weak one—I knew we had a shot. And you picked up on what I was doin' fast enough to jump, too."

"I figured if I didn't, he would kill me first and then go after you, maybe in a smarter way."

"Probably right." He pulled the flowers from behind his back and set them next to her bed. Her eyes widened.

"I'm not even going to try to guess what flowers cost you on the Moon."

"Not nearly enough. I wonder if you can tell me something, though."

"Of course."

"I still don't know why you came to me. Why didn't you go to Senator Tokash, or someone else?"

Her eyes drooped closed. "I suppose I ought to confess. When I was a little girl, I had a terrible crush on you. The hero of the Grissom colony. I suppose part of me still needed that hero. You didn't disappoint."

"That's the nicest thing anyone's said to me in a long while." He paused. "Much as I hate to cash in on hero worship, Dr. Kimbrell, I'd like to see you again. Without the thugs and the secrets and so forth."

"I think that can be arranged," she replied, eyes steady on him.

Back in his room, Lee opened the link and entered a number. After a few moments, an angry-looking Senator Vladmir Tokash appeared. His thin hair was mussed, and he seemed to be wearing a dressing robe.

"Crawford?" he said. "What possesses you to call me at this hour?"

Lee smiled. "That's no way to talk to your best friend, Vlad."

The senator's eyes nearly bulged out of his head. "What on earth are you talking about? If it's about the committee—"

"Oh, rest assured, Vlad—it *is* about the committee. It's about how you're gonna withdraw from it. You see, I just had a little talk with a friend of yours—a soul mate, you might say—and he told me quite a lot about you."

"I don't have the faintest idea what you're talking about."

"Do you have your signal scrambled at your end, Vlad? Because I've got some big news."

Tokash nodded.

"Good. You see, I've got a way to detect telepaths. Turns out there's a genetic marker. Now things get interesting, don't they? I'm going to announce it tomorrow. So there're two ways we can play this, and both

involve the Senate being the first ones to get tested. But how the tests get reported—that can make a difference."

Tokash pursed his lips. "I see."

"With me or against me, Vlad? You've tried playing against me, and three people are dead as a result. We can be buddies, you and I. How many of our colleagues are telepaths, do you think? Politics probably draw them—after all, half of politics is knowing what the other guy is thinkin'. Now, I personally believe it would be good to have a telepath point of view in the Senate—one and only one—but I'm afraid the voters won't see it that way. Still, what the voters don't know won't hurt 'em, will it? So. With me or against me, Vlad?"

Tokash put his head in his hands, and then looked back up, tiredly. "With you, Senator Crawford."

"Call me Lee. First thing in the morning, I want a list of every telepath you know, most especially those in your employ. They work for me now."

"Very well."

"Another thing, just in case you're still thinking about some sort of stunt. You realize that you are the product of genetic engineering?"

"What?"

"The genetic analysis makes it pretty obvious. I think it's best that that news not be made public, don't you?"

"Good God, yes."

"See? We think alike. Together, I think we can keep this little fact from getting out—that we can identify telepaths is one thing. *How* we do it is best kept a question of global security, one best controlled by the Committee on Metasensory Regulation. So while you won't be head, I'd of course like to have you as my right-hand man." He grinned. "Right where I can see you, that is.

"And get some rest, Vlad—you look like hell."

4

Publishers Weekly, 6 February 2117

In Senate hearings today, a spokesperson for Random House, Inc., alleged that telepathic literary agents may have done "incalculable damage" to the publishing industry as a whole, urging immediate genetic testing of all licensed and aspiring agents, with stiff penalties for offenders. Overseeing the Committee on Metasensory Regulation, Senator Lee Crawford said, "The implications are clear, and we appreciate the thoughtful testimony from all involved. This matter must be handled with intelligence and sensitivity, but hopefully not until we're done negotiating the advance for my biography." The senator later explained that this last was "just a joke."

The Boston Globe, 21 May 2117

Triana Neesom of Perth, Australia, today filed suit against her dentist, Graham McKay, D.D.S., for invasion of privacy. McKay—recently identified as a telepath—indignantly denied the allegation that he had "picked Neesom's bloody brains" while the plaintiff was under general anesthesia for root canal surgery.

Weekly World News, 15 June 2117

THEY WEREN'T ALONE IN BED!

Ladies, take warning! A young woman from Manchester, U.K. (at her request we withhold her name), recently experienced what might be the worst first date in history—at the hands—and we do mean "hands"— of telepaths.

A model student and virgin, Georgia (not her real name) celebrated her twenty-first birthday with some friends at a local night-

spot. Noticing that she had drawn the attention of a handsome young man, her girlfriends urged her to break her long bedroom fast. Encouraged by strong drink, the young woman relented to peer pressure and at the end of the night found herself in the young man's apartment. All seemed to be going well, when—at that tenderest of moments—she heard lascivious groans, moans, and even applause from the next room. On peeking through the bedroom door, she discovered five men and women, whose applause doubled when they saw her. To her horror, she realized that they—and the young man she had been with—were all telepaths, and had all taken part in her sexual initiation, seeing and feeling all in intimate, graphic detail. She had been the victim of a telepathic gang rape!

Lee sat back in the uncomfortable chair and watched the monitor. DiPeso was just starting his monologue, draped across an antique couch and twirling a martini glass.

". . . so he says, how *does* a telepath feed a dog? And I said, pretty well, if you grind him up fine enough."

He sipped his martini languidly as the crowd howled. There were a few boos, but they were of the "what a bad joke" variety.

"Oh, come *on*," DiPeso said, rolling his eyes at the audience. "My ex-wife was a telepath—when I wanted sex she gave *me* the headache.

"Anyway, we have a great big show for you tonight. We've got Anna Keck, here to talk about her most recent movie, *Arkansas Traveler*. Kuan Ping is going to play you his hit song 'Zoomorphia,' and basketball great Joel Transom will tell us all about slam dunks and sex—or is that redundant?—on the Moon.

"But first, we'll have a word with Senator Lee Crawford, hero of the Grissom colony and head of the Committee on Metasensory Regulation." He paused and lifted his martini again, cocking his head thoughtfully. "You know, it's been said that the senator never met a censoring he didn't like—but we'll ask him about that in just a minute, after a few words from your local—"

"Senator, you're on in three," a sprightly young woman in a bellhop uniform informed him.

"So I am," Lee said, straightening his collar.

The chairs onstage were uncomfortable, too, and Lee had to repress an urge to reach over and tweak DiPeso's ample nose—or better yet, punch it. Despite all that, he grinned and extended his hand.

"Well, Senator. You've been quite the man in the news lately. Let me start with the question that surely is preying on all of our minds. Consid-

ering that you and your committee control the fates of hundreds of peo-
ple—and knowing how careful you boys in Geneva are about abusing
your power—well, what *is* sex like with a telepath?"

"Well," Lee drawled, "I can't comment on that personally, but my
experts tell me it would be a lot like being interviewed by you."

"How's that, Senator—a sort of cosmic experience?"

"Not exactly. More like doing all of the work while the other person
has twice the fun."

"Ho—well, there's an image!" DiPeso said. "And not a pleasant one
for our audience, either. Now, seriously. How is this Metasensory thing
going?"

"Pretty well, now that we can identify telepaths—"

"Not all of them, though."

"No, but up to about seventy percent of them can be identified
through a brief medical exam. This is a substantial number—and a high
percentage of others come forth voluntarily."

DiPeso put on his "serious face." "Well, that's pretty good, isn't it?
But are you saying that you can't protect us from that other thirty per-
cent?"

Lee rubbed his hands together. "Actually, if you don't mind, I'd like
you to meet a few of these people I'm 'protecting' you from."

DiPeso's face showed a hint of dismay before he managed to cover it
with an "oh, really?" expression. "Well, I'm sure that if they're with you,
I've nothing to worry about. Bring 'em out. But folks, repeat after me—"
He then began rubbing his temples and murmuring, "Think clean
thoughts—think clean thoughts—no thoughts about Anna Keck—"

The audience was laughing, booing, and rubbing its collective tem-
ples as the five telepaths came out. But a hush settled when they saw the
first two.

DiPeso was the first to recover. "Anna, sweetie, you're jumping the
gun a little. Your segment is—"

"It's right now, dear," Anna replied. In early middle age, Anna Keck
still had the same grace and quiet sensuality that had made her, first, the
world's sweetheart, and then, one of its most respected actresses. "I've
been on your show—what is it, thirty times now—and never really had
anything important to say. Now I do."

For perhaps the first time in front of an audience, DiPeso was clearly
flabbergasted. He actually stuttered. "Are—are you saying—"

Lee stood up and let her have his seat. Anna took it, swept back her
luxuriant black hair, and gave DiPeso a little kiss on the cheek. "Just
keep thinking those clean thoughts, dear."

"Good Lord o'mighty!" DiPeso said, recovering. "It's a miracle you haven't slapped me thirty times by now. You've been—this whole time?"

She shrugged and smiled at the audience. "I didn't know until I took the new screening test. I always knew I was good at understanding people—at knowing how they felt—but I've never heard words or anything. Most telepaths can't, really—it's a false stereotype. I can't read your mind, Alex."

"Well, thank Buddha for small favors. Whew. 'Cause I'm sure there must be some sort of law. Well, this is—"

"This isn't about me," Anna interrupted. "We still have a segment for that, right? Because I *do* want to talk about *Arkansas Traveler*. But first I'd like to let the senator introduce everyone else."

"Well, by all means—but I think I know this young man," he said, gesturing at the twenty-something fellow with the Apollonian profile. "Aren't you that fireman . . . ?"

Lee clapped the young man on the shoulder. "This is Guy Guillory. Most of your viewers will remember him as the young man who saved thirty people in the San Francisco earthquake last year. Guy came to us voluntarily when—well, I'll get to that in a moment. Guy's telepathic ability enabled him to find those trapped on the collapsed sixth floor of Trombles. I might add that Guy is just now able to walk again—his body was covered with third-degree burns on his fifth trip in, two trips after the building caught fire."

Guy nodded nervously. Lee patted him on the back and moved down the line to a slight blonde with a pleasant, but not beautiful, face—the girl next door, the kid sister. "This is Clara Suarez. She used to be a stock trader until she voluntarily quit when she learned she had metasensory powers. She now uses her abilities for the International Trade Commission to find less honest telepaths still trading."

He moved to a boy of perhaps thirteen with flaming red hair. "Stephen Campbell. Stephen didn't know he was a telepath either, just that he had a lot of luck hitting what the pitcher threw. Steve was beaten within an inch of his life and left to die on the street in Edinburgh. And this—come here, sweetheart."

He held out his arms, and the last of the five ran into his arms, to the *awwwing* of the crowd. "This is Constance. Constance is five, and last year she watched her whole family slaughtered execution style. She herself was shot, hacked with a machete, and left for dead. We found her under the corpse of her mother."

Constance looked around the room. She was a living doll with huge, dark-bright eyes and brown hair done up in a little bob. She whispered

something in Lee's ear, and he laughed. "She wants to know if she can sit by you, Alex."

"I—yes, of course. I never turn a lady down."

Anna gave the little girl a hug as she came by. Then Constance hopped up into the seat and looked at Alex DiPeso with those huge eyes. There were some gasps from the audience, for on her left profile, a fading white scar started in her hairline, passed through her ear, and vanished at the neckline of her dress.

"Hello, Constance," DiPeso said. "What do you think of Los Angeles?"

She just looked at him and smiled, a bit sadly. "You're a nice man," she said. "I can tell you're a nice man. How come you say such mean things?"

DiPeso worked his jaw, and a profound silence stretched in the studio. Finally, finally, he reached over and took her hand, and his voice seemed caught in his throat as he said, "I don't know, honey. I can't explain it, can I?"

And upward of six billion viewers saw a teardrop glitter at the corner of his eye before the cut to commercial.

"Okay, we're back, and we're still talking to Senator Lee Crawford of the Committee on Metasensory Regulation. Frankly, I planned to have moved him off by now and brought someone entertaining on, but during the break he told me he had something important to tell us. So I think I'll just shut up for a moment and see what it is."

Lee nodded. "Thank you, Alex. I first want to thank you and your audience for giving me the chance to show you these special young people. Look, the face of the unknown is the face of a monster, and for most people telepathy is unknown. It's frightening. In our hearts, I think we all know that that doesn't excuse some of the things that have happened— certainly not the way people like Constance and Stephen have been treated. So I wanted to show you the face of the unknown, so you can see that there is no monster, no alien, just us.

"Now, my committee has gotten a lot of criticism from both ends of the spectrum. I've been criticized for taking away the rights of telepaths—an untrue accusation—and for not being 'hard enough' on them, which I'm happy to say *is* true. They don't deserve punishment simply for being born different. But they *are* different, aren't they—if not in most ways, then in this one special way."

He clasped his hands. "I'm being long-winded, so I'll try to get to the point, because I know you all want to hear more from Anna and the other guests Alex has lined up tonight. The point is this: over the past

year or so, I've had contact with a lot of telepaths, and one thing I know is that most of them have a strong desire to serve, to use their powers not for the good of themselves, not for the good of a single nation, but for the good of all humanity.

"To that end, I would like to announce that the president has given me the go-ahead to form a new government organization, made up of telepaths like Anna, Guy, Stephen, Clara, and Constance. We're all agreed that this is the best, most sensitive way to handle both the needs of telepaths and of the world at large. What people are really afraid of is not telepaths, I'm convinced, but the fear of not knowing *who* is a telepath. Most of us don't mind being naked, so to speak, but we don't want just anyone seeing us naked without our consent. The MRA—Metasensory Regulation Authority—will prevent that. We can identify seventy percent of all telepaths medically, but I think most people who know that they are telepaths will come to the MRA of their own free will, where they can be useful without fear of persecution."

"But what about those who don't want to join?"

"Well, naturally there will be some who want to continue with their normal lives. I'm happy to announce that Halotech has developed a new drug that shows great promise in inhibiting psionic abilities. It's still in the testing stage, but it looks good and, once approved, will be offered as an option for telepaths who want to preserve a normal lifestyle. Beyond that—well, there are criminals in every demographic. Just as in any group of people you choose to look at, there will be some minor fraction who simply have no social conscience, who will always take the easy way out. This is not a trait of telepaths, my friends—it is a trait common to humanity.

"However, as you might imagine, telepaths present special problems in incarceration. Because of this, we've proposed a set of separate rehabilitation facilities specially designed for the needs of telepaths, which will be overseen by MRA—which will, of course, all be overseen in turn by the Earth Alliance Senate. In short, it's high time that people step back and see what's being done.

"The Earth Alliance is the first true world government, and in just over thirty years look what we've accomplished. We have thriving colonies on the Moon, plans to move on to Mars, and we've detected what might be the first real murmurings of an alien civilization. All it took for those things was a little faith, a lot of ingenuity, and sweat.

"It's the same with the so-called telepath problem. In a hundred years, people will look back at this as the beginning of something wonderful." He spread his hands. "Of course, this is all pending Senate

approval, so if you like what you hear today, I urge you to message your senator."

DiPeso nodded as if in agreement and then did his famous double take. "Well, that's about as serious as my contract allows this show to get. I'd like to thank you, Senator, as I'm now marked for death by all of the news shows. I don't suppose you could spare a few of your, er, 'regulators'—to keep me safe?"

Lee shook his head dolefully. "I don't know—the Senate would likely deem that a misallocation of personnel—but I promise to look into it if you'll promise to invite me back sometime."

"Senator—that's an abacus. You can count on it."

"You have nice hands," he told Alice that evening in the Delacorte lounge. Onstage, the band was playing some oh-twenties revival piece, haunting and brisk all at once. Servers drifted by, ghostly in the pale veils and long dresses so popular along the Pacific Rim.

She dimpled, but skeptically. "You make weak spots in me where I had none," she said.

"Hmm. Tell me where they are so I can poke at 'em."

"You do a good enough job of that already. I sometimes wonder if *you* aren't a telepath."

"Not me, darlin'. You saw me get tested."

"Uh-huh. You did a good job on the DiPeso show, too. The man's never shown an honest feeling aside from disdain in twenty years, and you made him *weep*. That's bound to go down in the history books." She laid her hand on top of the one caressing hers. "Why did you break the news about the MRA on his show, though? Why not one of the news shows?"

"How many news shows do you know that have a viewership of six billion? *Live.* Twice that saved. When word gets around, everybody in the solar system will have seen it by tomorrow." He stopped. "God, I love sayin' that. The solar system. Ours is the first generation in history to really be able to say that."

"I don't know if I would go so far as to say we're in the same generation," she said, doubtfully.

"Am I an old man robbin' the cradle, Alice? Is that what you think of me?"

She looked surprised. "I must be naive. I didn't realize you were trying to steal anything."

He shrugged. "You are naive, then. I'd like to take you for everything you've got."

"Really."

"Really."

She avoided his eyes. "I can't be her, you know."

"You don't even look like her. When have I ever made you feel that way?"

"Never—never on purpose. But there's something—even when we're close, there's distance, Lee."

"Anything we can't build a bridge over?"

"I don't know."

"Well, why don't we get married and give it a go?"

"What?"

"You heard me."

She looked back up at him, as if he were one of those ancient inkblot things she kept as objets d'art in her office.

"Okay," she said, softly. "If you love me, okay."

"I love you."

"I love you, too, Lee." She took a sip of her drink, still looking a bit troubled. Then she smiled. "But what kind of honeymoon can compare to our first date?"

"Darlin', I'll do my best."

He left Los Angeles feeling good, but that sensation vanished on the red-eye back to Geneva, as the reactions started pouring in. All the usual stuff about his grandstanding—they all wished they could grandstand as well as he. That was trivial. But some of the responses to the MRA were troubling. Not unexpected, but troubling.

It was morning when he arrived in Geneva, and he went straight to work—best way to deal with jet lag.

Tom Nguyen was waiting for him.

"I thought you'd be in today."

"Yep. What's up?"

"The party called again."

"Screw 'em. What else is up?"

"I have a feeling you know."

Lee yawned, poured himself a cup of coffee, and rubbed the grit out of his eyes. "Yeah, but my brain's a little run-down. I imagine you've been on this with your usual efficiency. The vote?"

"Ten percent better than expected, our sources say."

"See? I told you I should go on DiPeso."

Tom nodded reluctantly. "It could have gone bad, though—well, it didn't. The tear made the top of the news everywhere."

Lee sipped his coffee. "Constance, God bless 'er. It's her gift. Not that she really needs it—she's so adorable and pathetic all at once any-

way—but our tests put her at P12, powerful enough to nudge a tear out of anyone, if need be."

Tom shook his head. "What did you tell her?"

"I told her to make 'im cry, and damned if she didn't. Hell, I got misty-eyed, too—I guess I was within the field of affect or whatever."

"This is really dangerous, Lee. If anyone suspects—"

"They won't suspect because they don't want to. The real bigots will say it, of course, and thereby set themselves apart. See, opinion wasn't really polarized, not most places. People were ambivalent about telepaths, now they aren't. They feel ashamed of themselves. They want to help. And best of all, they can help *and* keep the mind readers away from them all at the same time. They call their senators. The vote will go our way."

"The nonmember nations want your head. They say they won't give up their telepaths."

"We'll see about that—it's a human rights issue. What about the members?"

"Everybody wants to make their own policy. The Russian Consortium and Amazonia are being real pains. Both are going to vote against you—maybe China, too. You'll squeak by with a majority, but the MRA is on shaky ground. We can't afford to make a mistake here."

Lee studied his aide for a moment. "Tom, you gettin' any sleep at all?"

Tom blinked. "Not much."

"Take care of yourself. I need you." He took another sip of his coffee. "Any movement on the other front?"

"Vacuum. There were some experiments by various militaries trying to develop exploitable psionic powers in the twentieth, but none of them went anywhere. For the last hundred years, nothing."

"Damn it, *somebody* did it. If not a country, then a corporation. There has to be some evidence other than the telepaths themselves. Tokash's telepaths haven't come up with anything?"

"Nothing. Every telepath they've scanned had a normal enough childhood, their powers aside, and no connections other than what one would normally suspect. If they are part of some larger conspiracy, it's very well hidden."

"We're missing something."

"No doubt."

"This is important, Tom. I want to ride the tiger, not discover ten years down the road that I have my head in its mouth."

"You and me both, Senator."

5

Blood watched the DiPeso show with growing interest. A dry Arizona breeze blew in through the open door, and carried with it the throaty croak of a raven.

"I wonder if Crawford is one of us?" Teal murmured. "He seems too smart to be a normal."

"Normals aren't stupid," Blood said.

"That doesn't sound like you."

"And we aren't all that smart. I had a bad moment back there in Alaska. Don't remind me of it. Arrogance will get us killed."

Mercy shifted uncomfortably on the couch, curling up like a cat. "How can we hide, now that they have the test?"

Blood looked frankly at her. "The question is—do we really want to hide?"

Teal tilted his chair back against the wall. "What do you mean?"

Blood shrugged indifferently. *Where's Monkey, anyway?*

You know Monkey. Send him out for groceries, and he ends up with every cop in town on his tail. (pause) Why are you blocking? Aren't we family?

We are. I just don't know what I'm thinking, yet. I want to get it straight in my head before—

Someone was at the door. Monkey and someone else, someone locked and blocked tighter than anyone Blood had ever touched. She eased her hand onto the pistol in her jacket pocket.

Monkey poked his head through the door. *Howdy and salutations.*

Talk, Monkey. Mercy—

Right. Like you and Smoke weren't going on when I got here. He cleared his throat. "Look, folks, I've got someone with me. Come on, little fellah—"

A boy of perhaps six looked uncertainly through the door. The dark tone of his skin and shape of his face suggested Hispanic or Amerind

blood—not unusual in Flagstaff—but his brown hair was touched with golden highlights.

"Monkey, what are you doing?"

"Hey, Blood, he's one of us. And strong, too. Feel that block?"

"I feel it. Since when did you start picking up strays?"

"Since when did we *stop*?" Monkey growled, uncharacteristically indignant. "He was just wandering the street with an old Indian woman, real low level, but on the wind, all right. I tried to get her to come, too, but she just pushed the boy off on me. I scanned her, but she got pissed off, and I didn't learn much. I think she found the boy in the desert a few months ago."

"You want us to take care of a kid?"

"For G-God's sake," Mercy stuttered, unfolding herself from the couch. "Are you going to talk about him like he isn't here? Come here, son."

The boy hesitated for an instant, and then came forward and let Mercy gather him up.

"I'll get him something to eat," Teal said. *Jeez, Blood, c'mon. It's not like he's a normal kid. He's one of us. Didn't we make a vow that we would take anyone in we found, make them part of the family?*

Damn straight, Monkey said. *Look, Mercy is already playing mama—*

The boy jerked, stared at Monkey with wide eyes.

Hello, that got something—

Mercy frowned up at them. "I don't appreciate being left out."

"Sorry," Monkey said. "But the boy responded to our wind-talk just now."

"Be careful with him," Mercy said, stroking his head, touching his face. "He doesn't want to let us in, yet. Just give him some time."

Blood sighed and reached forward to tousle the boy's head. "Welcome to the family, kid."

She felt Monkey coming before she saw him, but she kept her eyes on the dark disk of the new moon.

The Night, the Wind, the Sorcerer, he said, as he eased up behind her. *Leave me alone.*

"Are you still mad about the kid?"

"I'm not mad, O'Hannlon—I'm worried."

"Don't use my mundane name. I never want to hear it again."

"We aren't kids anymore, Monkey. It's time to grow up. I'm not the Blood Woman any more than you're really Sun Wu Kong. We're just Desa Alexander and Jack O'Hannlon, just like when we met."

"No. Not like when we met. We've made each other better. We've

walked the wild paths and come through alive and kicking. You're lettin' the mundane world screw with you. We're above it. We're the future, Blood."

"I don't know if I see a future."

She felt his breath on her neck then. *Don't fool yourself, Blood. You're a tiger, not a herd beast. You're cobra. Blackhearted.*

She felt his desire like it was her own, a delight as dark and strange as her first taste of licorice. His nails trailed down her face, across the thin fabric of her shirt, her belly.

This is what I'm talking about, she managed. *We know how bad we are together—*

This is bad? He did something new with his hand.

(!!)No!

You think too much.

She whirled on him then, suddenly angry, almost hating him. But then she saw his eyes, and she knotted her fists in his copper hair, bit his lip, and for a time did not think at all.

Three months passed. Everyone got crummy normal jobs, Blood's crummier than most, waiting tables in a bar. Something of a comedown for the dark goddess. But telepath testing was working its way through the ranks of business and government jobs first—she figured it would be a while before they got around to waitresses.

Somebody noticed the kid, and a social worker came by. They told him he was Blood's sister's son, which seemed to satisfy, but they had to put him in school.

He seemed to improve a little, after that, though he was in special classes.

Mercy made her announcement at the dinner table. It was clear that something was bothering her. Her shields were up—they were as thin as paper, of course, and Blood could have poked through them anytime she wanted, but the family respected privacy. If Mercy wanted to shield, they let her.

But then she told them. "They tested me today."

Blood froze with the spoon halfway to her mouth, as the table became a sudden whirlwind of silent panic. The boy, whom they had taken to calling James, cringed.

"You let them test you?" Blood said, slowly.

"It was a surprise. They just came through the office and took some tissue."

"And?"

"And I'm a teep."

"Big surprise. Well, we've been here long enough. Time to—"

"No." Mercy's voice was as firm as Blood had ever heard it. The mind behind it was firm, too. "No, I can't keep moving like this. I'm not like the rest of you. I . . ." She stumbled off, and Blood caught some vague images—herself as the dark goddess, the mindscream of a hundred people dying when Monkey's bomb went off. "I like my job."

"You like being a secretary?"

"It's honest."

"But they'll never let you keep it, not now that they know. Christ, I knew this was going to happen."

"I'll take the injection," Mercy said, softly. "They said I could keep working there if I took the injection."

Smoke frowned. "Can't let them still your wind."

"Yes, I can. It doesn't matter. I'm not strong enough for it to matter anyway. What little use I get from my talent has only made me unhappy. Even with you guys. It's best."

They argued more, but Mercy was firm.

Mercy came back the next day like a dead woman. When Blood tried to touch her mind, she had to run for the toilet, and there she vomited for half an hour. Mercy curled on the couch, her normally lively eyes blank. She watched the vid with only sluggish interest. Tentatively, Blood scanned her again. She was reminded of Novocain, and also of heroin. It was as if Mercy only *remembered* being alive.

She locked Mercy in her room the next day, called her boss, and told him that the injection had made her sick. That would put them off for a day, maybe, but then they would come hunting for her. And when they came for her, they would find them all. But no one would do this to one of hers, ever again.

"I'm going to the school to get James," she told Teal and Smoke. "When Monkey gets back, don't let him wander. We leave tonight."

Outside, the thin air was fragile with autumn, Arizona's San Francisco Peaks challenging the clear, dark sky with their sun-dazzled starkness, and she struggled to see beauty, slow her breathing, still the desire to find Mercy's boss, rip open his mind, find out who had injected her friend. Mercy, the one who painted pictures, who wrote poetry, whose mind opened like a flower to beauty. Blood was their heart, sometimes fist; Teal, their intellect; Monkey, their passion and lunacy; Smoke, their quiet strength—but Mercy, Mercy was their *soul.* Now she was embalmed alive.

She should kill them. They knew what they were doing. If the drug had lasting effects, she would. She swore she would.

* * *

The secretary smiled briskly when Blood got to the office.

"Hello, I'm Ms. Nogales," she said. "I've come for my nephew, James. We've had a family emergency."

The secretary aimed her sharp nose at Blood. "Which grade is he in?" she asked, pleasantly.

"First. In the special class."

"Oh yes—I think they're being tested now."

"Tested?"

"Telepath screening."

Blood blinked. "Without my permission?"

"It's the law, Ms. Nogales. It's a painless procedure."

"Where?"

"The lunchroom. But you can't—"

Blood left her explaining what she couldn't do. She knew where the lunchroom was.

They were all lined up, as if for inoculations. Two competent-looking women in white coats were doing something to their arms with a steel cylinder, then inserting the cylinder into a black box. Blood scanned the line frantically, looking for James.

She finally found him on the other side, absently munching on a cookie. Milk and cookies for the good little children at the other end of the line.

She hurried over to him.

"Ms. Nogales?"

She turned to see Mr. Craig, James' teacher.

"What's going on here?" she demanded.

"Compulsory testing. There's nothing to worry about."

"James is delicate," she said heatedly.

"He did fine. Didn't you James? And you'll be happy to know, Ms. Nogales—he came up perfectly normal."

She touched Craig lightly. It was the truth.

"Well, thank God," she said.

"Most kids are normal. Only one in ten thousand tests out as a telepath. I doubt we'll even find one here today."

She nodded. "Well, I'm relieved. I came by to pick James up."

"Oh?" Suspicion leaked out under his words.

"Yes. His grandfather, I'm afraid."

"I'm terribly sorry to hear that. How long will he be out?"

"Only a few days, I hope. We have to go to Houston."

"Well, we'll miss you, James," he said to the boy.

James kept nibbling on the cookie. When she took his hand, Blood tasted the chocolate chips.

"Come on, James, we have to take a little trip."

Outside, in the car, she managed to relax a little. *Thirty percent,* she thought. *Thirty percent will get through. You're a lucky boy, James.*

But that was probably as much luck as her little family could count on. It was time for them to make their own luck.

6

"Ah, Senator Menshikov," Lee said. "So good of you to join me."

Out on the grounds, the party had quieted, though perhaps twenty people still played croquet as the fireflies trembled up from the grass. Lee sipped his bourbon and leaned over to kiss Alice on the cheek. "Alice, would you mind seeing how everyone else is doing?"

His wife disengaged herself from him and rose a little unsteadily to her feet. She had had a bit too much to drink, something that was beginning to worry him.

Menshikov waited silently, until she was gone. "Quite a place you have here," he commented, taking a seat in one of the large rocking chairs.

Lee gestured at the house and grounds with his bourbon. "Not my ancestral home," he remarked. "I grew up in one of the block tenements that used to stand just over that hill, on the outskirts of Natchez. My friends and I used to sneak over to admire this place, just to spend a few minutes in the gardens before the gardeners chased us out." He smiled at the recollection. "It was a big house, and I suppose we got big dreams from it. Antebellum revival, you know, built in 2064. Sturdy stuff."

"No slaves, I notice."

"Now, Senator, no need to be nasty. I don't provoke you with asides about human rights issues in your own past—and I believe the Russian Consortium boasts a few. We take the good from the past, you and I, and we leave the rest to rot. We aren't romantics, are we?"

Menshikov grinned sardonically. "I assumed you brought me—and the rest of your guests—to talk about the present?"

Lee shook his head. "The future. I'll be frank—I'd like to know why you're blocking me on the military issue."

"I don't believe telepaths have any legitimate function in the military."

Now it was Lee's turn to show a wolf's grin. "You mean in the Earth Alliance military, don't you? Because you have them in your own."

Menshikov leaned into the chair, his eyes widening slightly as it rocked back, but otherwise keeping his composure. "I deny that categorically. I hope you didn't invite me to your house to insult me."

"Quite the opposite. I'm tryin' to schmooze you. Can I get you another drink? Vodka. You're a traditional guy—you can't turn down a drink."

"No, I suppose I can't."

Lee signed for a servant, who already had the drink poured.

"To understanding," he toasted, and they drank.

The girl brought two more.

"Senator." Menshikov chuckled. "I seriously hope you don't intend to try to drink me under the table. Russians have evolved a higher capacity for drink through the simple process of natural selection."

"Senator," Lee replied, "You're talking to the end product of four hundred years of hybrid vigor when it comes to that. I'm descended from a long line of drunks from thirteen different countries. *Prosit.*"

They drank again, and Menshikov cocked his eye. "Aren't you satisfied? You've placed your MRA people in the business sector, in the judiciary system—now you want EarthForce to have them?"

"We need them to maintain stability, and you know it. Every Earth Alliance nation-state keeps its own stable of telepaths, despite the resolution against it. I know it and you know it, so let's not play that game—not here, not now, with no reporters around, just me and you. That's fine. But we can't go too far that way. If we aren't going to devolve into some twentieth-century nightmare—if EarthForce is to play its role as the peacekeeper and enforcer of the solar system—EarthForce needs telepaths."

More vodka appeared. Menshikov took the small crystal glass and held it between thumb and forefinger, staring speculatively at the cold, clear liquid. "You know," he said, "it isn't so much that I disagree with you. The problem, you see, is that anything we give to the MRA we also give to *you,* Senator. You have become entirely too powerful in entirely too short of a time, and to be frank, I do not like you. The fools in the Senate have given you telepaths—the only ones in the world legitimized to use their powers. Then they allowed you to place these people among the most powerful corporations on Earth, and to involve them in the process of the judiciary—"

"No one objected to that. Business begged for them, to monitor transactions, all on the up-and-up. The judicial system needed them, too, to help victims identify criminals. Bottom line was, I was asked to justify the existence of the MRA in monetary terms—by *you* among others, if I remember correctly."

Menshikov nodded sadly. "It was a mistake, I see that now. I won't compound my mistake by giving you the military, too."

"Don't you think you are being the least bit paranoid, Senator?"

"Hah. Russians have also been bred for paranoia. First, everyone in the world invaded us. The Mongols. Napoleon. Hitler. Then we put our trust in Stalin, in Khrushchev, in Yeltsin, in Kolishnikov. We reluctantly trusted the West once again to help us rebuild after the civil war, and found ourselves an economic colony for twenty years. So yes, I am paranoid, and history has taught me that I am right to be—that I would be a fool not to be. And I do not trust *you,* Senator Crawford. You are entirely too glib and entirely too strong. And I do not find that I want any more of your vodka." He set the glass down.

"Wait a moment, if you please, Senator."

"For what?"

"I didn't want to do this."

"What, for God's sake?"

"A girl named Lena. A pregnancy. A threat to go to your wife and the papers. A lonely corpse in a block of concrete in the ooze at the bottom of Lake Baikal. I know where she is."

Menshikov stared at him.

"You see, I don't like you either, Senator. I don't like old men who play with thirteen-year-old girls. I don't like men who have their playmates killed because they become inconvenient. Call me old-fashioned, but I just don't like it. I ought to throw you to the wolves, because it's what you deserve."

"You can't prove it. Damn you and your telepaths, anyway. But their testimony isn't admissible in court."

"It doesn't have to be. I have the body. You were thoughtful enough to preserve that body in concrete, so I have a dead child, and inside that dead child another with *your* DNA. I have the sworn testimony of your goons, who weren't quite as up on telepath court procedure as you. Even if you somehow beat the courts, you're finished, Menshikov."

"Unless I do what you say."

"Yes."

"And you do not think you have too much power."

"Don't you talk to me about power, you bastard. I don't use my power to rape little girls and have them murdered."

"Yet despite your outrage, you are willing to let me get away with it to further your own position."

Lee just smiled bitterly and tilted his head.

Menshikov shook his head and then laughed. "You have beaten me.

I concede." He lifted the vodka. *"Salute!"* And they drank again. "And now I go to my bed."

"Tell your wife I said hello."

Menshikov shuffled off into the darkness, and Lee set his empty glass down and breathed in the night air, syrupy with honeysuckle, fresh-cut grass, mimosa blossoms. He looked back out toward where he was born, remembering the tiny cubicles, the missed meals. Who would have thought that a boy who lived in that place would ever own this one, would ever gather the reins of heaven into his very hands?

But it was all falling into place.

"But you don't have everything you need."

He looked up. The vodka was just starting to flatten the world. The speaker was an attractive, dusky woman perhaps thirty years old, with almond eyes and hair that gleamed like obsidian. With her was a pale, long-jointed man; a giant with almost black skin; a nervous-looking brunette; and a small redhead with a sarcastic smirk that seemed a permanent part of his face.

"Who are you? How did you get past my guards?"

The woman laughed without humor. "We are the Night, the Wind, the Sorcerer."

"Telepaths."

"Indeed."

"Did you come here to kill me? Did Tokash send you?"

Now the smirking man laughed.

"No," the woman said. "We could, but what would be the point? No, we rather like what we've seen of you, Senator Crawford. Your exchange with the Russian senator just now. We liked that."

"Who are you?"

"I am Blood, and this is my kith. My family."

"And you say you have something I need?"

She nodded. "We've been around and about. We've been to Geneva, where you keep your little stable of telepaths. Did you know that the best of us have escaped you? The strongest. We can end that, because we're the best there is. You want your MRA to have the best and the brightest; it starts with us."

Lee wished he hadn't had so much to drink, now. He had thought his night over. "Why? Why come to me?"

"I want my family to have a home. We're tired of hiding. We want the same thing you want, Senator—a little power, a little control."

"How do I know that?"

"You just have to trust me, I suppose."

"Well," said Lee, tapping his fingers to the rhythm of the whippoor-wills that had just begun to sing. "Well. Welcome, then."

"That went well," Teal said, as they made their way back to where they had parked the car.

"Yes, it did," Blood said. But she noticed that Monkey had his blocks up. "Monkey? Do you have something to say?"

"Yes. Yes I do." He took a deep breath. "I'm not going."

Surprise all around, exploding like firecrackers. Anger.

"We all agreed—"

"No, you all agreed."

"We're a family, Monkey. We make decisions together."

"Maybe it's time I was orphaned then. I'm not going."

"What's the alternative?" Teal snapped. "Hiding for the rest of our lives? Becoming military slaves like our brothers in the Consortium?"

"I picked up that last from Menshikov, too," Blood admitted. "Another reason to join the MRA. We can not only reveal things like that, but be in a position to do something about it."

"Crawford doesn't give a good damn about us, you all saw that. He wants to use us just like everyone else," Monkey said.

"Not like everyone else. He doesn't want to kill us, as many do. And we can use him."

Monkey set his mouth stubbornly. "No machine was ever fixed from the inside. Don't make that mistake, Blood. We belong out here, with our brothers and sisters. Normals can't be allowed to tell teeps what to do. We can't put our lives in the hands of mundanes."

"Exactly. The MRA has to be a teep organization. It has to be ours. Who better to do that than us?"

"It shouldn't exist at all," Monkey said. "We can organize, build an army. People are going underground, going to the countries where they think we're holy. We can—"

"Monkey dreams," Blood said. "Don't confuse yourself with your namesake. You taunted me about *The Man Who Would Be King,* and you were right. But you want to be Sun Wu Kong, build up an army of monkeys, challenge the emperor of heaven, have your name stricken from the book of death." *We are too much alike, you and I. We are both too much like spoiled children. This is the real way, the realistic way. The Man Who Would Be King and Sun Wu Kong the Monkey King both ended badly. It's a stupid dream. All that matters now is the family. Grow up.*

Better to serve in heaven than to reign in hell, eh Blood? I remember when you were better than that. I'm not going.

"I'm not going," was all he repeated aloud, to the rest. "Who is coming with me?"

No response.

"Mercy?"

"I can't. If they catch me, if they make me take an injection again—" She broke off. "I can't."

Monkey nodded, bitterly. "I'm taking the kid," he said. "I won't let you drag him off to some fascist training camp."

"Since when do you care about the kid? Or about these 'brothers' you keep talking about us having?"

Monkey lifted his chin, and for once he did not smile. "Maybe you're wrong about me, Blood. Maybe I have grown up, just not the way you have. But I'm taking the kid. He doesn't even test as a teep. I won't let you give him up."

"Monkey—" Mercy began, but she never finished. Something inside her shut her up.

"Go then," Blood said, softly. "Go."

And Monkey went. That very night.

Good luck, she sent, after he was gone, on their own private wind. *I love you.*

But there was no reply. She knew there would not be.

PART 2

The Kith

PART 2

The Kith

1

He awoke choking off a scream, heart stumbling in his chest. The inchoate terror of his dream clung to him like a shroud, blinding him to where he was. The seat, the window, dim pools of light marching away from him. Where?

"Dad? Are you okay?"

The shroud tore, and he peered through to see his son, a boy with twelve years, his mother's blond hair, his own pointed chin. Beyond the boy he now recognized the darkened interior of a train, reading lamps, other passengers.

"It's okay, Len," he murmured. "Just a bit of a bad dream. Where are we?"

"I think we're coming up to Prague soon."

"We change trains there. I'm glad I woke up." He rubbed his eyes and patted Len on the cheek. The boy looked tired and worried. "We'll be okay. Is your mom awake?"

"Yah. She went back to the washroom," he said. *Dad, will we get to stay this time?*

"Don't do that, son. Especially don't do that when we're coming up to a station. Not until we get to India."

"Will we get to stay in India?"

"Yes. We'll have work permits there, and an apartment. You can go to school and make friends." He nodded at the booklet in Len's lap. "You've been checking it out?"

"Yah." He didn't sound very excited.

"Tell me something about it, then."

"Well—Calcutta is the third largest city in the world. And it has the tallest building, even though it was built fifty years ago . . ." He stumbled off. *(confusion, sadness, anger)*

Didier leaned over and kissed his son on the head, wrapped him in a hug. "It'll be all right this time. They can't come for us there."

They rode in silence for a time, and Didier tried to remember the

dream that had awakened him. Their old house in Antwerp, the house where he had grown up, collapsing. A dark woman he did not know, standing in the doorway, telling him something . . .

There.

It was faint, a whisper, but its triumph was undiminished by distance.

"Oh, no," he murmured.

His son looked at him again, questioning.

(block) He couldn't let him know. "I need to go do something," he said. "I need you to be the man for a little while. Can you do that?"

"Where are you going?"

"Just up a few cars. You may have to change trains without me. It's okay—just tell your mother I'll find you on the train. Don't mindspeak. We're almost there, son."

"Okay, Dad." But the boy was probing at his block.

"Don't do that. It isn't polite. Stay quiet."

"Okay, Dad."

"I love you." He kissed him again and stood up, his belly feeling like a pit.

As soon as he was out of the car, he let his block drop, opened his mind wide. Len wasn't strong enough to hear him this far away.

I'm alone. I'm scared. I'm in trouble. He kept that going in his mind, his very real panic sharpening it.

Alone. That was the important part.

Someone was still touching him—very carefully, but he could feel it. He had an image of a skull, laughing, of a cat approaching.

He went through the next car, wondering what time it was, missing his timepiece. It had been an heirloom, Japanese, more than a hundred years old. He'd sold it to buy their tickets. He looked at the info-strips, but they were busy advertising low, low rates to the Russian Consortium. But it must be well past midnight.

He moved on through the eerily silent train, until at last a soft bell tone sounded and the train said, "Prague. Praha."

He moved to the door. He could feel the triumph arriving like a storm, but from what direction he did not know. Maybe—maybe it was another refugee. Or a thief. He suppressed hysterical laughter—at himself, that he would be relieved if it was a thief, or a simple murderer. What a world. What a world.

The doors hissed open, and he stepped out onto the platform. The scents of city came to him on a chill wind, coppery and stale.

He walked quickly, until he could almost feel the breath on his neck, and then he began to run.

Got him! There!

Three other minds exploded into motion, somewhere near, and he almost screamed. They were everywhere—they were nowhere. He ran faster. He was in good shape—he was a runner, a Hash House Harrier.

A runner. It had been okay at first—the test hadn't revealed him, as a boy. Then he had met Mary. Mary had never been tested. Her father, a biochemist, had somehow faked the results. But he was gone now, and everyone knew the Mark came through the mother, and Len must have it. They had managed to avoid the test for twelve years, moving, running. And he had heard from a man that he should go to India, where they liked teeps, where they would look the other way.

He leapt down onto the tracks. One of the voices was fading. He was outdistancing them! Maybe he could find a Catholic church, get sanctuary. Did Prague have many Catholic churches? He could find one.

He ran hard up the tracks, and now there was a uniformed guard shouting at him, a normal, who thought his only crime was trying to get out of paying for something.

But no, his crime was deeper than that. His crime was existing.

He emerged from the station beneath a coffee sky with a hint of cream stirred into the east. Nearly morning. The tracks were sunken three meters below ground level, but a maintenance ladder climbed up one side. Once in the city he could disappear into a million minds, erase himself.

Alone. Lost. In trouble. Help!

Mary knew what to do from here on out. He just had to lead them off, keep them away from *Mary and Len.*

(block) Cursing himself. Had that slipped into his frontvoice?

"Stop!" the normal shouted.

But he was up, onto a nearly empty street.

And there she was, the woman from his dream, jet-and-argent hair bound in a tight queue, oriental eyes tightening with satisfaction. She wore black.

No more running. I'm here to help you.

He turned and ran the other way, just in time for him to see the flash of the guard's neural collapser. It struck him in the chest.

His limbs jerked, but he managed a few more steps back toward the retaining wall around the tracks.

Flash, as the baton struck him again. Slow motion, as his legs folded, as the tracks rushed up, as something quietly snapped in his neck and momentum turned him over. He couldn't move his head, but he could see the guard, looking down at him. He saw the angel of death join the normal.

"I got him for you," the guard said, in English, as they began to fade.

He felt her hatred. *Normals.* It was like a dagger.

An instant later—he didn't see what she did—the guard joined him on the tracks, his surprise fading into oblivion.

He tried to move again. He couldn't tell if he was breathing.

Woman: *(hint of sadness) Why did you run?*

He tried to stay focused. Was she really sending to him? How could she ask that?

(resignation, defiance, brandy and ice) Because I want my life.

Woman: *You can't have it, not around normals. You know that. They hate us, fear us. You can only be safe with us.*

(outrage) I've seen the camps.

Woman: *(exasperation, disdain) The camps are for fools.* She appeared, kneeling next to him. Another voice piped in, slender as a reed.

Reed voice: *Will he make it?*

Woman: *I don't know. His neck is broken. Ambulance coming?*

Reed voice: *Of course. Did he take out the normal?*

Woman; image: *The normal shooting Didier, woman striking the guard hard in the throat, the guard feeling his larynx crushed, surprise, sucking for air, the sort of !Pop! as his skull shattered against the concrete.*

Reed voice: *You'll go too far one day, Blood. You can't just kill normals.*

Woman: *He deserved it. Look what he did to our brother.*

A third voice, carrying the raw tones of youth. For this one he caught a name—Daria. *But the teep was running from us. The guard was helping us. Wouldn't we have killed the teep if we had to?*

Woman: *This is your first hunt, but from now on you must know. Teeps are ours. If they have to be killed, we kill them. They are ours. But no matter what—no matter what they've done, they don't deserve to be dirtied by a normal. Ever. Normals are the enemies, Daria, the real enemies. Teeps are our kith, our family, even if they deny us. Never forget that.*

Daria: *The kith is mother. The kith is father.*

Woman: *Those aren't just words, you see.*

Daria: *I do see.*

The woman knelt where he could see her. She touched his face so only he could hear. *I don't think you will live. I'm sorry. Is there anything you want me to tell your wife and boy?*

Please, no. Let them alone. You've killed me, let them alone.

That's not how it's going to be. But I'll take good care of them.

He felt like he was shivering, rattling apart, as if a train were arriving inside of him. *I love them. Will you tell them that?*

Of course. Their names?

Mary— He stopped. *You didn't know about them, did you?*

I wasn't sure. I see them now, on the train to India. Nice-looking boy. And now for another thing or two . . .

He would have wept, but he didn't have time. Death swallowed his tears along with the rest of him.

Blood shuddered as the world reasserted itself. She had followed him only to the threshold, and as far as she was concerned, that was too far. The sense of dislocation, the vague shadow of nightmare, would be with her for days.

She looked down at the still face. *A P9, maybe P10. What a pity. We could have used him. Did the rest of you get it? The face of the man who helped him get his passports?*

Yes, Teal answered. *But there was an afterimage behind him—somebody our friend here never saw, but that he picked up from his benefactor.*

Blood nodded grimly. *Exactly. Did you recognize him?*

Teal hesitated. *It might not be . . .*

Blood snorted, and said it out loud. "Bullshit. It was Monkey. I knew we would pick his trail up one of these days."

Teal reached to touch her, ignoring the bewilderment of the rookie beside them. *Well? What do we do?*

Blood shot him a weary glance. *What else? Catch him, of course.*

2

"Understand me, Senator. It's not just murder I'm investigating. It's the machine behind the murder. In short, Senator Crawford, I'm investigating the Metasensory Regulation Authority itself."

Lee shook his head as if at a child. "You've got all that backward, don't you, Senator?"

An ambiguous grin quirked Philip Lai's handsome, ascetic face. He folded his long fingers into the loose pockets of his grey suit. "I don't believe I follow you, Senator."

"Son, don't play games with me. I was in this business when you were still learning to count on your fingers. What I mean is, certain senators like yourself—most of them in the opposition party—have been hankering for a piece of me. Now they use a murder that they have absolutely no evidence for to try to hang the MRA out to dry. You see what I mean, son? You've not only already decided that the murder was committed, you've decided that it was committed by a member of the Authority, and that in turn the MRA is to blame, and thus me. But you've got not a single link in the chain of causality. So what that really means is that you want *me*—for purely political reasons—and you're willing to climb up the crummiest, shakiest ladder in the solar system to get to me. How'm I doin'?"

"*I* have not decided anything," Lai stated. "The president appointed me to this investigation. If you don't approve of that, I suggest you take it up with him. You are familiar with the president, aren't you? Contrary to what you might believe, he is not your subordinate."

Crawford actually laughed. "Yeah, I guess you're right. How could I suspect underhanded political motivations from a man who makes a comment like that? Or from a president I actively campaigned against?"

Lai's hands emerged from his pockets again and spidered out on Lee's desk. He leaned forward. "I will be clear, Senator. I don't like you, and I don't like the MRA, I don't like Teeptown, and I especially don't like your telepath goon squads. I think you've consistently abused your

position, and I think you've grossly misused the talents of the telepaths you keep incarcerated. Now, my feelings on these matters are one thing. They are my opinion, and that is neither here nor there. Except, Senator, that I can *prove* what I say."

"Son, you can certainly try."

Kevin Vacit heard the shouting quite clearly as he approached the door marked SENATOR LEE CRAWFORD. He paused. The secretary had said to go straight up and knock, that he was expected. But walking in on an altercation didn't seem the best way to meet his new boss.

Then again, ignoring instructions might be worse. He rapped. The shouting broke off.

"Come in!"

Kevin opened the door.

"Who the hell are you?"

Kevin recognized him, of course. He had grown up seeing Lee Crawford's face on the vids and in newspapers. It was a sort of shock to see him in person. He had expected Crawford to be bigger somehow, more godlike. In an intangible way, he was. There was an almost palpable sense of power that lay behind that seamed, angular face, that did not come across on a screen or in any photograph.

"Sir—Senator—I'm Kevin Vacit."

"My replacement," said the other man. Kevin recognized him, too—Tom Nguyen, who had interviewed him.

"Damn it, Tom, I don't need your replacement. I need *you*. You've been with me for almost twenty years."

"I'm sorry, Lee. It's what I feel I have to do."

The senator blinked, and his face relaxed. It was as if he had just realized his anger was showing and chose not to show it any longer. He sighed. "Very well, Tom. I guess I'm not going to talk you out of it. I'll miss you, though."

"I just think, under the circumstances—"

"Tom, I told you I don't hold any grudges."

"It's not you I'm worried about. It's me I can't live with." He seemed to remember Kevin was in the room.

"Sorry, Kevin. Kevin Vacit, meet Senator Lee Crawford."

Lee Crawford smiled, the avuncular hound's grin from a thousand images. "Good to see you, son. Hear good things about you. Have a seat, won't you?" He turned back to Tom Nguyen. "You will stay long enough to fill him in?"

"Of course. Two weeks, and then as needed."

"Good. Well, let's see here, Mr. Vacit—may I call you Kevin?"

"Of course, sir."

"Then you must call me Lee. In private. Outside of the office you should call me Senator for a while."

"I understand S—Lee."

"Good. So, Kevin. Bachelor of science in neurophysics from ASU, master's in the same from Harvard—and a degree in law. First in your class. Worked with the Houston special attorney for metasensory evidence—ah, Ernesto Perez, a good man." He looked up. "Son, how old are you?"

"I'll be twenty-four next month."

Lee smiled. "You'll stop countin' that way someday, son, I promise you. But damn impressive, to be where you are at your age. Precocious, even." He stood up. "Drink?"

"No, thank you."

Lee snorted. "Figures Tom would replace himself with another straight arrow." He went to a small cabinet and withdrew an earthenware bottle, poured an amber fluid into a small crystal flute.

"So you oversaw telepaths in the courtroom."

"I did."

"Well, tell me this. Some of my colleagues have been pushing to broaden the admissibility of teep testimony. What's your opinion?"

"My opinion is that things are best as they stand."

Lee nodded. "Well, at least you have an opinion. Now explain it."

"Spectral evidence."

"I'm afraid you've lost me, son."

"In the late seventeenth century, in North America, in Salem, Massachusetts, a number of people were tried and many hung for witchcraft. The court admitted testimony of spectral evidence—allegations that the accused had appeared in ghostly form to those they afflicted. One of the men involved—Cotton Mather—argued persuasively against the admissibility of such evidence. After all, the testimony wasn't verifiable—the witnesses could lie for any number of reasons, accusing innocent people. Despite Mather's objections, the testimony was admitted, and twenty-one people were executed. Later, there was a backlash, a big one. I think telepath testimony is comparable. It's good for establishing the possibility of guilt, but shouldn't be admitted without corroborating physical or overwhelming circumstantial evidence."

Lee cocked his head. "They teach you that in law school?"

"No. I'm something of a history buff."

"Write that up for me. It'll sound good on the floor. Can you think of other historical precedents?"

"Yes. In Nigeria, in 2002—"

"Just write it up." He held out his hand. "Good to see someone earning their pay on the first day. Now, why don't you have a talk with Tom? He can fill you in on the nastier aspects of working with me." He turned back to his vid, but called again before Kevin could get out the door. "Have you been screened?"

"Yes, S—ah, Lee. It should be in my vitae."

"We'll want to screen you again, in-house. Good to have you on board, Kevin."

"Good to be here, Lee."

Tom Nguyen stood as the third member of their party approached, a lean fellow the color of black coffee.

"Kevin Vacit, may I introduce Akimba Ironheart."

"Mr. Ironheart," Kevin said, taking the black-gloved hand.

"I hope you don't mind, but it's SOP to have a teep along for these sorts of things. To be candid, assisting Lee is an extremely sensitive position. Even the vice president doesn't have higher clearance."

"I understand completely. And I'm aware of Mr. Ironheart's reputation—you worked on the Knorozov trial, didn't you?"

Ironheart seemed pleased. "I did."

"That was good work."

"Thank you."

Tom drummed his fingers. "Another reason for Mr. Ironheart's joining us has to do with security above and beyond you. Some of the things I'm going to tell you can't be overheard, and there are a lot of people who would *like* to overhear, teep and normal alike."

Kevin nodded.

"The first thing I want to stress is that this job carries some risk. While it's not well known, there have been four attempts on the senator's life in the past fifteen years. None succeeded, and in each case after the first, teeps were able to identify the assassin before his attempt."

"I haven't heard about these."

"You wouldn't have. Cards on the table, Kevin—you've signed a disclosure document. That's to be taken seriously, and from here on out it comes into play. But I ask you again, for the record—do you swear to keep the things I tell you confidential?"

"I do."

He felt a sort of tickle among his thoughts, a faint alien presence. Ironheart nodded. "He's telling the truth."

Tom smiled thinly.

"Good. Let's go have a look at Teeptown, then."

* * *

Kevin took in the broad avenue, the carefully sculpted landscape. In the middle distance he could see a mass of scaffolding and lifters busily at work, and beyond that the sharp peaks of the Alps.

"Is that EarthDome?" he asked, pointing toward the distant construction.

Tom nodded. "It will be. What else could it be? It should be a wonder when it's done." For a moment, a brief regret seemed to flash across his face, then he turned in a slow circle.

"This is the metasensory compound."

"It looks more like a village."

"It is, Mr. Vacit. Some call it Teeptown, as a matter of fact. That's the square, there—bars, restaurants, a few shops. Those larger buildings on the hill there are the dormitories for the children and singles. Married housing is down that way."

"I thought it would be more like a military base."

"We try to minimize that feel. Teeps are not ordinary enlistees, as I'm sure you know. Most come from civilian backgrounds, and though they find themselves more comfortable here, with other teeps, than they did out in the 'mundane' world, we want them to have some of the comforts of the lives they've left behind. If you know the military, you know the people on military bases are always trying to get off base. Most teeps would rather stay here, though, where they are safe. But given that factor of isolation, we try to make life as—you'll excuse me, Akimba— 'normal' as possible."

Kevin nodded as they walked along. The buildings were mostly new and fresh, unpretentious ceramic brick, a hue removed from natural earth tones, topped with high, pitched roofs. More than anything, the complex resembled some of the self-towns that had sprung up in rural areas over the last few decades—homages to an earlier time. Simulated small towns, as it were.

He saw a lot of children, fewer adults, the occasional uniformed cop or functionary.

"Metasensory has four legs, as it were. First and foremost, its function is education. Teeps are taught how to use their powers and how to control them. The younger we get them, the better."

"What about the parents of the children?"

"It's something of a boarding school. The parents can visit, the kids can go home on holidays—if they're deemed able to control their powers. It's not perfect, but it works. Eventually, most kids end up feeling more at home here than with their parents—I suppose that's inevitable. Of course, most kids who are teeps have at least one parent who is also a teep, so we have whole families here, too. Many of the children were

born here. In fact, we'll be having our first secondary school graduating class in just three years. An exciting day."

"I look forward to it."

"Education goes beyond teep abilities, of course. All of the usual courses are offered, but we try to steer people toward careers for which they are best suited. Here, for instance, we have the school of law enforcement, and there the verbal arts college. And, of course we have a military prep academy.

"The Authority no longer draws on government funds—that makes it one of the most popular programs with taxpayers. We hire teeps out to private business, where they monitor deals—on a mutual-consent basis, of course; to the courts, which I know you are familiar with; and to EarthForce, where they mostly serve in Alliance security."

"And Senator Crawford oversees all of this."

"It was his dream—one of them, anyway. Lee has many dreams. Yes. Very little happens here without his knowing about it—which means *you* have to be up on it all. And so now you understand the precautions we are lavishing on you."

"I hope I'm found worthy. It's exciting."

"Some of our detractors don't think so," Tom said.

"I've heard some complain that the senator has too much influence."

Tom smiled sardonically. "I don't doubt he is the most powerful man on the planet. I think you're bright enough that I don't have to explain why."

"If—may I ask you something candid, Mr. Nguyen?"

"You can certainly ask."

"You've been his aide for a long time—since the beginning. Why are you—"

"It's personal. Very personal. I'll just say that I think Lee deserves a better aide than I." Tom looked down, seeming embarrassed. "He needs someone, Kevin. Someone he can trust. Someone who will always tell him the truth when he needs to hear it. Somewhere along the line, that stopped being me. If you can't do it, get out now. At this point, you haven't seen too much, you don't know too much. You can go your own way."

"Does that mean you can't?"

"My options are somewhat more limited, for reasons of security. Yours will be, too, if you stay long and then decide to quit. But if you want to be near the throne, there are prices to pay. I've been at the center of the world since back when it spun in a different direction. I can't stay here any longer, but I don't regret a moment of it."

Kevin nodded. "As long as we're being honest, can I ask another question?"

"Shoot."

"The stunfence. The concertina wire."

"Ah. You noticed that. Ostensibly, it's for the protection of the teeps. In reality, too—we've had many threats and a few isolated attacks on the complex. The local normals don't much like the teeps. But as with any boarding school, we also have our share of would-be runaways." He paused. "It's not a perfect world, and this isn't the perfect solution."

"I wasn't criticizing, just asking. If I'm to do this job, I need all the information."

"Just keep an open mind. And don't be fooled by Lee's country-boy act. He's a very sharp old fox, and he just keeps getting sharper." He swept his arms wide. "This is all yours now, Mr. Vacit, and welcome to it."

Kevin was left wondering if Tom Nguyen meant Teeptown—or the world.

3

Lee and Kevin found Blood sitting on a bench near the playground. Shrieking children swung, climbed, bounced, and ran through its brightly colored labyrinth.

"Mornin', Desa," Lee called, as they approached.

"Good morning, Senator. What can I do for you?"

"We need to have a talk, I think."

She nodded, focusing her dark eyes on Kevin expectantly. Lee took the hint.

"Kevin Vacit, this is Desa Alexander, chief field operative for the Metasensory Regulation Authority."

"We've met," Kevin said, stepping forward.

"You seem familiar." It sounded like a challenge.

"You were in Houston last year, on the Richter case."

"Yes, of course. That was a bad one."

Lee cleared his throat, and changed the subject. "The hearings start tomorrow. I think we need a game plan. What have we got on this guy?"

Desa turned her gaze back to the playground. "Nothing," she said. "Lai is so clean you can eat off of him."

"No one can be that clean."

"Yes, well, the problem is we can't deep scan him. He has teeps with him."

"That should make it even easier—"

"They aren't ours, Senator."

Lee's face went a little stony. "Ah," he said.

"Yes. But even without them, he would feel a deep scan. I'm no politician, but I think that would be a bad move just now, since involuntary scans are unlawful."

"Family? Friends?"

"Nothing we can use. This guy is one hundred percent career, Lee. Reminds me of someone else I know." She waved a diffident finger at

Lee, then brought it thoughtfully to her chin. "There are, of course, more extreme solutions."

Lee shook his head. "No. Too high profile. If Lai turned up his toes or went missing—in the public mind, it would only prove that he was onto something. Anyway, Lai is only the tip of the iceberg; I've got a sizable minority in the Senate against me, and making Lai go away won't make the problem go away. So we have to cover ourselves, then. That might be harder." He paused. "He says he has proof that you killed that railroad cop in Prague. Is that possible?"

Desa looked up with a faint smile on her lips. "Are you asking me if I'm guilty, Senator?"

"Hell, no. I don't care, and I certainly don't want to know. If they have teeps, that's the last thing I want picked out of my head. I just want to know if it's possible that they have some evidence against you."

She shrugged. "Anything is possible. But I very much doubt it."

Lee made a sour face. "It may be a bluff, a ploy to try to get us to do something stupid. Is everything else covered?"

She crossed her arms. "If you mean do we look legal, yes."

"That's not what I mean, and you know it." He turned to Kevin. "Do *you* know what I mean?"

Kevin casually pushed his hands into his pockets. "The way I see it," he began, "is that for the past fifteen years everyone has pretty much looked the other way. People wanted teeps regulated, and that's what they got. But times have changed—teeps have been a legitimate part of business and the courts for more than ten years. They have their sympathizers, now. And to be frank, Ms. Alexander, your people haven't always used as much restraint as they might have."

"Damn straight, son," Lee grumbled.

"Listen," Desa said, her voice flat and dangerous. "For fifteen years now, *Senator,* my people and I have been saving your ass. If people start to wonder why Menshikov went silent and quietly retired, why Karl Dressler had a nervous breakdown, why Muhammad Ifriqiya dropped mysteriously off the face of the Earth—you're going to blame that on *my* lack of restraint? Don't ever doubt we're married in this. Ever." She stabbed her gaze at Kevin. "And you, little boy. I know you want to make a real big impression on your boss, here, but don't *think* to do it at my expense. If the senator hasn't made this clear, let me spell it out for you. *Teeps* made Lee, Lee didn't make teeps. He knows that, I know that, and if you want to stay in this business, you better know that, too."

Kevin cocked his head and met her ferocious eyes.

"Ms. Alexander, I say what I see. Sometimes I don't see everything. All I'm saying is that times are changing. We've already established that

all our fates are linked. Mistakes have been made. It's my job to help you fix them. If either you or the senator have a problem with that, maybe I need a new job."

He looked significantly at both of them.

Desa turned her gaze thoughtfully toward Lee. "He has some guts, doesn't he? He might do."

"Yep." Lee sighed, joining her on the bench. "Maybe we needed some new blood." He was silent for a moment, then nodded at the playground. "Brenna out there?"

"Yes, watching the younger kids."

"You must be proud. I hear she tested P10."

"Which one is she?" Kevin asked.

"That one," Desa said, pointing. "The one with the reddish-brown hair. It's her birthday. Fifteen."

"The future," Lee said. "Makes me feel old."

Desa grunted, still watching her daughter. "You *are* old, Senator."

The din in the Senate chamber diminished to a hush as Lai cleared his throat.

"We'll come to order," he said. He waited another moment, then directed his gaze toward where Blood sat, all business in her neat, brown uniform.

"State your name, please?"

"Desa Alexander."

Lai nodded. "Also known as Blood?"

"That's my nickname, yes."

"Could you explain that, please?"

"It's personal, Senator, and I don't see how it has any bearing on these hearings."

Lai shrugged. "Just curious. It seems apt somehow."

Blood smiled.

Lai shuffled through a few sheets of paper. "Might it have anything to do with a religious cult known as the *Katun Prophecy*?"

Blood felt her eyes widen, and at the same moment, she felt a familiar tickle at the edge of her senses. Then she snapped up her guards, mental and facial. "I don't know what you mean by that."

"Ms. Alexander—Blood—weren't you the leader of a religious cult known as the Katun Prophecy?"

"Not to my knowledge."

Lai nodded, as if reluctant. "Perhaps my information is wrong, then. Ms. Alexander, can you tell us what you do?"

"I work for the MRA. I enforce the EA laws regarding telepaths."

"Do you? Do you do anything else?"

"I raise my daughter. I'm active socially. Is that what you mean?"

"Not exactly, but we'll get back to that. You say you enforce Earth Alliance laws. And yet I have three affidavits that claim you enforced these laws in non-Alliance countries. Again, I must confess that I'm very confused. How can Earth Alliance laws be enforced outside of the jurisdiction of the Earth Alliance?"

"They were criminals, Senator. I extradited them. It's a matter of record."

"Indeed it is. But the funny thing is that when I checked those records I found the extradition process occurred *after* you apprehended said criminals."

Blood shrugged. "I don't recall any such instance, but I wouldn't be surprised if that were the case. In many situations, the criminal is taken in the process of crossing borders, so jurisdiction becomes messy."

"I see. And so you consider, for instance, breaking into a private residence in Christchurch, New Zealand—a country with which the Alliance doesn't even *have* an extradition treaty—and abducting four people to be only a little 'messy'?"

This time, Blood managed to repress her shock entirely. "Senator, I have never done such a thing. None of my agents has ever done such a thing. Because I have not done these things, I know for certain that you have no evidence that I did—so why are you saying this?"

Lai took a sip of water. The floor was entirely still.

"Ms. Alexander, I never speak to things I cannot prove. I will demonstrate that you have, in fact, seized telepaths in decidedly unlawful ways. I will also prove that you willfully and maliciously have murdered civilians over whom you have no jurisdiction whatsoever. Furthermore, I will show that the anecdotal evidence of your own actions fits a larger pattern. One that represents an extraordinary abuse of power by your organization."

A single pair of hands clapping filled the silence that framed his pronouncement. Blood turned along with everyone else to see Lee Crawford, applauding.

"Well, that's entertainment, isn't it, folks?" he said. "It certainly is. High drama. But you know, I'm one of those fellahs you *hate* to sit by during a movie. The one who'll poke you every five minutes and say 'Now what just happened there?' and 'Who is he?' Because I like things to be kept real simple. So do you mind if I ask Ms. Alexander a few questions?"

"Senator—"

"Exactly. This is a Senate hearing, and I am a senator, or at least you seem to think so."

A few chuckles broke the stillness then, and Lai nodded reluctantly.

Lee clasped his hands in front of him. "Ms. Alexander, as an officer of the Metasensory Regulation Authority, perhaps you're aware of the history of your organization, more aware than someone outside of it. Did you study its charter?"

"Yes, Senator—it was required reading."

"And who created the MRA?"

"The Earth Alliance, Senator."

"More specifically."

"The Senate."

"You mean *this* Senate?"

"Yes, Senator."

"Hmm. My, my. And who oversees it?"

"The Senate."

"*This* Senate? You don't say? This whole time?"

"Yes, Senator."

"Why do you expect that all of a sudden this Senate pretends it has no idea what your organization does?"

Blood shrugged. "You've got me, Senator."

"Well, we're together on that. Let's talk about you, Ms. Alexander. You've been doing this job for a while?"

"Fifteen years."

"And in that time, you've often been accused of the sorts of things Senator Lai is talking about?"

"Senator, it's a matter of record that I have not."

"But you haven't been praised for your performance either, have you—oh, *wait*, Ms. Alexander! Are those medals I see on your uniform?"

"Yes, Senator. The Gold Shield and the Crossed Arrow."

"I seem to remember those are awarded for outstanding service to the Earth Alliance and for bravery, integrity, and honor."

"Yes, Senator."

"Who awarded those medals to you, Ms. Alexander?"

"The Senate, sir."

"What? *This* Senate?"

"Yes, Senator."

Lee nodded and looked over at Lai. "Senator Lai is sort of a young fellow. Do you think all of this happened before his time?"

"I like to think I'm not all that old, Senator," Blood replied, smiling faintly.

"Well, you don't look it—and neither do I, for that matter." That

drew a few chuckles, too. "Ms. Alexander, are you familiar with Senate hearings?"

"Yes."

"Are you aware that when charges are made, they are usually accompanied by evidence at the moment of the charge?"

"Yes, Senator, I've always been of the understanding that that's the usual procedure."

"How do you feel when you see an exception to that rule?"

"I think it's a bluff—grandstanding. I think the accuser is trying to get the media to pick up his unsubstantiated assertions—to create a perception of guilt in lieu of real evidence."

Lee nodded gravely. "That's how I've always felt. Senator Lai, how do you stand on the matter?"

Lai pursed his lips, and then flashed his enigmatic grin. "I'm just setting things up, Senator. Just making certain the issues are all clear. I thank you for clarifying them." He continued, addressing everyone in the room. "As I will show over the next several days, it is indeed the Senate that has made the pertinent mistakes here. It is the Senate that must correct them. In the next few days . . ."

Blood lost him, then, because she felt the touch again, and this time she recognized it. She swept her gaze around the audience, around, until . . .

He had dyed his hair brown, and surgery had changed his features more than age, but when she saw his eyes, she knew him. Even through her blocks she heard his soundless laughter.

Monkey. It is you. How have you been?

Hao. And you?

What are you up to Monkey? What do you have to do with this?

Everything, I'm afraid. End of the line, Blood. You took the wrong track. I'll give you one more chance to get off of it. I can help you disappear. But this is the end of it.

"Ms. Alexander?" Kevin repeated for the third time.

She finally looked up, gathering her thoughts, focusing on the myriad bright slices of sail and pennant that shifted out over the blue-silver surface of Lake Geneva.

"The senator asked me to speak with you," he repeated.

"Where is he?"

"He wanted to be here, but I insisted he stay out of it. He doesn't need to know the answers to the questions I'm going to ask you."

"Ah. Plausible deniability."

"Something like that."

"Maybe you don't want to know either, little boy."

"It is, of course, my job. So I'll take my chances. Let me start with the New Zealand thing—"

"He's bluffing," she said, sharply. "That was clean, I know it."

"Couldn't you be wrong?"

"No. It was clean."

"Then how does he know about it?"

She shrugged. "He has teeps with him. They could have picked the story from several minds."

"So it wasn't all that clean."

She quirked her mouth. "You're a lawyer, right? Didn't I hear that you've handled cases using teeps? Then you know that kind of evidence is completely inadmissible without corroborating data. And I'm telling you, there is none." She pressed her fists together. "Same with everything else he says. He has a teep working with him, a P12—"

"How do you know that?"

"What?"

"That he's a P12?"

She rolled her eyes. "It's a guess, based on what he can do. Do you want to hear this?"

"Sorry."

"He can know some of these things, but he can't prove any of it. I'm sure."

Kevin ticked his finger on the marble balustrade. "Then he can't—" He paused to think about it. "He isn't doing what we think he is, then. The hearings aren't the point. What *is* he up to?"

Blood leaned back. "I don't know." She looked more intently at him. "You have a strange mind, you know that? Mechanical, almost. Too— something. Almost doesn't feel real."

"That's rather impolite, don't you think?"

"I can't help it. A normal couldn't understand. This close, I can no more avoid seeing the shape of your mind than the shape of your nose. Does that bother you?"

"No. What I meant was—well, you wouldn't tell me I had a big nose or ugly eyes, would you? And yet you tell me I have an unattractive mind."

"I didn't say I find it unattractive. What do you think you would see if you could see my mind?"

He considered. "Wild horses. Knives. A whirlwind. I don't know. You certainly don't look like someone who ought to be wearing a uniform."

She shrugged. "I have something I have to do. It happens to coincide

with what the senator is doing. I have to wear this uniform for it all to work." She reached for his face with her gloved hand.

He flinched away, just slightly, and she sighed and lowered it. "So, what do we have? Hearings that must be a cover for something else. Something his teeps are doing?"

"Maybe. Listen, can you see the 'shape' of Lai's mind?"

"Yes."

"Do you sense any deception coming from him?"

Blood shook her head. "No. But that might be a screen put up by one of his teeps. I don't think so, though—I don't think even a P12 could do that to me. But I suppose it's possible."

"I'm not a teep, but I'm pretty good at reading people, and I don't think he's bluffing either. Which probably means someone else is using him. Which means . . . what *does* it mean?"

"I don't know," Blood said. "But I'm going to find out."

Kevin had never met Alice Kimbrell-Crawford before, but he recognized her immediately, despite her disheveled hair, the streaks in her no-streak makeup, her red eyes. Leaving Lee's office, she passed him in the corridor, obviously in a hurry.

He knocked on the door she had just closed. "Lee?"

"Get out."

"Lee, it's Kevin Vacit. It's important."

"I said *get out.*"

Instead he stepped in, and closed the door. The lights were set to minimum, and Lee Crawford was just a shadow behind his huge desk.

"Whaddyou want?"

"Lee—the hearing?"

"Th'hell withit."

"Lee, have you been drinking?"

The senator rose unsteadily, lifting a bottle of bourbon from behind the desk as he did so.

"Drinkin'? No. I've been changin' my blood for something better." He lifted the bottle and threw back another few swallows, stumbled over to the leather sofa, and wobbled down onto it. "Damn legs, don't work worth a damn anymore. Time was—time was—" He coughed. "You get old. Things stop working. People die. People *leave*—" He looked up at Kevin, a spark of anger in his eye. "What do you think of me now, eh? The great Crawford? The Moon hero, the teep savior—"

"I think you're drunk. That's about the size of it."

Lee wagged a finger at him. "I know about you. I looked into you. Zuni Indian—"

"No, only part—"

"Everyone's part somethin' these days. Part this, part that. 'S a good thing. People think they're pure they start killin' each other. I didn' mean nothin'—except you were like me. Grew up dirt-poor. Made somethin' of yourself. Pulled somethin' out of that bastard, the universe, that he never ever intended you to have. Am I right?"

Kevin was silent for a moment. "Something like that."

"Yeah. I can sense it. I can feel it. That's why you're still here. Tom didn't have that—little rich kid. But I liked him, anyhow. Can you believe that? I loved him, even after him and Alice—" He choked off a hoarse laugh and then took another drink. "I'll miss him more than her."

"Maybe that's why she did it."

Lee rose jerkily to his feet and stalked over to Kevin, stood there swaying in front of him. "You little shit," he whispered. "You little—" He swayed another second or two. "Shit. How *dare* you be right?"

"Why did you marry her?"

"Liked her. Part of the game. Good wife for a hero, all's well that ends well. *Loved* my first wife, look how that turned out. Thought it might go better this way. But damn—I think, in the end, I loved Alice, too. Funny how that kinda thing sneaks up on you." He stumbled back to the couch, then turned his dimming eyes up to Kevin.

"Thumb that switch, will ya? That 'un by the desk."

Kevin found the small plate and pressed it. Above, the ceiling became space and stars.

"Where are they, you think?" Crawford wondered. "I know they're there. When I was a little boy, I used to shine my flashlight at this star or that, thinkin' one day they'd see my message. All this other stuff—teeps, the Mars colony, everything—it's all just markin' time. The real thing is out there, the aliens that'll finally make us Human." He looked at Kevin. "You know what I mean?"

"I think so, Senator."

"It's the only thing I really dream about. I'm gonna be around when it happens. I'm gonna be there. The bastard can't stop me. Before I die, I'll see them, face-to-face." He took another swallow, sputtered on it. "We'll show him, won't we, Kevin? Show that bastard. I did pretty good today, didn't I? Made Lai look pretty silly. I've still got some left."

"Yes, sir."

"You're a good kid, Kevin. If I'd ever had a son—"

"Let me put this up, Lee." The bourbon bottle had dropped from Crawford's hands. What little remained in it was leaking onto the polished slate floor.

"Show 'im," Crawford mumbled, throwing his arm over his face. He might have been weeping.

Kevin put the bottle up, then returned to where Crawford had begun to snore. He turned him on his belly, in case he should become sick, and sat there beside him for a moment, the legend that stank of rotted corn and charcoal filtering.

"Don't worry, Senator," he said. "We'll show him. You just rest."

4

Blood glanced around the Senate chamber. *Where are you, Monkey?*

She couldn't feel him at all, today, but he could do that, if he wanted. Make himself a pane of glass. She didn't see him, either, but he might be disguised as anyone.

Lai was getting his notes in order.

Kevin Vacit was right. Something was up. But what?

Could it be so simple as getting the media stirred up? That didn't feel right, not with Monkey involved. Monkey was better than that. For years he had been the biggest thorn in her side, there again, gone again, clever and slippery as ever. If he was here now, where she might get her hands on him, he must be playing for very high stakes indeed.

And if he was here today, it would be a mistake. Ten MRA agents were planted in the crowd. Plainclothes. Good ones.

The room fell silent as Lai stood. She stole a glance at Lee Crawford, who looked a little green, and at Kevin, who seemed to be searching the crowd as much as she.

"I call to order," Lai said. "I would like to continue my questioning of Ms. Alexander, if it please the Senate."

Blood nodded. "I'm ready. Senator."

"Very well. Ms. Alexander, can you tell us where you were on August 16, 2132?"

"Of course. I was on train 1116 from Amsterdam to Prague. We had information that a family of illegals was trying to reach India."

"Why India?"

Something was strange. She couldn't place it at first.

"Ms. Alexander? Why India?"

"Hmm? Because they give refuge to illegals. Though an EA member state, they aren't signatories to the Crawford-Tokash act."

"I see. So you were chasing this 'dangerous criminal'—Didier Krijgsman, a traffic flow analyst—his wife, Mary, and their ten-year-old son, Len. Is that right?"

She had it now. The minds in the room were silent. Even her own operatives. Someone—or several someones—were blanketing the proceedings. Why?

"The law is very clear," she said. "They broke it. I was trying—"

Who could have told Lai about Prague? There were no witnesses, only Teal and the rookie—

She stabbed her eyes around the room.

"Ms. Alexander? You were saying?"

She saw Daria, six rows back, and sent her scan there, brutish, cutting through the film of silence like a knife through paper.

Felt Daria's hand, lifting something.

Then she saw it all.

"Ms. *Alexander*—"

"Senator Lai, get *down*." She shouted at the top of her lungs, at the same moment springing up from her seat. Daria's dismayed face settled into a mask of determination, and her hand jerked up. Blood would never get there in time.

But she didn't have to. The line was drawn, two eyes triangulating, and she punched her leg against her seat, launching herself into space, just as the weapon flashed. A wind blew through her, a strange feeling, and she hung for what seemed a long time in the suddenly bright air before slapping into the seats.

Pain filled her in a great rush, then, and screaming. She could not sort out the vocal from the shrieking of minds, but it didn't matter.

Agony continued to uncurl. She couldn't even tell where she had been hit.

Blood! It cut through everything.

Got you, Monkey. Got you, damn it.

Jesus, Blood. Jesus.

Come against me, you lose.

You're the one dying! Damn it, Blood, I didn't want . . .

"Ambulance!" Someone was screaming. Mind images of herself fell on her like rain. She was broken, lying across the seats, a hole punched through her chest.

You wanted to make it look like MRA did it. The rookie here, in plainclothes, but she would be caught trying to escape, and then they would discover she was one of our agents. They'd think we killed Lai because he really had some evidence. But now they'll dig deeper, find out she's one of your little rebels.

Just hang on, Blood. They've sent for an ambulance.

(laughter) You lose. You know I loved you, right?

(pause. sick feeling) No. How could I? God, don't die, Blood. If only you'd said something.

Skip it. We made better enemies than friends. Come here, though, I want to tell you something.

Everything else was slipping away. Only Monkey remained, his face as she remembered it, young, full of laughing mischief. *Come here. Let me give you a kiss.*

He came, closer, and when he was close enough, she seized him. Something was pulling her down—she had a weird image of herself flowing into a straw, a thirsty god sucking on the other end.

Blood, no!

Come along, old friend. Let's see this together. Let's go see the Sorcerer.

Down, farther, her thoughts tearing away from her one by one. It was as if she were made of fireflies, and now they were all free, spinning out into the maelstrom. And Monkey, terrified at last, squirming in her embrace, howling.

The last of her began to fall away, and Monkey went with it. Then her grip loosened. He rocketed up, out of the vortex, seeking life. She watched him go, no longer caring. Her last remembrance as the lights vanished was of her daughter, Brenna, and her last satisfaction was in knowing that Monkey would never know he was her father.

The Night, the Wind . . .

The Night.

UP wire service, 3 September 2133

In a desperate move to discredit the MRA, rogue telepaths last week tried to assassinate Senator Philip Lai. The attempt was made by Daria Beaudain, a rogue telepath who had infiltrated the ranks of the MRA. A full investigation has been launched into the matter, and there is some suggestion of involvement on the part of certain members of the Senate.

Senator Lai expressed his remorse over the death of Desa Alexander, who ironically sacrificed her life for his, even as he was accusing her of murder. Said Senator Lai, "A truly moral man knows when to admit he has made a mistake. I may not be truly moral, but I do strive to be, and I here, now, humbly admit a terrible error. One that cost the life of a courageous woman, and for which I can never forgive myself.

"I allowed myself to be deceived by people I thought I could trust. I have scrutinized the alleged evidence they supplied me, and now judge it to be unquestionably false. I only hope the public can

forgive me my haste to judge. The experience has left me wiser and much, much sadder."

When asked for his comment, Senator Lee Crawford, the head of the Senate oversight committee for MRA, said, "The loss of Ms. Alexander was a terrible one. She was like the daughter I never had, and my grief is too private and strong to commit to public record. As for Senator Lai, I'm only happy that the MRA was able to perform its function; without her metasensory powers, Desa would never have been able to detect and react to the assassin in time. Senator Lai is as bright a young man as the Senate has seen in a long time, and his concern is evident. If he will agree, I'd like to have him on board the oversight committee—the MRA needs men like him.

"Those who killed Desa, I must admit, make me very angry, but I try to control my anger. Desa Alexander would have wanted me to. What she wanted for her fellow telepaths was a life that was free of fear and violence, a productive and fulfilled life like her own.

"It is truly sad when people fight with such animal violence the very things that are best for them. They deserve our pity and our compassion."

Lee closed his eyes against the bright sun and savored the perfume of forest and water. The delta of the Kinabatangan River was perhaps his favorite in the world, its rickety stilt villages and dense mangroves somehow evoking the Mississippi of Mark Twain in a way that the modern Father of Waters could not. He journeyed halfway around the world to reconnect with the past of his own homeland. How odd, how myriad the ways men and women moved themselves through time.

"You did a good job, son," he told Kevin. "You had it figured close to the bone, close enough for old Blood to do what she needed to do. I will miss her, damn her eyes."

"Thanks, Lee. I wish I had figured it out quickly enough to save her."

Lee shrugged. "Better this way, really. More dramatic. And Blood was a loose cannon, would've gotten us in more trouble down the road. This problem is just sleepin' for a while, not going away. People have short memories, that much I've learned. In a few years, they'll make another try, don't you worry. Until we have the clout to make it global and uniform, the MRA is always going to have its enemies."

"Maybe now, while Blood is still a hero—"

"No. She's popular, but people are still a little too leery of the Authority. The Russian and Indonesian consortiums won't let go of their

own teeps until they're forced to. This won't change that, and we'd just raise issues best left under the loam for the time bein'."

He paused, took a sip of his tea. "I got pretty drunk the other night. Might've said some crazy things."

Kevin smiled, very slightly. "To tell you the truth, you were too drunk for me to make out anything you said. Your southern accent gets pretty thick when you drink."

Lee scratched his chin. "That's a fact? You know, they used us as code speakers in the Kamchatka war, like they used the Navajo in WW Two."

"I don't doubt it."

Lee nodded, then shaded his eyes and looked directly at him. "Anyway, thanks."

"You're most welcome."

Lee watched the flight of a rare hornbill, at peace for the moment.

5

Solar System Today, **18 January 2148**

Interplanetary Expeditions spokesperson Ezinma Roberts today reported the successful completion of an eighth experimental station on Mars, near Syria Planum. The IPX station was built to explore the Martian permafrost and refine the process of creating arable soil. "This takes us another step closer to the permanent colonization of Mars," Roberts proclaimed, "but we're still a long way off. Making a home for humanity on another planet will require the sustained will of the entire world."

"Kind of—as they say—a stuffed shirt, are you not?"

Kevin Vacit glanced sideways at the speaker, a young woman in her midtwenties seated to the left of him on the plane. In the right frame of mind, he might have summoned a mild admiration for her bronze hair, startling jade eyes, and generous lips. At the moment, he felt instead a mild irritation.

"Officer—Davion, is it?"

"*Elle-même.* That is absolutely correct. Ninon Davion, at your service."

"Yes. Well, Ms. Nina Davion—"

"Nin*on.* Use your nose, you know? Nin*on.*"

Suppressing a sigh, he tried another tack. "I'm attempting to read, Ms. Davion."

"And I'm bothering you?"

"You are—distracting me."

"What you are reading—it is important?"

"It is entertaining."

"Ah. As I am not, I suppose." She lifted the corner of his book and peered at the title. "*The Demolished Man.* Yes, it sounds very entertaining." She shrugged, looking away. "It is true, I suppose. They told me this

trip would be no fun at all. *I* said, *no* one can be no fun at all, but *they* said—"

"Who are 'they,' Ms. Davion?"

"Now you ask me a question? Yet how can someone so unentertaining as I provide an amusing answer? No, no—please. Go back to your book. I will sit here, silently."

He blinked. "Thank you."

He tried to read a few more lines, then closed the book. "Do they really say those things about me?"

She hesitated a moment. "You are speaking to me?"

"Ms. Davion, you know I am."

She turned back to him. "Well, they say you are very efficient, very serious, very dedicated—"

"And is there something wrong with that?"

"No, no, of course not." She rolled her eyes. "But look, have you ever been to San Diego before?"

"No, I can't say that I have."

"Neither have I. And what do you intend to do there?"

"I intend to solve the problem that you and I have been sent to solve."

"And?"

"And what?"

"I've heard San Diego is a beautiful place. Food. Wine. Tijuana a very short trolley ride away . . ."

"You do understand, Ms. Davion, that we are on a mission involving EA security? At the highest level?"

"I'm afraid that the level of security is so high that I have no idea why we are going there," she replied. "I certainly hope *you* do. I am just—as you say—the 'muscle.' "

"For muscle, you certainly talk a lot."

"Well! I was keeping silent until you—"

"Sorry. You're right. Look, I promise to debrief you when we reach San Diego."

She placed her hand on her chest. "Sir! I apologize for my opinion of you. You are very forward indeed!"

He actually felt his face warm. He was blushing.

With a little frown he returned to his book, silently cursing Lee Crawford, who had surely done this to him on purpose.

Phillip Stoddard, the head of research for Interplanetary Expeditions, fingered his rusty beard and addressed them with a sort of benign amusement. "I don't really understand what all of the fuss is about," he

said. "When the incident was reported, we imagined an officer of the Authority would drop by, but to have Senator Crawford's own aide here—maybe you fellows know something I don't."

Kevin smiled briefly. "That's always possible, I suppose. But the MRA always takes the death of one of its own seriously. That, coupled with the security breach in—" He stopped abruptly. "Doctor, is this a safe area?"

"Hmm? Yes, of course. The security breach was in lab 16, where the artifacts are housed. But that turned out to be nothing."

Davion cleared her throat, and to Kevin's vast surprise, her words came out very crisp, very professional. "Nothing? Yet it coincided so closely with Mr. Raskov's death."

"Look, I know you guys are paid to be suspicious—but you aren't *serious*, are you?"

"We would not be here otherwise," Davion said.

"Well, look. The autopsy confirms Mr. Raskov died of a stroke, and as for the security breach, that must have been some sort of glitch."

"I'm sure it was," Kevin soothed. "But we have to check it out, you see. Orders. Anything involving the artifacts—"

"Of course. Would you like to see them?"

"Very much so," Kevin replied.

Lab 16 was spacious, clean, white, probably as near the platonic ideal of "lab" as could be reached in reality. Stoddard talked about security as they moved through it. "Getting into the IPX building without authorization would be a problem," he informed them. "Reaching the thirtieth floor would be essentially impossible. Entering this lab—and these vaults—would require the direct intervention of an omnipotent deity."

As he spoke, the vault in question sighed open.

What was within reminded Kevin vaguely of a reptile house; a dark, cool corridor faced by brightly lit windows for the first thirty feet or so.

"When we aren't studying them, the artifacts are kept in the vacuum vaults," Stoddard said, gesturing toward the end of the corridor and a series of sealed lockers. "But you can see some on the tables, the ones we're working on now."

Kevin peered through the nearest window. On the table rested a rough torus mottled by raised bumps. In the next window there was an essentially cylindrical object exhibiting several knoblike protrusions.

"And these were found on Mars?" Davion asked.

"Yes, buried in Syria Planum."

"What have you discovered about them?"

"Nothing new, I'm afraid. They are clearly manufactured, though the

method of manufacture isn't obvious. They don't seem to be cast, or riveted, or welded together. They are made of highly organized alloys, some unknown. Some pieces, despite their appearance, are permeable to visible light, while others are almost opaque even to neutrinos." He smiled broadly. "In other words, we still don't know a damn thing about them except that they are of alien manufacture."

Kevin nodded, still staring. He was struck by an odd and impossible sense of familiarity.

"And the breach—"

"As I said, it must have been a glitch. None of the artifacts are missing—EA security cataloged them independently and prior to us, so I can prove that—nor have they been disturbed in any way."

"Yet the security system registers that there was a break-in."

"A ghost, perhaps. Nothing the cameras recorded."

"Well." With a growing sense of disquiet, Kevin surveyed the rest of the artifacts on display. "I think I would like to see Mr. Raskov's quarters, now."

They broke the security seal and entered Raskov's room. It was a jumbled mess, clearly the product of a disorganized mind.

"The quarters have been sealed since his death?"

"Other than to remove the body, yes."

Kevin paced about as Davion conducted her inspection, taking photographs from various angles, opening drawers.

"Do you have any idea what you're looking for?" Stoddard asked, mildly.

"Dr. Stoddard," Davion replied, "I wonder if you don't have more important things to do?"

He colored slightly and drew himself up. "Yes. As a matter of fact, I do. Buzz my link if you need me." He left.

When he was gone, Davion smiled. "He *is* hiding something, you know."

"Did you scan him?"

"Not a deep scan, no. But his surface thoughts showed some agitation and nervousness. Especially when he was talking about the artifacts. *Most* especially when he said that they had discovered nothing new."

"That's interesting." He shuffled though some papers on the desk. Among them there was a sketch pad, which he flipped open. The first ten pages or so were landscapes, impressionistic, drawn with pencils and pastels. Halfway through the book, however, the theme abruptly changed. First came numerous sketches of insects—a dragonfly, several beetles, many others Kevin did not recognize. On the second page was a

beetle done in pastels—a species he *did* recognize, though he didn't know its name—one of those iridescent green bugs that looked almost as if it were made of colored chrome. It was very well rendered.

The rest of the notebook was filled with similar drawings. Pushing through the loose papers on the desk, he found a few more. And then another notebook full.

"Was Mr. Raskov an entomologist, professional or otherwise?" he asked.

Davion shrugged. "I still have my briefs on, when it comes to that. There was nothing in the record you gave me to indicate it." She peered over his shoulder, her body just touching his. "It seems a recent interest. You see? He has dated his drawings."

Kevin flipped back through. While the landscapes had been done over a three-month period, the bug sketches had all been done in three days—May 3 through May 5.

"He must have drawn almost nonstop, those three days."

"The security breach in the lab was May 5. Raskov died on May 5."

"So you think he became so obsessed with bugs that he had a stroke?" Davion said.

"I don't know. A stroke is one of the easiest things to fake."

"You think he was murdered for an abrupt interest in bugs?"

Kevin tapped his finger in the pad. "Let's finish up here. I want to interview Mr. Raskov's supervisor."

"He was one of our most professional business telepaths," Freda Noy said. Her nearly round face pinched into a broad suggestion of sorrow. "It was such a terrible thing. Did you know him?"

"I did not," Kevin replied.

"Nor I," Davion added. "But can you tell us what friends he might have had here?"

"Not many, the poor man. He kept largely to himself. Telepath, you know." Her olive skin darkened a shade. "Oh, dear, I didn't mean—well, of course you know."

"Actually," Davion said, "Mr. Vacit is, of course, not a telepath. I am, but I take no offense. Many who work outside tend to be introverted. It becomes tiring, trying to *avoid* learning other people's secrets."

Kevin felt a certain inward appreciation. Davion played her bad cop part very well; she kept their interviewees off-balance with consummate skill.

People were worried by teeps, anyway, and by making certain her role was clear, she cast Kevin, by contrast, as the one the normals could identify with, perhaps even confide in.

Now if only he could play *his* part better . . .

"Ms. Noy," he said, softly. "I have here a record of the transactions Mr. Raskov monitored from the early part of May, and I thank you very much for providing it. There is only one I don't really understand—Kuchinsky-Behn?"

"Oh. It's a small biotech firm out of Canada."

"Part of the larger Tangent conglomerate?"

"I believe so, yes."

"The principals of the meeting—Kuchinsky of Kuchinsky-Behn, and Roland Hammerstein from this firm? Is Mr. Hammerstein available?"

"Oh—no, I'm sorry. Mr. Hammerstein has been reassigned to the Sandakan office."

"Perhaps later, then. But you have a transcript of the meeting."

"Oh, of course. Would you like a copy?"

"Please."

Turning to her computer, she called up the file, printed it out, and handed it to him.

"Thank you, Ms. Noy. That will be all for now. I'll probably want to speak to you again."

"And of course, I'll be happy to be of what help I can."

"We'll show ourselves out."

Back in the hall, with no one around, Davion put her smile back on. "I have decided you will take me to get something to eat, Mr. Vacit," she informed him.

"Ms. Davion, we have much to do. If you need something, I'm sure they have a dining room here, or you can order room service—"

"Look at the time, Mr. Vacit. Six o'clock. Work time is over, I believe, and you will find no one else here to interrogate. Now, please, you don't want me to confirm those rumors about you, do you? I had hoped to be able to laugh in their faces—tell everyone that it only took a French key to unlock the wit lurking inside of you."

"Ms. Davion, I'm working on what is proving to be a difficult matter. I am not, by training, a detective, and yet I am being asked to do the job of one. I—"

"You are frustrated. Your mind is as tightly wound as your ass. Unwind the one, and the other will uncoil as well. So said my grandfather, a very wise Andorran man. Really, I must insist—for the *good* of the investigation."

He nodded in sudden understanding. "For the good of the investigation."

* * *

Outside, strolling down a sunlit walkway, he glanced at her. "Okay. What didn't you want to say in the building?"

"You can be a bit thick at times, can't you, Mr. Vacit?"

"I suppose. I'm sorry it took me so long to catch on. So what was it?"

"I don't feel in the mood for conversation just yet. As I remember it, you've agreed to take me to dinner."

"I thought we'd just established that that was only to get us out of the building."

"Oh, no, I meant everything I said. And I think Italian will do quite nicely."

"Ms. Davion, I have no idea why you've become so fixated on this quest to 'unstuff' my shirt, but I assure you—it isn't at all appropriate."

Davion showed her dimples. "Not bad, for Italian wine. It has a certain primitive vitality."

"We could have found a French restaurant, I suppose," Kevin replied, steadily.

She made a face. "I do not eat 'French' food when I am abroad. It is too brutally disappointing. With Italian, the potential for disappointment is so much smaller."

"Ah."

"You do not like food, do you?"

"I eat it. It keeps me alive."

"As I said. You do not like it."

In response he took another bite of his cannelloni. "Oh, my God," he said. "Delicious. It makes me want to sing." He put his fork back on the plate. "Now, will you *please* tell me what you discovered back there?"

She rolled her eyes—yet again—and set her glass down. "You are so determined not to enjoy yourself. Here you have the company of a *very* beautiful woman—"

"Yes, I do."

She stopped, clearly surprised. "Really? You find me beautiful?"

"Of course. But you work for me, and—"

"Ah. And I am like the food, *n'est-ce pas*? Very well. Two things. First—do not bother to read the transcript of the transaction Raskov monitored—it is a fake."

"Really."

"Really. The second thing is this what's-his-name—Hammerstein—wasn't really assigned to the Sandakan office. She doesn't know *what* happened to him, and she's more than a little worried about herself."

"About her job?"

"Her life, I think."

He picked at his food, avoiding Davion's challenging eyes. "So we have a teep who monitors a business deal. It was a secret transaction, probably illegal, and they killed him."

"I think so. But we cannot prove any of it. We cannot prove the transaction is a fake. We likely will be unable to find either of the principals to subpoena, but if we do they will simply quote the forged transcript. A simple scan will show they are lying, but of course such information is not admissible in court."

"Spectral evidence," he murmured.

"Say again, please?"

"Nothing. But what has this to do with the security breach in lab 16?"

"Perhaps nothing. A coincidence."

"I have very little faith in coincidence."

"Or anything else, it seems," she mused. Her green eyes flickered devilishly. "I believe after dinner I should like to have a walk on the shore."

"Fine. I hope you enjoy yourself. I'll be in my room, trying to work this out."

"Take your shoes off," Davion said. "Get your feet wet in the surf." She was doing just that, playing tag with the edges of the breakers, shoes in hand, slacks rolled to her knees.

"I'm allergic to seawater."

"Yes, I'm sure you are." She came back to him, and to his alarm and discomfort, took his arm.

"You have an interesting mind, Mr. Vacit. Did you know that?"

"So I've been told."

"Oh, really? What was her name? Should I be jealous?"

When he didn't answer, she squeezed his arm. "Ah. A secret. *Another* secret. You are a man of secrets, Kevin Vacit. You are made of them. I do not even think a telepath could pry them out of you."

"Have you tried?"

She laughed. "Yes, of course, I'm trying right now. But I haven't scanned you. That's what I mean—I don't think I could. Certain normals have the equivalent of blocks—nothing telepathic, just a kind of order, of discipline. Your mind hums like a clock, Mr. Vacit. I would not dare try to scan it for fear of being pinched by a gear."

"Aside from the fact that such would be illegal," he reminded her.

"Besides that, yes. I like my job, and would not care to lose it."

"You do, don't you? And you do it well. I hardly recognize you when you are working."

She laughed and kicked at the spray. "I'll take that as a compliment. Two compliments from Mr. Kevin Vacit in a single day. Quite an accomplishment, you know." She let go his arm and ran back out into the surf. "I love the sea. It is very alive. I love the feel of it. All the little voices."

"Voices?"

"Well, not voices, actually, just a sort of—something. I suppose only a telepath would notice it. There's nothing to read there, of course, nothing intelligent—though I should like to scan a dolphin someday. No, it's just a kind of—loud quietness."

"But telepathic? You get impressions from non-Human life?" He knelt and ran his fingers in the water.

"I do not think it is my imagination. I suppose everything living must have a mind, in a way. I can sense animals, of course. Not understand them, really, unless it's something simple like hunger or fear. The ocean I don't understand at all, though I touch it and listen very hard, but something is there. It *is*." She considered him. "Poor normals. It must be like missing a sense of smell, or something."

"Yes," Kevin said absently. "Yes, it must. Thank you, Ms. Davion."

"What for?"

"The evening. And perhaps the solution to our puzzle."

"I don't understand," Dr. Stoddard said. "You've already seen them."

"I have. I wish to see them again. It's about the security breach."

"I've explained about that."

"Oh, yes, I know. Would you care to explain why the records of the hour during the breach were erased?"

"What? They weren't erased."

"Oh, yes, they were. Very professionally done, but when I had my own people go over them again, with finer analysis, we found evidence of it."

"But nothing's missing. Nothing was disturbed."

"No. No, I think that's correct. Tell me, Dr. Stoddard, what does one need to enter these vaults?"

"The right key codes. The right retinal prints."

"If someone entered the right key codes—but without the retinal prints—what would happen?"

"An alarm would go out."

"And that would register as a security breach."

"I—yes."

Kevin nodded distractedly. "Let me tell you what happened, Dr. Stoddard. On May 1 or thereabouts, you asked Mr. Raskov to do you a

favor, one somewhat outside his function as a business telepath. You had developed a suspicion about the Syria Planum artifacts, and on a lark you decided to test your hypothesis. You brought him in here, and he touched one of the artifacts."

"Why? Absurd."

Kevin ignored him. "Two days later, Mr. Raskov was contacted again, this time to monitor a business deal. He was chosen because the deal concerned the artifacts, and what he himself had discovered about them. Rather than expose another telepath to that discovery, you chose to use the one you had already tainted. This meeting was a secret negotiation—perhaps to sell technologies, perhaps to position certain stocks for what you think may be coming soon—and by 'you,' I mean both yourself and IPX, Dr. Stoddard."

Stoddard was turning pale. He wasn't good at this.

"In any event, it wasn't easy, but knowing what to look for, I was able to trace a flow of funds, so I can prove this part of my story, too.

"When Mr. Raskov conducted his monitoring task, perhaps someone grew concerned. He may have looked—drawn, fatigued, as if he hadn't slept in several nights. He may have said strange things, acted a bit unstable. Maybe he even demanded to touch the artifact again. Our records show he had a strong artistic—and somewhat romantic—streak. You probably refused. He lifted your key code from your mind and tried to break into the lab the night of May 5. He didn't succeed, of course, but that was alarming enough that someone here—perhaps you, perhaps a superior—thought it best that he quietly expire. And so he did."

Stoddard was still pale, but managed an insincere smile. "I don't believe you can prove *any* of that."

"I don't care if I can. Open this door. I want to see one of the artifacts."

"You don't have clearance—"

"Of course I do. I have presidential clearance. I've shown it you once. Do you want to see it again?"

"No."

"Then open the vault."

With obvious reluctance, he did so, and gestured for them to enter.

"No, you first, please."

Stoddard stepped in, and they followed behind him.

At his nod, Davion removed her gloves. She went to the strange torus, hesitated for an instant, then touched it lightly with her fingertips.

She jumped back as if stung. "Oh, my God, yes!" Her green eyes were the size of coins. She stepped forward again, tentatively, and

touched it again. Her face worked through a variety of strange expressions before she removed her hands.

"It is—it's very faint, you understand. My reaction was from the strangeness, not the intensity. But yes. This thing—I can feel it, as if it might be alive."

Stoddard looked as if he were very close to tears.

"Some men are coming up, with guns," Davion said, suddenly. "He signaled them with some kind of silent alarm on his link."

"How far do they have to come?"

She stared at Stoddard until a sweat broke out on her forehead. "A few floors."

"Five minutes or so?" He shrugged. "Dr. Stoddard, by that time our own team will have the building secured. You didn't think I would accuse you, here, without adequate preparation? You've played a violent card for no good reason."

Now Stoddard started to cry in earnest. Tears ran down his face.

"There, there," Kevin said, without any actual sympathy in his voice. "It isn't as bad as you think. Stand your troops down so we can avoid any unpleasant little firefights, and I'm going to explain to you how you're not only going to avoid prosecution, but retain your position, as well. Do you understand? Is this getting through? The only difference is that you will no longer be dealing with Kuchinsky-Behn, or anyone outside IPX. Anyone, that is, save *us*."

Stoddard's eyes were beginning to clear. "But Raskov—"

"Died of natural causes. Though I will insist that the Authority receive very high compensation for what was obviously a work-related accident. Am I clear on this?"

"Yes."

"Stand them down."

Stoddard went to a wall phone, punched in a number. "Code 4. Cancel," he said.

"There," Kevin said. "You see what happens when you jump to conclusions?" He looked back at the artifact. "Organic technology. It's been tinkered at for centuries, with no results. Do you really think you can reproduce it?"

"I—I honestly don't know."

"But it seemed worth the risk."

"Yes."

"Next time—when you want to take a risk—come to *us*. I think you will find it much less dangerous—and much more profitable—than any alternative. Do you understand this?"

"Yes, Mr. Vacit."

"Ms. Davion, will you walk Dr. Stoddard outside?"

"My pleasure, Mr. Vacit."

When they were gone, he regarded the artifact for a long moment. "Who made you?" he murmured quietly. He reached his fingers out and touched the surface. For a moment he felt the most profound wonderment he had ever known, a surge, accompanied by that nagging feeling of familiarity. And insects, beautiful, creatures of starlight and mist, seemed to dart behind his eyes.

He withdrew his fingers and went to join the others.

He had just removed his shoes when the knock came at his door. It was Davion, of course.

"Ms. Davion—"

"Now, now, Mr. Vacit. I have come to congratulate you."

"No need. It was you who gave me the solution."

"Ah, *oui,* but you put it all together so prettily. The biotech firm. The drawings. Wonderfully done—and I had begun to suspect you had no imagination. And your bluff—about our forces already being in the building—magnificent."

Somehow, as she was talking, she had slipped in the door, was standing very close. He could feel her breath on his face.

"Ms. Davion," he said, gently, "I really—"

But she stood on tiptoe and kissed him, very lightly, and it felt like lightning jolting though him.

"Really what?"

"I really don't think you know what you're getting into, with me."

Her smile went away, and her gaze crystallized on his.

"I'm very good with secrets, Mr. Vacit," she whispered. "Very, very good with secrets."

"You'd better be," he murmured, drawing her near, and gently pushing shut the door.

6

Beyond the straining oaks, a blue-white crack split the mottled, eggshell sky. It mended itself faster than the eye could blink. Over the wet spattering of marble-sized raindrops, a stuttering tearing sound shuddered the air.

Lee Crawford breathed deeply of the wind from the condensing storm, watching a canopy that was like some great cathedral made of a hundred variegated marbles, grey, black, milk, dark green, not still, but constantly grinding, sluggishly.

"Nothin' like a thunderstorm, by damn," he murmured. The wind whipped a spray of rain in under the eaves, and he gasped in pleasure as it flecked his face. The earth trembled as the sky hammered it somewhere not far away.

When the downpour truly came, it was less interesting—just a steady roar, with no sky to see—so he went back inside. This part of the storm was best enjoyed through the tattoo it beat on the roof.

He poured a tumbler of bourbon, savored its sharp, heady smoke, and stepped into the drawing room. It felt like he had pins in his knees and back. His body ached all the time—never with great pain, just all the time.

Kevin was there in the study, shuffling stacks of books and two monitors.

"How's it looking?" Lee asked.

Kevin glanced up. "It's been better, Lee." Kevin's hair had as much iron as ebony these days, but for an instant he looked to Lee as when he had first seen him, boyishly serious.

"Well. We've seen this before, haven't we?"

"Yes, we have. But there's no stopping the hearings this time. And this time they have the goods, I'm afraid. The Chiapas incident made too big a splash. Japan, the Indonesian Consortium, Amazonia, and New Zealand are all threatening to pull out of the EA if President Robinson pushes further for a universal MRA."

"It's just an excuse," Lee muttered. "The EA is hanging together by a thread anyway. Teeps are just one issue."

"That's true, but—do you remember the American Civil War?"

Lee rolled his eyes and waved his hands around at his mid-twenty-first-century antebellum revival house. "What do you think?" he snapped sarcastically.

Kevin chuckled. "I forgot where I was. Then you may remember that the war was brought about by a whole complex group of economic and social issues—but it was the moral issue of slavery that proved to be its focus. It's the same here—give the people something they can hang on to. You're right—the Earth Alliance is trying to tear itself apart for a thousand reasons, but the Chiapas incident has given it a popular voice. You have to admit, a hundred rogues dying, singing in a church, while our officers stood outside—"

"It's not like we set the damn fire." Lee sighed. "Damn psychopathic martyrs."

"But the perception that they would rather die than be regulated by the Authority, *that's* the point. People generally like martyrs."

"Don't they," Lee said, taking another sip. "Even if it means letting the world go to hell in a handbasket."

Thunder growled in the distance—the heaviest of the rain had already passed. The evening would be nice—damp, whippoorwills. He could fall asleep on the porch, rest . . .

He sighed and stood. "Vacation's over, Kevin. Call the airstrip and tell them we want to leave within the hour."

Kevin nodded. "It's already done," he said. "And Shell is waiting upstairs to help you pack."

"Good." He paused. "Kevin?"

"Yes, Lee?"

"Why are you still with me?"

Kevin frowned. "What kind of question is that?"

"A sensible one. Everyone else is gone. Alice. Tom. Those that didn't leave me are dead. You could've—hell, after that thing back in '43 you could have run for office yourself—yet thirteen years later, you're still workin' for me."

"And you could have run for president ten times and won. Why didn't you?"

Lee smiled. "And take a demotion?"

Kevin returned the grin. "And now you have *my* answer. Besides that—" He looked down at the table, then back at Lee. "Besides that, I'm proud to work with you, Lee."

Lee felt his eyes growing moist. Damn, but he was a sentimental old

fool. Was this what the first signs of senility were like? "I'm proud to have you with me, son. I can't even say how proud."

Shell Alexander flashed him a smile as he entered the room. She was placing his suits in a hanging bag. As with Kevin, he was stunned by a moment of déjà vu. It could have been Blood standing there.

But Shell was not Blood, and on second glance didn't even look much like her. Her thick tresses were brown rather than midnight, her skin pale. Her eyebrows flirted with being red, and her chin was longer and narrower than her grandmother's, tapered. No, Shell resembled Blood in much less tangible ways. The set of her stance, the flicker in her eyes, the way her hands moved. Like many in the "kith" of the Authority, she had kept her grandmother's name, as well. Mitochondrial descent, they called it.

"Hi, Uncle Lee."

"Afternoon, Shell. I'm sorry to have to ruin your day like this. I know it's goin' to be a terrible thing to have to see your fiancé back in Geneva."

She shrugged. "He's okay. They certainly could have picked someone worse for me to marry."

"I thought you fancied him. Michelle, just say the words, and I'll—"

"Hush, Uncle Lee. No. I don't want special treatment. My grandmother wouldn't have wanted that, nor my mother. I'm her daughter, and I'll set a good example."

Lee patted her shoulder. "You're a fine woman, Shell. A credit to your mother and her mother. You should be proud to bear their name."

"I am," Shell replied. "Now. Do you want all of these suits, or just—"

She was cut off by an inarticulate yell from below. For an instant, Lee felt his blood freeze. There hadn't been an attempt on his life in years, but—"

"No, it's okay," Shell said. "It's just Kevin. He's excited about something. I can't . . ." She trailed off as Kevin burst into view. He was grinning like a cat, something Kevin rarely did.

"Senator, you better get downstairs. You aren't going to believe it. You really aren't."

He put the image up for the tenth time.

"I knew they were there," Lee whispered. "By God, I knew they were there."

"That ship must be a kilometer long. At least."

"Where are they from?"

"We don't know. The guess going around is Proxima Centauri."

Lee nodded. His eyes felt damp. "Damned if I didn't do it. I lived to see it. The most important day in the history of humanity." He looked around at Kevin, Shell, the rest of his staff. "Remember this moment. Tell your children about it. Nothin' will ever be the same again."

Matthieson, G.

"The Alien Within, the Alien Without: Rethinking the MRA." In *Comprehensive Modern History: An Anthology.* Teller, Brahe, and Asanji, eds. Chicago: University of Chicago Press, 2210.

It is widely believed that the arrival of the Centauri saved the Earth Alliance from collapse, for on April 6, 2156, differences between the key nation-states seemed irreconcilable. By the evening of April 7, however, mankind had begun to unite in a way unknown in Human history. The differences between Arab and Israeli, Malay and Chinese, Japanese and Gaijin were suddenly understood as superficial and trivial in the face of the true unknown, the Centauri. Some may claim this overstates the case—after all, there are still social, religious, and status conflicts on Earth that sometimes turn violent. The true student of history, however, can see the difference. In 2156, a clear line was drawn that has never been crossed since—with one salient exception.

Out of all humanity, one group was suddenly elevated to a new status of persecution. When it was discovered that the Centauri—and the other alien races they spoke of—also had telepaths, many on Earth suddenly suspected Human telepaths of being part of some sinister alien design, perhaps of being aliens themselves.

Suspected of acting as spies, saboteurs, and agents of cultural subversion, telepaths were once again subjected to levels of violence not seen since the horrific year of 2115. Then a countering sentiment arose—that if aliens had telepaths, Earth most certainly needed them, too. This logic prevailed in the end, but only after much bitter loss of life.

President Elizabeth Robinson was not a physically big woman, but an immense sense of presence radiated from her steel-grey eyes. Her squarish, ebony face had character to spare, more so in person than what was portrayed on the nets.

"Senator Crawford, it's wonderful to see you again."

"The pleasure is most certainly all mine, Madam President," Lee said.

"Please, have a seat. Coffee?"

"Please."

She signed, and a man brought them each a cup. "Well, first, let's congratulate ourselves, shall we? I know you've worked for the formation of a universal registration and an independently chartered MRA since before I was born. Today, you got your wish."

"I couldn't have done it without your help."

She shrugged. "Thank William Karges for saving my life. Thank the Centauri for showing up. Thank the fates. After that, I'll accept your thanks." She took a sip of her coffee and set it down. She leaned back and peered at him over steepled fingers. "However, unlike those others, I have a favor to ask."

"I'm inclined toward favors, Madam President. What do you need?"

"I'd like you to resign from the Senate."

He blinked, but could find no answer. He was still searching for one when she went on.

"The charter for Psi Corps calls for its administrator to be appointed for life, by the president. I need you there. You have the know-how, the staff—you've been with the MRA since the beginning."

He grinned. "This won't make you popular with some of the folks in the Senate."

"This is my last term. The hell with them. You're the man for the job."

Lee pretended to muse for a moment. "I wasn't lookin' forward to another campaign anyway. Madam President, if you want me, you've got me."

"Perfect."

"Madam President, I was wondering . . ."

"Senator?"

"I realize that access to the Centauri is still very limited. Even the Senate has not yet been allowed to meet one of them. But—I'm an old man. I've waited my whole life to meet a real, live alien. I wonder if I might have my wish indulged."

She took up her coffee again. "I think it a matter of the highest security that the head of EA Psi Corps meet with the Centauri ambassador to discuss the telepaths of both races. After all, our visitors claim we are their long-lost colony, don't they?"

"You sound skeptical."

"That would be putting it mildly. But—the first permanent ambassador will be here in a month. I think I can arrange a meeting within the first week."

"Madam President, I will be eternally grateful."

* * *

"I'm sorry you can't come, Kevin."

Kevin shrugged. "It's okay. I'm just concerned about security."

"So are they, apparently. Your car can follow me to the compound, anyway. I doubt I'll be long inside."

"I'll be waiting outside when you're done. You can tell me all about it over a drink."

"As if you would have one." Lee started to get into the car, then turned back to face his aide. "I was damn sorry to hear about Ninon Davion, Kevin. I know you two were friends."

Kevin nodded almost imperceptibly. "She died doing her duty. She would have wanted that."

"I feel sorry for the little girl."

Kevin cleared his throat. "Better get going, Senator."

"Right. See you soon." He ducked into the car. A moment later, it began to move silently forward.

He watched the streets of Geneva as they glided by. Buildings a thousand years old side by side with offices that looked as though they had been built yesterday. He thought about the books he had read as a child—the classic twentieth- and twenty-first-century novels. How many times had first contact been written about? How many times had the future been imagined?

Sometimes you recognized that you were living in the future, and sometimes you did not. He had been the boy with the flashlight, standing beneath the stars, shining Morse code up, hoping it would be seen. He had traveled through time, eighty creaking years, to finally see what that boy dreamed of.

In the end, time travel had hurt more than he ever imagined it would, but it was worth it. Worth the old bones, the shortness of breath. It was worth it because he had kept his eye on the prize. It was worth it because, by damn, *his* journey would be remembered.

The car did something strange; a sort of hiccup, and then another. He watched with incomprehension as the window he was staring out was suddenly mottled by snowflake designs, accompanied by a vague vibration but no sound.

Then there was light, terrible, terrible light, and sound at last for an instant before his eardrums were gone. And then blackness.

He awoke, probably a few seconds later, to pain like he had never imagined. One of his eyes didn't seem to be working, but the other puzzled at what it saw for a few moments before recognizing blood, the sharp end of a bone sticking out of his thigh.

His breath was sucking in his chest, which felt as if syrup were filling it up.

Bastard, he thought. *You bastard.*

He meant, as always, the universe.

He lay there, as his breaths came shorter and shorter. Couldn't they have waited another hour? Just another hour?

He wondered where everyone was. Kendra, Alice, Tom, Blood, Shell—Kevin. He would like to see Kevin again.

He would like to have seen a Centauri, damn it.

And then Kevin *was* there, bending over him. He tried to reach the boy's face, wipe the tear from his eye, but his own blurred . . .

He blinked, and a Centauri was there. He must have heard the explosion, come out of his compound to see what all of the fuss was about. He looked exactly like they had on the nets, hair swept back, face Human—and yet not. Sharp teeth.

"Got you, you bastard," he told the universe.

And he died.

That was damn nice of you, Kid.

The voice came from the darkness; Kevin couldn't pinpoint quite where. If he concentrated he probably could locate the source, but it wasn't worth the effort. He wiped his eyes.

He deserved it, he sent back. *Despite it all, he deserved that, at least, to see a Centauri.*

I don't think I've ever seen you cry, Kid.

I haven't cried—I haven't cried since my mother died, holding me.

And now you get sentimental about some normal—not just any normal, but the bastard who was responsible for Psi Corps.

Monkey, you don't care about anything as long as you can blow things up.

I didn't see you objecting. You could have stopped me anytime. I'm strong, but there's never been anybody like you, Kid. Even Blood never recognized you. I'm the only one who has ever known, and that's only 'cause I raised you.

No, there was one other, Kevin sent. *Which reminds me . . .*

(slight resignation) You gonna do me now, Kid? You probably could, but I wish you wouldn't.

No. This has all worked out pretty well. You have the underground, and now I have Psi Corps. No, I need a favor. He sent Monkey the images. A woman, an infant.

Holy shit. When did you ever have time to get a baby on someone?

Kevin smiled at the bittersweet memory of precious hours and days

stolen here and there over the last ten years. Ninon had been required to marry a teep, of course, and Kevin had never been able to tell anyone but her his own true nature. He had worked too hard and too long to cover it.

She had understood. Ninon had been the greatest risk of his life, but she had been worth it. And the miracle that she had had his child, so shortly before he lost her . . .

There was time, was all Monkey got.

You don't want your kid in Psi Corps.

No. Some unpleasant things are going to happen in Psi Corps in the next few years, and I won't be able to protect her if she is there. But you can protect her.

I'm gettin' pretty old, Kid.

Not too old. Her name is Fiona. She's only two months old. Take good care of her.

I'll fight Psi Corps, Kid.

(shrug) I don't care. Just don't get my daughter killed.

What kind of game are you playing? I don't understand this at all.

Don't worry about it. Just do what you do. Help the rogues all you want. I may even be able to help you from time to time. But if you get caught—if you get caught, I may not be able to help you.

You were always a strange one, Kid. Good luck.

Good luck to you, too, Monkey. And Monkey?

Ook?

Don't tell her about me. She can't know.

And Monkey was gone. Kevin stayed with Lee until the police and the ambulances got there, and after. He touched the tears on his face and wondered at them.

"Goodbye, Lee," he whispered. "You showed him. You showed the bastard."

Then he straightened, and went out to do his job.

PART 3

Resistance

Resistance

1

The scream was her compass. Fiona kept it in her mind, as she had been taught, turning it around to see where it was clearest. That still gave her two corridors to choose from, so she took the left one.

It was an old school: floor, wall, and ceiling tiled with ugly but nearly indestructible Vibralite—what Grandpa Monkey referred to as "tech-nouveau riche" architecture. It was the logic of a whole era—you come up with a cool new synthetic and you build everything out of it, no matter what the cost to the senses.

Half the buildings in Malaysia were Vibralite. Architecture may have taken a more aesthetic turn, but Malaysians were pragmatic—if it was still in good shape, use it. It could have been the national motto. Vibralite would still be in good shape when the Sun went nova.

The best thing about the stuff was that it was like paper to psi powers. She whisked past roomfuls of normals and suppressed their uncontrolled babbling as background noise; the scream was still clear, the pain, the confusion. She had to hurry.

If she had known more about schools, she would have found him more quickly, but she had never been in one before—her education had always been dealt with on the go, through netlinks, home schooling, tutors.

But eventually, following the mental cry, she found the school nurse's office—or so the label on the door proclaimed. An agitated man in the uniform of a guard and a frowning woman in a brightly colored Muslim head scarf turned to scrutinize her as she arrived.

"Is that where he is?" she asked. "Is my brother in there? Please, I have to see him."

The look she got was rather peculiar, and a surface mindflash showed her why: the boy huddled inside, in tears, had features darkly Dravidian—an ethnic Indian. Her own skin was light, her hair auburn.

"He's adopted!" she said, desperately. "What's wrong with him?"

"We've called the doctor, young lady," the woman said. "I really think it best you wait until they arrive."

But Fiona knew that was a lie even without a surface scan. Grandpa Monkey's com mole had picked up their call to Psi Corps. Which was why she was here.

"You have to let me see him," she repeated.

"Young lady, do you have any identification?" the guard asked pointedly.

"Not with me."

The administrative type frowned. "Stay here with Mr. Bao," she said. "I'll be right back." *(suspicion)*

Right, Fiona thought. *You're going to call for more muscle. You know this kid doesn't have a sister.*

She had only a few seconds then, so she did something she really hadn't wanted to do. She walked toward the door, as if agitated, and then pretended to trip. The guard reached out to catch her—and she fugued him. His eyes went wide and blank, as whatever his last thought had been began suddenly repeating itself, freezing his mind in the moment. It wouldn't last long. It also left her worn-out, and her blocks slipped, so when she opened the door the boy's mental keening was almost too much for her.

He was there, curled up on the floor, maybe twelve years old, just like the image she had read from the guard's mind.

Come on. Come with me if you want to be free! she sent, as strongly as she could.

"Make it stop!" he shrieked hysterically. "Make them all stop! It's cutting me up!"

I'll make it stop, I promise, but first you have to come with me.

"Please—"

Come on!

He responded to the order, coming jerkily and uncertainly to his feet. She grabbed his hand and practically dragged him through the doorway.

By the time the guard started shouting, the boy finally got the idea. She put the thought in his mind that running would get him away from the voices in his head, and once he thought that, she had a hard time keeping up with him.

The front doors of the school had locked automatically by the time they reached them—except that she had propped one open, so the bolt poked impotently out into thin air.

After that, fifty steps got them to the scooter, and she had the boy on it, and they were racing away from the school. There was no pursuit.

The boy started calming down. He was strong, but not so strong that the voices of other children could follow him this far up the little road. They rode into hills and palm plantations, where stray thoughts were few.

But she needed to prepare him, for soon they would be among the sprawling factories and rise housing of Kuantan, where his newly opened and unprepared mind would be assaulted once again.

Look, she told him. *You're okay. There's nothing wrong with you. You're just special, that's all.*

I'm a demon. Auntie Po said—

You aren't a demon. You're just like me, a telepath. I'll take care of you. Now the first thing. You have click-builders?

That's for little kids.

But you had them?

Yeah.

Good. Pretend you have a whole pile of them. Pretend you're building a wall around yourself, one clickbrick at a time. See? Here, I can help you . . .

By the time they got to Kuantan, he had a thin but adequate block up.

She pulled into Lot 66 feeling triumphant. The restaurant was empty—they served only the evening meal, which gave them the daytime to transact their real business. Nearby, the South China Sea rolled crests of sunlight toward the shore. The scent of chili, ginger, and lemongrass mingled with salt wind. Grandpa Monkey stood in the kitchen, grinding the spices in a stone mortar.

What the holy hell did you do? Sounding just as pissed off as she thought he would. His ancient face looked like an apple shriveled around God's own frown.

You weren't here. We got the call. If I had waited for you, Psi Corps might have gotten him. (defiance) Besides, I'm a big girl now. Hell, I'm nineteen! How long are you going to try to keep me from doing my part?

You do your part, smartmouth, and don't argue with me. Of all the stupid—

Oh, yeah, I get to do tactical. Build bombs, but never set them off. Look at maps, but never make the steal-and-run. You train me and train me for everything, but all I do is sit behind a com-link. I'm—

The training is for emergencies, not so you can run off and get yourself killed—or worse, caught.

"Well," she said aloud, "I *didn't* get caught, did I? I'm not stupid. I know the nearest Psi Corps precinct is in KL! That's half an hour even by—"

But she stopped abruptly, as both she and Monkey turned to stare at

the boy. Her words had triggered a mindflash in him. All of their eyes went round as an image shouted itself, of a man in a black uniform, with a bronze and copper badge, bending over the child.

"Shit," Monkey said. "Psi Corps has already been at him. That means—" He stopped, staring upward. "Choppers! Go, Fiona. Take the kid and go. Get to the old temple." *Your father is going to—* Then the thought snapped off, as it always did, when it came to her father.

"Oh my God," she said. "I led them right here. I led them—"

He grabbed her in a rough hug. "Go. Now. You might make it. I have to crash the system, you get it? Go!" And he shoved her out the door and toward her parked scooter.

I can't leave you!

Damn straight you can. What did I teach you? Jeez, Fee, I'm over ninety! How much longer did you think I was going to make it, anyway? I can't run anymore, and I can't fight. But you can. Next to me, no one knows as much about things as you. So they can't have you. Too many people count on you. Go!

But you . . .

Not to worry. Love you, Kid. Now get the hell out of here.

She had been moving all along, almost propelled by his insistence. She mounted the scooter, got the boy up behind her, hit the switch, and whirred away.

Monkey sighed and looked about the restaurant. It was very old— once it had been open-air, but the heavy pollution and fires of the early twenty-first century had led the owners to close it in. He poured a glass of shaoxing, dropped in one of the little dried shrimp one drank with it, and raised the glass. "To you, Blood, whichever hell you're in. Teal, Smoke, Mercy—" He paused and shrugged. "—Kid." He took a drink of the wine, and waited.

He didn't have to wait long. The door burst inward, and four men in black, close-fitting armor jackets stepped in, eyes glittering with jubilant cruelty. Psi Corps Hounds, not exactly chosen for their table manners. Behind them followed two Psi Cops, pistols trained on his heart.

"Hello, folks," he said, raising his glass. "What can an old man do for you?"

The Hounds surged forward, but the lead Cop—a tough-looking black woman—restrained them.

"Jack O'Hannlon. I have many warrants for your arrest. And the confiscation of your property."

Monkey laughed. "Jack O'Hannlon. Now there's a name I haven't heard in a very, very long time. I don't much think I care for it."

"Please stand up. Slowly."

"Sure thing, sweetie. But to be fair, I have to tell you that what you have here is your typical 'beep-beep-zip-bang' kind of situation."

The Psi Cop nodded to her men, who started forward cautiously. "I don't follow you."

"Not a fan of twentieth-century vids, eh?"

"Can't say that I am."

"Well, here, I'll explain it. 'Beep-beep,' that's the call of a certain flightless bird. 'Zip' is the sound of something moving very fast. And 'bang,' well, bang—" He grinned and raised the glass.

Even two hundred yards away, the shock of the explosion twisted the scooter off the road. Fiona managed to take it on her leg, shielding the boy with her body, but they ended fetched up against the embankment. She turned her eyes in horror to the mushroom of black smoke rising into the blue Malaysian sky.

"Grandpa . . ." Her mouth worked soundlessly for a moment, and she began trying to crawl from beneath the cycle. Then she was suddenly paralyzed by whole new kind of pain. In dull incomprehension she looked at her grotesquely twisted leg. Her head suddenly felt very large, as if it were a balloon expanding. The last thing she saw was a black Tawanaka sedan pulling up a few yards away, the Greek letter "psi" plainly emblazoned on its doors.

2

Kevin Vacit sighed wearily as he settled behind his desk. At seventy, he had no right to feel and look as well as he did, but that didn't stop him from wishing he felt better.

He began going through the daily reports, and did feel better. Twenty new registered teeps, one a potential P12—and as good, some fourteen detected who had somehow slipped through the Corps' fingers. Evolution.

The somewhat rough birth of the Central African Block was finally smoothing out, and commercial teeps were once again profitable there. The rebuilding was going well on Mars, and EarthForce had requested five more telepaths to keep security tight on the Red Planet.

His desk link burred. "Sir?" his secretary asked.

"Yes?"

"One of the interns to see you."

"An intern?"

"Yes, sir."

"What does he want? I don't have any appointments, do I?"

"No, sir. But she says to tell you her name is Alexander. Natasha Alexander."

"Oh. Send her in."

A moment later the door cracked, and a young woman stepped through. He caught himself staring; the resemblance was striking. Oh, of course she was a woman—quite beautiful at that—but with that queue of flaming red hair and upturned nose, she so strongly resembled Monkey that he almost expected to hear his first mentor's taunting voice in his mind.

Then she turned, and he couldn't see it anymore.

"Sir?"

"Sorry, Intern," he said. "You reminded me of someone."

"That would be my mother, Michelle Alexander. I understand that

the two of you were friends—that you worked for Senator Crawford together."

He nodded. "Indeed. I was fond of your mother. I was sorry to hear about her death."

Natasha met his gaze levelly. "I miss her. She was a good friend, perhaps my best. But the Corps is mother and the Corps is father, sir."

"Yes," he replied. "I'm glad we can be a comfort to you. And I hope you further understand that the friendship between your mother and I was just that—between us."

"Oh—yes, sir. I've come to ask no favors of you."

"Good. I've followed your progress, of course. You've been a model student here and an exemplary intern. I wouldn't want to see you mar your record by seeking some sort of favoritism. After all, as you say, the Corps is mother and father—and good parents cannot play favorites."

"I understand completely. No, sir, I've come to you because of something I discovered in my research. I thought I should bring it to your attention, personally, myself."

"Why did you feel the need to do that, rather than passing it up through proper channels? I assure you, I review all research that's done here."

"Yes, sir. But some things my mother said led me to believe it was best I come to you directly. I tried to make an appointment—"

"—but the director doesn't see interns by appointment, I know. I have to admit, Ms. Alexander, you've piqued my curiosity. Exactly what did Michelle tell you?"

"That you and she shared a common curiosity about the origins of telepathy. It was almost an obsession of hers, and I gathered that you were—um—very interested in it, too."

He allowed himself a smile. "Yes. It's an important question, don't you think? Those in the know realized very early on that teeps must have been the product of genetic manipulation. That was before my time, of course, and the knowledge was suppressed to prevent panic. They were already killing teeps in those days, and the idea that some government or corporation had created teeps for some devious, sinister reason—" He broke off. "Are you saying that you have the answer?"

"Sir, I have the beginnings of an answer."

"What might those beginnings be?"

"That we've been looking in the wrong place. After sixty-five years, I think we can be certain that it was no corporation or government. For one thing, we still don't know exactly how telepathy—much less telekinesis—operates. On the genetic side, we've come to understand that the

level of sophistication required to engineer it would have produced spin-off technologies that we simply have never seen."

"Agreed. But this is nothing new."

"I've turned up something new, sir, but I don't know what to make of it. Perhaps you will."

"Go on."

"My specialty is actually in history and anthropology. I was hoping to be placed with the proposed applied social sciences division, but it never materialized."

Kevin shook his head. "No. Normals aren't quite ready to have their lives planned by teeps."

"Of course, and so I'm interning as a business teep. I'm only a P5—"

"Nothing to be ashamed of. Speaking as a P-aught."

"I know. Though I think Mom was disap—well, that's neither here nor there. My point, sir, was that I did a rather involved project on the syncretism and evolution of twenty-first-century religious cults."

He nodded for her to go on.

"You see, when times change rapidly—or catastrophically—there is a tendency for people to become dissatisfied with traditional religions and seek something new. Looked at historically, we see flashpoints in which hundreds of small religions arise—the two best examples I can think of are the early Christian era and the late twentieth century. And now, of course, in the wake of the Centauri and the perspective that brought . . ."

"I'm familiar with the phenomenon. Sort of a natural selection process, wouldn't you say? A variety of new religions are born, and those that best satisfy the needs of people survive. The rest vanish."

"Yes, sir. You can count on one hand the number of actually new religions in the last two thousand years that have lasted. Anyway, that's what I studied. Obscure, I know. I was looking at the twenty-first century, which for the most part was a period of winnowing—the hundreds of late twentieth cults were dying out and consolidating. But I ran across a small anomaly."

"That being?"

"A number of small cults floresced in the twenty-sixties. At first I thought they were hang-ons from some of the late twentieth astronaut/angel cults—"

"Astronaut/angels?"

"Yes, sir. That's really a glib label for a broad phenomenon. Velikovskians, Raeleans, Heaven's Gate—it was basically a belief that aliens had visited or were visiting Earth, that our cultures, religions, destinies, perhaps even our genetic makeup had been shaped by ancient, godlike as-

tronauts. Our legends of gods and angels and so forth were supposed to be race memories of those visitors. We now see the cults as an effort to syncretize science with ancient modes of belief, and most of these cults had waned by the twenty-twenties."

"But they came back in the twenty-sixties?"

"Briefly. That stands out because they all peaked in popularity during a three-year period between 2059 and 2062. After that they faded again, and by the end of the next decade, there is no record of them—as such."

"The timing aside, what's so odd about that?"

"If you excuse me, sir, I don't think the timing is aside—it's the point. My great-grandmother—this isn't well known, sir—before she joined the MRA, my great-grandmother Desa was something of a, ah . . ."

"She was a mercenary, a grifter, and at times a thief. I knew her well. Anything dubious she did in her youth was more than made up for by years of faithful service and her heroic death."

"Yes, sir. As you say. In the early twenty-one-teens she led a religious cult—purely a scam on her part, she never believed in it. It was a sort of Mayan-prophecy religion, but with very strong echoes of the astronaut/angel cults. So I checked, and sure enough, she had pieced her phony religion together from some of the things her father *really* believed."

Kevin leaned forward, frowning. "What are you saying?"

"I checked membership against the teep registration base, and did some basic genealogical extrapolation. I found that sixty percent of registered teeps are descended from a member of one of those cults. The other forty percent I don't have enough data for. I also ran the stats for the general population—only one person in two thousand living today had ancestors in one of the cults."

"So it's not a coincidence or an artifact. Teeps really are descended from these cultists."

"Yes, sir."

"How much further can you go with this?"

"Well, I was working on a synthesis—trying to pull together some of the common elements of the various cults. I've also got the locations of some of their worship locales—a cave in Yucatán, an old Buddhist temple in China, a mountaintop shrine in the Philippines. I think those bear checking out."

"You say you *were* working on this synthesis."

"Well, yes, sir. Now I'm an intern in the commercial division, so I won't have time to—"

"How would you like to work with my office? I could put you on this full-time."

She made no attempt to hide her joy at that suggestion. "That would be wonderful, sir."

"Good. I'll make the arrangements."

3

Fiona woke in pitch darkness. She was in a coffin. The walls were of some soft, padded substance that she could not tear.

Air sighed onto her face from a small tube. If she wiggled, she found she could move several inches in any direction. She could turn over, though it hurt her leg, which was encased in a heavy cast. She could not sit up—and she didn't quite have enough room to pull into a fetal position.

"Where am I?" she whispered.

A few instants later she was screaming it, as her limbs began to itch, and then her belly, and her brain. And then she couldn't stand it, the very thought that she couldn't move her limbs through their full range of motion.

She didn't know how long that panic lasted, but finally she grew calmer, used the relaxation techniques Grandpa Monkey had taught her. And she listened.

Almost, there was nothing—only the very vaguest chittering at the edge of perception. She pushed her mind out with everything she had.

Nothing.

She found two more tubes next to the air tube. One provided for water; the other, some sort of tasteless paste. So they weren't trying to starve her.

She tried to reach out again. If only she could find another mind, one that stood beneath the Sun, one that had some grasp on the passage of time—but there was nothing. It had been a faint hope, at best—without line of sight she could have contacted only a teep as powerful as herself.

She passed the time doing multiplication tables, telling herself stories, remembering the hundred landscapes of her life—the rocky hills of Andorra; the cold green beauty of Alaska; the bustling madness of Tokyo, Singapore, New York, Mexico City; a quiet, still night on the waters of Tasik Chini . . .

It all ended, eventually, with her pounding at the walls, screaming

just to hear something. Of all the places she had ever lived, none of them had ever been *silent,* both to the ear and the mind.

She awoke violently. Someone had been talking to her, hadn't they? Telling her something. There was a lingering feeling of comfort, of happiness, that tasted somehow plastic.

Fiona. It was a strong, clear voice. She grasped at it, ran toward it. It was everything.

Fiona, I can save you. But you have to do what I say.

Please, get me out of here.

I will. But first you have to do something for me. You have to promise you're going to be a good girl.

I promise!

There was a brief pause. *(skepticism, biting hard) I don't believe you. You shouldn't lie to me, Fiona. I'll come back when you mean it.*

And the voice vanished as if it had never been.

Hours, days, months, or years passed, she couldn't tell which. She clung to the hope that the voice would return. Just when she knew she was at the edge of madness, it did.

Hello, Fiona.

"Please don't go again. Please."

Are you ready to be a good girl?

I'll do anything you want.

You've been involved with some very bad people. The man you called Grandpa Monkey—Jack O'Hannlon—was a murderer. He raised you, so you can't be held responsible for your feelings toward him, for the crimes you yourself committed at his behest. I can wipe all of that clean. I want to be your friend, Fiona, truly I do, but you have to help me.

How?

You've seen things. You know things. These people are not your friends, Fiona. They are criminals and killers. They planted a bomb, Fiona, in Geneva. They killed a lot of people.

Psi Corps, she answered. *We bombed Psi Corps . . .*

Images suddenly burst into her head. A girl of perhaps thirteen years, most of her face gone. An old man, moaning, reaching for something with a hand he no longer had. A cloud of pain, exquisite and complex. *What do you imagine Psi Corps is, Fiona? They are the villains your brave, heroic underground murdered. Your own kind. People just like you, trying to find a safe place, a place where the normals won't hate them, fear them, kill them. And when they find that safe place, what happens?*

More murder, this time by their own kind. That's what you've been a part of, Fiona.

She didn't want the voice to go away. She didn't. She didn't like what it was saying, but it was far better than silence. She felt as if she were on the edge of a precipice with nothing, nothing at all below her. Only the voice kept her from plunging over.

You lie, she said. *You lie. Psi Corps is slavery.*

The scan hit her hard and fast, the most powerful, brutal attack she had ever experienced. For an instant she nearly surrendered, but Monkey had taught her well. She punched the invading mind back, first by inches, then by yards, threw up levees, dikes, and finally walls that enclosed her. Weeping, she touched the sky of her tiny world, trying to prove herself real, and almost failing.

Her greatest fear was that soon she *would* fail.

She slept again, and the voice came back. Her walls went up automatically, woke her. As soon as she dozed again, the voice came back. It went on, and on, until something in her exploded, leapt out of her, a whip, a blade, and she felt a terrible satisfaction at the cry of pain.

For a time they left her alone again.

And then—so faint she thought at first she was making it up—she heard another voice. When she understood it was real, she first thought it was another trick. But it was too weak, groping in the dark, as frightened as she. And it could not reach her without her help.

Still suspicious, she ignored it as long as she could, then reached out again.

Who are you? she asked.

Who? Who?

Are you an owl, then?

(something like laughter) No. I'm a prisoner, like you. In a little box. I've been here—

The voice weakened, fluttering in her mind like a candle in a draft. She nursed it, as she might a little flame. *My name is Fiona.*

I'm Matt. Matthew. (pause) I think I'm losing my mind. I think I'm making you up.

Maybe I'm making you *up.*

(pause) We have to resolve this, don't we? Matthew said. *Tell me something I don't know.*

That would prove nothing. Descartes said—

Please, no philosophy. That's the last thing we need, some dead Frenchman trying to convince us we aren't real.

I think you may be another one of these Psi Corps goons. What do you think about that?

I may be. Or we may be each other. Maybe we're both insane. All I know is, I feel better now.

Me, too. I—Matthew? Matthew?

But he was gone.

Fiona?

Where have you been? she angrily demanded.

They tried to scan me. I think I passed out.

You're even weaker than before.

I'm okay. I'm just worried that they'll—they'll find out about us.

You mean that wild night we had on the beach in Santa Cruz?

(laughter) Hell, I'd *like to know more about that.*

You picked me up at a party, she began. *It was boring. The host had this ugly little dog he kept trying to make do tricks—*

—and we went to the carnival, and rode all of the rides, until we noticed a dwarf and a giant following us—

—but we got away from them, and when the chase was over, we were on the beach, and I was cold so you gave me your coat—

It was sweater, actually. Then you told me how big and strong I was, and asked if I'd ever been swimming in the Pacific—

Hey, hold it, buddy, Fiona said. *I don't go that far on a first fantasy. Straighten up.*

Sorry. What if we just walk hand in hand and look for starfish?

Better. Much better.

Then we can go back to my place—

And eat pizza. God, I could use a pizza. And a beer.

The next day the other voice was back, but she shut it out. She no longer needed it as she had. What was more, she had no intention of opening even a crack for them to learn about Matthew. It was clear her captors had made some sort of mistake; they had taken pains to isolate her so that the only contact she had was with *them.* They had underestimated her, or Matthew, or both.

"Come on," Matthew said. "I've got something to show you."

They stood in darkness, a thin, cold wind whipping around them.

"Where are we?"

"Just wait."

Over time, their illusions had gained clarity as each surrendered control to the other. It was not exactly like reality, or even like a dream, but like the sharpest of memories.

They sat on a pinnacle of stone, and the sky gradually began to grey.

A line appeared, far away, darkness separating from light, and then, with breathtaking suddenness, a thumbnail of brilliant orange appeared, and a plain of copper. She gasped with the intensity of it.

"That's the Sulu Sea," he said, quietly. "See those dark places? The Philippines."

"It's beautiful."

"This is one of my favorite moments. I climbed up here in the dark. I almost got sick from the altitude, and I sat here, not believing it would be worth it. I almost went back down, while it was still night. Then this . . ." He trailed off as the liquid sun separated from the waters, and the whole world emerged in shades of gold.

"Where are we?"

"Mount Kinabalu, on Borneo. I wish I could see your face," he murmured.

"Oh, if you could see it you might not say that," she said. "It's funny, isn't it? We carry such clear pictures of everything but ourselves." His face, an indistinct oval, nevertheless seemed sad.

"Wait," she said, and concentrated. She brought up the image of a model she had seen on the vids, in magazines.

"Oh!" he said, and then, "No. That isn't you. Put her away. I can wait."

"Wait? Wait for what?" she asked, bitterly.

"We'll meet," he said. "We'll meet, and I'll know you."

"Sure," she murmured. "Sure we will." She looked back out at the flaming waters. "Thanks. Thanks for showing me this."

He nodded. "You're welcome, Fiona." She felt something like an arm going around her, and a flood of warmth, tenderness—

And then searing light, so bright it was painful. She coughed back a shriek as Matthew and the Sulu Sea vanished, replaced by the hideous brilliance and the sudden clashing of metal. She shut her eyes, tightly.

"Get her out," a voice—a real voice, made of quivering air—said. "Put her in compound five."

She was out. Out of the box. They lifted her up, but her legs would not, of course, support her. Two men dragged her along, and still she could not open her eyes.

Matthew? But he was gone, not even a whisper of him left.

4

Stephen Walters grinned toothily at the look of outrage on the secretary's face.

"Mr. Walters," she said, "I'll thank you not do to that."

"It was just a thought, darlin'," he replied.

"Yes. *Your* thought, and quite at home in your foul little head. Please keep it there."

"Hey. Your loss. Is he ready to see me?"

"In a moment."

He put his hands behind his back and took one with the other, glancing aimlessly around the office. Despite his bravado, he was intensely curious. What could the director want with him?

The door opened up, and Walters put on a cocky smile when he saw who came out. "Well, if it isn't my old friend Fedor!"

Fedor's return grin was froglike, so wide was his mouth, and his black eyes shone with good humor. "Hello, *moi droog*. What terrible thing have you done, to be called before the director himself? It wasn't that Turkish girl, was it? I warned you they were funny about such things there."

"I can't imagine what you're talking about, Fedor. And I might ask you the same, you know."

The secretary coughed for attention. "Mr. Walters. The director will see you now."

"Well, it's been nice knowing you, Stephen," the little Russian said. "If you have a moment before they lock you in prison and throw away the key, come by my place. And bring that bottle of vodka you owe me. Potato, not grain, for God's sake."

"I'll do that, friend," Stephen said. He clasped Fedor's hand warmly and watched him go. He brushed his uniform and straightened it, combed his fingers through dirty blond hair, shot the secretary a final leer, and entered the director's office.

"Hello, Mr. Director," he said. "What is it today?"

Kevin Vacit looked up at him. Walters tried not to show it, but Vacit gave him the creeps sometimes. The director had a mind that ran on tachyons, always on top of everything—but behind the now-and-then smile and the benign expression, there was something more alien than even the few Centauri he had met. Something extra—or something missing. It was a good thing, he reflected, that Vacit was not a teep—then he mentally blushed, realizing that the director might have any number of teeps around monitoring him anyway.

"Stephen Walters," Vacit said, glancing at the contents of a file folder. "Born June 15, 2155, in Casper, Wyoming, U.S.A. Joined EarthForce in 2172—served in the 355th North American. Won the EA Silver Star for bravery at the Battle of Douala. Because of this you weren't court-martialed the very next year, in 2173, for striking a superior officer. Served as a mercenary soldier in the CAB until 2175, when you manifested latent telepathic abilities. Eventually rated P8—very surprising for such a late bloomer. Joined the Corps voluntarily that same year. You've been in the special ops division since then."

"That all sounds right, sir."

"You've done mostly undercover work, is that right?"

"Yes, sir. I'm not strong enough to be a Psi Cop, so I do what I do best."

"And I hear you do that very well—except that you are perhaps too enthusiastic." Vacit pulled a new page from the file. "Others are unwilling to work with you. They say you take too many chances."

"I just prefer to work without a net, sir. You can't win a race without getting on the fastest horse."

Vacit locked his hands together and put them before him on the table. "Well, Mr. Walters. I'm going to give you a chance to do what you do best, and I assure you, this time you will be very much without a net."

"The Corps is mom and dad, sir. I'm up for it."

"I'm glad to hear it." Vacit lifted a packet and passed it to him. "Those are the files on one Fiona Temple. She's presently in our internment camp near Kuala Lumpur. I want you to break her out."

"Sir?" He shuffled through the photos. They depicted a young woman, maybe twenty. She was pretty, with auburn hair, high cheekbones, and large, blue-green eyes.

"Ms. Temple was, until recently, a member of one of the most powerful cells in the resistance. We haven't been able to learn much from her; she's a P12, and very good at blocking even the most determined scans. We could dig until she broke, but I think we would lose far too much that way. In the end, I think she would be more useful to us free than interned."

Walters nodded. "I see. The old buddy game. Yes, sir, I'm up to it."

Vacit nodded. "Again, good. But Walters, you speak of this to no one. You report only to me, in the field or anywhere else. As far as the Corps goes, you don't exist anymore, is that understood?"

"Yes, sir."

"And Walters?"

"Yes, sir."

"This woman is important. I don't want anything to happen to her."

"Yes, sir."

"You will have some help in escaping from the reeducation camp—I'll give you the details later. But understand, no one in the camp will know about you. If you misstep, you're just as dead as any rogue trying to escape."

"I sort of figured that, sir."

Vacit nodded. "That's all that need be said just now, then. You'll be flown there in two days. I suggest in the meantime you familiarize yourself with the area and work on your story. Make it close to the facts so your surface thoughts don't contradict what you say. She's good enough to do light scans without you noticing."

"With all due respect, Director—*that* you don't have to tell me. Like I said, I do what I do best, and this is it."

"It had better be, Mr. Walters. It had better be."

Kevin watched Walters go with some misgivings.

Monkey's death had come as something of a blow—he somehow never thought the old man would die, but there could be no doubt this time. It had taken days to find a fragment of him large enough to identify, but forensics not only had confirmed that it was him, but had enough of him to prove he was dead. Of course, it might have been a clone—

No. Monkey would not be able to stand the thought of another *him*.

And Fiona had been captured. He had always known it was a possibility. Monkey had never put her on the front lines, so to speak, but Monkey himself was never far from danger, and Fiona was never far from Monkey.

He had to be careful, very careful. He was sure some of the more powerful teeps suspected him, and perhaps a few senators. One got old, after all. And though none of his enemies was in much of a position to touch him, it wouldn't do to underestimate them. If they were to discover that he had nurtured the resistance, even as he made the Corps stronger—well, he doubted any explanation would save him. Worse, everything he had done would be for nothing.

He would do what he could for Fiona, but daughter or no daughter, there was only so far he could go.

He looked down at his agenda. All routine, all things he had done a thousand times and would do a thousand more.

Then he looked at the new report on his desk, and thumbing through it, felt an itch he hadn't felt in a long while.

He chimed his secretary's comlink. "Has the travel office put together the equipment I asked for?"

"Yes, Director. The team will be ready to leave Thursday."

"Inform them that I will be joining them. Notify Mufwene that he will be in charge for a few days. And get me Ms. Alexander. I want to talk to her."

And there was another thing he had been putting off. "Get me a meeting with the Centauri ambassador, as well."

5

Fiona fell into the filthy water for the third time, choking on the fetor of human waste and dead fish. An involuntary breath sucked the filthy muck into her mouth and nose. Her stomach tried to vomit, but there was nothing in it.

She tried to push up on trembling limbs. Though her broken leg was healed, more than a month in the isolation tube had left her with the resilience of a boiled noodle. The Malaysian sun had raised moonscapes of blisters on her back and arms. The fever that caused—and the lack of food—were no help to her atrophied muscles.

Her arms gave out, and she collapsed back into the flooded rice paddy.

"Get up, you lazy bitch!" The voice sounded far away. She understood that her head was underwater, and that she might well be drowning. She couldn't muster the energy to care.

"Bitch!" And then a jolt that yanked her whole body into a ball, cramped with agony.

Ah, yes, agony. Leave it to real pain to show how sunburn, starvation, and fatigue were nothing but pretenders.

She came out of her ball like one of the cobras that hung around the paddies, uncoiling each screaming muscle in a single motion that ended with her fist displacing the guard's jaw four inches upward. Not a big man anyway, he went back into the sludge, flattening rice as he did so.

She stood there, glaring down at him, as other guards began shouting and a couple of shots were fired.

The downed guard stood, his eyes full of a piggy sort of hatred. She balled her fists.

He advanced, raising his shock stick. She snarled and assumed a boxing stance. Kicking would be useless in this gunk.

The guard regarded her, and then exchanged the baton for a pistol.

"Hey! Hey!" One of the other prisoners was slogging through the water toward them. "Don't!"

The guard quickly shifted his aim.

"Hey! Just wait a minute, fellah!" The man was tall, strong-looking, a dirty blond, even dirtier now.

"You. Shut up."

"Just—hey, listen, man! Look at her tattoo. P12. You know what that means?"

"Shut up!" He cocked the hammer back.

"Okay, okay. But how do you think the Psi Cops are going to react when they come around and find you've scragged one of their possible recruits? How many P12s do you think there are anyway? It's not like she was trying to escape."

The guard narrowed his eyes. "You aren't a P12," he observed.

"No."

The guard slammed his pistol back in its case and strode toward the big man. He hit him in the neck with the shock stick. The prisoner gurgled and folded, but did not fall. Fiona started forward, but two more guards grabbed her from behind. The guard hit the blond man again, and again, and again, until he was still in the mud.

"You mindwitches. You make me sick. You think you are so much better than us. But Osman Taheng will show you who is better. You'll learn that, if nothing else."

He turned back to Fiona. "You will carry him back to the camp. Whether he is dead or alive, you will carry him."

The fellow began to groan about halfway back to the camp, which meant they only had five more kilometers of torturous mountain ridge to negotiate. She had wrapped his arms around her neck, and was dragging him behind her. Fiona had lost count of the times she had collapsed under the man's awkward weight. Worse, the guards were holding the rest of the work gang to her pace. This meant they would be as delayed as she, quite possibly beyond the evening meal, which was meager enough as it was.

All in all, it was better than the isolation tube. Except—

Except she missed Matthew. She hadn't found him since she emerged. For all she knew he was still in his hole. Or dead. For the briefest instant she had thought the man she carried—who had come charging to her rescue—might be he. But a glimpse of his mind was enough to dash that hope.

"Hey—woddja—th' bulls loose mom—" He sucked a long, shuddering breath, and she stumbled again, this time just to her knees.

"'Ey, no—" he said, a little more strongly. "I c'n walggh—" He gagged into silence.

"I doubt that. He hit you seven or eight times. You shouldn't even still be alive."

"Hell, my momma used to do me more times than that every morning."

"Oh. So this is just nostalgia for you. And I was going to thank you."

"Walk!" A guard jabbed her in the back with a stunstick, but it wasn't charged.

"Oh-kay, here we go—" She draped his arm back around her shoulders and heaved him up. His legs kicked a little at the ground.

"Be—still," she grunted. "That's—not—helping."

"Sorry."

A few minutes later, he did manage to get his legs under him again, and she felt more than half of his weight come off of her shoulder. At that point the guard hit him with his stunstick again.

"You son of a—" She choked, as her charge collapsed once more. "I said carry him. *Carry.*"

Which she did, from there on out. If the fellow regained consciousness, he was smart enough not to reveal it this time.

Fiona finished her bowl of rice and cast a longing glance at the one on the ground, a few feet from the unconscious man. She had, after all, carried him for almost ten kilometers. She had burned her calories and his, too.

But that would be what they wanted, and she wouldn't give them the satisfaction, even to fill her still-growling stomach. Instead she sighed and took a look at his wounds. None of the burns looked particularly serious.

At her touch, though, he stirred and hesitantly opened his eyes. They focused on her, and for a moment he looked at her without recognition.

"Oh," he mumbled. "You. Sorry."

"You probably saved my life. No reason to be sorry for that."

"Yes, but you had to carry me."

She shrugged.

"What's your name?"

"Fiona."

"Irish name. Good name."

"Hasn't brought any luck with it that I can see." She considered him for a moment. "On the other hand, maybe it has. I could be dead now. Been here long?"

"A few weeks, I think. Time flies when you're having fun." He held out his hand. "Stephen Walters."

She took it. His handshake was weak, the fingers still trembling. "Nice to meet you, Stephen Walters."

"And you? You just got here, right? I never saw you before last week."

"I was here. They just had me in a hole."

He managed a weak whistle. "What did you do to deserve a hole?"

"I've no idea, but I'm going to try not to do it again." She shifted on her haunches. "Better eat that. They'll take up the bowls soon."

"Thanks for saving it for me." He lifted the bowl and began pawing the rice out, first gingerly, then with greater gusto.

"Where did they catch you?" she asked quietly.

"Angola, in the CAB. The Corps came in the same day they changed the laws. I thought I could slip past 'em. I heard there was some sort of underground, but I didn't have time to make the connection. You?"

"Not far from here, I think. Kuantan."

He seemed to expect a little more, but she left it at that.

He finished his rice, and then glanced back at her. "Maybe I should've gone to Psi Corps." He sighed.

She bit off a harsh laugh.

"Well, it's gotta be better than this."

She frowned. "Is this a recruitment speech?"

He snuffled out what may have been a chuckle and pushed himself, hissing, into a sitting position. "Not hardly. That's not my style either. Not that they would take me now, anyway. You, on the other hand—"

"Yes, you said something about that. What did you mean?"

"I was in another camp, somewhere in the CAB. We had a P12, guy named Tycho. They put him in a hole for a while—then the Psi Cops came and took him. Maybe that's why they put you in a hole—to break you down, get you to join the Corps. That was my guess, anyway, and I saw your rating tattoo, and—"

"Not from where you were standing, you didn't. The rating's too small. How did you know?"

He flashed her a reluctant smile. "I've been watching you, I guess."

"Really?" Her voice sounded a trifle cold, and she was glad.

"Not—not what you think. I mean, you've got a nice face and a sweet smile, but that outfit has to go. And you could use more than a little cleaning up."

"Look who's talking. Look, vacbrain, I appreciate what you did, but—"

"Hey, hey. I'm just kidding. That's not why I've been watching you. Well, maybe it's what got my attention, but it's not what kept it."

"What then?"

"Fire, that's what. You've got some real fire in you. Enough, maybe—maybe to . . ." He trailed off. "Never mind. Guards are coming

anyway, and there may be teep-snitches out there. Some people'll do anything for a little extra food, even sell out their own kind."

She nodded. "Yep. Well. Be seeing you around, Stephen Walters."

"Abacus."

Over the next few days, as they cut ditches to flood several new paddies, she began to feel stronger. The viscous, clinging heat of the Malaysian day was no stranger to her, and her muscles were finally adjusting to being used again. She saw Steve for a few minutes each day, but they mostly just exchanged pleasantries. She searched more for Matthew, but if he was out there, he wasn't letting on. She held on to the images—the sunrise, the house where he grew up, the beach at Santa Cruz. None of it real, of course, and yet somehow more real than what she was going through now.

Monkey was dead. She had tried not to think about it in the hole, but it had come at her in nightmares. Back out here, in the world where he died, she could no longer deny it. He had gone out like she always knew he would, in a big fat blaze of glory.

She hated him for it. More, she hated herself, because it had been her fault. She had led them there.

She jammed her shovel into the ground. My fault. My fault. My fault. A thousand spades of dirt like that. She could fill the world and it would still be true. Sweat stung her eyes, but not tears.

Two days later she burst out laughing, because "my fault my fault my fault" had somehow become *maaf faud,* Malay for "forgiveness heart." Just the kind of stupid pun Monkey would have loved to make. For that matter, it could be *maya faud,* "illusory heart"; or, better, *mawa faud,* "monkey heart"; or *mawa foti,* "monkey photograph" . . .

Now she was crying, but the tears held something of joy in them. What would her grandpa Monkey say? "Fine, you feel guilty. Makes you feel all moral, right? Kid, there's nothin' less moral than guilt. You screwed up? Okay. You want to do something about it or just shoot yourself in the head? Because for a *thinking* being, there are no other choices."

She came to with cold water on her face, thinking that there seemed to be a damn lot of coming to in concentration camps. She opened her eyes to Stephen's grey ones.

"Water break," he said. "You went out, but I don't think anyone noticed. The heat?"

"No. Epiphonic shock."

He blinked. "You say the damndest things, sometimes."

"So do you. What did you mean about me having fire the other day?"

"This isn't a good time—"

"Because if you mean you want help getting out of here, let's do it."

He grinned. "Now?"

"Now."

The grin faded. "You're serious."

"Yep."

He gave her the water cup. "Okay. We'll talk tonight."

They left the food line, moving toward the village "square." The camp was an old *kampung* village—tin and concrete buildings, a few old-style houses up on stilts. Beyond that were the fences, three rows of them, stunfences with concertina wire strung along the top. There were supposed to be mines in between.

"I do have a plan," Stephen said. "But I figured—"

"You need a P12 to do it."

"You aren't scanning me, are you?"

"You'd know. No, it's just obvious."

He shook his head. "No. You've got what it takes to escape, and most of these don't, sorry to say. I need a P12—I need someone like you even more."

"I'm listening."

"Just be ready. Stay on your toes. You'll know when the time comes."

6

Ambassador Vitari grinned his sharp-toothed grin and took a drink of the Evan Williams. He made a face.

"Director, that is a most unfortunate substance."

Kevin nodded. "An old friend of mine used to favor it. I don't drink, myself."

"I am sorry to hear that. Is it serious, this medical condition? It sounds quite serious to me, not being able to drink."

"It's a matter of perspective, I suppose."

He watched as the Centauri downed the rest of the drink, his back-swept hair briefly replaced by his several chins. Vitari's face was somewhat less contorted when it reappeared.

"I begin to warm to it," he allowed. "Now, then. You wished to speak about telepaths. Nasty creatures, I think. Always at your back, you know, helping your enemies to plot your downfall. Still, a great house cannot hope to succeed without at least a few. And the women can do quite interesting things when they put their minds to it." He cackled, slapping Kevin's shoulder. "Did you hear what I said? Put their *minds* to it."

"That's very funny, Ambassador." He tried to sound as if he really meant it, but that sort of thing had never really been his forte. It didn't seem to matter. The Centauri, still delighted by his own remark, was pouring himself a full snifter of the bourbon.

"Yes, telepaths," he mused. "What is it you want to know?"

"Well. Ambassador—I was wondering if you can tell me something of the history of telepaths in the Centaurum. Have you always had them?"

"Aha! You ask a very interesting question. The answer, of course, is no. When we were less evolved as a race, no significant part of our population was telepathic."

"They are the product of evolution then?"

"Not as such. They are an indicator of evolution. I will tell you a peculiar thing, Director. It is a little known—but not particularly secret—

fact that all of the more advanced races have telepaths. The lower ones do not. And so, in the not too distant past, it occurred to us to wonder why this might be so. And do you know something?"

He sloshed a little of the bourbon from the overfilled glass, gesturing obscurely. "We found a sort of marker in the DNA of telepaths, quite remarkably the same among the various higher races. Now, you understand, of course, I mean among races that evolved from quite different sorts of creatures."

Kevin blinked, but otherwise did not show his surprise. "That's interesting," he said. "I wonder that I've never heard that."

"I presume because you've never *asked*, Director."

"What do you make of this peculiarity, Ambassador?"

"Well, it's quite obvious, isn't it?"

"Not to me."

"As I said, it's a sign of favor—from the Great Maker or the gods if you wish, or the universe itself if you don't. Once a race reaches a certain point in its evolution, telepaths inevitably appear. It is a law of the universe!" He emphasized this by half draining the glass.

"Is there any proof for this—spontaneous process?"

"Proof, proof. Always you Human people desire proof. The Narn have *no* telepaths! That is proof enough! Narn are a primitive, underevolved, childlike race. What further proof do you need?"

"I understood that the Narn once had telepaths."

"Yes, I'm sure. And your Earth-dogs once had wings and built amazing statues of glass bricks on mountaintops and destroyed them all to the last molecule of silica that you should never, never know. Director, the Narn will say anything to create the impression that they are anything other than what they are—semisapients who are happiest when laboring for their betters. I give their so-called civilization another decade on its own before the inertia of the Centauri presence among them dissipates itself. Then they will beg to have us back. So you see? The Narn have no telepaths. They are not evolved enough to have them. What further proof do you need of my thesis?"

"None, I suppose."

"Now you sound *skeptical*, Director. What hypothesis do you propose, eh?"

"I have no hypothesis, Ambassador—"

"Come. You have something on your mind. Please, tell me."

Kevin frowned. How far did he want to go with this? But the Centauri, despite some rather—exaggerated—claims in the past, had known other races for a long time. This one was drunk, and from what he could tell, only partially believed what he was saying about telepaths.

"Suppose . . . Is it possible that some more ancient spacefaring race might have—tinkered—with all of our evolutions?"

A brief look of displeasure crossed the Centauri's face, an indefinable sense of some unsettling emotion that lay behind it. Then the alien bared his teeth in simulated humor. "Director. As well ask if the fairies from your folktales were responsible. We Centauri are the oldest, most evolved race in the galaxy. There are, perhaps, a few others who approach us in age, but none who surpass us. I'm aware that some rather unpleasant incident occurred because of a paranoid belief that we had somehow saddled your people with telepaths. Surely you are not bringing this up again, now that it has all finally quieted down?"

"No, Ambassador," Kevin replied. "That would be a terrible mistake, and I thank you for pointing it out to me. It was only, after all, an idle thought."

"Well, idle thoughts are better than none at all, Director, so long as we learn not to *speak* them." He patted his hand upon Kevin's. "I will see to it that all of our information on telepaths reaches your hands, Director."

"That would be most kind."

Natasha Alexander was waiting in the hall outside. He shook his head, a silent *no*.

"Do we proceed to Yucatán then, sir?"

"Yes. And Ms. Alexander—"

"Sir?"

"I'm going with you. I've seen to the arrangements."

The daylight behind them had thinned to a pearly film, and the darkness ahead exhaled a peculiar scent, resiny, pinelike.

"What is that?" Kevin asked their guide, a spindly little man named Roberto.

"Copal," he said. "It's what they burn to please God."

"It comes from a tree," Natasha added. "Legend says that, once, the lords of death craved human hearts, but the hero twins tricked them into feeding on the smoke of copal, instead."

Kevin nodded absently. He was remembering a time when he was very young, before his mother died. When they lived in the ancient, sprawling Zuni pueblo, filled with the scent of sage burning, of piñon crackling in the *horno* ovens. The clarity of the memory startled him. It had been a very long time since he had thought about that time in his life.

"Did Blood ever come here? Your great-grandmother?"

Natasha shook her head. "I don't think so. She didn't believe in this stuff."

Kevin nodded to the Psi Cops with them. "I think it's time for the torches," he told them.

Harsh electric light flooded the cave, and now he could see the faint curls of smoke, the faded paintings on the walls. He made out a creature with the body of a man but the head of a crawfish, something that might have been a serpent, rows of glyphs he recognized as Mayan writing. The rest was patchier—a hand here, part of a headdress there, a goggling eye that did not look remotely Human. He wondered how old the paintings were—if they dated to pre-Columbian times or if they were the product of more recent cultists.

"Sir," Natasha began hesitantly, "are you certain you want to proceed? I don't really think the director of Psi Corps should risk—"

"Thanks for your concern, Ms. Alexander. If this becomes too taxing physically, I will let you know."

"Yes, sir."

They descended through the narrowing tunnel, and after a time, heard singing. Again, Kevin experienced an odd sense of displacement. The song—and the language of the song—was unknown to him. But the rhythm of it, the intervals between its four notes, struck sparks in his oldest memories. Shalako spirits, dancing into the square to the sound of rattles and chanting. The taste of fresh bread, the crisp scent of an open cooler full of ice and soft drinks in a general store. Fumes of old-style gasoline engines.

His mother dying. The dark waters. The dance hall of the dead. The gift . . .

He blinked, and the tunnel had widened into a chamber. The singing stopped, and he heard their guide begin speaking in a language he did not know. He could circumvent language to get to meaning with a scan, but was reluctant to do so.

As it turned out, there was no need.

The singer was a wrinkled man of many years. He wore a colorful headdress something like a turban, and a red loincloth. The rest of his body was bare, and black with tattoos. In one hand swung a censer, from which the pungent copal smoke drifted. He squinted into the electric torches.

"Put out the lights," Kevin ordered.

In the gentler glow of candles clustered on a sort of altar, the old man's eyes were opalescent.

"You come for me?" he croaked, in English, reaching to finger Natasha's Psi Corps badge. She backed up a pace.

"We came to ask questions," Kevin replied. "May I ask your name?"

"I am the priest. This place is in my care."

"I am Kevin Vacit. This is Natasha Alexander, a telepath with Psi Corps."

"He's a teep, too, sir," Natasha said. She turned toward the priest. "Are you aware, sir, that you are required by law to register with EarthGov and Psi Corps?"

"I am aware. I did not do so. I am registered with a higher authority."

"There is no—" Natasha began, but Kevin waved her to silence.

"The priest before you. Was he a telepath, too?"

"Yes. And him before him, and so on—back to when time began."

"And how do you know this?"

The priest cocked his head. "It is spoken, it is written. These things remember themselves."

"You have written records of every priest of this place back to the beginning of time?" Natasha asked, skeptically.

"Yes."

"May I see?"

The priest flushed darker, but then he shrugged and went to a wooden box. He lifted from it a folding-screen book, opened it, and pointed to columns of hieroglyphic characters.

"That is Blood Woman, the first," he said, "Then Cedar Jaguar, Jaguar Night—"

"I only count seven names," Kevin interrupted.

"Yes. I am the seventh priest."

"I don't understand—"

"Excuse me, sir, if I may?"

"Go ahead, Ms. Alexander."

She turned back to the priest. "When did time begin?"

The priest consulted his book. "It began six *katun,* seven *tun,* two *uinal,* seven *kin* ago."

"What? In English, please."

"Time began May 11, 2055," the priest replied, with what might have been a sneer.

Kevin blinked. "I see." He glanced at Natasha. "Consonant with the beginnings of your cults."

"Yes."

He again confronted the priest. "What else do you have in these caves? Any workrooms, laboratories, storage rooms?"

"Below here, nothing, only the dark of Xibalba where live the lords of death. Perhaps it is the place for you."

"Is he telling the truth, Ms. Alexander?"

"He's blocking me, sir."

"Sir!" It was one of the Psi Cops, a very dark young man named Okonkwo. "Sir, I'm getting other teeps, somewhere near—"

"How many?"

"Hard to say. Something was hiding them before, but—" Okonkwo suddenly froze in place as a chant began, this time sounding from many throats. The priest was suddenly transformed, a thing part man and part jaguar, and from the deeper depths of the cave came more *things*. With them blew a dark wind of power, the greatest Kevin had ever felt.

7

They came for Fiona early in the night, two women with shotguns. They took her to the showers, cleaned her up, and put her in a crisp cotton dress, dark green. After that they escorted her to one of the larger buildings—one that the prisoners were never allowed near, though it was still within the gate. She noted the small helicopter outside—a Foyle 350, with ground effect jets—as black as the starless sky. The air was heavy with the scent of gathering monsoon rains.

Her guards walked her to the door, rapped, and stepped back.

Come in. It was a strong voice, one she recognized.

A gust of cool air met her as she opened the door, the breath of a benevolent god after days in the stifling dormitory buildings.

"Ms. Temple. Come in." The Psi Cop was a tall man with an equally long face, pleasing to the eye. He motioned her toward a couch. "Can I get you anything? Water? Wine? Sake?"

She didn't answer.

"I think I'll have some wine, myself." He considered, taking a decanter from the small table in front of the couch and pouring a glass of deep red. "You're sure you won't join me?"

"I would sooner drink with Adolf Hitler, Pol Pot, or Hiriam Tower," she said, sweetly.

The Psi Cop shrugged, and indicated the couch again. "Sit. Please."

She did, and he took the chair on the other side of the table, swirled his wine and sniffed it, took a small sip.

"Aren't you on duty?" Fiona asked.

He lifted a hand in a "so what" sort of gesture. "Not as such. I'm not out performing genocide at the moment, which—by your references—you seem to think is my business. For the moment I'm here to chat with you, and in that capacity I'm inclined to indulge myself. But I've been rude, haven't I? My name is Joseph Teal-Montoya."

"Nice to meet you, Joe. Again."

"You recognize me. I'm pleased."

"How could I forget your little brainwashing operation? Tell me, what do you wear when you've got a girl trapped in a tube, poking at her mind? What's appropriate for rape?" She glanced significantly at his uniform. "But I suppose I'm about to find that out, aren't I?"

She thought she caught a glimmer of discomfort from him, but he covered it well. "Ms. Temple, I do not enjoy that part of my job, but I do it because I must. Do you think I like letting these—these *normals* torture my people? Because that's whose hands you are in. Normals. And not just any normals, but the ones who hate our kind so much that they volunteer to torture them. Do you understand? It's part of a very old compromise in the EA. Telepaths get two chances to escape the persecution of the ignorant, Ms. Temple. If they take the sleeper injections, deny their heritage, and become part of the cowlike herd, they get left alone. If they join the Corps, they get to live, love, and serve among their own kind. Besides that, there is only this. Normals cannot bear the thought of us hiding among them. They will not tolerate it, and when they catch you, this is what they do to you."

"I remember being captured by Psi Cops."

He made a face. "Yes. You've committed crimes, Ms. Temple. Even Psi Corps must mollify the government."

"Just tell me why I'm here."

"Because you are a P12, of course, and I think you know that. You are, whether you like it or not, special, and so we are allowed extra latitude in trying to teach you reason. Your crimes won't be remitted, but you can serve your time as parole, study, learn to use your talents more effectively. In time, you can begin to serve. I offered you this once, and I admit that I did so in a dishonest way. But, Ms. Temple, I've seen too many of my brothers and sisters slip away—dying filthy deaths in these camps—from malaria, infection, at the hands of these thugs they call guards. I will do everything in my power to save who I can. With you, I failed once. I get one more chance. Won't you please help me?"

Fiona leaned back and clapped her hands lightly. "Very moving. Have you ever thought of doing Shakespeare?" She leaned forward intently. "Let's get a few things clear, shall we? I am *not* 'your kind.' I am not your sister. I've spent my life fighting you jackboots, and I'm not about to stop now. And this good-cop-bad-cop drivel isn't fooling me. But you know what? I don't think you got me all spiffed up and poured into this dress so you could invite me to be one of your storm troopers. So why don't we skip the vacuum and get straight to Mars?"

He took another sip of his wine and set it down. "I was afraid that would be your response. O'Hannlon had nineteen years to condition you, and next to that I have had very little time to make you see the truth."

"O'Hannlon?"

He smiled. "You never even knew his name. Monkey, he called himself. I believe he took the name from Sun Wu Kong, the Monkey King of Chinese legend. Monkey, the brash trickster, who thumbed his nose at all gods, all conventions, all law, who fought heaven and hell and won—for a time. It was a grandiose appellation your grandfather took, disguised as a joke. But if you've read the story of Sun Wu Kong, you know that that brashness and pride finally led the Monkey King to ruin, to face himself, to at last submit to his better angels, seek wisdom and service to others. The true story of the Monkey King is that he abandoned his selfish nature. Our old friend O'Hannlon never learned that." He took another sip of wine. "Perhaps he got bored with that part of the book and quit reading it. You—you, Fiona, are his legacy. You are the part of him that continues—who can at last learn the wisdom that eluded him."

Fiona smiled. "Strike two."

He shrugged. "For you, not me. Very well, Ms. Temple. You will go back to the camp, as you seem to wish, and doubtless die young. That should give you a great deal of satisfaction. First, however, you will repay your crimes. Many in the Corps lost their lives due to your actions—oh, I don't think you killed anyone directly, but everyone in your resistance cell is equally guilty."

"Isn't my rotting in this camp good enough for you?"

"Good enough for the normals, yes, but not for the Corps. We require a different sort of payment. A life for a life, if you will. Ms. Temple, as a P12 your life is very dear to us. You wish to throw it away—that is your prerogative. I cannot stop you. But your genes are another matter. They belong to us all." He clasped his hands over one knee. "Again, you have two choices. One involves certain mechanical devices. The other is much more pleasant, and would probably require you staying here, in comfort, for quite some time."

"With you, you mean."

"Yes. I am a P12 also, of course. I've had the genetics run. Our child would be a P11 or P12."

"No."

"Understand. Either way, you will have my child. This is not my choice nor yours, but the choice of the Corps. The Corps is mother, the Corps is father. They were to me, and they will be to my child. Our child."

"No."

"You cannot say no. You can be restrained, you can be sedated, you can be artificially inseminated—but none of these would be very pleasant for you. I can make things very nice for you indeed. I would prefer it."

"No."

He sighed. "Let me add just one more, very small incentive before I give up. I can be very persistent, you see." He clapped loudly, and the door opened again. Two Hounds pushed through, holding a man she had never seen before between them. He was emaciated, filthy, his black hair long, tangled, hiding his face.

Fiona?

Oh my God, she thought. *Matthew!*

She watched as they pushed Matthew roughly into a chair.

"Yes, we discovered your little liaisons," Teal-Montoya said, returning to his chair. "Not, unfortunately, in time. I was puzzled by your resistance—and his. After we gave up on you and pulled you out, he eventually succumbed to a scan. His feelings about you were quite plain."

"But he wouldn't join you, either."

"No. And do not worry—he will also make his contribution to the gene pool. There are a variety of ways he might do so, some very unpleasant indeed. I think I will leave it up to you to decide exactly how unpleasant it gets for him."

Fiona. It was Matthew. *Fiona. Don't* . . . His mind dissolved into chaos as the nearest guard struck him with a shock stick.

"You bastard!" Fiona snarled, standing, hurling hate and pain at the Psi Cop with every ampere of will she possessed. His eyes widened, and he dropped his glass, reeling back. Then he recovered, his blocks shutting against her, a grim look appearing on his face.

"Perhaps, after all, this is just a waste of my time," he said. "You two—" He gestured toward his Hounds, froze, and looked extremely puzzled as he toppled and fell. First one, then the other Hound followed him to the floor. Fiona stared, not quite understanding, and then noticed the thin sliver of bamboo, ending in a little cone of latex, standing out from Teal-Montoya's carotid artery. Then a motion beyond the half-open window.

A moment later, Stephen Walters eased through the door. In his hand he carried a bamboo tube a few feet long.

"What—" she started.

"No, *shh.* Time to go."

"Why didn't you tell me?"

"Because he might have picked it up from you, and then we would have both been done."

"But you said you needed me."

"Yes. They wouldn't have brought anybody but a P12 in here. And

after they brought you in here, and I got this far—I needed you on my side."

"What. What do you need me for?"

He pointed to the downed Psi Cop. "He isn't dead. I hit him with a nerve toxin."

"Where in the hell did you get a nerve toxin?"

"Modified cobra venom—plenty of those around here. Fiona, I'll explain in detail later. Right now I need to know if you can do something."

"What?"

"His chopper won't work without him at the stick—unless he authorizes a change in bioident. We need that to happen. I've heard some wild stuff about what P12's can do. Can you plant a suggestion in him that he turn his chopper over to me?"

She frowned. "I can't control him, if that's what you mean."

He shook his head. "No. The toxin will wear off fast, but when he comes out of it he'll be confused. If he wakes up with a strong urge to transfer idents—maybe to someone he thinks is one of his Hounds, because he's sick or injured, maybe dying—"

"Yes." She shook her head vigorously. "I think—yes, I think I can do that."

"You do it while I take care of the guards." He paused, looking at Matthew. "Who's he?"

"He's going with us."

"Look at him, Fiona—he'll be deadweight. What's going on here?"

"He's going with us, or I don't do this."

"Damn it—" He blew out a breath. "Fine. That means we have to carry two people out to the chopper undetected."

"I carried you, remember? I can carry Matthew."

Teal-Montoya was beginning to stir as Stephen pushed him into the pilot's seat. A commotion had also begun at the other end of the camp.

"They've noticed I'm gone." Stephen gritted his teeth. "Get him *in*."

She heaved Matthew into the backseat less gently than she meant to. "Okay."

"Get in."

They closed the doors and sat in the cabin, each with a pistol, as they watched dark figures moving back and forth across the square. After a moment, bright lights snapped on, flooding the entire compound.

"C'mon, wake up," Fiona said, patting Teal-Montoya's face. Then, when that failed to produce results, she slapped him.

His eyes slitted open.

"You're hurt, sir," she hissed. "Remember? They shot you? We have to get you to a medic. But I can't fly your chopper."

She had deep scanned him, found an old incident in which he had been wounded, doctored it. There had been no helicopter or transfer of bioident that time, but he had to stay confused only for a moment—

Steve tapped her on the shoulder. From the corner of her eye, Fiona noticed two guards entering the building they had just left.

"Sir, hurry. You're bleeding."

"Ah. Yes." He groaned weakly. "Computer—transfer bioident and voice recognition from Joseph Teal-Montoya, 49-156667349—to—what was your name?"

"Lenya Kolkin, 60-234637586," Fiona said. One of her aliases, hopefully one that was still active. The door to the house banged back open, and two men came out, both with rifles, looking around wildly.

Teal-Montoya was looking at her oddly. "Do I know you?"

"Hurry, sir!"

"Is your hand on the plate?"

"Yessir."

"Car, transfer. Go." He looked at her again. "I do know you, don't I?"

Stephen hit him in the jaw with a right cross—the Psi Cop gagged and slammed against the window. Fiona scrambled over his body, grabbing at the controls.

"You were supposed to transfer it to *me,*" Stephen hissed.

"Tough. Hang on."

"You know how to fly one of these?"

"I'm about to learn. If you have any tips . . ."

If Stephen had any, they stayed in him, bottled there by the sudden g-force as quick-jump ground effect jets kicked them straight up, away, to freedom.

8

Kevin closed his eyes against the nightmare that had battered its way through his blocks. It was an unfamiliar experience, shocking. No one had ever gotten in there, behind his mask.

Nor did he want them there. The force was clearer to him now. This wasn't one very strong mind, but many weaker ones bound together.

And yet not entirely together; their *gestalt* was like an octopus, separate tendrils supporting one another, working in unison to pry him and the others apart. Their monstrous forms were, of course, illusion.

He took his own mind from its box, a keen, razor-edged saber, a sleek and deadly thing. He cut in small slices at first, but with precision, one tentacle at a time.

Panic. They hadn't considered him a threat—hadn't been able to see, even, that he was a teep. It was his mother's parting gift, this invisibility.

Whick, whick—snicker-snack. They fell away, but his mind was starting to ache, like a muscle clenched too tightly for too long.

One of the Psi Cops shook loose, saw what was happening, and his pistol barked. The priest went down. Again, and what remained of the octopus flew apart, worms wriggling away, trying to burrow into the earth. In a few minutes it was over; those who were not dead had surrendered. Kevin surveyed them. No longer monsters, they were old men and women, children.

"As I said," he breathed, trying not to sound weak, "search the cave."

Something sweet touched his lips.

"Sir!" Natasha whispered.

His nose was bleeding, and he was weeping tears of blood.

"Sir, I didn't know—"

"I did not intend for you to know, Ms. Alexander. Or anyone else for that matter. If the normals ever discover that the director of Psi Corps is a telepath . . ."

"Yes, sir. No one will know, sir."

He nodded wearily. "It's our destiny, not theirs, Ms. Alexander. Never forget that."

"I never will, sir."

"This is all we found, sir."

It was like metal, smooth and hard, but with a faint shimmering and shifting that was not like metal at all. He recognized it instantly as being like the artifacts from Mars. When he touched it, he felt a vague shock, and for an instant he was back in the storm of his mother's death, staring up at the Shalako in fear and wonderment.

He handed the small shard back to Natasha, watching for a reaction. If she felt anything, she did not show it.

"It was on the altar, sir. There was no sign of any equipment that might have been used to manipulate genes."

"They subradared the whole place?"

"Yes, sir. Nothing."

"Well. For the moment, at least, we seem to have reached a dead end. There are more sites like this?"

"A few."

"Check them out. Take more people this time, and if the places have guardians, take no chances. Use gas or nerve collapsers. There are questions I want answers to."

It took him a good long while to stop gritting his teeth. Fiona was managing the chopper pretty well for someone who had never flown one—which was to say that every moment he spent looking at the windows sent his life flashing before his eyes.

So he concentrated on other things. Binding and gagging Teal-Montoya, for instance. He uplinked long enough to get a fix on their location and a map of the area, then cut the satellite link, after which he methodically shut off anything else which might help Psi Corps, local cops, or anyone else following them. Fiona made exactly one call on the local link, spoke in what sounded like gibberish for ten seconds or so, and then let him shut it down, too.

Half an hour later, she landed the craft in a small clearing next to a lake.

"We get out here," she said.

"In the jungle?"

"Yes."

"What about the Psi Cop?"

In answer, she opened the door and dumped the now-conscious Psi Cop onto the ground. He lay there, glaring at them. Fiona ignored that, ran to the back door, and opened it.

"Matthew?" he heard her say.

"How is he?" Stephen asked, scanning the surrounding jungle. Teal-Montoya's gun felt good in his hand.

"Still unconscious."

"He's got a pulse, though."

"Yes," she snapped, a little irritably.

"Listen," he said, "not that I want any thanks, or anything . . ."

She softened. "I'm sorry, Stephen. I'm just worried about him. That was—what you did back there was wonderful. You saved me from something very unpleasant, and I don't know how I'll ever make it up to you."

She smiled, and it was a very nice smile. She held out her hand, and he took it, felt the tingle of her gratitude.

"We make a good team," he managed, wondering why the words sounded so thick and dumb in his throat. "Of course, I'm fresh out of plans, now."

"Don't worry about that. I think I can pick up the ball for a while." She cocked her head winsomely. "You'll have to explain about the nerve toxin someday."

"Oh. I was a chemist, hard as that may be to believe, and I worked for a pharmaceutical company. Cobra venom is a nerve toxin, and with that and a few handy prison-camp supplies you can make some pretty interesting things."

"Apparently so." He liked the sound of her admiration. Too bad about the half-truth—he had studied chemistry, and had even made the nerve toxin, but with items Vacit had had smuggled to him. Oh, well— praise based on false accomplishments was better than no praise at all.

"So," he asked. "What now?"

"Now? Now I would suggest lowering your pistol, at least for the moment."

Stephen followed her gaze, and realized he was staring down the barrel of a rifle. All around him, the forest whispered as a small army appeared.

"Stephen Walters, I want you to meet Helang."

Helang was a small man with the quick black eyes of a predatory bird. Like the rest of his twenty-some-odd people, he wore camouflage. "I don't know you," Helang said.

"He helped me escape," Fiona said. "I vouch for him."

Helang considered for another moment or two, then nodded briskly. "This way, then." He motioned out into the forest.

"What about the chopper?" Stephen protested.

"We'll take care of that," Helang replied.

"You'll ditch it?"

"No, Mr. Walters. We'll use it. But first we will lead your pursuers on a merry chase."

"What about the Psi Cop?"

"Don't worry about him, either," Helang said, his smile a little nasty.

Stephen glanced at Teal-Montoya. *Serves you right, you son of a bitch,* he thought. *I wanted to snap your neck myself when—* He suddenly realized that he might be sending and cut himself off. Fiona didn't seem to have noticed, anyway—she had turned to Helang and begun chatting in a language he didn't know.

I'm just along for the ride, now, he reminded himself.

They followed a trail through the jungle for a few hundred feet, two of Helang's men carrying Matthew. They came to the bank of a river, where several very long canoes were tied up. The unconscious Matthew went in one, between the two men who were carrying him. Fiona, three of Helang's men, and he crowded into another. Someone handed him a paddle.

"We're going to paddle? Paddle away from Psi Cops with helicopters?"

"Paddles don't leave chemical trails or send out EM pulses or even generate heat," Fiona pointed out. "And the canopy will keep us from visual sightings from the air. Have a little faith, Stephen. We'll be using faster transportation soon enough."

"What now?" he asked, about an hour later as they put in at a small kampung. Fiona got out of her canoe and went to check on Matthew, and Stephen followed.

"There's a link here," she explained. "They're just checking in to see where the cops are—where it is and isn't safe to go."

"Who the hell are these guys?"

"They call themselves the *Orang Asli,*" she said. "It's an old term for the aboriginal people."

"Some of these guys don't look aboriginal to me. That one's blond."

Fiona nodded, wiping Matthew's face with a damp rag. "It's just a name. They have different backgrounds."

"But they aren't telepaths."

"No. They're revolutionaries, of a sort, mostly refugees from Sarawak and Kalimantan. The Indonesian Consortium forcibly resettled them here back in the thirties, when they controlled Malaysia. They want their homeland back."

"And this has what to do with us?" Stephen asked.

"The telepath underground has worked with them before," Fiona said. "We supply them with our special kind of information; they help us move people along the underground railroad in this part of the world."

"Whoa. 'We've worked with them before'? Underground railroad? What have I fallen into, here?"

"Welcome to the resistance, Stephen." She considered for a moment. "You have two choices now. I can do my best to get you away from here—to somewhere safe. Change your identity, have some fake test results forged. Or—" She turned her gaze on him. "We need people like you, Stephen."

He had known the offer would come, of course—it was what Vacit

had counted on—but somehow it was still a jolt. Fiona was sincere, fiercely so, and though she wasn't trying to broadcast, her passion leaked.

"I'll—ah—can I think about it?"

"Of course."

Helang came back and squatted down near them. "Problem," he said. "The usual connection in Singapore won't fly. In a week or so, maybe—"

"In a week or so, they'll find us."

A little cough interrupted them, and they turned to see that Matthew had opened his eyes. They were fixed on Fiona, as if she were the only thing he could see, but he spoke to all of them. "I know another way," he said. "At least, I think I do."

A giant opened the door. His ebony features swayed over them for an instant before a huge grin nearly bisected them.

"Brother Matthew!"

Matthew clasped the giant in a hug, then held him at arm's length. "Still growing, I see!" he said.

"Only in my heart, I hope. The beds here are too short for me as it is." A frown crossed his features. "We thought you had been taken."

"I was. Brother Justin, please meet Fiona Temple and Stephen Walters, my earthly saviors."

Fiona found herself gaping at the whole exchange, as she took in the giant's brown robes, the crucifix and rosary about his long neck. "You— you're a *priest*?" she asked Matthew.

Matthew placed a hand on her shoulder. "No. I *was* a monk, for a time, here. But—"

"But Brother Matthew was not content to let trouble come to him," Justin finished. "He would rather go into the world and find trouble. And *bring* it here, apparently. Please, all of you, be welcome." He made the sign of the cross, and they stepped into what seemed a limestone cathedral. It was a natural cave, or mostly natural. They had climbed for almost two hours up the steep side of a sort of mesa before finding the little door—still some two hundred feet or so short of the top. They could see out the top, now—a shaft of sunlight speared into the chamber from a natural opening above, its light falling near an altar.

"You know why I came here?" Matthew asked. "I hate to put the order in danger, but—"

"But you have need of us. I understand, Matthew."

Another monk approached them, this one considerably shorter than Brother Justin. Older, too. He had a round, pleasant face.

"This is Brother William," Justin told them. "He can be trusted."

Brother William smiled glowingly at each, as they were introduced. "Brother Matthew! I have heard so much about you, and it's a pleasure to finally meet."

Matthew nodded, but as he reached to take the monk's hand, his legs wobbled.

"Please, our pardon!" Brother Justin said, reaching for Matthew. "Of course you need rest, food, medical care."

"No time," Matthew said.

"It will take time to arrange your travel," Brother William soothed, "certainly a few hours. You will be safe here until then."

Matthew nodded reluctantly.

"Come, Matthew," Brother Justin said. "Let me take you and Stephen to clean up and eat. Brother William will make certain Ms. Temple has the privacy to do the same."

"Thank you, Brother Justin," Matthew said. He took Fiona's hand. "It's okay. You can trust them."

She nodded, and turned to follow William. They left the sanctuary and began moving though Human-cut corridors.

Brother William glanced over at her. "I was sorry to hear about Monkey."

"Thank you." She wasn't really surprised. The Church was one of their staunchest allies, though very cautious of the aid it gave them. Monkey had dealt often with them.

"Well. He left something here for you. Would you like to see it?"

"Left it? When?"

"Long ago."

"Please. I'd like to see it now, if I may."

"First bathe and eat. I'll bring it to you soon."

"Now, please."

William shrugged. "If you wish."

"Damn, that feels good," Stephen said, easing into the steaming water. "Double damn."

"I agree," Matthew murmured from his own tub a few yards away. He closed his eyes and lay back. "Thank you."

"For?"

"Helping Fiona. Stopping the Psi Cop from—"

"Hey, my pleasure, believe me. So, Matthew. Are you a part of this resistance, too?"

"Sometimes."

"Is that how you and Fiona met?"

"No. We met in the holes."

Stephen sat up. "I thought the holes were isolation cells."

Matthew nodded. "They put us too close."

Matthew's tattoo was just showing. A P12. At the sight of it he felt a surge of resentment, and Matthew noticed it. "Sorry," Stephen said. "I'm just a lousy P8."

"None of us can help how he is born," Matthew said. "It's what we do with what we have that's important. And you—without you, things would be very bad for Fiona and me right now. Very bad."

"I don't know. Fiona's quite a gal. She would've come up with somethin'."

"She is amazing," Matthew agreed, and Stephen found himself disliking his tone, too.

The image was a little blurry, as if the crystal was not quite compatible with the reader. Or perhaps it was the film of tears she kept wiping away.

Grandpa Monkey's face filled the screen.

"Fee, if you're lookin' at me here, it means I'm dead. I've left a few of these around for you, not knowin' when and where you'll come across 'em, but I do know they won't get handed out till I'm on the slab. So.

"I've raised two kids in my life, Fee, neither of 'em my own. The first one was your father, the second one was you. I'm sorry you missed your father—I know I haven't talked much about him. When I found him, he was just a little thing. It took me years to learn what happened to him, what made him like he was. His mother died holding him, killed by normals. They were both telepaths, and I think . . . I think she took something with her when she left, and left something else behind. I've never known anyone so driven and so passionless all at the same time. Anyway.

"I lost him for a while, and when I saw him again he gave me you. I don't know anything about your mother at all, Fee. And your father—" He scrunched his face in unaccustomed lines of pain, or regret, or both. "Your father didn't want you in Psi Corps. He was absolutely clear about that. Clear. And you know how I feel about the whole thing. Anyway, I promised him I would take care of you, though the last thing I wanted was to raise another brat.

"You turned out to be a good brat, though. You're everything your father wasn't. You have passion, kindness, love, honesty. Your pop wasn't a bad guy—just cold, very cold. I think him givin' you to me was the closest thing to love he's ever been able to do—well, maybe the second closest thing. So take it as a compliment.

"I'm rambling, and I hate thinking about my own mortality, which this damn morbid business is doin'—so, two things.

"One: If I'm dead, and you're not—surprise, kid, you're the leader of the resistance. I've been puttin' this damned thing together for umpty years, and it's finally gettin' a little steam behind it. So I'm goin' to tell you where to find all the information I probably just blew up—the cells and their contacts, the underground railroad routes, all the good restaurants along the way, yada-yada-yada. You may want to do this or you may not. If not, pass it on to someone else—I'm dead, I don't care."

He paused again, and his brows arched in amazement. "Well, whadaya know, I *do.* Look, Fiona, this is important. A hundred and fifty years ago, there were no telepaths. This is still the start of things, but things have a tendency to get set in their ways in the beginning. Listen, Fee. Telepaths are from every country, every ethnic group, every religion. But they are *your* people. We are *becoming* a people, that's inevitable, because normals will never accept us entirely. We have to find a way to hang together. Psi Corps—they found one answer to that, but it's the wrong answer. Very wrong.

"The resistance isn't an answer, Fiona. It's the search for answers. It's an effort to create possibilities, to give us many roads to choose from. When I was young, I didn't think anything was important. I just loved to cause trouble. I thought of myself as chaos, spreadin' anarchy just for the hell of it. Live and learn. Now I want my people to have choices. Given choices, some of us will eventually hit on the right path for teeps. There's a very simple word for what I'm talking about, but simple words tend to lose their meanings when you say them too much. Freedom. That pretty much sums it up, when you do the addition.

"So, there, that was One, and a very long One at that. Here's Two, not quite so long.

"Two: I love you, Kid. Go get 'em."

Stephen lay looking at the ceiling, unable to sleep. Everything seemed to be going according to plan, but something was bothering him, something itching in the back of his brain.

A few moments later, he gave up, stepped into the loose pants the monks had provided him, and padded out into the corridor. He found the sanctuary again. It was night, and the only light was cast by the candles at the altar.

So far, so good. He had accomplished his first two goals—won Fiona's confidence and gotten them out of the reeducation camp. He was as good as in with the underground. So what was bothering him?

The camp had gotten to him, maybe more than he wanted to admit.

He didn't really have sympathy for rogues, but nobody deserved that kind of treatment. Still, when the Corps was stronger, they would surely correct the situation. The camps were bad because they were controlled by normals. Teal-Montoya—he was just a bad apple, a typical petty chieftain, exercising what he saw as his prerogative. Hell, if he had been in Montoya's place, ordered to get a child on Fiona, wouldn't he have done the same thing?

He felt a sudden flush of anger and shame at the thought, and that took him by surprise. He liked to think of himself as a pragmatic fellow, who did the things that needed to be done. He had rarely felt guilty in his life, most certainly not for a lascivious thought. But Fiona—he sighed. He was no dummy. He had to admit that he liked her, perhaps more than liked her. He had been ordered to protect her, but he would have done it regardless, because it felt right.

Which would make it tough to betray her, when the time came. But according to the game plan, that time was still in the future, perhaps the distant future. He could worry about that later, couldn't he?

None of that was what bothered him. He was still trying to trace the source of his unease when he saw shadows moving among the candles.

Fiona rose and dressed, followed the silent call in near darkness. She found Matthew waiting for her at the head of the corridor, just outside of the sanctuary. For a long moment, they stood a yard or so apart, just looking at each other, saying nothing. His eyes were polished iron, translucent jewels—

That's your own reflection, his mind wisped.

She felt her blocks snap up, shutting him out.

"It's funny, isn't it?" he whispered aloud. "How our faces and bodies get in the way?"

"It's just—I mean, it's all so fast. This is the first time we've really met."

"No. It's the first time we've drawn apart." He held out his hand, his gaze so steady on hers she couldn't bear it, so she closed her eyes. But his were still there, only brighter, deeper, and then she really did see herself in them. Her own features, the ones she hadn't been able to picture clearly in the hole. She had seen them in mirrors, of course, evaluated them, wondered if her nose was too small or her eyes too wide apart—but now her face blazed, and it was beautiful, and she wondered how she could have ever forgotten what it looked like.

Gently, like silk sliding to the floor, her blocks went down, and she touched his hand. He stepped forward, his hand cupping gently behind

her head, but she was hardly aware of that. They were already kissing when his lips touched hers.

A hundred feet away, Stephen felt the kiss like a knife in his heart. *Pretty damn good for a guy who did nothing but lay there while I saved her,* he thought. He nurtured the anger for a moment, turned it this way and that until it made sense. Fine. This would just keep him from being a damn fool. It would allow him to do what he had to do.

But it still hurt.

He was turning to go when he noticed someone else moving in the sanctuary. At first he thought it was one of the priests, but something about the way he moved, pantherlike, triggered something in him, and it all clicked into place.

Brother William. He had seen the monk before, at the academy. He was Corps.

10

He snaked across the sanctuary, wishing he hadn't left the pistol with his other stuff. Where the hell was his mind, anyway? The only saps bigger than he were Fiona and Matthew, obliviously locked in their French hello as at least three Hounds converged on them.

He was still ten yards away from the Hounds when they noticed him.

The Corps is mother, the Corps is father, he sent.

They paused, and he leapt, muscles exploding like uncoiling springs. A pistol flashed, a silencer masking its deadly bark, and he felt a sirocco breathe past his ear, but then he was there, driving his fist straight into the Hound's face. He let his momentum carry him over with the toppling man, as another gun whistled. He rolled, came up in a crouch, and launched himself at the second shadow, chopping hard at the extended wrist and spinning to throw the full weight of his charge into his elbow. He felt it crush larynx, and then—

Stop or die.

The thought was so certain, he did, actually feeling the aim on his heart. He turned, slowly, to see "Brother" William, pistol in hand. A third Hound was covering Fiona and Matthew. The two he had hit still lay on the ground.

"That's enough," Brother William said. "I don't want to kill any of you, but I certainly will if I have to."

"Don't do this," Matthew said.

William laughed harshly. "Spare me. And don't count on Justin or any of the rest for help. They are—indisposed."

"If you've hurt them, I'll—" Matthew stepped forward, fists balled.

"You'll nothing." He gestured with the gun. "But not to worry. Justin and the others are safe, for the time being. They'll stand trial for their crimes, of course, and in the end may wish I had killed them here and now."

"How long?" Fiona asked. "How long have you—"

"It seems like an eternity, my dear, and not an eternity I've enjoyed.

I hold you and O'Hannlon responsible, damn you both. We had hoped to get him when he ran, but of course the miserable creature blew himself and one of our best officers to kingdom come. Still, we knew he'd left the crystal for you. It was keyed to your bioident, of course, so we couldn't open it. We were going to send it to the reeducation camp—but you've solved that problem very nicely. The terminal you read it on copied the pertinent information. Now, I would prefer to keep you alive, in case the other information is similarly protected."

"The hell with you."

"Not yet, my dear, and I don't believe your defiance will last very long. I've read Teal-Montoya's report on you and Mr. Dexter here, but your little display of a moment ago made it quite unnecessary. You'll cooperate or I'll take Mr. Dexter apart, a bit at a time, and I'll make sure you feel it as he comes to hate you for what you've done."

"That won't happen, Fee," Matthew said, low. "He can do anything he wants to me—I'll never hate you. Protect the resistance."

William shrugged. "You'd be very surprised what changes sufficient pain can incite in a person's personality. It's no matter, really. There are other things we can do if that fails. With proper drugs and deep scanning, Ms. Temple will do whatever we want her to do, though it might not leave much of her mind. A pity, but she's proven she's unredeemable, anyway, so—"

Then Stephen felt it, like a hole opening in his heart. Fiona was tensing to spring, to make the Hound kill her. The Hound felt it, too, and his finger tightened on the trigger. Stephen leapt, hurling himself at the Hound, knowing he would be too late—

And something caught at his limbs, froze them, and he crashed to earth.

An instant later, his limbs unfroze, and he climbed slowly to his feet.

William stood like a statue. So did the Hound. For a moment he didn't understand, but then he saw Matthew, eyes like glass, his whole body shuddering.

"Hurry," he said, gritting his teeth. "I can't—only a second or two—"

Stephen and Fiona understood at about the same time. She leapt for the Hound, and he jumped William just as Matthew groaned and staggered back. William swung the pistol straight and true, but he just didn't have time to fire it. He might be a Psi Cop, but the monastery had made him slow and lazy. Stephen hit him very hard, went down with him, and made sure his neck snapped before he rose.

When he was finished, Fiona had two guns and the Hounds were all on the floor.

"You killed him," Fiona whispered.

"Damn straight," Stephen hissed. "He knew, right? Where this information about the underground could be found? Now he doesn't. We have to do the rest of these, too."

"No," Matthew said, voice shaky. "We can't kill them in cold blood. Brother Justin—Brother Justin and the rest will find something to do with them."

Stephen wanted them all dead—what if one of them had recognized him? But he brusquely agreed.

"Fine. What now, then?"

"Find Justin and the rest," Fiona said. "Destroy the terminal. Then—" She grinned. "The information Monkey left me is in the U.S. Five will get you a hundred that 'Brother William' there has a jet somewhere and has already registered a flight plan with Psi Corps to go pick it up. The whole operation will be covert, so he won't be scheduled to check in again until he gets there. He probably has border clearances, everything."

"Maybe, maybe not. And we can't fly his plane if it's keyed to him."

"That we can get around," Matthew said. "Brother Justin has the equipment for that, and to transfer the clearances to our fake idents. Fiona, you may be right."

"We'll see, won't we? Matthew, are you okay?"

"A little drained. I'll be fine."

"Stephen?"

"I'm okay." He paused. "Thanks to Matthew."

"Sorry I caught you in the freeze, there, for a second. It's hard to be selective."

He nodded curtly. "Well. Let's get to work, shall we?"

An hour later, they were high over the South China Sea, streaking eastward toward America.

11

Natasha Alexander joined him at the start of his second mile, looking trim in her black bodysuit. She slowed her pace to match his.

"Good morning, sir."

"Good morning, Ms. Alexander. I hope you won't run me to death today."

"I'll try not to—sir."

"You have something to tell me."

A look of dismay crossed her features. "Am I leaking? I hoped I had learned better control than that."

"You have fine control of your blocks and guards," he said. "It's your face and voice that give you away."

"Oh."

"We spend so much time here teaching you to deal with other telepaths, we forget the more ancient forms of mind reading. The late Senator Crawford—now there was a man who could read minds, though he had no trace of telepathic ability. Until my forced display in Yucatán, even the most powerful telepaths failed to detect me, nor did I really fear that they would. Crawford, I worried about."

Their pace had slowed even more, he noted. Time was, he could run at a good clip and still have wind for a conversation, at least this early in the run. "Don't let an old man bore you," he said. "What do you have for me?"

"As you know, we've learned very little from the various cult shrines. Though there is one peculiar thing I ought to mention."

"That being?"

"A myth. When we questioned the survivors of the Qahsah cave site in Yucatán about the metal—or what we thought was metal, anyway—they all told the same story. It's a variant of an ancient Mayan myth. The upshot of it is that there were twin brothers who descended into the underworld to battle the lords of death by playing a sort of ball game against them. The lords of death won and killed the brothers. Their

heads were cut off and buried. From one of those heads, a tree grew, and the tree produced a fruit that looked like a human skull. A daughter of one of the lords of death came by. Her name was Blood Woman—"

"Blood Woman?"

"Yes. I think that's where my great-grandmother got her name."

"Likely. Go on."

"Anyway—this part is strange—the skull spit into her palm. She became pregnant and gave birth to another set of twins, identical to the first. When they grew up, they, too, went to battle the lords of death. They defeated the lords of death, but one of the twins was killed. The other rose up into the sky and became the morning star. The one who died did something similar to his father—a tree grew from him, and then a skull grew from the tree. But this one spit in the palms of many women, and was reborn in small pieces all over the world. Finally, a special woman took the skull itself. That piece of—of whatever it was we found in Yucatán is supposed to be part of the skull.

"To make this more interesting, I've found variants of this story at some of the other cult sites. The names and details change—at the Indonesian site, for instance, the two brothers were shining *diwas*—sort of like angels."

He mulled that over as they reached an incline, and he didn't have the breath to talk, anyway. On the downhill slope, he glanced over at her. "That could encode some memory of genetic manipulation. The twin brothers—clones? The spitting in the palm, some sort of injection?" He sighed. "Sometimes I think Humans go way out of their way to make the comprehensible as incomprehensible as possible. Do you have any thoughts on this?"

"The lab boys think that 'metal' is really organic—that it might have been somehow alive at one time."

"Yes." He nodded to himself.

She gave him a puzzled look before going on. "I know that various corporations experimented with that sort of thing earlier this century, but none of them got anywhere. Even the Centauri don't have anything like it."

"That we know of," he cautioned.

"Have you considered asking the Centauri about it—the artifact, I mean?"

"No. I somehow think that would be a very bad idea."

"I think I see your point, sir."

"You have something besides all of this, don't you?"

Fresh excitement tinged her voice. "Yes, sir. I went back to my demographic database, the one I used to make the teep/cult connection—

I've improved the base, and I thought I might have missed something. I had."

"Oh?"

"Yes, sir. We place the first generation of teeps born in the twenty-fifties and early twenty-sixties—"

"About the time the priest told us the world began."

"Yes. And I've tied a very high percentage of teeps to original members of those cults. But I started running random checks against other demographic bases, chosen by stratified random sampling, and I found an even stronger correlation to both cult membership and teep ancestry."

"That being?"

"At one time or another, they all visited or lived in Antarctica."

"Antarctica?"

"Yes, sir. Despite a few military incidents and the Chilean war of 2035, Antarctica has been international territory since the late twentieth. Every major country has a base, if not a colony, there."

"And there are a lot of tourists. Are you saying every tourist or colonist in Antarctica is a teep ancestor?"

"No, sir, only a very small fraction. It's just the conjunction of that with the other data sets that is suspicious. That's not all, though—"

He chuckled, and that forced him to stop running altogether. Natasha slowed with him.

"Sir?"

"At the Mountains of Madness," he said.

"Sir?" she repeated.

"An old story, by an author named Lovecraft. Never mind. Is there more?"

"Yes, sir, there is. I checked the logs of the various colonies and tourist expeditions. All the teep ancestors we have records of—and that's not many from the total, sir—but of the ones I have, all of them seem to have gone missing for a few days. They claimed to have been lost, but showed few signs of frostbite or malnutrition."

"That," Kevin allowed, "is very interesting indeed. Did they all vanish near a common location?"

"Yes, sir, they did."

"Curiouser and curiouser. And you have that location, I presume."

"Yes, sir."

"Well. Let's go, then."

He stepped out for some air. The air was ninety below. Kevin Vacit had twice been to the Moon and once to Mars, but in its own way the bottom of the Earth was more desolate than either, and certainly more

dangerous. Anabatic winds that whipped up to a hundred and twenty miles per hour and temperatures that dove to a hundred and thirty below made it the solar system's harshest, coldest desert with an oxygen atmosphere.

Small wonder that, after almost three centuries of settlement, Antarctica still had only a few more inhabitants than Mars.

At the moment, the winds were a mere thirty miles per hour, so he could see most of the Vostok colony—a series of domes and covered walkways, some caked with ice, others freshly thawed. An ugly place with a population of less than a hundred.

"It is a cold place, but I find it beautiful," a muffled voice said behind him.

Kevin turned to regard Sergei Zviyagin, a middle-aged man bundled, like himself, in a heavy parka. "Hello, Commander," he said.

"It is a big place with little motions. I call it a white book of a thousand pages—and hidden in those pages are a few haiku, written, perhaps, in invisible ink."

"That seems apt," Kevin remarked.

"Well, my thanks, Director. I aspire to be a poet, you know. A poet-detective. And I must wonder—as a poet-detective—what haiku are you looking for, written out there on the sastrugi, around the subglacial Gamburtsev Mountains, at the Pole of Inaccessibility? What could be of interest out there to your organization?"

"We're searching for a colony of rogue telepaths."

Zviyagin stared at him for a moment, and then burst into deep belly laughter. "You see, Director! You see how wise I can be, in my way? I've waited, waited, waited for a chance to speak to you out here, where ears and microphones hear nothing but snowy hiss, unless you stand very close. And now none of your people—or mine—will know that I laughed at you. Nor will my people know that you insulted me.

"You want me to think you believe there are telepaths, burrowed down in the ice that covers the Gamburtsevs, gradually evolving into creatures of crystal? Come, Director. Your people—your Psi Cops and soldiers and scientists—they have put a strain on our existence here. Our once orderly lives have been disrupted, and you wish to repay me only with something I can laugh at?"

Kevin turned his face back out toward the white plain. "EarthGov has approved my stay here, and our business is a matter of internal security. That will have to be enough for you, I'm afraid."

"I see." He paused, rubbing his mittened hands together. "You search for something, a dark spot in a satellite photograph. Remote sens-

ing registered a gravitational anomaly there a hundred years ago. Now it is gone."

"You know something of this?"

"I know there are a thousand dark spots in the snow—mines that didn't work out, homesteads, craters dug by missiles during the conflicts. But I think I know the one you are looking for."

"Why didn't you say this when I asked for information earlier?"

"Because I do not care to be kept in the dark on my own command. Because I do not care to be lied to. But—I will take you to it. I will see what you see. You need tell me nothing."

The wind picked up. The snow tickled his nose like dust. "Very well," Kevin said, finally. "But, as you say—I can tell you nothing."

The power sleds bumped painfully over a sea of frozen waves, formed where wind scoured away the softest ice, leaving behind jagged drifts. Sastrugi, they called it. It was something he could have done without, but the wind was too unpredictable to trust planes or helicopters. Even flyovers were canceled, and Kevin did not want to use the satellite systems. Too many people might notice his scrutiny of this place if he diverted orbital gazes.

The Sun was out today, spilling a fury of heatless light upon the plain. His goggles helped—and would certainly filter out the high UV levels—but still, when he shut his eyes, he saw only flat redness.

After many hours, a sort of blue-grey lens appeared in the heretofore uniform brightness, growing larger as they approached it.

"There you go, Director," Zviyagin shouted. "Your hole."

It was, indeed, a hole.

They stood at the rim of it, staring down. He could not see the bottom; a mist of snow dust obscured vision after a few hundred feet.

"How deep is the ice here?" he asked Zviyagin.

"Two kilometers. Maybe more."

He measured the diameter with his eye. A hundred meters? Two hundred? It was hard to say.

"The wind is better for flying right now?" he asked.

"Well, yes, right now, but that can change very abruptly—"

"We'll risk it. Natasha?"

"Yes, sir?"

"Have one of the Garuda-class choppers meet us here."

"Yes, sir. Can I tell them why?"

"I have to go down there."

* * *

They descended through a cyclone of their own making, descended through time, past ice laid down when Lincoln was president of a fractured United States, when Alexander marched, when the Great Wall of China was built. Below waters that had last been clouds when Sumer was founded, when the first grains were planted, when Neanderthal and Homo sapiens shared the same forests in Europe, until at last they settled once again on the snows of their own century, a few inches that had drifted down to coat the hard earth, the foothills of the Gamburtsev Mountains, whose highest peaks never felt the Sun.

"Floods," Kevin ordered, and the world became light.

Ice gleamed around them. Not the familiar ice of the world they knew, but ice bruised by two kilometers of its own weight. It was striated, black, aquamarine, subtle pearl, milk, jade. Chunks the size of cars had spilled from the walls, from here and higher up. Some seemed to have exploded like bombs.

"This hole can't be too old," Natasha whispered. "The ice shifts— not a lot, but it's always moving." He got a chill from her that had nothing to do with temperature.

"Sir, it's not safe. Another piece could fall anytime. The whole thing could collapse."

"I know." He turned, walking in a circle around the chopper, feeling something—a trace of something. He kept walking.

"Sir, radar doesn't show anything but ice. I really think—"

He didn't hear the rest, as light and sound exploded around him, wrapped him in vision.

When someone died, something of them lingered. Their thoughts and memories, what they had been, what they might have been. Not for long—most often for fleeting moments only—but it did linger. A sort of shadow of the mind, cast upon the particles of creation itself, perhaps, fading as the universe moved without it. No one knew how it worked— any more than they knew how telepathy itself really worked—but it was, like telepathy, an observed phenomenon.

Someone had died here. Something was left.

A thing, a structure—a ship, huge, scintillating, alive. He saw chambers, corridors—people, floating in transparent, fluid-filled tubes. Voices, throbbing below the level of understanding, voices like the grinding of worlds against one another. And duty—an important one.

And pain. An enemy, a darkness. Pain and sorrow, memories of a thousand years, hopes for a thousand more. The air shattering. Life shattering. Gone.

* * *

He became aware of his own breathing, harsh, like a runner in panic. Sweat had filmed over his face and was beginning to freeze there, and Natasha was holding his hand, shaking it, mindscreaming at him.

Director! Mr. Vacit! Kevin!

"I'm here," he murmured.

"Oh, God. Thank God!" She buried herself against him, and he felt her concern and—love?—rush over him like a wave.

He pushed her gently back. "It's okay. I'm okay, Ms. Alexander. Did you feel it?"

She mastered herself quickly. "Feel what, sir? You just started staring into space, shaking. You were blaring static. I thought something was wrong with you."

"It was like a death-trace, but—" He couldn't find it. "Is this where I was standing? The whole time?"

"Yes."

"And when you came over to me, you felt nothing?"

"No, sir. I'm sorry."

"No. It's okay. There's nothing here, you say?"

"Radar and sonics show nothing. Very slight lingering background radiation. It's an empty hole, sir."

"It is," he agreed. "It is now."

PART 4

Legacy

PART 4

Legacy

1

Stephen jerked his head back from around the corner of the stable. Inside, a horse snorted uncertainly.

"Damn!" he snarled. "They've already got him. I count—holy Moses!—three Psi Cops and a goon squad of maybe ten. All of this for one kid?"

"Block!" Matthew hissed. "They're sweeping!"

Stephen snapped his guard up, felt his companion's stronger power settle over both of them—not just blocking, but making them transparent to a searching scan—hopefully. He swallowed his resentment and checked the rounds in his clip.

After a moment, Matthew relaxed. "Okay," he said. "That was tough."

"Well, now what? Two against thirteen, three of them Psi Cops."

Matthew sighed. "I guess we can't win them all. Better pull out before they *do* notice us."

Stephen nodded affirmation and stood, slowly. "Still—" he said. "Three Psi Cops. If this kid rates that much attention—" He scratched his head. "What did the report say again?"

"We didn't get much of it, and parts of it were garbled. The Corps has a new code, and about twenty percent still comes through scrambled. A boy, age thirteen—Remy Ligeau. The usual stuff—freaked out in church, somebody passed it on."

"I'm surprised," Stephen remarked. "I've never seen a more close-mouthed community."

"Yes, but the reward for turning in a teep can be pretty steep."

"I guess. There must be more. This just doesn't smell right. Three Psi Cops in Wherethefrag, Canada, two hundred miles from anyplace with a population higher than a dachshund's IQ? Uh-uh. Head for the woods. I'll meet you in town, at the café, say about ten o'clock or not at all."

"What? Stephen, wait—"

But he was already gone, sprinting along the edge of the trees. He waited a few moments, to give Matthew a head start, then began firing short, controlled bursts. The tableau seemed frozen for a moment—the Psi Cops, two with their hands on the shoulders of a boy; a man and woman, presumably the boy's parents, standing on the porch of a cabin, looking worried; a perimeter of guards, way too relaxed.

His first three shots hit the wagon they had come in, and by the third he was sure he had taken out the power system. Then he started in on the guards. By that time it was self-defense, as bullets laced the air around him. He ducked back into the woods, dove behind a downed spruce. He popped back up and fired again, hitting a second man in the shoulder. At about the same time, the man on the porch—the father— was somehow holding a shotgun. It roared and belched a cloud of smoke, and one of the Psi Cops mindscreamed as he sprawled among the chickens pecking around the yard. Then both the father and mother went down as the remaining Psi Cops opened up. Stephen calmly shot another Psi Cop and the nearest guard, as an inch from his head the bole of a spruce tree opened a smoking eye. He ducked again, but not before he noticed the boy running into the woods. The remaining guards and cops seemed not to notice—they had sights only for him, now, and things became very violent around his log.

The house sat at the top of a mountainous ridge that ran to his left and right. The road he and Matthew had come up on went right—the boy was going left.

He started wiggling backward, down the incline, raising his arm high for a shot now and then. When he thought he had enough of an angle, he jumped up and ran, paralleling the ridgetop.

As he ran, he counted what he had last seen. One Psi Cop left and four grunts. Still not good odds—but he should have a little time now. Psi Cops weren't usually wilderness types. His original plan had been to take out the car and then pick them off one by one as they headed to town on foot, but this was better, if he could catch up with the boy before they did.

Reaction was setting in, and his legs felt a little quivery. What the hell was he doing? Matthew had a way of bringing out the stupid in him, like no one else besides Fiona. But of course, the two were very much corollary.

Puffing, he worked his way back to the top of the ridge, tearing through a stand of dense secondary growth, and then back into clearer woods. He did a quick pivot, but no one was following yet.

He found the boy's track easily enough, and took off after him.

* * *

He found the boy huddled against a tree at the edge of a ravine, watching him approach with wild eyes.

Easy, Remy. I'm here to help you. It'll be okay. He glanced behind him again, feeling imaginary crosshairs on his back.

Remy Ligeau inched closer to the abyss, whimpering. Stephen walked a few steps closer, hand outstretched. *C'mon. We have to hurry.*

Bad, bad. Run hide run hide papa says don't don't just, no not ever dark angel touch me but still my boy love redeemer please just a little thing didn't mean to papa papa . . .

Stephen slapped his hands to his ears involuntarily, but of course it didn't help, though his blocks did. He felt disoriented, not so much by the words as by the stream of images and feelings that bellowed from the boy's mind like a bullhorn turned up to the point of distortion.

"Good Lord . . ."

A bullet spanged from a nearby rock, and he dove forward, grabbing the boy and yanking him down. Remy thrashed like a wildcat, and for a moment, the two of them hung at the edge of the cliff before falling.

Stephen's gut floated empty for an instant, and then they hit a talus slope, rolling, skittering down about thirty feet before he caught hold of a scraggly cedar. A good thing, too, for another ten feet and the slope of loose stone spilled over the final lip of the crevasse. Swearing, he hung on to the boy with one hand and the shallow-rooted cedar with the other. The rifle lay perhaps five feet upslope.

"Grab a tree, boy," he snapped. *Grab a tree!* The boy looked at him, uncomprehending.

Two, then three figures appeared at the top of the ridge.

"Bring us the boy," one shouted down.

"Shoot me, and we both fall."

Bring us the boy! It had the force of command, and Stephen had to fight the sudden instinct to do exactly what the Psi Cop demanded. But he couldn't anyway.

The Psi Cop seemed to dive off the edge, followed by the man next to him. The third turned, raised his rifle, and did a back flip. The first two bodies bumped down the slope and off into space, while the third fetched up against a large boulder.

Matthew appeared, staring down at them, and then he, too, fell. The reports of rifles clapped in the chasm, loud, then faint, then loud again . . .

Grab a tree! Stephen flung again, furiously. *Papa says grab a tree!*

Eyes still clouded, the boy finally did, and Stephen scrambled free. Matthew had fallen at a strange angle, and was out of sight. Stephen got the rifle and crawled upslope on his belly.

Stones began dancing around him, and more applause rose from the ravine. Breathing slowly and evenly, he tuned that out as distraction, sighted the head he could just barely make out, focused on its barely discernible thoughts, fired, fired, fired as something hot scored his shoulder—

He felt it, a rush of horror, surprise, resignation, nothing. The shooting from the top of the ridge stopped.

There was one more out there. Or would they have sent one to get help?

Matthew? Matthew, are you there?

Nothing. He glanced back at the boy, who seemed to have finally grasped the notion that he would fall if he didn't hold on to something. Five minutes crawled by, and he repeated his call to Matthew, with the same negative results.

Ah, well. Good riddance. It would make all sorts of things easier.

He was surprised to feel a bit of self-loathing at that thought. But self-loathing was a feeling he had come to terms with. Like every time he sent the director a memo.

He began inching toward where he had last seen Matthew. It paid to be sure.

He found the other man scarcely a yard from the edge. His shoulder was bleeding and his eyes were closed, but this close Stephen could feel the life still in him. One little push could fix that. A very small push, indeed.

He let himself down toward Matthew, cocking his leg back to kick him. The leg was shaking.

He didn't know how long he lay like that, but in the end he gave up, grabbed Matthew, and hauled him up the slope to safety. The wound was bad, but shouldn't be fatal; the purpling spot on Matthew's head was a better explanation for his little nap. He lifted the eyelids and found the pupils were the same size, so no concussion.

He went back down and helped Remy up. The boy had gone silent—almost catatonic, in fact. When he returned, Matthew was raised up on one elbow.

"What happened?"

"You saved my life," Stephen told him, brusquely. "Then one winged you from behind. It was pretty funny, really. Like you were all just walking up to the cliff's edge and falling over. Like lemmings, or something." When Matthew didn't laugh, he continued, "I guess you had to be there."

"Are they all dead?"

"There's one more, I think."

"I shot one back at the house," Matthew said.

"Oh. No, we're jake then. But we should get out of here. We'll go back up to the old farmstead, and then I'll go down and get the car."

He found them in the barn, Matthew seeming woozy and the kid looking as crazy as ever.

"C'mon, Matthew, up and at 'em. I don't know what this kid did—swallow the president's secret résumé or what—but there's another squad of cops in town, gettin' ready to come up as we speak. They already found our car."

"Oh, no."

"Oh, yes. I don't know how long we have, but I'd say not too long. I'm going to grab some food and things from the house—do you know how to saddle a horse?"

"You're kidding, right?"

"I like to saddle Jisabelle."

They both turned in astonishment to behold Remy, stroking one of the horses.

"You get the food, Matthew. I'll help Remy—I haven't ridden in a while, but I think I can remember the basics."

"There's only two horses."

"Remy can ride double with one of us."

As it turned out, it was Matthew riding up behind Remy, because once on the horse, the boy suddenly seemed to come alive, the voices bubbling out of his head reduced to a sort of rhythm-mantra, wordless. Was he in the horse's head? If he could do that, it certainly would make him valuable to Psi Corps.

It felt good to ride again. He had spent considerable time galloping the plateau around Casper when he was a kid. Riding a horse wasn't exactly like riding a bike, but it did come back to you.

They found a back way down the mountain, went up a creek for a time, starting the occasional false trail. Sundown found them in an elevated pass, with a good view back toward where they had come from.

"They'll bring helicopters soon, with microdoppler and infrared. Tomorrow, maybe, the next day at the latest." Matthew sighed, leaning back against a stone.

"Better have a fire now, then, while we still can," Stephen reasoned. He gathered the wood and soon had one going. Remy had at first refused to dismount, but did so when he saw the fire, coming to watch the flames in fascination. Matthew broke out some food—homemade bread and goat cheese.

"What was with those folks, anyway?" Stephen asked, after swallowing a bite of his sandwich. "I mean, we liked things kind of old-fashioned back in Wyoming, but Remy's people didn't even have a refrigerator." He hunched closer to the fire. "Not that they need one, I suppose." A deep chill had fallen with the night, reminding him that October in these latitudes could be murderous.

"I think they were Pareilists," Matthew said. "Sort of like the Amish."

"Huh. Weird that anyone would choose to live like that."

"Weird to me that anyone gets to *choose* how they live. Have you ever tried to imagine it, Stephen? Being able to pick where you want to live, how you want to live, what you want to do?"

"I don't have to imagine it," Stephen remarked. "I didn't get my stuff until I was twenty-two. For a while, the whole world was open to me."

"Maybe that's worse, then—to have freedom and then lose it."

Stephen laughed a little bitterly. "I was doing a damn good job of narrowing my choices before I went teep. No one has real freedom."

"Being able to make your own mistakes *is* freedom. Freedom isn't about making the right choices, or about everything working out fine. It's about getting to decide for yourself and taking the blame yourself if you blow it."

"That last is a right a lot of people don't really want."

Matthew chuckled painfully. "Sometimes, Stephen, I wonder what keeps you with us. You don't seem to really believe in what we're doing."

Stephen stirred the fire with a stick, and a nebula of sparks lifted toward their stellar cousins. "Believe? I just like a good fight. Have I ever given you cause to doubt my enthusiasm?"

"No. I just don't understand you. You're always closed to me."

"I'm a private kind of guy."

Matthew was silent for a moment. "Do we know where we're headed?"

Stephen nodded. "Dena country isn't far. The underground has a cell there."

"Dena country? That's more than a hundred miles."

"You have a better idea?"

"No—Stephen, look at that!"

Something funny was happening with the fire. The sparks were forming odd patterns, clumping here and there. As Stephen watched, a small chunk of glowing wood joined its smaller, fiery brethren in a weird cyclonic dance.

"Holy Moses," Stephen breathed.

Matthew nodded. "A telekinetic."

"No wonder Psi Corps sent the A team."

Intent on the coal, Remy seemed not to notice them at all.

"That means they won't turn loose, either. Not that they would, anyway, after we killed those Psi Cops, but—Jesus. This is the first teek I've ever seen. Are they really all like this—a little soft in the head? That's what I've heard."

"He *can* hear you, you know, even if he doesn't respond."

"Yeah. Sorry, Remy. Man, look at that." He took a swallow of water, still watching the display. "Think of what he could do. Throw switches. Jam guns. Maybe even do things inside a man, like monkey with blood vessels, or whatever." He paused. "I guess they want to breed him, huh?"

"Or dissect him. Or both."

They paused, as the thought set in. It was Stephen who broke the silence.

"Okay, Matthew. You don't understand me—I don't understand *you*. We keep fighting this fight, but where is it all going? Eventually, even friendly countries are going to say enough is enough. Right now we just shuffle people around, from here to there, but in the end nothing really changes, does it?"

Matthew leaned back on his elbow. "Maybe we are the same, in a way. It's not about winning—not right now, at least—it's about the fight. As long as we let them know we won't go quietly, we keep the idea on the table that we *are* people, that we have rights, that there should be a place for us. I don't know where. Maybe here, maybe in the stars—all I know is, when you give in, when you let them put you in a hole, it can take a long time to claw your way back out. So we stay out, make them take notice of us, keep the idea of freedom alive until we can see a way to fill the hole in."

"By which 'hole' you mean Psi Corps."

"By which I mean *all* of it. The normals who won't accommodate their lives to fit us in. The senators who only use us as chits in a political game. The corporations who exploit us, the bigots who kill us. And yes, Psi Corps, who would try to forge us into mindless weapons."

"We're beatin' ourselves into weapons. We kill, Matthew."

"Yes. That's the problem, isn't it? Trying to keep from becoming the thing we hate."

Stephen didn't answer. What could he say? The show was over—Remy had somehow dropped off to sleep in a sitting position. "Poor kid. He doesn't know what kind of life he's in for, does he?"

"Sometimes," Matthew replied, softly, "not knowing is better than knowing."

Stephen snorted. "That's the kind of thing I've come to expect to hear you say. Makes me want to twist your head off, sometimes."

The next day the clouds blew in, along with a few snow flurries. It got colder, and they drew the blankets they had taken from Remy's house tight around them. They didn't see any choppers until nearly sundown, when Matthew spotted one near the horizon. By that time they had worked their way down out of the mountains and were in high plateau, a mix of spruce forest and open grassland. It made for better time, but when the choppers expanded their search pattern, hiding would be a lot harder.

"Fire?" Remy asked, hopefully, as the dark drew down upon them.

"Sorry, Remy," Matthew told him. "The bad guys will see it." As he said it, he listed in his saddle a bit.

"We better halt here," Stephen said. "You need the rest."

The Moon drizzled milky light into the clouds, but beneath the high trees, darkness lay unchallenged. Remy huddled against Matthew. Everybody loved Matthew.

"How did you end up being a priest?" Stephen asked, to distract himself from the marrow-chilling cold.

"Monk," Matthew corrected. "You've never asked me that. You've never asked me much of anything, Stephen. Five years we've worked together, and yet we've never become friends."

"Yeah? But you keep tryin'. Too hard sometimes. Why?"

"Because Fiona loves you."

Stephen knew he didn't hide his shock, not all of it. He felt his throat close up. "What?"

"She cares deeply about you. You're important to her, and I trust that."

"That's no good reason to trust somebody."

The wind hissed in the trees, and his body began to shiver uncontrollably.

"We're all going to have to huddle together or freeze," Matthew said. "Come over here with us."

"No, thanks."

"Not just for you. Remy and I need you."

"Maybe I will in a minute."

"You really don't like me, do you?" Matthew said.

"What's brought all this up?"

"You don't want to answer?"

Stephen gnawed his lip for a moment, and then he said, "All right, no, I don't like you. You took advantage of Fiona, and you won't let her

out of it. You've used her to make yourself a big man—everyone in the resistance loves you, and it's because you're married to *her*. Hell, the whole underground would fall apart without you guys. Everyone does what they do for you, not because it's right, or best, or sensible—but because they want to *be* you."

"What are you talking about? How did I 'take advantage' of Fiona?"

"They were brainwashing her. It's an old technique. Cut someone off from everything outside, wait till they start to go crazy in their own heads, then step in with a sweet voice and nice promises. They fixate on you like a baby bird. Only you got to her instead of Psi Corps, didn't you? She would have fallen in love with anyone in that state."

"You forget I was in that state, too. When I lost her—when they took her out of the hole—it nearly killed me. I broke. I'll break again without her. Think what you want, Stephen, but if you think all we have is fixation, then you haven't been paying attention for five years."

"Shut up."

"Or maybe it's something else. Maybe you wish it had been *you,* there in the hole with her. You jumped like a scared cat when I told you she loved you. Have you ever admitted just how much *you* love *her*?"

"Shut up."

"Why didn't you kill me back there? You could have. You know you wanted to."

Blinding, murderous rage pulsed through Stephen, came and went like a flash of lightning. "You *scanned* me?"

"No need. Why didn't you kill me? I think that's a fair question."

Stephen stared up at the grey clouds. His voice felt oddly detached from his throat, as if it were a bird flown from it, singing on its own now. "I didn't kill you because it wouldn't have changed anything. Believe me, if I thought killing you would get me Fiona, I'd do it so fast—" He broke off, started again. "But it wouldn't, you see? She wouldn't love me any more than she does, and maybe she would hate me for lettin' you get killed. So you're safe with me."

Matthew reached over and laid a hand on his shoulder. "I know that, Stephen. I knew it before I asked the question. I'm just not sure you did. Now, please, come over here and keep us from freezing."

"Please?" Remy added.

He awoke, crouched against them in the grey dawn. Quietly, quietly he untangled himself from Remy's arm, stood and walked off among the trees and mist so they wouldn't see him cry.

It had been a long time since he had slept with anyone.

Oh, yes, sex he had had. He wasn't worshiped like Fiona and Mat-

thew, but he was a hero of the revolution, and there were always women passing through willing to bed a hero. But he had never *slept* with them, never stayed the night.

Telepaths dream. And when telepaths touch, and dream, they dream together . . .

Remy. His mind was a kaleidoscope, broken, each thought refracted so many times it made no sense. But he knew he had lost his papa and mama, knew it in his bones, and his loss was no less terrible because he couldn't express it. No, it was more terrible.

And Matthew—Matthew dreamed only of Fiona, of her dark red tresses, the sweetness of her lips, of melting against her body, of the worlds within worlds they shared. All of the things Stephen could never have. But those things were nothing—even hair and skin and flesh were just things, things he might possess if he killed Matthew and stole her away, despite what he had said the night before.

But he could never have what Matthew *felt*. Stephen had believed he loved Fiona, but compared with Matthew he was a firefly hovering next to a supernova. What Matthew felt was so big, so powerful, so absolutely real it made him ashamed of his own pale emotion.

It's what she felt, too. Thousands of miles apart, in their dreams, they still somehow touched—lighter than a ghost's eyelash, below the level of thought and image. Maybe even they weren't aware of it. But *he* was, now.

And so he wept, there among the spruce, as a new snow began to fall, and it felt as if his heart were contracting, understanding suddenly how empty it was. Collapsing, fading—even his hatred of Matthew was a lie. Even, really, his love for Fiona.

And so he had nothing left, did he? Except his mission.

He should have kept that knowledge close to him all of the time, kept focused on his mission. The problem was, he didn't know what his mission was anymore. To stay with the underground forever, always the traitor, yet always doing his best for them, too? Would he never be released, taken back into the Corps? Couldn't he just end it now, turn Matthew and the kid in, go back *home*? It wasn't what the director wanted, but who knew what that crazy old man was up to?

A thought more chill than the weather struck him. What if the old man was *dead*? What if his reports were going into nothingness, and no one even knew who Stephen Walters had been, that he was undercover, *any* of it?

The snow answered none of his questions, so he went back and woke Matthew and Remy. With luck, they could finish the trip by the end of the day.

* * *

Midday they sighted a mile or so of glittering train on the horizon, watched it vanish in the distance. They rode parallel to the tracks, knowing that would bring them to a town.

It did, though not much of one. Matthew, of course, managed to remember the name of the contact. Stephen—the least suspicious of the lot, being unwounded and capable of speech—walked into the local general store, a thirty-year-old prefab building crusted in antlers, furs, and old traffic signs. A vid blared loudly as he walked in. The owner was a bored-looking man with a seamed, square face the color of old leather. He wore a baseball cap.

Stephen told the man he was looking for Russ Telling, whom the man didn't seem to remember until he bought a pickled egg for twenty-five Northam dollars. He got directions, and by a few hours after sundown, they had followed them to the end of a dirt road, a log cabin, and a yard full of dogs that were suspiciously close to wolves in appearance.

"You guys are in a lot of trouble." The man peered down at them from his front porch, a shotgun slung casually under one arm. He was old, with close-cropped silver hair and the nose of an eagle.

"You know who we are?"

"Murdered a bunch of Psi Cops up in the hills, I hear. Is that you?"

Matthew cleared his throat. "Yes. That's us."

"Did you kill 'em?"

"Yes."

"Come on in, then."

He gave them hot coffee and roast venison. "I'm called Russ Telling," he said, as they ate. "It ain't my name, but it's something to call me. I don't much care for those guys, the Psi Corps. They got my wife. Tried to get my sons."

"Did you send your sons away?"

"Yes. Into the hills. There's plenty of land here to hide in. The only reason they got my wife is because one of our people went over and helped track her down. We killed him, though, so now they don't have nobody that knows the land. It costs too much to hunt them down." He wagged a finger at them. "*You,* they will hunt down, whatever it costs. We'll hide you for a while, move you around—but in the end you'll have to go.

"In the morning, the brushmen will come for you, keep you safe. You got here just in time, you know. There's a Psi Cop in town, waiting on you. We've been giving him the runaround."

"You knew we were coming here?"

"The brushmen felt the boy. He's a loud one. He can move things, can't he?"

"I move things," Remy confirmed.

"We don't want 'em to have you, do we? No, not you."

He turned back toward them. "We'll set something up, don't you worry."

The "brushmen" turned out to be twins, two young men about twenty years old. They wore heavy coats made of some kind of animal skin and looked like they came out of some ancient book. They ate eggs and hash with the old man, saying little—little out loud, anyway, and Stephen kept a polite distance. No point pissing these people off.

"Here you go," one of the brushmen said, dumping a bundle out on the floor. "You guys change into this."

Matthew went through the stuff. It consisted of long underwear, jeans, shirts, and heavy coats like the boys wore.

"We have our own coats," he pointed out.

"Not warm enough, and too much metal in them. You want to hide from helicopters, you'd better listen to us."

So they changed, and headed out into the woods.

"Why do they call you brushmen?" Matthew asked the boys, as they walked along.

"An old legend," one of them said. "The brushmen were sort of supernatural people who went off to live in the wilderness. They didn't live in houses. People were sort of scared of them, but also came to them when they needed favors. That's us. Teeps. When we get word that the Psi Cops are around, we just hit the woods, hunt for a while."

He turned to confront Matthew. "You're Matthew Dexter, right?"

"Yes."

"It's an honor to have you here. We—" The two seemed to confer for a moment. "We admire you a lot."

"You're the admirable ones," Matthew said. "Taking in strangers, eluding the Psi Cops."

The twins laughed, in tandem. "I'm Mike—this is Jimmy. How many strangers have we taken in? A few. We've helped some get from one coast to another. But *you,* Mr. Dexter—you and Fiona make it all happen. All of it."

Stephen just listened, dully. Even here, among the last of the hunter-gatherers, he couldn't escape. At least he didn't care anymore.

Real snow came, and they moved from shelter to shelter. He and Matthew spoke little—it seemed they had exhausted everything they

might say to each other. After you admitted to a man that you wouldn't mind killing him, what else could you say?

The brushmen, sensitive to his moods, sent him out to hunt, alone. He rarely got anything, but then that wasn't the purpose of his expeditions.

His modern rifle notwithstanding, he fell into a Paleolithic rhythm. Alone, in the woods, tracking prey, he found a purpose to keep the emptiness at bay.

Until the call came. The first day it was only the merest whisper, but by the second it had gained strength. Clarity came on the third day, when the touch resolved into his name.

Walters. I'm alone, unarmed. I need to talk to you.

He scanned the valley below, searching for the source. Whoever it was probably had him in line of sight, and he didn't like that.

By the river. Morning.

The man approached with his hands open, a gesture as ancient as humanity. Stephen did not reciprocate—he kept his gun up. Thirty paces away the stranger stopped, pushed back the hood of his parka.

"Fedor?"

"Yes, of course. Who else would they send to find you?"

"You crazy Siberian. I'm amazed you're still alive."

"I love you, too, my friend. How are you?"

He regarded the dark-haired man for a moment. "You tell me, Fedor. Have you come to kill me."

"The Corps is mother, the Corps is father, Stephen. I've come to bring you back, not kill you. The director sent me."

"Did he? What does the director care about me?"

"Come, come, moi droog. I know your mission. I know, also, that you must be near—how is it in English?—near the end of your rope. You've been out far too long, too long away from the family. But now it's over at last."

"Over? Or do they just want the boy?"

"He belongs with us—you know that. Only the Corps can care for him properly. We tried to get word to you before, before the bloodshed—"

"Yes, what about that? I've killed my own kind, Fedor. I—it was part of my orders, but—"

"It's forgiven. No one will even know."

Stephen lowered the rifle. "I can go home?"

"Yes. It remains only to get the boy, and this Matthew Dexter. Then—"

Fedor understood what was happening even before Stephen did himself. Before he could lift the nose of his rifle, the Russian was reaching behind him. As his hand snapped back over, now holding a pistol, Stephen's own muzzle finally came up, and the explosions rang together.

Together, they pitched backward into the snow.

Son of a bitch! Stephen sent. He couldn't move his body at all, but there was no pain, either.

Fedor's touch was losing strength fast. *You love them. Why didn't you tell me, moi droog? I wouldn't have—*

You shot me! Stephen sent, angrily.

Self-defense. I saw it coming. Your mind—

Stephen understood, now. *It's true. Fedor, I'm sorry. You can't understand.*

I understand you have killed me. What else is there to understand. Ah, God! It's so stupid for me to die because you were in love and didn't know it.

Stephen tried once more to rise, but couldn't. *I'm sorry Fedor,* he said again.

I wish I had some vodka. And a smoke. I wish . . .

Stephen had the impression of a door swinging open, slamming shut, light, then silence.

He lay there, just he and the sky, and for the first time in his life he thought he felt truly at peace.

He awoke on a sledge. Matthew was pulling it, the brushmen and Remy walking on either side.

"Matthew—" he managed

"*Shh,* Stephen, you've lost a lot of blood."

"Not important. I've got to tell you some things."

"It can wait."

"Maybe not. I—I'm sorry, Matthew. I didn't understand."

"Understand what?" Matthew stopped, turned toward him.

"A while ago I said that the resistance only worked because of you and Fiona. I made it sound like an insult. The thing is, you guys—" He clenched his teeth at a hard, deep pain. "The thing is, most teeps turn rogue not for some abstract cause, not for some high ideal, but because life is stacked against them. Their lives are misery—hunted, hurt, never anywhere long enough to make friends. Searching for just a minute of happiness in years of pain. They go on because they *hope.* If they had no hope, they'd join Psi Corps or take the sleepers.

"But hope is so fragile, Matthew. It's the easiest thing to kill. And yet there you two are, in the eye of the storm, and everyone can see how you

feel, *feel* how you feel. They can see it's not stupid to hope. You love each other, and so they love you. I—I think I've known it for a long time, I just didn't want to see it."

"Because I destroyed your hope," Matthew whispered.

"No. No. Listen to me, Matthew. I *wanted* Fiona. She gave me desire, not hope. Only you guys together gave me that. Only the both of you." He licked his cracked lips. "There's something else. I want you to scan me. I want you to know everything."

"You aren't strong enough for that."

"But if I die—"

"You won't die," Matthew said. "We've got our connection. Baraka Industries sent a chopper three hours ago. We're going home."

"Where—" He coughed on what felt like a live coal. "Where is home this week?"

"You know. Wherever Fiona is."

2

Senator Khalid Ahmed of the United Islamic Nations (UIN) had a sleek face, the eyes of a tiger, and a smile that meant nothing at all. That he appeared on the comscreen and not in person diminished his presence not in the slightest.

"Director Vacit," he said. "I hope you are well today."

"Very well, thank you, Senator. What can I do for you?"

"You can explain to me why you are preparing the *Varona* for a Venus run. Correct me if I'm wrong, Director, but I'm fairly certain that—as lead boils on its surface—there are no rogue telepaths on Venus."

"You never know where you will find rogues, Senator."

"Mr. Vacit, you have never been known for your humor. I respectfully suggest that it is too late in your career to begin trying to build a reputation for it. We both know where rogues can be found—here, on Earth, on every continent, in every country. And yet, oddly enough, though you direct a well-funded, highly organized institution with broader discretionary powers than any similar organization on or off Earth, these rogues seem to not only be thriving, but doing more damage each day. Bombings all over the globe. Schoolchildren snatched from testing lines. Three reeducation camps 'liberated' in as many months. And here you want to jaunt off to Venus."

"There's been a murder there, on the orbiting station."

"Fine. Send a telepath—on the next supply transport."

"The killer may have been a rogue telepath, as I told you, and thus the matter requires Psi Corps investigation."

"In that case, I require the details of the case."

"You will have them. When I return. I'm already on Station Prime, and our departure window draws near."

"Perhaps you can simply tell me why the director of Psi Corps needs to go along on a simple murder investigation."

"It's within my boundaries as director."

"Yes, it is. But that isn't a reason."

Kevin replied with a simple shrug.

Ahmed turned a shade darker. "I have to tell you, Director, many of us have grown concerned over leadership at Psi Corps. You might want to keep that in mind."

In other words, some of you have begun to think yourselves powerful enough to retire me, Kevin thought, as he acknowledged the statement by inclining his head and severing the link.

"Sir?"

"Yes, Ms. Alexander?" He turned and immediately had to catch himself as his Earth-born reflexes again betrayed him in the zero gravity. They still had an hour or so of turnaround—it was always wise to run a few tests on the fusion drive before kicking it back on for the deceleration leg of the journey. Even though he understood that, he would be happier when he had weight again, even if it was the result of confused inertia rather than the product of real gravity.

"May I ask a question?"

"You've been my assistant for what—fifteen years now? I suppose you may."

"Why are we going to Venus?"

"Such impertinence," he responded wryly.

"Yes, sir, I know, but after four days in a ship, one begins to wonder these things."

"Aren't you enjoying your book? Isn't it keeping your interest?"

"Yes, sir. I mean, I suppose. Did this Bester ever write anything else?"

"Yes, he did, and it is probably the second-best work of twentieth-century speculative fiction. The one you're reading is the best. You don't agree?"

"I haven't read much science fiction, modern or ancient. It's—well, the language is strange. It's amusing that they refer to 'scanning' as 'peeping,' though. I suppose I don't really see the point in the literature as a whole. All in all, Bester did a poor job of forecasting the future."

Vacit fingered his chin. "The point of science fiction isn't to predict the future, but to *imagine* it. Those are two very different things. I didn't understand either, when Senator Crawford introduced me to the subject, but over time I finally *grokked* it."

"Sir?"

"Never mind."

"I'll keep reading, sir." She hesitated. "And if you can't answer the

question, sir—about why we're going to Venus—you can just tell me so, rather than distracting me."

"We're going to Venus to find what was in the hole in Antarctica," he said.

Her eyes went very wide, not something he often saw them do anymore. It reminded him of the much younger intern who had walked into his office, long ago.

"What makes you—why Venus, sir?"

He composed himself, reached out to make certain that no one else was within ear- or mindshot. No one was. Besides himself and Natasha, there was the flight crew—all P3s or under—and two Psi Cops, both presently asleep aft. As for electronic spies, his personal team had debugged the *Varona*.

"This is for you only. Do you understand?"

"Yes, sir."

"Years ago—before you were born—I touched an alien artifact, one IPX had found on Mars. Not Centauri, not Narn, but produced by a technology like we've never seen—until that fragment you and I found in Yucatán. The same technology, Ms. Alexander. Organic in nature, very advanced."

"I see. Sir, you might have told me about this—"

"The artifacts of which I speak are among EarthGov's most highly classified secrets, Ms. Alexander. I shouldn't be telling you about them even now. I do so only because of the great trust I have in you."

"Yes, sir. I appreciate that, sir."

"Then you will appreciate that what I tell you next is more than classified—it is unknown to everyone except me."

She nodded.

"The fragment from Yucatán—did you perceive anything unusual when you handled it?"

"Not really, sir—but I'm only a P5."

"The artifact from Mars had a certain—signature. When I touched it, I felt—I suppose I must call it *awe*. Ms. Alexander, you must know me well enough to know that I despise the unempirical, the untestable, particularly when considering them as a basis for action. I distrust what cannot be objectively verified.

"Perhaps that is why I have waited all these years to act, to do anything about this, to even try to verify what I suspect—because the basis of my suspicions are so—questionable." He paused to let that sink in. She *did* know him well. She didn't prompt or cajole him, but waited for him to continue, knowing he would.

"I must digress again. When I was *very* young—eighty years ago,

when I was four—my mother died. She was holding me. She was a powerful teep, and I was, too, even at that age. I went with her, when she died, via a sort of involuntary deathbed scan. I went beyond the doorway, and I think I almost stayed there. I saw a Shalako—a sort of spirit my mother's people believe in. I felt it was good, and kind, and very powerful. And then it became my mother, giving me a gift.

"I've always believed that the gift was real, in some sense. I think she gave me some of her strength, enhanced my abilities. As you know, the scales can't rate me, but I think I'm at least a P13. But since Antarctica, I have begun to question whether that is all that happened."

"You felt something in Antarctica, I remember."

"Yes. I felt a death-trace, one so old that it shouldn't have been there. I've sent P12s back to that site since—without telling them, of course, what to expect—and they felt only a faint presence, nothing like what I perceived. The same with the artifacts—while P12s feel *something*, they seem to receive no impressions as clear as my own."

"But, as you say, sir, you are stronger than they. And at least you've obtained objective confirmation that your experience was the result of some external cause."

He nodded reluctantly. "The death-trace in Antarctica was—*familiar* to me. It was something like the Shalako, from when I was young. And like the artifact from Mars and the fragment we found, but stronger—stranger, and yet, more familiar. It was"—he struggled—"almost as though this was a piece of *me*. A part of myself I recognized."

"That's not an uncommon phenomenon, sir, especially with teeps."

"No, it's not, but in most cases it is an illusion, a trick of the mind. And so I wish to test this, as best I can. You asked what this has to do with Venus. The impression I got in Antarctica was of two beings, two Shalako, two—whatever they were. One had died, and it was *his* trace I felt. You remember the story you told me? About the two brothers who battled the lords of death? One died, and his essence remained on Earth, the other lived and became the morning star?"

"Yes, sir."

"The morning star is Venus."

Natasha finally looked a little troubled. "Sir, I hope you have more to go on than that."

"I do," he said, feeling frustrated. "But it's in here." He tapped his skull. "It's like I've known it for a long time. Like it's always been there. Yet it took you, and fifteen years, to convince me to actually trust it."

She considered that for a moment, then looked at him frankly. "Sir, if you say you trust a feeling—well, I trust it, too."

"Thank you, Ms. Alexander. There *is* a bit more—something a little

more substantial. You remember that satellites had, in times past, mapped a gravitational and magnetic anomaly at the Antarctic site? Well, I've located a similar anomaly on Venus—so similar that it matches to within ninety-eight percent both in strength and dimensions. It's at the Venusian south pole. So it may be that I'm not entirely crazy. Nonetheless . . ." He paused.

"Yes?"

"Ms. Alexander, if you ever suspect I *have* gone mad, or even senile—I count on you to tell me."

He expected her to laugh it off, but instead she pursed her lips thoughtfully.

"Sir—I don't think you're mad, or senile. I've never thought so. But there *is* something I don't understand. It's been bothering me for some time now."

"That being?"

He felt her scanning—not him, but for "peepers."

"Don't worry," he assured her. "Nothing is leaving this cabin unless we want it to."

Even so, she lowered her voice to a whisper. "You could have shut the underground down ten years ago, shut it down cold. I'm certain of it. But you didn't, and I think you've even helped them a little. Why?"

He cracked a rare grin. "I *thought* you had figured that out," he said. "I leaked it to you very slowly, watching you carefully the whole time."

"But the risk—what would you have done had I tried to betray you?"

"I honestly didn't think you would, but if you had—I don't really have to tell you, do I?"

"No, sir."

"And you really want the answer to this question? Even knowing that you may not like what you learn?"

"Yes, sir. Very much."

"When I first became Senator Crawford's aide, I was infiltrating the MRA organization—not to sabotage it, necessarily, but to understand it from the inside, to form an opinion of it. Over time, my opinion of it grew, and I began to see its importance.

"When I touched the artifacts from Mars, I came to understand something else. Something truly profound. There are beings out there in the cosmos, Ms. Alexander, beside whom even the Centauri look like cavemen. Some, I'm certain, are benevolent—those who made the artifacts on Mars, for instance. At least so it seems. But I also have the impression—no, the *certainty*—that there are others, who could and would destroy our race with no more thought or effort than you and I would expend to kill a bug on our kitchen floor.

"When we meet those beings, we will need every weapon we can get our hands on, and among those weapons I include ourselves. We will need the most powerful teeps we can find—more powerful than any we presently have, I think. P14s, P30s, if such a thing is possible. And stable telekinetics." He heaved a sigh. "I can't even tell you why I think that, exactly, and for some reason it angers me when I examine it closely. But I *am* certain."

"So the arranged marriages were your idea. To prepare us to fight these aliens, if they truly exist?"

"Oh, they exist. But no, the genetic matching was already in place when I started working for Crawford. I encouraged it."

"And the underground? How does that fit?"

"Evolution. Think about it. Which teeps escape the grasp of the Corps? The smartest, the strongest, those who best know how to work together and alone. The underground is the gene pool that we draw from. If it were to disappear—if there was no underground—we would lose the selective process. Intentional selection—breeding—can produce faster results, but evolution does the unexpected. I think—I thought, anyway—that we would need both to produce our best future."

Natasha turned her book over in her hand a few times, clearly disturbed by what had been said.

"Speak your mind, Ms. Alexander."

"I never—sir, I've always understood that you had some deeper agenda, some purpose that drove your actions. I've always admired you, always trusted your judgment. You've always seemed to be completely rational, governed by reason . . ." She stopped, apparently unable to finish.

"You never imagined that, at the bottom of it all, there was an article of faith? I don't blame you for being disturbed, Ms. Alexander. I would be disappointed in you if you weren't. I've struggled with this for years myself." He turned for a moment to the small port, gazing out at the enigmatic stars beyond.

"Let me put it another way, Ms. Alexander," he continued. "One you may find more palatable. Assume I'm wrong about our powerful, alien enemies, and my intuitions are proved just so much fantasy. We still have the normals to deal with. Right now, however much we hate to admit it, they are our masters. I am the director of Psi Corps only because they do not know what I am. The next director will probably be a mundane, and who can guess what direction politics might take in the future?

"I have seen our situation shift too many times in my life. It will shift again. Perhaps one day they will decide that Earth would be better off

without our kind altogether. If they have us all registered, all in the Corps, all in one place—well, that will make their job the easier, won't it?

"Personally, I think the Corps is our best chance—already we have more power than EarthGov suspects. And one day—one fine day— normals will awaken to find that it is *we* who are the masters, as it should be. But that day is not yet come, and until it does, I think it wise not to keep all of our eggs in one basket. The underground is not the enemy, Ms. Alexander. Normals are the enemy."

He turned away from the stars. "I've never said these things to anyone, Ms. Alexander. I once loved a woman, and I never even said them to her. But I grow old, now. And I know you—I know you understand me."

Her gaze was steady on his again. "I think I understand you perfectly, sir. And agree completely."

"And what do you think of my sanity now?"

"I think," she replied, matter-of-factly, "that I have never met a saner man in my life."

"Thank you. I trust you mean that. You've asked why we are going to Venus. The answer is that I think we'll find an answer there. We'll find our past, and in so doing—our future."

The station commander pretended outrage when the *Varona* came into dock, but there was little he could do about it. There *had,* in fact, been a murder on board the *Lucifer.* It was unlikely in the extreme that a rogue teep had been involved, but Officers Trout and Sasaki—the two Psi Cops they had brought along—had their orders. When the *Varona* left Venus orbit, it would be with the corpse of a verified rogue, P10.

In the meantime, Kevin had places to be. He had one of the *Varona*'s two shuttles outfitted for an orbital jaunt, so Natasha and he left only a few hours after their arrival.

As he watched the wheel-shaped station vanish against the marbled immensity of Venus, Kevin's confidence began to wane. Not his faith in his people, but in himself. He had come an awfully long way and risked a great deal for—for what? What did he really expect to find?

There was no question of landing on Venus to investigate the anomaly. Oh, ships had gone down there, twice, and both times had discovered that reaching the surface was no problem. Leaving again was. Their own shuttle wouldn't even make it through the clouds of sulfuric acid that veiled the goddess of love, much less endure the nine-hundred-degree, ninety-bar kiss of her surface.

Nevertheless, Natasha piloted the shuttle into geosynchronic—no, he supposed that was Aphroditosynchronic—orbit over the south pole,

where they waited, watching hurricanes chase one another through the roiling upper atmosphere.

"We have oxygen enough to stay two more days. Lucifer Station keeps calling to ask if we need assistance."

"Tell them no, again," he replied, wearily. "Continue to hail the surface."

Natasha did so. He didn't sense any doubt from her, despite the two fruitless days they had spent, hovering above the planet. Her trust in him seemed in inverse proportion to his trust in himself.

Another day passed. He sent down the second of the surface probes—he'd sent one the first day. He beamed messages in all languages and on all wavelengths, from modulated radar to gamma bursts.

He remembered Lee Crawford, trying to speak to the stars with a flashlight.

In the dark, two Shalakos came to him. Kevin could just make out the outlines of the surrounding pueblo, the ladder emerging from the kiva, where the great mysteries were kept. The Shalakos gestured, and he followed them into the deeper dark of the kiva.

There they danced, and sang of the days when his people had been creatures with webbed toes and feet, of the days when they had lived far beneath the earth. As they danced, they became the twin war gods, the children of the Sun, shining with all of their father's brightness. They sang of leading his ancestors from darkness to the world above.

The world was overrun with monsters, dark and terrible, but the twins went among the monsters, killed them with lightning and fire. On they sang, these masked dancers, of evils over which they triumphed, and of greater evils still to come.

In the end, they had to go. In the end, they could leave only a wonderful gift for the children, whom they had brought from the depths of the Earth, raised from slimy things living in the waters to the five-fingered people of the pueblo.

In the end, one of the twins died, and the other danced away. Kevin approached the corpse, still shining with terrible beauty, still masked. He removed the mask.

He saw beneath it his own face.

"Sir!" He lurched awake, the dream stripping away from him, thoughts and feelings he hadn't experienced in eighty years remaining at the edge of his mind. He had rarely thought of and never believed those

things so dear to his mother, that world of spirit and faith she inhabited. For eighty years, his mother's teachings had been nearly silent in him.

Now they were awake.

"Sir, there's something happening."

"What, Ms. Alexander?" Waking was harder at his age, as if his body demanded practice for death. He rubbed grit from his eyes.

"All of our sensors went down a few minutes ago," she said with remarkable calm. "All of them."

"Tap into the satellite net."

"That's down, too, and I suspect Lucifer Station is down. Something is jamming everything."

Kevin pulled himself forward to the cockpit. The nose of the shuttle was pointed directly at the planet. Night bisected the view, clotted cream and darkness. Against the white and yellow arabesques, something was growing. A dot, a circle, not just coming closer, but blooming like an orchid, or perhaps like a beetle unfolding its wings.

It was a ship, but a ship unlike any he had ever seen, and it continued to grow until there was no Venus, only the ship, its carapace scintillating, shifting vaguely and constantly.

It opened a mouth and took them in.

COME. The voice coalesced out of sudden static, as order emerging from chaos. It was impossible to tell if it was a voice of sound or the mind.

He glanced at Natasha, who had gone alabaster. "Did you hear it?"

"Yes, sir. Sir, hull sensors are back up. It's an oxygen/nitrogen atmosphere outside, and pressure has equalized."

He peered through the port, but beyond lay only darkness.

"Well, Ms. Alexander," he said softly. "Let's go see your astronaut/ angels."

As he set foot on the floor, faint patterns began to appear—like a phosphorescence he had once seen on the surface of the ocean at night. The light gradually rose, mother-of-pearl, glints flashing from a dragon-fly's wing. It reminded him, too, somehow, of the kiva. So many echoes. And to the ear there was no sound, but below the level of sound—what Monkey used to sometimes call the "wind"—a faint modulated humming. Kevin couldn't actually discern anything specific—no thought, no emotion. Instead what he got was a sense of perfection, like seeing the best solution to a problem, of suddenly understanding the symmetry in a pattern that had—an instant before—seemed elusive and chaotic.

Gaining confidence, he reached his mind out further. Again an overwhelming feeling of familiarity surged through him like a wave.

I've been here.

YES. A hundred times stronger than before, the voice filled everything.

Where are you? Who are you? Kevin asked.

I AM HERE. I HAVE ALWAYS BEEN HERE.

And the Shalako stood before him, blazing light and glory, its headdress like the rays of the Sun. A sense of awe—worship even—smote him so hard he almost tumbled to his knees. And something sounded inside of him, as a string sounds when a like-tuned string vibrates nearby. Vision engulfed him.

He saw a war, fought on a scale beyond imagining. The enemy was darkness; the ships, black spiders. Worlds fell before them, whole races perished. They were entropy, they were the end of everything, they were the monsters out of the birth of time . . . An explosion of images, too much to understand.

The war ended, but only for a while. They were not gone, the monsters, only waiting. Their enemies waited, too, these things that looked to him like Shalakos, like angels, like gods because it was the only way he could understand them. They waited, and they prepared the younger races for what was to come. Even the race so young it knew only the vaguest echo of the last war. Humanity. Two came, together, to prepare them. One died . . .

The experience devolved into images, so fiercely bright and alien that he felt himself slipping away. He was dying, all that was *him* hurtling into nothing. But there was a way, a piece that could remain, a container that had been prepared for it. A place to wait, and sleep, and one day wake. He went into that place and rested.

He was back in the cave, in his mother's arms, and he felt her slipping away, and himself along with her, and the storm, the light, the Shalako, the gift.

The moments became one, the death, the resting, the gift. The images became one. And he understood—some of it.

You made us, he told the Shalako. *Took some of us, altered us for centuries, brought our genes back to Earth, implanted them in people.*

YES.

To stand against these monsters. To save ourselves.

YES.

The gift—my gift—it was from you, somehow. What was it? Why do I see your—brother? Why do I feel what he felt?

THE MIRROR NEVER SEES ITSELF. THE REFLECTION NEVER IS ITSELF.

Kevin wanted to rephrase his questions, but there was a silent punc-

tuation to the Shalako's reply, a certainty that this vague riddle was his last word on the subject.

You—led me here.

YES.

Why? What am I supposed to do?

A momentary pause, like looking over the edge of a very high cliff.

EVOLUTION CRAWLS TO IMPERFECTION. IT ENDS IN EXTINCTION.

And it was gone. The light faded.

GO NOW.

Back on the shuttle, surrounded once again only by space, Kevin stared out at the stars, seeing now the terror that lurked between them. The Enemy. He felt a hatred for it that was and wasn't his. He heard the words of the Shalako.

Natasha coughed softly behind him.

"Sir?"

"Yes, Ms. Alexander?"

"When you— What did it look like to you?"

"A bright spirit. My mother. Myself."

"I saw an angel."

"I suspect it isn't so much *what* you see as what the thing you see represents."

"It was—it was wonderful."

"Yes."

"What do you think he meant, at the end? It sounded almost like he was telling us to do something."

"Evolution crawls to imperfection." Kevin sighed. "I should have seen it long ago, but I didn't. I've wasted time."

"I don't understand."

"I was right, about the need to produce powerful telepaths. You saw the enemy?"

"I saw—terrible things. Creatures of darkness."

"Yes. But we can hurt them, somehow—or our children can. I think that's why one of the—angels—died. I think the enemy found them on Earth, saw what they were up to. They had to fight, then, to protect the secret. Protect us. They made us, Ms. Alexander. They took the raw stuff of humanity and made something better. I think they started very long ago, helping us along, guiding us. But just over a century ago, they gave us the final push, the final gift. Now it's up to us. The ship is gone, isn't it? And the anomaly?"

"Yes, sir."

"Yes. He stayed here until we found him. Now he's gone."

"Evolution crawls to imperfection?"

"Yes, of course. Evolution is about reproduction, nothing else. It never produces anything 'better' except in that sense. It evens out extremes in preference to flexibility. What we want is an extreme—the best telepaths possible. Evolution is a blind process. Natural selection can't plan for anything, it can only respond—with glacial slowness—to present conditions. But sentient beings can plan and design. We are outside of evolution now, beyond it, free of its limitations. Telepaths weren't produced by evolution; better telepaths won't be produced by it either. Not fast enough, anyway. It's up to us to take up the work where our creators left off. It's up to Psi Corps." He smiled faintly. "The mirror never sees itself."

They were silent for a time, and Natasha fell asleep. He held himself up against the gentle pressure of their acceleration, gazing down thoughtfully at her. She had been a good aide. A good friend, even. He trusted her more than any living person.

But he didn't trust her this much. He didn't trust her with *this*. This was his mission, his burden. He still had life enough and time to do the things that needed to be done.

Psi Corps was already on the right course—he had done most of the right things. He had known. How was still unclear—had the dead Shalako somehow passed a piece of its soul to his grandfather, thence to his mother, finally to himself? Or was it more subtle than that, an imprint on the genes that formed neurons, a program, software that would lie dormant until triggered by certain input?

He didn't know, and didn't really care. All he really knew was that he no longer had any doubts.

His mistake had been the underground, and there he had let emotion cloud his judgment. For Psi Corps to be what it had to be, some unpleasant things had to happen to its members. His love for Ninon Davion and her daughter—*his* daughter, Fiona—had led him to rationalize a wrong and almost disastrous course. Ninon would not have wanted to see her daughter in the Psi Corps he was creating.

But his sentiment was as nothing when measured against the greater need. If humanity fell, was extinguished, the struggle of teep against mundane was meaningless. Only an organized force could stand against the coming darkness, and only the Psi Corps could create it. He would spare Fiona if he could, but the resistance had to end. And it would, very soon.

His mission. His burden.

He extended his fingers until they lightly touched Natasha's face.

And recoiled. The Shalako—or whatever it really was—had left something there. Something small, almost unnoticeable, but something in her brain. Like a seed.

He brought his fingers back down and did his work very lightly. She would remember everything, but never desire to speak of it, save to him. When he died and she died, then no one would know.

But the machine would have been built by then. The machine would run without knowing why. It was best that way—a machine that knew its purpose, its destiny, might fight against it, try to steer its own way. Humanity—and telepaths—no longer had the luxury of that sort of spurious freedom.

He settled back into his own couch, weary, seeking sleep without dreams.

In her own dreams, Natasha Alexander saw the being of light, and it looked back at her with a light that illuminated thought and bone and blood and marrow; it looked upon her genetic structure and was pleased. **IT WILL BE YOU, IF THE DARKNESS COMES SOON,** the light said, **OR ONE IN YOUR LINE, IF THE DARKNESS COMES LATER. YOU, OR THE ECHO OF YOU, WILL HEAR THE CALL, AND YOU WILL COME TO US, AND WE WILL FINISH THE WORK WE BEGAN IN YOU.**

And as the light faded, Natasha Alexander wept tears of ultimate love, and dreamed of being finished: gleaming, indestructible, *whole*.

And she knew one thing: They would meet again.

3

Fiona put on her winningest smile for the young doorman. He looked uncertainly back down at his clipboard.

"I still don't see your name on the list."

"Sure you do. Miriam Soto."

"Oh. That's funny, I thought you said a different name. Must've heard wrong. You can go in, then."

"Thanks, handsome."

She left him blushing at the door. She had plucked the name from his mind easily enough—along with the fact that he didn't know what this Soto looked like—but when the real Miriam showed up, that would make things sticky, so she had best hurry.

The Four Seasons ballroom was just starting to fill up, so it was still easy to pick people out at a distance. She spotted the tall, elegant figure of Holden Waters right away, surrounded by a small flock of pretty young things. Trying to sashay—not quite sure she knew how, and not at all happy in her strapless evening gown—she went to join the flock, waiting at the edge until she caught his eye.

"Oh, my," he said, "I don't believe I've met *you.*"

"How soon they forget," she replied.

"But don't tell me that we have! I couldn't forget such a face."

"Well, perhaps it isn't my face you would remember," Fiona said, sweetly. This prompted huffs of outrage from the other women around Waters, and two of them drifted off.

"Young lady—" he began, more than a trace of irritation rising in his voice.

"Yes—Daddy?" She raised her voice on the last.

"Young lady, I don't know who you are—"

"That's okay, Daddy, the paternity test knows who *you* are, and—"

"Could we have a word in private?" He glanced around the room. Like neutrons caroming through plutonium, the first girls to huff off had begun a chain reaction, and attention was shifting their way. She smiled

and waved languidly as Waters led her off, gripping her arm gently but firmly.

A few moments later, they were in a small lounge.

"Now. Young lady. I don't know whether we've really met or not—"

"Daddy, you might want to turn the camera off, if there is one in here."

"Stop calling me that!"

He said nothing about a monitor, and she understood from his surface reaction that there actually wasn't one—as far as he knew.

So she smiled sweetly, pulled a molded plastic gun from her purse, and shot him. There was only a suspiration—the pistol used CO_2—and a little blood as the flechette pricked into his throat. His expression was just turning to horrified shock when his legs went. She caught him on the way down, eased him into a chair.

"Here we go!" she said, removing her long-sleeved gloves. She placed her hands on his temples and scanned. When she had everything she needed, she planted a very firm, clear thought in his mind. When he awoke, he would know for certain that one of his factories was about to explode, which one, and when. He would have just enough time to evacuate his workers, and no more.

She put her gloves on, reached back into her purse, and pulled out a black marker. She left him with LIVE FREE printed across his forehead.

She didn't go back through the ballroom, but slipped out a back door she had been informed of—it could be exited, but not entered.

She returned to her van—a late-model Cortez—drove a few blocks, parked, and shucked out of the dress, exchanging it for jeans, T-shirt, light chest armor, and a sweatshirt. Then she resumed driving.

She pulled onto I-5 and headed south toward Tacoma, past Boeing-Mitsubishi Field, and took an exit into the grey heart of an industrial park. She parked outside the outer fence, retrieved an assault rifle and wire cutters from a compartment under the seat, and got out.

The outer fence was mostly symbol, there to keep kids out—the real security precautions were farther in, and were someone else's responsibility. She cut through the mesh in a few minutes, checked her watch, stepped through the gap, and waited, watching the blinking lights perched on the high vents of the Waters complex. She tried to remain collected, but the sight of the sleeper factory tightened angry cords in her chest. No one who had met one of the zombies the antitelepathy drug eventually produced could really imagine it was a legitimate option. Yet it was manufactured by the ton, wasn't it? Normals watched their neighbors take the injection twice a week, without blinking.

After this, maybe they would blink.

At 10:00, klaxons started wailing. Hopefully this meant only that Waters had awakened and done the right thing.

Fifteen minutes later, she heard the sound of several people running toward her and raised her rifle to greet them, just in case they weren't who she expected.

Matthew?

It's us!

At about that same moment, three small suns appeared in the Waters complex, and an instant later the shock of the explosion blew over her. Hard on its heels came Matthew, Stephen, Cinnamon, Adam, and Phoebe, and she threw herself into Matthew's arms, allowing herself the luxury of a quick embrace.

"You did it!"

"Perfect plan!" Stephen said, slapping her on the back. "Perfect, that is, if we don't get caught. Let's move, people!"

They piled into the van and Stephen took the wheel. He gunned the engine, and they streaked out of the lot.

"Any problems?" Matthew asked, squeezing her hand.

"Only the walking-in-high-heels part."

The van rattled from the shock of another, greater explosion.

"*That* was the sleepers," Stephen remarked. "Had to clear the building away first in order to get maximum dispersal."

"The weather is holding," Matthew observed. "The cloud should drift right through Seattle. Maybe after normals get a taste of the stuff, they won't be so eager to inject it into us."

The evacuation rush—and the related panic that swept through the nearby areas—covered their escape nicely. They got back on I-5, exited again a few miles later, and made a quick stop at a friendly house in Renton. There Cinnamon, Adam, and Phoebe piled into a green Makarov Bogatyr utility and headed due south toward Portland. Fiona, Matthew, and Stephen continued in the van, driving for six hours on back roads, rounding the imposing Mount Rainier, out through the Yakima valley, until they at last reached a private airstrip belonging to Rentech Corporation.

A dapper young man in a black three-piece suit met them at the gate.

"You aren't looking for the wine country, are you?" he asked.

"Yup," Stephen replied, "I'm lookin' for a bottle of '61 Chaldee."

The fellow nodded in satisfaction. "Welcome, Mr. and Ms. Dexter, Mr. Walters. Your travel arrangements have been made. Your plane is

boarding now. My name is Rinaldo D'Aguila, and it will be my pleasure
to accompany you on your journey."

"Pleased, I'm sure," Stephen replied.

Fiona bounced twice on the bed, experimentally. "I think I've forgot-
ten exactly what this *is*," she remarked, collapsing spread-eagle on the
huge four-poster.

"It gets better," Matthew said, peering into the next room. "A
shower. Shall we get clean before we get dirty, Mrs. Dexter?"

"Why compartmentalize?" she asked, arching an eyebrow. She took
one more bounce on the bed to catapult her toward Matthew.

Later, as they lay sweaty and gripped together, Fiona glanced sleep-
ily around the room. "Y'know, I didn't even think about whether there
might be a camera in here."

"Too late to worry about that now."

Do you trust these people?

*I'm naked in one of their suites, which doesn't say much about my
intelligence, because no, I don't. But they've always played well by us. We
would have had a hell of a time blowing the sleeper factory without their
help, and even more trouble getting away. Now we're in a nice room, we've
got a day or two to amble around the French Quarter while they get us ready
for the next leg. It beats our usual travel arrangements.* He smoothed his
hand across her belly.

*(skepticism) They helped us because Waters competes with them in
pharmaceuticals, not because they care about teeps,* Fiona replied.

*True enough. But if the underground ran exclusively on altruism, we'd
be in pretty bad shape.*

Which she couldn't disagree with.

Fiona slept restlessly. The bed was *too* comfortable, the room *too*
nice. Some of her people were sleeping on the streets tonight, some in
concentration camps. It didn't seem right that she should be surrounded
by such luxury.

But that wasn't all of it. She eased out of bed and went to the
window, gazing out at the lights of New Orleans. The new French Quar-
ter stretched out below, rebuilt after the terrible flood of 2092. It didn't
look so new anymore. So much of the city had been destroyed in the
flood that many had wanted to call it New New Orleans, but it hadn't
been a very popular suggestion.

Deep down, she wondered if she didn't need a New Fiona.

She loved her cause, but she had changed a great deal in the four-
teen years or so since she had taken Monkey's place. At first, she had

believed she could somehow win, change the whole world. That had been a good feeling, the best. The little victories were good—when they snatched a kid from Psi Corps or blew up a sleeper factory—but in the old days those all had been garnishes to the main course, the dream of that last battle, after which everything would be okay.

The years had gnawed at that dream, and without knowing exactly when or how, she one day had realized that winning small battles was all there was, because the war—the war could not be won. They were bailing water from a hulled lifeboat.

Eventually she came to where she could admit this to herself, and even make a little peace with it. The problem was that she could not even begin to speak of it to others, not even Matthew. What recruited people and kept them going through everything was the very simple belief that one day it would be over, and they could all step into the sun. What kept them going was hope.

And she and Matthew, for better or worse, for richer or poorer, had become the center of that hope, the axis of it. How would the rest feel if they knew she, Fiona, the mother of the revolution, had no real hope left in her own heart?

Her musings were interrupted by a soft knock on the door. She found her jeans and pulled them on, tugged the sweatshirt over her head, and went to the peephole.

It was D'Aguila. What could he want?

She opened the door a crack.

"Ms. Dexter?"

"That's me."

"I hope I didn't wake you, but a matter of some importance has come up, and we rather hoped we could request your services."

"You need a scan done? *Now?*"

"Please."

She considered. This was one of the prices they paid, when they got corporate help. Rentech probably had a hundred teeps in their employ, but they were all Psi Corps, which meant they wouldn't do illegal scans.

Already feeling dirty, she nodded. Matthew was still asleep, and she didn't wake him.

The "matter of some importance" was a young man—perhaps twenty-five—with curly blond hair and a pleasant, round face. It would have been even more pleasant, she imagined, without the split lip and bleeding nose. She regarded him through a one-way mirror, beyond which he sat in a grey room with a small table and two chairs.

"He's a teep," she told D'Aguila. "A strong one."

"Strong enough to be a Psi Cop?"

"Yes."

D'Aguila made a sort of grating noise. "He started working in our technical support department about a year ago. We caught him trying to send files out to somewhere, but he was able to erase both the files and the intended destination before we caught him."

"What do you want with me?"

"I want you to tell me what he's doing here—whether he knows about our arrangements with the underground, and so on."

"It won't be easy. He'll block."

"Do what is necessary."

"He may be stronger than I am."

"We can only ask you to try."

She nodded, feeling sick to her stomach. But she went inside.

She felt his touch leap to her immediately.

"You're one of us," he said, softly.

"I doubt that very much," she replied. "I make you for a Psi Cop. What about it?"

Yes, I'm Corps. I'm proud of it. What I meant was, you're one of us, a teep. In or out of the Corps, we are the same. Kith.

"Speak aloud," she said.

You don't want me to speak what I know aloud. You're with the underground, I guess.

Good guess, she replied.

You do a lot of business with these people. They're just using you, you know.

And we use them. To fight you jackboots. What's the difference?

That's what I'm wondering. (pause) They're going to kill me.

That's not my concern, Fiona said. *You dug your own grave. But if you cooperate, let me scan you, I might be able to get you out of here in one piece. I don't know what I'll do with you then, but I won't kill you.*

(laugh) If you find out what I know and tell them, they will most certainly kill me. And you, too.

"Let me scan you."

You want it? You got it.

Her mind filled with images. How long, she could not say, but at the end of it she was trembling.

Stay quiet, she told him, when it was done. *I'm going to tell them I couldn't scan you.*

He nodded, and she left the room.

"Well?" D'Aguila asked.

"Too tough. For now. Keep him in there and don't let him sleep. I can get it in the morning."

D'Aguila shifted uncomfortably. "I'm supposed to have the results by ten o'clock."

"You will. I promise you. Matthew can help me."

"Very well." She felt a touch of suspicion. Not, she hoped, too much. "I'll find my way back, if you don't mind. Having someone near me right now is—uncomfortable." She tapped her head.

"I understand."

On the way back to her room, she stopped and knocked on Stephen's door. After a few moments—and some muffled curses—he peered blearily out.

"Hey. What's up?"

"Come over to the room for some coffee." *It's important. Bring your stuff.*

"Early day, eh? Okay. Be there momentarily."

They paced on the balcony, waiting for Stephen to finish.

"Nothin' out here," he finally said, stashing the bug sweeper back in his bag. "I think we can talk."

"Good. I've already told Matthew that they asked me to do an illegal scan on a Psi Cop."

"Son of a bitch. Did you?"

"Yep. Didn't have to try hard, though, he gave it up. I pretended I couldn't nail him, told 'em we'd all come back for another try in the morning."

"Okay. I'll bite. Why the Japanese opera?"

"Because the Psi Cop wasn't here to investigate the underground. He was here to investigate a slavery racket."

"What?"

She abruptly swung her fist into the wall, almost taking pleasure in the sudden sharp pain in her knuckles.

"Jeez, Fee—"

"For every three teeps Rentech moves for us, one vanishes. We thought Psi Corps was doing it. They weren't. We've been helping these bastards enslave telepaths."

"Holy Joe."

"You're certain about this?" Matthew asked.

"*You* scan him."

"No, no, of course I believe—damn. What now?"

"This cop has all of the major locations for the trade in his head. We

can track them down, one by one, get 'em back. But first we need the cop. I'm not leaving him here for these monsters."

"He's a Psi Cop," Stephen rumbled. "He'll betray us first chance he gets."

"I'm not going to adopt him," Fiona said, "just get him out of *here.*"

Matthew was nodding. "Fiona's right. This is our fault—we sent those people to Rentech, and now they're slaves. Our problem. We get the cop."

"I'm not arguing this one," Stephen said. "But we can get what the cop knows and then—"

"Then what?" Matthew demanded. "Kill him in cold blood? I've killed Psi Cops when they were shooting at me, sure, but this? No."

"Okay, okay. We get the cop."

They took the guards with Fiona's flechettes. They never knew what hit them. D'Aguila—and the burly man standing beside him wielding a street sweeper—proved to be bigger problems. Opening the door must have triggered some sort of alarm; the big man already had the shotgun raised as they entered, and D'Aguila was pulling a Browning.

Fiona hit the bodyguard with everything she had, fugueing him even as his finger tightened on the trigger. D'Aguila got a shot off, which hit Stephen square in the chest. Though the impact must have hurt considerably, even through his body armor, Stephen's charge did not slow. He slammed D'Aguila into the wall so hard that cracks spidered in the plaster. Matthew, meanwhile, calmly shot the frozen guard with the flechette.

The Psi Cop was right where she had left him, though he had been beaten some more.

"Knew you'd come around," he said, lisping on a freshly broken tooth.

"Shut up. How well do you know this building?"

"Well enough to get us out. But they have four teeps here, in the building, ready to transport."

"And you know where."

"Yeah, sort of. What we have to do is get to a link, call Psi Corps—"

"No," Stephen grated, cocking D'Aguila's confiscated Browning. "No, you show us where they are. Letting Psi Corps have them is no better than leaving them here."

"You don't believe that."

"Shut up and do it."

"Okay. You're the ones with guns."

"Damn straight."

"Wake D'Aguila up."

That took a little doing. They finally had to reach into his mind and pull him out of it.

"Wha . . . ?" he said groggily.

"Here's what," Matthew said. "You have four teeps held in this building. You'll take us to them and then get us all out of here."

"Impossible. The whole complex must be on alert by now."

Stephen jerked him by the collar. "You'd better hope that isn't true, or if it is, that you can do something about it. Because if you *are* right, you're a dead man. And don't try to lie to us, either, or walk us into a trap, because you know you can't. Now be a good boy, okay?"

D'Aguila's eyes flicked from one to the other, perhaps searching for some sign of mercy. If so, he found none.

"There is a way, maybe," he allowed. "The esps are on D level. We might be able to get from there to the helipad by using the executive elevator. Might."

"Might makes right," Stephen replied. "Can you access the system to set off some false alarms in another part of the building?"

"Yes."

"Do it."

They avoided the guards in the halls by sensing them ahead of time, but motion detectors were harder to fool. By the time they reached D level, Fiona had a definite sense that the noose was tightening. As the elevator opened, her suspicions were confirmed by the bright, metallic smacking of bullets near her head.

Stephen bellowed and opened up with the street sweeper, spraying lead pellets as if with a hose. Two men screamed and crumpled in bloody ruin.

"End of the hall," D'Aguila said, staring and obviously trying not to vomit.

"Fine. Matthew and I will go. Stephen, watch the elevator."

"Roger."

"You could give me a gun," the Psi Cop said. "I could help."

"Very fat chance," Stephen replied.

The doors were locked, of course, but D'Aguila's card opened them. Two African-looking girls—twins, maybe twelve years old—a red-haired boy who might have been five, and a thin young woman in her early twenties turned listless eyes up at Fiona as the door slid open. She could feel their numbed minds and it almost made her retch.

"Sleepers. Damn them to hell."

"Come on. Come on all of you. We're getting out of here," Matthew said.

More gunfire sounded from down the hall.

"Damndamndamn," Stephen swore, as they approached. He was bleeding from a score on his arm. "Children?"

"We have to get out. You, D'Aguila. Which way?"

"The rest of this level is storage. The elevator is across the warehouses."

"Lead."

Suddenly the doors to the stairs banged open, and two egg-shaped objects bounced through, spinning near Matthew's feet.

"Matthew!" Fiona shrieked as Stephen yanked her down to cover.

But there was no explosion. An instant later, Matthew came hurtling by. "Gas! Go!"

They wove in and out of what seemed a rabbit warren of small workstations and storage areas, Matthew running point with D'Aguila, Stephen bringing up the rear, she and the Psi Cop in between, encouraging the fleeing teeps to run faster.

Stephen was fighting a rearguard action as they moved through a large warehouse area and at last reached a small elevator. D'Aguila's card and bioident got them in, and they had perhaps twenty seconds of breathing time before the doors opened again.

Unbelievably, the rooftop was empty when they exited. A chopper stood empty on a large pad, but they had crossed only half the distance to it when bullets cracked the concrete around their feet. With no cover, Stephen threw himself flat and unloaded the street sweeper again. Matthew was right beside him, firing six shots and then changing clips.

Three guards in heavy body armor were crouched behind a large antenna, firing Naga nine-millimeter submachine guns in controlled, professional bursts. They had a clear view of the fugitives all the way to the helicopter.

Fiona made her decision. She knelt and took careful aim at the guard she could see best, squeezed off a round.

Get 'em in the copter, Psi Cop. We'll be there when we can.

You won't make it.

None of us will make it without cover fire. Go!

She fired again and didn't watch the Psi Cop and his charges as they broke for the flier. She was too busy. She counted slowly, estimating how long it would take them to make it.

After thirty seconds, the guards found some nerve. Two started forward from cover, as the other two stood and fired almost nonstop.

Matthew had to roll to avoid being cut in half, and sparks struck inches from Fiona's face. Desperately, she reached for their minds, but they were too far away to get a decent lock on amid all the commotion.

Stephen roared, bounced up, and charged toward the nearest man. He'd dropped the empty street sweeper and was snapping off fast rounds from a pistol he'd picked up, probably back on D level. One guard pitched back, his teeth blown down into his neck.

The elevator door opened. Fiona spun desperately, firing between her knees. She hit two of the five newcomers, but the bullets spanged from body armor. She pulled the trigger again, and the piston cracked on an empty chamber.

She kicked back from the return fire, knowing as she did so that it was over.

Then the elevator and everything near it ceased to exist. It was replaced by a flare of painfully white light and as quickly by an ugly black cloud.

She had no idea what had happened, but she leapt up anyway, spinning just in time to see the Psi Cop turn the grenade launcher—sling mounted in the chopper—on the men at the antenna array.

He grinned at her as she leapt aboard, followed closely by Stephen and Matthew.

They ditched the chopper in the Atchafalaya basin, stole a battered Volkswagen truck from a used car lot, and drove west toward Mexico. Stephen and Matthew took the cab, while Fiona, the Psi Cop, and the rescued teeps piled into the back. Fiona checked them all for wounds. They seemed okay, but Fiona was by now certain that they had been given more than sleepers. They probably weren't even aware yet of what had happened.

The Psi Cop grinned around broken teeth at her.

"We make a good team," he said. "I make you to be a P12. You'd be a hell of a Psi Cop."

"Say that again, and I'll open you another set of eyes," Fiona replied pleasantly.

He shrugged resignedly. "What now, then?"

"First, I thank you for saving our lives back there. After that, you tell us which other Rentech installations have teeps."

"Most of them aren't at Rentech sites. They're rented out, sold to private citizens, to criminal syndicates, kula rings, you name it."

"But you know how to get the records of those sales."

"Yes I do."

"I want them."

"Why? So you can fight a war on two fronts? One against Psi Corps, the other against Rentech? I doubt you have the resources for that."

"You have no idea what we have. We'll do it."

"Worse, Rentech is one of your allies. Will you examine all of the 'friends' of the underground more carefully now? Once you start turning over these rocks, you never know what you'll find. If you get too picky, the underground won't have any allies left at all."

"Give me the locations."

"I won't."

Fiona snorted. "Oh, yes you will."

"No. What kind of life can you offer these kids? Always on the run, at risk of this same thing happening again? Out here, among the normals, our people will never be anything but victims."

"And with Psi Corps we'll never be anything but slaves."

He shook his head. "I pity you if you really believe that. This is what we do—protect teeps. Normals hate us. They'll never see us as anything but something to use for their own ends. Psi Corps is the only place we can be safe, free. I won't give you the locations."

"We'll tear them out of you."

"You would do that to one of your own kind? Then everything they said about you fanatics is true."

"Look—what's your name?"

"Heckman. Claude Heckman."

"Claude, I've been in the camps. I've seen what the sleepers do. I know what Psi Corps is, and I want no part of it. You can't see it because they brainwashed you. You're a good little soldier. But don't expect me to buy any of it, okay? You take away people's most basic human rights, and that opens the door to the kind of crap Rentech is doing. Nobody cares because teeps have no rights, and Psi Corps keeps it that way, makes it okay."

"Psi Corps cares. I was almost killed proving that." He raised his chin toward the sleeping children. "You talk about freedom. Ask them which *they* want. The freedom to be abused—or to be protected, cared about, among their own kind?"

"I'm not arguing this with you."

"What *will* you do with me? After you fry my brain?"

Fiona watched the thick-footed rows of cypress go by for a while without answering.

"Here's the deal," she finally said. "You give us the locations for half and keep half. We hold on to you long enough to be sure you told us the truth, then we let you go be a good little soldier some more. Half for us, half for Psi Corps. If you don't like that, we tear it out of your head and finish you off with a bullet."

Claude considered. "It's a mistake," he said, finally. "But yes."

"Fine."

One of the twins rubbed her eyes, sat up, and hesitantly approached. "Come here," Fiona said, opening her arm. The girl nestled under it and closed her eyes.

Fiona closed her own, over a wave of tenderness that quickly became anger, both surprising in their intensity. The Psi Cop thought he had a family, but she knew what family was, and Psi Corps wasn't it.

But neither was the resistance—it was just the hope of a family, someday. The prayer for one.

And suddenly she understood where her own hope had gone, and maybe—just maybe—how to get it back.

4

Jenny Winters' Diary

July 21, 2189

Dear Diary:

I can't say it, so I have to write it. Fiona told me I should start a diary. I didn't think it was a smart idea. What if the Psi Cops found it, and it had all of this information in it? But she told me about another girl, long ago, named Anne Frank. She said sometimes it was worth the risk, and what if a Nazi had found her diary and read it; maybe it would have broken his heart, rid the world of at least one evil man the best way. Not by killing him, but by making him good.

I wish I had started it earlier, so I could have written down the happy things.

Because Fiona is dead. And Matthew is dead. And Stephen is dead. And if you are a Psi Cop, reading this, I hope it breaks your heart. Because they were people so good I don't have any words for them. They gave us love, and hope, and dreams that no one can take away from us.

I hope they aren't dead, but I know they are, because no one has heard from them, and they wouldn't be gone so long without letting us know they were okay. I hope they aren't dead, but they are.

I should introduce myself, I guess, since this is my diary. My name is Jenny Winters, and I'm thirteen. I was born in the United States, in Vermont, but I don't remember Vermont. My mom was a teep, like me, and her and dad had to move a lot. She won't tell me, but I know what happened to dad. He got tired of it, and he left her, and he turned her in, but she took me and ran. That was in England, I think. And we went from there to India, and then to Amazonia. Mom got a job there working for a corporation. I won't write down the name, or even the city, because they knew she was a teep, and

they hired her to do illegal scans. They didn't pay her much, and we had to live where they said.

Where we lived wasn't much, just a sort of dark little room with one bed and a kitchenette. But we had plates there. Me and Mom bought them together, and she let me pick out the design. We never had real plates before that. My neighborhood was nice, with a park and even a beach not far away. I learned Portuguese pretty fast, and had a few friends—Mily, Paolo, Rex.

They never T-tested me in school. Mom said her company fixed that for us. I think that was the main reason she worked for them, because I think she didn't like what she had to do very much.

I'll write some more tomorrow.

July 24, 2189

Dear Diary:

I almost didn't write in this anymore. I listened in on one of the meetings the other day. I'm not supposed to, but I'm practicing being stealthy. I've heard all of the stories about Fiona and Matthew and Stephen, and I know to be a good resistance leader you have to be as good at sneaking around as at fighting.

That's what I want to be, too. I don't want to just ride the railroad to someplace safe. I want to fight. I want to blow Psi Corps up completely, and maybe EarthDome, too. Fiona and Matthew said not to think that way, that we only should blow things up when we have to. I think Stephen likes to hear me say it, though.

I like Stephen. Matthew is great, but he's married to Fiona of course, but maybe I'll marry Stephen someday.

Except he's dead. It's just that I can't imagine anything that could kill Stephen. He's been shot about sixty times, and he always gets back up.

I'm losing track of this. I almost didn't write anymore, because at the meeting (no, Mr. Psi Cop, I won't tell you who was at it) at the meeting they said we were losing heart. They said that some people in the underground never liked Fiona and Matthew anyway, and now they're going to do as they please. And other people are losing hope. I think a lot more people have been captured since F and M and S disappeared.

Anyway, Mom died in Amazonia. I don't know exactly what happened, because at first I wouldn't listen to them, and then I didn't believe them. Some men came from the company Mom worked for,

and they told me she was dead, and that they would take care of me. I was about ten, then.

What they did was, they sold me to Mr. Farber. Yes, Mr. Psi Cop, I am telling you his name, and I didn't slip up. I don't care what happens to Mr. Achilles Robert Farber. I worked in his house. I got my voices when I was nine, and he knew that. He made me listen in on things. He made me feel things that other people were feeling, and then made him feel that. Bad things, like people getting stabbed and beaten up. Other things that maybe felt better but which Fiona says ought to be private.

Sometimes he did things to me, and made me make him feel it at the same time. I won't tell you all of the things, but Fiona said I should talk about it. That I shouldn't be ashamed or anything because it wasn't my fault. So I'm not ashamed. I wish I could forget some of it, though. I used to drink and sniff paint and that kind of thing, hoping I might forget, but Fiona put a stop to that. I used to like drinking, especially vodka or whisky when I could get it, but now I don't miss it at all.

July 25, 2189

They were like king Auther and Guinever and Lancelot. Well, not exactly, but I thought I should make a literary reference, like you're supposed to in school. I knew how to read when I came here, but Fiona taught me to like reading. What I mean is that they are like a king and queen and the perfect Knight, even more perfect than Lancelot, because Stephen would never betray Matthew, and neither would Fiona.

Maybe they're more like the three Musketeers.

A few months ago, they got word that a boat getting teeps out of China was going to be boarded and searched by the Psi Cops in Capetown. They got down there in time, tied up the Port Authorities, and disguised themselves as them. Then they led the Psi Cops onto the wrong ship, which was owned by a certain Tong lieutenant who shanghaied the Psi Cops and put them to work in the poppy fields someplace. I guess they're still there. Serves them right.

Another time Fiona and Matthew got captured in the Central African Block. Stephen just walked into the holding station and killed everyone there, like an avenging angel.

See, leaders don't have to put themselves in danger. You didn't see president Indrasingh leading the troops during the Quebec riots,

did you? But They do. They won't send any of us to do a job they wouldn't do themselves.

They say that king Auther isn't really dead, but just waiting until he is needed. If that's where F & M & S are now, waiting till they're needed—we need them.

I don't think the three Musketeers are supposed to be waiting anywhere, but we could use them, too.

August 2, 2189

I'm pissed. Me and one of the boys went to the market, and we played the deception game. It's good practice for being stealthy. And we got a bottle of something that tastes bad (I can't read the writing here) but man, is it strong.

Well, so what. If Fiona didn't want me to drink, she shouldn't have got killed. I hate her.

I have to go. I think I have to throw up.

August 4, 2189

I didn't mean to say I hate Fiona. I don't. Sometimes I get mad when I drink.

I didn't tell you how we first met. They found me at Mr. Farber's house. Mr. Farber helped them sometimes, but when they found out about some of the things he does, they hit his house hard, anyway. He must have got wind about it, because he wasn't there when they came. Stephen found me in my room. I thought he was part of another game, but he got me dressed and told me we were leaving. Then Fiona came, and when she saw me she cried. Her tears almost filled up my head.

Stephen wanted to kill Mr. Farber, but they couldn't find him.

I think the resistance is going to hell. They blew up a train station, and a lot of normals were killed. Fiona and Matthew wouldn't have let that happen. They would have hated it.

Anyway, we have to move now. I don't know when I'll be able to write again.

September 3, 2189

I can't believe it. I don't think I've ever been this happy.

Fiona and Matthew and Stephen aren't dead. They're here. And the best thing, the very best thing of all, is why they were gone. It wasn't because they were captured or because they didn't care any-

more. They were gone because Fiona was having a baby! They named him Stephen, of course, "Stee" for short, so they don't confuse him with big Stephen. I can't even write here how happy I am. It's like the Sun went away for a long time, but then came back even brighter and better than before.

I can tell Stephen is proud. He actually holds the baby, as goofy as that looks. He told everyone he was the godfather. But they still had time for me! Stephen gave me a big hug as soon as he saw me, and asked how I had been running the revolution while he was gone. I didn't tell him things were going wrong, because it doesn't matter anymore. Fiona and Matthew hugged me, too, although they are very busy. Everyone wants to see them, and they have the baby. I think Fiona was sad, because I think she smelled the stuff on my breath, but now that she's back I'll stop, of course. I'm just going tonight, because my friends say we should celebrate, and they know where we can steal some real whisky, not that stuff we've been drinking.

I can't believe I'm so happy. Everyone else is, too. A baby! In Psi Corps they make you marry people you don't want to, because they breed people like they breed dogs to get poodles and things. And out here, they steal babies, take them off, and raise them. But Fiona and Matthew had a baby, a real, fine beautiful *free* baby.

Every time we give up hope, they bring us more. I heard one of the older women say that.

So, mister Psi Cop, if you are reading this. You lose. You can't keep us down, no matter what you do. You can't.

Kevin Vacit thumbed through the rest of the pages in the little book, but they were all blank.

"So I'm a grandfather," he murmured. "Imagine that."

He hit his com. "Send Ms. Alexander in, now."

"Yes, sir."

Natasha entered a few moments later.

"How is the girl?" he asked.

"She'll be okay, poor thing. They had to deep scan her, of course, but she'll recover." She shifted uncomfortably. "She isn't going to a camp, is she?"

Kevin shook his head, tapped the little diary. "No. She's already suffered enough at the hands of normals. We have everything she needs to straighten out right here. Structure, authority, and a family. She's confused and damaged, but it's not too late for her."

"The Corps is mother, the Corps is father."

"And we need that, we orphans. She'll see in time. Tell her teachers to use extra patience."

"Yes, sir."

"And this other matter. You have the location of the eastern base of operations?"

"Yes. And they won't shift because we planted a cover to make it appear the girl was picked up by local mundanes for stealing. They don't know we have her."

He nodded. "It's been a long wait, but I think it's time to move. The underground is completely out of hand. Even their supporters in the Senate have to admit that. It's time to clean it up. And this Fiona and Matthew Dexter, they seem to be the heart of it. I want them alive— martyrs we don't need. When they join the Corps and come out against the underground, whatever remains of it after tonight will dry up and blow away."

"Yes, sir. But what if they won't join, sir?"

"They will, because we need them to. The people in the psych department have made a few breakthroughs in conditioning techniques. I hope to convince them with reason, but if we can't, then we can't." He smiled dryly. "First we have to get them, of course. I want double the necessary strike team. Oh—and the girl's diary confirms the rumor— there is a child. Be certain it is not harmed."

"Will do, sir."

She left, and he thumbed back through the book. A card he hadn't noticed fell out. Someone—presumably the girl—had sketched a picture on it in colored pencils. A king and queen, each wearing a crown, a knight in golden armor, and in front of them a manger. Beneath it she had written, "Gallahad is Born."

On the inside it said, "Happy Birthday, Stephen Kevin Dexter."

5

Fiona padded to the crib, unsure what had awakened her. Little Stee was asleep—miraculously. By this time of the morning he was usually either bawling or sandwiched between Matthew and her.

She knelt, gazing at him in renewed wonder, feeling his small dreams of color and smell. She did not even have to reach to find them; he was broadcasting already. Not for him the sudden, jarring transformation of later life.

"Everything okay?" Matthew asked.

"Sorry. I didn't mean to wake you."

"You didn't. I was awake when you got up."

He swung his feet over the bed and came to join her. "He is beautiful, isn't he?"

"When he isn't crying, you mean?"

"Even when he is crying. When he chooses to cry, my son is the best damn crier in the world." He yawned. "Doesn't really do it that much, though."

She kissed him, a quick peck, and thinking better of that gave him a firmer buss on the lips. He returned it.

I love you, as the kiss lingered.

Sometime afterward, when they were back on the bed, Stee began to snuffle a little, and Fiona went and got him.

"Vacation's over," Matthew said, tickling her belly.

"Vacation? I don't remember a vacation. I remember weighing a standard metric ton and—"

"I stand corrected. I meant—I wonder if we made a mistake, dropping out of sight like that. Things are pretty shaky around here."

"We had to do it," Fiona said. "We needed it. Our son needed it. We took a little breather, and now we're ready to start again." She paused for a moment. "I'm worried about Jenny. Did you see her? She's drinking again."

"I—"

"What?"

"I was waiting for the right time to tell you. This isn't it, but—"

"It's about Jenny?"

"Yes. She's missing—apparently about three days now. Not Psi Corps; the local sheriff picked her up for shoplifting."

"And you didn't tell me this?"

"I only found out a few hours before bed. I was going to tell you in the morning, after you got some sleep. Fiona, I set some of our best people on it. We'll get her back."

"Three days? What about bail? Why didn't I notice?"

"You're a little busy now," he said, tapping Stee on his soft head. "And the problem with bail is *finding* her. She went into the juvie system, and that gets confusing. We have to play someone as a relative, and for that we have to wait on documents."

"We should have taken Jenny into hiding with us. I knew better than to leave her here."

"If we'd followed that logic, we would have had everyone with us," he murmured.

"I know. I know. Poor Jenny."

"We'll find her. Stephen's going out tomorrow."

"Okay." But she lay on her back, worrying, and could not sleep again.

And then, suddenly, Stee gave a weird little cry. It did not sound like any noise he had ever made before, not like a baby at all. It sounded like an adult, somehow—not the quality of the sound, which, after all, came from immature vocal cords—but something about the tone and inflection. It was a cry of terror and despair, and it sent up all of the hairs on the back of her neck.

He did it again, and now she felt his mindcry behind it.

"Matthew? Matthew."

He came awake just as Stee screamed like a torture victim.

"What's wrong with him?"

"He's feeling something. Hearing something and—" She sprang out of bed and ran to the wall com, snapped it on, thumbed the number one switch. A primitive system, built of spare parts, with no AI, but it worked and the parts weren't traceable. They had had trouble with AIs having hidden instructions, betraying them when linked to nets.

The panel lit to clean static.

She thumbed number two. More of the same.

Number three flickered on, and there was Chin Hsung and Ned Kowalewski, chatting. They looked at her in surprise.

"Hey, little mama," Kowalewski said. "What's up?"

"Ned, One and Two perimeters aren't responding. What's going on up there?"

"What?" He began punching at his control panel. "Ah, shit. You're right. Might be a malfunction—"

"No. Ned, Hsung, fall back, get out of there!"

Hsung was lifting his rifle when the door behind them suddenly crumpled inward. The first instant of the explosion must have overloaded the audio sensor, because after a quick *crack* it was soundless. From the smoke, two black-clad Psi Cops emerged, weapons spitting flame. Hsung never got off a shot; Ned got off two, but didn't seem to hit anyone. Then one of the Psi Cops took aim at the camera and the screen went solid.

"Oh, my God."

She hit the alarm, and then the fifth switch. Behind her, she heard Matthew swearing and jerking his clothes on.

The screen lit again, this time to Terrence Enoch's square, serious face. "Yes?"

"Terr, it's a raid. They've taken out One, Two, and Three perimeters already—at least. I'm on my way. Blow the Neck and start the evacuation." She reached for her clothes.

No revolution could be entirely mobile. There had to be bases of operation, nodes, vaults, resting places. The underground railroad circulated people from house to house, from country to country, and for the most part, that was the underground. But they had a couple of fortresses that shifted only every few years, nerve centers that no one should be able to find—not without their knowing they were found.

This was one of them—a series of caverns beneath Tennessee. A hundred and thirty years ago it had been a hotel, a tourist attraction, but had gone broke. It had been quietly purchased by a mining company, but if one followed the maze of paper to the actual source of the money, it led to one Josiah Tozer, a very wealthy man who had lost his only son to Psi Corps.

This was his memorial to his lost son, his revenge against Psi Corps, his gift to those still free. Periodically abandoned and reoccupied, it had been one of their best centers of organization. Tozer had been dead for ten years. He would never know that his legacy had finally failed.

When Fiona and Matthew reached the ops room, it was a strange combination of bedlam and grim efficiency.

"They're hitting everywhere," Enoch told them. "Andorra, Singapore, Salt Lake City—every major house, node, fortress. We've lost all of them."

"Couldn't they just be jamming us?"

"Oh, they are. But we have antennas twenty miles from here and

cables snaked through solid bedrock they don't know about. You want to watch the Colin Bateman show, you can. You want to raise the safe house in Norway—no."

"How? How?"

"It's been coming for a long time," said a voice behind them. They turned to find Stephen Walters.

"That bastard, Vacit. I thought I had him figured out, thought I had cut him off cold when I came clean with you guys. But he's been playing with us all along. He could have done this anytime. Back when I was his man, he had all of the information he needed to shut the whole thing down—I know, 'cause I gave it to him."

"Why now, then?"

"Something's changed. I don't know. Back then, it almost seemed like he *wanted* the underground to survive."

"That makes no sense."

"Vacit's a strange old man."

"It doesn't matter now. What matters is getting out of here and salvaging what we can of the situation."

"We have to get Stee out," Fiona hissed fiercely, hugging the infant to her chest. "My son won't grow up in Psi Corps. He *won't*."

"Okay, folks!" Matthew raised his voice. "It's the scatter! It looks like they only know about the front way in, so we need to start bleeding people out through the back doors. They've probably got satellites lookin' for that, so the first out will have the best chance. Run like hell— don't go anywhere right away, just travel. We'll set back up somewhere and let you know what and where is still safe." He paused for a moment.

"I love all of you," he said. "You've been champions. Just hang on, wherever you go. They can pound us but they can't keep us down. Now go, get safe!"

He turned back to Enoch at ops.

"Are you tracking them?"

"Yes. They overrode the AI somehow, but I've got them with the motion detectors. They're still consolidating Vestibule section."

"That mean they aren't past the Neck yet."

"That's right."

"Why haven't you blown it, then?"

"Two reasons, related. The motion detectors are hardwired here, but everything else goes through the AI. They've crashed that."

"Monkey's number one rule," Fiona said. "Always hardwire the explosives. Why didn't we?"

"I think Kim did that. She wanted the AI to be able to do it while we ran."

"Stupid. Or maybe she was a Psi Corps sleeper. Damn it."

"Another thing—for the same reason, we haven't been able to alert the people staying in the Ballroom."

"How many?"

"About twenty."

"No!" Stephen roared. "That tears it! The hardwiring goes as far as the relay, right? So I can set off the charges from the Grand Ballroom and get them out at the same time."

"Except that you aren't going to," Fiona said.

"What? Fee—"

"No. I'm making this quick, Stephen. You have to get out, now. Because you're taking your godson."

"No, see, that's what *you* should be doing."

"Can't. Look at them, Stephen, they're falling apart. We have to pull them together, or Psi Corps will get them all. And we have to do it here, now. We'll go to the Neck, blow it, get those people out. That'll give us lots of time."

"Great. Plenty of time. Then you wait here, with Stee, and—"

"Stephen!" Fiona's voice rose to its loudest. "For the love of God, get my son out of here! Can you really think of anyone here he would be safer with?"

Stephen opened his mouth, but nothing came out.

"It's true," Matthew said, lower. "You're the only one we really trust, Stephen. And you're the only one who can keep the underground going if something happens to Fiona and me." He grasped Stephen's hand and dropped subvocal. *If Fiona and I cut and run now, it's all over. You called it, ten years ago. I didn't believe—didn't want to believe it—but since we've been gone, I can see it. Too many people trust us. Too many people depend on us. This is bigger than our lives, Stephen, but I'm selfish enough to want you and my son safe. That's the most important thing, period.*

Fiona joined them. *Please, Stephen, don't drag this out. You know we love you. Now go—we'll see you in a few days. We'll meet at the place in Missouri.* She reached to embrace him, kissed him on the cheek, and then, very carefully, handed him the sling carrier and Stee. "And I'll see you soon, too." She kissed her son, and then quickly turned away.

"Okay!" she shouted. "I need ten volunteers! We're going to blow those Psi Cops back to Geneva!"

A ragged chorus of cheers went up, and a good deal more than ten stepped forward.

For a moment, Stephen stood paralyzed, but then he dropped his gaze down to his godson, and he suddenly understood. Enough of this— he had orders. Time to be the soldier, no matter how wrong it felt.

* * *

Once, the two main galleries of the cave had been connected only by a crawl space a foot or so high. The entrepreneurs who had decided to create the Styx Hotel had enhanced that to create a grand hallway reminiscent of Gothic arches. The "rooms" of the hotel varied, one side to the other. The Vestibule chambers, accessible to the outside for centuries, had been something of a mess. Stalagmites and stalactites had been broken off or blown from the ceiling by centuries of teens with shotguns.

As a result, the outer sections were made up of small rooms and old administrative offices. Now they served as perimeter guard posts, with a maze of small mines and coded gates that it would take the Psi Cops a while to work through. The inner gallery was the Grand Ballroom, a glittering cyst of mineral wonders.

Far beyond that, in the maze of smaller, water-carved passages that snaked down below, were the nerve centers of the resistance. But transients stayed in the comfortable rooms—cabins, really, carved into the living rock, tier upon tier of them stacked up around the ballroom. Some called it the Kobold Condominiums.

The Psi Cops were still working their way through the outer rooms, the staccato bursts of their weapons drifting far ahead of them.

Fiona ran into the Grand Ballroom. It was full of people, the residents of the Kobold Condominiums, wondering what was going on.

"All of you!" she shouted. "We're under attack by Psi Corps. I need you to clear the gallery, head back toward the dispersal stations. We'll give you the time you need, but you have to go now. Leave your things."

She left Jean and Wen to organize that, and then quick-timed the rest to the AI terminal node. She put two from her team to the task of finding the hardwiring for the charges, and took her remaining six up the grandiose Neck. There they fanned out, took positions, and waited.

They did not have to wait as long as she had hoped. The invaders weren't all Psi Cops—most were probably Hounds and special ops, probably with a few EarthForce normals thrown in to fill out the cannon fodder.

Matthew came up beside her and took her hand.

"Ready?"

"Let's go."

Their minds came together almost seamlessly, organizing and focusing the lesser talents of the others who accompanied them, painting the picture they wanted those who were approaching to see.

The invaders arrived in her mind's eye, and she felt their confusion at what they saw. The image she and Matthew projected was reflected back from their minds, and she enhanced it, added it to the original

illusion, created a loop. The Hounds stopped, staring. They saw the Neck already shattered and collapsed, water cascading down the debris, filling the chamber they stood in. In point of fact, there *was* a river above them. Part of it had once flowed through the caves, but its bed had shifted, leaving the caverns dry. The charges had been laid to open a long seam to it, however. Once Psi Corps found a fortress, it could never be used again. Monkey, who originally set the caves up, had been a firm believer in scorched—or in this case drowned—earth.

The illusion held for a minute, as the Psi Corps troops doubled in number. Among them she now felt very powerful minds, the Psi Cops themselves. Their doubt slammed against her will like a sledgehammer, pounding almost physically in her skull. She gritted her teeth, gripped Matthew's hand more tightly. If they could hold it long enough, even the Psi Cops might begin to believe it. Once belief was firm, they could keep the illusion up for hours.

Another minute or so passed, as the attackers began discussing the situation. One fired a burst at the debris, and imaginary sparks flared on the stone. The imaginary water level rose.

A Psi Cop fired another burst, and that broke someone, probably Mikko. Fiona felt him shake loose, weakening the rest, and sudden thunder to the right revealed his panicked alternative.

That was it. She yanked out her Naga, aimed around the column of stone she crouched behind, and began to fire.

The cavern filled with the whine and ricochet of bullets.

Surrender! We don't want to harm you! The combined urging of the Psi Cops battered her, and for an instant she considered it. At least she would be alive, and Matthew would be alive . . .

She clenched her jaw and fired again. Her life was hers to win or lose, not Psi Corps' to give her. "Live free!" she yelled. "Live free!"

Limestone spalled all around her.

They must have it by now. Start the retreat.

Mikko was already down—she'd heard his death scream. Mustapha and Chapman—something was making them sleep.

"Gas!" she hissed. *Go!*

The remaining three ran back down the Neck as she and Matthew lay down cover fire. Then she tossed a grenade and ran herself, just as something struck her oddly, made her head whirl and her body seem far away.

Matthew was dragging her, almost, and suddenly the whole situation seemed more than a little ridiculous. She giggled.

Her grenade went off, and she felt someone die, and that snapped her out of it. She must have come in contact with the gas they were using.

As she ran, she could feel it wearing off—it must have a short life, sensible in a cave. Had the cops been wearing masks? She hadn't been able to see.

By the time she reached the end of the corridor, she felt almost sober again. They reached the team at the AI at a dead run.

"Got it?"

"Got it."

"Blow, then."

An instant later, very near, the sky fell. There was no sound of explosion, just a dull sort of vibration in the stone, and then a low, grinding crash followed by the gush of water. A ragged cheer went up, and Fiona recognized her own voice in it.

Ops was on skeleton crew when they got back.

"How is it?" Matthew asked Enoch.

"Not good. They had Two and Six staked out. I don't think anyone got through. They found One and Four about three minutes ago. We've sealed them all and diverted everyone to Five, Seven, and Eight."

"Which way did Stephen go?"

"Eight, I think."

"Good. Good. How many do we still have in here?"

"Us, and maybe thirty more." He hesitated. "We've lost every major nexus now. They've shut the railroad down. There's nowhere to go, even if we get out."

"We've got time to breathe, though."

"Sure. We've teams at all the other entrances. We can blow 'em as we find 'em. But you two better go, now, while you can. They're picking off our exits pretty fast."

"I'm not leaving until everyone else is out," Matthew insisted.

"That won't happen," Enoch said. "Because *I'm* not leaving with you two here. *Capische?*" He glanced at a sudden glare from his board. "There went Seven."

"We still have Eight, though?"

"Yes," Enoch replied. "Stephen should be out by now."

"Eight, then," Matthew said. "The caves are filling up. Time to go, and all of us are going together."

6

Stephen emerged on a mountainside, stepping into the cool night air. His namesake was awake, but quiet, almost as if he understood the need for it. Perhaps he did. The kid was already a powerful teep. Stephen scanned the valley and hillside through his night goggles, but noticed nothing peculiar.

"Okay," he said, to the other five or so in his group. "Spread out. I know you want to stay together, but you can't. Stay away from the highways and small towns—go cross-country when you can. Time works for you, so put as much of it as you can between now and when you have to put yourself in danger again. If you hear choppers, hide under something, and don't move. Try to get to Chattanooga or head south. Keep your ears to the ground; we'll get the railroad back together, but it could take a little while."

They nodded solemnly, and reluctantly started away. All but one, that is, a fifteen-year-old girl named Valerie. She stood as if petrified, staring at the cave mouth.

"Where are Fiona and Matthew? Why aren't they coming out?"

"They'll be out, don't worry."

"I'm going to wait for them."

"If you wait here, you'll only tip off any air surveillance the Psi Cops have, Valerie. Go!"

"I'll wait for them inside of the cave," she said stubbornly.

"No. They *will* find this entrance, it's just a matter of when. You're one of the lucky ones, so don't be stupid and blow a chance others would kill for."

She turned her terrified gaze on him. "I've never been in the woods. I don't know what to do."

He sighed. "Come with me, then. You can help me with the kid."

She brightened a little at that.

He watched where the others went—mostly down into the valley,

which made sense. It was narrow, almost a gorge, and sparsely populated, with heavy cover and a stream.

So, of course, the cops would look there first. He turned and started up the mountain, Valerie in tow.

It was harder even than he thought it would be, leaving Fiona and Matthew. He strained to find their thoughts, though he knew it was impossible, through the layers of ancient stone. He kept catching himself dragging. *Think of the kid,* he would remind himself.

He was so preoccupied that he almost missed the choppers. They were running nearly silent, without lights, but they blotted the stars at the edge of his vision, and through the night goggles he could see that they left a faint trail.

"C'mon!" he told the girl, urging her up the next slope. There was nowhere to hide, here, nothing that would provide shelter from infrared sweeps, or from radar so refined it could detect a heartbeat. The choppers weren't close enough yet, but they would be soon. Odds weren't good that he could take a chopper with his rifle, much less the three he counted.

Valerie began to whimper; she had noticed them, too.

The rise brought them to a small road, one that hadn't seen use for a while, judging by the high weeds thrusting through the black pebbles that remained from the ancient asphalt. Over the centuries, rural populations had continued to contract toward cities, as fuel prices rose and private cars gave way to trains and monorails. The cheap fuel cells that powered cars now had done a bit to reverse the trend, and people kept predicting—as they had for two hundred years—that cheap communication and AI nets would eventually decentralize civilization. But cities had become a habit with humanity, a hard one to break, and the countrysides had been given over to national parks and big industry. For the most part, people liked things that way. The Appalachian Mountains were littered with ghost towns.

They didn't find a whole town, but the remains of a house, its slate-tiled roof mostly intact. It would have to do. He hustled Valerie into it, found that it had a cellar that had been dug into the rock. Even better.

The girl was near panic, and Stee was picking up on it, starting to wail.

"Here," he murmured. "Watch Stee, will you? I'm not so good at it. That's what you can do for Fiona and Matthew. Watch their baby. It's the biggest job there is."

Taking the baby seemed to calm her down. He crawled back to where he could see a sliver of sky and waited.

The helicopters went over, and kept going, making a beeline toward entrance Eight.

"Okay," Fiona hissed. "Matthew and I will scout point. Terrence, China, you watch our flanks. They might be out there and they might not, but we should be ready for a fight."

She could feel their tension, and nothing else. If there were cops outside, they were quiet, well shielded.

She poked the nose of her rifle into the air, looked around carefully, and followed it out. Matthew was right beside her.

Okay, Fee?

Seems okay. I just—no! Above us!

Almost too late, her night visor showed her the faint pools of heat. Metal began clanging all around them. Bombs! But no explosions—

Gas! She sent it as loudly as she could. *Masks!* She pulled her own on, hoping the invaders weren't using a nerve agent. Some of her group either didn't hear or weren't fast enough, but most got them on by the time ropes began snaking from the sky. She lifted her rifle and fired at the dark shapes that were sliding down.

A man screamed and thrashed to the ground.

Out! OUT AND RUN.

She put her back to Matthew's, and they both kept firing up, their tracers cutting loops in the sky. Men poured out of the helicopters like rain from a thunderstorm. She hit another, and another—

The choppers began to fire back. The tracers ate toward them, as Fiona pumped bullets toward the gunner. Behind her, the rest of their group were doing as ordered, fleeing through the holes as Matthew and she opened them.

They both dove flat as the fire from the choppers thuttered the earth where they had been standing.

The gunfire was tiny, almost inaudible in the distance, and Stephen shook his head. Poor bastards. He wondered who it was.

But then, in a terrible flash, he knew, because he caught a hint of Fiona, mindscreaming.

Too far. Way to far. Your imagination, he told himself.

But he knew it wasn't.

It didn't usually take Stephen long to make decisions. It didn't now.

"Watch Stee," he grunted to Valerie. "I'll be back for both of you. Stay here and do *not* move."

* * *

Fiona had seen movies in which one or a small handful of commandos or cowboys or policemen fought against fifty times their number, and won. The way the scenes were shot, it seemed credible. The method was to break the action down into a lot of smaller confrontations. What the films generally left out, purposefully, was the big picture, the aerial views, because this would show the fights for the fantasies that they were and leave the audience wondering why all of the bad guys to the sides, behind, and above the hero were holding their fire so said hero had to shoot only those in front of him.

She and Matthew survived in such a situation about as long as one could, perhaps twenty seconds.

Then a mule kicked her in the back.

Fee! But then several somethings hit Matthew, too, somethings that hurt him a lot more than a mule.

The only place they could go was back into the cave, and the muffled *whump!* that greeted them as they stumbled into it—more charges farther down, sealing it shut—reminded them that they couldn't go far that way, either.

Matthew had dropped flat next to Fiona, continuing to fire methodically, despite the pain she felt radiating from him. She stood straddling him, because she knew if she squatted or lay down she wouldn't get back up. Her breath came painfully—the impact of the bullet on her vest must have broken ribs.

She fired all of her rounds and then ducked around the corner. Matthew gurgled, and she grabbed his foot and dragged him around, too, tossed her last grenade so that it bounced out into the clearing, then began changing clips.

Stephen tore down the hill, stumbling often. Once he fell a full thirty feet, and his head cracked against rock, but he kept going, blood welling along the rims of his goggles. The helicopters bobbed in and out of sight. He couldn't hear gunfire anymore, but that might be because of the blood pounding in his ears.

When she peeked around the corner to fire again, the tunnel filled with lead. She got off only a shot before something tore the rifle and most of her shoulder away. She grunted in surprise and fell back against Matthew, where he lay bubbling blood from a hole in his throat.

Take them alive, you idiots!

That from a Psi Cop outside.

"Alive?" she muttered. "Alive."

Fiona . . .

She stripped off her goggles and mask, pushed his up, and bent to kiss him. She didn't need to see his face anymore, or her own.

Surrender, Fiona, he managed.

And go back to one of those camps? No. They can use us, program us, make us betray ourselves . . .

She felt them getting close outside. She hunted on Matthew's belt and found his last grenade.

Remember that wild night in Santa Cruz?

The boring party? The carnival? The midget and the dwarf?

And we went walking on the beach.

I remember you were shy. You wouldn't go skinny-dipping. Wouldn't go that far on a first—He coughed, and something broke loose inside of him. *I love you, Fiona.*

I love you, too. She pulled the pin.

The last thing she saw was sunrise over the Sulu Sea.

Stephen was still eighty feet up the hillside when a tongue of flame curled out of the cave mouth below, and he felt them go.

He screamed. He screamed and he began to fire. Sparks flew from the nearest chopper, hovering at about his own level, and it turned, sluggishly, its sixty-millimeter barking to life. He stood, watching the fire hunt him, squeezing the trigger of his rifle in metronome bursts.

The gunner fell back.

He was empty. He put in armor-piercing rounds and started again. It took eight shots to crack the cockpit, another three to take out the pilot. The craft dove into the mountainside, its rotors exploding as they dug at rock.

He walked farther down the hill, took the time to shoot a couple of men coming up it, but now the other two choppers were after him.

He stepped behind a tree, felt it shiver like a drumhead under the impacts. He pulled the pin on a grenade, counted six, and then stepped out and flung it as far and high as he could.

It detonated short, but the blast picked the chopper up a few feet. He pulled, counted five, threw again. This time he got the rotors.

He realized that he was still screaming, that he almost couldn't see for the blood and the tears. Fiona and Matthew were dead. He would kill every one of the bastards. Every last one.

Of course he was out of ammo, and grenades, too.

He pulled his knife, and then the tiniest bit of sanity crept back into his head.

Stee. If he died, who would take care of Stee? It was their last wish, the only thing they had asked of him.

So he sheathed the knife, as the last chopper rose like a death angel above him, and he began to run, weaving through the trees. The stupidest thing he could do was lead them straight back to the kid, so he wouldn't do that. He would lose them first, then go back. If only Valerie kept her head.

He plunged down the hill, leaves kicking behind him. They couldn't possibly see him anymore; they were hunting him on radar and infrared. He stayed in the tallest stands, to make them keep their distance.

He took a bullet anyway. Coming straight down, it shattered his clavicle, wobbled along his ribs and dug into his hip. Shocked, he ran headlong into a tree, rolled, and plunged into freezing cold water. Gritting his teeth against the pain, he managed to kick himself up under a mass of debris that choked the stream to one side.

The chopper flew on.

He stayed there a few more moments, breathing hard, then tore two strips from his shirt, plugged the entry and exit wounds on his shoulder, tore a third strip, and tied it tightly around both.

The arm hung uselessly.

He drew the knife again, and waited.

He didn't have to wait long. In what seemed only a matter of moments, he saw two dark forms, stalking down the stream, moving their rifles in careful arcs. He stayed still, blocking, until they were fifty feet away, thirty. He felt their minds and realized that he was lucky; they were bloodhounds, not Psi Cops.

Twenty feet and one suddenly stiffened, turning his head this way and that.

He couldn't charge from where he was. He just stood up, very slowly.

"Hello," he said.

The first man snapped his rifle up and fired. The bullet went wide, hissing into the water a yard to his left. The second man did the wise thing; spun in search of ambushers from another direction. Stephen surged into motion.

The next round caught him in the chest, and the impact against his vest nearly toppled him backward, but he felt huge, massive, a neutron star, and an awful laughter bubbled up from his chest. The boy—and it was a boy, no more than twenty—fired again, missed—

—and Stephen drove the knife through his throat. The second Hound opened up on full automatic as Stephen turned again, using the impaled Hound as a shield. A bullet blew through the body and scored along his head, another weirdly smashed into his thigh, but by then he had gone cold, and all that meant nothing. He dropped with the body,

pulling a pistol free from its belt, and shot the second Hound between the eyes.

Then the river was silent. In the silvery moonlight, the blood was only one more shadow.

Grunting, he pushed up, stripped the Psi Corps uniform from the larger man, and changed into it, no easy matter with a shattered shoulder. The chopper whirred over again, but it didn't fire. Now there was no way of knowing who was friend and who was foe—the cops must be everywhere.

Grimly he set out up the hill.

He encountered only one more Hound, and his stolen uniform allowed him to get close enough to kill silently.

But when he at last reached the abandoned house, there was no one there. Shell casings littered the ground, and the tall weeds had been trampled by boots.

He slid against the wall, too tired to weep, too tired to think. He went to sleep, praying silently not to awaken.

EPILOGUE

It is a fact that the time it takes the Earth to orbit the Sun is—with a tolerance of a few nanoseconds—the same each revolution.

It is nevertheless a fact that each year passes more quickly than the one before.

Kevin Vacit tried to measure his footsteps, as he could not the years. Tried to make them even, regular. But in his memory, the real rhythm of his life would not be fooled. Eternal days in the New Mexico sun, playing tag with Monkey, chasing lizards, and watching ants build jeweled hills. The bright, strong years with Lee, each day like a new epic, each moment condensed with peril and potential. Ninon Davion, and the years coming quicker, never time enough for anything. The last two decades—what were they? Mayflies laughing briefly at him as he tried to make it all last, create something that would continue after him, somehow.

He approached a door, and the guards, knowing him instantly, simply stood aside, asking no questions. His steps carried him on, past painfully young, clean-scrubbed nurses, smiling nervously as he entered the crèche.

He strolled past the rows of infants, some silent in sleep, some crying stridently, some noticing him vaguely as he walked by. He approached one, one particular one, that stared at him with wide, dark eyes.

He touched the wrinkled parchment of his hand against the child's new skin, and closed his eyes.

For the child, each day was still a universe, almost infinite, shaped by desires as simple as gravity, modulated by incomprehensible curiosities.

Life should be lived backward, so we can end like this, merging gradually into the background unconscious of the universe. Instead, we grow more self-aware, more disconnected, the better to scream our terror and loss as we plunge into the abyss, unable to recognize that the abyss is just something we are a part of, an eddy in space that becomes, for just a moment, unique from all other things.

He blinked. Philosophy. Lee would have called it a damned waste of time. Lee would be right.

He sighed and smiled in gentle self-mockery, and removed his hand from the brow of his grandchild. *I'm sorry, Ninon. I'm sorry, Fiona. But this was the way it had to be. You can be proud, though. He's a P12.*

"You are my legacy," he said to the child, his voice so faint even he wasn't sure he was using it. "You are the part of me that will go on. You are Psi Corps."

He moved to the end of the little crib, to the blank tag there, and considered his decision. For this child, the Corps would truly be mother and father. He was no longer the child of Fiona and Matthew Dexter. He was no longer the grandson of Ninon Davion and Kevin Vacit. He was a future still to be imagined.

He paused an instant longer, and with a rare, wry smile, took a pen from his pocket and wrote a name on the tag. Then, measuring his footsteps, he walked away.

Freda liked the children, even when they were trouble. That was a good thing about Psi Corps—if you didn't like what you did, everyone knew it. You couldn't get away with neglecting the children, here.

She cooed to her older charges and introduced herself to the new ones. She was most curious about the one the director had come to see, but she checked the children in the order she came to them. It wouldn't do to go out of order, perhaps miss one.

When she finally reached the child, he was asleep. A very handsome boy, with a good head of hair already.

"Well, *hello* there, Alfred," she said, very softly, looking to see what name was on the tag. "Welcome home, Alfred Bester."

Deadly Relations

Bester Ascendant

Deadly Relations

Bester Ascendant

For Gene, Gina, John, Pat, and Robert

ACKNOWLEDGMENTS

Thanks to Steve Saffel and Jenna Scott McCaffrey for insightful editing; Kari Magee, Betina Pavri, and Chris Luchini, and other folks at JPL for their technical expertise (my mistakes are not theirs); and Joseph Cochran for help on the Mars and Beta colonies.

ACKNOWLEDGMENTS

Thanks to Steve Saffel and Jenna Scott McCaffrey for insightful editing; to Kurt Mhyee, Parker Parry and Chris Lucian, and other folks at TPI, for the technical expertise (my mistakes are not theirs); and Joseph Osbahn for help on the Mars and Beta colonies.

PART 1

Thesis

1

Al Bester strained his small body to its limit, reaching on tiptoe for the next branch. The tips of his fingers just brushed it. Above, the waxy leaves of the oak danced in a sudden warm breeze, tantalizing him with glimpses of the beckoning sky beyond. Al loved the sky. In the shapes of clouds—sometimes in the stars at night—he thought he could see the faces of his parents.

He steadied himself and looked down. The ground seemed unreasonably far away. Maybe he should be happy he had managed to get this far—most kids his age couldn't. After all, two branches down, you had to swing around the trunk, hang in space by one hand for a moment to grip the next limb up.

This limb he simply couldn't reach, and the trunk was still too thick to shimmy up. He was stuck. He would have to wait until he grew taller. If he ever did.

Or—he looked up again, speculatively. Or he could jump. The branch was thick, and he would have to jump pretty high, but if he could snag it, he might be able to pull himself up.

But if he missed, he would probably fall.

He was still staring wistfully up at the unattainable heights when he felt minds stirring below.

Hey, Alfie! Come down! We're gonna play cops 'n' blips.

Why were they bothering him? Couldn't they see he was busy?

C'mon, Alfie!

He looked down reluctantly. Seven kids from his cadre stood below. *Way* below. He suddenly felt a little dizzy.

"Give it up, Alfie," their leader—Brett—called up. "Even *I* can't get that one."

Like Al, Brett was six years old, but Brett was a good head taller. And everyone liked Brett.

Yeah, come on. Before you hurt yourself. That was Milla. Milla was his

height, and he secretly—*very* secretly—admired her golden hair and blue eyes. He liked the way she laughed—when she wasn't laughing at *him.*

"Oh, Milla is worried about Alfie," another girl—Keefa—said. "Woops. Anyone catch that? What she was just thinking?"

Al strained, but caught nothing. He would love to know what Milla thought about him.

But then he did catch something. An interweaving *mant* from below.

<div align="center">

ALFIE & MILLA
SITTING
went *IN*
up
A
TREE
to
fetch
a
pail
of
K
I
S
S
I
N
uGh!

</div>

He turned his face to the bark, so they wouldn't see his angry and embarrassed blush. His feelings were harder to hide, but he squeezed them in tightly, balling his left fist as he did so, for concentration.

He wouldn't be a baby. He wasn't a baby—he was too old to wet the bed, too old to go in his pants, too old to bloop his feelings all over the place. If the teachers caught you blooping, they made sure everyone knew. That was the next worst thing to being punished by the Grins.

Frowning, he looked determinedly back up at the branch and jumped as hard as he could. That would show them.

But his timing was a little off. He got his arms around the branch all right, but his fingers never quite met up around the thick bough. There was nothing to grab onto, and only pressure and his nails in the bark kept him there—pressure he couldn't keep up for long.

He looked down, and that was worse. He was hanging above and off to the side of the limb he had been standing on. He would never land

square if he dropped—no, he'd fall the whole way, and probably break something.

One nice thing, at least—he had shut the others up. Or rather, stopped their stupid manting. Now what he got was a *shim*-shimmer of worry and excitement, with at least two strong desires to see what would happen when he fell.

"Hang on, Alfie, I'm coming up to get you!"

Brett. Brett was coming to save him and be the hero. The taller boy was already clambering up the tree.

No way, Al thought. *No way.*

He swung himself and dropped. The kids below gasped like a crowd watching a circus performer as he hit the branch feet first, teetered for a long, terrible moment, and then found his balance. He stood there, fighting the urge to hug the branch, breathing hard. Below, he sensed a restless pause.

"Wow."

He peered down. That had been a girl. Milla? He wasn't sure.

"You were lucky. You should have waited for me to help you," Brett said. "You shouldn't even be trying to climb it alone—this is *constructive* play time. We're supposed to play *together.* Will you come down now?"

Al bit back an urge to dare Brett to duplicate his feat. It would be great if Brett tried and failed, but what if he managed it—or did better? Right now, at least somebody was impressed with Al Bester. A girl somebody.

"Okay," he said. "But I won't be the Blip this time." He started the descent.

He had played a Blip many times, and that part offered no real challenges.

He reached the soft grass of Alpha Quad and turned to face the others.

"You get to be the Blip, Alfie," Azmun said. Azmun was an ugly boy, with a face like a bat.

"I said I didn't want to be the Blip."

"We voted, Alfie. You have to do what we say."

"Yeah. It's for the greater good of the Corps," Milla put in.

So Milla *didn't* like him. His momentary elation vanished, but his stubbornness remained. "I didn't get to vote," he complained, stubbornly.

"Okay," Brett interjected. "All in favor of Alfie being the Blip, raise your hands."

All hands went up except his own. Of course.

"All against—"

"I was the Blip last time. This time I get to be a cop," Al insisted.

"But you were a *good* Blip. You'll probably grow *up* to be a Blip," Azmun argued.

Anger boiled through Al so fast it felt like his scalp would pop off. His fist actually seemed to ache with a need to punch Azmun's stupid bat-face. "You take that back. You take that right back right now," he said.

Azmun hesitated. Al realized his demand had come out calmly, not like he was really mad at all. The way Teacher Hua's voice did, when *he* was mad. It had a similar effect, too, because the anger behind his words was clear, despite his blocks. Weird, and scarier than someone acting mad.

He would have to remember that.

Basically, Azmun was a coward. Unless someone joined in with him and gave him courage, which could easily . . .

"Hey, Azmun, don't say things like that," Brett interposed. "Apologize, or I'll tell the teachers, and they'll send the Grins after you."

An involuntary thrill of fear ran around the circle.

"I'm sorry," Azmun mumbled reluctantly. "What I meant was, you're good at playin' the Blip. 'Cause you've got strong blocks 'n stuff."

"C'mon, it'll be dark soon," Brett said, "and we've already blown most of constructive play time. What if Teacher Hua or Ms. Chastain—or the *Grins*—scan us and find out we didn't play anything approved?

"Tell you what. Alfie and I will *both* be Blips. Okay? Alfie?"

Al blinked at the older boy. What was Brett—oh. That was it. He hadn't saved him in the tree, so he would save him now. That was Brett, always trying to be the older brother.

"Okay," he said, having no choice at all.

"Three goals," Azmun said. "The statue of the Grabber, the spout at the fish pond, and the red knob at the rail station is the third. But you both have to choose the same one. Okay? But if one of us touches you, you're caught."

"No problem," Brett said. "You'll never catch us, Psi Cops. Count to fifty. No cheating. C'mon, Alfie."

"We should say the pledge first," Al pointed out.

"Oh. Yeah." Brett looked a little sheepish and cleared his throat. He hurried through the pledge, and the other kids followed, some just mumbling.

"I pledge my body, heart, soul, and mind to the service of Earth Alliance, and the people who dwell on her myriad spheres. I promise to

keep the laws, to keep the faith, to keep my eyes on the truth. I pledge to serve my comrades, my cadre, and the Corps. The Corps teaches, guides, and provides. The Corps is mother, the Corps is father. We are the children of the Corps."

"Now, catch us if you can!" Brett said, and he started off. Al followed, counting under his breath. Despite himself, he began to feel the excitement. He loved hunting, but it was more challenging when the odds were against you. People were more impressed when you won. He edged nearer Brett, so they were almost touching. *Which goal?*

The statue would be the hardest, Brett responded. *I say that one.*

Okay. I'll lead them off toward the rail station and then double back, Al told him.

No! Brett shook his head. *We should stick together.*

Why? Blips wouldn't.

Yes they would. Blips are dumb. That's why they're Blips.

You want to get caught? Al glyphed the other kids laughing at them.

No. But Blips are supposed to stick together.

That's not a real rule, Al 'cast.

No. But it's what we're supposed to do.

Right. So let's do something different.

Brett considered for a moment. *Okay*, he 'cast, after a moment. *Listen, we'll hide and make a quiet place. When we figure out which way they think we went, we'll go to the other.*

Why not split up, like I said? He was beginning to get irritated. *Then at least one of us makes it.*

That's not *how Blips think. Blips are selfish—that's why they're Blips. We have to act like Blips.*

I thought Blips were Blips because they were stupid, Al rejoined, sarcastically.

Stupid, selfish—same thing. Didn't you watch John Trakker last night?

He couldn't argue with that. John Trakker, Psi Cop, often made that very point each week, as he led captured rogues off to be re-educated into productive citizens. And week after week, Blips showed how stupid they really were. Al never missed that vid—they showed it in the common room, complete with popcorn. And he had read all of the books, too.

Still, it seemed to him that *some* Blips might be smarter than those John Trakker came up against—like, what if a Psi Cop went Blip, one who knew all the tricks? That had happened once on the show, to John's partner Heng, but only after he had been drugged by an evil rogue, so that wasn't really the same.

No, a Psi Cop would never turn rogue while he was in his right mind. Well, he wasn't a rogue anyway, and he didn't want to be one, even in a game. He was going to change the rules. He was going to pretend that he was a Psi Cop and that those chasing him were rogues. And Brett . . .

Brett might be a Psi Cop, or he might be a rogue, pretending to be his friend. He would have to keep his eye on Brett. The tell-tell would be if Brett seemed to be trying to get them both caught . . .

They wound their way past the 3–5 cadre house, where he had lived the year before, and it struck Al how small it was, compared to the 6–10 house where he lived now. Of course, his cadre was bigger now, too—thirty instead of the twelve last year. And there were more cadres in the 6–10 house.

Ms. Chastain said that was because some teeps didn't join cadres until they were older. They were late bloomers and had to stay in the *latents'* dorm. The other kids called the latents' dorm the "Basement," and nobody ever went there unless they had to.

Al couldn't imagine not having any psi. How could you have a real cadre without psi? The kids from the Basement were good at playing normals in the games, but everyone made fun of them. Mostly they kept to themselves until they got their psi and could join a real cadre. Some got really old before that happened.

Brett had gone silent, but his blue eyes darted here and there, searching for a hiding place.

The two of them ran up one of the duracrete drainage ditches past the new construction site. Brett trotted a couple of feet out into the mud and leaped up on a fresh foundation. Then, with a running jump, he returned to the ditch, leaving what looked like a one-way trail. Al had to admit it appeared convincing. Maybe Brett was on the level after all.

From the ditch they hopped over to the lawn in front of the infirmary, and then around back.

"Quick," Brett whispered. "Let's get up on the roof, here. We'll be able to see and p'see and hear and p'hear them from way off."

Al nodded, and the two of them went quickly up the slightly creaky metal ladder attached to the corner of the building. They crawled across the roof and lay peering over the raised edge, minds alert for the faintest shim of their pursuers.

The paths of Teeptown were relatively empty, at two o'clock on a Sunday afternoon. He saw a couple of women in grey suits—they weren't teachers or cops or boots, so they were probably busybodies, teeps not strong enough to be cops. There was old man Tareq, cleaning up the

quad. A boot in EarthForce uniform—Al p'squinted the shim of each, and his eyes widened. The boot was a normal.

You didn't see many normals in Teeptown. But when you did, they were usually important.

"Hey, Al," Brett whispered. "Make a quiet place, remember?"

Brett was already doing it, glyphing himself as a part of the building. Al, slightly red-faced, joined him in the illusion.

"You're not a bad guy, Alfie, just a little weird," Brett confided.

"I'm not weird."

"You're always playing alone, always have, even when we were really little. And you don't get excited about anything. If Azmun had mouthed off like that to me, I'd have punched him, good."

"It's wrong to hit someone in your cadre," Al replied. " 'What hurts one hurts us all.' "

"Yeah, but sometimes you have to show a guy. You've just gotta—I mean—I don't know. People want to like you—the cadre's gotta hang together—but you're just a little too weird. You need to act more regular, you know?"

Al shrugged. He didn't care what Brett or anyone else thought.

Yeah. If he kept telling himself that, it might eventually be true.

"There," Brett whispered, suddenly.

P'squinting, Al could make them out—Keefa, anyway. Keefa was a weak blocker—she'd probably end up a busybody or a boot, but never a cop.

A few moments later, they came into sight—but only Keefa, Jon, and Roberto. That was a little worrisome. Where were the rest?

"That's to distract us, I bet," Al whispered. "They know Keefa bloops like a teek!"

"Maybe." They watched the three move up to Brett's false trail, mill about for a moment, then follow it.

"All right," Brett said. "They think we went to the rail station. So we'll go to the Grabber." He started crawling toward the ladder. Reluctantly, Al followed.

Halfway down the ladder, Al caught it. A shim-shimmer of triumph.

"They're here!" he shouted.

Cursing, Brett hurried down the ladder, just as Azmun, Ekko, and Milla came around the corner.

Brett made it to the ground in time to run, but Al had to jump. He hit hard enough that breath whoofed out of him and his chest hurt. Nevertheless, he ran after Brett.

He had made up his mind now. Brett was a traitor—one of the rogues. He'd been planted in Psi Corps to betray Al. No Psi Cop would

be as stupid as Brett. John Trakker would *never* have ignored Heng's advice, not the way Brett had ignored him.

Brett was playing his part well, though, running so hard that Al had trouble keeping up—as if Brett really didn't want to get caught.

As he ran, Al tried to drop distracting glyphs: Scooters about to cross the road, Grins stepping out of the shadows, ladders falling on their pursuers. He couldn't be sure if they were doing any good—it was hard to form the images while concentrating on running. But he sensed that Brett and he were pulling ahead.

Brett sensed it, too, because as they came to the corner of one of the dorms, he suddenly changed course, ducking down stairs that went to the lower, back side of the building. From their hiding place, Brett glyphed an illusion that had them still running, and despite his suspicion, Al joined him.

It worked. Azmun and the others whizzed past.

"Ha," Brett said. "Now"

But Al p'heard something Brett didn't—the other three pursuers coming close behind. And Brett didn't notice Al slipping into a recessed doorway.

There, under cover, Al steeled himself, then closed his eyes tightly, calling up an image of Brett's face. He imagined himself as Brett. In his mind, he merged his own face and Brett's into one, then changed Brett's into his.

It wasn't easy, and he didn't think it was working, until he suddenly heard Milla shout, "Hey! We've got Al!"

To clinch it, he blew sparks in Brett's mind—not a nice thing to do, but then, Brett was a traitor. So instead of running, Brett just stood there stupidly, long enough for them to catch him.

Then Al bolted, feeling their confusion paralyze them as they suddenly saw two Als.

They were all behind him now. No one stood between him and the statue of the Grabber. All he had to do was run, and he could run faster than any of them except Brett.

But as he reached the statue, he slowed uncertainly. Standing nearby, looking up at it, was the normal he had noticed earlier, in the EarthForce uniform. As Al approached, the man turned his gaze from the statue to him. There was something very unpleasant about that gaze—the man's eyes were the color of pencil lead, his face very pale. When he saw Al, he seemed to not like what he saw. But when he spoke, his tone was mildly friendly.

"A little out of breath, young man?"

"Yessir."

"You look like the devil's chasing you."

"Yessir."

"Some kind of game, I hope?"

"Yessir—cops and blips."

"Oh, very good—that's one of the approved games, yes?"

"Yessir."

"Is this statue your goal?"

"Yessir."

"Better touch it, then."

Al hesitated another instant, then did so.

The uniformed man looked up at the statue again. It portrayed a man, leaping, with outstretched arms, a look of noble determination on his face.

"Tell me about this statue."

"It's the Gr—I mean, it's William Karges. He was the bodyguard for—uh—President Robinson. Nobody knew he was a teep, but one day he p'heard—I mean heard with his mind—someone who wanted to kill the president, an' he got shot warning her. Nobody liked teeps—I mean telepaths—back then, and they weren't supposed to have jobs or rights or anything. But because of what Mr. Karges did, President Robinson made Psi Corps, to reward us, so teeps would have a place they could be safe and productive."

The man smiled gently. "They taught you that in school?"

"Yessir. And we watch the movie every Birthday."

"Did they also teach you that Washington chopped down the cherry tree?"

"Sir?"

"Never mind. Here come your friends. What's your name, son?"

"Alfred Bester, sir."

He nodded, then returned his gaze to the approaching mob of children, led by Brett. Al could feel the anger shimming from all of them. He had expected Brett to be angry, but why the rest?

"Looks like he won," the normal remarked. "Better congratulate him."

Brett hesitated an instant. Al could tell that, if the normal weren't around, they would all be shouting at him now. But no telepath was ever allowed to fight with another telepath around normals. Never.

So Brett held out his hand. "Good goin'," he mumbled. But as their hands touched, he 'cast something very different. *We're gonna get you, Alfie, you slug.*

That was bad, but it wasn't the worst thing. For a second, Al felt an intense flash of anger, hatred even. And it wasn't coming from anyone in his cadre.

It was coming from the normal.

2

Teacher Hua was explaining that the Earth Alliance had been founded so there could never be a World War IV, and had just asked a question about the importance of the Psi Corps in the Alliance, when three Grins entered the room. Al knew with cold and immediate dread that they had come for him.

Despite their nickname, they weren't grinning. Their masks were smooth plastic, with no visible openings for eyes, nose, or mouth—but like vid or AI units, they could be used to display images. The icons were usually simple—a bright yellow grin appeared when they brought awards, medals, or presents; a threatening, downturned mouth when they came to correct or punish.

"It seems someone has been bad," Teacher Hua said, noting the expressions on the "faces" of the three silent, grey-robed figures. "Now who in *my* class might have been bad? Who has brought shame upon the Corps?"

Al sensed a mild wave of panic rippling around him. Most everyone in the room had been bad, of course, at one time or the other—but bad enough for this? The Grins gave no clue as to who they might have come for—they just stood there, while Teacher Hua surveyed the room with grim speculation.

Al glanced at Brett, whose triumphant expression struck him like a snake. Brett had told. The Grins *were* after him. Knees shaking a little, Al rose from his seat.

"Alfred Bester," Teacher Hua said, softly. "And what do you think you might have done wrong, Mr. Bester?"

"I—I don't know, sir. I mean I'm not sure. But I think it was me."

In response to that, the three figures rustled toward him, hands lifting. As one, they stripped off their black gloves. The sight was worse, far worse, than seeing a nurse preparing a needle to take blood. His scalp tingled with a rush of terror.

They laid their hands on him, and he tried not to block, he really did,

but it was like trying not to blink when someone swung at your face. And so it hurt even more as they tunneled into his mind, found his sins, dragged them out in bright glyphs, mindcasting them for everyone to see.

When they finally let him go, he came to himself again, gasping, sweat pouring down his face. The whole class had witnessed his misery.

They had to help him up because he was trembling too violently to walk. Tears welled behind his eyes, but he would not cry, could not, not on top of everything else.

Their gloves were still off. They weren't done yet.

They took him, alone, to where he had done it, where the others had caught Brett. They stood him in the very spot, in the door frame, and stepped back to regard him. Their masks were unadorned now—blank ovals of plastic.

"What did you do?" The Grins had strange voices, inflectionless, like an Artificial Intelligence. Some thought that's exactly what they were, robots, though robots were supposed to be illegal.

"I . . . I betrayed Brett."

A sharp stab into his mind. "You don't believe that. Why?"

"He was playing dumb. He was going to get us caught. I wanted to win the game."

"You betrayed a member of the Corps. You cannot win—not at that cost."

"We were pretending to be Blips. Blips betray each other."

They crowded nearer, and one pointed an ungloved hand at him. "That is a lie. The others were pretending you two were rogues. *You* were not. You imagined yourself a Psi Cop, *chased* by rogues.

"But it runs deeper than that, Mr. Bester. No matter what any of you were pretending, you are all members of the Corps. Whatever you pretend in the course of constructive—or unconstructive—play, Brett is your brother. You share the same mother and father. Do you understand?"

"Yessir," Al replied, bowing his head. "The Corps is mother. The Corps is father."

"You can't forget that Brett is your brother without forgetting that the Corps is your mother and your father. Do you understand?"

"Yessir."

"You won't forget."

It wasn't a question, but a promise. The three stepped forward and laid hands on him again, one behind him and one to each side.

For an instant, nothing happened, and then, suddenly, the world grew brighter.

The steps where Brett had hidden suddenly came alive, each grain in the stone became a universe of significance. The buildings, the lawn, the trees—all burned into his mind with terrifying, hyperreal clarity. Shame shaped the light; fear framed the image, permeated it.

The Grins lowered their hands. They put their gloves on and led him back to class.

The trek from the classroom door to his seat was one of the longest he had ever taken. He felt like the corpse of a cat they had once found. It had somehow fallen from one of the buildings. Splattered, guts hanging out, fascinating because it was so horrible.

He avoided the questioning glances of the students as the subject switched to math, kept his head down, trying to pretend nothing had happened. It was hard; the image of the place where he betrayed Brett lingered in his mind, like an afterimage of the sun on retinas. But he made it through the day and trudged back to the cadre house, wishing he didn't share a room with Brett.

At the meal in the common room, everyone avoided him. Probably worried that if they spoke to him the Grins would come for them next. When it was time for *John Trakker, Psi Cop,* he had no enthusiasm for watching it and quietly slipped off, seeking solitude.

He almost bumped into Ms. Chastain. The tall, thin brunette wore a dark brown skirt and turquoise blouse. She looked down at him over the tip of her rather pointy nose. He liked Ms. Chastain—maybe not as much as he liked Mr. King, who had been his house father at 3–5, but that might just be because he missed Mr. King.

"Al, did you have a bad day? You always watch *John Trakker.*"

He nodded, sullenly.

She reached down and lifted his chin with her fingers. "Grins came for you, didn't they?"

"Yes, ma'am."

"Did you deserve it?"

"Yes, ma'am."

"Well." She seemed to study him for a moment. "I was just going to have some tea in the kitchen. Would you care to join me?" Her voice was kind.

"Yes, ma'am."

"May I tell you a story, Al?" Ms. Chastain sipped her lemon tea and nudged the plate of gingersnaps toward him. He took one.

"Yes, please."

"This is about my grandmother. She was a telepath, like me. Not as strong as me—she was maybe a P3 at best, though she was never rated."

"What do you mean? Everyone is rated, 'cept maybe Bli—" He broke off, suddenly embarrassed.

But Ms. Chastain smiled gently. "No, Al, she wasn't a Blip. She never got to join Psi Corps, you see. She was born in 2035. She never registered because she lived in New Zealand, and they didn't require it there—it was before universal registration. She was a good person, though. She didn't try to use her abilities for personal gain, but worked with the Catholic church, helping the needy.

"But one day, when my mother was just five years old, some normals came to the church and they burned it. And they took all of the priests who were teeps, and they took my grandmother, and they tied heavy weights on all of them and dropped them in the ocean. My mother was there, but she was hiding, and from where she was, she felt my grandmother drown.

"She kept that feeling in her heart, and when I got old enough, she passed it on to me. It was awful, Alfred, but I know why she did it. She did it to remind me, always, that we aren't like normal people. Even if we try to pretend we are, the normals will remind us." She smiled, and then abruptly laid her hand on his and switched to 'casting.

We're special, Al, all of us. The normals know it, and they hate us for it. And there are so many more of them than there are of us, so many. If we don't stand together, all of us—if we aren't stronger and smarter and better than them—they'll do it again, like they did to my grandmother.

So when you think you've been treated harshly, remember that. It's to make you strong and good, to get you ready for the challenges that come later. Because even though many normals hate us, it's still our job to protect them, too. From themselves, from enemies out in the stars. And you, Al— you're really strong—you test P12, and if you train well you can live up to that potential. You will have to be more responsible than most. You'll look back one day and understand everything that happened to you. You'll see that it was for the greater good. Do you understand?

He managed a little smile. *Yes.*

Good. How about another cookie?

That night, in his nightmares, he saw the steps again, and watched himself as he betrayed Brett. But when he woke up, heart pounding, he remembered Ms. Chastain's words. *I have to be better than I am,* he thought to himself. *I have to be the best, and I have to do it right.*

But he had a hard time getting back to sleep. After a while he rose and went to the window.

Their room was on the third floor, faced away from most of the city lights of Geneva, and he had a good view of the stars. He started picking out the ones he knew, trying to remember what he had heard about them, which were the homes of men. And in the corners of his eyes—where the stars were strangely brightest—he thought he saw the faces.

When he focused on them, they always went away, so he could never see them directly. He knew the woman had dark red hair, and the man had black hair. They were the faces of the Corps, the mother and father. Sometimes, when he was alone, he would talk to them, ask them questions, but they never answered. He heard their voices sometimes, when he was asleep, but when he woke up he was never sure what they had said. Only that they loved him.

But of course they did. They were the Corps.

Sometimes he wondered what he would see if a Grin took off its mask. Would he see those faces, but clearly? Where were they, if not behind the Grins?

Maybe in the big buildings. Maybe the director was his mother.

A soft rustling behind him interrupted his thoughts.

"You okay, Alfie?"

It was Brett.

"Yeah."

"Alfie— Look, I'm sorry. I didn't know it would be so bad. The way you looked when they brought you back—I'm sorry I told."

"No," Al replied. "No, you did right. I shouldn't have done that to you."

There followed an awkward pause. "I just wanted you to know," Brett finished. Then he brightened. "Anyway, Birthday coming up. What do you think you'll get this year?"

"I don't know. I don't really want anything."

"I do. I hope I get a John Trakker PPG. Wouldn't that be cool?"

"Yeah." He tried on a smile. "We better get some sleep. 'Sleepy boys are no good to the Corps.' "

"Yeah. Good night, Alfie."

By the time it came, Al was excited about Birthday, though not for the same reason as Brett. It was Birthday, naturally, when new kids joined the cadre. Al had mixed feelings about it—things had been easier when the cadre was smaller—but there was always the hope that someone really neat would join. Maybe a girl who would like him.

He knew he really wasn't supposed to like girls, but he did, and he couldn't help it. The problem was getting them to like you back. And hiding the fact that you liked them from the others . . .

He still liked Milla, but had sort of given up on her.

Anyway, Birthday was always a lot of fun, and there wasn't any schoolwork on Birthday.

Birthday started at seven, but everyone was up well before that, eagerly awaiting the opening of the common-room doors. When they finally swung wide, there was whooping and cheering at the decorations that festooned the room, especially the piñatas. Al got to break one of those—it was easy, even blindfolded, because everyone glyphed to you where it was. After that, some kids from another cadre—an *older* one, from the 11–13 house—came in and did a play for them. It was a story they all knew, from one of their world readers, but it was still fun to see it acted out.

There were only four new kids, a girl and three boys. The girl was pretty, with dark hair and green eyes. Brett was already talking to her, though, as they watched the play.

"They aren't saying anything," she noted.

"They won't," Brett said. "You have to p'hear."

She shut her eyes. "I can almost hear . . ."

"P'hear," Brett corrected.

"I've never met another mind reader until a few days ago," she said, softly—apologetically.

"It's okay. We call ourselves 'teeps,' though. Link hands with me and Alfie. We'll help you. Alfie?"

She looked at him with her mossy eyes, and when he took her hand, his face felt funny. Warm.

Al focused on the play. The story was from the Central African Block, he remembered, from the Wayo tribe, or something like that. There were two main characters, Hornbill and the Elder, and besides them, three villagers—though the audience was supposed to play villagers, too.

Hornbill was lying down. The actors wore little in the way of costumes, instead glyphing their appearances. Hornbill was a bird with a very small beak.

Hornbill: *I don't feel like going to a funeral today. It's such a long business, with the procession and all. I would much rather lie in my hammock and take a nap.*

Village: *LAZY HORNBILL! HE DOESN'T CARE ABOUT THE VILLAGE!*

> **HE** don't do nothin' for us
> **ONLY** what **HIS**
> **CARES** he **PEOPLE!**
> **ABOUT** should
> **HIMSELF** *is selfish!*

Elder: *Shame!*

Hornbill: *No, no, you go ahead.*

Village: **WE ARE YOUR BROTHERS AND SISTERS! DO RIGHT BY US!**

> mother father obey
> kith kin respect

(Glyph of the calendar flipping, days passing.)

Hornbill: *Ah, no, my own son has died! Surely the people of the village will come to help me bury him!*

Village:

> C
> F H
> FAT CHANCE!
> T N
> C
> E
> !

Elder: *You have never helped in a funeral. Now no one will help you!*

Hornbill: *But I don't even know where the graveyard is!*

Village: *BECAUSE YOU NEVER CARED BEFORE!*

Elder: *Find it yourself, lazy Hornbill!*

(The actor mimed the hornbill, carrying his son's coffin on his back, a heavy burden, searching for the graveyard. Glyphs of calendars flipping, days, months, years passing. Putrid ooze leaking out of the coffin as it gradually transformed into the hornbill's cumbersome beak.)

Hornbill: *Where is the graveyard? Where is the graveyard?*

But the words were a cry, the sound of the hornbill's call, repeated forever as he paid for his sin. The sin of standing apart from the village, the sin of selfishness.

The play ended, and they clapped. The older kids took a bow.

At that moment, four Grins walked in through the open door.

For a moment, Al felt a cold spot form in the pit of his belly, but then he saw that this time, the robed figures *were* grinning, huge happy smiles, and each carried a large sack. It was time for presents!

Brett got his PPG—not a real one, of course, but it looked real and whined like one warming up. Al got a book on John Carter, the founder of the Mars colony, and they all got plastic Psi Corps badges. After that there was cake and cookies, and pin-the-tail-on-the-donkey with half the cadre trying to help the blindfolded player and the other half trying to hinder him.

For supper they had a picnic on the lawn and watched the stars come out in the evening sky, while Ms. Chastain played the autoharp and sang from the cadre songbook.

Al was enjoying himself. Everything seemed right. The Grins had brought him a present, so his own sin must have been forgiven. He wasn't going to be like Hornbill, cursed forever.

Maybe it was time to try the tree again. He walked toward it, humming *Happy Birthday to Us.*

At the base of the oak, he noticed he was being followed. It was the new girl.

"Hi," he said. "So what's your name?"

"Hi." she answered. "My name is Julia." She pronounced it *hoo-lee-yah.*

"My name is Al."

"I thought it was Al-fee."

"That's what they call me. I like Al better."

"Okay. I just wanted to thank you for helping me with the play."

He nodded, unable to meet her green eyes. " 'S okay."

And then she just *stood* there, smiling, and he was supposed to think of something to say. But he couldn't. And in a minute she would get bored and leave.

"Watch this!" he said, and without waiting for a response, he ran over to the tree and started to climb it. He got to the swing-around branch and kept going. He felt strong, like he could do anything. Higher, and he found himself under the branch again.

He didn't look down this time, but he imagined Julia, watching him as he climbed higher and higher. He steadied himself, bent his knees, and jumped as high as he could. His hands came together—

And caught around the branch. Grunting, grinning, he pulled himself up and over the branch, tempted to shout to the others, to let them see that he had done it. He looked down to see how Julia was taking it.

She wasn't there. She was walking off, hand in hand with Brett.

His feeling of triumph evaporated like rubbing alcohol.

What's the use, he thought. That was it. He was giving up on girls. What did they know? Here he had climbed the tree for her, risked his life . . .

And he was just realizing how much farther down it was from here. Birthday stank.

He awoke with a hand over his mouth and a Grin staring down at him. He tried to scream, but the hand and a fierce psi command stopped him. He breathed hard, the chemical scent of the glove in his nose.

The Grin was blank, expressionless—no smile, no frown. When his breathing slowed, it motioned him to silence, removed the hand from his mouth, and handed him a robe.

Follow, it commanded.

They moved through the empty streets of Teeptown like will-o'-the-wisps, passing familiar places made strange by the hour.

Teeptown was just that, a small town. It had a Common—a center with shops and such—and lots of quads, each with their own, smaller commons. Al really only knew Alpha Quad. When he was a baby, of course, he had lived in the crèche, in the hospital quad, but he didn't remember that. He got his psi early—again, before he could remember—and so he had never lived in the Basement, but had gone straight to the first cadre house. Though he had twice changed houses as he got older, they were all in Alpha quad.

Now he and the Grin moved out of that familiar quarter and into the quad with the Minor Academy. Off that—farther right—was the Major Academy; Al had never had the nerve to go that far afield, but he had wandered the grounds of the Minor, watching the older kids, trying to figure it out. He still wasn't clear exactly how it was put together, though he heard cadres got broken up there, and people were reassigned to

"schools." That didn't sound like much fun, but nobody went to the Minor Academy until they were twelve or so, so he had a while before he had to worry about it.

Once they had passed through the academy grounds, he found himself in territory he *really* didn't know. There was a sort of invisible line, past the stanchion field, that kids knew they weren't supposed to cross, and for the most part, they didn't. There were apartments for the married couples, and for the grownups who ran Teeptown—some of them *normals*. And government buildings, he guessed.

The Grin led him on through the no-kids land. Al worried that it might be a trick—that the Grin's mask would change to a frown, and he would be chastised, suddenly, for crossing the unseen demarcation.

But through his fear, he began to feel a new sort of excitement. *Maybe I'm going to see the mother and father,* he thought. *The faces from my dreams.*

The Grin took him into a large building, through winding corridors of dull pearl, to a large office of nearly the same shade—or which probably would be, if the lights were turned up. Tonight, they were very dim. The Grin ushered him through the door and left, closing the portal behind him. Al was left standing uncertainly in the near darkness.

"Come forward, Alfred Bester."

There was someone behind the big desk. He noticed, as his eyes adjusted, that the room had many shelves, filled with paper books—and not a whole lot else. No pictures, like the painting Ms. Chastain had in her office, nothing like that. Books, and walls, and a desk.

And behind the desk was the oldest man Al had ever seen.

His hair was cut so close to his head, the only way Al knew he wasn't bald was because it was whiter than milk, whereas the rest of his head was like a brown paper bag that had been crumpled, smoothed, crumpled again, smoothed again, then stretched tight over a skull. Al found himself wishing that he could touch that face, to see what it would feel like. Would it be hard, like leather—or delicate, like tissue paper?

"Do you know who I am, Mr. Bester?"

"No, sir."

"My name is Kevin Vacit. I am the director of Psi Corps."

The director. "Pleased to meet you, sir. The Corps is mother. The Corps is father."

"Indeed. And it seems that mother and father had to discipline you, a few days ago."

"Yessir." The vague fear in his chest tightened.

"Come closer."

Al stepped even closer, and suddenly he saw the director's eyes, cold gems, colorless. Like—like he didn't know what.

And he felt a shadow go through his mind. It wasn't like a scan, not even a light one. He wasn't even sure it was real.

But the director smiled. "You felt something?"

"Yessir."

"Interesting. Most don't."

Al waited for the director to explain what it was that most people didn't notice, but instead the old man leaned forward and clasped his hands together. "Listen to me, Alfred," he said, his voice rather low and scratchy, but still perfectly intelligible. "What do you want to be?"

That was easy. "I want to be a Psi Cop, sir."

"Why?"

That was harder, and Al thought about it for an instant. He had heard that the director of Psi Corps was always supposed to be a normal, appointed by the EA senate. So he might be able to get away with lying—

No. He had already shamed the Corps once, he would not do it again.

"I know I'm supposed to want to be a Psi Cop so I can serve and defend, and all of that. And I want to do all that, I really do, but—"

"It's not the real reason."

"No, sir. It's because to be a Psi Cop you have to be the best. The very best."

"And you want people to know you are the best."

"Yes, sir."

"You know that's the wrong answer, don't you, Alfred?"

"Yessir."

The old man nodded thoughtfully. "Everyone has different strengths, you know. No one is better than anyone else. A good business telepath, a good military telepath—as long as you perform to the best of your abilities, it's all the same."

Al could think of no reply, so he said nothing.

"You don't believe that, do you?" the director asked.

"I . . . no, sir."

"Well."

The silence stretched so long and thin, Al was afraid something would break. Then the old man sighed. "Don't tell anyone you came to see me, Alfred. You can return to your bed now." He made a sign, and the door opened again. The Grin was waiting for him.

"Sir?" Al asked, as the masked person moved to lead him away.

"Yes?"

"Will I get to be a Psi Cop?"

"That remains to be seen, Mr. Bester. But—" He paused. "Do not think that being the best will make you happy. The very qualities that allow the one, preclude the other."

"I don't understand, sir."

"I know. You're too young. When you do understand, it will be too late, won't it?" His face wrinkled up, oddly. "It's been a pleasure meeting you, Alfred. I think—yes, in a way I think you would have made your parents proud."

"My parents, sir? You mean the Corps?"

The ancient face smoothed out again. "I mean your parents, your mother and your father."

"My mother and father are the Corps, sir."

"Quite right." He sighed. "And I knew them all."

"Sir?"

"Never mind me, Mr. Bester. I am an old man, and my mind wanders. In fact, I don't expect we'll meet again—I'm going away soon, and someone else will become director in my place. The Corps is your mother and father, as you said. And the Corps is proud of you. That's all I meant."

But it wasn't, and Al knew it. For just an instant, he thought he had seen a woman's face—*the* woman's face . . .

But he retreated from that thought. If anyone suspected he had read the *director's* mind, even accidentally, there was no telling what would happen to him.

"One other thing, Alfred."

Al's throat tightened. Had he been caught?

"Sir?"

"Things may—change—after I'm gone. Remember who you are. Remember how you were raised. It's important. The Corps is important. It has a purpose more important than anyone can possibly dream. Can you remember that?"

"Of course, sir."

"Remember this, too, then. *Watch for the Shadows. Watch, and beware.*" When the director said *Shadows,* something seemed to form in Al's brain, an image, kind of like a spider. Then it sank into something and was gone.

"Good night, Alfred. And good-bye."

3

"Hey, Alfie," Brett called from across the common room. "What do *you* think the Grins really are?"

Al looked up from his book toward the little knot of kids around the table. He had been trying to tune their conversation out.

"What? How should I know?"

Brett shrugged and Julia giggled.

"What's funny?"

Julia seemed to sober, but it was Milla that said, "Because you're kind of *like* a Grin, Alfie. Nobody can ever tell what's up with you."

Al sighed and laid his book down. He decided to ignore the comment. "First of all, they're called *monitors,* not Grins—"

"Vidflash!" Brett snorted. "We all know what they're called. That's not the question."

"Well, it's not for us to wonder about who they are," Al said. "They're Corps, and they're here to help us. That's all that matters."

"See what I mean?" Milla said.

"Okay. What do *you* think they are?" Al responded, drawing himself up. At twelve, he was still the shortest boy in the room, and shorter than most of the girls, but he knew some of the others still found him physically intimidating. He had given some of them reason to.

"Robots," Julia opined.

"Humaniform robots are illegal. The Corps wouldn't have robots."

"That's what I say," Brett agreed. "Besides, who ever heard of a telepathic AI? So what are they?"

Al considered them all for a moment, then lowered his voice. "I think they're brain-wiped criminals."

"Huh?"

"Rogues who couldn't be reeducated. Students that asked too many of the wrong questions. They wipe their brains and program them to do what they do."

Julia shuddered. "You really think so?"

"What I think is that we shouldn't be talking about it," Al responded. "It's not our business. If the Corps wants us to know what they are, they'll tell us."

"Maybe we're supposed to figure out what they are. Maybe it's another test—did you ever consider that?"

There had been a lot of tests lately, with Minor Academy admissions coming up.

"I think I know a test when I see one. Unlike some of you."

Julia and Azmun paled. They knew who he was talking about.

"That wasn't nice, Alfie," Brett said. "You don't have to be such an ass about things."

Like any of you are nice to me, Al thought. *Like any of you care how I feel.* But he kept it blocked and locked. He wouldn't give them the satisfaction of knowing that they could hurt him. After all, they were just jealous. Even Brett couldn't outdo him on the tests—except in some of the *normal* stuff, like running, and then only just barely.

He just shrugged, knowing that would annoy them more than any verbal response.

The final tests started tomorrow. Those who passed would move to the Minor Academy. He would be one of them, and he would finally be where he ought to be. In the Minor Academy people would *appreciate* him. He wouldn't let Brett and the rest distract him from that goal. From finally escaping them.

"Take a few minutes to get ready, Alfred. Simon," Teacher Roberts said, with an absent air. He made a few marks on his notepad.

Al opened his envelope and glanced at the photograph inside. It depicted a brick-red groundcar, a Cortez JumpPoint. He closed his eyes, held the image for a moment to make sure he had it, then sealed the envelope and laid it on the desk in front of him. Ten meters away, across the room, Simon did the same. Al took a moment to size Simon up. He was the same age, twelve, but from a different cadre. Fox-faced, auburn hair to match.

Al closed his eyes again and took deep, slow breaths as he shut the world down. The telepathic white noise was the first to go, that sort of distant ocean sound produced by the millions of minds in the Greater Geneva area. Layered above that were the hundreds of thoughts near enough to be half intelligible—a word here, a few brushstrokes from a landscape there, traces of mood like aromas, some sharp, some subtle.

Gone. Leaving only the nearest thoughts, investing themselves in his brain almost with the ease of his own thoughts. He remembered himself as a child, wondering, *Am I really thinking that, or is it someone else?*

It was the most dangerous confusion a telepath could face.

Deep slow breath in, deep slow breath out. The voices going out like stars at sunrise, till only one was left—Simon's. You couldn't really see a mind, of course, but to Al, Simon's appeared for the moment as a hard black sphere, encased by larger, silver-translucent balls, nested within one another.

Al had never really imagined this required any sort of explanation, but Teacher Roberts had talked about it often enough. He liked explaining things that didn't seem to need explanations.

"Basically, we're just fancy monkeys," he'd told them, the first day of class. "Our ancestors didn't evolve like wolves, or horses, or whales, specializing their digits into claws or hooves or flippers. Nope, evolution left us with the same feeble five digits that our reptilian ancestors had. General, not specialized. All of the primates followed that pattern— never committing to specialization, always trying to stay the jacks-of-all-trades.

"The only real change from the lizard hand to the monkey hand was opposability, the ability to grasp—and we needed that, running around in treetops. The other thing we needed were eyes in the front of our heads, bifocal, so we could triangulate, see depth—be able to actually *catch* that next branch when we jumped at it.

"But that turned out to be a big change, after all. Our bifocal eyes needed all this new hardware to run. As a result, primate brains got bigger. Sight got better, hand-to-eye coordination got better, and the other senses suffered, but so what? Because with those big brains came unexpected benefits.

"For sixty million years or so, primate brains have been built around vision—vision and manipulation of our generalized, lizard hands. As a consequence, we learned to express ourselves with pictures first. Words came later.

"Telepathy is a very new evolutionary step, and evolution always has to work with what it's given. Birds didn't just grow wings—their forelimbs were modified. Likewise, we do telepathy with those same old monkey brains, and the primary modality is still visual. So we 'see' the unseeable, picture the unpicturable.

"Think about dreaming. Dreaming is caused by random surges in neuroelectricity. These jolts go through the brain and release images; our brains then try to organize these images, make sense of them, release or build more images to fill in the gaps. When we awaken, we try to assign linear, logical meaning to them. We don't 'see' random surges of electric-

ity jolting into our brains—we see ourselves, sitting in class in our underwear or running in slow motion from angry Grins.

"When a rogue tries to fry your brain with a mindblast, you won't 'see' an inchoate, deadly force, or a pattern of electrochemical reactions triggered in your neural net. You'll see a sword coming to cut your head in two, a car about to run you down, the sky falling. That's fine, because that's how we work, we fancy monkeys.

"The trick is to not get confused, and that's a big deal. We relate to things we *don't* know in terms of things we *do* know—by analogy. If you've never seen a snake, but you do know worms, you will see the snake and think, 'Aha! It's like a big worm.' But if you make the mistake of thinking that a cobra is an earthworm, you make a very foolish—and terminal—mistake. If you actually think that a mindblast *is* a sword— well, I can take you to see some people who made that very mistake. You can take turns spoon-feeding them and changing their diapers."

He tried to keep that in mind, as he focused on the sphere that signified Simon's psyche. As he watched, the translucent shells began opaquing.

He was confident that his own blocks were in place. They were familiar friends. Still, general blocks were of only so much use in this test.

"Proceed," Teacher Roberts said.

Simon came at him in a storm front, a roaring, crackling mass. Amused by the crudity of that approach, Al met him force for force, and they collided like twin hurricanes. Jagged blue-white bolts condensed into coruscating ball lightnings, eddying, sputtering out, sometimes erupting into whirls of purple fire. Simon couldn't beat him like this, and he must know it. What was he up to?

A terrible fear gripped him. Then a sense of defeat. The test was already over. Somehow Simon had already found his hidden image, was about to tell Teacher Roberts what it was . . .

No. Simon had been clever. The frontal assault was a feint; the real attack was this awful despondency, sneaking down the slow, tropical river of his limbic system. Emotion so basic and colorless he hadn't recognized it wasn't his own.

But to project despair so well, Simon must own some of it.

Al tightened the feelings, intensified them, and launched them back to their source, in a fluid bolt that dug quickly through the outer shells of Simon's mind. It stopped short of the inner sphere, but like an oil strike in reverse, started pooling there, flooding and poisoning Simon's outer blocks with gloom. As his own false sense of failure faded, Al caught a surge of panic from Simon.

He worried for a moment this might be another feint—an attempt to exaggerate his confidence—but his deepest instinct told him it was real. The acid of Simon's attack was dissolving his own guards.

Simon's psionic thunderhead boiled away, but Al's was still there, and finding itself suddenly unchecked, it hurled toward the deconstructing blocks. One, two, three shells cracked and sublimated, and Al snatched greedily at the glyphs leaking through, as bright and effervescent as oil on a sunlit pool. Simon attempted to distract him one last time by triggering an involuntary motor response—a desperate move because if discovered, it was easily reversed. It was a clumsy attack, and Al simply reflected it without knowing what it was.

The last of Simon's blocks shattered, and his secret stood revealed: a photograph of a knight in armor.

Laughable. Al opened his eyes.

"It was a photograph of a knight," he said, briskly. "Fourteenth century, I think."

Simon's eyes were wide and dazed. He was looking vaguely at his lap, and as Al caught the scent of ammonia, he suddenly realized what motor response Simon had been trying to provoke.

Served him right, then.

"Very good, Alfred," Teacher Roberts said. "And good try, Simon."

"May I be excused, sir?" Simon choked out.

"Yes, perhaps you'd better."

When Simon was gone, Teacher Roberts' lips twitched in a little grin. "That was well done," he said. "Now, I didn't see what was in the envelope you chose. I still don't know what your image was."

"Yes, sir."

"I'm coming for it. Now."

Before Al could blink, an egg of molten pain cracked against the nape of his neck. He had already relaxed his battle guards, of course, and this smashed through his habitual ones as if they weren't there. Desperately, he tried to enfold the pain, but Teacher Roberts' Humpty-Dumpty would not be put together again.

Instead, he just gritted his teeth and swallowed it. It was only pain, and nothing real was happening to his body. Nothing real, though he felt his hands clutch and spasm with the force of it.

Teacher Roberts' mind didn't look much like Simon's. It was part spider and part octopus, spinning out a hundred tentacle-legs of black concertina wire. One of these was already wrapped around his neck, razoring into it, and more were enveloping him.

Vision and manipulation. The two shaping forces of telepathy. He pushed back his fear and hesitation, grasping the scalpel strands with

imaginary hands, knotting them to each other. Many faded as he did so, but not quickly enough. More came, splitting like roots digging into loose soil, now tipped with throbbing green scorpion stings. He couldn't stop them all, and he knew it. More wrapped around him, and pain was a hot filament through his axis.

Don't be confused. He was letting Teacher Roberts control the imago. The instructor's mind was no more a monster than Simon's had been a spherical fortress, but Al had let himself be convinced it was, tried to fight the metaphor on its own terms—treating the tentacles as if they were *real.*

He twisted his perspective, twisted it again, and the radial monster collapsed around itself, formed the knight from Simon's photograph, save that it had four arms instead of two, each equipped with a massive sword. This was a perception he could deal with a bit more easily; one of the weapons was buried in his neck, but he slid off of it, made each of his fingers a rapier and flicked them out.

The knight fell back beneath the onslaught, sparks striking on his armor from Al's needlelike fingers, then lashed back even stronger than before. Three of the blades grew longer and heavier as the fourth condensed away. They hammered at his rapiers, shattered them, and Al was forced to replace them with bucklers just to fend off the merciless battering.

Still, he was planning a new attack when he suddenly noticed that the fourth "sword" hadn't vanished at all, but merely reshaped itself into a gun. It winked a red eye, as Al threw everything he had—everything—into a final, impossible defense. Something in his skull seemed to explode, and silence followed.

He blinked his lids open. Someone was patting him on the cheek. The rasping in his head was his own breath, and his lips had a salty taste on them. The bright copper smell of blood clogged his nose.

"Sorry about that, Alfred." It was Teacher Roberts, with a concerned look on his face. "I let you push yourself too hard."

Al swallowed shakily. He noticed that he was on a gurney, that not far away a nurse was fussing about.

"Where am I? That was . . ." Words failed him.

"This is the infirmary. You're okay, they just wanted to watch you for a little while. You've been out for about two hours." He hesitated, then gripped Al's hand. "I want you to understand that I wasn't trying to hurt you, Al. But in your contest with Simon, I noticed a certain self-congratulatory smugness. You're good for your age, and you push yourself harder than anyone I've ever seen—too hard, in fact, as this incident demon-

strates—but there are mind rippers out there who can make what just happened to you seem like a thump on the nose. It would be a disservice for me not to help you understand that, now, before you make a habit of overconfidence."

"I think I understand, sir."

"I don't think you do. But it's a start." He paused. "You grasped part of my lessons, Al. You tried to control the imago, the metaphorical construct I attacked you with, and did a good job. It's one approach, but it has its dangers. It's a sort of a shaman game—"

"Sir?"

"Shamans. Tribal doctors and magicians. Worldwide, they were said to go into trances and fight battles of imago, transforming as their opponents transformed. One would be a wolf, the other would become a lion. Then the first would become a bear, his opponent a—*T. rex* or something. Often it was even more subtle than that; one becomes fire, the other becomes rain, the drowned fire rises as a mist—and so on.

"The winner is the one whose form plays most cleverly and convincingly against his opponent's form. It only works because both combatants allow their minds to accept the rules, to be bound by what they know of the normal world. And that brings me to one last point. Have you ever played paper, scissors, rock?"

"Yes, sir." Al was mystified by the sudden change of direction.

"Let's play. On three."

They shook their closed fists three times. Al kept his clenched—rock. Teacher Roberts' came out two fingers—scissors.

"Well?" the teacher said.

"I win. Rock smashes scissors."

Teacher Roberts reached out, very quickly, and grabbed Al's hand at thumb and little finger, twisting it around. Al yelped, involuntarily, in surprise and pain.

"*I* win," Roberts said. "I win because I don't acknowledge that there was a rock or scissors. Only our hands. And my hand is bigger, faster, stronger, more skillful than yours. You see?" He released Al's hand as quickly as he had taken it.

"Yes. I see," Al said. *You cheated. You broke the rules.*

Teacher Roberts caught that, and his eyes glittered. *Exactly, Al. Exactly. You have a decision coming. This is the end of this session, and you'll be going to the Minor Academy next, if you pass. If you aren't comfortable with breaking rules, I suggest you take business prep courses. If you want to be a Psi Cop, though . . .*

He smiled and stood up. "I'll see you tomorrow for your written final. It's a take-home. Discuss—let's see—I want you to compare Yakut

shamanic battles, the Flight of Loki, and the exploits of the lively Lemminkainen. And be ready to transpose them in action, should I ask. Yes?"

"Yes, sir." Though he had not the faintest idea what a Yakut was—or who "Loki" or "Lemminkainen" were. That kind of assignment was typical of Teacher Roberts.

"How'd you do?" Brett asked, as Al came into the room with an armload of books.

"I stunk. And he gave me a take-home." Al closed his eyes for an instant; his psi contest with Teacher Roberts had left him feeling as if he hadn't slept in days.

"Hmm. Well, don't wear out—we have the intercadre tournament day after tomorrow. I think we've got a good chance."

"Sure we do."

Brett turned back to whatever it was he was doing. Al opened his books and began trying to sort out what to skim through first. Brett was only sucking up to him because he *did* want the cadre to win. That was Brett, always thinking about his position as leader.

Not that anyone had ever elected him, or anything. They just accepted it, which was all wrong. Brett was neither the smartest nor psionically the strongest. Why should he be the one everyone paid attention to?

But that was the way it was, wasn't it? For now, anyway. When they got to the academy, where positions were officially awarded by merit and ability, he would come into his own.

He had just a week to wait.

He focused his attention on the book, and to his surprise, he found himself enjoying it. He was entirely absorbed in the weird duel of two Yakut shamans when the door suddenly burst open.

He hadn't heard or felt them coming. You never did.

Grins. Angry Grins.

What have I done this time? He was afraid he'd let it slip out. Fear mingled freely with his anger, and he certainly wanted to keep *that* in.

In the last year or so, the Grins had become more and more arbitrary with their punishments and scans. It should be obvious to everyone how unfair it was, but the adults never seemed to notice the change, even when it went on right in front of them.

He tried to remember what he had maintained that very morning, that they had no business questioning the Grins, but it was hard, very hard.

"Take off your clothes. All of them," the Grins commanded, in their flat, less-than-Human voices.

He and Brett complied. Al might resent them, but there was never any question of obeying them. They were a fact of life.

It got worse. The Grins herded the two of them, naked, from their room into the common room, and there was the rest of the cadre, all naked as slugs, girls and boys alike. Al had always supposed he might like to see some of the girls without their clothes on—especially Milla, who had taken on an intriguing shape in the last year or so—but he found that faced with it, like this, he was horrified. They didn't seem pretty, or sexy, or whatever—they seemed like sea creatures, yanked from their shells, left to shiver and die naked on the beach.

In other words, they looked exactly as he felt. Sick.

From the common room, they were all forced outside. The expressions on the masks of their tormentors became less pleasant by the second.

4

The Grins led them down what seemed miles of sidewalk, surrounded on every side by older kids, academy students, adults. Al felt himself being measured, weighed, scrutinized. Though the watching crowd uttered not a single sound, telepathic gibes and insults made it clear they found him wanting.

Little guy, isn't he? A little rat.

Hey, kid, what's a six-year-old doing, doing the walk?

Are those your arms, or soda straws?

And now the Grins were grinning, and Al suddenly realized that all along their smiles had been ironic—even when they were bringing presents or awards, they had always been smiling *at* him, not for him. Laughing at him, behind their masks.

At last the "walk" was over, and they were led into a darkened room, spacious, a little musty. It wasn't so dark that he couldn't see the others, who, like him, were starting to shiver with the cold, wanting to huddle together. But they were kept apart by nakedness and terror. A lot of them were crying, and many were blooping like crazy, all their lessons drowned by shame and humiliation.

But they couldn't do that to him. Not to Alfred Bester. He didn't know what was going on here—whether the Grins had gone insane, or whether this was some horrible plot somehow perpetrated by mundanes—but when the Psi Cops found out about this, somebody would pay. They would pay, and he would be there to see it.

He jerked, suddenly, like the fish he had once seen a man pull out of Lake Geneva. A scan blasted through his defenses as if they weren't there. He rallied a defense—and let it drop. No one was allowed to challenge the Grins.

But if the Grins had gone insane . . .

It was too late, anyway. They were dragging glyphs from his mind, scattering them to the other kids: Him looking longingly at Julia. Wetting his pants when he was six. Stealing a candy when no one was looking.

The things he kept locked away—black spiders in secret jars, bright hopes he hoarded like jewels. All were torn from him and thrown into the air like confetti shredded from his soul.

And the air was suffocating with such confetti. There was Brett, peeking through a cracked door at Ms. Chastain as she bathed. There was Milla, bleeding between her legs and crying, so humiliated she couldn't think straight. Azmun, sitting in class, suddenly losing control of his bowels, afraid to let anyone know, unable to admit what he had done, as the smell got stronger and stronger . . .

It went on and on, the wailing and bawling worse and worse, until finally, something cracked in Al. He stood up, and it was like his mind was on fire, like he was shooting comets out of his brain instead of thoughts.

STOP IT! STOP IT! STOP IT! YOU STINKING GRINS, STOP IT!

The other kids took it up, first one, then another, then all of them, screaming at the Grins to stop. Al felt suddenly as if he were an atom of water in a huge wave, a tsunami of anger and justice.

And the Grins—stopped. But the kids didn't—the wave grew and grew, crushing down on the Grins, as they psionically gorged on each other's anguish, fear, and hatred.

Then a terrible white light filled the room, blinding, and everything broke off into confusion again. When the light came back down, when they could see again, they were so stunned that no one said or psied anything.

Because the Grins had taken off their masks. Al knew them.

Teacher Roberts. Teacher Hua. Ms. Chastain. Ms. Kitsuru. Teacher Alverado. Mr. King. Nurse Childress, who had held him and talked softly to him, sung him bedtime stories. They were all Grins. All of the adults. All of the people who had raised him. The Corps.

Teacher Hua, the oldest, stepped forward into the stunned silence.

"Now you see," he said, gently. "And now, hopefully, you understand. The Corps is mother and father—and we are all mother and father to one another. We are the ones who raised you, taught you right from wrong, pleased you—and yes, frightened you. This is all to the good, and in the future you shall understand, even if you don't now.

"You are Cadre Prime. All telepaths are special, but you are the most special. The powers of most children do not bloom until they are eleven, twelve, older. Most of you manifested almost as you were born. Only five percent manifest before puberty. You are all rare.

"Cadre Prime. Telepaths born, and you have raised each other as much as we have raised you. When you move from here, from cadre dorms and into the academies—it will be different. You will live and

work beside those who were raised as normals who realized their abilities later in life, who do not understand the Corps as you do. They say the words but do not understand in their hearts what it *is* to be Corps. It is your special gift to be able to teach them that, to show them by the example of how you live, how you learn, how you work together and apart.

"All of us—all of us who stand before you—we were once members of Cadre Prime. We are your mothers and fathers, we are your sisters and brothers. We stood before our elders as you now stand before us. We were frightened, humiliated, angry—as you are. And together, as you did, we took up the cry, threw off the yoke, became mothers and fathers ourselves. Then they revealed themselves to us, as we have to you.

"Now it comes full circle. You were children. Now I say, you are not. You are us, and we are you."

Teacher Hua began taking off his clothes. The others did, too. Without the grey robes, teacher Hua was a scrawny old man with a potbelly. He did not look scary at all. He knelt before them, and the other adults followed suit.

"A moment ago, your minds were violated. That was to show you one reason the Corps was formed, why one must never invade the mind of another without their permission. That law must be inviolate. It will not be done to you again, and you must not do it to others, except in very special circumstances.

"One of those is now. Our minds are open. Our barriers are down. Do what you will."

For a long moment, it was impossible to believe. No one moved. They just stared at the kneeling adults, their teachers and friends, who were also their tormentors.

Then some began reaching out, understanding that it was true, that the barriers were indeed down. That the adults would do nothing to stop them. First one, then another of the kids nibbled at the unprotected minds, darting in to find some secret, and then out again, as if they feared some trap might be sprung.

Then, with the suddenness of critical mass, the room exploded, once again, with pain and shame. But this time, it came from the adults.

Al found he couldn't participate. He stood there, blinking at the world turned upside down, his heart clattering weirdly in his chest. Why were the adults allowing this? They were the ones in control—who would give that up?

But then he caught something, a presence—watching. Approving. The director?

It didn't matter, because he suddenly understood. The teachers

weren't in charge, any more than he was. The *Corps* was mother and father, not any of the individuals in it. Teacher Hua's words began to make more sense.

When it was over, they were given black robes to wear, and more important—gloves. Al pulled his on, felt them close about his fingers. Gloves, at long last.

He was no longer a child.

Teacher Hua had said a lot, some of which Al understood, some of which he did not. But the thing he understood most clearly of all was something Teacher Hua had *not* said. It was a very simple thing, really, something he should have known all along.

Adults were no different from kids. They were not to be trusted, not as individuals. Teacher Hua could not be trusted. Ms. Chastain, despite all of her kindness, could not be trusted.

Only the Corps itself could be trusted, and only the Corps itself—its laws, its institutions, its entirety—deserved his loyalty.

He trusted the Corps. He would never trust another human being again.

That night, when he looked at the stars—when he dreamed—he looked for the face of his mother, with her dark red hair; he looked for his black-haired father. The ones he had always pictured when he said, "The Corps is mother, the Corps is father." Maybe they *were* his parents, his biological ones—he knew other kids had them. Milla's even came to visit, though not very often anymore.

He had asked about his own, once, and was told they had been killed when rogues bombed Teeptown. Maybe his infant mind remembered them, or maybe he had made them up, or lifted them from another kid.

Whoever they were or had been or had never been, they were gone now. There was nothing in the night sky but stars, nothing in his dreams but silence.

PART 2

Antithesis

PART 2

Antithesis

1

The backfist snapped to within an inch of his face, but Al didn't blink. He had known before Jackson flung it out that it would never connect.

The reverse punch was another story; that was the real attack, and Jackson drove it at Al's solar plexus with every ounce of his considerable strength and weight. Al wasn't there, though. He stepped aside and 'cast his next move: a ridge-hand to the back of his opponent's head. Jackson caught the thought—Al meant him to—and twisted to avoid the blow he knew was coming.

Al dropped into a crouch, both palms flat on the floor, extended his back leg like a boom, and spun. Since he was turning to avoid a blow to his head, Jackson's first indication of this came when his feet were clipped neatly from beneath him. A head taller and twenty pounds heavier than Al, he made a satisfying thud as he landed on the mat.

"Halt!" Sensei Kaplan called, stepping onto the mat. Jackson was struggling to his feet. Al could feel his frustration and hostility, and hoped the match would go on; Jackson lost all control of his strategy when he was like this.

But Kaplan ended the match. "Take note," he said. "Mr. Bester used the minimum motion necessary. He fought the battle where it really takes place—in the mind. He won before he began his attack. Mr. Jackson is a bigger man, but his mind is weaker." He gazed around at the group—all second-year students in the Minor Academy. "Attention. Class dismissed." They all bowed in unison.

Jackson glowered at Al before walking off, and Al answered with a thin smile. He could afford to be generous.

"Nice match, Al," said Raphael, a wiry young man with luminous black eyes.

"Thanks." He paused for an instant, trying to think how he might expand on the other's overture. It was an instant too long.

"Raphael," called Susan, from across the room. "How about some lunch?"

"Sure. See you tomorrow, Al."

"See you." He shrugged mentally. He had a class next hour anyway, and Raphael probably knew that. Probably that was why he didn't ask Al along for lunch.

Probably. Al headed for the showers. He didn't have time for a lot of socializing, anyway. Standing in the Minor Academy was absolutely critical, if he wanted to get into the MetaPol prep classes in the Major. That was just three years away.

Al was so deep in thought he almost bumped into Julia in the hall. He caught her signature just about the time he found himself face-to-face with the deep brown of her startled eyes.

"Oh—hi, Al," she said.

"Hi, Julia." Her face had narrowed, her features sharpened, though at fifteen the curves evident beneath her gold-and-umber uniform still hesitated between girl and woman. "How—how are things?"

"Pretty good," she allowed, her eyes straying around the white, almost antiseptic hall, as if searching for someone else in the hurried mass of students. "How about with you? I heard that you won the Karges award last year."

"Yes, I guess I did."

"I'm not really surprised. You were always the best in the cadre. We were wondering about you the other day . . ." She trailed off, probably just realizing that she had said "we." He knew, of course. The Minor Academy was large, but not that large. He had often noticed Julia, Milla, Brett, Azmun, Ekko, and most of the others from the cadre having lunch or playing soccer on the quads.

"Have you decided yet?" he asked. "Which school you might end up in?"

"Oh, well—yeah, I'm looking at the business school. Guess I'll be a busybody, like you always said. And you? You still want to be a Psi Cop?"

Al nodded. "Yes."

"Well—good luck at that. It won't be easy."

"Thanks. I . . ." As with Raphael, he wanted to say something else, but he wasn't sure what. It was a distinctly unpleasant feeling.

"I have to get to class," Julia said. "I guess I'll see you."

"Yeah. Me too. Well, nice running into you." He flashed her a smile he didn't feel, then started off.

"Hey, Al?" He turned, surprised to find her still regarding him.

"Yes?"

"I—some of the old Cadre Prime is going on a hike, up in the Alps. Sort of an unofficial reunion. You're welcome to come, if you want."

He blinked. "Sure," he said. "That might be fun."

She smiled, a bit shyly. "Saturday? We're going to meet out by the Grabber, about seven in the morning."

"Okay. Okay, I'll be there."

She hurried off, and he went on to statistics, wondering why his step felt a little lighter.

He made it through class, and managed to absorb a moderate amount of what Professor Diebold said. When the buzzer sounded, he headed, as usual, down to the West End MetaPol station.

The MetaPol Central Station was in the administrative complex. Students weren't barred from the area, but they were discouraged from it unless they had a specific assignment. The West End office was smaller, more intimate, and much more accessible. There were usually only six cops stationed there, and three of them were on assignment at any given moment.

A long-boned man with a heavy, angular face one shade lighter than ebony greeted him with a fierce, somewhat disconcerting smile. "Ah, Mr. Bester. And how are you on this fine day? Come to make your usual rounds?"

"Yes, sir, Lieutenant Van Ark. Do you mind?"

"Not at all. But—ah—I'll let you in on a little something."

"Sir?"

"We don't call each other by rank. That's for normals. We teeps, we know who we are."

"Oh. But on the vids—"

"Well, yes. But a lot of normals watch vids, stuff like *John Trakker.* They feel more comfortable with titles and ranks and that kind of thing, so we leave them to their illusions."

"Got you," Al said. It made sense. "So what do I call you?"

"Mr. Van Ark will do."

"Okay. Mr. Van Ark."

Van Ark chuckled. "How long have you been coming in here anyway, Mr. Bester? Four years now? You follow these Blips like some kids follow baseball or soccer."

"Yes, sir. When I become a Psi Cop, I want to know who they are."

"When? Not if? You've certainly got no problem with confidence, Mr. Bester. Anyway, it's good to see a youngster taking such an active interest. You're a good example. Still—" he widened his hands expressively "—you're in here every day, rain or shine! Don't you ever just take a day off? Fly a kite, take a girl on a picnic? When you get to be my age, you'll regret it."

Al reflected—very carefully, very controlled—that when he got as old as Van Ark, he intended to have a much higher rank than lieutenant, whether the title was spoken or not.

"I'm going hiking this weekend," he remarked, to cover any hint of his reaction.

"Hah. Sounds like more work to me. But to each his own." Then he glanced at his computer screen. "Well, the monitors are there, if you want to look." It seemed to Al that the big man had adopted a devilish look on his face.

"Wow," Al said, his eyes widening as he scanned down the list of names. "They got Kashiwada, D'Amico, and Enoch. They've been on the hunt lists forever."

"Enoch since before you were born," Van Ark observed.

"All at the same time, too, it looks like. This morning. Hey, and there's Deitz, too." He frowned at the screen. "Something's up, isn't it? Something big."

Van Ark's laughter boomed for a few beats. "Well, I shouldn't be telling you this before it hits the vids, but I will if you swear to keep it quiet."

"The Corps is mother, the Corps is father," Al observed. "I would never betray the Corps."

Van Ark lowered his voice a bit. "They just hit a big underground cell in the United Islamic Nations—Kazakhstan, I think. The reports are still coming in. That's where they got those three."

"Can I see some more of it? Some of the reports?"

"Sure. Provided your oath of silence covers this, too."

"It does."

Van Ark reached his indenticard over and slid it through a slot. "Okay," he said. "You have access. Have fun."

Al nodded, and Van Ark moved to a seat nearby. What appeared before him was a précis of the strike, a list of Blips suspected to be at the site, and then a progress report. It was only level 4, of course, so all of the really nifty details were missing—sources, casualty reports, detailed tactical information and the like. Nonetheless, it was instructive to compare the projected list against those registered captured. Enoch and Kashiwada they had expected to find; D'Amico had been a bonus. Those were the big boys.

On the second tier he recognized Klassen, Brazg, and Nielsson, all of whom had been on the general hunt lists for more than five years. Of these, only Klassen seemed to have been captured in today's raid. Did that mean that Brazg and Nielsson had slipped through the Corps' fingers, or that they had never been there in the first place?

Interesting. With a nod from the lieutenant he called up their individual files, wondering if their histories would provide a clue.

Lara Brazg was thirty and had been born in Canada. She had registered with Psi Corps at the age of fourteen, a P5, and gone on the sleepers. Disappeared at twenty-one. She was implicated in two assassination attempts and one package bombing, and had kidnapped at least two teeps from reeducation facilities. A classic type A Blip, she might even be a good person who had been led astray, brainwashed by some highly organized and cynical underground.

Her type could be shown the truth, saved, reeducated, and end up a useful member of the Corps. It had happened more than once. In her picture she looked pretty, a dirty blonde with a face smudged by light freckles.

Portis Nielsson was a different story. Born in the UK, he was a year younger than Brazg, but had a much longer rap sheet. Several felonies: two murders during a holdup, one count of manslaughter from a bar fight in Madrid, numerous petty and two grand theft indictments. He had spent six years in jail as a juvenile, but had never tested positive for telepathy.

Toward the end of his stay, the prison psychologist nevertheless had become convinced that Nielsson had psi abilities, but simply did not have the mitochondrial marker—not that unusual; after all, thirty percent of telepaths lacked it.

En route to a reeducation facility, Nielsson had escaped and had been at large ever since. In the past four years, his criminal activities had shifted focus to underground-related offenses. Nielsson looked like a type C Blip, a sociopath who had found an organization to validate him. While any teep could be brought around by reeducation, Nielsson's type—a born criminal, used to abusing his powers—was the toughest to change.

His photo seemed to confirm that—even on the vid screen, his eyes 'cast malice, and his square jaw was set in an intractable smirk.

"A nasty customer," Van Ark remarked, walking up behind him. "You'd be pressed to find even a mundane as ruthless as that one."

"The cops will get him," Al said.

"You'll be interested in another little tidbit I picked up, too," Van Ark said, a bit conspiratorially.

"What's that, sir?"

"Stephen Walters has resurfaced."

Al scrunched a skeptical face. "He's been dead for twelve years."

"That's what we thought, but he was clever. He should be, he's the only Psi Cop to ever go rogue—"

"—only after he was mindblasted and reprogrammed by the Dexters," Al reminded him.

"Ah—yes," Van Ark replied. "Anyway, those bits of him they found at the blast site in Nicaragua must have been cultured tissue, because they just found some strands of his hair in this UIN raid."

"But not the man himself."

"No."

"Couldn't the hairs be pretty old?"

Van Ark wagged his head. "Living skin cells attached. Walters was there."

"Wow. The legend lives."

"Looks like it."

Al squared his jaw. "I almost hope he hangs in there until *I'm* a cop. I'll get him."

"Mr. Bester," Lieutenant Van Ark said, "I would never put it past you."

Al thought about rogues as he ran, a little later. He was trying to push his run to ten kilometers at six minutes a klick. He was on the third klick—always the worst—so he pushed himself faster and tried to occupy his mind with something other than the pounding of flesh and bone against duracrete.

Why would anyone go Blip? What did they hope to gain? Oh, men like Nielsson were easy to explain—they were just criminals using fellow criminals to help them stay out of jail. But what about the others? What could they possibly hope to find that Psi Corps couldn't give them?

He tried to picture himself, outside the Corps, a *later,* raised like a normal. Say he was twelve when he got his psi—what would he do out there in the mundane world? Take the sleeper drugs? That way he could hide his abilities, keep leading the life he was accustomed to—except that normals would find out, through personnel records, or official files. He couldn't get a job or even get housing without disclosing his nature, and the normals would still hate him, sleepers or no.

Or he could join Psi Corps, get a free education, room, board, job placement, protection from mundanes, the company of others like himself.

So rogues didn't want the sort of life normals had, and they didn't want the opportunity to hone their powers to the utmost, to live and work as telepaths. *They don't want to be normals and they don't want to be teeps. What do they want?*

Well, they blew things up. Maybe that's all there was to it. They just wanted to cause trouble. There were certainly people like that.

He mulled it over more, but he seemed to have hit a wall. The answer was probably something pretty obvious, he mused. The problem was, you didn't want to go around asking questions like this about Blips—not if you wanted to be a Psi Cop. You were supposed to catch them, not understand them. Yet—wouldn't it be easier to catch them if you *did* understand them?

He was starting to feel his second wind coming, and that was always nice. He shelved the internal discussion in favor of the view, as his trail reached the top of the hill. He could see beyond the walls and wire that protected Teeptown to where the Rhone was leafed with sunset gold. A small smile on his face, he pushed himself into a sprint, felt like a galloping horse or a charging bull, invincible, immortal. Eventually he had to slow, but the feeling remained. And wedded to it, a pleasant-sounding name—Julia.

"Al! It's good to see you. I'm glad you could make it." Brett's smile was dazzling.

Al smiled thinly and took the other boy's glove in his own for a brief, firm handshake. "I haven't been hiking in a while," he said. "It sounded like fun."

"Did Julia tell you where we're going? Up near Mont Blanc. Ever been there?" He paused. "You did manage to get a pass, right?"

"Yes—to the pass. Not to Mont Blanc."

"We aren't actually going on Mont Blanc—but pretty near. You'll like the hike. The place where we camp has a great view, and we might be able to catch a few fish."

Al nodded, since that didn't seem to require any other response. Brett had grown in the bone—he was two heads taller than Al, with the sort of ruggedly handsome face one saw on Psi Corps recruitment posters.

Al took note of the "we" and the past tense in Brett's comment. These guys had made the hike before, maybe often. It wasn't, as Julia said, a reunion. They were already unified; it was only Al Bester, the outsider, who was rejoining them. But why? What did they want with him?

The others—Milla, Azmun, Ekko—greeted him, but their enthusiasm was guarded, and this sharpened his suspicions, but Julia was all smiles. He allowed himself, reluctantly, to consider what he hoped to be the truth: that Julia liked him and had invited him on her own, even knowing that the others might not be all that happy about it.

"We'll take the train up to Chamonix, and hike from there," Brett

was explaining, as they moved on line to purchase their tickets. "When we come down, we can get another train back at St. Gervais."

"Sounds good."

"And, um—did you bring anything else to wear?"

Al glanced briefly at his standard issue brown outdoor pants, gold shirt, and light academy jacket.

"Sure, I have a change."

"No, I mean—you know, not issue?"

"Why shouldn't I wear issue?" Al asked, noticing, suddenly, that none of the rest of them were.

"In case we run into normals," Milla said, very simply.

Al shrugged. "What if we do? I'm not ashamed of the Corps."

"It's not *that*," Brett said. "It's just better—I mean, you can never tell what normals will do."

"Hey," Al said, with a rare burst of old pride. "We're Cadre Prime. Let them do their worst."

The moment he said it, it rang wrong, awkward, and he was sorry he'd said it. But Brett's eyes widened, and he said, "Well, yeah! Darn right! I forgot, we've got the winner of the Karges award with us. With you, we can handle anything."

"Come on, Al, you sit by me," Julia said, as they went through the sliding door and onto the train.

The first leg of the hike was a breeze, though Al found he had to pace himself down so the others could keep up. As a result, he found himself springing up slopes, then waiting for the others. It was clear that, even physically, he trained harder than they did.

As the day wore on, a little of the awkwardness wore off. After all, they had grown up together, even if he hadn't seen them a lot lately. They were cadre. They had faced the Grins together. He was used to them.

The same couldn't be said for the other academy students. Oh, some were from the secundus or tertius cadres, but even they had grown up mostly as normals or in the Basement. Most of them—almost all of those in his classes—were actually laters, hadn't gotten their psi until they were twelve or older. He hadn't really tried to make friends with most of them; they thought he was weird, he could tell, or were maybe even a little afraid of him. That was probably for the best—it left him more time to train, to better prepare himself for the Major Academy.

The hike was pleasant. Wildflowers spangled the sunlit meadows and upland pastures, and the forest was an evergreen cathedral. Al had rarely been in the woods—a few picnics and field trips when they had been kids,

not once since entering the Minor Academy. It was something he kept meaning to do, but never quite felt he had the time for.

They were taking a rest against an old stone wall—for a moment silent, perhaps in appreciation of the day—when they heard voices coming up the trail behind them. Al could sense weak, undisciplined minds—normals, of course. He started to shut them out, then out of curiosity he didn't. He hadn't had much contact with normals.

They came over the hill soon enough. Five young men, maybe a few years older than he. Two were tall and lanky, enough alike that they might be brothers. One was no taller than Al, but a good deal thicker, almost bulldoglike, with a single, long, black eyebrow. The other two were of middle build, a redhead and a blond. They were chattering cheerfully about something in French, and briefly acknowledged the telepaths with almost imperceptible nods as they passed.

All but one, Bulldog-boy, whose gaze, tracking with interest over the girls, suddenly fastened on Al.

"Q'est-ce que c'est que ça?" he asked, rather abruptly. He was pointing at Al's academy clothing. "Eh?" He jabbed the finger as if spearing something. "What's the matter, you? Can't read my mind in French?"

His friends had turned now. "Viens, Antoine," one of the lanky ones said.

"No, no," Antoine snapped, waving them back. "For so long I have wanted to meet one of these little prodigies. Are all of you mindscrewers, or do you just carry this one as a pet?" he asked Brett and the others.

Al tightened his lips and said nothing, but Brett answered him in French. "Look, fellows, we're just on a hike. We don't want any trouble."

"Trouble? Are you saying we're trouble?"

"No. I didn't say that."

"Just go on your way," Al advised.

"Oh, is that an order, Captain Mindscrewer?"

"It's a suggestion," Al said. He noticed his knees felt funny. The whole scene had become a little unreal, as if the light had abruptly changed. His heart was beating faster. Almost without thinking, he flexed his knees.

"Oh, a suggestion. Well, I have a couple of those myself," Bulldog-boy said. "I suggest that you stay in your kennels back in Geneva, and not wander up here where decent folk might have to see you. I suggest you stay out of my damned mind."

"Psi Corps regulations forbid unauthorized scans," Al pointed out. He paused a beat, and then was surprised to hear himself continue. "Besides, I wouldn't read your mind any more than I would step in dogshit on purpose."

Bulldog-boy—Antoine—grinned, revealing teeth like piano ivories. "Aw, that's cute. *P*si-Ko made a joke." He pronounced the *p*.

Julia attempted a smile. "Come on, guys—"

"Hey, boys, the *p*slut can talk. What else can you do, *p*slut?"

Al gave the boy a curious look, reached out, and thumped him on the nose.

What happened next was a blur. Al expected the boy to attack him— he had been working up to that anyway, that was clear. He had expected to know where the blow was coming from, like when he did a karate or fencing drill with a weaker teep.

But this wasn't a drill, and Antoine didn't think at all about what he did next—a javelin of pure rage speared Al in the brain, blinding his mind, and sledgehammer fists were just an instant behind, slamming into Al without focus, but with amazing violence. He pulled his arms up reflexively, so his forearms took most of the percussion meant for his head, but he still reeled back, was still backpedaling when his opponent's head butted into him and slammed him into a tree. Then Antoine was on top of him, battering down with those hamlike fists—

And then he was off, howling and gasping for air. Al blinked his eyes open to see Brett standing by, fists balled, radiating a cold determination.

"Leave," Brett said.

Bulldog-boy's friends had him now. "C'mon, Antoine," one of the tall ones said. "He isn't worth it. He'll get you arrested, and then what?"

Antoine glowered and came slowly to his feet. Al managed to climb shakily to his own. His breath was choppy, and he tried to slow it, as he had been taught.

Antoine grimaced a terrible, smilelike expression. "Bet you don't think you're so hot now, do you, mindscrewer? If it hadn't been for your friend, I'd have pounded you senseless, eh?"

Al reached out with his psi. He could feel the hot, stupid little mind. He could do almost anything with it. Push it any way he wanted. He could give Antoine a seizure, he could fill his mind with nightmare, he could rip his thoughts to . . .

But no, that was against the rules—it would be betraying the Corps. So he had to watch as the boys hiked on, Antoine sneering back at him until they were out of sight. He could p'hear their coarse laughter well after he couldn't hear it anymore.

2

"Don't let it get to you, Al," Julia soothed. Al watched new wood starting to scorch on the campfire, unconsoled. How could a normal have beaten him? In front of Julia, in front of everyone?

If he had planned to humiliate himself, he couldn't have done a better job.

"I felt his mind," she went on. "He was like an animal."

"Yes," Al replied, "he was. A dumb animal. One I should have beaten."

"Hey," Brett interjected, "bullfighters have to be *trained* to fight bulls. We haven't had much practice against normals."

"*You* beat him."

"I blindsided him. And I wasn't trying to beat him, just get him off of you. Come on, cheer up. You'll know better next time."

"I could have mindblasted him in a second," Milla grumbled. "We could have taken them all. What's the point of having superior brains if we can't use them?"

"Because that would be selfish," Al muttered. "We're supposed to protect and serve, not use our powers to satisfy our own needs."

"You believe that?"

Al looked up at her, startled. Not so much that she had thought it, but that she had said it. "Yes," he replied.

"We're supposed to protect and serve guys like Antoine? Give me a break."

"Look it up," Al said. "It's in the handbook."

"Normals *wrote* the handbook, Al."

"The Corps wrote the handbook. The rules are good." *I just screwed up,* he thought. *I could have taken him. Next time . . .* He sighed. He had already replayed the fight in his head a hundred times. It wasn't helping. What stayed with him was the sick feeling of fear, the awful realization that there was a real difference between facing someone on the dojo floor and facing someone who really wanted to *hurt* you. The

physical blows hadn't really damaged him—he doubted that he would even bruise. But the memory of his fear was like a dead star in his belly, and everything in him was falling into it.

He looked up at Brett. "Anyway, thank you." He hated saying it.

"We have to hang together," Brett said. "Cadre Prime."

Al remembered his boast, earlier that day, about Cadre Prime being able to handle anything, and Brett's remark about how they *must* be invincible if they had Al Bester, winner of the Karges award, along with them.

The dead star ate another bite, and Al suddenly felt queasy. "I'm going for a walk," he murmured. "I'll be back soon."

He wound his way up through the trees, skirting the edge of a twilight meadow, found a spot in the violet-brocaded field and lay on his back, watching a cloud skewered by twin contrails with dull eyes. It was vaguely heart-shaped, salmon bruised mauve by the shadow of the Earth crushing down upon it. For a moment he felt absolutely still, and there were no voices at all. He experienced an unexpected, melancholy peace, watching the sky fade. His body felt heavy, as if he were becoming stone, and as he petrified he could sense the ponderous, slow wheeling of the Earth through space.

He had lost track of time, somewhat hypnotized by the feeling, when he heard voices near, hushed ones, whispering. The sounds were too faint, but he knew from their surface thoughts that it was Brett and Julia. They were excited about something. Looking for him? Worried? He closed his eyes, trying to get them clearer, and suddenly—

Warm lips, pressing against his, and arms reaching around. A body, prickly-warm, slim, a joy in the arms, breath tickling against his neck—

He shut it out, blocked and locked, returning to a now artificial silence. Julia and Brett. Of course.

The stars came out, and still he didn't move or relax his blocks. He did not want to feel, even for an instant, what he had just felt or what might follow. He waited until he was sure, as the air chilled, and his rock body lost even its Human warmth.

Finally, tentatively, he opened again, blessedly to silence. Feeling sore and weary, he stood and made his way back toward camp.

He stopped when he saw the firelight. They were all there, their faces picked out in fine detail, even at this distance, like a faraway painting by a Dutch master. They were smiling and laughing, and he could sense something emanating from them. He tightened his control, and suddenly knew beauty.

He could never explain it to a normal. He could barely explain it to himself. He could sense the signature of each individual, but there was

something more, a tapestry of thought and feeling they wove together, impossibly intricate and familiar. Like the mants they had done as kids, but infinitely more complex, more practiced, and yet at the same time more natural. They were different, each of them, but they were also one in the thing they created together.

And in all of those weaving lines, in the subtle word-and-image play, in the shared secrets and emotion, there was not a single empty space. They were full, complete, a living organism. There was no place or need for Al Bester.

It's always going to be like this, he thought. *Me, out here, in the dark. Sometimes I can look into a window, see people in love, see people with friends. But I'll always be out here.*

He also realized that it was okay. One had to be stronger out here. His allegiance to the Corps could remain untainted. How could he really protect and serve all humanity if he went in there, inside? If he loved anyone—if anyone loved him—it would only serve to weaken him. If he were a part of their tapestry, of their song, their power to betray him would be almost infinite.

But they *were* beautiful. He would protect them—Julia, Milla—yes, even Brett. He would protect all of them, all of his people. But to do that, he had to be what he had been tonight. Stone.

Antoine couldn't have hurt stone. Julia couldn't have hurt stone.

I'm glad I feel this way. I'm glad to admit it's over.

But he did have a question to ask.

"That must have been some walk," Julia said the next morning, as they packed up the camp. "You didn't come in until we were all asleep."

"I was just—thinking," Al told her. He took a deep breath. "And wondering."

"About what?"

"About why you asked me along on this trip."

"Because you're our friend, Al. Because we miss you."

He paused. "I don't think that's the truth. Won't you tell me the truth?"

She wouldn't meet his gaze. "I—Al, we were worried about you."

"Why?"

"Your professors are worried about you. They don't think you have any friends. And you didn't stay in touch with us—"

"You didn't stay in touch with *me,*" he corrected.

"Al, you never liked us. We never thought you did. We thought you were happy to be away from us. But the teachers worried, and—"

"—and they asked you to do something with me. You bumped into me on purpose, didn't you?"

She nodded. "Are you angry?"

"No." It was the truth—he didn't feel angry at all. "No, I'm grateful. I used to worry about having friends—everyone else seems to. Sometimes I think it would be nice to have people to talk to—" He broke off, remembering watching them the night before, remembering also the stolen feel of Julia's lips. "Anyway, I don't care about that anymore. I'm over it. And you can tell the teachers not to worry."

"Al . . ."

"It's okay, Julia. Thanks for asking me along. I've learned a lot."

He didn't speak anymore on the trip down the mountain, and after a while nobody really tried to speak to him. When they reached the train station at St. Gervais, he broke his silence to say that he would buy their tickets if they wanted to grab some lunch at the restaurant on the corner, and he would join them there. They accepted the offer; he knew they would talk, and Julia would tell them everything he had said. He didn't really care.

The line was surprisingly long, but he supposed it was Sunday—there must be a lot of people returning from the country.

Surrounded by normals, he felt a little dirty. He almost imagined that they smelled different, earthier. He caught an older woman in a black shirt buttoned to the top staring at his clothes, her distaste undisguised by what, a moment before, he had taken for pleasant features. A dark, rotund man, who had also taken note of him, wore a stonier expression. Al returned the old woman's gaze, narrowed his eyes, then smiled faintly, nodding as if to himself. She reddened and looked away. He had not scanned her—not even touched her surface thoughts—but he let her wonder about that, about what dirty little secret he might have uncovered.

He found himself slightly cheered by this.

He was three back in the line now, and the longhaired woman buying tickets turned and hurried off, preoccupied. She didn't see him at all, but he caught a vague whiff of—fear?

He glanced after her. He knew her, he was certain, he just couldn't quite place the face. Something about the hair wasn't right, and the eyes.

He felt a little catch in his throat, an acrid taste on his tongue. It was Lara Brazg. A rogue. A Blip.

The raid had been in the UIN. He pictured those who had escaped, radiating outward, rats fleeing a sinking ship, searching for another place to hide.

Brazg had been there after all, and gotten away. And now here she was, hurrying off to catch a train.

He didn't hesitate for an instant. It all seemed so clear, what he should do. The next person was done, and he stepped up to the window.

"Five for Geneva, please," he said, and at the same time, lightly, glyphed the image of Brazg at the woman. She didn't seem to notice anything unusual—probably because Brazg had been there so recently—but the information bounced right out of the ticket seller's surface thoughts. Paris. Brazg's ticket was for Paris.

"And one for Paris," Al finished. He passed her his card. This would nearly clean out his meager allowance, but what better way to spend it?

At the restaurant, he paused for an instant, wondering if he should tell them, but no. Brett, at least, might want to go along—or more likely would call the Corps. That didn't fit Al's version of the immediate future. So he smiled and put the tickets on the table.

"We got you a sandwich," Julia said, a little too brightly.

"Thanks. Just let me go wash up."

But he went straight past the washroom, hoping there was a rear door and finding it. He went out and jogged quickly back to the station. There, he used the few credits left in his chit to buy a black overshirt and pulled it on, hiding his academy garb. Then he was off to catch the train to Paris.

He felt a peculiar humming in his blood, a sort of fierce joy that washed through his disappointments like a cold, cleansing stream.

He was on the hunt.

Al watched the farmland of Bourgogne whip by, startled by the quality and quantity of green, intrigued by the small hamlets with their ancient churches, by the antique feel of the landscape. A hundred years ago—three hundred years ago, if he had taken this same train ride, how different would it have been?

It made him feel smaller. His own history began and ended with Teeptown. His biological parents had died in a terrorist bombing, and he had never known them. His earliest memories were of the crèche. For Al, Teeptown was like an album of memories; any route he took through it jogged constant reminders of his childhood and the lessons he had learned. He still flushed with shame when he passed the steps where he'd betrayed Brett—that place haunted him. Crossing the sidewalk between the old cadre dorms and the Minor Academy never failed to remind him of that terrible and wonderful day when the Grins revealed themselves. The statue of William Karges held new significance each time he saw it, as did the parade ground, the quads. His personal story was a thread in the tapestry of Psi Corps history.

But out here, he felt unraveled, a strand drifting on an ocean of time. A million years of normal history, a landscape that held no clear meaning for him, a huge book written in a foreign tongue.

He found he did not entirely dislike the feeling. It was frightening, but it was a challenge, as well.

He found Lara Brazg the old-fashioned way, by walking up the train until he spotted her. She sat pressed against the glass like a fish in an aquarium, seemingly oblivious to the interior of the train. Al was not deceived; even with his blocks as tight and subtle as they could be, he sensed that she was watching quite carefully through the eyes of those around her. He passed on through the car at a measured pace, trailing a faint—hopefully "normal"—feeling that he was in search of an unoccupied toilet.

Two cars up, he relaxed a bit. Teeps could often sense each other over great distances, especially if they wanted to, but it required a mutual and cooperative effort to exchange any real information without line of sight.

Well, he knew where she was, what now? The safest thing would be to call the Corps station in Paris and have cops waiting to pick her up. But that would defeat his whole purpose in following her. He wanted to catch her himself. He wanted the Corps to know that they had done a good job in training and raising him. He wanted Cadre Prime to know what he gained when he lost them—and thus what *they* had lost. He couldn't bear the thought of Brett and the rest feeling sorry for him, which at the moment they almost certainly did.

But how to collar her? Psi Cops carried weapons, which he didn't have. He might be able to subdue her physically, but his encounter with Antoine had left him a little dubious of his abilities. That left psi attacks, and he knew several that ought to work—she was, after all, only a P5. He could push her, or maybe spark out her cortex and while she was out of it, tie her hands behind her back with the cord in his backpack—

While a bunch of normals screamed bloody murder. She would keel over and they would see him start tying her up. He didn't have a badge or anything other than his Psi Corps ID. Probably he would end up getting arrested himself, by railroad security.

Maybe he should just have a talk with security first, explain who he was, and all of that. That seemed like a good compromise. He would still be the representative of Psi Corps, making the collar, because the train cop would be a normal, and a normal couldn't risk going up against a Blip by himself. Even a P5 could make a mess out of a normal.

He continued toward the front of the train. The security man wasn't hard to spot, a middle-aged fellow whose balding head was nearly hidden by his long-billed cap. Al sucked up his confidence and approached him.

"Sir?"

Watery blue eyes met his gaze. "Yes, son?"

Al lowered his voice. "Sir, my name is Alfred Bester. Is there someplace we can talk in private? I think there may be trouble on the train, and I don't want to panic anyone."

Al didn't need surface thoughts to catch the mixture of skepticism and concern on the man's face, but after a moment, the cop nodded. "Up here, in my office."

A few moments later, they closed a narrow door behind them and stood in a cabin with a coffeemaker, a surveillance camera system, a table with an AI and a half-eaten sandwich on a plastic dish, and a narrow bunk. "What's this about, son?"

"You have a rogue telepath on the train."

"A rogue?" His eyes widened perceptibly.

"Yessir. I'm a student at the Psi Corps academy in Geneva, and I recognized her from her picture. She's been on the hunt lists for some time, and she's considered dangerous."

"Well. Have you called ahead to the Psi Cops in Paris?"

"No, sir. I think that the two of us could take her—I'm a P12, and I can run interference with pretty much anything she might try, while you take her into custody. Do you carry a side arm?"

"I have a shock stick. Here, you know her name? Can you pull her up on my database? We need to find a match with her ticket."

"Yessir." Al turned to the keyboard and began shifting to the requisite screen, hoping the cop would go along with him, rather than calling the Corps station in Paris.

Paris? This train had half a hundred stops, some before Paris, some after. How had the security man known Brazg was getting off in Paris? Al hadn't mentioned that he even knew where Brazg was going.

Without that thought, what he sensed next might have come too late. As it was, everything clicked at once, and he hurled himself to the side, crashing into the bulkhead, as a shock stick crackled through the space he had just occupied.

This time, his first reaction wasn't fear but anger. Mauled by two normals in as many days? *No.*

The train cop lifted the shock stick for another try. Al noticed, with the odd clarity of adrenaline-heightened perceptions, the pucker of wrinkled skin on the cop's elbows, the storm-tang ozone scent of the weapon.

He struck. The normal had no guards at all. His mind was watery and open and—delicious. It was as if Al had been shelling walnuts his entire life and was suddenly offered a plate of them, already shelled . . .

What he did wasn't fancy—he just sparked him, sent a powerful jolt into the cop's ancient, limbic, lizard backbrain, the first rock in an avalanche that roared forward toward consciousness, gathering fears, images, and pains in an unstoppable cascade of waking nightmares that obliterated his thinking mind in an instant. He groaned like a lost soul, his pupils suddenly became pinpricks, and he dropped the shock stick, lurched back against the door.

Al grasped and lifted the shock stick carefully, and touched it to the man's temple. The cop jerked, fell prone, and kept jerking. Al found a pair of handcuffs in the man's back pocket and snapped them onto the unresisting wrists.

Now what?

For a moment he didn't care. He felt like the unstoppable Jugger-

naut of Hindu legend, an elemental force that had been contained for too long. He just stood there, grinning, hands clenching and unclenching, wishing another normal would come at him, just *try* something. He felt—

He sipped in a deep, calming breath. He felt *too* good. This was exactly why Psi Corps had the rules it did. He had always considered himself controlled, strong—compared to most he knew, he was. And yet this could be addictive, more addictive than a drug. Only his training had saved him, and the strong principles taught by the Corps.

It suddenly occurred to Al that he now understood some of what it might be that rogues desired—freedom to exercise their abilities whenever and however, on whomever they wished. That could be a powerful incentive, as he had just learned—but not an admirable one.

So indeed, what now?

He took off the cop's shoes, then his socks, balling up the last and placing them in the fellow's mouth. The cop was starting to come around, and once his eyes were somewhat clear, Al came to the painful decision that he was going to have to break a regulation. He probably had already—pushing a normal, even in self-defense. Still, at this point it would probably be for the greater good if Al Bester survived.

"Why did you do that?" he asked, aloud, and then scanned for both the willing and unwilling response.

He got it, and nodded grimly. The cop's name was Alistor Hech, and he was a rogue sympathizer. That's why Brazg was on this train to begin with. Even so, if he turned Hech in, the cop likely would report him for unauthorized scanning.

Well, that was for later. He probed a little more, but the normal didn't know anything else, or if he did it would take a deep scan to find it. Even under the circumstances Al wasn't willing to go that far.

What Al knew was what he had started with: Brazg would get off in Paris, and from there on out only she knew her plans.

The door rattled, suddenly, and Hech started making frantic gagging noises. Gripping the shock stick, Al dithered for an instant. The door was locked, but if the person on the other side had a key—

He placed his fingers against the door and concentrated.

"Hech?" he heard, muffled.

He's not in here. No one is in here (glyph of the room, empty; glyph of Hech, walking though the aisles of the train). No one is in here. The room is empty.

He kept it going, his limbs beginning to shake with the effort.

"Huh." Someone on the other side of the door grunted, finally, and Al heard footsteps receding.

Hech glared up at him from the floor.

"Make noise again, and I'll be forced to make *certain* you are silent," Al said, quietly. He wasn't at all sure what that meant, but he let the normal think the worst, for now.

His legs had gone noodly, so he sat down at one of the small chairs. He was going to have to stay in here, with Hech, until they reached Paris, that much was clear. If he left the compartment, someone would find the cop and they would then find him. Despite some vids he had seen to the contrary, he didn't think anyone could hide effectively on a train.

Al began to regain some of his strength and all of his confidence. A little more searching of Hech turned up a pocket phone and a 9mm snub-nosed Dayak. He had a pistol and shock stick now, and he had proven that he could handle a trained security man without the aid of any weapon at all.

He could handle a Blip, too.

An almost imperceptible deceleration—and the info-strip on the wall—alerted him when the next stop was Paris. He tucked the pistol in the waistband of his pants, folded a day-old copy of *Universe Today* around the shock stick, took a deep breath, and started for the door.

He paused before opening it, staring down at Hech. He knelt by him, wondering if he could plant a compunction to keep the fellow from talking about him. Maybe, but probably not. Anyway, that would be going way, way too far. He was in trouble enough as it was. But perception could be as powerful as the real thing, couldn't it?

"I'm planting a compunction in your mind," he told Hech. "You won't feel it, or know it's there—unless you try to talk about me or this incident. If you do that, you will find yourself having a nasty recurring nightmare each and every time you close your eyes. It won't be pleasant."

Then he just probed a bit, ran his mental fingers over the contours of Hech's mind—enough so the cop could feel him. Almost as an afterthought, he touched him with the shock stick again. That should keep him quiet for the next few minutes, anyway.

He opened the door, saw and felt no one in the corridor. He went out and locked the door behind him. Then, straightening, he walked back the way they had come, trying to exude confidence. "Act like you belong somewhere, and people will think you do." Teacher Diebold had told him that, years ago.

Outside, city rushed by, the jumble of the industrial district, with buildings like giant pipes and vast, rusted machines—and glimpses of the skyline now and then. He made his way to where he had spotted Brazg, and his heart fell.

She was nowhere to be seen.

For a moment he stood rigid. Had she been warned somehow? She might have detected him the instant he walked past her on the train, gotten off five stops back while he was hiding in Hech's cabin.

Suddenly things were a lot less promising than they had been. He had assaulted a train cop and had nothing to show for it. Once Hech figured out that Brazg was gone—and his connection to her as unprovable as his assault on Al—he could bring charges with impunity. Scans weren't admissible in the courtroom, so it was just Al's word against his. Any jury would favor a mundane—after all, teeps weren't allowed to serve on juries.

The relief was almost dizzying when he realized that Brazg had left her seat only to join the impatient crowd waiting to deboard.

Got you, he thought, breathing for the first time in a significant number of moments. And he followed her off of the train into a chaos he could never, in his wildest dreams, have imagined.

Al had read about Paris, of course, the City of Light. He had imagined it as a place of ancient, eldritch beauty, a sort of fairyland of beret-capped artists and thinkers basking leisurely and thoughtfully in the gentle glory of the past. At night it would be a city made of stars, a constellation brought to Earth. That was what he had imagined. It wasn't what he saw.

The Gare de Lyon was a severe and spacious building, rebuilt sometime after the last World War, when it—like much of the city—had been blasted by terrorists. Al's first impression was of a large oven full of rats, just beginning to warm up. The rodents—instinctively beginning to understand their fate—were squirming, writhing, clamoring to get out. Except their dim little rat brains didn't know where "out" was, so they just formed a struggling mass.

He had never encountered struggling masses before—not in Teeptown, not in Geneva. He lost sight of Brazg within seconds, caught a

glimpse of her moving quickly, lost her again. She was in a hurry. Al picked up his pace, trying to weave through the crowd. He cracked his blocks so he could get a telepathic whiff of Brazg.

It was as if a thousand people all tried to shriek something very important at once. He gasped, involuntarily slapping his hands to his head, his head which was expanding like a balloon, stretching thinner, thinner. The crowd became a series of vid stills, each different, the thousand motions between each unseen. The mindroar went in and out, as if he were a radio with poor reception.

Then he managed to shut it all down and realized he had slumped to his knees. People glanced at him with expressions ranging from neutral to irritated as they made their way around him.

He shook his head and stood again. That had been stupid. And he had no idea how long he had fugued. Probably only seconds, but—he glanced at his watch, then remembered he had not glanced at it before, so he still didn't how much time had passed.

He looked wildly around, wondering what to do. He had two options—he could descend the escalators into the underground, or exit up to the street. If he chose the wrong direction, he would certainly lose any chance that remained of finding Lara Brazg.

He glanced at the torrent of people passing into the depths below the city and shuddered. He could not go that way, not right now.

He came out of the station on the Rue de Lyon, a narrow, bustling cobblestone street surrounded by dirty grey buildings that looked as if they should have crumbled long ago. It had just rained, and a peculiar stench mingled with the tang of wet stones, a stink made of a thousand stinks, as if somehow, impossibly, the city remembered open sewers, burning diesel and petrol, the sulfur of ancient gunfire—every chemical that had ever oozed or diffused on it since the beginning of time.

It was another alien scene, more threatening by far than the countryside—and yet somehow thrilling, as well.

More exciting still was his glimpse of Lara Brazg, vanishing around a curve. This time, better prepared, he telescoped a tight, tunnel-like probe in her direction and got it, an impression of her mind as individual as a fingerprint, or perhaps more appropriately, as a scent to a bloodhound. He wished he could risk a light scan, to maybe catch where she was headed if he lost her again, but he couldn't. A teep of Brazg's abilities would never notice him tracking her, but anything more blatant might set off some alarms in her head.

Al hurried up the street, on the hunt again. He followed her sign, crossed a deeply recessed canal on a small iron footbridge. To his faint

surprise, the canal vanished into a vaulted tunnel not far to his right, running underneath a broad plaza. An emerald pleasure boat arabesqued with gilded lilies was just passing beneath the arch. He stared into it for a moment, but had no sense that she had gone there, either on the boat or the narrow footpaths flanking the waterway.

He looked around for street signs, and realized, with the surprise of a tourist who happens upon a place he's heard of, that it was the Place de la Bastille, where once had stood the city's most famous prison. It was gone now, the square now dominated by the looming Opéra Bastille, itself nearly three hundred years old. The plaza seemed to have been built over the canal.

Where once the prisoners of the French kings had languished, vendors hawked trinkets and souvenirs, and tacky shops and cafés looked inward to the July Column with its gilded statue of Liberty. A small cluster of Centauri tourists—dressed in immaculate and ornate garb, and accompanied by what looked like an armored guard with a *sword*—picked their way through the shops. It was hard not to be distracted by them—he had never seen a live extraterrestrial before—but he tried to keep his mind on the task at hand. Nonetheless, once again the Blip had vanished from sight.

But not from mind. She was here, somewhere—he could feel her.

He stood for a while trying to sort her out of the colorful crowd of tourists and entrepreneurs. He managed the roar better this time—people were farther apart, but more, he was quickly adapting to the new conditions. He caught the catlike thoughts of a pickpocket, moving up on unsuspecting marks; the passion of two young lovers; the hatred an old woman harbored for holiday season and the locustlike swarms of gawkers it brought. The slightly odd feel of the Centauri minds, their amused disdain at almost everything they saw. Still he couldn't pinpoint Brazg. She was still, cocooned, probably in one of the buildings.

And he must look a little suspicious, he realized, standing in the open, staring like this.

He walked around the edge of the square, and when he thought he felt her strongest, he took a seat at a small sidewalk café. He tried to cultivate a relaxed appearance, to separate his expression and body language from his purpose.

He nearly jumped out of his skin when a fluid male voice said, "What do you want?" nearly in his ear. It was French, harsher than the gentle dialect of Switzerland, but still perfectly intelligible.

"A cup of coffee, please," Al said, in the same language. "And what else do you have?"

"Eh?" the waiter said.

"A cup of coffee," Al repeated, "and I would like to see a menu."

"I *am* sorry, sir," the waiter said, "I do not speak German, or whatever that is. I speak only French."

Al frowned up at the man. He had Brazg's scent as firm as a beacon in his mind, now, and it still wasn't going anywhere. He could spare a moment to touch the surface thoughts of the waiter. And the waiter was lying.

"You understand me perfectly well," Al said. "If you don't want to serve me, fine, but I'm going to sit here, nevertheless. Play your games with some tourist—not with me."

The waiter's lips pinched tight, and then he twitched a Gallic shrug. "As you say, monsieur," he growled, and stalked back into the café.

Al returned his attention to the square. He gazed up at the little statue of Liberty, covered with pigeons and the white streaks of their droppings. Evening had arrived on pastel wings, and as it came lower and darker there was a vague sense of being in a city sunken beneath the waves. Everything had a bluish tint, a sense of depth, a little melancholy. Over the rooftops and beyond, a great ivory cathedral was visible—the Sacré Coeur? It might have been an Atlantean temple. Across the square, a trio of musicians started playing Peruvian music, the soft but insistent trills of their *quenas* twining up from a solid foundation of guitar.

The minds around him were still busy, but the city seemed to be taking a long, deep breath. As if Paris and its inhabitants weren't quite the same thing. It seemed, too, that once he had tuned out the particular thoughts of those around him there was a sort of pattern, or series of patterns, quite beautiful in their own way.

He thought once again of the moment he had spied upon, only the day before, the manting of Brett, Julia, and the others. This was so much more vast, and so much more unconscious.

Geneva had always been there, in the background. Not something he had noticed, really, or thought of as singular. But Paris was—different from Geneva, its psychic air as distinct in flavor as its physical atmosphere. Did cities have a sort of mental gestalt, a psionic fingerprint, as identifiable as a person, once apprehended?

It was an intriguing thought. Beautiful, even.

His coffee came, and he sipped it. He ordered a sort of sandwich of thick bread and oysters. He waited, and like so many before him, tried to understand Paris.

* * *

The waiter had begun to glare at him for overstaying his welcome at the café, and it was quite dark, when he suddenly became certain that Brazg was on the move again. He let the waiter credit his account, but remained sitting for the moment.

The city was alive with light now, but once again, Paris didn't meet his expectations. That was okay, he mused. He had found his fairy constellation in the subtle mind of the city, if not in its lamps.

A figure passed through the shadows on the plaza and then through a streetlight. To the eye, it might have been a man or woman, in shapeless sweater and baggy pants. The hair was short and looked black.

The mind was Brazg, though. He was certain of it.

He rose as she reached the far side of the square, where she vanished, bit by bit, into the ground—first feet, then knees, then shoulders, finally head.

The canal. She had gone down the steps into the canal.

He followed, trying to keep his pace casual, but feeling it quicken anyway. He did not want to lose her again.

Centuries of feet had worn a shallow trough down the steps. He almost stopped to stare at it, astonished by the signatures of age. There was nothing like this in Teeptown. Were there such places in Geneva? Not where he usually went.

As he reached the walkway, Brazg was moving out of the circle of one of the lights picketing the canal. The shadow she moved into stretched some hundred feet or so, and beyond that lights on the ceiling of the tunnel picked up again. The ones nearest the tunnel mouth seemed to be malfunctioning.

There were only a few people out, and they were walking far ahead of Brazg. He made out three small craft coasting silently down the waterway.

Now was the perfect time to apprehend her.

Or maybe he should wait and see where she was going? He might find an entire underground cell.

He slipped into the darkness, trying to decide.

A soft sound, a whisper of mind—he whirled, adrenaline stabbing through his heart. Something weighty and fast jacked up the point of his chin, and he hurled back. The stone wall caught him. As he steadied himself against it, still amazed at the weird *click* his teeth had made when they snapped together, he reached for the pistol in his waistband.

Ah—no. Stay very still, or I will bleed you like a pig.

It was strongly 'cast, and Al found himself looking a bit cross-eyed down the narrow tube of a fléchette pistol.

Behind it, a half-shadowed face grinned at him. Though he had seen it only in photographs, he recognized it instantly by its scars, by its stone killer eyes.

Portis Nielsson.

5

"Look, Lara," Nielsson said. "Got ourselves a regular John Trakker, here."

Brazg approached from the left. Even in the dim light, her face seemed haggard, with crescents under her eyes nearly as dark as her newly dyed hair.

"Why have you been following me?" she asked wearily, then frowned. "Port, he's just a boy."

"But what kind of boy?" Nielsson wondered, following the question with a quick, brutal scan.

Al met the scan and brushed it aside. Nielsson gritted his teeth and went again, using his mind like a sledgehammer. It was strong, but nothing Al couldn't handle.

When Portis stopped, his breathing had quickened noticeably. His breath stank.

"I guess that answers that question," he said, grimly. "Boy's a regular prodigy. So what are you doin' followin' my good friend, Prodigy? I don't take kindly to it."

"I—ah—I want to join the underground."

"The what?"

"You know. The underground. I want to be a Blip."

"A Blip, huh? Funny thing about that word—only people I've ever heard use it were from Psi Corps."

"I was raised in the Corps," Al said, trying to hide his dismay at the blunder. "I ran away."

"Did you."

"Port, he's just a kid," Brazg repeated.

"Yeah. Ramie was just a kid, and Jio, and what did the Psi Cops do to them?"

"Can't we just—tie him up or something?"

"He's a pup, but he's got a hell of a mind. Can you be sure he didn't pick your brain? Can you be sure what he knows?"

Brazg regarded Al for a long moment. Her eyes were unreadable. "Let's get in the boat," she said at last.

Nielsson nodded and gestured with the weapon. A small powerboat drifted at the edge of the canal. Not seeing that he had any options, Al stepped into the rocking craft.

In a few moments, Brazg had the motor humming, and they plowed quietly down the canal, away from the tunnel, leaving a wake like ripples of black glass.

"What's your name?" Brazg asked.

"Al."

"Al, if you really want to join the underground, you'll have to let us scan you. You know that, don't you?" Her voice took on a slightly pleading tone. "If you don't—well, Port is right, we can't really risk letting you go."

"No, we can't," Nielsson affirmed.

"I just wanted . . ."

"Let us scan you. Let us see what you wanted for ourselves."

The boat was leaving the end of the canal, joining some larger waterway. The Seine? The quays along it were broad, tree-lined. Farther down he could make out crowds of people. Would they hear him if he shouted? Would they pay attention? Probably Nielsson would just shoot him.

"I guess I have to, huh?" he asked.

"Yeah, Al, y'do," Nielsson answered, grinning in a thoroughly humorless fashion.

"Okay, then. I'm ready." He had one very small chance. He tried not to think about what would happen if he failed. Nielsson was a killer— they both were, really, but Nielsson probably enjoyed it.

Al dropped his guards.

They both came in.

Al knew full well that if they combined their efforts, they likely more than doubled the strength of their probe. It took training, but some telepaths could weave their minds together, intensifying the results. And he might be able to use that against them.

These two would have to be compatible with him *and* with each other. What he had in mind he had to do against their will, and it still might be for nothing.

Oddly, he was calm. His heart was beating just like a clock, though he might be an instant away from floating dead in the river. Part of him was distantly amazed at his composure.

As Al dropped his guard, he pulled something else up.

Help me. Help me. I fear the Corps. The Corps is chasing me. And I'm afraid of you. I have no one.

A trained P12 would see through that in a nanosecond. He was hoping it would take Brazg and Nielsson just a bit longer.

It did, and Brazg actually moved to meet him, which was good. *We'll help you . . .* she thought—

And then the three of them howled like the damned, as Al fused their minds to his and screamed. Amplified through two minds, he sent a shock wave racing into the night, carrying on its crest a single word.

HELP.

The wave rang out for a quantum's worth of time only, then their guards snapped down, severing the brief union with what felt like twin lightning bolts to his brain. He had been as open to them as they were to him.

He used the pain, rode it up to take command of his muscles, and jumped.

Arcing toward the water, he gulped a deep breath, which went somehow wrong, as if he had sucked in an icicle. They were only about thirty feet from the bank, and as he plunged into the chilling wet, he felt something burn his ear, a crescendo of rage—from Nielsson—and shocked betrayal from Brazg. And something else, something that had come out of the fusion with them.

A place.

He swam frantically, unwilling to come up because he felt Nielsson trying to find him, knew that he had the fléchette gun. Normally he could hold his breath for quite a long time, but his lungs hurt already, which didn't seem at all right. In fact, the pain was really, really bad.

He managed the quay, though, and glyphed himself rising from the water, back nearer the mouth of the canal. He didn't know if it was enough, but he couldn't wait: he heaved himself from the water.

Something whined by him, struck sparks from a wall. He bounced to his feet and ran, suddenly filled with an almost electric energy. He hadn't gotten very far when he heard the boat bump behind him, and then footsteps pounding on stone.

He sprinted down an alleyway, turned a corner, took a right, a left. Nielsson was still behind him, but Al was drawing farther away, he could feel it.

Cops and blips again, just like when he was a kid. He could do this. He could win.

He wondered where the Paris Psi Corps station was. He should know that, shouldn't he? He should have checked during the train ride. He didn't have the faintest idea where he was running, only that he had to lose Nielsson or die.

His lungs felt full of molten tar, some of which was bubbling out of

his nose, so he had to open his mouth to get enough air. But he couldn't get enough, not nearly enough . . .

He came hurtling down the end of the street and found himself back at the broad, tree-lined quay along the river. He almost ran headlong into a group of revelers, toasting one another with champagne. They laughed curiously at him as he staggered past, found his stride again, and dug in.

He stayed on the quay because there were a lot of people on this section, walking dogs, jogging, going from bar to bar and coffeehouse to coffeehouse. He tried to quiet his mind, draw the seared edges of his blocks back together, knowing they were leaking, knowing also that if Nielsson could get a clear shot he would take it, even with all of the witnesses. The fléchette gun was silent, and besides, Nielsson was a psychopath.

He felt as if he ran on a rapidly spinning disk now. The lights of Paris weren't points, but the tails of orbiting comets. His feet were becoming slabs of duracrete.

He no longer had any idea where Nielsson was.

He passed through a large crowd, ducked up a street into an alley, and finally, wheezing, hid in a recessed doorway.

As he collapsed against the brick wall, the dark alley strobed, and another—sunlit—scene replaced it. He was back in Teeptown, at the spot the Grins had burned into his mind. The vision shivered with unnatural color, as if the walls, trees, grass, and sky were producing light instead of reflecting it, as if their very atoms were tiny arc lamps . . .

The specter faded, and he was in the alley again, trying to be quiet, to make a quiet place . . .

Quiet, quiet . . .

He could barely inhale now. Water was still bubbling out of his nose. He wiped at it. It was sticky.

He was never sure if it was the realization that what he was exhaling wasn't water at all, or a simple lack of oxygen that took him out. One moment he was sitting, back to the wall, trying to brace himself to face Nielsson. The next his face was pressed hard against the street. Then nothing.

A conversation woke him. Two black rats were discussing where their morsel had gone off to.

"A tasty corpse it looked, not long dead. It was here somewhere."

"Maybe not dead at all. Maybe he'll squirm a little when we start chewin' on him."

Then he really woke. His face was in a sticky puddle on the stone.

The rats from his nightmare were still talking, though their conversation was a bit different.

I can feel him. I think he's out of it. This way. Nielsson.

Let's just get out of here, Port. That call . . .

No. You felt him get it, the safe house. He knows where it is. He's here, somewhere. He won't be any trouble.

He's already been too much trouble. This is taking too long.

And he could hear their footsteps now, not through their ears, but through his own. This wasn't good. He had to get up, to run some more.

He told his muscles to do so. They told him they had the night off.

He dimmed his mind, made it seem as if it were going out, as if he were dying. He was, of course. That seemed obvious. Still, he had no intention of going peacefully.

He wondered what Cadre Prime would think of him now. Stupid or brave or just—suicidal?

They came closer. He held imagoes of their minds, now. Nielsson's was simple, and if he had to draw it, it would be a knife. Brazg's was her face, simplified almost as much as a Grin's, mournful, hopeless.

Closer, closer he let them come. But once they saw him he would have to—

They saw him. He used every bit of will he had left to raise his head and establish line of sight. Nielsson was a blurry shadow, but that was plenty. He hit him with everything he had, just a simple burst to the pain center. Nielsson screeched, his knees buckled, then straightened. He laughed harshly. "Still got some left, eh? This ends it. Tell the Devil I said hello."

Then a confusing thing happened. Nielsson spun on his heel and fired the fléchette *away* from Al.

At the same moment, the alley flickered yellow—like someone lighting a cigarette—and the walls seemed to slap together like giant stone cymbals. That was the sound he heard, anyway.

Then Nielsson's knife mind was shattered. Al saw what looked like a door crack open, and white light stabbed through, and something yanked at him—

He yanked back. The door slammed, the light went out. There were some scuffling sounds. Al coughed, and something large and wet came up.

Then a hand touched him, warm, and he suddenly felt reassured.

"Ambulance. Now." A man's voice, a rich baritone, very precisely articulated. What sounded like a British accent.

"You'll be all right," the voice said, gripping Al's hand. "Don't worry, son. You'll be okay."

* * *

Al opened his eyes to see sterile, white walls, comforting and familiar. At first he thought he was back in the academy, until he raised his head enough to see an unfamiliar skyline beyond the window.

"Well," a man's voice said. "I wondered if you had gone into some sort of hibernation cycle." The voice he remembered, the cultivated baritone from his fevered nightmare. He started trying to turn his head, but then the speaker walked into view.

The first thing Al noticed about him, of course, was the black uniform and brass-and-copper badge. A smile quirked seams in a dusky, broad face with a nose as large and proud as the beak on an eagle. A salt and pepper—mostly salt—mustache and goatee gave him a look that Al tentatively assigned as Shakespearean. Few Psi Cops had facial hair.

"Sir?"

"My name is Sandoval Bey, Mr. Bester. You may call me Mr. Bey."

That name rang a bell. Bey—Dr. Bey, if he remembered correctly—was a high-level instructor. Why was he in the uniform of a Psi Cop?

"What happened, sir?"

"Not a very precise question, Mr. Bester. What happened today, yesterday, a thousand years ago? Here, in Spain, on the moon?" Al detected no actual remonstrance in his gentle, jovial tone or merry eyes.

"I mean, what happened with the Blips, sir." He paused an instant and then modified that. "Lara Brazg and Portis Nielsson. I was chasing them—"

"Yes, yes, Mr. Bester. I think I can guess what you meant from context. Lara Brazg is in custody, thanks to you, on her way, hopefully, to be reeducated. Portis Nielsson—well, I'm afraid he didn't make it."

"I'm sorry to hear that, sir."

"Are you? He did try to kill you. Put a neat hole through your left lung with that fléchette pistol of his."

"Yes, sir. But he might have been reeducated, if . . ."

"If what, Mr. Bester? If we had captured him alive? Yes, the odds of that would have been increased greatly if you had done the proper thing, and called Psi Corps the moment you picked up their trail."

Al winced. Then it dawned on him. "Will I get a reprimand on my record, sir?"

"That would seem to be appropriate, wouldn't it?" An ambiguous smile ghosted Bey's lips. "But no, the test of intelligence is in the evaluating of its mistakes. That test is one you must take now, but it won't be Psi Corps that judges your score—it will be the universe, and her executioner, evolution."

Al smiled weakly. "Yes, sir. Natural selection almost got me, I suppose."

"Almost, Mr. Bester. But don't forget—whatever doesn't kill you makes you stronger." He cocked his head thoughtfully. "Of course, in actual fact something that almost kills you can leave you crippled for life, mentally and physically, and greatly hasten your death. I find that Nietzsche engaged in a lot of wishful thinking, not a trait I associate with strength, really." Despite the grim topic, he smiled broadly.

That made Al's head swim, ever so slightly. In that queasy at-sea state he remembered something, however. "Sir, I got something from them. They were headed for a safe house on the rue—the Rue de Pepin. 1412, Rue de Pepin."

"I see. Well, very good, Mr. Bester. That will be seen to, and your cooperation noted, I'm sure. You're a very lucky fellow."

"I'm lucky you found me. Thank you, sir, for saving my life."

"Well, that *is* the function of the aged, Mr. Bester. Once we can no longer contribute to the race in a direct, genetic way, we keep our eyes on the young. But you helped yourself a great deal, with that distress call of yours. If not for that, we would have certainly been too late. We were looking in a whole different quarter of the city."

"Then you already knew that Brazg and Nielsson were here?"

"What? Oh, no, Mr. Bester. We had no idea those two were in Paris. The Blip *we* were looking for was you. Did I happen to mention that you are under arrest?"

6

Al straightened his uniform and tried not to appear nervous. He stared at the heavy door for a moment, steadied his breathing, forced the rhythm of his heart to slow from improvised jazz to a brisk march. He pushed the door open and stepped into a room he had never yet had the misfortune to see.

Most of the classrooms and dorms were spare, white, clean, designed to keep the mind free from distraction. This room was just as minimal—starkly so—but was weighty and dark, as if cut and burnished from a basalt cave. A single shaft of light awaited him, and beyond—raised above, behind a long bench—he could make out the five members of the review board, faces spectral in the dim, amber light of reading lamps.

"Alfred Bester, come forward."

He stepped into the light, resisting the urge to squint. Of those regarding him, he recognized only two. One was Dr. Hatathli, the principal of the Minor Academy; the other was Rebbekah Chance, the ranking Teeptown Psi Cop. Seated in the center was a third, who looked familiar, but Al couldn't quite place him. Someone important, probably from the director's office. Maybe even one of the assistant directors.

"Mr. Bester," Dr. Hatathli began, "is accused of unregistered and unsanctioned travel. He applied for and was granted a two-day leave in the Alps. At the end of those two days, instead of returning on schedule, he purchased a one-way ticket to Paris."

Ms. Chance cleared her throat. "This fact registered with our monitoring system, but as he is an exemplary cadet we gave Mr. Bester the benefit of the doubt. When—after several hours—he did not contact us, we dispatched a special detail to investigate. An officer with the Paris office went to the train terminal to meet Mr. Bester. He was found murdered a day later. We suspect he was killed by rogue telepaths or their agents."

Dr. Hatathli took all this in, glancing down occasionally at the display in front of him. Now he turned his craggy, square face toward Al. In

the dim lighting, he resembled vids Al had seen of the statues on Easter Island, his eyes invisible in shadowed sockets. "Mr. Bester?"

"Yes, sir. I did apply for a two-day leave to go hiking with my old cadre. When we were coming home, at the train station, I recognized Lara Brazg."

"And why didn't you report this immediately?" Hatathli replied.

Al started to answer, but the man in the center cut him off with a raised finger.

"I have a better question. Mr. Bester, how did you so easily recognize this rogue telepath?"

Al suddenly remembered himself, long ago, when he and Cadre Prime had played that fateful game of cops and blips. The normal in a military uniform, at the statue of William Karges. Al remembered speaking to him. He remembered the flash of hatred . . .

This was that man. Al took a deep breath. "Sir, I hope to be a Psi Cop one day. I like to go to the West End station and look at the hunt lists."

Ms. Chance nodded. "That's confirmed by the officers there."

The normal didn't turn toward her. His voice, however, was of deep winter. "When I require information, Ms. Chance, I will ask for it."

"Yes, Director."

Al felt his face twitch and damned himself. *It's the director himself. And not the one I knew.* He remembered his conversation with Director Vacit only vaguely, but it had seemed to be some sort of warning, about things to come. About this man?

"Mr. Bester. Let us dispense with parceling out details. You went AWOL. You did so in the apparent company of a rogue telepath. The security officer of the train was found bound and gagged, and the Psi Cop who was to arrest you at the Lyon station murdered. You disappeared for several hours in Paris and were found, wounded, in the company of not one rogue telepath, but two. A scan while you were unconscious revealed that you knew the location of an underground safe house." He paused to glare at Al.

"Well?" the director said, after a moment.

"I'm sorry, sir," Al replied. "I was not aware I had been asked to speak."

"Speak," the director said, disgustedly, waving his hands.

"Sir, if I was scanned, and the information passed to you, then you must also be aware that I never had—nor ever could have—any intention of becoming a Blip. My allegiance is first, last, always to the Corps. The Corps is mother, the Corps is father."

As he said it, he heard Chance and Hatathli murmur it along with

him. He felt suddenly more confident. "You must know, sir, that my intention was to apprehend Lara Brazg myself. I see now that it was foolish, but with all respect, sir, it was not the act of treason you seem to suggest."

"Don't tell me what I suggest, Mr. Bester."

"Yes, sir. Shall I continue, sir?"

"Please. I'm aching to hear what you have to say."

"I followed Brazg onto the train. The train cop was her accomplice. By the time I was actually on the train, I started to think I ought to get help. When I told him of her presence, he tried to hit me with a shock stick. A scan of the cop will show that."

"We cannot scan *him* without his permission. He will not give it."

But you can scan me anytime you like, despite the law, Al thought. And it was clear that the director had intentionally underlined that point, emphasizing that Al had only those rights the director allowed him to have.

Al decided that there was nothing to do but continue. "I never saw the officer from Paris, and I have no idea who murdered him, though it might have been Nielsson. I knew nothing about Nielsson—"

"Except his name, it seems."

"Yes, sir. The same way I knew Brazg's."

He outlined the rest of his story, while the director sat in stony silence. "As I said, sir," he said, in finishing, "if I was scanned, you will know I am speaking the truth. If the scan was incomplete, of course I volunteer to be scanned again, as deeply as necessary."

"I don't know that you are speaking the truth. I am not a telepath. I can only judge the facts at hand and testimony given."

Al felt a wave of shocked outrage emanate from the other review board members, and he suddenly understood.

The director hated telepaths. He did not trust them. And perhaps— for some unknown reason—he hated Al Bester in particular. The thought wasn't his alone, but filtered lightly through the room, and Al understood that some or all of the panel members were sending him a signal. *It's us against him. You are with us. Be careful.*

A throat cleared behind him. "Director, Mr. Bester was injured try-ing to apprehend Nielsson and Brazg. That he was shot by Nielsson is absolutely clear. That Nielsson planned to shoot him again is absolutely clear. I fail to understand the relevance of this entire line of—" he paused and finished with faint note of sarcasm "—'questioning.'"

Al didn't turn, but he knew the voice, and it felt like solid ground suddenly appearing beneath the feet of a drowning man. Sandoval Bey.

The director aimed his ice-chip eyes behind Al.

"Are you advocating for him, Dr. Bey?"

"Absolutely. He is impetuous. He is also fifteen. Neither of those qualities, last time I checked, is considered criminal. Insubordinate, yes. Punishable, yes. Criminal, no."

"Indeed? Very well, Dr. Bey. You think he should be punished, punish him. I command him to your custody, and will hold you responsible for any future transgressions on Mr. Bester's part."

"That's fine with me, Director."

"I did not ask for your approval." He turned a withering glance upon Al. "In the future, Mr. Bester, I urge you to remember your place. You are a student, not a Psi Cop. The Corps cannot abide even the appearance of disloyalty. Do I make myself clear?"

"Very clear, sir."

"This panel is dismissed."

In the hall, Al closed his eyes and felt his limbs tremble, ever so slightly. He wasn't sure he ought to, but he paced for a time, until Bey came through the door and nodded at him.

"Dr. Bey—"

"Walk with me, Mr. Bester."

They stepped out into the morning sunlight. Bey gestured across the lawn, and they started across it.

"I just wanted to thank you, sir."

Bey's head chopped in a nod. "Don't thank me yet, Mr. Bester. Despite what I told the director, your behavior was inexcusable. Your unthinking actions resulted in the death of a Psi Cop and of another telepath. I should have let him have you."

"Why didn't you, sir?"

"Because, Mr. Bester, the director is a mundane. Because he has no sense of justice. Rest assured—I do."

With near hatred, Al watched the children coming across the parade ground. Teacher Hua led them, but he knew that wouldn't entitle him to any mercy. No, he remembered these field trips well, back when he was in Hua's class.

If I live long enough, he wondered, *will I see every situation from every perspective? I've been the child, now I'm the statue. Will I one day be the teacher?*

He was irritated by the thought. But what else did he have right now, except to think and suffer humiliation?

Yes, the children had seen him, but they were still acting puzzled. It was their first trip to see the "statue of the day," then.

"That's a real man," one of the kids noted. "He isn't a statue at all." She was a freckle-powdered girl with dirty blond hair. Her name tag proclaimed her "Vicky."

"Hey, yeah," a boy agreed.

Vicky put her hands on her hips. "How come he isn't moving? How come he just stands there, like the Grabber? How come, Teacher Hua?"

"Ask him," Teacher Hua said.

Vicky looked up at Al. "Why are you just standing there, Mr. Statue?"

Al wet his lips, wishing it were time for one of his five five-minute breaks so he could get a drink of water.

"My name is Alfred Bester. I stand here because of pride. In my pride, I believed I did not need to observe the wisdom of my elders. I acted without regard for the Corps. I stand here to warn against the rule of pride. The Corps is mother, the Corps is father."

He stopped. Those were the only words he was allowed to say to anyone.

"Wow," Vicky said. "How long does he have to stand there? How long do you have to stand there, Mr. Alfred Bester?"

He wasn't allowed to answer that, but he didn't know the answer

anyway. This was the beginning of his third day, and Dr. Bey had not informed him how long it would go on.

"Hey!" Vicky said. "How long do you have to stay standing like that?"

He remained impassive. He had become rather good at impassive. Vicky pouted.

"Look at him, and learn your lesson well," Teacher Hua admonished. "Now, if no one has anything else to say, come along."

They started off. Al was just allowing himself a deep breath and a bit of relief when Vicky turned back, a determined look on her face. "*Why* do you have to stand here like a statue?" she asked.

Damn. "My name is Alfred Bester. I stand here because of pride. In my pride, I believed I did not need to observe the wisdom of my elders. I acted without regard for the Corps. I stand here to warn against the rule of pride. The Corps is mother, the Corps is father."

The other kids had paused, and some still looked confused. But Vicky's face held sheer, malicious triumph. "Don't you get it?" she said. "He *has* to answer *that* question."

"Why are you standing there?" asked a dark-eyed boy whose tag identified him as Tali.

Al repeated his speech. Then they all started in, asking him one after another, fast, so that he had to speed up. And they laughed at him, the little jerks, and they kept asking, and they started improvising mants around him, making fun of him.

Normally children this age had short attention spans. Not when they had a chance to be cruel, though, especially to an elder.

But if this was the worst he saw today, he would be lucky.

It was finally Teacher Hua who broke it up, though Al suspected he wasn't supposed to. As they vanished from his view, he felt the lightest touch from the old man. *Hang in there, Alfred. You may suffer from too much pride, but some of us are proud of you, too.*

It left him feeling a much taller statue.

The brief good feeling vanished at the lunch period, when academy students had their way with him. He had thought, after three days, that he had inured himself to their taunts. They always seemed to think it was funny to dress him up. Today it was a leprechaun outfit—green hat, a little Kerry vest, a pipe he had to hold clamped between his teeth. They ate in front of him, too, first passing the food beneath his nose and then 'casting the very taste of it to him as they ate. He didn't block it; he had blocked all day the first day, and paid for it all night and the next day with a seething headache.

They finished their meal, and one of them—a girl maybe sixteen years old—got up and strode toward him.

"Look what we have, my friends," she said. Her vowels had a crisp purity, an accent he couldn't place. She was beautiful, with hair and skin nearly the same shade of cinnamon-brown, amber-tinted eyes. He had noticed her before. She stepped closer, looking up at him.

"Preach us a sermon, Mr. Cadre Prime. Tell us how great you are, how you are the heart and soul of the Corps, how everything we poor *laters* do is just catch-up."

She waited a second or two. "No sermon, huh? But you look like one, a living sermon, your jaw all stuck up in the air, a regular portrait of a preacher. The Corps is mama, and you are a *mama's* boy, aren't you? Run back to mama, little boy, and she'll tell you how great and strong and wonderful you are, how *proud* she is of you—after she makes you stand out here for a few weeks." She suddenly jumped up on the podium next to him.

"My name is Alfred Bester!" she shouted. "I'm up here because I'm such a short, scrawny, tight-assed little fellow that I thought I would impress everyone by being a big, brave Psi Cop! I thought they would be so impressed, and yet look what they did to me! And so I see now that I really *am* a short, scrawny, tight-assed, self-important little fellow!"

Her companions hooted and cheered, and she did a little curtsy.

His body hummed like a tuning fork, he was so angry. It was a flavor of anger he had never tasted before, savage, visionary. He saw himself punching the girl in the face, again, and again, until that smug smile went away, until she admitted that she was wrong, until she understood that— he was *better* than her. That she should be praising him.

Another group was coming. He could already tell they were excited about what she had done, were planning their own loud speeches under his name.

Screw it. She would pay. Let them prove it.

He formed a telegraph of intense pain, addressed it to the girl's now-distant back, and prepared to send.

Don't.

His anger congealed at the touch, but did not cool.

Do. Not. It was Bey, probably behind him. Sandoval Bey. Dr. Sandoval Bey, who had scanned him, who—despite his claims—knew nothing of justice but everything about torturing Alfred Bester.

But he let the attack sigh away. He let the anger form cysts under his flesh. He could dig it out easily enough later. He would show everyone, Bey included. They would all regret treating him this way.

So he stood there, and endured.

At eight o'clock, his day as a statue was over, but his punishment was not. He returned, not to his room, but to a special detention cell, all white. He was allowed no books, no vid, nothing. He couldn't study and he couldn't entertain himself.

Not studying was bad. Exams weren't that far away, and it didn't take long to get behind. He couldn't afford failure now, not with the Major Academy within reach.

One thing he knew: normally those who were punished as statues were allowed to at least study when their day was done. This stipulation of Bey's was more than unusual. Did he want Al to fail? Probably.

For the first time, he considered the unthinkable—that he might wind up as a business telepath or in the courts. In the courts, where he would have to lick the boots of the Psi Cops who brought the criminals in . . .

The thought was intolerable. He got up, angry, restless, and cramped. He ran through a series of punches, kicks, blocks, and kata. He ran in place to work the knots out of his legs. He went back to punches and kicks, and suddenly found himself battering against the wall, flecking it with red from his knuckles. He backed up, breathing hard.

He threw himself on the bed and closed his eyes, trying to calm himself by listening to Geneva.

Geneva had been his project since the punishment began. Intrigued by what he had noticed in Paris, he used much of his time as a statue— and here, alone, in this room—to further study the background noise he had always taken for granted, to listen for the nuances.

It was a vague, impressionistic swirl. At times it almost seemed orderly, but the instant he thought he had a pattern, it vanished. Not unlike watching clouds, always changing, passing briefly and coincidentally through forms that seemed familiar.

The real difference was night and day, for at night most people slept, and the white noise became vivid, less connected. It was—he struggled for an analogy to explain it to himself.

With a quiet suddenness, one appeared. He saw a painting, a street scene, a woman in big skirts. His viewpoint approached the painting, zooming in, magnifying. What had been clear images lost sharpness, dissolved . . . then, as he got nearer and nearer, the canvas resolved once more into a multitude of tiny dots of different colors.

Yes. It's like that, he returned. *At night the picture becomes dots. Except that each dot is a picture, too . . .*

The image—and the mindtouch that had brought it—vanished. He knew it had been Bey, though. Another overture of kindness, another trick.

You aren't supposed to scan me. It is against the regulations and against the law.

No answer. He might as well have imagined it.

The next day, they took to putting peanut butter in his hair, to attract the pigeons. He tried to stand still with them perched all over him, shitting on him. He discovered that pigeon brains were too small and stupid to credibly frighten with Psi powers. They would flap off, but always return.

People would remember this forever. When he was a Psi Cop—if they ever let such a laughingstock become a Psi Cop—with twenty years behind him, people would still point at his back and snicker, remembering him with birds, birdshit, and peanut butter all over him. How could he ever be effective like that? Bey had ruined his future.

At eight o'clock, he didn't go to his cell. Instead he broke into a run, fell down because his legs were clumsy and stiff from standing all day, but got back up. It was just beginning to rain, a cold October drizzle dripping over the mountains that soon became a downpour. He felt as if it were becoming steam as it hit his skin, so feverish his anger seemed.

He knew where Bey's office was. He found it and pounded on the door. His fury made him a giant, but he was beginning to lose height when the door finally swung open.

Sandoval Bey looked at him mildly. "Mr. Bester, I believe you should be in your room now. The watch will be wondering where you are."

"Why are you doing this to me? Why? This is worse than anything the director would have done."

Bey's eyes crinkled, and he suddenly bellowed a laugh. "Mr. Bester," he said, "in some ways you are pitifully naive."

"Sir, how can I ever—I mean, if I don't have any respect, how can I . . .?"

"Come in, Mr. Bester. I don't want anyone to see you standing in the hall."

Al stepped in, and Bey shut the door behind him. In an instant, everything seemed to change. He suddenly saw himself, wet, covered in birdshit, standing in the office of one of the most powerful men in Psi Corps.

"Now, Mr. Bester. You broke the trust of the Corps. You have been given a lenient punishment, considering. What is your complaint?"

"My complaint is that—that— Why does my punishment have to be so—so—"

"Public?"

Al just stood there trembling for a moment. "Sir, I thought you were my friend."

A peculiar expression passed over Bey's face then.

"Al," he said softly. "I *am* your friend. I'm trying to save your life."

"Sir?"

"Mr. Bester, I have done many scans of the dead and dying. I have likewise, in my time, come upon the scene of a death, many times so close on the heels of the reaper that I could still feel the trace of the dead person, their last thoughts, echoing away. When I come upon the body of someone who has slit their own wrists, swallowed handfuls of pills, hung themselves—when I come upon a suicide, Mr. Bester, do you know what thought I find most often, hanging in the air, glowing for me to see?"

"No, sir."

"This will show them. This will show them." He paused and rested his lambent gaze on Al. "Does that sound familiar, Mr. Bester? It should."

"Sir, I have *never* considered—"

"Suicide is a frame of mind, Mr. Bester, not an act. It is a deluded, contemptible state."

Al was beginning to feel cold. He was starting to shiver. He saw how his pursuit of Brazg and Nielsson might look like an attempt at—"Sir, I realize I made a mistake, but—"

"It isn't about one mistake, Mr. Bester. It's about your life. I've been watching you."

"Sir?"

"You are an outstanding student. Too outstanding, really. In seven out of the last ten training exercises, you exceeded safe tolerances."

"I strive for excellence, sir."

"Why?"

"Because the Corps deserves only the best."

"The Corps deserves cadets who live to pay it back for their training, who don't end up dead or as mewling idiots in a hospital ward. That *is* where you are headed, Mr. Bester. You have no friends. You run, you practice martial arts, you drill unsupervised in your 'spare' time. All solitary activities. And this is how you've lived, as far as I can tell, for your entire short life."

"I don't really get along with others very well, sir."

"No, you don't. That's exactly the problem. Mr. Bester, a Psi Cop has the hardest job in the world. He has to hunt down his own people. For their own good, yes, but hunt them he must, and sometimes kill them. His own people, and they hate him for it because they do not understand. The normals who benefit from his work do not understand him either, of course—at the best they tolerate him, see him as one sort of smelly

animal useful only for ridding them of even smellier ones. At worst, they fear and loathe him.

"Mr. Bester, no one is strong enough to handle that on their own, and especially not someone with the mind of a suicide. *'I'll show them!'* Who will you show, Mr. Bester? The only people you have who might love you, support you through all of that, keep you sane, make you feel as if you have accomplished something—the *only* ones—are your brothers and sisters in the Corps. You need them, Mr. Bester, as badly as you need the ability to block a scan. How did it feel at the inquiry, when I was suddenly behind you, supporting you? When the adults on the board secretly encouraged you?"

"It felt good, sir." *But not as good as defeating the railroad cop, all by myself,* he added, in silent defiance.

"Did it strengthen your resolve, make you feel as if you could face anything?"

"I suppose, sir."

"You suppose. Sit, Mr. Bester." He motioned toward a padded leather chair. "Sit. The damp won't hurt it. You love the Corps, but that isn't enough. You must love those *in* the Corps, and they must love you. You must love the Blips you hunt. You must love the world you live in, Mr. Bester. You must broaden your passions. You must find art, and music, and poetry that stirs your soul as much as duty. Duty in and of itself is weaker than you think, Mr. Bester. It can betray you. It almost betrayed you in front of the review board." He paused. "Do you understand this? Do you understand any of it?"

"I'm not sure, sir."

"You have appetites, Mr. Bester. You want to show that you are the best, in the vague hope that someone will like you—or be sorry they didn't pay more attention to you earlier. It is a logic that defeats itself, that assures that the thing you want most will always elude you. Do you know what you really want, Mr. Bester?"

"I want to be a good Psi Cop."

The blow came so fast it seemed like Bey's hand merely materialized on his face. It stung, all the way to his soul.

"That's for lying," Bey snapped. His face was very dark. "You presume to know what makes a good Psi Cop? Do you? You know nothing. The Psi Cop who *died* because of you was a good Psi Cop. I trained him. He had friends, people that loved him. He is mourned. Will anyone mourn you, Mr. Bester?"

"I don't think so, sir," he said, face flushing hot. "I don't really . . ." He broke off.

"You were going to say you don't care, weren't you? But that isn't true, is it?"

"Sir, don't—" His throat was constricting. The last few days suddenly seemed piled upon him like so many rocks, but above those a whole mountain was crumbling.

"How was the trip with Cadre Prime, Al?"

"I thought—they only took me with them because—" What was happening to him?

"Because I told them to, as a matter of fact. But you hoped, didn't you? Hoped that you would belong?"

"I've never belonged, sir. I've only ever belonged to the Corps. I don't understand why you're so mad at me. I don't understand why the director said those things, called me a traitor, because I *love* the Corps. I don't understand ANY OF IT!" He was shouting now, and hot, salty tears etched streams down his face. It seemed as if the bones in his chest were melting and squirting up through his eyes.

Bey stared at him for a moment, then sighed. He laid a hand on Al's shoulder and squeezed.

Al didn't want to. It felt stupid and stiff and weak, but that simple Human gesture burst the dams behind his eyes, and though he still did not understand why, he wept uncontrollably, gritting his teeth. He couldn't remember another person touching him with kindness, with care, in so very, very long. It hurt terribly. He couldn't trust it, didn't Bey see that? It was stupid to trust, stupider to need. Bey was just another kind of Grin, subtler. His face was his mask.

But his tears didn't know that, and he wept for what seemed a long time. The older man made no move, just kept his hand on his shoulder, neither drawing him nearer nor pushing him away.

"Don't worry," Bey told him. "Don't worry. It *will* be all right. Now go back to your room. I'll make it seem as if I sent for you, to reprimand you. Go."

Once back in his room, Al no longer knew what he felt. He felt as if a gulf had been torn through him, and it was filling with waters he did not recognize in the slightest.

He lay on his back and tried to contemplate Geneva again.

And a touch came, feather-light. He knew that one of the walls must have a disguised window. Before that had made him feel like a fish in a tank, but now it was suddenly, oddly comforting.

You were wondering about perspective the other day, the voice said.

Dr. Bey?

Yes.

Sir, what—

When the children came by, you were wondering if you would one day see the same situation from all perspectives.

Yes, sir.

Was there some point to that speculation?

Yes, sir.

What was it?

I'm not sure, sir. I'm still thinking about it. Actually, he wasn't. The thought had come and gone. Bey probably knew that, and he was suddenly sorry he had lied.

Good. There is something I want you to see.

Suddenly, a section of wall came to life. It flickered in stark shades of grey and black, sputtering white sparks streaking like comets. Then images appeared, as colorless as the beginning pyrotechnics. A half-destroyed building—ancient Japanese, maybe, and some men, talking. A title came up, in English and in Japanese.

RASHOMON

Blinking wearily, Al sat on his narrow bunk and began to watch.

He thought about the film all the next day. The premise was actually quite simple: a rape and a murder, seen from four points of view—a bandit, a woman, her husband, a woodcutter. They all agreed on a few facts—but in the end, the stories were all very different, each altered to put the teller in the best light. As it turned out, even the murder victim—the husband—wasn't a reliable witness when his spirit was called up from the dead. Only the woodcutter—who seemed to be merely an observer—had anything approaching an objective view.

And yet the film cast doubt on even *his* version of the story, leaving Al with the frustrated revelation that he could never know for certain the truth of what had happened.

If a telepath had been there, to scan everyone, would it have helped? Maybe not, because the characters seemed to have convinced themselves that things really happened the way they said they did. It would make it very difficult, at best, to investigate the matter. And the telepath would be like the woodcutter, a seemingly objective observer who really wasn't. Couldn't be.

Obviously, at some level of reality, there was only one set of events that really happened.

But no observer could be objective.

He certainly couldn't be, standing, looking foolish, humiliated, and

angry. He could see the story only from his own point of view, the point of view of the victim.

In *Rashomon,* it was arguably the victim's story that in the end proved most doubtful.

And so, since he had nothing better to do, and since he was tired of looking through the eyes of a victim, he tried to imagine himself from the point of view of his tormentors. In a general sense, that was easy. He found he could understand the children—after all, he had once stood in their place—and he found, quite surprisingly, that this dissolved much of his anger toward them.

The older students were different. He had never been in their place. When he was older, he had simply ignored the "statues" on the parade ground. He hadn't been interested in them. It was thus harder for him to imagine what an academy student, who should have better things to do, would gain from the experience of taunting a helpless fellow.

Of course, he didn't have to imagine, entirely. He gleaned clues from their surface thoughts, from the surface thoughts of their friends. Little Rashomon images to sift through, to piece together into biographies.

It was hard at first, because he fought understanding them—he would have rather despised them—but once he learned a certain simple truth, he quickly got into the spirit of it.

Fatima Cristoban, for instance, the woman who had taunted him so cruelly two days ago, was a later, hadn't come into her psi until she was thirteen. Raised as a normal, she missed the mundane world, was uncomfortable in the academy, and had a deep dislike for anyone who grew up in a cadre, especially Cadre Prime.

One day Brett and the others passed in the distance and waved at him. Fatima was there—putting lipstick on him, actually—and she noticed them. The thin compression of her lips was perfectly consistent with the sudden spike of anger in her surface thoughts.

No, it wasn't just him Fatima hated.

Jeffer Powylles. He wished he had the guts to do what Al had done. On another level, he knew he would never have the guts, and if he couldn't, then nobody should exist who did.

Jiri Belden. He liked helpless things. It made him feel less helpless.

The simple truth was that the joke was on *them.* Each thing they did, each insult, was simply another clue for Al to puzzle at, another instrument he could use to dissect them.

Nothing could be very threatening, once dissected. They became his victims; not he, theirs. He had the power of knowing them, and that was a terrific power, indeed.

At night, Bey's lessons continued. They weren't like any lessons he

had ever experienced before. Bey would present him with a vid, or a short story, or a poem, or a painting. The significance of the selection often escaped Al for a day or more. But in the end, each piece was like a distorted mirror, reflecting some thought of his own, a thought carried to conclusions he himself would have never reached, and sometimes could not agree with. He argued with Joyce, Nietzsche, Heinlein, Voltaire, Card, Blake. Bey had a particular fondness for great thinkers from the past. He argued with Bey, too.

It was a peculiar kind of learning. It filled him with a strange excitement. He began to see ways he could use it, too. It started to make some of the things he had already learned make a certain sort of sense.

On the tenth day of his punishment, he saw a girl approaching him, her dark, bobbed hair bouncing with her ambitious stride. She looked to be about his own age. She was pretty, but not entirely conventionally so—her mouth was wide, her eyes black in the bright sun. He began composing her biography, and then understood that she wasn't really approaching him at all, but merely walking in his direction.

That was actually too bad. He had looked forward to picking her apart. Maybe—he tightened his control, touching on her surface thoughts, not a real scan. She seemed deep in thought, and probably wouldn't notice a very slight—

She stopped, rather abruptly, and her gaze darted to his. Blocks shut out everything. She cocked her head thoughtfully.

Well, he had her attention, anyway. He felt an embarrassed flush color his face and wished he could control his body as well as he could his mind. She came toward him, sauntering almost.

She was planning something now, or wanted him to think she was. She was slim, her arms long and coppery. Her gaze stayed fastened on his. He thought briefly of a cobra, swaying toward its prey. Her lips were slightly quirked. He tried to put himself in her place, to see the scene as she saw it, but came up blank.

She stepped up on the podium with him, cocking her head this way and that as he noticed they were the same height. He could smell her now, a scent with some flower in it.

She kissed him on the lips. Twice. The second time she took his lower lip between hers and stretched it, so that the contact lingered sensuously. His knees actually buckled. Her eyes flashed dangerously, and then she abruptly laughed. She walked away, still laughing. It took every ounce of willpower he had not to turn his head and follow her.

Biography? His mind was blank. About this girl, he didn't know one damn thing, except—she was fire inside, combustion thinly disguised by skin.

He would like to know a lot more.

But she didn't show up the next day, or indeed for the next four. But Bey did, on the fourteenth day. He came across the green, smiled conspiratorially, and said, "Your time is up, Mr. Bester. You may rejoin the animate."

"Thank you, sir." He paused awkwardly. "Sir?"

"Yes?"

"Thank you for everything."

"You are quite welcome, Mr. Bester. Good day." He placed his hands behind his back and started away.

"Sir?" Al said again.

"Yes, Mr. Bester?"

"I was wondering—could we—ah—talk sometime? Face-to-face?"

"Of course, Mr. Bester. Why don't we meet in my office, tomorrow, about 0600?"

"Thank you, sir."

"Go on, Mr. Bester. You have a lot of catching up to do. Fourteen days will set you back considerably, and exams are only a month away."

"I'll manage, sir."

"I'm sure you will. I'll see you tomorrow."

8

Al looked forward to his meetings with Sandoval Bey. He never knew what the older man was going to say, but it was almost always something interesting, offering a perspective he hadn't considered. Bey's thoughts had mass, inertia—they were bodies in motion. Sometimes they entered Al's brain like bullet trains, sometimes like stealthy thieves, but they always seemed to find a place.

He liked Bey's office, with its odor of coffee and cigar smoke, shelves packed with books, some with crumbling spines, some so new he could still smell the ink. He liked the Gauguin print with its wide-eyed beasts and cavernous jungle. He liked the faint baroque interplay of Bach or Telemann that underscored most of their conversations, or the occasional, surprising days when instead it was Wagner or—on one startling occasion—the wild discords of Stravinsky.

"This one started a riot when it was first played in Paris, you know," Bey had murmured that day. He had been a little strange, subdued—and yet somehow more taut—than usual. Al later discovered that Bey had been forced to kill a Blip that morning.

He was curious about Bey—he wanted to know everything about him, but he took things as they were revealed, relishing the small details and broad strokes as he built his portrait of the man.

He didn't look at Bey's public record, or even search for articles about him in publications. Most of Al's life was spent in a whistling gale, frantically struggling to win this contest or pass that test, but his time with Bey was the eye of the storm, a place for long, deep breaths. He didn't want to spoil that by making Bey into another project.

What he did know was that Sandoval Bey was an important man. He knew that because his office was in the administrative building, because even high officers deferred to him, because he had challenged the director and still had his job. He had once been an executive officer in MetaPol—maybe the chief—but had retired from the position after only

two years, to become station chief of Geneva. He was an instructor at the Major Academy, teaching advanced criminology.

As station chief, he still wore the MetaPol uniform sometimes—internally for certain purposes, but also when a member of the Corps went Blip. That was why he had been called in on Al's case. Usually he just directed operations, and it was rare for him to actually take to the field. Al felt most fortunate that he had benefited from one such unusual event.

Bey's father was Turkish, from the hill country, a poor boy who rose to political prominence. His mother had been the British ambassador to Turkey, and they had lived there until he was six, when his father was murdered by a political dissident. Thereafter, Bey had been raised in London, and had spent long summers with a grandfather who lived near Madrid. He had joined Psi Corps as a teen—Al really wasn't sure exactly when or under what circumstances. He was a widower, and it was a subject he studiously avoided.

Today the music was Wagner, the overture to *Tristan und Isolde*. Brave brass sang out over the storm growl of low strings as Al approached the door. He rapped the heavy wood, wondering what they would discuss. He had just read Hobbes' *Leviathan* and wanted to talk about it, but Bey would most likely surprise him again.

He did.

"Good morning, Mr. Bester. What does the rest of your day look like?"

"I . . ." He had a test to study for, an important one, but Bey was dressed in black Psi Cop garb, smiling enigmatically. "I've an open flight plan, sir."

"Good, good. How would you like to accompany me on a hunt? See how it ought to be done?"

"I would like that very much, Dr. Bey."

"I thought you might."

"Are we leaving now?"

"As soon as we prepare." He handed Al a photograph. "This is the runaway."

Al took the picture, then gave a vague start. It was Fatima Cristoban.

"You know her?"

"Sort of. She used to come by and bother me when I was the statue of the day. Put lipstick on me, and such."

"But you aren't friends."

"No."

Bey nodded. "Good. I'll leave you to prepare."

Al looked up, a bit startled. "Sir? How do I do that? We haven't been taught that."

"Yes you have. I taught you, in fact. You may use my office. I'll be outside when you're done."

Al watched him go, a bit perplexed, then looked back down at fawn-colored Fatima Cristoban. He remembered her self-satisfied sneer, and the deep uncertainty it hid.

Why? he silently asked the portrait. *Why would you betray the Corps? They offered you everything.*

But he knew part of the answer. After all, he had assembled a biography of her, in his mind. He tried to recall her telepathic signature, impose it upon the photo. He tried to imagine her speaking the anger and fear she felt, her insecurities about the Corps.

Was this what Bey meant by preparing? To try to remember Cristoban's "scent," the better to track her?

Somehow, he thought Bey wanted something more of him than that. He concentrated more deeply on the photo, willing himself to understand Fatima Cristoban, to be able to anticipate her movements. The hunter becoming the prey.

After a few moments, he closed his eyes in frustration, aware that Bey was outside, aware that he still had not done whatever it was the older man imagined he should have learned by now. Cristoban remained a photograph.

You have to love those you hunt, Bey had once said. And that recalled something else, something from long ago. When he had played cops and blips with Brett and the rest. When Brett had insisted a Blip could only act in certain ways because they were stupid or evil . . .

But that wasn't the case. To kids, Blips had no motive: the point of view was always that of the cop, even when you played the Blip. You never really stepped into the Blip's shoes. That was why, that day, he had chosen to pretend he was really a Psi Cop being chased, rather than accept the role of a rogue.

Think of Rashomon.

As insane as it seemed, Fatima wanted to escape the Corps. To understand any of it, he had to look not *at* her eyes, but through them.

He turned slowly in Bey's office, and his gaze came to rest on something he had always considered odd—a small mirror in a frame of plain, polished wood. Bey kept a neat appearance—his mustache, in particular, was always elegant and trimmed. But he had never seen the station chief preening in front of that mirror, or even glancing in it. In fact, he couldn't imagine Bey doing so. Bey was not, Al was sure, a vain man.

But there was the mirror, out of place in the cluttered, scholarly office, hung almost like an icon. He felt a flutter of excitement.

Know your enemy. Love your enemy. Be your enemy.

He held up the photo so he could see it and his own reflection in the glass. He remembered Fatima again, but this time placed those memories and perceptions into his own reflection. Long ago, he had projected himself onto Brett, to fool the others. Now he projected Fatima Cristoban onto himself. Concentrating. The room beyond the focus of his gaze began to blur. For a long moment he felt as if he were pushing against some flexible but impenetrable membrane, a tension on some surface of the universe he had never imagined existed before—and then, subtly, he seemed to slip through.

The image in the glass was no longer his own. It was Fatima Cristoban's.

The Corps is not my mother or my father, she said, defiantly. *I have a mother and father. I won't go see them, because that's the first place they will look for me. I'm choking here, I'm hemmed in. I want a bigger sky. I want things to be as they were before I got my psi. They will be.*

He blinked his eyes, slowly, resting them for a few heartbeats in the dark before returning them to use. He was looking at himself again. But inside, in his head, he felt a sort of compass now, a lodestone swinging always north.

And north was Fatima Cristoban.

Taking a deep breath, he left Bey's office and found him outside of the building, smoking a long cigar.

"I'm ready," he said.

Bey studied him through oily curls of smoke.

"So you are," he said, approvingly.

Al watched the Earth below with fascination. He had never flown before. The helicopter made almost no sound, and it seemed as if they were gliding along, fifty meters or so above the trees. Like flying in a dream.

"We have her as far as Amsterdam," Bey explained. "She used a forged ident—not a bad job, but not so good that we didn't catch it, after a few hours."

"I don't think—" Al broke off, not wanting to speak out of turn.

"Mr. Bester?"

"I don't think she could have forged an identicard."

"On what do you base that, Mr. Bester?"

"I could be wrong. That just wasn't my impression of her."

Bey stroked his goatee. "I tend to agree with you. You think she had an underground railroad connection?"

Al shrugged. "Sir, I don't know that much about the underground."

"Well, we'll be met by other cops and some bloodhounds in Amsterdam, in case things get hairy. My guess is they won't—the resistance is weak these days, and laying low. I think she got the ident from a forger in Geneva and is hoping to find the underground railroad in Amsterdam. It's a city with that sort of reputation."

Al nodded. They were over countryside now, and it occurred to Al that it was probably some of the same territory he had covered by train not long ago. Then it had seemed somehow overwhelming; now he saw it as a hawk might, a big place full of small things at his mercy.

It was a feeling he liked a great deal.

"Mr. Bester, I want to be clear about your position here. You are a student, and an observer. This sort of thing is not usual—I usually select advanced students from my class to accompany me, if anyone."

"I'm honored, sir, but may I ask—why me?"

"Think of it as a reward. You've pleased me, these past few months. I think you've come a long way. The Corps needs Psi Cops who know what they are doing, not—" He broke off and twiddled with his mustache, frowning, before continuing. "*Anyway*. I had to pull considerable strings for this. No one thought it was very wise, not after your last little excursion. There are some who will be watching this whole enterprise very closely. I want them to know you are now the levelheaded lad I say you are. Do you think we can convince them of that?"

"Yes, sir."

"Good. I chose this hunt because I don't think there will be much danger, but that is never a given, so pay attention to me. If I say go, you go. If I say sit, you sit."

"Understood, sir."

"I also thought you might like to see Amsterdam. You enjoyed Paris, didn't you?"

"Well, sir, I was shot and nearly killed, so I'm not sure 'enjoyed' would be the best word—"

"Hah. I scanned you. You were fascinated by Paris, and well you should have been. You will be fascinated by Amsterdam, too. With any luck, we can make time for a brief tour. Educational, of course."

"She was here," Bey said, surveying the dingy little room. "Not long ago."

Al felt it, too, the vague imprint of Cristoban's psyche. It didn't belong here, in this narrow space, on that wretched tiny bed. It be-

longed—*out* somewhere, with a wide sky. He thought back to her file, which he had reviewed on the helicopter ride. She was from Argentina. Was it a spacious place?

He shook the feeling off. Ever since he had "prepared" himself with the photograph, it was as if a ghost hung near his shoulders, entering his eyes now and then and rendering them alien. Was it possible that he was actually in touch with the Blip somehow? Sharing her actual thoughts? He asked Bey.

Bey was still walking slowly around the room, as if surveying each molecule in it. He didn't look at Al.

"I don't know," he replied simply. "Telepathy and distance are very strange things. Once, in the Belt, a construction worker went missing. We didn't find him for hours, and when we did it was first with radar and then with a telescope. He was in an EVA suit, twenty miles away, drifting. No response from his comlink, nothing. All of the shuttles were out, but we knew we could rig up a sled in pretty short order—if it was worth it. They asked me if I could tell whether he was alive or dead. He was a little dot in the sky, but once I established line of sight, I had him. I scanned him, and he was alive, though unconscious. Turns out it was attempted murder, but that's a longer story. Twenty miles and clear as a bell. I even got who the would-be killer was from him, then and there. We had him detained before the sled even rescued the castaway.

"On the other hand, I've been unable to pull surface thoughts from someone hiding in a closet ten feet away." He paused. "I know they teach line of sight, but I could tell you some stories—" He looked at Al, finally. "It comes down to this: We still don't know exactly how telepathy works. I sometimes wonder if its limitations aren't more psychosomatic or perceptual than anything else. Why else should I be able to scan someone twenty miles away, simply because I can see a tiny silver dot?"

"So it's possible I might have established some link with her?"

"I wouldn't count on it. It's more likely closure—your mind putting things together from a number of facts and sensations. Your memory of her signature, the traces of her left in this room, the details you know about her—the Human mind is a strange machine, even without telepathy. The main thing, Mr. Bester, is that it *works*. 'Why' is usually a fine question to ask, but in this case—" He stopped, smiling. "Have you ever seen the animated vids?"

"Yes. I used to like *Roadrunner*."

"Hmm—the roadrunner was the Blip, right? And the coyote, the Psi Cop?"

"Yes, sir. The roadrunner was clever, but he always got caught in the end."

"Did he ever run off of a cliff, and not know it? Just hang there in the air until he realized that he wasn't standing on anything?"

"Yes, sir. That's when he would fall."

"Sometimes our abilities are like that. Convince yourself that something shouldn't work, and sometimes it doesn't."

"In that case, sir, I'd like to tell you something I really shouldn't know."

"What's that, Mr. Bester?"

"She's out in a park, somewhere, or a field. Someplace open."

Bey nodded thoughtfully. "Well. An intuition. And you may be right—that may be where she *wants* to be. That's very different from knowing where she is."

"Yes, sir."

"Let us suppose she is trying to reach such a place. I assure you, it is not in Amsterdam. What will she need to get there?"

"Credits. Her own chit is no good now, and she must know that."

"Exactly. Let's interview the manager."

Cloe Lyster was a stringy woman in her late forties, with hair like a white tumbleweed. Her beaklike mouth clacked out brief, acerbic answers to their questions. No, of course she didn't know where the girl was. She had checked in the day before, gone out, and hadn't returned. Yes, of course she'd run an ident check, but there were problems with the system just now. No, she hadn't required a retina scan—she didn't even have the equipment. Young? Yes, but a million young people came through Amsterdam on holiday. Why should that be suspicious?

"If she was on holiday, why did she ask you about jobs?" Bey asked, not looking up from his notebook.

"Lots of kids get part-time—" She froze, realizing that this was the first mention of jobs thus far. Bey looked at her, a bit archly.

"I know the law," she said, sullenly. "You aren't allowed to do that."

"Do what? Ask you a question? Madame, of course I am."

"You aren't allowed to read my mind."

"I didn't," he said mildly. "I guessed, and you obliged by being stupid. That's at least twice you've been stupid with us, Madame. Once when you lied to us, again when you let me trick you. Please, do not be stupid again. I now have probable cause to do a scan, if I wish. I can have the authority in less than an hour. Have you ever been scanned, Ms. Lyster? I assure you, you won't like it. Personally, I'd prefer not to do one—I don't imagine I would like the inside of your mind." He leaned on the antique, polished wood of the counter. "Why not just tell me what I want to know? I will find out, one way or the other."

Lyster's eyes seemed to dull, and she reached for a slip of paper and a pen. She wrote down a name and an address.

"It's nothing to do with me," she said, softly. "I warn them."

Bey looked at the scrap for an instant, then back at Lyster. "Nothing to do with you?" he said, softly. He pulled out his tel-phone and flipped it open.

"This is Bey," he said. "I need an elite squad to meet me at the following address," he said, then read the street and building number from the manager's note. "At least ten bloodhounds. Keep it quiet, but come armed for bear." He paused. "Send an ambulance to 21 Lagendijk Street, too. A Ms. Lyster has had some sort of attack."

He closed the phone. Lyster was backing away, blinking rapidly. She turned and tried to run.

"Sir?" Al asked, as their car sped through the city. "Why did you—"

"You'll see why I did it soon enough," Bey said, grimly. "Don't worry about her. She'll wake up with a headache and have bad dreams for the next six months. Better than she deserves."

"She works with the underground?"

Bey shook his head. "Most runaways like Ms. Cristoban don't find the underground. They find people like Saskia Grijs."

"Grijs?"

"Yes. That's who our sweet little old landlady referred Ms. Cristoban to."

Bey parked on the street, near an ancient-looking three-story building. Lights were flashing in the upper story, and a crowd was gathered on the street, staring upward.

"No!" Bey shouted. "I told them to wait!" He bolted from the car and sped toward the house, PPG in hand, black coat flapping behind him.

Al sat stunned for a moment, staring up at the flashing lights, before noticing two men in MetaPol uniforms lying facedown in the street.

Bey hadn't told him to stay in the car. Hadn't told him anything.

In a few heartbeats he was with one of the downed men. He knew in an instant the fellow was dead. It wasn't the gallon or so of blood pooled beneath him, or even the film forming on his wide eyes—it was the *nothing* that was in his mind.

The other man was dead, too. For a moment Al felt disoriented, as if the whole world had come apart at the atomic level, and then come back together slightly different.

Dead. This was real. They had been people, and now they weren't.

Above, he could hear weapons conversing. That's where Bey had gone. Bey, who could be dead, too.

The dead man was still clutching a PPG. Gingerly, Al took it from his still-warm fingers and slowly, quite slowly, followed Bey up the stairs.

He continued to pass bodies. One on the stairs, one on the first landing. Outside, sirens were approaching—regular police, he imagined. He thumbed the PPG on, found that it was already charged. The man outside must have died shooting, at least.

The corpse trail led to an open door. Al noticed that the gunfire seemed to have stopped.

He glanced through, and found himself face-to-face with the muzzle of a PPG.

"Don't!" Bey said, from somewhere. "He's with me!"

Al's heart was well toward the front of his mouth. The face staring into his was intense, almost mad-looking—but beneath it was the familiar Psi Corps badge.

You should be more careful, kid.

Al nodded vigorously, still not capable of saying anything.

Bey was across the room. Five other cops had taken up positions. Bodies littered the floor, perhaps fifteen, and only one wore a badge.

"Search the whole thing," Bey snapped. "Rip up what you have to. Where is the girl?"

As his eyes adjusted to the darkened room, Al realized that Bey was speaking to a woman, thirtyish. Her platinum hair shone against her dark brown business suit.

"I want my lawyer," she said.

Bey's expression didn't change, but hers did. Her eyes rolled back in her head and her back arched, hands spasming. She made a sort of clucking sound and fell wetly to the hardwood floor.

He nodded. "Three of you come with me. Al, I thought I told you—" He paused for an instant. "No, I guess I didn't, did I? My mistake. Come along then." He broke into a trot.

They wound up another tight corridor, old wood. Oddly enough, the air had a strange, antiseptic smell.

Bey approached a door and motioned. Two of the hounds kicked it in.

"Hey!" The man inside was large, broad-shouldered, with aquiline features. He was just putting on a white shirt. The rest of his clothes lay in a heap on the floor. "Listen, I paid good—" then he saw who they were.

PPGs whined.

"No," Bey commanded. "I want *this* one to go to trial. Take photographs."

One of the hounds walked over to the man and kicked him in the crotch. When he doubled, he slammed the butt of his PPG into the base of his skull. The fellow went down, groaning.

Bey ignored all of that and went to the bed. That was where Cristoban was. Al followed, almost unaware that he was doing so. There was blood everywhere. He noted, dully, that it had beaded on the sheets rather than soaking in, as if the sheets had been made with—this—in mind.

She was still alive, tied spread-eagle. Naked. One eye was swollen shut, and her face was battered beyond recognition.

Help me . . .

Bey cut the bonds with a small knife.

"The ambulance just arrived, sir," one of the bloodhounds said.

"Tell them to hurry."

Am I—I'm in trouble.

"Don't worry about it," Bey said, softly. "Don't worry about anything. Just hang on, okay?"

I just didn't want—I wanted it to be like it was . . .

"It will be. Just like it was. We've called your parents. They're coming to get you."

Really?

"Really."

And then she wasn't there anymore.

Bey bowed his head, then straightened and stood. He looked terrible, like an angry god, a single tear trickling down one cheek.

God damn them. Damn them to hell, Al suddenly caught, from Bey. It had a strange subtext, almost as if he weren't talking about the criminals who had raped and murdered Cristoban at all, as if he meant—

But that was impossible.

"Come on, Mr. Bester," he said, softly. "It's time we left, you and I."

Bey swirled his coffee and gazed out at the creamy morning light on the canal. A paddleboat with a young couple in bright yellow shirts disturbed a family of ducks. A third-story window opened, and a beautiful girl with long, white hair leaned out to enjoy the hint of breeze.

"I'm sorry, sir," Al said, sipping his own coffee.

"What are you sorry about, Mr. Bester?"

"I know it upsets you when someone gets killed."

Bey seemed to consider that for a long while, as Amsterdam quickened, and the streets began filling with men and women in business suits,

the fronts of restaurants and shops rolling up. The older man's eyes took all of that in, and his face was placid, but Al was certain that if he dared to scan him, he would hear Stravinsky playing.

"A fellow goes out to the country one day," Bey began, "and he stops in at this farm. He's talking to the farmer, when he notices this pig with three peg legs. Three wooden legs and one real one. He asks the farmer about it.

" 'Let me tell you about this pig,' the farmer says. 'This is *some* pig. This pig saved my life once. The house was on fire, and this pig charged right in, dragged the wife and me out.'

" 'That's pretty amazing,' the fellow said.

" 'That's not all. This pig can do calculus and all kinds of mathematical whatnot. Why, some say he's even solved Fermat's last theorem.'

" 'Seems I read that in the papers a few years ago,' the city fellow said.

" 'Yep. Reporters came out for that one. Also, this pig can play the piano—he prefers Chopin. He really is *some* pig.'

" 'Well, I have to agree,' the city fellow replied, 'but what happened to his legs?'

" 'Well,' says the farmer, 'when you've got a pig this special, you don't want to eat him all at once.' "

Al blinked, felt his lips lift up involuntarily.

"Yes, it was a joke, Mr. Bester," Bey replied. "You are permitted to laugh."

"Yes, sir. It was an awful joke, if I may say so, sir."

"Mr. Bester, somehow I don't think of you as a connoisseur of humor, so I will take that as a compliment. Cultivate a sense of humor, Mr. Bester. You will need it to survive. And if you use it correctly, you might even be able to convince mundanes that you are almost Human." He finished off his coffee.

"What do we do now, sir?"

"I'll have to go to the arraignment this afternoon. I was thinking of sending you back to Geneva."

"If I'm in the way, I understand."

"On the other hand, I have most of the day free, so instead I considered we might take in a few museums—there is a very nice modern art museum here, you know. We can eat some frites and mayonnaise, wander along the waterfront, check out what was the red-light district, before the neo-Lutheran purge last century. Beautiful buildings that have seen centuries of the best and worst that Humans can do. We can remind

ourselves that we are still alive, and that that is a fine thing indeed. What do you say, Mr. Bester?"

Al thought about all the studying he had backed up because of this trip.

"That sounds fine to me, sir."

9

The blade flicked out in what seemed to be a straight lunge, but Al knew it was a feint-disengage. He went for the parry anyway, but instead of staying put or advancing to riposte as his opponent expected, he took a brisk retreat, caught the elusive steel with a second parry in *prime,* slid neatly inside the enemy point, and riposted at last—a difficult move, but it looked very elegant if you could pull it off.

He pulled it off. Green light, his point.

The score was fourteen–fourteen. Al returned to the en garde line and pulled off his mask. He saluted his opponent, a long-jawed, big-boned fellow named Emory. Al flashed Emory a smile. "One more. Loser buys lunch."

Emory nodded a little nervously.

Perfectly relaxed, Al flexed his legs and dropped his foil to absence. They began to dance.

Emory was a bit predictable. He beat, advanced quickly in a low line, lunged, disengaged. He 'cast his next move—or what he wanted Al to think was his next move, a retreat-crossback-fléche—and instead did a lunge-and-duck, hoping Al would be suckered into running onto his blade.

Al went for it. Give the guy a break—he hadn't won a match all day, and this was, after, all, only practice. If they ever faced each other in an official bout, Emory would learn, to his dismay, that Al had been fencing about five notches below his best.

"Well done," Al said, taking off his mask and saluting. He strode forward enthusiastically to shake Emory's hand.

"It was a good bout," Emory said. "I'm surprised I beat you."

"Don't sell yourself short. You've got some good attacks. You sure suckered me with that last one. I guess I'm buying lunch."

Emory grinned. "I guess so. I—ah—I promised some friends I would meet them in the sandwich shop on the square. Would you mind being in company?"

"Not at all," Al replied. "Any friend of yours is a friend of mine."

* * *

". . . and the farmer says, 'Well, when you have a pig this special, you don't want to eat him all at once,' " Al finished.

All five made faces. Emory aside, Al hadn't met any of them before—they were all sophomores, and he was a senior.

"Thanks a lot, Al," one of the girls—Alemba—said. "Makes my ham sandwich all the tastier."

"I strive to give pleasure," Al replied. They were all still chuckling, Alemba included.

"So tell us, Al," Emory said, after the moment had passed, "what was it like, tracking down Brazg and Nielsson?"

Al put on a sober face. "You heard about that?"

"Everyone heard about that. A lot of us were rooting for you, when you had to be the statue of the week, but we were afraid to say so. The older kids—"

"I appreciate that, but it's just as well you kept quiet. The Corps doesn't punish without good reason. Going after those two was the dumbest thing I ever did in my life. I genuinely appreciated my punishment."

"Still, some people went too far. Fatima—"

"I felt sorry for her," Al said. "I still do. I wish I had understood at the time how disturbed she was. Maybe I could have done something." He was surprised to realize that he really meant this. "What she did to me was a symptom of her own problems. It didn't really have much to do with me."

"That's right, you were there, weren't you—when she, you know . . ."

Al nodded. "That hunt was part of my punishment, my lesson. The Corps really wanted me to understand the evil that's out there, the kinds of things that can happen to telepaths in the mundane world. Believe me, when I saw what that sick pervert did to her—" He broke off, strategically.

"It must have been awful," Dierdra said, her violet eyes round.

"Let's talk about more pleasant things," Al suggested.

"Yeah," Emory replied. "Like our trip on the lake next weekend— Al, would you be interested?"

"That sounds nice," Al said. "Can I let you know in the next day or so?"

"Sure."

Later, when he and Emory were alone, the taller boy looked a little sidewise at him. "Did you let me have that last point, in the gym today?"

Al chuckled. "I never let anyone 'have' anything. Haven't you heard that about me?"

"The older kids talk like that about you," Emory said, cautiously. "I have to say, you aren't what I expected."

Al chose his words carefully. "It's not their fault. I used to be a little too competitive. I've—learned a few life lessons."

"Well," Emory said, a little awkwardly, "you're okay by me."

"Thank you, Emory. That means a lot to me. See you in fencing tomorrow?"

"Count on it."

"You won't fool me with that duck again."

"We'll see!"

Al watched him go, surprised at the warmth in his chest.

He was still at the top of his class. He still tested highest in psi-tests. And he had—friends? Almost friends, anyway. People who liked having him around.

"Good morning, Al." Bey shuffled some papers from his desk. "What can I do for you?"

"I was wondering if I could take a rain check on the Geru exhibition this weekend."

Bey nodded. He seemed a little stiff. "I was going to talk to you about that. It was a little problematic anyway. Some things have come up. You have some other engagement?"

"Some of the sophomores asked me if I'd like to go out on the lake with them."

"Go, go by all means. This is what I've encouraged in you, eh? You should be out with the other students—for your own sake, and because it makes a good impression." He glanced at his watch. "If you have time for a walk, though . . ."

"Right now, sir?"

"Yes. Is that a problem?"

"No, sir." But Bey never went out this time of day.

"Forgive me that little subterfuge, Mr. Bester," Bey said, as they strolled along the parklike north quad. "I wanted to mention something to you, and I wanted to do it where no one was likely to overhear."

"No problem, sir."

"Matters have come to my attention that will impinge on our talks."

A little hollow seemed to appear in Al's throat. "Oh. Anything important, sir?"

"Yes, but I can't talk about it. And that's not what I . . ."

Bey paused for a second, uncertainly, and for no reason he could name—Bey's thoughts were, as always, carefully guarded—Al felt a slight dread. "Mr. Bester, did you ever meet with Director Vacit?"

"Why—yes. Yes, sir. When I was six years old. He called me to his office after that incident with the Grins I told you about."

"Hmm."

"Why do you ask?"

"Mr. Bester, I worked closely with Director Vacit in his last years here. He took few into his confidence, but he confided in me now and then. Those of us who knew him well were aware that—he took a certain interest in you, Mr. Bester. Over all of the other students. None of us ever knew why, not even Natasha, who was closest to him."

"I . . . *me,* sir?"

"Yes. It was one reason I was keeping my eye on you, out of respect for him, though as I think you know, I've found reasons of my own to be concerned for you."

"Thank you," Al said, almost at a loss for words. "I—I know you've saved my life, in more than one—"

"No, let me finish. I don't want to get sidetracked. The present director—Johnston, the one you met at your hearing—has done everything he can to remove the influence of Vacit. All of Vacit's former aides are elsewhere, retired, or—well, Director Johnston has certain ambitions. And a certain vision for the Corps, which is—which some feel is untraditional."

This uncertain speech was not like Bey at all. "But you're still here," Al noticed.

"Indeed." Bey plucked at his beard. "He knows, Mr. Bester—Johnston knows that Director Vacit took an interest in you. Like me, he doesn't know why. That bothers him a lot. And so he keeps a close eye on you, Mr. Bester. And those you associate with. You have a bright future ahead of you, Mr. Bester, but you have an enemy. He will be the more your enemy if you and I continue our association, especially now."

"Now, sir?"

"I really can't speak of it."

"But, sir—Dr. Bey, I don't care about that."

"Yes, you do. You will. And you don't have all of the facts before you, from which to predict consequences. Mr. Bester—" his voice softened "—*Al.* I don't want to hear from you. Don't come by to see me. Don't message me. Respect my wishes in this." He turned, put a hand on his shoulder. "But know that I am proud of you. You've learned a lot—"

"I've learned everything important from you, sir."

"You were an apt pupil. I will consider you a perfect one if you obey me now."

"I—" His chest was tight. "I will, if you tell me to, sir."

"Good. Perfect." He reached into his pocket.

"I want you to have this." He withdrew something, something that fit into his palm. Al held out his hand stupidly and felt something cool pressed there.

"This was my first. It always brought me luck. Hang on to it. On the day you have earned the right to wear it—and that day will come, Al, I do not doubt it in the least—I would be proud to see it on your uniform."

He paused, as if to say something else, shook his head, and suddenly turned and walked away. "*À bientôt,* Mr. Bester."

Only when he was gone did Al open his fingers to stare at what he already knew was there—the brass and copper of a MetaPol badge.

Two steps to your right, Al, Emory 'cast. He glyphed, too. Al saw himself approaching a shallow pit. It was perhaps a yard across. He paused for an instant, trying to will himself the ability to see through the blindfold, but of course that was impossible. He could only see through the eyes of his teammates. That was the point of the contest, really. One reason he had avoided such team events in the past—it meant trusting one's teammates completely.

Trust. It came hard.

He flexed his knees and leapt. The floor found his feet a little sooner than he expected, and he almost stumbled. Emory must not have noticed that, the extra height beyond the trench. Sloppy, but he probably hadn't imagined Al would jump, thinking he would edge around instead.

Shooter, Al, two o'clock! That was Indira, and Indira was always precise. He dropped and rolled sideways, came up with his own simulator held level. Indira, on one side of the course, and Abraham, on the other, glyphed simultaneously. The two images were confusing, but necessary. With them he was able to triangulate where his opponent—also blindfolded, also coached by his team—stood. Al squeezed the contact, and was rewarded with a small ringing sound.

A cheer went up from his side.

You did it, Al! Emory 'cast.

No, Al replied. *We did it together.*

There was a celebration, of course. The victory had advanced them to the semifinals, and they all thought their chances looked good. For Al, it was a sort of revelation, this shared victory. It was mixed—when he failed he let everyone down, and when he succeeded he had to share the glory. But being part of a team had its rewards, as well. For the first time,

he felt he was at the center of something, rather than clinging to a rapidly rotating edge.

Something was still missing, though, and that something was Sandoval Bey. Al had struggled to understand the feeling of loss that had only seemed to mount as the months marched by. Three months, and not a word from the station chief.

Part of him felt ashamed for missing Bey, because he was bright enough to understand the implications of what he felt.

Most of his new companions were laters—most had been raised for years by biological parents. They were all loyal to the Corps, all thought of the Corps as mother and father—but as *surrogate* mother and father, as replacements for their birth parents.

For Al, the Corps had been his first mother, first father, yet despite that, his feelings toward Bey were—if he was honest with himself—filial. The primitive instincts that even the best telepaths inherited from their mundane ancestors still lived in him, urged him to focus on human individuals as parents.

The faces he had once seen in his dreams were gone, left behind with childhood and the Grins—but Bey's face had taken their place.

It was wrong. *We are all mothers and fathers to one another.* That had been the lesson imported by the Grins. That was the lesson of the Corps.

It didn't comfort him much. He missed Bey.

He shook his head. The excited conversation around him had shifted, and he tried to focus, to catch up. He didn't want them to think he wasn't paying attention to them, that he didn't value them. It was one of Bey's lessons—if you show someone they have value to you, it automatically makes you valuable to them.

So he joined in the conversation, pushing Sandoval Bey to the back of his mind.

Half an hour later, a Psi Cop walked into the bar. He glanced around, and when his gaze met Al's, recognition kindled. He came over.

"Alfred Bester?"

"Sir? Yes, sir, that's me, sir."

"Would you come with me?"

"Of course." He turned to the others. "See you guys for practice in the morning?"

"Sure thing, Al. You were great today."

"You guys, too. See you."

The Psi Cop set a brisk pace. "Sir? May I ask where we're headed?"

"The director's office," the cop told him. "Director Johnston wants to see you."

* * *

"Mr. Bester."

Al had never heard his own name sound so threatening. The director maintained his familiar, thin smile as he appeared to review something on the desktop display.

"Sir."

"I've heard good things about you, of late. You may know that many of your teachers had concerns about you. I did myself, after that little incident in Paris. I'm very pleased to say, no one has had the slightest complaint about you since that time."

"Thank you, sir. I believe I learned a valuable lesson."

The director nodded. "You will graduate the Minor Academy this year?"

"Yes, sir, if I meet the requirements set by the Corps."

"Oh, I'm sure you will have no problems there, Mr. Bester. All of your instructors seem quite certain of you."

"That's gratifying to hear, sir, but of course I take nothing for granted."

"No, I'm sure you don't." He paused, took a small tumbler half full of what appeared to be water, and relaxed back into the arms of his padded chair. "Have you seen Dr. Sandoval Bey, recently?"

Al felt it then, a faint touch, a prickling of the skin. Someone, somewhere, was scanning him, a very light scan, like a business teep.

"No, sir. Not in months."

"You two spent quite some time together. You even went on a raid with him, I seem to remember. No, no—don't fear to admit it, he cleared it through this office."

"So he told me at the time," Al replied.

"Do you know why he took such an interest in you? He advocated for you at the hearing, took you under his wing. You two met regularly for months."

"I can't say, sir. He saved my life in Paris, I suppose that had something to do with it. He thought my education was incomplete."

"Really? He said that? In what way does he feel the Corps is not doing its job as educator?"

Al felt, suddenly, as if he had walked into a trap. "That's not what I meant, sir. It wasn't the Corps that failed, but myself. The lessons Dr. Bey thought I should learn were there for me all along—I just didn't learn them."

"And what lessons might those be?"

"I—" Al realized that it was hard to articulate what Bey had given him. "He taught me to appreciate other people. To work with them, to try to understand their point of view."

"I see. And this Blip you chased together, this Fatima Cristoban—did he teach you to understand *her* point of view? Did he teach you compassion for rogue telepaths?"

Al's mouth suddenly felt very dry. There was something—some subtext to this conversation—that was leaking from the director. He tried desperately to shut it out. "I—she was confused, sir. Very confused. I suppose I did feel sorry for her."

"Tell me, Mr. Bester," the director said, very softly. "If you had to choose between a rogue telepath and a—*mundane*—who was loyal to EarthGov and to the principles of the Corps, which would you choose?"

"I am loyal to the Corps, sir. A rogue is a rogue."

"I see. A commendable attitude. Do you think Dr. Sandoval Bey shares that attitude?"

"Of course, sir." But he felt a flicker of doubt at that. Bey might—just might—under the right circumstances—put the telepath first.

And he knew, with sinking heart, that his doubt had been heard and noted by someone he could not see.

"Very well. That will be all, Mr. Bester."

And as he left, he felt the same flash of hatred he had felt all those years ago, when he had first seen this ice-eyed man. And there was something else—a danger, a threat. Not to himself, but to Bey. And it was mixed with a feeling of terrible triumph.

He fought to control his breathing all the way back to the dorms. Bey was in danger—grave danger, of that he was sure. He should warn him, go to his office— No, that was crazy; send him an anonymous message.

But what if Bey really had betrayed the Corps? Wouldn't warning him be an act of treason, too?

Yet it was plainly impossible. Bey *was* the Corps, represented everything good about it. Even if he had sympathy for some rogues, that didn't mean—

The director was a mundane, a jealous, power-mad mundane, who—

He crushed those thoughts, but they kept coming back. Bey was in danger. How could he do nothing?

Then he turned a certain corner and for just an instant didn't understand where he was, how his feet had led him there, why the world had suddenly become so vivid. Why he was six years old again and all life since a dream.

It was the *place*. The place that the Grins had branded into his mind. It all came back—the fear, the shame—mostly the shame. He felt a sob jerk in his chest, but he grabbed it with his heart, kept it there, tight and cold and awful. Grinding his teeth, eyelids twitching, he closed his hand in a fist, hurried on, until the feeling faded, became a memory again.

They were trying to trick him. That's what they were trying to do. The director had intentionally made him think Bey was in danger, to test his loyalty, his commitment to the Corps. If he went to Bey now, it was all over, everything. No Major Academy, no future with MetaPol, nothing.

Bey was fine. Maybe—he shied away from the thought, but couldn't entirely dismiss it—maybe Bey was even *in* on it. Since his foolhardy pursuit of Brazg and Nielsson, everything had been leading to this—a test to make sure Alfred Bester really was Psi Cop material.

Now his breath smoothed out, and his heart found a reasonable pace. He went back to his dorm, he took out his books, and he studied.

Three days later he stood on closely trimmed grass, his legs like wood.

It should be raining, he thought. *The sky should be black.*

It wasn't. The sun dazzled, a jewel on a vast pillow of blue velvet and white lace. The leaves of the trees glistened with dew. Birds were singing, though the music—the music in his head—nearly drowned their song.

He was the only one there, at the grave. No one else had come. They said he was lucky to even be buried here, considering.

"They say—" He couldn't speak, he found—not with his throat. *They say you were helping the rogues, that you sympathized with them. They issued a warrant for your arrest, and when they came, they found you . . .*

He couldn't picture it, Bey standing on a chair, a rope around his neck, calmly kicking the chair from beneath him. It didn't fit. Bey hated suicides.

I've heard—whispers—that they killed you. That they gave you a choice, and rather than disgrace the Corps you—you did it while they watched. Like a samurai. Is it true, Dr. Bey? I trusted you.

(Anger, sudden, somehow like hiccups.) The director was right, or half right, wasn't he? You may never have helped the rogues, but you did sympathize with them. If you were given the same choice they gave me—good mundane or bad telepath—you would always choose the telepath, wouldn't you? What have your philosophies gotten you? Your jokes? How could you betray me by dying?

The grave did not answer, of course. Al stood there, staring at the fresh earth—smelling it, like the flower beds after the ground crews broke them for planting—and he wondered if he would live. He wondered if a Human heart could just tear itself in half, if his life could simply vomit out of him, as anything he ate did, each time he pictured Bey hanging there, face purple, his beard still neatly trimmed.

I could have warned you. I didn't. I'm sorry. I'm sorry, even if you really were a traitor.

It should be raining. The sky should be black. He closed his hand on the badge in his pocket, and it felt like a smooth piece of bone, long dead. His head was full of music, discordant, mocking.

Stravinsky.

10

Al admired Freja Magnussunsdottir's face. It was like carved ivory, fixed, expressionless. She seemed to speak and blink without using muscles; despite her advanced years, the only wrinkles were precise, incised lines that never bunched and neither lengthened nor shortened.

"The field test," she was saying, "will not comprise any fraction of your grade—it will comprise *all* of it. Those of you who do not have a B average or above will not be allowed to participate. As of now, you have effectively failed the course."

"But that's—we weren't told that at the beginning of the class. It wasn't in the syllabus!" The protester was Roger Fieldstone, a burly, weak-chinned senior.

"Mr. Fieldstone, sit down. I did not give you permission to speak."

"I'm sorry, Instructor, but this is simply not fair. If we were required to maintain a B average, we should have been told so."

"Mr. Fieldstone, you feel you could have done better if you had known it was required of you?"

"Yes, ma'am."

"I see." She nodded thoughtfully. "Then the Corps has no use for you. Excellence should not be conditional, it should not arise from necessity—but from desire. You have admitted that you took my class less than seriously, Mr. Fieldstone. If we were to give you a badge and a PPG and make you a Psi Cop, why should we expect any more of you? I'm recommending you be dropped from the program entirely."

"But I'm a senior," Fieldstone said, his voice panicky. "I can't—you can't—" He stood there, mouth open, and then collapsed back into his seat, burying his face in his hands.

Serves you right, Fieldstone, Al thought, but did not 'cast.

"Now. As I was saying before Mr. Fieldstone's unfortunate interruption—" On the very word, the door suddenly creaked open. Magnussunsdottir chopped off in midsentence and turned her uninflected face to see who it was. "Ah. Ms. Montoya. How nice of you to join us."

"Sorry, ma'am, I was arrested."

"Arrested."

"Yes. By the sight of the interns jogging by. The men wear these tight little—"

"Sit *down*, Ms. Montoya."

Montoya smiled, shrugged, and did so. On the way she caught Al staring at her and arched her eyebrows. He looked quickly away.

He remembered Elizabeth Montoya, had recognized her the first day of class. She was the dark beauty who had kissed him four years ago, when he had been the statue of the day. He had considered reminding her of the incident, but didn't really see the point. Montoya was a capricious creature, always flirting, usually outrageous, rarely more than a single word away from being thrown out of class—and yet somehow, she never quite seemed to say that word. It irritated him that she got away with such behavior. Her attitude was not, in his opinion, fitting for a Psi Corps cadet.

"If I am finally free of interruption," the instructor began again, "I will finish what I was saying. For those of you to whom the field test is still a concern—you will be assigned to four-person teams. You should be ready to go at 0500 tomorrow. The location, duration, and nature of your exam will not be disclosed. You will be provided with no tools, equipment, or clothing. You are free to confer among yourselves between now and then. Group assignments will be posted after class. Now, if you will all refer to diagram one of your text, we can begin a discussion of today's assignment."

"Well, Alfie, looks like we're on the same team," Montoya chirped, peering over his shoulder at the posted list.

"I prefer Alfred," he said.

"I prefer Alfie. Alfred sounds like a butler. Anyway, where do we meet to go over strategy? Uh-oh—we've got Vetsch and Nhan on our team. Couple of lowlifes."

"Hey!" Thuy Nhan said, behind them.

"No offense."

"So, where are we meeting, Captain Alfie?"

"Hiking boots," Al said.

"Right. Best to be overprepared in the footwear department. Unless they dump us in the middle of a black-tie formal."

"I hadn't thought of that," Vetsch said, resting his rounded chin on folded arms.

"No," Al said. "It can't be anything that specific. If it is, there will be

opportunities for us to acquire the right clothing. We should start with survival gear."

"Swiss army knives," Nhan offered. "Water."

"It won't be a simple survival test," Montoya said, doodling on her list. "We'll have to track, I'm sure of it."

"Or avoid being tracked," Al replied.

"How so? It's a class on detection techniques."

"Right. Nothing teaches you to hunt like being prey."

"Ah! Words of wisdom from the master."

"Look," Al said, starting to feel really irritated, "I take this seriously. I *want* to be a Psi Cop."

"Hey, we all do," Montoya gave back, "but can't you have a little fun with it? Relax! We're the best of that class."

"I know we are," Al said. Actually, he didn't agree. Nhan was smart, but she had no stamina. Vetsch tended toward the bottom end of P12—he ought to have been rated a high-end P11. And Montoya—Montoya had no discipline.

Still, if they thought *he* thought he was better than they, they wouldn't follow him. "We are the best, but that just leads to overconfidence. Now, I say lightweight parkas—we can always dump them if they put us on the equator or in the Sahara."

"Wear pretty underwear, in case we have to strip all the way down," Montoya added. "I have a nice set with Narn-head mottle."

Inwardly, Al sighed. It would be a long afternoon.

They were in a jet for a while, or perhaps a jet simulator. They might have been on a train, and they were certainly in a helicopter toward the end. A lot of time passed, though thanks to the blackout conditions they traveled under, it was uncertain exactly how much time—their watches had been taken from them before the trip began.

When they finally stood again on the ground, still blindfolded, Al took a deep, slow breath. The air was brittle with cold, and he was glad he had insisted on the jackets. Rich scents of earth, hay, the memory of smoke surrounded them, and he felt tall grass brushing his pants. It was resoundingly silent—no traffic noises, no distant voices. The same was true of the psychic wind. They were somewhere far away, remote.

Someone removed his blindfold—a tough-looking woman with close-cropped hair. Everything remained dark, but it was a darkness with stars, and a moon.

Once they and their packs were out of the chopper, it left again on nearly silent rotors. Al sleepily blinked the nightscape in a series of still lifes with eyes gritty from fatigue.

"Well, here we are," Montoya observed. "Wherever 'here' is."

"Now what?" That from Nhan, who was hugging herself against the cold.

No one move. There might be clues as to what we're supposed to do almost at our feet. And don't speak aloud unless you have to. He glanced slowly around them. He could make out a horizon, some clumps that might be trees, houses, buildings. A few lights, very distant. *First we listen to see if anyone is out there.* He already had, but now they had line of sight.

Right, Captain Alfie.

They all concentrated, scanning their limited view.

After five minutes, *Anything?*

The answer was a uniform no. Following that, two of them kept watch, while the other two looked more carefully, switching on the two sets of infrared goggles they had between them. *Like meerkats,* Montoya said, one of many annoying references Al didn't get.

When infrared showed them nothing, they switched to flashlights.

"This is getting us nowhere," Montoya hissed, after a quarter of an hour. "We need to really look around. We don't know that we have time for this kind of lollygagging."

Al didn't want to agree with her, but he had to. He was impatient.

Fine. Let's do a clockwise sweep, about ten feet apart, with flashlights.

"Wait!" Montoya said. "Look there!"

Maybe half a mile away, maybe much farther, a string of light raced through the darkness. At times it resolved into circles or arcs. A ground-car, or something similar.

"You think that's it?"

Al stared at the car, keeping line of sight, reaching out, trying to find—

There. He had it. Someone in the car and they were thinking—

Catch me if you can!

Al opened his mouth to repeat it, aloud, but Montoya was already gone, loping off into the near darkness with amazing speed. Vetsch and Nhan looked to him.

Damn it.

"You two follow. Walk thirty feet apart and try to keep us in sight. 'Cast if you notice anything. Watch our backs." Then he ran after Montoya.

It took a minute of hard running to catch her, and she was barely slowing down. He could've passed her, but didn't.

What the hell are you doing? he 'cast. *We have to work together on this. C'mon, Alfie. You aren't the cautious type. You're overthinking this*

whole thing. It's a game of tag. We're it. If we sit on our hands, we'll get nowhere.

We can't catch it!

We sure as hell can't if we don't try.

He had no argument for that. Besides, he liked running. The grass hissed against their thighs, and he was just getting the wonderful burn in his belly. In the moonlight, Montoya looked fierce and free. She might have been a lioness.

So for the moment, he surrendered to the joy of motion, the gratifying feel of his muscles, the night air. Even when the light vanished over the horizon, they didn't slacken.

A dawn sky like diluted milk revealed a flat plain that met all four corners of the world. Light transformed the landscape in unexpected ways, awakening a severe, bruised beauty.

The psionic landscape had altered, too—subtly—throughout the night. It had seemed at first totally silent, but that was because Al had been immersed in the background growl of Geneva for all of his life. Here, in the quiet hours of morning, faint impressions began emerging— heartbeats a hundred times faster than human, sharp hungers unburdened by denial or need for justification, occasional, almost vivid, flashes of color and structure.

The steppes, too, had a mind. At first he enjoyed it, but after a time it became a little distracting—too strange to completely dismiss but of no use in accomplishing his task.

It was Montoya who found two lines of bruised grass that must be the tire tracks. They followed them for hours, alternating between fast walking and trotting, as the sky rapidly filled with light.

Call a halt, Captain Alfie. He looked up to see Montoya, winking at him.

Tired?

No, but Nhan is. She's just too proud to say so. If we keep going at this pace, she won't be any use to us when we get wherever the hell we're going.

He looked at Nhan, and realized that Montoya was right.

"Let's take a rest," he said.

"Fine with me. I'm bushed," Montoya replied, aloud.

They dropped their packs. Al walked up toward the next rise. The plain wasn't as flat as it seemed; it had a gentle roll that hid subtle valleys. They had seen a few structures—houses, factories maybe—but as the tracks didn't go near them, they hadn't approached them either.

He felt Montoya come up behind him.

"North Dakota? Mongolia? Where do you think we are?" she asked.

Looking at the huge sky, Al remembered Cristoban, and Argentina. And Bey.

"Right now it doesn't matter much," he said. "Right now, our job is very simple—we follow these tracks. We're on the hunt."

"Uh-huh. Hey, Alfie—*Alfred*. Aren't you even going to ask me?"

"Ask you what?"

"Why I kissed you that day."

He considered that for a moment. "No."

"Why not?"

"It doesn't matter. Whatever the reason was, it had to do with a moment a long time ago. It's got nothing to do with now."

"You're a hard case, you know that? They say you had about a year when you unplugged your ass. You even went to semifinals in a team competition, then dumped your friends like a load of smelly shit."

"They weren't my friends. They just wanted to win the games."

"They thought you were their friend. Emory in particular was pretty torn up about it. He said it was like you had just cut them out of your head. He understood you were upset about Dr. Bey, and no one expected you to finish the games. They did sort of imagine you would *talk* to them again, though."

A sudden suspicion came over Al. "Who put you up to this?"

"What? Put me up to what?"

"This. Trying to talk to me."

She stared at him for maybe ten seconds, and then burst out laughing. Still laughing, she walked back to join the others.

Two hours later the tire tracks vanished into a river, one of the oldest tricks in the book. They split into teams, two up, two down, examining both banks. Al took Nhan with him.

They met again four hours later. The news wasn't good—in each direction the river was bounded by bluffs too steep for even the most rugged groundcar, and to the south the channel got too deep to drive in, anyway. Where they stood was essentially the only place their quarry could have forded the river. And night was opaquing the pearly sky.

What wood they found was too damp to start a fire with, so they ended up huddled in sleeping skins, jackets on. Al turned the problem over and over in his mind, but got nowhere.

He awoke to a sharp jab in the ribs, and looked up blearily to see a smiling Montoya.

"Found the car," she said. She was dripping wet.

"In the river, sunken," Al guessed.

"Yep. Half mile downstream. Found some footprints in the mud, too."

He shucked himself out of the sleeping skin. "I'm impressed."

"Are you? I didn't think anything could impress you."

"I'm impressed by a lot of things. The mathematical precision of Bach. The prose of Joyce—"

She squatted next to him. "*Are* you? Or do you just say things like that?"

That hit him oddly. He remembered—in sudden vivid clarity—the feel of her lips, a moment of impossible intimacy in the midst of humiliation, and for a nanosecond it seemed he *knew* Montoya, had always known her. And she knew him, saw straight through to the middle of him. For that flicker of time, it seemed a pretense to act like they were strangers.

"Let's go," he mumbled.

Montoya led them to the car, and, taking turns diving in the uncomfortably cold water, they did a hurried search of it. Again, Al felt the faint fingerprint of the same person who had challenged them two nights before. That made it easier to follow the footprints, which were almost imperceptible in the grass. After a time, however, it seemed pretty clear where the trail was leading; in the vast distance they could make out a small town, roads converging from several directions, including from slightly south of their own path. Soon they were walking on blacktop, and the sign of their prey was gone entirely.

"This is very bad," Al confided to Montoya, as they approached the town. "Two, maybe three thousand people in that town. How do we find him?"

"Or her. You've got me. But we'll think of something."

"Confident, aren't you?"

"No more so than you."

She shrugged, but he could tell the comment pleased her.

"You were raised in the Corps, weren't you."

"Yes. My biological parents were Corps, but they died when I was very young."

"You sure about that?"

"What's that supposed to mean?"

"I don't know. Have you ever seen any evidence that they really existed?"

"Are you questioning the Corps?"

"No. Yes. We should question everything, shouldn't we? Even if only for form's sake? How can we be good detectives if we make a habit of accepting assumptions blindly?"

"Why should the Corps lie to me about my parents? There's nothing even faintly logical about that." The very thought was sickening. Mon-

toya just didn't know—couldn't know. She was a later who had been raised as a normal. Normals lived in a world of suspicion and violence, and it tainted them.

"Look," he said mildly, "my parents don't matter. They wouldn't if they were alive, except that the Corps would have two more valuable members."

"I'm sorry I brought it up." She touched his shoulder with her gloved hand.

A galvanic shock ran through him, as if he were a discharged battery suddenly exposed to current again. Again he remembered her approaching him, noticing him on the parade ground.

"Why, then?" he asked, trying to keep his voice flat, nonchalant. Trying not to inflect it with surrender.

"Why what?"

"Why did you kiss me?"

A smile pulled at her lips, but somehow it wasn't a capricious one. There was something honest about it, something personal.

"To thank you," she said.

"For what?"

"It's hard to explain. I—I had just come into the Corps. You have to understand, it's different that way. Harder. It's very different from the outside world, and everyone is already broken out into cliques. I was— well, I was having my doubts. Frankly, I was considering running away."

"That would have been foolish. Another girl—"

"Fatima. Yes, I heard about her. But by that time I was okay, because I saw you."

"I don't understand."

"I had seen you there for days. When I walked past, you were dressed like—like Santa Claus with lipstick. And there was shaving cream all over you. You looked ridiculous—I couldn't have stood there, like that. I couldn't have borne it. And the way everyone talked about you—what you were going through was worse than anything that I could imagine.

"And yet when you reached to touch my mind, and I felt you—you weren't angry, or ashamed. You were curious. You were just standing there, taking it all, and you were okay. That's when I knew I would be okay, too." Now her grin became mischievous. "And you were kind of cute. And I could tell that you thought I was beautiful."

"I didn't—"

"You still do. I see you looking at me. Why haven't you done anything about it?"

"Because—" *Because what's the point? What will it get me? Another*

chance to be hurt, another chance to be distracted. Excellence I can have, because it depends only on me. Happiness is an illusion, and for me not even that. He didn't say it, didn't 'cast it. It was the first time he had even thought it. Montoya's presence brought back that year of joy and sorrow, and it felt like remembering madness. He had seemed so full of—something—back then. Something hot and alive, like—well, like Montoya herself. Her mind was like a furnace.

And she was threatening to bring it all back, the madness, the weakness, the pain.

He noticed that they had entered the town. "We had better get to work," he said.

11

"This is hopeless," Nhan said.

"Nothing is hopeless," Al replied, though he could not for a moment imagine in which direction hope might lie. They knew, at least, where they were—Tuulu, a small town in the Altai Federation.

"We aren't going to find him just walking up and down the street," Vetsch said.

"No. I thought I might catch a scent of his signature, but—" He furrowed his brow. "This is like a game of cops and blips, right?"

"A game of what?" Montoya asked.

Al blinked. "You never played Psi Cops and blips when you were little?"

But all three were looking at him in puzzlement. Laters, every one. They had no idea what he was talking about.

He remembered the Grins, each heavy word they had impressed upon him.

The others were pretending you two were rogues. You were not. You imagined yourself a Psi Cop, chased by rogues. But it is deeper than that, Mr. Bester. Whatever any of you were pretending, you are all members of the Corps.

Could it be that simple?

"In cops and blips there are multiple goals, usually arbitrary. In this case, though, the goal should have to make some sort of sense."

"We've already checked the train station, the bus station, the car sales and rental lots—"

"Right. So maybe the goal is arbitrary, after all."

"I don't get it."

"Remember, this is a test, not a real hunt, or even a contest. Maybe—maybe it isn't about catching the Blip, but about doing everything right."

"But a Psi Cop's job is to catch rogues."

"Sure. But sometimes you fail. Then what? Then you put out the word, report what you know, and trust the rest of the Corps to help you out. Where is the one place we haven't gone since we've been here?"

They looked at him blankly, and despite himself, he felt a smile crawl sluggishly across his face. "The local Corps station."

"Holy Moses," Montoya said. "Why didn't we think of that earlier?"

"Because we were thinking of this as a contest. We thought we were competing with the Corps. Real Psi Cops don't compete with the Corps—not even in training."

Montoya's eyes were wide. "I wouldn't have thought of that."

No, he thought to himself. *None of the rest of you could. Only me, only someone who grew up in a cadre. And I should have thought of it much, much earlier.*

A huge grin spread across the Psi Cop's already broad face. "Well," he said, in precise Anglic. "Are you here to give up?"

"No, sir," Al said. "We are here to notify the local station chief that a Blip recently passed through here."

"Catch me if you can," the cop said. "Congratulations."

"Thank you, sir."

"Holy smokes, you were right!" Montoya let out a war whoop and started dancing with Vetsch and Nhan. Al just stood there, feeling proud and stiff—and somehow, despite it all, a little left out.

"Unfortunately," the cop said, "for logistical reasons, it'll be morning before we can get you a connection back to Geneva. I've got rooms for you about three blocks from here."

"What's the drinking age in this 'grad?"

"Drinking age?" The cop pretended blank-faced incomprehension, then shrugged his shoulders.

"Heh!" Montoya replied.

"To Alfie," Montoya said, raising her shot glass high.

Al looked dubiously at the amber fluid in his own glass. But the toast was for him . . .

He sputtered on it, nearly blew it back up through his nose, and they laughed at him, but it was good-natured laughter, and Montoya was pressing a crescent of lime into his fingers.

"Suck on this," she said.

He did, and that made things better.

"Whew!" he managed. He stared at their grinning faces. Sure it was illusion, sure it was temporary, but . . .

He poured them all shots. "To all of us," he toasted. This time it wasn't nearly so hard to drink it down.

Later, they lurched back to their rooms, singing. He would never remember exactly what. The air had become a honeyed syrup—it almost

seemed he should be swimming through it—and he was acutely aware of Montoya clinging to his arm. Aware of her fire, of it eating up his own limbs, perhaps attracted there by the heat of the tequila in his belly.

At the rooms, there was a round of good nights, of jokes—all hazy— and then suddenly he was alone with Montoya, very near her opalescent eyes. She wore the same mischievous smile he had first seen on her.

"Right," she said softly. "And why haven't you asked me to kiss you again?"

"I—because I—" He furrowed his brow. "I don't understand the question."

"You're a smart fellow, Alfred Bester, but in some ways you're as dumb as a stick."

"Look, this isn't smart," he tried to say, though it came out as "shmarr," " 'cause we're drunk, an'—" He stared at her suddenly. "We *are* drunk, aren't we?"

"Never been drunk before, hey?"

"Well—no. The Corps doesn't—"

"Hush." And then she kissed him. It wasn't like the first time; it was an explosion. It was as if all of the universal constants had just changed by a factor of two. From his classes in astrophysics, he knew what that meant: all the stars flying apart as fusion became impossible, whole galaxies disintegrating—

Of course, he didn't care. He felt her lips, the taste of tequila and salt, and he felt her feeling his lips. He brought his hand up to press the cool satin of her hair and kissed back. He was, perhaps, overeager, and neither were in good control of their bodies. They overbalanced and thudded into the door, slid in a heap to the sidewalk. Montoya laughed and kissed him some more. There was nothing even remotely playful about it anymore. He saw her, saw himself through her, and in that instant he wanted to *really* know her, everything about her, to make the illusion of the day before into a prophecy. He wanted to learn the shape of her toes. The names of her childhood pets. Her hopes and dreams.

How to unfasten her bra—

She laughed as she unlocked the door, but she didn't fool him. She was as nervous as he was—it was only that she was braver, brave and fierce and lovely in a way he could never be. But he wanted it, to hold it, to plunge into her heat.

"Vetsch—Nhan—"

"In the other room, Alfie," she whispered. "In the other room." Then she brushed the warm petals of her lips along his neck, and he stopped worrying about it. About anything.

12

"Hey, champ!" Elizabeth Montoya said, looking up from her books just as he came through the trees. She bounced up and into his arms, but when she darted her face forward to kiss him, her hair came between them. She laughed and pushed it out of the way, and her face materialized, right there. He seized the initiative and kissed her.

A year. A year and she hadn't realized her mistake, let him find someone nicer, taller, better for her.

He had expected it. From the first moment they came together in the motel in Tuulu, he had expected her to evaporate like every other happy thing in his life. He had stared at the beauty of her face in the dawn, and had mourned the passage of time and the pain it would bring him when she finally awoke. Instead, when her eyes had opened, she had grimaced at her hangover, but kissed him anyway. They ate breakfast together, and she used the pronoun "we" a lot. Any questions had somehow been asked and answered in the night.

A year of furtive meetings, of time stolen. Each and every time he saw her, he feared it would be the last.

But now . . .

"So what's this big news?" she asked, leaning back so their bellies pressed together, but he could see her whole face, undistorted.

He cleared his throat, suddenly feeling shy.

"We're a match," he said.

"I'm a match. You're dry wood. Ya wanna get together?"

"No, I'm serious. I mean we're a—ah—we're a genetic match."

"Al, you're shaking."

"Ah—yes, I guess I am."

Her eyebrows steepled. "Are you saying you had our genetic profiles run? To see whether we can have Corps-certified babies?"

"Yes."

"Oh. Um. Can I ask why?"

"Well, because—well, I thought—look, I'm not trying to rush you,

Liz. I know things might change, I know you might not want me by the time we finish our training. We'll both be interning soon enough. But I love you, Elizabeth Montoya, and now we know—"

"What's all this got to do with genetics? Alfred Bester, I love you, too. And you damn well know I'm going to be with you when we finish our training. But I'll be damned if I need the Corps' permission to make babies with you, if that's what I want."

"I—Liz, I understand your feeling about it, but we have to be realistic, right? And anyway, this is perfect! There's no way they can object now."

She looked as if she was going to argue more with him, but then her face cleared, she shrugged, and she kissed him again. She drew back, comets dancing in her eyes. "You do love me, don't you? You wouldn't have checked if you didn't. I'm sorry, Al. I feel so close to you, sometimes I forget that we grew up in such different worlds. This means a lot to you."

He nodded solemnly. She mussed his hair and then kissed him once more, a slow, languorous kiss that spoke more than words.

The virtue of a kiss, he had learned, was just that. In and of itself, it was no large thing; flesh pressing together, a somehow always-unanticipated tickle. But when he and Liz kissed, it was expression, an attempt to communicate the incommunicable. To show—with the care one took, with this or that slight inflection in the grammar of lip, cheek, tongue, chin—what lay in their hearts. For the first time he pitied—truly, deeply pitied—mundanes, who could never possibly know how powerful and deep a kiss could be, much less lovemaking.

No wonder they were mean. They were like he had been, without Liz. Unfinished, half-made things, angry because they understood they were missing something important, that other people had it—but never, never able to know it themselves.

"Let's go somewhere," she said, when they left. "Let's celebrate." But he felt it, in the kiss. He could no longer pretend that it was his imagination. Finally, something had gone wrong.

A year ago, that would have been enough for him. He would have cut his losses, as he had the loss of Cadre Prime, of Bey, of Emory and the rest. But he could no longer imagine life without Liz Montoya. He couldn't see his future without her eyes, her smile, her soul near his.

She was covering it for his sake, but the genetic matching bothered her, and it bothered other things in her he had been trying to ignore. Still, this time, he couldn't give up. He had to know what was coming between them. Because he had no doubt that she loved him. He could

feel her affections like a fixed star. Couldn't he? Or had he become that big a fool?

"A celebration it is," he said softly.

He took her hand across the table and studied her candlelit face. "I thought the news would make you happy."

She smiled, but it seemed a little forced. There was a rhythm to their communication—at certain times, they would settle for words; at others, they would share all of themselves. The last was so powerful it couldn't be borne continuously. The cycle was necessary, but sometimes it was frustrating not to know exactly what she was thinking.

Yet he would never violate their trust; he would wait for the invitation. It was like lovemaking—it had to happen by mutual consent and in mutual delight, or not at all.

"I was happy, Alfie. I am. It's just that—it bothers me that we had to check at all. That you felt we had to. This is *us* we're talking about. It's our lives. Why should anyone else even have a say?"

"It's the way it is," he said. "And, our feelings aside, it's the way it ought to be. I love you, Liz, and you are the most important person in the world to me. But the world is bigger than we are, and there are things more important than the two of us. I know it in my heart, and you do, too."

"I know you believe that, Alfie. I can feel it. And I respect it because I love you. But there are some things I just can't accept. This is one of them. I'm happy we can get married when we want to—and someday I do want to marry you, Alfred Bester, I do. You know I do. It just upsets me that it isn't our choice."

"It is now. So why are you still upset about it?"

She shrugged. "I guess I'm not. Maybe I can't believe that we were so lucky. Maybe, deep down, I was so worried I still don't believe it."

"I know that feeling," Al said. "I have it every time you look at me. Every time I touch your hand."

"Careful, Alfie. You have to stay the sensible one, remember? You are my axis. Without you, I think I would fly off into space."

"And without you, I would be a cold, dead planet. No life, no heat"

"Let's get out of here. I want to go for a walk."

They paid their bill and left the restaurant. They had passes for the whole night—hard to get—and they tripped up and down the streets and lanes of Geneva. They decided to go on an impromptu tour of churches and bars—one church, one bar, one church, two bars. Al was careful; he had learned that drunkenness was not for him, even with Liz. Alcohol

took his control. He felt out of control enough when he was with Liz, but in a giddy, wonderful way. Add too much strong drink, and it was like *he* was flying off into space. Liz was right—one of them had to keep one foot on the ground, and it was natural for it to be him.

But it was hard, so hard with her. He wanted to lose himself in her, enter the bright blaze that lived in her breast, even if it should consume them both.

They found themselves in a park, on a hill overlooking the lights of the city. Teeptown wasn't even visible, though the topaz immensity of EarthDome was. They sat on the hill and watched starships land at Port Thiessen. They talked about the universe.

"Mars, that's where I'd like to go," Liz said. "And after that, Kalevala. They say the wind there smells like a thunderstorm all the time, that there is always lightning in the upper atmosphere, like burning spiderwebs. I want to see it all. Narn. Centauri Prime."

"We will. Once we're Psi Cops we can put in for transfers. If we're married, they might even assign us together. Even if they don't, we'll be able to take our vacations together, with the jumpgate time we earn. We can go anywhere. Anywhere, as long as we're together."

She wrapped her arms tighter about him, and their languid comfort suddenly grew more electric. She began kissing him, insistent.

"Not here," he managed. "This is a park—"

"We don't have enough time as it is. Neither of us has any leave for three more months."

"I can sneak in to your dorm, when your roommate is out—"

"I hate doing it there, in Teeptown. People can hear—"

"They wouldn't if you weren't so loud—"

You like me loud.

Ha. It hurts my ears and what—what are you—

She was on top of him, her long, pleated skirt settled around them like a collapsed parachute. She was working at his pants.

Better cover your ears, she told him.

They stayed there until dawn, and he watched her sleep again, loving each angle of her face with his gaze, tracing her jawline with his finger. *I love you,* he 'cast, and in her sleep she smiled.

A week later, they found time again. His roommate had leave, and they lay together twisted in his sheets. He knew how she felt, but he liked having her in his room. When they were away, in Geneva or farther afield, it was like a strange dream. Here, she seemed part of his life. It was comfortable, real. It helped him imagine their future together and make that real, too.

Tonight she was restless, more restless than she had been a week before. Her unease felt like a rotten spot in his own chest.

"Alfie—have you ever considered—have you ever considered not joining the Corps?"

"Not joining? I'm already in the Corps."

"Only until you finish the academy. Then you can choose."

"Choose what? The sleepers?"

"I know. It's just that—you can't see it, Alfie. You remember that movie you showed me? *Rashomon?*"

"Sure."

"You grew up in the Corps. I know you love it. But—you know, you *must* know—that they only showed you one side of the story, don't you? You know that there's a whole world out there that has nothing to do with the Corps."

"What happened, Liz? Did one of the instructors—"

"Nothing in particular happened, Alfie. It's just that I don't like being *controlled*, and the Corps is all about control. It's about—"

"It's about being telepaths," Al said. "Liz, that's what we are. There isn't any place out there for us. Nothing. The Corps is all there is, and I know there are some things about it you don't like, but—"

"How do you know that there's nothing else? How *would* you know? All of your life you've been taught one thing—that the Corps is the only way. Don't you see how that serves them?"

"What 'them'? There is no them. The Corps is *us,* Liz—"

"Oh yeah?" She sat up in bed. "When did 'we' ever get a vote about the breeding regulations? When did 'we' get any say whatsoever? When did *we* get to decide that we can never be lawyers, or stockbrokers, or politicians—"

"That's EA law, Liz."

"It's all the same, Alfie. It's all control, and we just do what they say."

"Are you saying that I don't have the brains to know I'm being controlled?" Al asked, suddenly feeling a little angry. "That I believe the Corps is best only because I've been told it is? Liz, I've *been* out there. I've seen what happens to our kind without the Corps. I saw—"

"You still saw only what they wanted you to see."

"No. I went after Brazg and Nielsson on my own. Nielsson was sick. He would have killed me. The whole underground is like that."

"So much from a single example! You were trying to take his freedom. Of course he—"

"Nielsson was a criminal. What freedom do you think a criminal should have?"

She looked down at him, her eyes ablaze, and he was suddenly, terribly frightened. Not *of* her, but *for* her. But then she bent and kissed his forehead. "I'm sorry, Alfie. I upset you, and I didn't mean to do that. It's just that sometimes I want you to see more than you do, just for a moment."

"And I want you to understand," Al said. "I know it's hard. They always told us in Cadre Prime that it was our job to make laters understand—"

"Is that all you're doing with me?" she said, flaring again. "Making me *understand*? Doing your duty to integrate laters into good Corps members?"

"You know better than that, Elizabeth Montoya. You know how I feel about you."

Her face had hardened, but now it relaxed again. "I do know." She sighed. "Sometimes I wish I didn't. You're the best thing that's ever happened to me, though. I love you." And she came back to him, and they spooned together perfectly. Soon she was asleep. It took Al longer. He felt a sort of breathlessness he never had before, a little like he had been punched in the solar plexus. Light-headed. And he didn't know what it meant.

Weeks passed, and Liz seemed to calm down. The final examinations were approaching, which meant that they saw less of each other, but when they did sneak an hour or most of a night, it was good. She still seemed a bit distracted, but then, so was he. In less than a month, the long ordeal of the academy would be over, and they would finally be Psi Cops—interns, anyway.

A week before finals, he met with her for lunch, and she asked him to meet her in her room that night.

He went, a little after nine. Liaisons like this were ambiguous territory—essentially everyone knew that students went to each other's rooms, and ostensibly it was forbidden. As long as you were careful, as long as appearances were maintained, no one really cared. Like a good parent, the Corps knew that sometimes it was best to be a little blind in one eye.

So sneaking in was a just ritual, though there were penalties for being caught. He might be forbidden to associate with Liz for a time; leave, always difficult to get, might be entirely restricted.

Al liked the window. It was traditional, and gave him a chance to hone his climbing skills.

He rapped on the pane. After an instant the curtain drew back, and there was Liz. She flashed him a halfhearted smile and let him in.

He saw immediately that something odd was going on. Clothes were folded neatly on the bed, and her backpack was out and already half full.

"What's up? Did you get leave?"

She paused and bit her lip, and he suddenly knew what she was going to tell him. That she had met someone else. That they were taking leave together.

No, she 'cast. *I don't have leave.*

Why are you packing?

I don't have leave. I am *leaving.*

That's not a good idea. I went AWOL once, remember—

She rushed suddenly into his arms, wrapped him up so tight it actually restricted his breathing. *Not AWOL, Al. I'm leaving. Leaving the Corps.* She pushed back a bit, so he could see her eyes, see that she was serious.

No you aren't. You're just upset about something. You aren't thinking straight. You're afraid of the exams—

Yes. I'm afraid I'll pass them. I checked, Al. No one who passed the exams ever left the Corps.

Of course not. Why would they?

Some tried. They were sent to the rehab centers. I'm going now, before someone picks up on how I feel, before they send me *there.*

He could feel her heart ticking against him. He couldn't feel his own at all. It was very strange.

Liz, I love you.

And I love you, Al. That's why I'm asking you—I'm begging you—come with me. We can be together. Not when we get leave, but all the time. We can do everything we said we were going to do, and more. We can be free.

We would be criminals, Liz. The same criminals we've been trained to hunt.

Right. We know all of the tricks. They'd never catch us. And we could go to the outer worlds, where they don't care, where the Corps doesn't reach.

"My God," he whispered. He couldn't stand. He sat on the bed next to her.

"I'm doing it, Al. I have to, and I want you to understand. I want you with me. But if I stay here I'll wither. I'll suffocate. You are the only reason I have to stay, and if I do it, I'll end up hating you. I don't want to hate you."

He put his head in his hands. He couldn't think.

"Just—wait a few more days. Give me time to think."

"No. Al, if I give you time to think, you'll never go. Right now, deep down, you know this is right. I can feel it. You know this is the best thing

for us. For you. What has the Corps ever given you but pain? You think you belong, but when have you ever belonged?"

"Only to you," he murmured. "Only you and Bey ever made me feel that way."

"You see? For once in your life, Al, act from your heart. From the passion I know you have in you."

"You can't ask this of me. It's too much."

"I know. But I have to. If I didn't love you so much, I would have just gone. But I do, so I had to see you." She took his chin in her fingers. "I want you to go, now. I want you to meet me where we made love, in the park, at midnight. If you don't, I'll never see you again. It's the way it has to be."

He wandered, trying to think. Past the statue of William Karges, into the cadre quad, where he hadn't been in years. Without ever consciously deciding to, he found himself at the base of the oak, the one he had spent so much time trying to climb.

He could reach the lowest branch now. He didn't have to jump for it. He leaned against the bark, feeling its familiar roughness, like an old friend.

In a way, when he had lived here, the tree had been his only friend. The kids and the cadre had never been, and the adults he had imagined as caring for him had been the same Grins who punished him so terribly. Only the tree had been the same, day in and day out, always challenging him to climb higher, never changing the rules. Like the Corps itself.

He swung himself up onto the branch and began to climb.

The rules *had* changed. He was bigger. The stretches and gaps in the branches that had once been such a problem weren't impediments at all anymore. He kept going, effortlessly, past the high-water mark of his youth. Up and up, to where he had never been, to where the branches were narrow, to where he could feel the tree actually swaying with his weight, and the limbs themselves trembled with the effort of supporting him.

And he could see the stars above, those same stars in which he had seen the faces of his parents, the stars he and Liz had dreamed of seeing much closer, together.

Yes, the rules had changed, hadn't they? Bey, and now Liz. And *he* had changed.

He sat in those new and dangerous branches for a long while, thinking, playing futures in his mind, like vids. Dangerous, uncertain futures. Futures with rules yet to be defined.

* * *

She rushed into his arms with a gasp, crushed his lips with her own, and they swayed together on the hilltop like saplings twining together for strength.

"I knew you would come," she said, breathlessly. Her face was shining, the fire in her burning brighter than he had ever seen it. In that instant, he loved her more than he ever had, more than he even knew he could.

And in that instant, too, she knew. He felt her body stiffen, and now he had to grip her harder, because if she ran it would only be worse. He expected her to fight. He wanted her to.

But she didn't. She just went dead in his arms. Her mind went away from him, shuttered behind bars and doors he hadn't felt since they had been together.

When the cops came out of the trees and took her away, she never even looked at him. She just stared at the ground.

He stayed where he was, rooted by the ghost of their last embrace, savoring it.

"Are you okay?" He looked up to see one of the cops. It was Van Ark, the old fellow from the West End precinct. His dark face was gathered with concern. "You did the right thing, Mr. Bester. I know it must have been hard for you."

Al nodded wordlessly.

"Give you a lift back to the dorms?"

"Sure."

"Don't worry about her. She'll be okay. They do a good job at the reeducation camps. Some day she'll even thank you."

"I know."

"You did the right thing."

"I know. 'The Corps is mother, the Corps is father.' " Al looked into the Psi Cop's eyes. "It's the only thing we really have, isn't it? The only permanent thing. The only thing that won't die or abandon us." He didn't know why he should explain this to Van Ark. Because the other would understand, he supposed.

Van Ark nodded and patted him on the shoulder. "Let's go home," he said.

Al nodded. He did have exams to study for.

PART 3

Synthesis

1

Thoughts slipped about him like eels through dark waters, mostly tail and fin, but here and there the occasional glimmer of an eye, the flash of moray teeth. He wasn't among friends, which meant he was surely in the right place, after all.

That was good, because coming here had been a big risk, and justifying it to the travel authority had been no easy matter, especially to follow a trail that had reached an official dead end three months ago.

Blips had gotten good at making the sorts of journeys most peoples had abandoned in their respective stone ages. Horseback. Raft. In this case, a Polynesian double canoe. A reproduction, incorporating almost no metal. A satellite would have actually had to look for it in order to find it.

Three months ago, no one had thought to do that, himself included. Jonathan Stone, rogue telepath, had gone once again on the hunt lists with the designation "whereabouts unknown." Most had more or less forgotten about him.

Alfred Bester had not. Alfred Bester hated to look foolish. Most of all, he hated to lose. It chilled him to think how close he had come, this time. Another day, and it would have been too late.

It might still be, he reminded himself.

He smiled pleasantly at the dark faces, often tattooed, watching him stroll up the beach. They did not smile back, made no attempt to hide their objection to his presence. Most had probably figured out why he was here. Some would act. Even now, someone was probably realizing that his tel-phone wasn't working, that the local system had been shut down. At the same time, they were also noticing that he was a lone Psi Cop, without backup.

Yes, he was the gardener, turning over the rock, and soon enough things would start to squirm out.

Soon enough they did, and in doing so did him a favor. All of their scuttling about, just beyond his sight, actually directed him to the right

building. He knew for certain that it was the right place when six large men planted themselves on the porch, between him and the door.

"Hello," he said, pleasantly. "How are you gentlemen today?"

They were all dark, dressed in sarongs or shorts. All but two had facial tattoos.

"Pretty well," one of them answered, his New Zealander lilt melodic despite the subtle hint of danger built into it. "And you?"

"I'm just great. Salt air, a beautiful beach—"

"Private property," one of the men noted.

"Government business," Al returned, pleasantly. "I'm looking for a fellow named Jonathan Stone."

"I had a cousin named Jonathan Stone," one of the men volunteered. "He went down at sea, some time ago. Kind of a crazy fellow, him."

"He's in there, isn't he?"

"Nah. Or he's everywhere, I guess, depending on your religion."

"My religion says he's alive, right in there," Al maintained, nodding his chin up behind them.

"What's your religion say about an afterlife?" another of the men growled.

"Tell him to come out," Al said. "Tell him to come out, and I won't have to call in the choppers."

"You don't want to do that. All kinds of political trouble there."

"Yes, I know. In fact, I think if choppers come in, at least one faction here will open fire. That means the EA troops will move in—something they've been looking for an excuse to do for a long time. That's why I walked in here alone—I want to spare everyone that. Now, somebody here might take it into their head to do me harm. I can stop a few of you, maybe most of you, but in the end you'll probably get me. I understand that. I'm here because I'm betting you have more sense than to do it, and because I think your cousin Jonathan has enough regard for his family and his people not to put them through it. He made a brave run. He almost beat me. But I'm the best there is, and I won. It's time for him to acknowledge that."

"What's your name, Mr. Best-That-There-Is?"

"Alfred Bester."

"Bester-That-There-Is," the speaker said. "Okay. I'll go with you."

"Mr. Stone?"

"Yep."

"Don't do it, Johnny," another argued.

"Nah, he's right. If they'd never caught on, that would've been one thing. But he got me fair and square." He stood up.

"Do you have anything you'd like to bring?"

"Nope. Don't insult my intelligence, okay? I know I'm going to a reeducation center. I've seen them. So let's not pretend you're taking me off to summer camp."

Al shrugged. "Very well."

They started back up the shore, walking up the long spit of land. Stone kept stopping to gaze out at the sea.

"Do you mind?" he said. "I didn't give you a hard time. Do you mind if I look, for a moment? Might be a while before I see the ocean again."

"Go ahead."

Stone set his eyes on the distant horizon. "My ancestors—some of 'em, anyway—sailed thousands of miles out there, without compasses, without astrolabes or computers or satellites—well, except the moon, of course. Just guts and the stars and dead reckoning."

"You did it, too," Al said.

"Oh—yeah, knowing it could be done. That's not the same as sailing out into an unknown ocean, not knowing if anything at all is there, with only so much in the way of supplies . . ." He smiled faintly. "I always wanted to do that, out where that kind of thing is still done, in the stars. But they wouldn't let me, you know, when they found out what I was. They wouldn't let me be."

"That's life," Al told him. "We can't have everything we want. I'd like to be taller. I'm not."

"Yeah."

"Anyway, you could've joined the Corps. That can take you out there, to the stars."

"Oh, yeah. As a cop, or a hunter, or the pet magician of some general. That's not what I wanted." He looked at Al. "Why do you do it, Bester-That-There-Is? What did the underground ever do to you?"

"Killed my parents. Ruined everyone I ever loved. Not a lot, I guess, but I can be as petty as the next man about having my life ruined. The underground is a lie, and a destructive lie. The Corps is the truth. It may not be perfect, but it is the truth."

Stone shrugged. "Guess I'll see how truthful it is in the camps. Are you gonna check on me a year from now and see if I'm still alive? See if they beat me to death or drove me crazy with punishment scans? Or are you just going to turn me in and forget I ever existed?"

"I'm just doing my job."

Stone laughed. "Yeah. Okay, I'm ready to go."

Al caught something then, a bitter sardonic humor. He looked sharply at Stone. Stone saw that he knew and smiled.

"Got you, Mr. Bester-That-There-Is. You stopped to catch a minnow and the whale got away. Too late now."

Al blinked at him, then hit him with a scan. He should have done it to start with, even though it was illegal. Sure, they could never use it in court, but—

Stone fought him, tooth and nail. He was strong, maybe a P10. They stood on that headland by the sea, a storm whipping up. The sea and sky bled together, the earth thinned to nothing. Shark-headed beasts and bird-headed men stormed his defenses.

Shaman battles, Al remembered.

It lasted a long time. Stone was clever and determined, but in the end Al was stronger and more skilled. The big man slumped to the earth, unconscious, and Al had three things from him that were important. A name, a signature, a destination.

He turned and ran back up the beach as fast as he could, PPG drawn.

"Get the hell out of my way!" he snarled, as he came back up to the house. They didn't try to stop him; they stepped aside and let him go in.

He didn't find much—a blanket, the faint residue of a telepathic signature, the same one Stone had been carrying in his mind.

He should have known Stone had given up too easily, that he was sacrificing himself for someone else. He should have known there was someone else in that damned canoe.

The biggest fish of all. The leader of the underground since 2190, for more than thirty years. Stephen Walters.

Al had missed him. But he had his signature, and he knew where he was going.

This hunt was just beginning.

2

"Tell me why I should give you this assignment, Mr. Bester," station chief Niles Ramanashah said mildly.

Bester lifted his chin a tad. "Sir. Because I'm the one who found the lead, sir."

"We are all one in the Corps, Mr. Bester. Didn't you know that? If it's a matter of pride—if you just want to prove you can catch this guy, that's not reason enough."

"No, sir, that's not it. I'm the one who found the lead, so I'm the one who has his scent. This isn't just any Blip—this is Stephen Walters, and I think we'll need every edge we can get. If you check my records—"

"Oh, I've checked your records, Mr. Bester, no need to worry on that account. And of course your reputation precedes you. You've made quite the name for yourself for such a young man. You're—what? Thirty?"

"Thirty-three, sir."

Ramanashah glanced at the display on his desk. "Interned with Olivia Vong, where you showed outstanding courage under fire. First assigned to the Saint Petersburg office—you made lieutenant in just under four years. I won't even bother to read your list of arrests." He paused. "There are some notes. A number of civilian-related incidents."

"Only two official complaints, sir, and in both cases the individuals were eventually convicted of aiding and abetting, so of course they kicked and screamed."

"I can see that, Mr. Bester. Most of the worrisome comments are from your superiors, in particular Geoffrey de Vries, who had you transferred from his command. You seem to have made him nervous."

"Commander de Vries is a good man, sir."

"Indeed. But perhaps a little timid?"

"I can't speak to that."

"Huh. Mr. Bester, if I send you to Mars, it will be me who takes the heat for any incidents there. I am not timid, and to be perfectly candid, I have little sympathy for mundanes who get in the way of a Psi Corps

investigation. On the other hand, the Corps itself has taken some political heat in the last few years, so for the good of us all, there is some need for a certain—decorum. Do you follow me?"

"Yes, sir. Does that mean—"

I have another piece of information, Mr. Bester, one not written in your record. Director Johnston—he doesn't like you. Do you know why?

Not exactly, sir. Something about his predecessor taking an interest in me.

Well, you are something of a loose cannon, Mr. Bester, but I haven't seen a more gifted young officer in a long time. And, as you say, you are the logical man for the job. I'm having you transferred to my station immediately. The director won't like it, but then that isn't your concern. I'll detach you to Mars as soon as that's done. Pack warm, Mr. Bester. I hear Mars can get a bit chilly.

"Holy mother of God," Erik Andersen choked out, closing his eyes. The hull of the lander had begun to hum in a tone that couldn't possibly be good, and the distant rusty curve of the planet was flattening with uncomfortable speed. "Doesn't this bother you at all, Al?"

"It's not the fall that worries me," Al replied. "It's that quick stop at the bottom."

But Al had to admit he wasn't exactly thrilled. He had never been afraid of flying, but then he had never dropped like a stone for hundreds of miles. Over the last few days he had watched Mars go from marble to baseball to basketball, but it had always been *out*.

Now it was *down*, with a vengeance. He remembered Teacher Roberts' long-ago lesson about the primate origins of human sensibilities. He could appreciate that ancient tree-dweller in him right now—it was *bad, bad, bad* to be up this high without a single branch to hold on to.

Nope, this wasn't flying, it was falling.

It got worse, of course, as they hit the unpredictable lower atmosphere, which was thickened, wetted, and—it seemed—angered by terraforming. Just as you were telling yourself that you were safe in the belly of superior technology—that such landings were routine—your gut would drop, inertia would yank you in some unnatural direction, and it would seem thoroughly implausible that survival was even remotely possible.

He kept his breathing steady and let Erik do the moaning for both of them. Being frightened sometimes had utility, sometimes not. He was in someone else's hands and would either survive or not. Nothing his backbrain screamed at him would change that.

Still, when the ship was finally motionless, his body felt like a wet

towel, snapped too many times by some kid in a locker room. He deboarded on wobbling legs and queued up for the security check.

There was a woman in line in front of him with a little boy in tow. The boy, fidgety—and seemingly unperturbed by the landing—looked around restlessly before noticing Al and Erik behind him. When he did, he started tugging on the woman's sleeve. "Mommy," he said, "there's one a them mindfrickers behind us."

The woman turned, her face darkening from copper to dark brown. "Jeremy!" she snapped. "I never want to hear you use that kind of language again." She looked apologetically at Al. "I don't know where kids hear these things, I honestly don't. I'm very sorry."

She was lying, and Al knew it. He smiled. "Well, you can only control what they get at home," he replied.

"I try to teach him the right things," she said, her voice a bit defensive. She knelt down. "Look, Jeremy, I want you to apologize to the nice man. He's Psi Cop—one of the good kind of telepaths. He helps protect us from the bad ones."

The boy peeked around her leg.

"Hello, Jeremy," Al said. "My name is Mr. Bester. As your mother said, I'm the *good* kind of telepath."

"Oh." The boy reached uncertainly for his hand. "How come you wear gloves?"

"Because if I didn't, I might accidentally burn your brain all up," Al said, still smiling. "We wouldn't want that to happen to such a nice little boy." He looked back at the mother, whose face had done an odd about-face and was now rather pale. "I believe," he said, pointing beyond her, "that the customs man is waving you over." He cast a knowing look at her bag. "May I help you with your luggage?"

He hadn't scanned her, so her bright flicker of panic was all the more amusing. Everyone had something to hide, some dirty little exception they imagined themselves entitled to.

"No, thank you," she said quickly.

Al shrugged. But as she left, he whispered a subtle, subliminal suggestion to the customs agent that he search her bags with more than usual thoroughness.

"You ever get used to that crap?" Erik asked.

"What crap?"

"The bigotry. The hatred."

Al shrugged. "The dinosaurs had their moment, too," he observed.

"Meaning?"

"Nothing, Erik, nothing. Look, now it's our turn."

A man and woman in MetaPol uniforms greeted them as they left

the terminal. One—a tall blond with a prematurely receded hairline—stepped up. "Welcome to Mars. I'm Faren McCleod, and this is my associate Roxanna Durst." He indicated a thick-boned young woman with handsome cheekbones and green eyes.

"Pleased to meet you both. I'm Alfred Bester, and this is Erik Andersen."

Polite bows went around.

"Well, once we get your luggage, we can move on to the briefing, if the both of you are up to it."

"Absolutely," Al said. "I'm eager to get started."

Judit Uhl settled into her chair with a look of contemptuous amusement playing across her somewhat catlike face. "So you know that *the* Stephen Walters is on Mars, eh, Mr. Bester? On Mars. On the planet somewhere. And that is the extent of your knowledge?"

"Almost. I will recognize my quarry, of course, by his signature. But I've studied Walters. If he's here, he's not alone. In fact, it's a good bet that there is a large, highly organized resistance cell on the planet somewhere. That should be hard to hide, now that we know it's here. Am I wrong?"

Uhl smiled with an obviously false sincerity. "Yes, Mr. Bester, you are. And Geneva was aware of that when they sent you."

"I'm sure they weren't, or they wouldn't have sent me."

"Let me explain something to you, Mr. Bester," Uhl said, motioning toward the window. She came out of her seat as if propelled by springs and clattered to the view with staccato grace. Al rose and joined her in regarding the landscape.

What looked like crushed brick spread to a horizon of low mountains. They were looking east, and a small, sickly looking sun was just starting to crawl through a long Martian day. The sky was a dark salmon—not that different from the land—bordered on the northern horizon by dirty red and black lenses that Al assumed were clouds.

"Looks forbidding, doesn't it? It is, but people are not easily forbidden, Mr. Bester. What we have here is a planet with more land area than Earth. To keep watch on that, we have forty trained Psi Cops. Forty."

"So few?" Al said. "Still, no matter how much land area there is here, the situation can hardly be the same as on Earth. After all, even the air isn't free here. Your population is more constrained, by necessity. The places they can arrive and leave from are few in number—the spaceports, the city air locks—"

She interrupted him with a small laugh. "Ah. Mr. Bester, it must be wonderful to live in such a dreamworld. Ships land on Mars every day, all

over the place, unmonitored and uncontrolled. We have three large cities, two hundred and thirty experiment and mining stations—most privately owned—and about three thousand registered hinterland colonists. Add to that at least as many unregistered squatters—religious extremists, utopianists, criminals, rugged individualists, cowboy-and-Indian wannabes. Oh, EarthForce stops transports and mining vehicles which try to slip things on and off planet without paying taxes and tariffs—but don't imagine we have the same kind of satellite net that Earth does, or the same number of ships. Maybe a tenth of such illegal activity is discovered.

"In other words, Mr. Bester, planetary security stinks, and no one really gives a damn. Marsies certainly don't. Marsies *like* freedom. They *like* the sodbusters, even the squatters. People leave the cities and join them all the time, some with permits, some without. The fact is, settlement permits are so cheap, the government mostly looks the other way if you don't have one. Mars is trying to attract settlers, not scare them off.

"So your rogues could be anywhere out there. Anywhere. Unless you have some idea where you want to start looking, you've wasted your time and the Corps' money." She waved dismissively at the landscape and returned to her chair.

"Well. I presume that you have at least a list I can start with, and transportation."

She nodded, smirking, and pushed a stylus tablet across the desk toward him.

Erik's eyes widened as he stared at the list.

"There's a hundred and fifty sites listed here. Scattered all over Mars. This will take forever."

"Yes," Al said, scrolling through another database.

"I guess we can narrow it down, some. I mean, the Blips are probably disguised as the last group we would imagine, right? Like maybe the Adamists, or some other 'Human purist' organization."

"Maybe. But there are still too many of them, and the local office won't give us more than two or three men at a time. Suppose we do stumble on them, what then? We vanish into the Martian desert, you and I. And when we start searching, word will get out, so they'll be ready. No, we have to pick the right spot the first time out, or get there darn quickly."

"And how do we do that?"

Al leaned back on his chair, looking around their cramped quarters. "Uhl talks as if there are hundreds of thousands of independent settlements out there. But there can't be."

"What do you mean? Here they are." He waved the tablet.

"They aren't independent. They can't produce everything they need, and they certainly can't produce everything that they want. Have you ever studied central place theory?"

"Not that I know of."

"Human beings don't settle randomly. Central place theory is one way of modeling where people live. Here, let me show you something." He cleared the desktop and then took up a stylus. Erik leaned over to watch as Al drew a large dot and filled it in. "This is a city—let's call it *Metro*." He labeled it. "Cities produce finished products. Computers. Phones. Stylish clothing. Art objects. Processed food. Entertainment. Anything you need or desire, you can probably find in the city."

"Okay. But all of the raw materials for that stuff have to come from somewhere else, right?"

"Yes, but leave that aside for a moment. Just think like a consumer. In the universe of things you might want or need, the city is the center."

"Okay."

"Now." He drew four smaller dots in a circle around Metro, and labeled them clockwise—*1, 2, 3, 4.* All were two inches from Metro, and about two inches from each other. "These we'll call towns. Each is about the same size. Let's pretend each produces something different—this one iron ore, this one corn, this one cotton textiles. You live in town 1, which grows wheat. So if you want bread, you just stay home. What if you want the iron tools produced in town 2 or the textiles produced in town 4?"

Erik studied the diagram. "Metro," he said.

"Why?"

"Towns 2 and 4 are no farther than Metro, but they are in opposite directions. The other towns are even farther. I can make one trip to the big city and get everything, plus catch a show and eat a fancy meal."

"Right. Now, in reality, you can still get lots of goods and services in your hometown—it's small, but it still has grocery stores, shopping centers, and so forth. Now let's add even smaller places." He quickly drew a series of even smaller dots around the town markers, four around each. "Those are villages. They have fewer goods and services than the towns because they are smaller."

"I get it. I go to town now and then for things I can't get in my own village, and I go to Metro for the things I can't get in town."

"Yes. And if we add even smaller dots—call them hamlets—and smaller ones—homesteads— You get the picture. If you live in a hamlet you go to the village a lot, to the town less often, to Metro, which is farthest away, only when it's really necessary." He tapped the tablet.

"These are all hamlets and homesteads. But each one is connected through a hierarchy of larger and larger places to Metro—or MarsDome 1. And MarsDome 1, in turn, is connected to an even more cosmopolitan place, Earth.

"In fact, on Mars, this model works even better.

"Consider the things each of these hamlets absolutely must have: the equipment to produce and maintain a breathable atmosphere and drinking water, and the parts and tools to maintain the equipment, for starters. Eventually, all of that must come from MarsDome 1 or Earth. Heavy metals aren't readily available here. Food is hard to produce in quantity. Maybe some of that comes directly from Earth in smuggler's ships, but the cost would be enormous, made even worse by its illegality. No, there must be a tight network of trade, and it all leads back here, to the Metro, the central place."

"I get it. The trail to wherever the underground is hiding—"

"—Starts right here. We don't start with that list of settlements. We start in Syria Planum and work our way out."

"Hold it. What about Olympus Mons and Solis Planum? Couldn't one of those be 'Metro'?"

"Sure. Three central places on Mars, which still makes things pretty simple. I guess we could throw in Xanthe Terra, too, though it's too small and young to really compete with the big three. But we start here, because this is where we are."

"So how do we find the outward trail?"

"Think of this. These people in the hinterlands—what do they *trade* for machined parts, for food, for new molecular filters, for power cells? There isn't that much out there, is there? I've checked into it; most do some sort of mining or local processing—iron, aluminum, various rare earths. Others produce curiosities—the Mennonites make polished hematite bowls that are sold back on Earth to the very rich, for instance. But it's hard going, very hard. Any valuable commodity you possessed would have to be used, simply to survive. Now, think. What commodity would the underground have to trade that would set them apart from everyone else?"

Erik got it. His eyes shone with understanding and admiration. "Illegal scans."

"Of course. So we don't need a list of these hamlets at all. What we need is a list of persons in Syria Planum who need Psi services that Corps members are forbidden to provide." He grinned evilly. "Which, I might add, I've nearly finished."

"I am in awe, Mr. Bester."

"I appreciate the compliment, but it's only common sense. And Erik?"

"Yes?"

"We won't mention this to the local office right away?"

"Surely you don't think—"

"I'd rather leave nothing to chance," Al said, dryly. "Anyone who actually lives on Mars should know what we just discussed without even having to think it through. Uhl didn't even bother to point it out to me. For whatever reason, she wants us to fail—or at the very least have a difficult time."

"Okay. Where do we start?"

"Shadiest element first. There's a certain man who seems to win an awful lot at poker."

"Look at that." Erik grunted, pointing across the crowded casino. "It's McCleod and Durst."

"Yes," Al agreed, spotting the two local Psi Cops. "And that's our man Cheo they're questioning. Very interesting. They're one step ahead of us."

"But they aren't sharing. Want me to eavesdrop?"

"I'll do it. You keep us quiet."

"Gotcha."

Al focused his vision on Cheo, an overweight fellow with rather nondescript features and hair coiffed in intricately bound braids. He was sitting at a card table that everyone else seemed to have deserted—there were three other hands, in any event, all lying discarded. The hundred or so minds in the casino created a palpable murk, but as Al narrowed his attention, he began feeling the cadence of the man's speech. When normals spoke aloud, their surface thoughts—that is, what they were saying—were strong enough to detect within line of sight without scanning.

. . . know nothin', he was saying. With a stubborn expression, he then listened to the reply. It seemed to be Durst doing the talking; he could make out her fiercely determined features. Al couldn't listen in on her, though. She would almost certainly notice if he did. And at this distance, without a direct scan, he couldn't get the "reflection" of her words off of Cheo's mind, only a sort of an impression. It was like hearing only half of a phone conversation.

I'm just a lucky son of a bitch, la, Cheo said. *I don't need a 'sicky to win, so I don't keep one around. Besides, what's it to you guys? You never cared about the 'sickies before . . .*

Al suddenly felt as if nails had been driven into his head, many of them. He gasped and clutched at his temples, closing his eyes.

That shouldn't have helped, but it did. Immediately the pain dimmed, which, after an instant, he realized meant that the brutal scan hadn't been aimed at him, but at Cheo, and that Cheo's pain had just run up his connection. He resolutely forced his eyes open, renewing the contact. Cheo was jerking in his chair as if being electrocuted, and the patrons of the casino, already keeping a respectful distance, quickly drew even farther away.

Al got it when they got it. A name, an address, the sketchy glyph of an appearance.

"Erik. Let's go. Now!"

"You okay?"

"Yes. Come on, before they notice us."

"So this is one of the 'towns' we're going to?"

Al grimaced, hand on his forehead. He felt as if he had a monstrous hangover. The train gave little sense of motion other than acceleration, but when he opened his eyes it was to a chalky red landscape hurtling by with nauseating speed. "Yes. A second-tier settlement. The next step on the trail."

"What if Durst and McCleod beat us?"

Al shrugged. "I'm not sure what would get them there faster than a train. A hoverjet, maybe, but there aren't many of those. Helicopters don't work here, obviously. An ATV would be far too slow. My guess is that they're on this train or will be on the next."

"This is crazy, working against other cops."

"I agree. But we don't know what's going on. They did an illegal scan—a hard, deep, obvious one—on Cheo in full public view. If you did something like that on Earth—anywhere—you'd be up on charges, at the very least. It seems that the Psi Corps enjoys a somewhat different status here. Cheo also implied that the cops don't normally care about Blips."

"You think they're in with them? That the cops here are traitors, helping the underground?"

Al held up his hands in a shrug. "Something's going on. They might just want us out of the loop so they can grab credit for the bust themselves."

"Durst and McCleod, you mean."

"Or the local office. If they get credit for a successful hunt without the aid of hotshot outsiders, they might be able to resist future investigators being sent here."

"But even that implies they have something to hide."

"You catch on quick, Mr. Andersen."

They got off the tube car in New Harappa, a settlement of about six hundred people. A billion or so years ago, when Mars was young and wet, rushing water had carved a canyon almost a quarter of a mile deep. When the water flew off into space as ions, or locked itself beneath the planet's skin, the fossil of that flood remained. Its narrow, almost sheer walls served as a reminder of how active the planet once was, and how silent and still it had been ever since.

Until now, of course. Today the polar ice caps were being melted, and carefully engineered microorganisms bred and metabolized in soils that made Antarctic permafrost seem hospitable. The canyon had been roofed over with the same macromolecular glass that the domes were made of. Its soil had been chewed by machines, cut with organic compounds, seeded with bacteria, planted in peanuts, potatoes, and vetch. Wells had been drilled to find where the last of the once plentiful water rested in crystalline form. The settlement would then quicken it to liquid and vapor and component gases.

The town perched above them, vertical, dug into the red cliffs, built on ledges. Exotic and striking, it seemed Middle Eastern, somehow, or like the ancient pueblos of North America that Al had only seen in photographs.

He didn't have time to gawk, however. "We want to go there," he said, pointing to a spot halfway up the right side. "There should be an elevator down this walkway."

At first glance, New Harappa seemed to be laid out like a termite mound, a chaos of tunnels, but in reality it wasn't that hard to navigate. Elevators and steep-angled stairs had street names—sidewalks running along the cliff face were avenues. All were glassed in—Marsies had a well-earned historical mistrust of canyon roofs and domes.

Al and Erik rode an elevator up Easy Street to Lowell Avenue and went quickly from there toward number 12, the address Durst and McCleod had torn from Cheo's mind.

Al led the way, with Erik a few paces behind. He slowed when he identified number 11 and was just turning to give Erik final instructions when a bolt of superheated helium scorched past his ear.

3

Al's reflexes took him down in a shoulder roll. His PPG was already out, and he brought it whining to life, its muzzle scenting wildly for a target as he spun on his stomach to face the direction of the attack. A second shot tortured another protest from the air, and then a third. Al felt a mind wishing to kill him, pointed at it, fired the PPG.

Erik was on his belly, shooting. Al's brain was meanwhile assembling the whole picture from fast-motion glimpses. Erik had fired first, over Al's shoulder, at a man stepping into the avenue from a recessed foyer. Probably Erik had actually felt him—the Swede was good at that, scenting impending mayhem. It was Erik's shot that had galvanized Al into his evasive maneuver, and it was a good thing—because there really were people behind them.

Al and Erik were caught in a cross fire, two behind them, two in front still on their feet, and one down from Erik's first strike.

Al's first shot hit the shoulder of one of those coming up behind them. The fellow staggered into the transparent avenue wall, and Al fired again. The burst of plasma hit the glass two feet in front of the man. Like the fluid it was, the PPG shot deformed a bit and slid on into him. Rapidly cooling, the helium was still hotter than the boiling point of lead, and the unfortunate fellow got it full in the face.

The other two were taking careful aim at Al.

I'm not here. He hit them with the glyph of the empty avenue, hard, and hoped they weren't teeps.

They weren't. They looked uniformly astonished, whipping their heads about.

Mundanes! Al shot one in the heart and the gun hand off of the other. He spun, came up in a crouch—

—and found himself confronting Erik's PPG.

Each took a step to the left, sweeping the corridor. All three on Erik's side were down.

"Keep me covered," Al said. The man whose hand he had shot off

was climbing to his feet, breath coming in hiccups. Al shot him in the back of the knee, then in the other. The bursts of plasma seared through tissue and tendon, scorching the bones beneath.

"You could have cuffed him," Erik noted.

"This is quicker. There may be more."

The first shooter had stepped from the foyer of apartment 12. Covered by Erik, PPG held in both hands, Al kicked the slightly open door with the side of his foot.

McCleod sat against the wall, one side of his uniform drenched in blood. He tried to raise one arm weakly—the one still clenching his side arm.

"Keep it down," Al growled.

"No, you put yours down."

It was Durst, to his left. He hadn't noticed her.

Al kept the weapon aimed. "Kill me, and my friend kills you. Probably I'll kill McCleod, if he isn't already dead. Why don't we just calm down and talk this over?"

"Because I don't trust you," Durst explained, tightly.

"You don't trust *me*? That's very funny, Ms. Durst. *I'm* just doing my job. I can't imagine what *you're* doing. Withholding information—"

"Not very well, it seems."

"Attempting to murder Mr. Andersen and myself."

"I've done no such thing."

"Please. Your men, then."

"You idiot. They aren't my men. Who do you think shot McCleod?"

"Not me, that's all I can be certain of," Al replied. "Drop your gun."

"No. I—"

Al hit her with a mindflash. She was almost ready for it and almost strong enough to resist. She even managed to finger the PPG contact, but too sluggishly to hit Al as he dropped straight to the floor. Erik was a whirlwind spinning past him. By the time Al got up, the younger cop had disarmed the stunned Durst.

"Now," Al said, smoothing out his uniform. "Where is Chandler?"

"There," Durst managed, pointing. Al followed her direction and saw a light-haired man sprawled on a couch.

"Dead?"

"No. Shocked out. Will you let me help McCleod?"

"Mr. Andersen, will you see to Mr. McCleod?"

"On it."

"So these men attacked you, then us, you say?"

"It would seem."

"Do you think we're safe for the moment? Don't block."

She didn't. "I think so." He didn't think she was good enough to fool him. She was telling the truth.

"Okay. I'm putting this up." He slid the PPG into its holster. "You're going to tell me what's going on, now—right?"

Durst nodded. "Right." She sat down heavily, rubbed her eyes with one hand, then rested her forehead on her fists and her elbows on her knees. She spoke to the floor.

"Things are different on Mars," she said. "It's a frontier. Things get rough. A lot of bad people end up here. Someone has to keep order."

"And that someone is you. That's fine. I have no objection to that."

"We're more respected here than on Earth. Marsies don't care much if we get a little rough, a little heavy-handed—as long as in the end we protect them from the bad guys."

"I'm with you so far. Sounds like a nice place, one I might come to like. So why are people shooting at *me*?" He plucked his shirt. "See? Same uniform."

"Because for Marsies, a lot of the bad guys are back on Earth. Earth sent you."

"Psi Corps sent me," Al corrected. "I'm sure you know the difference."

"Barsoom Autonomous doesn't, however."

"The terrorist organization?"

"Some are terrorists—most are businessmen, scientists, average citizens. Whatever you may have heard on Earth, most Marsies are in favor of independence. Most don't advocate violence, but you know how that goes."

"Those dead men outside weren't firing rhetoric at us."

"Or us," Durst snapped. "Because we were trying to find your rogue telepaths."

"Uh-huh. Tell me about that."

"There are Blips on Mars. Mostly we look the other way because they help the cause. They—"

"Wait. You just made a logical leap that I find hard to follow. Last I heard, Psi Corps had no position on Mars independence."

Durst nodded. "That is correct."

"But the local office does? Is that what you're saying?"

"I'm saying we're only effective here because people see we aren't *harming* that cause. Mr. Bester, there are only forty of us—"

"This song I've heard sung before. Is Uhl with Barsoom Autonomous?"

"Not officially."

"Which means 'yes.' Who else?"

"Most of her officers."

"But not you?"

"Sir, the Corps is mother and the Corps is father. McCleod and I were protecting the Corps."

"You wanted to find the underground before we did, because you knew if we waded through to them we would find all of this out."

"Yes, sir. And disgrace the Corps."

"Wrong. Uhl and anyone else who ignores a Blip for reasons of local politics has forgotten what their job is. The Corps would take pleasure in dealing with them, and setting an example. They deserve what they get."

"Sir, I think you might be surprised. My orders were explicit—locate the underground before you did and—ah, pacify it."

"But your orders were from Uhl."

"No, sir. Uhl probably tipped BA to ambush us here. We tried to hide our activities, but apparently we failed."

"You're talking nonsense. Geneva sent me, so your orders didn't come from there. If they didn't come from Geneva, and they didn't come from Uhl, who does that leave?"

"It leaves Department Sigma."

For a moment Al was stunned into silence. "Department Sigma?"

"Yes. McCleod and I were both placed here by the department."

"Can you verify that?"

"I think you know what a stupid question that is, Mr. Bester—if you'll pardon my saying so."

"What were you supposed to do when you found the underground cell?"

"Contact the department. They were going to send reinforcements."

"All the way from Earth?"

She averted her eyes and said nothing.

Oh, he thought. *So the rumors must be true.* Of a secret base on Mars, one which few even in the high command knew of. Even across interplanetary space, the director maintained a tight grip.

He nodded thoughtfully. "Mr. Andersen, how is Mr. McCleod?"

"He'll live, I think."

Al looked back at Durst. "Did you get anything out of him?" He motioned toward the unconscious telepath.

"Yes. He lives out here, but he goes into the city twice a week to get supplies for the underground and arrange contacts. He makes his money helping out gamblers, certain businessmen, and politicians. They rotate them in and out of here—it's his turn right now, but in another week he was going to switch with someone else."

"Does he know where the main base is?"

"Yes. But I can't get it out of him."

Bester quirked a sharkish grin. "Let me see what *I* can do," he whispered.

There was not, unfortunately, much left of Chandler when Al got through. Reeducation would be able to do something with him—possibly even return him to full sentience, make him a working human being. But however that turned out, he would never again be Thurston Chandler.

It upset Al more than he thought it would. Yes, the underground was misguided, and criminally so. Directly or indirectly they had cost him the only two people he had ever loved, and for that they would pay until they didn't exist anymore.

But still, they were his own kind. Still, they were telepaths. They should all be on the same side—the mundanes were the real enemy.

He brushed the unwelcome remorse off, treating it as a distraction.

"Here's the deal," he told Durst. "I know where the rogues are. You know how to contact the reinforcements we may need. I suggest we work together."

"And McCleod?"

"We put him in an infirmary. He can't travel."

She nodded reluctantly.

"Can we obtain an ATV, without the order going straight to Uhl?"

"I think so," Durst replied.

"Good. Because I'm ready to get this over with."

Night on Mars. A few high, thin ribbons of cloud frosted some of the stars, but most were almost as clear and sharp as the constellations seen from the vacuum. Phobos was the ghostly skull of a moon, dim, irregular. The smaller Deimos had sped around the horizon some hours earlier.

Durst was asleep, and Al confirmed it with a brief touch. REM sleep had a signature all its own, almost impossible to fake. Dreams drifted from her like vapor, but he ignored them.

"Why are you so hot for this one, Al? I mean, you have a reputation for busting rogues, but what you did to Chandler—you really want these guys, don't you?"

Al nodded. "When I was a kid—when I was just in the Minor Academy—I used to hang out around the West End precinct, check the hunt and capture lists. Underground leaders come and go, but there are a few—ever heard of Stephen Walters?"

"The Black Fox. The traitor Psi Cop."

"He was never actually a cop—he was in covert ops. Not even a P12. But of all the underground leaders, he's the only one who's survived from

before the purge of '89. It's all about him, Erik. If it weren't for Stephen Walters, the resistance would have died with Fiona and Matthew Dexter. It would have all been over thirty-three years ago. Just think what we could do if we weren't burdened with having to hunt our own kind—if we weren't divided. We were so close."

And Bey would still be alive, he added silently, *because there would have been no underground for him to sympathize with. And Liz would still be mine because she wouldn't have tried to go Blip, not without the underground out there, urging her, promising her something impossible . . .*

"So, yes," he went on, in a low voice, "I'm hot for this one. Walters has set the cause of the telepaths back a century. It's time for the legend of the Black Fox to end."

At Martian dawn, they came to the location Chandler had relinquished. A thin rim of rose appeared along the too-near horizon. They woke Durst, and the three of them bundled into surface suits and breathers, then broke the seal on the ATV. For the first time, Al stepped onto the true, unadorned surface of the red planet.

It was cold. The chill seeped through the body-hugging pressure skin, through the parka, and Al tightened the hood around his face. His thermometer read −50 Fahrenheit. His skin prickled. Here, in the lowlands, terraforming had already produced an atmosphere dense enough to make a full pressure suit unnecessary, and they had lowered the cabin pressure of the ATV slowly over the night to prevent the bends. Still, the air somehow felt thinner when one was actually in it.

It was, of course, poison—mostly carbon dioxide, so they still relied on the oxygen in the tanks on their backs, tanks that quickly became heavy even in the low Martian gravity.

But they didn't have far to go. Though it was dark, the landscape Al had ripped from Chandler's mind fit well against what he now saw. The entrance to the buried complex should be simple to find—and he had found the passwords, the keys to the front door, in a hiding place in a chair cushion.

Durst had placed her call, and even as their feet set down on what looked and felt through his booted feet like compact, wet beach sand, Al noticed fliers, coming from the sunrise. Four of them, black-hulled, unmarked, their bizarrely large airfoils making them resemble dragonflies.

Al checked his PPG as the vehicles settled, and heavily armed figures began pouring out.

A trio of them made their way toward Al. Close up, they all looked pretty much the same, faces almost totally obscured by breathers, physiques encrusted in heavy parkas.

Mr. Bester, I take it?

Yes, sir.

My name is Natasha Alexander. Department Sigma is my command.

An honor to meet you. He remembered the name—Bey had mentioned her. One of Vacit's old aides.

We'll see about that. In any event, you've had your part in this. We'll take it from here.

Not to argue with you, ma'am, but that's not what my orders say. I am to find and apprehend the members of the underground on Mars. My authorization comes from EarthGov, and says nothing about twiddling my thumbs during the raid.

The faceless figure seemed to contemplate him, and he felt fear stalking him as he was reminded of a Grin. The moment passed.

Very well, Mr. Bester. Indeed, it might be better this way. While this needs to be done, I have no desire to officially involve Department Sigma. The raid is officially yours.

Beneath his own mask he allowed himself a small, triumphant smile.

There was no need for stealth. The fliers took back to the air for surveillance purposes; they deep-radared the installation, dropped men at anything their tactical schematics suggested might be an exit, and started blowing things up. In the thin air, the first string of charges sounded like firecrackers, and the smoke blew out in a long exhalation as the first corridor, apparently slightly above outside pressure, surrendered a few millibars.

Al was one of the first inside, just behind four bloodhounds who were worked into a near frenzy, blasting everything that moved. The walls and floor were slick with sudden layers of frost, and clouds of still-condensing moisture and smoke from explosives fluoresced like nebula in the PPG bursts.

In this surreal atmosphere, Al had the detached impression of invading an anthill, and the insectlike masks of the defenders heightened that impression. He had his weapon set on low—after all, these were telepaths, and he didn't want to kill them. The mule-kick and surface burns of the first setting were sufficient to stop most people.

The installation defenders didn't pay him the same courtesy. A bloodhound next to him went down with a fist-sized hole bored in his neck.

They fought their way through corridors booby-trapped with explosives; two of the bloodhounds went down in an ambush from ceiling vents, but the rest worked their way in, for what seemed like hours.

The rogues made a last stand in some sort of control room, full of computers and uplink equipment. Barricades had been thrown against

the doors. The Department Sigma people were terribly thorough; they radared, set off charges, and then fired through the breaches. Several fell there, and Al was virtually swept into the room by those rushing from behind.

He fell into a crouch behind a console as plasma and old-fashioned lead slugs hissed and hammered around him.

And that's when he caught it, the signature. Suddenly he had the overwhelming sensation of familiarity, of warmth. A weird memory of being held, and certain smells—

He stuck his arm around the corner, fired. Somewhere near, God slammed the palm of one hand into the world and flipped off the light switch with the other.

He came to moments later, in the dark, struggling for breath. The explosion had broken the seal on his mask, and though his lungs gulped, the air they sucked wasn't nourishing them. He pressed the seal back into place.

His ears rang as if the tympana had been replaced with brass gongs, but that didn't stop the groans of the dead and dying from reaching his brain.

He pushed himself up, roughly. Something was wrong with one of his legs, but he couldn't tell what. It hurt, that much was certain, and it didn't work well. His nose was bleeding, too, the blood beginning to pool in his breather. The cavern was lit by a few dim emergency lights and a few console indicators that miraculously still worked.

He could still feel the signature nearby, attached to a great deal of anguish. He stumbled toward it.

He found Stephen Walters crushed against a bulkhead, one leg bent under him in a very strange way, one arm missing at the elbow. He still had his mask on, but Al had the distinct impression the eyes behind it were open.

I know you.

The hairs on the back of Al's neck stood up. *I was on New Zealand,* Al replied. *I tracked you here.*

No. Before that. I know you. Oh, God in heaven. It's my fault. Fiona, Matthew, forgive—

It paralyzed Al. The sense of familiarity was like a drug. It wasn't pleasant, it was horrible, but he needed it somehow. Somehow—somehow it was a piece of him that was missing.

What are you talking about?

I know the feel of you. I saw you born—after all I had done, after all the

blood on my hands, but they let me watch you come into the world, and you were so beautiful I cried. You were our hope, our dream—

My name is Alfred Bester.

We called you Stee, so you wouldn't be confused with me. They gave you my name, made me your godfather. Your mother, Fiona, how I loved her. Matthew, I loved him, too, but God— A terrible spasm of pain stopped him and almost stopped his heart. Al felt it tremble. *It was me that lost you. I thought I could save them, but they knew they wouldn't make it. All they asked was for me to get you out, keep you free, and I failed them. Failed—*

Matthew and Fiona Dexter were terrorists. They died when the bomb they were planting in a housing compound went off early. The bomb they set off killed my parents.

Lies. His voice was getting weak. *They fed you lies. You are Stephen Kevin Dexter.*

No.

Walters cocked his head wearily, and then he reached up to his face. With a trembling hand he pulled his breather up and off. In the gloom, his eyes were colorless, but Al knew they were blue. Bright blue, like the sky. A woman with dark red hair and changeable eyes, a black-tressed man, both all smiles. He knew them. Had always known them, but he hadn't seen their faces since the Grins had banished them. They were looking down at a baby in a crib, talking baby talk. And he could feel a love so strong—was it love? He had never felt anything just like it, because there was no hint of physical desire, no desperate need, just deep, abiding affection, and hope . . .

He was seeing through Walters' eyes, through the filter of Walters' heart. But then, horribly, another image superimposed itself. The same two people, but looking down at him, and he was the baby in the crib, and behind Mother and Father stood another man, a man with bright blue eyes, as bright as the sun . . .

They loved you. I loved you. I love you still. Psi Corps killed them and they took you away. I tried to find you . . .

Al wasn't aware of finding the PPG. Suddenly it was there, in his left hand and in front of him. His hand clenched on it, and Walters' face turned bright green, uncomprehending.

Shut up.

His hand clenched again, another viridian flare.

Shut up.

The mind images were dropping away, but not fast enough. He tried to shoot again, but the charge was gone. He tried and tried, squeezing the contact, throttling the lying glyphs in his brain.

Fiona . . . Matthew . . . Walters was still there, pulling the images about him in a blazing cloak. His eyes were still there, too, resigned, full of gentle reprimand. He stood near a gate, the doors of which were just beginning to crack open. *You can't destroy the truth.*

And he was gone, and finally the images shredded, a thousand visions of his parents, dancing, fighting, embracing, holding him . . .

No! He took it all in his fist and he squeezed until it went away.

The next thing he knew, Erik was kneeling by him.

"Al? Al? C'mon, let go, he's dead." Erik was trying to pry the PPG from his hand. He didn't seem to understand that Al couldn't let go. He couldn't.

4

Natasha Alexander was both older and more striking than Al had imagined. Her hair—the sort of grey that suggested it had once been red or blond—was clipped to just below her ears, framing a powerful, handsome face. Her black uniform—unmarked save for the usual Psi Corps badge—sheathed a lean, trim body.

"Mr. Bester. You are feeling well, I hope."

"I won't lie, Ms. Alexander—I've certainly felt better."

"If it's any consolation, I'm sure a day will come when you'll feel worse," she said wryly.

"I'm afraid I don't find that reassuring," he admitted. He tried to sit up, failed, and settled for raising the back of the bed a few inches. "What's even less reassuring is that they won't tell me when I will get out of here. I don't suppose they told you anything?"

"Only that your physical injuries will take a few weeks to heal. But they're likely to keep you longer than that, I think."

"I don't understand."

"You were in a bad state when we found you. Fugueing, as a matter of fact."

"So I'm told."

"And I gather you've been unwilling to tell the doctors exactly what occurred during your encounter with Walters."

"Ms. Alexander, that's because I don't remember," he lied.

She nodded, slightly. "How's the hand?"

He held up the knotted fingers. "It doesn't hurt, but I can't—" He stared at the useless digits, then shrugged. That he was crippled was self-evident.

"Did you know," Alexander asked conversationally, "that they can't find a physical reason for your disability?"

"That's not all that unusual, is it?" Al asked. "Nerve damage can be subtle, they tell me. Undetectable, even."

Alexander sighed. "Mr. Bester, you are, without doubt, one of the

finest young officers in the Corps. Your record documents it, and I've seen you in action. Your performance was exemplary, and I'm putting you in for a commendation. But Walters did something to you, and you won't tell us what. That's . . . not good for you."

"Ma'am, I told you—"

"Yes, Mr. Bester, I know what you told the doctors, and I know what you told me. That's unfortunate.

"Imagine our position—a highly trained, upper-end P12 suffers some sort of mind attack by one of the most notorious rogues of all time, is left with certain debilitating injuries, and can't remember anything at all about it. Mr. Bester, we want to help you, but you have to help us."

"You think I'm lying?"

"Not necessarily. Partial amnesia is common after a severe mind-blast. What I would like is for you to allow some diagnostic scanning. We might be able to reconstruct what really happened."

Al tried to keep his face expressionless. "Is that an order?"

She gazed at him for a moment, then sighed. *No. It should be. But the old director took a great interest in you and I . . . honor him.* Her eyes shifted away, then back. *I know you've suffered from being his favorite— you might as well benefit this once. Even though I'm not certain this is a benefit—I think you should have the scans. But it's your decision. I'm probably the only person who will give you such consideration.*

Ma'am—can you tell me why Director Vacit was interested in me?

He never told me. I never knew.

"No, I'm not ordering it," she said aloud. "But you should consider it."

"I will."

She nodded briskly and started to go. Then she turned back, regarding him oddly for a moment.

"Ma'am?"

"It's nothing. You just remind me of someone."

"Perhaps you knew my parents."

That drew a peculiar reaction from her, a sort of mental hiccup that she quickly covered up. "You are certain," she asked very softly, "that you don't remember anything Walters said or did?"

"Nothing."

"That's probably for the best. Good day, Mr. Bester. And good luck to you."

He watched her go. The fact was, he knew exactly what Walters had done. The sick old man had reached down into Al's deepest memories— to the parents he barely remembered—and he had twisted them. Ex-

pertly, cruelly, precisely. He had probably even known them, before he had turned traitor to the Corps.

In a desperate effort to save his own life, Walters had tainted those memories of Matthew and Fiona Dexter with his own, trying to confuse him.

It had worked. Now Al doubted his own mind. It made him sick.

If letting them scan him would help matters . . . but no. Walters had been skillful. Anyone examining him might actually think it was the truth—that he really *was* the son of the Dexters. If anyone in the Corps suspected that, for even a second, his career would be over.

Of course, they should be able to check, right? There must be genetic records in the data files that would prove conclusively that he was unrelated to the Dexters.

But if he checked himself, it might be noticed, and as Alexander had pointed out, there were people who did not care for him. And what if Walters—or someone else, someone on the inside—had tampered with the records? He couldn't rule out the possibility.

This whole thing felt like a time bomb, waiting to blow up in his face. He had to be careful not to trip it himself, not until he had the resources to defuse it.

After about a week they let him get out of bed but continued to stall as to when he could leave the hospital. Alexander had been right—they wanted to keep him under observation. They ran him through a battery of mental and psionic tests and exercises and seemed satisifed with the results. There were a lot of tests on his hand and arm, too, but nothing conclusive ever seemed to come of them.

Before long he was going stir crazy. He had never spent more than a week in his life doing absolutely nothing, and he didn't like it. What's more, the constant implicit questioning of his abilities made him nervous—they would never find anything, of course, but the longer he stayed in the hospital, the more suspicious it was going to look on his record.

There had to be something he could do, something that would convince them he was not only well but capable.

His third day up and around, he discovered that three of the rogues were in the hospital, too, in high-security wards. To occupy himself, he visited them, called up their files, learned what he could.

He discovered that two of them were nobodies, but the third was Anthony Selto, one of Walter's lieutenants.

Selto wasn't in a good way; he had been in cardiac arrest twice. They

hadn't questioned him yet because he wasn't strong enough. Probably he never would be.

Al immediately put in his formal request to do the deathbed scan. They came to get him the next day.

"I don't like this," Dr. Mandle told him, "but we don't have a choice. There isn't another P12 who can get here fast enough, and you did volunteer. I hope you know what you're in for."

"Tell me what to do." Al remembered the brief taste of death with Walters, the door opening and slamming. It had made him wonder, Did the universe remember people? Was there anything on the other side?

Probably not, but it was worth exploring.

"Just make contact with him. Talk to him. A violent scan will push him over the edge and you may get nothing. Be his friend, play along with whatever illusion his mind has constructed to help him die. At some point you will see a liminality—it may appear as a door or the mouth of a cavern. You'll know it when you see it. That's when you break off. Don't follow him beyond the liminality."

"Why?"

"Because we might lose you, too. It's happened before."

"Oh."

Al removed his gloves and reached out to touch Selto's face.

Then he was on a plain made of black clouds, beneath a sky teeming with ravens. The sun hung eclipsed in the sky. He sat on a black horse; Selto was beside him on another. Selto was a short, fierce-looking fellow dressed like a Napoleonic hussar.

"Well," the fellow said, leaning on the pommel of his saddle. "Are you death?"

"No," Al replied cautiously. He was inside of Selto's dying dream, and Selto didn't know him. Perhaps he could play off his confusion. "No," he said, "I'm Stephen Dexter." The lie clung, weird and bitter in his throat, and he was sorry he had said it. Saying it made it feel real.

It had the desired effect, however.

"Holy smokes! Walters found you! He's been looking for you for years. At times he thought you were dead." He cocked his head. "You look like your mother—the pictures anyway."

Al ignored the chill that sent up his spine. "He sent me to talk to you. He escaped, but he was mindblasted. He's forgotten a lot about the locations and ID codes of some of the cells. He's hoping you'll remember."

Selto shrugged. "I only know the one, the Baltimore cell through the Retrograde Hotel, room 661. Does that help?"

"Yes. Thank you."

They were approaching the gate, a sort of trilithon made of gigantic stone slabs. The horses kept the same pace but somehow seemed to approach the gate with exponentially greater speed. Selto drew a saber. "This is it," he said. "Into the valley of death rode the six hundred, and all of that. Are you going with me?"

"No, I have to go back and talk to Walters."

"Tell him I went down swinging, will you?"

There was no time to answer. He was rushing at the portal at breakneck speed. Selto was actually charging through, saber held high, the wind from his ride sucking Al along like a leaf behind a tornado. He fought to disengage, but a blinding light suddenly burst forth from the liminality. Selto stretched toward it, his saber becoming a line infinitely long, a shadow falling in the wrong direction . . . and he was gone.

Al had caught a glimpse of something beyond—there *was* something there—and then the portal had slammed shut. The world dissolved, and he was back in the hospital, his trembling fingers still on the dead man's face.

5

He awoke screaming, as he often did. The phantasms of night came with him to the waking world, and for long moments he remained surrounded by them, frantically trying to understand where he was, to banish the faces he had never known, the memories that weren't his.

In time, he succeeded, as well as he could. He rose, went to the sink, filled a glass with water and drank it. He stretched his arms, legs, and back until blood warmed his sleep-stiffened muscles and was silently thankful that he now rated quarters of his own. That no one but he himself was witness to these shameful awakenings. He closed his eyes, trying to feel the motions of the city outside, but behind his lids the nightmare still lurked, so at last he bundled into a coat and went outside to watch the sun kiss the snow-cloaked Alps awake.

The doctor—a long-faced man with a mustache that might have been penciled in by a mischievous child—looked him over with clinical suspicion. "Have you slept, Mr. Bester?"

"Some. I've had a little trouble with sleep, lately."

"Do you want me to prescribe something?"

"No, thank you. I prefer to make do without drugs. I'm sure in time my body will sort things out. I'm probably still readjusting to the day length on Earth."

"Unlikely. How's the hand?"

Al held up the useless club his left hand had become. The knuckles were white. "No change. Nerves don't heal, I guess."

"The nerves are not damaged, Mr. Bester, so far as I can tell. We've been through this before."

"Maybe you should go through it with my hand, then," Al replied, lightly.

"There are a few more tests we can do," the doctor said. "But as it stands, you seem to be in perfect health. Your leg has healed up nicely, and the minor burn on your arm shows no sign of having caused your

paralysis." He consulted his chart. "I see you've been doing deathbed scans."

"Yes. I started them on Mars, when I was confined to the hospital. It seemed a useful thing to do."

"Yes, but you're still doing them."

"I am. Someone has to."

The doctor set the chart down on the examination table. "Deathbed scans—are something we don't understand very well, Mr. Bester. The one thing we do understand, from experience and observation, is that it isn't healthy to do very many. You've done four already, which is three more than most will do willingly and as many as most can stand without suffering permanent disability. I suggest it's time for you to retire from this particular activity."

"Is that an order?"

"No, Mr. Bester, it is a heartfelt suggestion. You don't show the usual signs of stress associated with multiple scans, unless—tell me—is your insomnia due to nightmares?"

"No," Al lied.

"Hmm. Well, until you show clear signs of debility, I can't write you off, because willing scanners are hard to come by. But they can't *make* you do them."

"No one is trying to. I just feel it's my duty to the Corps."

"There are safer ways to suck up to command, Mr. Bester."

"I resent that implication," Al replied tersely. "Is my examination over? May I go?"

The doctor rolled his eyes. "Yes, Mr. Bester. But I'm making a note of my objections."

"What is it, Al?"

"I'm just tired. I did another deathbed scan this morning. Poor girl— but I got a clear image of her killer. I hope they catch the bastard."

"That's number five, isn't it?" Erik picked at his food and kept his eyes down, but Al felt the concern behind his words—and maybe something else.

"You aren't going to start, too?"

"Al, nobody does five necroscans."

Al shrugged and poked his fork into his pierogi.

"What are they like? The scans?"

"It's always a little different," he replied. "There's always a threshold of some sort—a door, the edge of a cliff—a sort of event horizon. The dying person hangs there for a time, and then—they go. They recede infinitely."

"Recede infinitely?"

"An illusion, I guess, since it only takes a short time. But that's the only way I can describe it."

"But it's like they pass through a doorway."

"Something like that."

"Can you—can you ever see what's beyond? Where they go?"

"No. Some fear it, some welcome it, but they don't know either, because they're still on this side when I'm with them. When they leave the liminality, I lose them."

"Don't you wonder what's there? I mean, if there is a door, it implies something on the other side."

"I wonder, I suppose. But as to the symbolism of the doorway, it doesn't necessarily mean anything. It's a mental construction, a way of conceiving of what's happening. It could well be wishful thinking—none of us can conceive of just ending, of not *being* anymore. What's more natural for a dying person than to pretend they're going somewhere else, even if they don't know what they will find there?"

"Or maybe they *are*—going somewhere else."

"Sure. Maybe."

"I know you, Al. You're looking for something, beyond that doorway. You think something's there, or you wouldn't keep doing it. What are you looking for?"

Al uttered a harsh chuckle. "I'm not looking for anything. What's got you so interested in this? Why all the questions?"

They've been asking about you. The evaluators.

Asking what?

Leading questions. They're worried about you.

Al swirled a chunk of the potato and cheese dumpling in sour cream and brought it to his mouth. He remembered his first taste of pierogi, his delight at its simplicity, its unexpected mixture of textures and taste. This one didn't seem to taste like anything at all.

"You get the impression people fear I'm unstable?"

"Yes. And that's not good, Al. I'm telling you this as a friend."

"A friend who perhaps hasn't been promoted as much as he would like?" Al asked, mildly. "Who thinks maybe I've been promoted too often? What did you *tell* them about my stability, Erik?"

Erik could turn an amazing shade of red at times. This was one of those times. "Look here, Al, I'm trying to save your career, not ruin it. You know the Corps won't risk an unstable cop. Why do you think all of your assignments since Mars have been domestic? Why do you think they've been keeping you away from the underground, or *any* shooting assignment?

"And lest you forget, it was *me* who covered your ass in the IA investigation of that mess on Mars. If it had been anyone else who'd found you, raving, shooting a drained PPG over and over at an unarmed dead man—hell, a *one*-armed, unarmed dead man—you'd be in area 5 even as we speak. So don't you *dare*—" He broke off. Al had never seen him so furious. "Screw you, Al, I don't need this." He pushed his chair back violently and stalked off.

Al frowned and, after a bit of consideration, took another bite of his pierogi. It tasted no better than the last.

Al wasn't particularly surprised when Assistant Director Babineau called him into his office a few weeks later. If he had been both observant and honest with himself, he would never have doubted Erik's word. But over the years, Al had gained the knack of ignoring—no, not ignoring, but disregarding—the opinions of those around him when they concerned him. When he worried about what people thought of him, it invariably led to grief. He sought excellence, and that rubbed people the wrong way—people didn't want you to be excellent, they wanted you to be mediocre, to keep expectations low, and make life easier for them.

This time, though, he should have been paying attention. The Corps could tolerate a lot in an officer if he was efficient—but it could not tolerate instability.

He half expected that Babineau was going to announce a hearing to determine his fitness to serve. In his mind, he was already preparing his defense.

But for today, at least, it was just Babineau, his diminutive form doll-like behind an overlarge desk.

"Ah. Mr. Bester. If you would?" He gestured to a chair, which Al stiffly accommodated to.

"Mr. Bester, I am a plainspoken man, and a busy one, so I'll come to the point, if you don't mind. Do you know Alisha Ross?"

"Sir? Yes, sir, we've met."

"What do you think of her?"

"Think of her, sir?"

"Did you find her attractive? Ugly? Interesting? Boring? Flaky?"

"She is not unattractive, sir. I can't say whether I find her interesting or not—we've never really spoken, and I know very little about her."

"Well, I'll tell you a bit. She's a P12, like yourself. Doesn't have the temperament for fieldwork, so she mostly does forensics, building psychological profiles, that sort of thing. She's a decent soccer player, twenty-four years old, single. Do I have to draw you a picture, Mr. Bester?"

"I see," Al said, feeling more than a little disoriented. "She and I—we have a good genetic match?"

"Very good. Mr. Bester, we've already spoken to Ms. Ross. She's agreed, in principle, to consider a match."

"And you want me to . . ."

"First you should meet, I should think. Talk about it. But quite honestly, Mr. Bester, there are many who think marriage would be good for you at this time. If it isn't hate at first sight, the Corps is much in favor of a union between you and Ms. Ross. Such thorough genetic compatibility is actually quite rare."

"Yes, sir. I would be happy to meet Ms. Ross."

"You're a credit to the Corps, Mr. Bester. I expected nothing less from you."

They met in a restaurant in the city, having been assured that the bill was on the Corps.

It was a somewhat awkward moment, the first in a series.

Alisha was quiet. She had a conventionally pretty face, with hair not assertive enough to be called either chestnut or auburn, and eyes that could be called nothing but brown.

"I heard you were on Mars," she attempted.

"Yes."

"How did you find it?"

"Well, once we were near enough, it was pretty easy," Al replied. "We just fell onto it." She smiled at the joke and took a rather large sip of her rosé. "And you?" he continued. "Have you been off planet?"

"Twice to the Moon," she answered. "No farther than that, I'm afraid. I really don't do well with zero gravity."

"Oh. That's too bad." He sat there trying to think of something else to say, wishing the food would hurry up. "I—ahm—you're from the United States—from Seattle?"

She nodded. "Yes. I don't remember much about it, though. I was brought into the Corps when I was eight. Have you been there? Seattle?"

"Oh. No. Almost, once—Portland. It rained a lot."

"That's what I remember."

The appetizers chose that moment to arrive, for which Al was grateful. He picked at his mussels, trying to make them last and keep his mouth too busy to talk at the same time. With someone you knew, that wouldn't stop conversation, of course—you could psi with a full mouth—but by mutual consent, neither of them initiated mind-to-mind communication. It seemed too intimate.

Al noticed as Alisha finished her wine and poured her some more.

"Thank you."

"You're welcome."

"So—are you horrified?" she asked.

"Horrified of what?"

"Of marrying me."

A mussel went down the wrong way, somehow ended up halfway into his nose. He took some wine to try to clear up the problem and nearly choked a second time. In the end it was quite a mess, and Alisha was laughing—a soft, appealing, genuine laugh.

"Sorry," he said, when he could speak. "I suppose I thought we would avoid that subject for a while longer."

"I did, too. I guess the wine went to my head faster than I thought."

"The wine went *in* my head," Al said, and smiled again. It felt real on his face, an unfamiliar sensation. He looked curiously into her eyes. "I'm not horrified, I find. I always knew that the Corps would eventually suggest marriage, I just suppose I never thought it would be so soon."

"Well, you *are* over thirty."

"You've seen my file."

"I'm in forensics, remember? I can tell you what your cholesterol level is, if you want."

"Hmm. Well, at least you go in with eyes wide open."

"Are you in love with anyone else?" she asked.

"No. If I were, it wouldn't make any difference, not with a match approved by the Corps." He thought of Elizabeth, remembered her objections to all of that, despite their compatibility.

"What?" Alisha asked, reading something from his face or surface thoughts. "I don't mean to pry—"

"An old girlfriend," he said. "Very old. To be honest, it's been a long time since I thought about anything but my career."

"The two of you weren't compatible."

"Yes and no. Genetically we were, and I thought we were in other ways." He smiled, and this time it felt normal—that is to say, false. "We were very young."

"I'm sorry it didn't work out for you, especially since you were genetically matched. I think that's really the most important thing, don't you?"

He remembered Montoya, the flame in her that had nearly consumed him. There had been ecstasy, yes, and excitement, and love. It had made him stupid, nearly ruined him. "Yes," he said softly. "Yes I do."

She smiled back, and Al realized that he *liked* Alisha Ross, that he might manage to like her very much. But he would never love her.

That was fine. That was more than fine. He didn't want to be in love again.

*　*　*

They were married in April. Alisha's parents came, but they seemed lost among her Corps friends. Erik agreed to stand for Al, but it was clearly out of duty—whatever friendship might have been developing between them was gone.

They went on their honeymoon to Bali. They climbed mountains and sunned on beaches. For Al, it was mostly a boring business, vacationing, but at times he genuinely enjoyed himself. Alisha wasn't bad company, even if she wasn't exciting company. Their lovemaking was pleasant and companionable, if not inventive. He grew to like the idea of a wife more and more—the comfort of having someone to go home to.

And his nightmares retreated, though they didn't go away. Alisha didn't ask about them, though he was sure she knew.

They changed, his nightmares, even as they lessened in intensity. For some time he had been haunted by fragments of the lives of those he scanned. Now he dreamed that he himself stood on the liminality, alone. In this case the threshold was the pinnacle of a mountaintop, terribly high, and low mountains receding to every horizon, fading with distance but never actually ending. It was almost pleasant.

He would stand there, feeling that all of the answers were somehow out there. He would hear familiar voices, just below the level of intelligibility.

A woman's voice, low and soothing. A man's voice.

The voice of the rogue on Mars. Of Bey. In the drifting clouds, from the corner of his eye, he would catch hints of the faces, but when he focused on them they dissolved, even as he felt his left arm stiffen, his fingers fusing together into a single mass.

He would wake, not screaming, but indescribably sad. And then he would find Alisha's warm body next to his, a living thing among his dreams of the dead. A warmth. And he would fold against her in the night. And he was grateful—to her, to the Corps. To the Corps, which had seen what he needed and had given it to him.

6

"Here's to Mr. Bester, who took us to the lair, who smoked out the quarry, who made us well and truly hunters!" Gavriil Kichgelkhut's face split in a wide grin as he raised his glass.

Al acknowledged the toast with a modest bow of his head. Gavriil was a romantic who imagined himself in the days of his Koryak ancestors, but he was a good hunter for all of that. Al would teach him to be a great one.

Al raised his own glass. "To the Corps, our mother and our father!" he said, and they all drank again. Al, of course, drank very little.

After that they rehashed the hunt, the long chase through the elaborate and crumbling subways of Brasilia, the moment when they had almost lost the quarry, the final firefight. Gavriil sang a Koryak hunting song, and they got even louder as the patrons of the Common Flamingo gradually drifted out of the place. Al watched them go with quiet pride. Early on, a few of the bar patrons had looked as if they might become belligerent toward the telepaths in their midst. Al had fixed that with a dark stare and a thought. Even with their crippled senses, mundanes knew he was a cobra while they were mice.

The last of them was leaving as his tel-phone vibrated for his attention. He pulled it out and thumbed the contact. "Bester here."

"Mr. Bester? This is Dr. Juan Koabawa. The Blip is dying."

"I see."

"We've been cleared for a deathbed scan. I understand you have some experience with them."

"Indeed I do."

"Your record shows that you've already done six, so I'll understand if you don't want to do another. But the brain damage is extensive, and she's going fast. Ms. Calderon was unable to make good contact—"

"Say no more, Doctor. I'll be there in five minutes."

He closed the phone, stood, and took a bow. "Duty calls, gentlemen.

Enjoy yourselves, but I want to see you all clearheaded by ten-hundred. Is that clear?"

He left, buoyed by their earnest cheers. Ten-hundred gave them three hours of sleep more than they had any right to expect. He knew his men—they would drink, but they would not get drunk. To do so would be to put themselves at the mercy of normals, and he had taught them better than that.

He felt good. It was good to be back in the hunt.

Another scan, though—since his marriage to Alisha, his desire to do them had waned. Erik had been right—he had been looking for something that lay beyond the liminality, though he wasn't sure what it was. Something missing, a lost piece of himself.

Yet every time he stood with the dying at that doorway, he saw less and less. He came back feeling not more whole, but diminished, as if part of him had gone with the dead.

Each time the liminality manifested differently, depending, apparently, on the person who was dying and the person who was scanning. The truth of the threshold was probably beyond human understanding, but it was that old primate brain again, operating by analogy, trying to make sense out of the inconceivable.

He would not have gone out of his way to volunteer for another, but when the Corps called, he answered. Especially as he was coming up for promotion, soon, to senior detective. Seven deathbed scans would make him a legend, after a fashion.

Her mind was shredded by approaching death. She had not allowed them to take her gently. Al had hated to use such force against another telepath, but she had been very strong, and in the end—whether the younger man knew it or not—it had been her or Gavriil. She could have shattered his mind. In such a case, you had to make decisions.

Gavriil had mindblasted her, not subtly but with all of his strength. Vessels had shattered in her brain, and the once life-giving blood now drowned all she had ever been.

She stood, quivering, at the liminality, a sort of storm front in which each of many lightning bolts was a dying memory, blazing out one last time. In the storm, a black eye was opening, waiting to swallow her forever.

Khol, he said softly. *Khol. I have to know why you went rogue. I have to know who led you to your death.*

She turned toward him. Her face came and went like a bad transmission. It shifted from large-eyed child to the hollow, gaunt visage they had

hunted. It distorted from abstract—like the face of a Grin—to photographic as she tried to hang on to herself. She wasn't succeeding.

I was a good cop. I was.

I know. You loved the Corps. What happened?

I was—I was good . . .

A shrieking, then, a terrible inhuman sound that tore into him, that set his teeth on edge, that threatened to rip open *his* mind. For an instant he knew a terrible attraction in despair, in destruction, and yearned for oblivion so much that if he had had a PPG in his hand he might have turned it on himself.

Lightning struck, and he was on Mars. The sky was still a hurricane, the eye bigger than ever.

It struck again, and they were fingering a small object, a black fragment of something—

—which was now somehow huge, arachnoid, hideous, looming over him—

Together, he and Khol screamed, and she was shrieking away from him, into eternity, and he was following, grasping the trail of her dying mind, riding the current of her spent life toward—toward—

Something that called him. A woman's face. A man's voice. Answers . . .

Answers he no longer wanted. He felt his ruined hand spasm with the effort of wrenching free, of abandoning Khol's desperate flight into nothing. She wanted to die, and he did, too, to know what was beyond, oblivion or solace. The storm had him, he had gone in too far, and he was glad—

Then the eye dilated, rushed away, and she was gone. Too late, he redoubled his efforts to catch it, but it was like the old problem of taking half a step toward a door, and then half of that step, and half of that. He could get closer, but never reach it.

And he was withdrawing his bare, trembling fingers from her dead face. He was weeping.

"I'm sorry, Mr. Bester," Dr. Koabawa said. "I shouldn't have asked this of you."

"No," he managed. "I'll be all right in a moment. Just—give me a moment." It felt as if something had been cut out of him, something he couldn't even remember anymore. Was it true, what they said? That a part of your soul went with those who died? How much of him was left?

Later, on the plane back to Geneva, he felt better. It was Khol's loss he felt, her trauma. The illusion of damage had been just that, an illusion.

Still, he didn't think he would do another deathbed scan. They wouldn't ask him again, not after seven. They probably wouldn't let him if he wanted to, after this performance.

He took deep, calming breaths, as Bey had taught him. He would be better soon.

He distracted himself by thinking of Alisha, how good it would be to see her, to not be alone.

Maybe this time she would conceive. That would please everyone. He knew she wanted a child, and he himself had begun to think of it as more than a duty. He had seen a lot of death—a bit of life would be nice. A new life that was a part of him, a continuation of him.

The liminality represented the past, threatening to draw him to his doom. Alisha, children—life—they were the future, and for the first time in many years it was the future that he wanted. His future, Alfred Bester's future, not some vague and nameless legacy of parents he had never known.

He squeezed that thought away even as it formed. He had no parents. The Corps was his parents, and that was all he needed, all he cared for.

He slept. There were nightmares, of course, but when he awoke, it was to hope.

Back in Teeptown, he bought some flowers and headed straight for his apartment. Alisha probably wouldn't be there—he was too early for her to expect him, and he didn't remember her work schedule—but she might be in. If she wasn't, he would put them in a vase and see what he could do about making a meal, something Alisha would like. Coq au vin, maybe, or duck with olives.

Smiling in anticipation of her reaction, he keyed the door open. He was so distracted by his plans, he didn't catch what was in the air until too late. Then he saw the table settings, the wine, and smiled. The smile faded as he understood that the bottle was empty, the food eaten, and only then did he feel the faint palpitations coming from the next room.

In one jarring instant he was a child again, on that mountain, eavesdropping on Julia and Brett, feeling their lips brushing as if against his own. But this time he already knew the feel of one of the pair, the peculiar way she knotted her hands together across a back. It was *his*—had been his . . .

The flowers slipped to the floor. He looked down at them dumbly for a time, then knelt to gather them up. He placed them in a vase and left, closing the door quietly behind him.

* * *

He didn't look down when he heard the approaching footsteps. He kept his eyes on the stars, on the thin films of clouds, on the vague secrets the patterns of light and darkness implied. Mysteries, cryptograms. Secrets.

"I'm—I'm sorry, Al."

He shrugged. "I suppose I should have expected it. I had no right not to."

"You don't believe that."

"No," he admitted. Then he asked, "Why did you marry me?"

"You know why."

"No. There was no need to marry. We could have conceived a child for the Corps—through artificial insemination, even. It's done every day. But you wanted to marry. Why?"

"Because they asked me to."

He sat back against the pedestal that supported the statue of William Karges. "I see. Another attempt to save poor Alfie Bester. To put him on the right track."

"They said you were becoming—erratic. And I—I admire you, Al. I like you. I wanted to help."

"What's his name?"

"Do you really need to—"

"What is his name?" Now he met her eyes. She had been crying, but he found he didn't care.

"Jared. Jared Dawson."

"Well. Another P12, at least."

"I knew him long ago, Al. We were lovers before I ever met you, but our genetic profiles showed a lower compatibility. And—" She broke off. "Al, you don't love me. We both know that."

"That doesn't mean you have to make a fool out of me. A laughing-stock in front of the whole Corps."

"Is that what worries you? I've been very careful about that, Al. No one knows. I swear it." She knelt in front of him, reached her hand to touch his chin. "It won't happen again, Al. I swear. I told him it was over."

"Spare me your pity, Alisha. You're right—I don't love you any more than you love me. I just thought—I just thought we could be friends. I thought we could trust each other."

"I'm sorry. It's all I can say. I won't do it again."

"Oh. Good. Now I trust you completely. That was easy."

"Al—"

"Go home, Alisha. Go home. I'll be there after a while."

* * *

Their words served only to ease them from one silence to another over the next week. They lived in the spaces. Al tried to come home as seldom as he could, but it was a slow week. The underground was quiet, and all incidents were local enough not to require the intervention of an external investigator. Al kept his feelers out, waiting, hoping for a distraction.

Alisha tried—he could tell she was trying. For the moment, at least, she was sincere about making their "marriage" work. But he knew he couldn't trust her, knew he never should have. The Grins had taught him that, long ago. Why did he keep forgetting? Was it some animal instinct, this blind desire to trust? Some chemical necessity?

It was ten days before he got the call he had been waiting for. Alisha was in the kitchenette.

"Who was that?" she asked.

He left without a word.

"His name is Karl Jovovich," the young medic said. "Massive trauma; his heart took a bullet. We have him on a mechanical pump, but he's rejecting. We've got a heart for him, but I don't expect—well, the collateral damage is extensive. He took five hits in the upper chest."

"So you want me to stand by during the operation."

"Yes. A scan right now would kill him for certain, and would violate his rights—"

"I'm aware of the law," Al said softly.

"I'm sure you are." The medic was a normal. He didn't like Al, that much was clear. He didn't like the whole situation.

"I'll wait," Al assured him. "I'll wait until you give the word."

"If I give the word." *Goddamn vulture.*

Al smiled, very thinly. "You have your job, and I have mine. I hope your man lives. But if he doesn't, isn't it better that we catch his killer?" He was lying. The man in the bed was a mundane. Al didn't care if he recovered. If he had been shot by another mundane—well, what better justice than that they should all kill one another? But, in these situations, it was best to be diplomatic. Mundanes were better off believing that the Corps was, as advertised, their friend.

He waited impatiently as the fellow was taken into surgery. He had chosen a mundane, in a mundane hospital, volunteering through the court system. That likely meant that MetaPol didn't yet know he was doing this. If they did, they might try to stop him, and he couldn't have that. Every moment he had to wait increased the chances someone in his division would realize what he was up to.

No matter what, this was the last time. The Corps couldn't possibly

risk one of their best—and yes, he was one of their best, there was no need for false humility—on an eighth deathbed scan.

That was okay. One more was all he needed.

They worked hard, deep into the night. He watched the earnest young surgeons, tasted their desperate faith, their passion for saving life, and wanted to laugh at them. Everyone died. Who did they think they were? But they sweated and cursed and finally wept when the heartbeat went flat, and they reluctantly called him over.

He worked fast. Once the pulse was gone, there was no time to spare. He pulled off the resuscitator, stripped the glove from his right hand, and touched the clammy brow. The man was young, a little weak-chinned. He had crow's-feet, despite his youth—perhaps he had laughed a lot.

Al closed his eyes, and set foot on a dark highway. He was walking next to the young man, who turned to face him.

"You the angel of death?"

"Maybe. You know you're dying?"

"I know. I can feel it. You see the end up ahead?" He laughed bitterly. "End of the road."

"Anything you want to tell me first? Who killed you?"

"No. Why does it matter?"

"I would think you would want revenge."

The young man shook his head. "You know that poem? I forget exactly how it goes. Death is the enemy, not my fellow man. I won't betray someone else to death."

"Even the one who killed you?"

"Nope."

"How noble. But you *are* scared."

"I'm terrified. Who wouldn't be?" The road had begun to move beneath them, like a slidewalk. Landscape whipped by them—sights, sounds, events—Al ignored them. The young man didn't care who had killed him, and neither did Al. That's not what he was here for.

"You dying, too?" the fellow asked.

"No. But I'm going with you."

"How 'bout you just take my place, if you're so damn eager?"

"I thought death was the enemy."

"Yeah. But you seem so all-fired anxious."

"I am."

"Why?"

"I want to see what's out there. Beyond that."

The liminality was approaching; Al had come to recognize it, whatever its form. The road was curling up at the edges as it raced along,

black walls going higher and higher, and finally closing, becoming a tunnel of nothing. Their pace was fantastic now, and the young man was starting to blur, to coruscate. Bits of his form were streaming behind him like the tail of a comet.

"This isn't so bad," the young man whispered. "I guess I can use the company. You want to take my hand?"

Al didn't want to, but that seemed the surest way. He reached out and did so, just as direction seemed to change, as horizontal motion became vertical—down, like falling toward Mars, like falling in a nightmare. For an instant he knew the sheerest terror he had ever known. Then the universe seemed to flatten, as all of him squeezed into a ribbon, a globe, a single, dimensionless point—then, nothing, save a humming like wind, and lights like stars, and the most interesting sensation of turning inside out, like a sock.

The young man was gone. Everything was gone. But he wasn't. He remained, somehow. And he spoke to himself.

He spoke to himself, but he spoke in voices. He spoke first in the voice of Sandoval Bey.

What did I hope to find here?

And he answered in the voice of Elizabeth Montoya.

The truth. The truth about my parents.

But I know that truth, Bey's voice replied. *I didn't have to come here for that. And it doesn't matter. It doesn't matter who or what my parents were.*

And now he spoke in the voice of Stephen Walters, the rogue he had killed. *There is nothing here. The only thing here is what I bring with me.*

And in the most ancient voice he knew, the voice of a woman. Of his mother. *I only bring what is in my heart. That is all that survives beyond the liminality, the contents of the heart.*

And finally, in his own voice. *And there is nothing here. There is nothing left in my heart at all.*

There wasn't. There wasn't. His skin was all that remained, inside out, empty.

He awoke with his back arched, the surgeon standing over him, sweating, mask down. A sparkling numbness was just working through his toes, presumably from the heart-lung stimulator on his chest.

"Got you," the surgeon said. "Goddamn it, I *got* you."

"Congratulations, Doctor," Al said, weakly. "You seem to have saved my life."

They still wouldn't let him out of bed the next day, when Alisha came to see him.

"Hello, my dear," he said, pushing himself upright against the pillows.

"Are you okay? What happened?"

"Oh—nothing much. I lost control of the scan. I guess I shouldn't have tried to do it so soon after the last one."

"You shouldn't have tried another one at all."

He patted her hand. "Your concern is touching. It really is. But there's nothing to fear—I won't be doing it again."

"I hope not."

"How did you get here so quickly?"

"The hospital called the Corps, and they informed me. I took the first flight."

"Yes. They informed my loving wife, of course."

"Al—"

"No, I'm sorry. That was inappropriate of me. Thank you for coming." He took her hand again, and sensed—something more.

"You have something to tell me?" he asked.

"I was going to wait—"

"No time like the present. I'm *fine,* Alisha."

She nodded. "Very well. Alfred, I'm pregnant."

He blinked. "Wonderful." Was it his? Probably he would never know. Nor did he really care.

"I hoped you would be happy."

"A fine, strong P12 for the Corps? Of course I'm happy."

She attempted a smile. "I'm glad. I'm glad you're okay. I was worried that you might want—"

He shook his head, reached up, and pecked her on the cheek. "You're my wife. That's how it should be. And now we have a child on the way. The timing isn't what it could have been, but we'll work it out."

"What do you mean?"

"Didn't I tell you? I requested a transfer to Mars. Babineau was in here just before you, to tell me it was approved. It's a great opportunity, darling, for all of us. All of the big stuff is happening on Mars. I can't turn it down. I think you understand."

She drew back a little. "I—think I do."

"I knew you would. But I'll write, of course, and send vids, and come home on leave every chance I get."

"I can get a transfer, too. I can go with you—"

"In your condition? And I know how upsetting space travel is to you. No, I can't ask you to do that." He said it firmly, finally, and she understood.

"If that's what you want."

"What we want doesn't matter. We do what we must." He smiled. "Thank you for coming to see me. I think I would like to rest again."

"Okay. Rest well."

He could feel her relief. If his heart weren't empty, it might have bothered him.

He slept like a baby.

PART 4

Ascendance

PART 4

Ascendance

1

"I hate the way they look at us," Ysidra Tapia said, lifting her chin incrementally at the crowd waiting on the train platform. Most looked like miners, though there were a few white-collar types. All stared at Al and Tapia with varying degrees of vehemence.

He shrugged. "I take comfort in the little things," he told her. "Things that give me a sense of security, of permanency. The sun rises and sets every day, objects in a gravity well fall down and not up, and normals hate telepaths. It's comforting, really, when you get to my age. It tells you that God is in heaven and all is right with the world."

Tapia smiled nervously. She was dreadfully young, a P12 at the start of her internship. She was slim and tall and dark. She reminded him uncomfortably of Elizabeth Montoya.

"Stinking mindfrikkers."

He didn't need his psi to hear that. It had been meant for his ears and for everyone on the platform.

It was easy, too, to single out the individual who had spoken—a tough-looking miner of about forty. Her muscular arms hung almost gorillalike at her sides. "You heard me," she said, dangerously. "Mind-frikker."

"Good day to you, too," Al said, with exaggerated brightness.

"Come on, Endra." Another miner—a younger woman—tugged on her arm.

"Come on?" she snapped. "Have you forgotten starving? The food riots? These mindfrikkers, fat and lazy, watching us starve?"

"Maybe you should have thought of that before you decided to sit out the Earth-Minbari War," Tapia snapped, suddenly. Al was mildly surprised. Apparently the trainee had some of Montoya's fire, as well.

"Wasn't our war. We didn't start it."

"Wasn't your war?" Tapia snapped. "You cowards. My father died on the Line. And my brother. Earth boiled a million gallons of blood into a

vacuum to save the Human race while you guys sat here like the Marsie cowards you are."

"You better keep your little pup on the curb, Mr. P-sicko," Endra said. Her voice moved into what Al recognized as a red zone. A murmer rose among the rest of the crowd—they were getting angrier by the second. He knew he ought to do something.

But he wanted to see how Tapia would handle it. She, in turn, seemed to think she had overstepped her bounds and suddenly became quiet.

Then the tube car arrived.

"Take the next one, mindfrikkers," the woman named Endra said, as the doors sighed open.

"I don't think we will," Tapia said. In the lull, some of her confidence had flagged, but Al could tell she was going to bluff it on out, now that she was committed.

"Yeah? Well, just come on." A silicon cutter appeared in the miner's hand, a wicked tool with an edge only a few molecules wide. She brandished it, and with her other hand made a gesture of contempt at least as old as ancient Rome. "Next time you freaks'll know to travel in a real pack, rather than just one old scrag and his little puppy-bitch."

"That's illegal possession of a weapon, under Earth Provisional Government regulation—" Tapia was still reciting the regs and reaching for her PPG when Endra threw the knife.

The years had taken away some of Bester's speed, but the same years of training had helped wear neural grooves deeper than reflexes. Al managed to knock Tapia far enough aside to save her life, but the spinning blade nevertheless slipped almost frictionlessly through her biceps. For an instant, it almost seemed as if it had missed, and then Tapia's arm sagged halfway off, blood fountaining out.

Cursing himself for not stepping in sooner, Al jammed Endra's mind and watched her drop. Then he pulled his PPG and shot four other miners in the legs as the rest, howling with fear, crushed onto the train.

Ignoring the groans of the injured mundanes, Al knelt quickly, used Endra's knife to cut a tourniquet from his shirt, then called for medics on his link. He laid Tapia's head back gently.

She had gone into shock, eyes glassy, but he had seen a lot of wounds in his time and suspected she would live.

So would those he had shot. He turned to them.

"I want you to remember something," he said, very softly, but very distinctly. "I want you to watch this, and remember it, and I want you to tell your friends." He stood up and walked toward where Endra lay puddled. Her eyes were starting to clear. "First of all, this isn't Earth.

You people turned your backs on Earth, remember? The officers who run the provisional government here—men and woman who fought in the war for you—well, they don't really care so much if you Marsies don't receive the full protection of Earth law.

"So, for instance, if something like *this* were to happen—" He pushed, and Endra screamed, trying, it seemed, to touch the back of her head to the heels of her feet. "Well, on Earth someone might wonder why I did it. They might even bring it up in a court of law. Not here. Or maybe—" Just for form's sake, he hit the woman with a deep, hard scan. Unearthed her hatred of the Corps, saw how she had lost a child in the food riots, found—something else. Something buried, encrypted, hidden.

It was entombed in her hatred, but she hadn't repressed the memory by herself. He recognized the signs—a P12 had cauterized a memory. A sloppy job, though, and it was still half there.

He yanked it out, like a rotten tooth, set it aside, and got back to the business at hand. He sparked her mind and then diced it. It was so easy to do to normals. When he was done, she just lay there, drooling, staring at the ceiling and making gagging noises.

Then he pushed each of the other four, just a little, so they would worry about what he *might* have done to them. "Touch one of my telepaths again, and what I've done to her will seem a kindness," he promised. "Are you all quite clear on that?"

The four nodded vigorously, and about that time the medical team arrived.

Satisfied that Tapia would live, he went back to his apartment and carefully unwrapped the thing he had torn from Endra's mind. Not surprisingly, it had Psi Corps in it, everywhere, all around her. Department Sigma.

Interested, he sifted the broken strands, weaving here, extrapolating there. He had worked with Department Sigma on a number of occasions, and was aware of some of their projects, but to a large extent they were still a black box to him. He didn't like that.

He saw Endra working for them, running a backhoe, cutting blocks of rust-red permafrost with a silicon knife—that's where she had come by it. Digging for something in the Martian dirt.

The digging was just the frame of the picture. Endra Nadja had been digging most of her adult life. No, it was where she was digging—and why—that they had cut out.

He carefully worked his way to the core of the burned memories, and in the ashes, in the powdery place between what is forgotten and

what was never known, he found spiders. Spiders boiling out of her flesh, spiders crowded on her eyeballs, spiders invading her mouth.

Strange. The records showed that Endra Nadja had been born on Mars and had never been off planet.

Where would she have seen spiders?

He supposed someone in the Corps might have planted the images there, as some sort of punishment, but that seemed unlikely—this was the part of the memory that was most damaged, that had been most viciously suppressed.

Anyway, it explained Endra's bolder-than-normal hatred. She didn't remember being hurt by a Psi Cop, but one had hurt her a great deal, doing this. The buried memory had fed her natural antipathy. Whoever had done this deserved a reprimand for such a half-assed job.

It wasn't a signature he recognized. He shrugged and started to file it away again, but paused for a long moment.

There was something familiar about this. But what?

He stood with his eternally clenched hand pressed against the macromolecular glass, staring out over the battered surface of Mars. His mind traced back through the years, in search of the feeling of spiders, of an alien touch . . .

The rogue in Brasilia. What was it, more than twenty years ago? She had had some sort of thing going with spiders. And hadn't she come from Mars?

Yes, this certainly went into the "to be considered" file.

Tapia dimpled at the flowers. "Thank you, Mr. Bester."

"Don't mention it. Next time, though, you should try to catch the knife by the hilt."

"I'll try to remember that. If it weren't for you, I'd be dead now. I guess—I guess I lost control."

"We all do that now and then," Al said. "It's perfectly natural to get frustrated, especially with mundanes. They can't understand us, any more than a blind man can understand a roomful of painters discussing a landscape."

"I know." She looked at him very seriously. "May I ask you a personal question? How have you been able to stand it all of these years?"

He looked her dead level in the eye. "It's very simple," he said. "I always have the Corps behind me. My family. And then, of course, I have my loving wife, and my son—"

"They live here, on Mars?"

"My wife is still on Earth—though she's thinking about moving up here, next year, now that the kid's out of the house. She doesn't deal with

space travel very well. My son is grown and in the Corps back on Earth, I'm happy to say."

"You must be lonely. Haven't you ever considered requesting assignment on Earth?"

"It's hard, but I feel I'm needed here, on Mars, and with my Black Omega Squadron. As much as it hurts, we do what we must."

"It's romantic, in a way," Tapia said.

"Yes. In a way. And now I want you to get some rest, because when you get out of here, you'll have some hard training ahead of you. No slackers in the Black Omegas, I promise you."

"Yes, Mr. Bester."

He made his way to his office, put off combing through a year's worth of backed-up paperwork in favor of glancing at the *Universe Today* headlines. He took notes on two items of mild interest.

The first concerned telepaths on Io who had cooperated in a union work shutdown. This wasn't news to Al, and the idiots had been dealt with already. After all, telepaths had a union, Psi Corps—they had no business entangling their allegiances, officially or unofficially. For Al, the article was noteworthy because of its very existence—the whole affair was supposed to have been stifled.

Again, someone had been sloppy.

A little more interesting was a profile of William Edgars, an up-and-coming billionaire in the pharmaceutical industry. Edgars was one of the contractors who produced sleepers, so anything concerning him was of interest. The article was typical Fortune 500 stuff, though—hobbies, carefully chosen political views, photos with the dog. When asked about business teeps, he seemed to avoid the question, an interesting thing in and of itself.

He moved from the paper to the revised hunt list but had only read a page when his vidcom belled.

"Answer," he told it. "Bester here."

A face appeared, a receding blond hairline, strong jaw, very white teeth. He had the momentary disorientation that came from recognizing someone once well-known, but transformed.

"Brett?" he asked, a little incredulously.

"Hello, Al. I was wondering if you'd remember me."

"Of course I do. Cadre Prime. What can I do for you?"

Brett hesitated for an instant. "Al, I'm on Mars. I wondered if I might look you up?"

That was—odd. He and Brett hadn't seen each other except in passing, in the halls back in Geneva, for more than thirty years. Thirty.

"Yes, of course. Where would you like to meet?"

"Well, I've never been on Mars before, and I don't have long here. I was thinking about hiking a little around the slopes of Olympus Mons."

"You're kidding."

"No, not at all."

"I can tell you're a tourist. Not all the way up, I trust."

"Probably not. Are you game?"

"I—" Something was wrong here. "Sure."

"Great. When are you free?"

Al didn't much like being outside on Mars. He didn't like trusting his life to canned air. And he didn't like the distant horizons, with no walls to put his back to. How many ways could you kill a man outside? It was easy enough on Earth: a hidden marksman, a well-timed avalanche, a falling accident. On Mars, it was so much simpler. A cracked air valve and a faulty gauge. A few molecules of any of a number of nerve toxins placed in the breathing mix.

Sure, it was the same inside the domes, but written on a larger page, and scale did make a difference. Few people would blow up a whole dome, or poison the entire colonial air system just to kill Alfred Bester. He could think of many who wouldn't mind waiting in a fissure on Olympus Mons, even for hours, peering through a telescopic sight.

A lot of people stood between him and death. That made him very uncomfortable.

Brett could well be one of those people. They had always been rivals. He had left Brett in the dust, rankwise, many years ago. Was he here to beg a recommendation—or earn one from Al's enemies?

"Ever climbed this whole thing?" Brett gestured at Olympus Mons, which dominated not just the sky, but the world. The tallest volcano in the solar system, its fifteen miles of height were difficult for the mind to comprehend. They were only about a mile up from the base, and already the puny horizon of Mars made the planet seem smaller, while the endless slope rose above them.

"C'mon, Brett." Al paused on a ledge. "We haven't spoken in more years than I can remember. Let's be honest. We were never friends, not really. You didn't bring me out here to renew an old acquaintance or to chat about our childhoods."

Brett stared up the vast slope. "Okay, Al. It's true. You were always the strange one in the cadre. I always did sort of like you, whether you knew it or not. We all did. You were just—you wanted more than we did, maybe. But you were Cadre Prime, Al, and I was Cadre Prime. We are alike in a way that others can't be."

Here it came. Brett wanted something, all right, and he was hoping

to key in on the only thing he could, the only thing the two of them had in common.

"Even after all of these years? You really think we share that much? Twelve years out of sixty-four?"

"Yes, I do. If I didn't, I wouldn't be here. We were never friends, Al, but we were brothers."

"So we were taught. But isn't everyone in the Corps brother and sister?"

Brett shook his head and started forward on the slope. He moved with greater ease than Bester. After years in the Martian gravity, Al's muscles had weakened somewhat. Brett was still used to the heavier pull of their home planet. "You remember what they told us? The Grins? That we, Cadre Prime, had a special duty?"

Al laughed harshly. "How could I forget?"

"Al, we were *born* in the Corps. Everyone else in our cadre joined before they were seven, and all of them were born manifested. Between us, we celebrated only one birthday. Remember? I still celebrate it. I'll bet you still do, too—and I'll bet you never tried to find out what day you were actually born."

Al shrugged.

"You don't think that makes us different? We see things, Al, in a way that those who joined the Corps when they were twelve, or fifteen, or twenty simply can't. They grew up as mundanes, then learned to be Corps. We grew up as the real thing."

"I'll grant you that. What's your point?"

"My point is that the director is a mundane."

"*Very* good, Brett. Perhaps that's because the Corps' charter states that the director will be assigned by the EA senate and shall always be a normal?"

"Yes. But Director Vacit was a telepath, you know."

"*What?*"

"You heard me. He was a telepath. He put the Corps together, him and Senator Crawford. It's not what they taught us as kids, but—"

"Yes, yes, of course I knew the William Karges story was a fairy tale—but Vacit?"

"You met him once."

"Yes." He could picture him, too, that fine, wrinkled skin and white, close-cropped hair. The faint feeling, like a wind. *"You felt something?"* Vacit had asked. *"Interesting. Most don't."*

And then Director Johnston's interest in him, because *Vacit* had been interested . . .

"How do you know?"

"Al, you've been in the field. I've mostly been in administration. You hear things there. A few people knew all along. Johnston suspects it, if he can't prove it."

"I fail to see what any of this has to do with me," Al said.

"Have you been to Teeptown lately, Al? Have you been in the classrooms, seen what they're teaching the kids? It's not the same as what we learned." He considered, for a moment. "On the surface it is. But underneath, the message has changed."

"Changed how?"

"We always learned that we were special—better than mundanes. That all telepaths were brothers, even the Blips we have to track down. Now it's—it's just the Corps, Al. Blips are enemies. They *do* things to them—"

"We always did things to them," Al said. "Have you ever seen a reeducation camp? Or someone on sleepers?"

"Have you ever seen one telepath *dissect* another?" Brett countered. "Have you ever seen one driven mad, when they tried to push him past P12 with drugs?"

"I've heard of such things, of course. Sometimes they may be necessary. You know as well as I do that one day there will be a war against the mundanes, Brett, a war we *cannot* lose. I, for one, am willing to make a few sacrifices to see that my people aren't slaughtered."

"Of course. I don't question that, Al. Any of us should be happy to sacrifice anything and everything for the others. What I'm trying to tell you is that this isn't being done for us—for *teeps*—it's being done *to* us. By mundanes.

"When Vacit was in charge—and for years after—the Corps was controlled by telepaths. Now it's not. They aren't experimenting for our own benefit, but to make us better weapons. Hell, surely you've heard about dust?"

"Yes. What's wrong with trying to enhance our powers?"

"Bull. Dust was developed to give mundanes psi, Al. To undercut us completely." He stopped, picked up a Martian rock, turned it at a few angles, then let it drop. "It's a matter of control, Al. In the old days, Cadre Primers were placed in strategic positions. The low-level ones became instructors, but the P12s went on to high command. Now there's a black box out there that they won't let any of us into. Because we're all suspect. Do you know how many of us have died?"

"No."

"*Most* of us, Al. Milla's gone. And Menno. Ekko. And I went back through the older generations. You met Natasha Alexander once?"

"Yes. Here, on Mars. She was the commander of Department Sigma."

"One of the first from Cadre Prime, and her mother and her mother's mother were both in the Metasensory Regulation Authority before it became Psi Corps. She was assassinated. She used to be Vacit's aide, did you know that? No Primers in Department Sigma, Al. Or in top Admin. She was in the black box and so they got her out. You should have been promoted all the way to the top, years ago. You know it, I know it.

"Oh, they let you have your Black Omega Squadron to keep you busy, but you know you're still on the outside. You have to. I should be higher up, too, though I never had the ambition you did. They've held us down, Al. And if they ever think they can't, they'll kill us."

"They? Who is *they*?" Al demanded angrily. Montoya had spoken of *they*.

"Johnston and his cronies, his pet telepaths, laters all— And behind them, a select group of senators, governors, industrialists—IPX especially. Mundanes, Al, mundanes. They're taking it away from us. From our children." He grabbed Al's arm. "Don't you know why Sandoval Bey was killed? You were his friend, don't you want to know?"

"Enough!" Al shouted. Despite his full-throated roar, his voice was surrealistically thin in the Martian air. "What are you here for? Are you trying to talk me into some kind of revolution? Assuming all you say is true, you think the two of us can just—"

But Brett was shaking his head. "No, Al. I'm just trying to save your life. I've already given up on mine."

"What?"

"I investigated. I left a trail. They'll find me."

"Oh. Wonderful. And you've led them right to me. It's *so* good to have friends."

"No, I promise you, I've fixed that. Anyway, they may have already been coming for you. Whether they were or not, something is happening here, on Mars, in Department Sigma. Something very big and very nasty."

"And what would that be?"

"They found something. Lots of somethings, actually, out there on Syria Planum—some of it long, long ago. Hell, the facility has been there since '73! Some of it we now think is Vorlon—organic technology, anyway. More recently, though, they found other things—" He stopped and took Al by both shoulders. "Some very bad things have been happening to telepaths on Mars, Al."

"You have proof of any of this?"

"No. But look—look very carefully—and you'll find it. You're better placed than I, smarter than I, stronger than I. You have your Black Omega Squadron and bloodhound units loyal to you. Al, whether you know it or not, you're the most powerful man on our side. You're the Black Pope."

"What side is that, Brett?"

"The only side that really matters, Al. The teep side. Don't you see, they've played you against the rogues, kept you occupied so you don't ask questions. But soon now, very soon, they won't be able to hide all of it from you. Then they'll have to do something about you. Something permanent."

"If what you say is true, they have their excuse now—you're talking to me."

"No. As I said, I've fixed that."

Brett was good. Al caught his intent an instant too late. The larger man's fist drove into his face, ripping the breather half off. His sharp intake of breath was already in progress, but it was almost all CO_2, and his head swam. Brett helped out by hitting him again, and his knees buckled, but Brett took him down gently to the jagged rocks.

"Sorry, Al." Brett yanked Al's PPG from its holster. "Just make sure you pick this up," he said. "And don't forget what I said. You're the one, Al. The only one who can save us. The Corps is mother. The Corps is father."

Brett shot himself in the face.

Al fumbled his mask into place and stood shakily, staring at Brett's corpse, determined not to move again until he had worked out exactly what to do. On consideration, he unholstered Brett's weapon and fired it—once into the side of the mountain, once so that it scorched his arm. PPGs had faintly different signatures and the weapons were registered—an investigation would tell who had fired which.

Then he took his own weapon from Brett's outstretched hand and replaced it with the other. He closed the dead fingers and squeezed them, and he remembered, so, so long ago, playing cops and blips, pretending Brett wasn't a good guy. Betraying him. His brother.

"I'm sorry, Brett," he said softly. "I really am."

And for the first time in a very, very long time he felt something that might have been a tear start in the corner of his eye.

He cracked the mask, let the desiccated Martian atmosphere have it. He had no time for that.

He could hardly doubt that Brett believed what he said—he had died for it. Brett might be wrong, but too much of what he said fit too well with what Al already suspected. He had known about Johnston for years.

Indeed, he and Johnston would have a personal meeting one day, to discuss purely personal matters—that was certain.

But the larger conspiracy—he hadn't exactly seen the shape of it until now.

If Brett was right, this amounted to much more than a political game inside the Corps. His telepaths were in danger. Alfred Bester's telepaths. They were all he had, all he cared about.

God help anyone who got in his way.

2

Glass shattered, and though it was up ahead somewhere, Bester ducked reflexively. He signaled his bloodhounds, and they spread out around him, their excitement barely contained.

They relayed their impressions back toward him in a chain. He loved it, hunting with his hounds. It was like being the conductor of a symphony. For the moment he conducted them like bassoons and low strings, plucked, as they crept like thieves through ruined corridors of antique white and aquamarine.

A hundred yards ahead, they came across a normal. Like the others they had found, he was curled against the wall, his expression slack. Blood seeped through a crack in his faceplate, but he was still alive. One eye was a bloody ruin, but the normal didn't care. He was more occupied with the nightmare his remaining eye saw, wherever it tried to look.

I don't understand, Tapia mused. *Why is he doing this?*

"Shh. Don't 'cast," Bester warned. He noted that she seemed to have recovered most—but not all—of the use of her arm. He had heard that she was proud of the injury, because it made her more like him. She was a good cop, and one of the few he was certain he could trust, especially now.

"Yes, sir. But McDwyer is smarter than this. I trained with him. If he were going Blip, he wouldn't—"

"No, no, Ms. Tapia. He hasn't gone Blip. That's not what's going on here."

His link quietly vibrated. He touched it on. "Bester."

"Sir, this is Donne. Sir, I've been watching like you said. Another team just came in. Looks like Sigma, all right."

"Good work, Ms. Donne. You know the plan. I'm sending a few back to help. Just keep them busy for a few minutes. Nothing overt, nothing we can't plausibly deny."

"On it, sir."

He motioned to a couple of the bloodhounds, and they turned and raced the way they had come.

"What's going on, sir?" Tapia asked.

"Better you don't know right now," he told her. "If everything goes as I want it to, I'll tell you. Meantime, our job is to concentrate on catching McDwyer. Alive."

"Yes, sir."

They passed through a high-ceilinged chamber that must have once been the resort's ballroom. Modest in size by Earth standards, by Martian standards it was lavish.

And in ruins. No one had even bothered to loot it—the shattered crystal of candelabras littered the floor, and once plush, real-leather sofas cracked in the dry Martian air. A fine coat of red dust covered everything, puffing up as they moved through it.

The Earth-Minbari War, the embargo that had followed, and the provisional Mars government hadn't done much to help the old tourist industry. New Vegas had survived, as had the upper-crust entertainments of Olympus Mons, but none of the more exclusive—and isolated—imitators. This one, the hotel Tharsis, would likely never open again. It was home to fifty or so squatters, some fugitives from the EPG, some just half-crazed outbackers.

McDwyer had made a sizable dent in their active population—the trail of bodies was even clearer than his footprints in the Martian dust.

Something else, breaking ahead, and three of his bloodhounds bolted forward. As per orders, they didn't draw their PPGs. Bester hurried his own pace, through the ballroom and into a wing of suites.

The hounds were already down when he entered, clutching their heads in stunned agony.

McDwyer sat across the room, balanced on the high back of a chair, feet in the seat. He was leaning forward, posed like a cross between a gargoyle and Rodin's *Thinker*. Behind him there was a large picture window, threaded with cracks. A dune of rusty sand piled against the outside, obscuring more than half the view. The plain beyond was lit by a rare, amber sky. The light from the window tinged everything in the room with a faintly sulfurous hue.

"Hello," McDwyer said, not looking up.

"Hello, Mr. McDwyer," Bester said. "I've come to help you."

He couldn't see the man's face behind the respirator, but a shim of glee drifted up from him, though it had an odd quality to it. Like honey with an aftertaste of anise. McDwyer's mind imago resembled a blob of caviar, a thousand little black bubbles, shifting this way and that.

McDwyer slowly shook a finger at him. "You know that pi doesn't

resolve. But neither does two plus two. It's just an approximation, you know?"

"No, I don't. Help me understand."

A muffled laugh. "You just want me to go back. But I'm already back, that's what you don't know. They're everywhere. Scratch the fabric of space, and you find their eyes, looking at you. You know? So why should I go back? I just wait, I wait, sometimes I forget, but then they return, because they never left—" He shook his head. "You want to see? You wanted *me* to see, and now *you* don't want to see? You still think pi resolves? You—"

"All right," Bester said. "Show me."

McDwyer clutched at his head. "Oh, sure—"

The caviar-mass of his mind suddenly jiggled, and each tiny egg split open—no, slitted open, like an eye. The whole thing had changed, become like the compound eye of an insect. Glyphs swarmed out. *Madness* swarmed out. Things like spiders, like black sea urchins, stinging things, poison ampoules. But that was only the beginning—it was the tide of feeling that hurt so, brought emotions like the scent of formaldehyde, the taste of rotted meat, the sound of a drill in a tooth. Passions that felt like skin tearing between fingers, a paper cut on an eyeball, the almost-pleasurable rupturing of a pus-filled wound. Desires that meant nothing, could mean nothing, to a warm-blooded mammal.

All of that hit Bester in under a second, and he snapped his guards up. Nonetheless, he was stunned by the intensity of the wave.

"No!" McDwyer screamed. His head jerked up. "You said you wanted to see!" He slammed the glyphs back at Bester, who countered, though he was still weakened by the experience of McDwyer's insanity.

Things from McDwyer's nightmare attacked him; chitinous stings bristling with hairs, and each hair an eye. The clacking mandibles of a spider, or a mantis. Ropes of maggoty sinews. Bester fell back before the onslaught. Drawing McDwyer out, a bullfighter waving his cloak.

When the attack thinned, when it seemed overextended, Bester struck back, a hard spark to the backbrain, meant to disable.

But the madman's defenses were too powerful, too *alien*. It was as if McDwyer's brain had been imprinted with something not Human at all—it didn't react like a Human brain, or even like the Minbari prisoners Bester had scanned during the war.

McDwyer renewed his assault, and it was all snapping in like a bear trap. For the first time it occurred to Bester that he might lose this battle. After all, he was strong, but not the strongest by far—

He couldn't get out the way he had come in—it was a sort of Chinese

finger-puzzle—so he plunged forward and burrowed out. Blood vessels exploded like water balloons, and he had no idea whose they were.

Then he was outside, looking through his own eyes. McDwyer sighed and fell off of the chair. *Thank you,* he said, very faintly. Then massive hemorrhaging took him away.

Bester wasn't remotely interested in following. Whatever hell McDwyer was off to couldn't compare to the one he had just been in.

"Whoof," he muttered, sitting down in another chair—a hardwood that creaked dangerously. Someone came into the room behind him.

"Are you all right, sir?"

"Quite all right. I—"

"Then what the *hell* is going on here?"

Bester turned to regard a tall, almost gigantic frame filling the doorway. Behind him there were at least ten men in black uniforms and hoods, not unlike Bester's own bloodhound units.

"We apprehended a rogue," Bester said, indicating the dead McDwyer. "I'm Alfred Bester, attached to the MarsDome precinct. And you are . . . ?"

"Who *I* am is of no concern. *You,* Mr. Bester, are a long way from home, and this is Department Sigma business."

"Well, it wasn't specified as such on the distress signal we received from the hotel."

"Hotel? There is no hotel—this is a ruin! Who notified you that McDwyer was here?"

"One of the residents—one of the dead ones, I believe. He called MarsDome and they patched it to me. What's the problem?"

"One problem is that this man was carrying classified information. The other is that I have a deep suspicion that some of your bloodhounds laid false trails, to slow me and my people up."

Bester shrugged dispassionately. "Well. As you may or may not know—I'm sorry, I still haven't caught your name—I am cleared up to level A."

"Yes? Well—"

"Surely this matter couldn't require clearance above that? What's *your* clearance? And, again, your name?"

"Ah—I'm Joseph Talmedge. My clearance is B."

"So you see? There is no problem. I have higher clearance than you do."

"Sir—I'm afraid you'll still have to be debriefed."

"No doubt. I was prepared for that. I'll follow you to Syria Planum— don't worry, I know the way."

* * *

"As I told your man, I have the clearance. Now I want to exercise it."

"Yes, in theory you have the clearance, Mr. Bester," Aubrey Pierre-Louis replied, bushy grey eyebrows sinking lower and lower on his forehead. "But this is a singular situation, and in *fact,* you may not be cleared for this."

Bester crossed his left hand across his belly and fingered his chin with the right. "I don't see how that can be, Mr. Pierre-Louis. Maybe you can explain it to me. Perhaps this is a need-to-know situation? Well, then, I have a need to know.

"In case you were asleep when it happened, one of our better P12s just went completely berserk. He was driven berserk by something right here. A new drug? A new technique to push past P12? Was he a volunteer? I don't *care.* But to do my job, and to keep things like this from leaking out—to the provisional government, for instance—*I. Need. To. Know.* Keeping me in the dark is simply stupid, and is a greater threat to Corps security than telling me."

"Al—"

"Don't 'Al' me, Aubrey, unless you plan to do something here."

"Al, you have every right to be upset—"

"Wrong. I have every right to know what the *hell* is going on. I have the *obligation* to be upset. Now are you going to tell me, or do I keep going over your head?"

Here was where his bluff rested on a fine line. Bester had worked for almost two months, keeping careful watch on Sigma's movements, waiting for something like the McDwyer breakout, an event that would allow him to claim privilege. He had even cultivated Pierre-Louis as best he could, hanging out in the chief's favorite bar, swapping war stories.

If Brett was right, and this went much higher, he was likely to hit a stone wall. His security clearance might even be in jeopardy. He had called in half a dozen favors just to get where he was at this moment.

If Pierre-Louis didn't cave, it was over.

"Very well," the older man sighed. "I suppose you should see. But this—this is top secret, you have to understand that. This goes way beyond clearance."

"I understand," Bester said. "I will be the soul of discretion."

"My God," Bester said. "What is it?"

"We aren't sure. We think it's a ship."

It was more than he had ever imagined. Ship? No. It was a fallen angel. Just the sight of it ate at his backbrain, at the part of him that remembered the days before life crawled out of the oceans, when things like *this* ate his wormlike, notochord ancestors. This is what had bred

spiders in Endra, who had never seen a spider. It was what had driven McDwyer as mad as the hatter in *Alice*.

A scene flashed behind his retinas, so vivid and disorienting that he nearly stumbled. Suddenly he was six years old, facing Director Vacit. Every detail was as clear as a photograph. *Watch for the Shadows,* Vacit had said. *Watch and beware.*

It chilled him to the marrow.

The ship was huge, even only half excavated. Its skin was black, but all shades of black—not the absence of color, but the maiming of it. It moved, it shifted. And he could *feel* it.

"Is it alive?"

"Yes. It is. Or we think it is, anyway."

"Sentient?"

"That's what we were trying to find out when McDwyer touched it. You saw the answer we got."

"Yes, I suppose I did. How long has it been here?"

"We don't know. It was buried, not covered by natural deposition. We think maybe two thousand years, maybe more."

"It's beautiful, in a way."

"It gives me the shakes," Pierre-Louis confessed.

"Beauty should shake you up, Aubrey. It should shake you to the core."

"Very nice philosophy, but if that's the case, I'll stick to the plain and ugly, thank you. I can do without the nightmares."

"What are you going to do with it?"

"Study it. See what makes it tick. It's clearly more advanced than anything any of the races we know possesses, with the possible exception of the Vorlons—and there, of course, we only go on rumor."

"And the Corps has it. Wonderful. Does EarthGov know?"

"Al—you really don't want to know who knows about this thing. You really, really don't."

"I'll take your word for it. But—can we work a little more closely from now on? You're the administrator. It's your job to provide the Corps with a future. It's my job to catch rogues, solve crimes, keep the peace. When those things overlap, as they did today, we should talk. Otherwise, I'll try to stay out of your hair. Agreed?"

"Agreed."

Bester looked back at the ship. "I think I'm starting to agree with you about this thing. Why don't I buy you a drink?"

"Not a bad suggestion."

Bester left with the feeling that he had approached the edge of a very deep canyon, teetered on the rim, and then withdrawn safely.

It was time to lay low. Brett had voiced suspicions, about a mundane-backed hegemony in the upper ranks of the Corps. Even if they were unfounded—and Bester didn't think they were—it still wasn't wise to attract undue attention. Especially now. Because it was clear that Brett was right about at least one thing: big happenings were afoot, very big. Bester was determined to be a part of them, but he would have to be patient.

A few days will tell if I've gone too far, he thought. Mentally, he crossed his fingers.

3

Three days later, he got a call from assistant director Menendez. There were four assistant directors—Bester usually dealt with Kaufman, in the Mars office. Menendez he had never spoken to. On the vid he looked awfully young, almost baby-faced.

"Beta Colony?" Bester repeated, politely.

"Yes. It's priority one."

Bester considered Menendez for a moment. "I can have my Black Omega Squadron ready in four hours."

"Negative on that. Black Omega Squadron is needed on Mars."

Bester blinked. "She's my squadron. I fought for years to form her."

"Mr. Bester, whatever role you had in the formation of the Black Omegas, they—like you—belong to the Corps."

"Of course. But I command them. Are you relieving me of that command?"

"No, Mr. Bester, I am not. These are delicate times. We need you at Beta Colony and we need your squadron near Mars, on standby."

"You're expecting trouble."

"Maybe."

"Very well, then. How do I get to Beta Colony?"

"The way anyone else would, Mr. Bester. We bought you tickets on a commercial transport."

"And how many of my bloodhounds may I take?"

"What's needed on Beta is an investigator, not a whole unit. Beta is not particularly—friendly—to the Corps, so we have to do this without much intrusion. The local office will supply you all the people you need."

"With all respect, I work better with my own people."

"I'm sure you do. But it's not going to happen."

Bester shrugged. "If that's the way the ball bounces . . . When do I leave?"

"You have two hours."

* * *

All the way to his quarters, and even while packing, he fought through his outrage, looking for perspective. They wanted him alone, far from his troops. If they had just sent him to Beta Colony, he would have considered it a distraction, something to get him away from Mars—and the black ship—for a time. But this—well, he must have miscalculated. He must have gone too far, after all.

He regretted, for a moment, putting off the appointment he had been planning. True, he had wanted to find precisely the right time, but . . .

No matter. He would survive this. The time would come, soon enough. It was inevitable; it was destiny.

There were a lot of things Al Bester might not have—true love, deep friendships, a beatific relationship with a happy cosmos—but if there was one thing he *did* have, it was a destiny.

"Well, place-names go through fashions," Bester was explaining to his fellow passenger. He was a man in early middle age, who identified himself as an insurance broker. "You have to consider the historical context."

"What historical context could there be for there to be fourteen 'Beta' colonies in Human space?"

"Well, you're from North America, right?"

"The United States," he said, a trace of pride in his voice.

Ah. A romantic, potentially even a national separatist, Bester thought, and filed it away for future reference. You never knew, with mundanes.

"Well, think. Almost every state in the United States has at least one 'Columbus' or 'Columbia,' one 'Franklin,' one 'Madison'—usually more than one. These names crop up everywhere because they were a part of the collective unconscious of the European-American settlers."

"Yeah, but those places are named after people."

"Well, consider the Springdales, the Oaklands, the Lake Cities."

"Still, Beta . . . ?"

"I think it's two things. First, we keep coming back to Greek. It symbolizes certain things to us—democracy, learning, literature, education. Never mind that Greeks were, for the most part, very undemocratic and not particularly literary or advanced compared to, say, China at the time—the symbolism remains. Oh, Greek went out of fashion—Sanskrit and Mandarin were all the rage in the last century. At the beginning of this century, Centauri had a brief heyday. Then, yet another Greek revival—I think in response to the fear of having our culture swamped by alien influences. Greek, Latin, Sumerian—all became very popular

again. I'll bet you had at least one grandfather named Achilles and one named Gilgamesh."

The fellow nodded.

"The funny thing is," Bester continued, "the Centauri picked up on that, too. If you'll remember, at the time they were trying to convince us we were a lost Centauri colony. They started using Greek and Roman names and their derivatives to translate the names of their planets and star systems. Oddly enough, a bunch of *their* colony worlds ended up being 'Beta' this and that, because in their settlement system there could be only one 'Alpha'—Centauri Prime.

"That's the second thing, of course. By the time we started setting up colonies, 'Beta' had almost become a slang word for 'less important colony.' It's not systematic—look at any star system with more than one colony. Odds are you won't see an Alpha, Gamma, or Delta colony—but it's even odds that at least a city somewhere will be named 'Beta.' "

"That makes sense, I guess. Do you teach geography or something in the Psi Corps?" His eye was drawn, as it had been several times, to Bester's badge.

"Oh, no. But the last guy I sat next to on a ship was a geography professor."

"And he told you all of this?"

Bester forced his face into a puzzled frown. "No. Why would you ask that?"

He loved the expression on their faces when he said things like that. Some men liked fine cigars, some liked French brandy. He preferred the man next to him, trying to laugh it off as a joke—and in the end, failing. In point of fact, he had read everything he just said in a standard tourist guide, but he wasn't going to tell his seatmate that.

An hour later he set foot for the first time on Beta Colony. This particular Beta was one in a system of only two colonies—unless you counted the minor settlements in the metal-rich asteroids. In that case, there were four.

The system's largest colony was on the fourth planet from the star, a world called simply Sheffer 4 on the star charts, and Aztlan by its inhabitants.

Beta was the third planet. Smaller than Aztlan, it still boasted almost half as many settlers as Mars—one million, two-thirds of them located in the polar industrial city, also called Beta. Only the poles were cool enough to be habitable, but that was greatly outweighed by the fact that the atmosphere had free oxygen in quantities sufficient to sustain Human life, and plenty of nitrogen, necessary for food crops.

Bester found Beta City to be quite impressive. The buildings had a

massive, muscular feel—after all, they had to cope with the same gravity that was nagging Bester at the moment, nearly one and a quarter times that of Earth. A hot, blustery wind combed through them—which after his years in the thin, frigid air of Mars, proved more than welcome. The wind smelled something like ginger.

Around the city, what looked like tall-grass prairie flowed off to mountains—distant except to the north, where a long row of them scraped at the sky. The sun looked almost exactly like the sun of Earth, and the sky was a velvety blue.

"Mr. Bester, I presume?"

He turned his attention from the view to a really quite attractive young woman—early twenties—with coppery hair cut in a Dutch bob.

"Yes?"

"I'm Lyta Alexander. I'll be your assistant while you're here."

"Well, a pleasure to meet you, Ms. Alexander. How long have you worked here?"

She blushed. "Actually, only a few weeks. I came here to intern with MetaPol—not as a cop, because I'm only a P5—but as a profiler. Unfortunately, the department is shorthanded, so they couldn't spare a real cop—or someone with more experience on the planet—to assist you."

"Why are they so shorthanded?"

"We've lost two men in the last two weeks, and their replacements haven't arrived."

"Lost?"

"Killed. By the Blinder."

"Blinder?"

"It's what we call the serial killer."

"Ah. My quarry."

"Yes, sir."

"Well. Let's get started, then."

"Let me get your bag."

"No. I've got it. Though it seems like it weighs twice what it did when I left home. I must learn to resist those duty-free shops."

"Well," Lyta began, tentatively. "You're aware the gravity is a little higher here . . ."

"It was a joke, Lyta. May I call you Lyta?"

"Oh. I—I'm sorry, yes, please do."

"For some reason, no one ever expects me to have a sense of humor," he mused. He noticed her smile hesitantly. "Alexander," he mused. "Any relation to Natasha Alexander?"

"My grandmother," she said, a bit surprised.

"I met her once."

Lyta smiled. "When I was a little girl, she used to bring me presents—well, they came through the Grins, of course, but I always knew they really came from Grandma."

"You were in Cadre Prime?"

She nodded affirmatively. "My mother was the only woman in our line in the last four generations who wasn't. She was only a P2, so she was in the Basement at first, but when she was still pretty young, Grandma arranged for some relatives to raise her outside Teeptown. She was monitored, of course, but never actively attached to the Corps."

"Four generations?"

"Six, really—all the way back to Desa Alexander, back before it was even Psi Corps."

"Yes, I guessed you were from one of the old families, since you kept your mitochondrial name. I was a Cadre Primer myself, you know."

She nodded again, and they went a few steps in silence.

"Lyta, I'm a little slight on the details of this case. The killer isn't a telepath?"

"No, sir—we don't think so."

"So I was brought in because he killed Psi Cops?"

"Oh, no, sir. That's only happened in the past two days. He's killed four other telepaths. He *only* kills telepaths."

"I see. Well, I suppose I should get briefed on the forensics data, then have a look at the crime scenes—"

"Actually, sir, I have some bad news. We found another body just a few hours before you arrived. Looks like the same killer. Our station chief is out of town, and local law enforcement has been wanting to go in, but we've been trying to hold it for you. I don't know how much longer we can."

"Oh. By all means, then—let's go."

They took a surface car, something Bester hadn't done in quite some time. They kept the top down, driving through the hot wind past rows of single-story buildings made of cut and dressed volcanic stone, with pitched metal roofs. Most of the houses had gardens. This was a roomy city, lots of space. Wide streets. Not like Mars—or many places on Earth, for that matter.

They stopped at a house that—in most cities on Earth—would have been a mansion. On Mars it would have been quite simply unthinkable. Here it seemed to be better than modest.

The street out front was swarming with police cars, reporters, gawkers.

"Oh, no," Lyta said. "It looks like they've gone in." She opened her

door, jumped out, and came around to let him out, but he was already out, staring at the house.

They pushed quickly through the crowd and up to the police line. A young fellow was manning it—his uniform was unfamiliar in detail, but obvious in type. He was a deputy or the equivalent. He looked at Bester and Lyta and clearly didn't like what he saw, but he let them in, if reluctantly.

"It's time to clear up a few things," Bester confided to Lyta.

There was blood—and a body—but for the moment he ignored them, and instead picked the man who looked to be in charge and walked up to him.

"You're the detective in charge?" he asked.

The fellow looked away from his notepad and down at Bester. Physically, he gave Bester the impression of a snowman made of ground beef, with two olives for eyes. Bester had once seen such an atrocity at the Museum of Modern Art on Mars. "Yer a regular mind reader," the detective said, eyeing Bester's badge and grinning broadly at his own joke.

"That's terribly funny," Bester said. "And I do mean terribly. My name is Alfred Bester. You are aware that this investigation has come under Psi Corps jurisdiction?"

"I know that the Blinder killings are under Psi Corps jurisdiction, yeah. I had no way of knowing this was one of his without investigating, though. Do I need to draw you a picture, or can you just suck it right out of me?"

Bester frowned slightly and turned to survey the crime scene. "She was a registered telepath?"

"Yep. Business esper, pretty well-to-do. They all are."

"What?"

"Your business telepaths. All pretty well-to-do."

"Ah. You don't care for telepaths, Mr. . . ."

"Stesco. *Captain* Stesco. No, I can't say that I do. Most of us immigrated here to get away from 'em, and—"

"Really? You came all this way just to get away from telepaths? And everyone else on the planet did, too?"

He kept talking because he was looking at the body. He kept talking to stay detached.

The most obvious thing about the dead woman was that her eyes were gone.

"Not just telepaths," Stesco modified. "There were lots of things we didn't like about Earth. Hey, don't get me wrong—I'm no bigot. I've got nothing against any of you personally. It's just—I just think if a fellow

wants to live someplace with no fear his mind is gonna be picked over by somebody, he ought to have the right."

"Separate but equal, Mr. Stesco?"

"Sounds good to me."

"Why don't you have local laws against the use of business telepaths?"

"We did, until a few years ago."

"So who let the snake into your little garden?"

"A coalition of businesses. Recent immigrants. Beta's changed a lot in the past few years, not for the better. There's your proof." He waved at the corpse.

"I don't see what your complaint is," Bester said. "Up until now, you people could only daydream about killing telepaths. Now you have real, live ones to play out your fantasies with."

"Hey, like I said—"

"You aren't a bigot. Yes, I heard you the first time. How many legs does a dog have, if you count the tail as a leg?"

"Huh?"

"How many legs does a dog have if you count the tail as a leg?"

"I—five, I guess."

"Wrong. Four. Because a tail is not a leg, even if you say it is."

"Hilarious." Stesco looked as if he thought it was anything but.

"Thank you. What are these marks on her arms?"

"When we found her she was tied up and hanging from the ceiling. We cut her down."

"You *what*?"

"Wasn't decent, a naked woman hanging up like that. The reporters might have taken her picture."

"What a charming little world this is," Bester remarked acidly. "You didn't sew her mouth up for some reason, did you?"

"No, she was like that when we found her."

"Like this—but hanging from the ceiling."

"I told you."

"Could you clear the rest of your men out? I need to talk to you alone."

"Why alone?"

"Detective, I'm in charge here now, whether you like it or not. You know it. And I assure you, it's best that this next conversation take place without your men around."

Stesco frowned, but went over to talk to his men. Bester continued his inspection of the body.

"Were the rest like this?" he asked Lyta, who stood to one side, looking very pale.

"Yes. Eyes gouged out, mouth sewn shut. He poured something in their ears, a kind of fast-hardening epoxy."

"What was the actual cause of death?"

"Suffocation. We think that after—sealing up—everything, he pinched their noses shut."

"Yes. Maybe he did it many times? Tortured them? Brought them nearly to death and then let them breathe, repeated the process? Deprived them of their senses so they could see only through his eyes, hear only through his ears as he was killing them?"

"Maybe. The MO was a little different on the two cops."

"We'll get to that in a moment," Bester said. The door was closing, Stesco returning.

"Now what?" Stesco said. "You gonna chew me out for stepping on your investigation? You could've done that in front of my men."

"Yes, I could have," Bester replied, flashing Stesco a little smile. "But I couldn't have done this."

He hit Stesco with a fugue to hold him and then a midrange scan. The big man's knees went rubbery and he swayed there, mouth twitching, drool running down his chin. When Bester was finished, he murmured, "And now, let's make sure you don't remember our little moment together—" and he made a few more adjustments. A moment later, Stesco's glazed eyes suddenly began seeing again.

"Whoa!" he grumbled. "Got dizzy for a second there."

"I advise you to watch your blood pressure, Captain Stesco," Bester said, helpfully. "You don't seem like a well man."

"Well, what didja want, anyway?"

"Just to thank you for your time and to assure you that I'll report whatever I come up with directly to you."

"Oh. Well, thanks. Guess I'll be goin' now."

"I guess you will."

After he was gone, he turned to Lyta and found her staring at him in undisguised horror.

"You have something to say, Lyta?"

"I—sir, that was illegal."

"Yes, well—I was tired of talking to him. The man had a foul mouth. A foul mind, too, but a scan is over with more quickly than a long conversation. Besides, it was a fairly cursory scan, with minimal damage—and he won't remember a thing."

"But sir—"

"Look at her, Lyta." He pointed toward the corpse. "Look at her.

There she lies, dead and mutilated. She's not the first, but by God we can make sure she's the last. If I have to scan a few small-minded bigots to speed up the process of catching this monster and protecting our people, I'm not above it."

Her face struggled to find an expression and settled for a dead neutral.

He sighed. "Lyta, when I was younger I believed in doing things by the book. I still do, when it makes sense. But in cases like these, I've become more interested in justice than in procedure. Sue me."

"Yes, sir," she said, though it was clear to him she still did not agree. "Did you learn anything from him?"

"As it happens—yes. He isn't the killer, and he doesn't know who the killer was. He doesn't *want* to know who the killer was—he thinks our man is doing a fine job, ridding his planet of teeps. Which is perhaps why he hasn't mentioned to the Corps what he *does* know."

"Which is?"

"There was another killing a week ago that he thinks has something to do with this. A mundane named Jack Finn."

"It's not in the record."

"I didn't think it would be. You have a summary report of all of this for me?"

"Yes, sir."

"I'll want that first. I also want you to look up anything you can find on Jack Finn." He looked around. "What about the security system?"

"Our killer has some way around it. We almost caught him, the first time, because a call did go out. Response time was slow, probably because the house belonged to a telepath. Still, we think the patrol only missed the killer by a few minutes."

"That only happened the first time? Since then there have been no calls?"

"That's correct, sir. Umm, excuse me, sir—my tel-phone—" She unfolded the small device. "Alexander here. Oh, yes—we're at the crime scene. Yes, of course, Ms. Mallory, I'll ask." She lowered the phone. "Our station chief is back and would like to see you at your earliest convenience."

"Mallory? Would that be Anne Mallory?"

"Yes, sir."

"Tell her we'll be right there."

Lyta did so, then closed the phone. "You know Ms. Mallory?"

"Sure, we worked together some back on Earth. A good cop."

"Would you like to put your things in your room, before going to the office?"

"No, plenty of time for that. I don't want to keep Anne waiting."

"Al. So pleased to see you again."

"You haven't changed since we served together under de Vries, Anne. I had no idea you were out here on Beta."

"Oh, I'm here, all right. I'm sorry I couldn't join you at the crime scene—I was on the other side of the pole zone, checking out some leads to another case when we got the word. I knew your ship was getting in about that time, and I knew you were competent to handle it. Any trouble?"

"The scene had been disturbed."

"By Captain Stesco?" Her face colored. "I left definite orders—"

"Captain Stesco seems to have some problems with authority—when the authority is a teep. Don't worry—I think next time you'll find him a bit more—pliant."

Anne Mallory's narrow face took on a sudden worried caste. "Al, you didn't. I know your reputation—"

"And so does the Corps. They wouldn't have sent me, Anne, if they didn't think my methods were needed here." At least he hoped that was the case.

"Al, this isn't Mars, that's all I'm saying. The locals are sometimes—narrow-minded."

"I'm used to that. Don't worry. I'll be discreet. But I'll find the killer. You don't kill seven of my people and just walk away. How many officers can you give me?"

"For walking around? Just Ms. Alexander, I'm afraid. When you really need them, three." She leaned forward and clasped her hands. "I was wondering—why didn't you bring your bloodhound units?"

Bester gave her a wan smile. "You'll have to ask the central office. Personally, I think they believe I've become lazy—that I can't work a case without my minions anymore. I'll be happy to prove them wrong." He didn't tell her his deeper suspicion—that there were probably those in the Corps who would be just as happy if he didn't return from this assignment.

"Tell me about your cops—Ran and Farmer? Ms. Alexander said the MO was different."

"A little. Sort of a quickie version. Their eyes were scooped out, but he just taped and glued their mouths shut."

"I've looked at the reports on the other victims. At first I thought we had something fairly typical, here—the victim forced to look through the

eyes of the killer as the deed is done. I worked a case in Buenos Aires like that. Every mundane psycho who comes up with it thinks he's the Thomas Edison of serial killings, when in fact it's so *obvious* . . ." He trailed off. "But I didn't notice the rest of it right away. All of the other body orifices were sewn up, too—the cops?"

"Epoxied," she corrected, with a slight quiver in her voice.

"So it's something more ritualistic. Something to do with the soul, the life force. Our killer has religious beliefs."

"Are you familiar with the religion?" she asked.

"No. Nor do I intend to become familiar with it."

"What do you mean?"

"One of my first lessons as an investigator was to learn to see things from my quarry's point of view. If you can understand your enemy, you can defeat him. But Anne—I'm getting old. I don't want to understand this sick son of a bitch. I just want to find him and punish him. Is that all right with you?"

She looked at him for a long moment, then nodded, grimly, a new determination settling upon her features.

"Good," he said. "And now, I think I'll go put my bags in my room and freshen up a bit. Then I'll want to go over the evidence in more detail. Do you have a list of suspects, witnesses?"

"No."

"No? That was a big house. Didn't she have any servants?"

"She had a houseboy, a maid, and a cook. None of them remember anything useful."

"Did you scan them?"

"No. None of them would agree to it. As you may have gathered, the locals are squeamish about telepathy."

"I want to see them anyway. You can promise them they won't be scanned, if you wish."

"Will I be lying?"

"Anne. What you don't know for sure, you can't lie about."

"Good enough."

"I'm glad to see you coming around. I think I'll go to my room now. See you later."

Lyta was waiting for him outside the office. "You're ready to go to the hotel?"

"Hotel?"

"Unless you'd like to spend the night in a holding cell. The local office doesn't have dorms—everyone lives in private homes."

"And you, Ms. Alexander?"

"I'm still in the hotel. Since I'm an intern, I'm allowed to comp it."

"I see. Well, the hotel it is."

Bester meant to drop his bags and get straight to work, but the room seduced him. The high gravity was already wearing out its welcome with his knees and lower back. The bed was huge—bigger, almost, than his entire bedroom on Mars.

But it was the tub that brought him to at least a conditional surrender. It was enormous, with massage jets.

The guidebooks all said off-worlders from lower-gravity worlds should bathe often, to give their skeletons and muscles a break.

He started running the water, then went to a terminal and used his access code to call up and execute a notepad copy of the report Alexander had given him. He took his usual security precautions and then, with the pad in his good right hand, he sank thankfully into the buoyant waters.

With the exception of the two cops, all of the victims had been business teeps. Some good basic work had been done already, including a list of clients for each victim going back several months, cross-referenced in several ways—by company, association, type of transaction. Several firms showed up more than once, but that was to be expected in a community of this size. Interestingly, all of the victims had been freelancers, rather than being attached to a particular corporation.

He looked over the list carefully. The victims had been chosen because they were telepaths, and business teeps were the easiest to come by. They made their livings by being accessible. Most likely, the killer had called them, set up an appointment, met them, killed them.

But in the lists of meetings, phone calls, and correspondence, no common denominator had turned up that checked out.

So try it from another angle. The bodies of the business teeps were all found in their homes. A servant? Some sort of maintenance worker?

He closed his eyes. He was tired, more tired than he had any right to be. The water felt very, very good.

No. He couldn't rest yet. Miles to go and all of that. He opened his eyes and focused on the report again. The letters seemed to swim. Too tired. He closed them again, and let his mind flow out. It had been a long time, he realized, since he had listened to a new city. He had never listened to one in another star system. For a moment, he felt an almost youthful excitement at the idea.

And yet there was nothing.

He concentrated, and more nothing.

Something in the stone the building was made of? In the atmo-

sphere? In the solar wind? And yet he had had no trouble earlier, when he scanned Stesco. Indeed, he had been in fine form.

His head bumped back into the edge of the tub, and he suddenly realized how slow and stupid he felt. Too slow, too stupid to be explained by fatigue.

With a snarl that came out only as a snort, he started trying to lever himself out of the tub. He was only halfway out when the man in the black hood stepped into the bathroom.

4

Bester sat back down in the tub. "I don't suppose you came to scrub my back?" he asked.

The black-hooded figure didn't answer, but he did raise a wicked-looking weapon, rather unhurriedly. Bester thought it might be a Narn hunting pistol.

Bester raised his own PPG out of the tub in something more of a hurry. His first shot missed, as the water dripping from the muzzle of the weapon vaporized and distorted the path of the phased plasma. His second shot was dead on target and caught the black-clad man in the right shoulder. Something spattered against the tile behind him—presumably something fired from the pistol—and he quickly scrambled out of the tub, for fear that the ampoule had contained enough nerve toxin to affect him even though it had diffused in the water. He kept his own weapon level.

The hooded man moaned, leaning against the door frame and obviously in pain. There was a good bit of blood.

"Yes, I know I'm a bit old to keep toys in the tub." Bester held up the PPG. "My version of a rubber ducky, I suppose. Push that weapon toward me, will you?"

The fellow managed to, though it wasn't easy for him. He sank to the floor. "Don't kill me," he said.

"Hurt a poor, disturbed serial killer like you?" Bester said, taking a robe down from its hook on the wall and slipping into it. "Now why should I do that? You want to pull that mask off, or shall I shoot it off?"

Struggling into a sitting position against the commode, the would-be assassin managed to pull the hood off with his left hand. The face beneath was unfamiliar, the green eyes startling jewels in a nearly ebony setting.

"You got something into my bathwater? Something like sleepers? I'm guessing that because I'm feeling better already." It was a lie, but at least he wasn't feeling any woozier. When he tried to scan the fellow,

though, all he got was a frustrating sensation of needing to sneeze, almost being able to sneeze—but not quite sneezing.

"Yes. In your water. May I tie a tourniquet?"

"Not just yet. You aren't the serial killer, are you? I'm guessing your bag has all of the right tools—needle and thread, epoxy, rope—but you aren't him. You came here to kill me, and with equipment I seriously doubt anyone outside of Psi Corps could get their hands on."

The man just looked at him sullenly.

"Okay. Get up. We're going in the next room, where we can have a civilized conversation." He motioned with the weapon.

"I've lost too much blood. I can't stand up."

"Shall I cauterize that wound for you? Sometimes, at the medium setting, if you hit *just* right—"

The fellow shook his head and climbed reluctantly to his feet. At Bester's direction he stumbled out onto the balcony and into a chair.

"There," Bester said. "This is tiled, too, so the maid won't have a lot of trouble cleaning it up. Now, why did you try to kill me? No, let me make it simpler for you. Who sent you to kill me?"

"Scan me and find out."

"I will, in due time. What did you hit me with? Sleepers don't work that quickly, certainly not absorbed through the skin. Something new Department Sigma is developing?"

"You're letting me bleed to death. Let me tie this off and I'll tell you everything."

"Very well. I'll call for some help." He backed into the room and picked up the tel-phone that lay on the counter.

The assassin bolted out of his chair. Bester dropped the muzzle of the PPG, to aim at his knees—

Too late. He had misjudged the man. Helped him, even.

Disgusted, he walked back to the balcony. Here, six stories was more like eight or nine on Earth. The broken body was already starting to draw a crowd. He sighed, punched a code into the phone. After an instant, a female voice answered from the other end.

"Lyta, could you come up to my room? I need you."

From the tone of her affirmative answer, he could guess at least one thing she might be imagining. He didn't have the energy to care.

They had coffee the next morning in the hotel restaurant, and a local breakfast specialty called *poksh,* a sort of heavy, steamed, sweet bread.

"But how can you be sure, sir, that this Koste wasn't the killer we're after?"

"First off because that's not his real name," Bester said. The coffee

was heavy and pungent, and left a complex aftertaste. Not exactly like any he'd had on Earth or Mars. He wondered if it was one of Beta Colony's exports—if it wasn't, it ought to be. "I tracked him through two aliases before I lost him. No, he was a professional assassin, and other than wishing to make it look as if I was killed by our local hero, I'm afraid he brings us no closer to resolving the case."

"I see. But who would want to kill you, sir?"

Bester laughed, his first genuine laugh in a long time. "You don't know me very well, Lyta." He took another sip of the coffee and a bite of the poksh. He found the bread less inspiring than the coffee. "What did you find out about Jack Finn?"

"Well, only that he disappeared a week ago, about the same time the Psi Cops were killed. They found his body two days ago, in a field about twenty klicks from town. I don't see a connection. He wasn't a teep, and he wasn't killed like the others. He was stabbed in the heart, very simple."

"Huh. Yet there was a clear connection in Stesco's mind."

"Maybe it was simple association."

"Maybe. What did Finn do?"

"He was the chief information ecologist for the city. That is, he monitored the way flows of information—in computer networks, telphone and link calls, and so on—related to power flow in the city."

"That's interesting. What else do we know about him?"

"He was an Adamist."

That got Bester's attention. "In other words, he was a Teep-hater."

"Yes, sir. But about half the population of Beta has Adamist leanings."

"Yes, what a surprise. But still—think about it. Were he still alive, Finn would be a prime suspect."

"How do you figure that?"

"All of the security systems in the victims' houses were linked to a citywide system. Finn was in a position to put kinks in that, if he wanted to. To block calls at the metropolitan level long enough to gain entry."

"Maybe. I think it would be more complicated than that, if you don't mind my saying so. He would still need the particular code, retina and fingerprint information, and so on for each house in question."

"It's worth checking into."

"You think he might have been working with the killer?"

"That would be highly unusual—if our killer is really a serial killer. They usually work alone." He ticked his finger against the table. "Our good friend Captain Stesco thinks Finn's murder is connected, doesn't

he? But he doesn't know why he thinks that, or I would know. It's a gut instinct, on his part."

"Anyway," Lyta said, "even if Finn was working with our killer, he couldn't have been in on the last murder. He was already dead."

"True. Ah, well. Today I want to do a series of interviews. Domestics, servicemen—anyone recorded as going near the houses in question. Also—I'm assuming the reports regarding the two cops are in a separate file?"

"Oh—yes, sir. I was going to give them to you when you finished the first. It's procedure here, I guess—"

"Right now what I want to know is this—where were the cops found?"

"In their homes, like the others."

"And yet, they were 'quickie' versions. Serial killers like to be in control, and their rituals put them in control. They tend to follow scripts to the letter. The cops must have been getting close to him—but if he went so far as to kill them in their homes, why not go all the way and do it right?"

"Maybe he felt pressed for time, having to do two in one night. Maybe he has some arbitrary deadline he wants to be done by."

"Good thinking. But the time of death of the other victims doesn't seem to confirm that—at least, I don't see any obvious pattern. Would you run an analysis? Just search for any patterning in the time of death. Meanwhile, I have some interviews to conduct."

Bester glanced at Lyta every now and then during the "questioning." For the most part she kept her eyes fixed firmly on her notepad, undoubtedly working on the time-of-death problems, but just as certainly trying to pretend she wasn't aware of what was happening.

Anne was better, and even helped him. A few years of isolation from the rest of the Corps might have made her a little timid, but she remembered who she was. She understood that minor damage to some mundanes wasn't important compared to saving the life of every teep the killer might have targeted.

He got quite a lot from the interviewees—images of deliverymen, repairmen, details about their own household duties. None seemed to have an explicit knowledge of the murders.

He scanned them, erased the knowledge of the scan, and sent them out. Let them worry about the blank places in their memories—he didn't have time to.

By the afternoon he was tired and frustrated, but Lyta managed to cheer him up.

"Sir, I think I have something."

"What's that, Lyta?"

"There *is* a regularity in the time of murder—it was so *obvious*—I don't know why it took me so long to get it."

"Well?"

"The murders are all on record in local time."

"Of course."

"The first murder happened around 10 P.M. The next happened a week later a little after 3 P.M. The next was two days later around 8 P.M."

"And you see a pattern in this?"

"Yes, sir. If you add a little wiggle-room for the forensic uncertainty, you get a factor of 2.5—that is, for each day after the first murder, you add 2.5 hours."

He got it. "The local day is 2.5 hours shorter than Earth's day."

"Exactly, sir," she said, triumphantly. "He's killing them all between midnight and one o'clock in the morning—Earth time."

"The witching hour."

"Yes, sir."

"And he had to rush the cops—he had to do one, then drive to the house of the other and do him, too, before the clock struck one. Brilliant, Lyta. I'm impressed." He rubbed his chin. "So far that doesn't tell us any more about who our killer is. But that settles one problem—he didn't pick the cops as victims because they were teeps, but because they were cops. He followed his MO as best he could—because they were teeps. I'll bet he imagines he feeds on their souls, or sends them to hell—something like that. That would explain why Finn was killed without the ritual—he wasn't a teep. Check the station log. See if either or both cops had paid a visit to Finn."

She nodded and worked at her terminal for a moment. "No, sir— but—" She looked up, excitedly. "But they did visit the information ecology office. Something about the flow grids."

"That's it. That's it." He clapped his hands together. "Finn was helping him, all right—but they weren't accomplices."

"I—don't get it."

"Imagine you're Finn. You hate telepaths, despise them. Your father came all of the way to Beta Colony to keep you away from them, and you grew up in a religion that preaches their destruction. And now, suddenly, in your own lifetime, the colony council votes to start letting business teeps in. You watch them become wealthy while you, a public servant, have to scrape by on what you always have. You hate them, but you're too timid to do anything about it, so your frustration builds up.

"Then you read about the first killing. You understand this killer—

oh, he's a little wacko, what with the *way* he kills them—but you don't really care. At least somebody is *doing* something. Only, when you go back over your information flow records for that night, you notice he almost got caught.

"Well, this is your job, this is what you do. You can help him. You can fix it so the security calls just disappear somewhere."

"But Finn was dead, for the last murder—"

"Yes, but it doesn't matter. You were right about the difficulty of breaking individual systems—that's not what he did. After the first few murders, Finn figured out the same thing you did—that the time for the killings was always midnight, Earth time. He put the whole city on a timer. I'll guarantee you that when we check, we'll find that at twelve midnight, Earth time, the whole system does a little hiccup—goes off-line for just a second, then comes back on. In other words, Finn opened every house for a minute or so every night, knowing that only one person would take advantage of it—the killer."

"No one noticed this?"

"No reason to. It didn't shut down banks or businesses—their systems are smart enough to know when they aren't online. Most home systems aren't.

"On the other hand, our two cops did figure it out. So did Detective Stesco. He knows why Finn died."

"But he doesn't know who killed him. Or care." Her eyes widened. "We could set a trap!"

"We could, but it's risky. We might still not know the whole story. How did the killer find out he was being helped? How did he know to kill the cops after they went to the office of information ecology? That's the missing piece, Lyta. If we know that, I think we know who our killer is."

"Well, it could just be someone Finn knew. In the end, they might still have been in it together."

"I don't believe it. And how did Stesco know these killings were connected?"

"That part's simple. He knew Finn was covering for the killer."

"Which means that either Stesco is a better detective than I gave him credit for or—"

"—or Finn bragged. To someone. Somewhere."

Bester smiled slowly. "He was an Adamite. Who might an Adamite brag to?"

"Other Adamites—people he was certain wouldn't tell."

Bester nodded grimly. "I think it's time we see our friend Detective Stesco one more time."

5

Bester glanced at Stesco's quivering body. "He'll need to be cleaned up, this time," he said.

Lyta—ashen—nodded.

"He heard Finn bragging in a bar—I'll make you good odds that it's an Adamite bar and that the killer frequents it, too." He thought for just a moment, then flipped open his tel-phone and entered a code.

"Annie?" he said when the station chief picked up. "Why don't you let me buy you a drink?"

The bar fell silent like a scene from a bad western. The place didn't really look much like a saloon—it was a scrubbed-clean-looking place. There were perhaps thirty patrons. Some of them looked tough enough to play the cowpoke role—most did not. They all watched Bester and Lyta with less-than-friendly expressions.

"Stop me if you've heard this one," Bester said, loudly enough for everyone to hear him. "A telepath walks into a bar. He goes up to the bartender and says, 'I want to talk with each of your patrons, one at a time, in the back room, starting right now.'"

The bartender, a tall, slight man with a thin horseshoe of hair, frowned, gaped, then said, "Hey, you can't just come in here and—and . . ."

"Replied the very articulate barkeep," Bester continued. "'But the place is surrounded,' the telepath—that would be me—responded. 'And if you don't do what I say, you're going to be very, very sorry. On the other hand, all I want to do is to ask each of you a few questions, out of earshot of the rest. It won't take long.'"

They commandeered the bartender's office. Bester and Anne started with the bartender. They didn't waste time asking him anything—they just scanned him. Then they started working through the patrons, taking turns to keep from wearing out.

Lyta, he noticed, seemed more and more uncomfortable. He began

wondering, again, if she might be a problem. Sometimes it took a little nudge to get someone to see the big picture. A bit of personal involvement.

"Lyta," he said, as patron number six exited. "Would you scan the next informant, please? I need to catch my breath."

Her eyes widened, and for a moment he thought she would refuse, until Anne added, quietly, *"Intern."*

She did it, though Bester monitored the whole thing and helped her excise the memory.

"Next."

The next fellow was a middle-aged, paunchy fellow. He drew a PPG almost as soon as he entered.

"Well, hello," Bester said softly. "We were expecting you."

The man looked at the three of them with curious eyes. "I had to do it, you know," he said.

"Of course you did," Bester replied. "Nasty telepaths, always screwing around with your head."

"It's not like that," the fellow said. "I want you to understand, I *loved* them."

"Oh, I don't really care to understand that," Bester said. "I don't care about that in the least."

The killer turned and pointed the PPG at Bester's face. Bester seized his nervous system, felt him trying to depress the contact. Such a little motion, one that would close the gap between life and death.

For a second, he thought he might lose the contest—the man's thoughts were like greased roaches, disgusting, slippery, distracting. But he held firm, which was unfortunate, because that put him far enough in to see the life going out of their eyes, the victims, one by one, feel an almost crushing affection—

"This is really him," he said. "Lyta, if you could take his gun?"

Lyta gingerly removed the weapon. The hand stayed out, trembling.

"Anne, could you cuff him?"

As soon as that was done, Bester blacked him out.

"Let's take him to the station," Bester said. "I want to take my time."

"What do you mean?" Lyta asked. "Don't we turn him over to Earth security now?"

"Lyta, surely you understand that all of the evidence we have indicating this man's guilt—all of the evidence leading to us even finding him— was obtained illegally. He won't be going to trial." He patted the man on the head. "No, I have very special plans for him."

* * *

"What did you do?" Lyta asked, staring at the prisoner. He wore a straitjacket, and his eyes bulged. His breath came in quick, animal pants—then he would go an entire minute without inhaling at all. Now and again his eyes would dart exactly like those of a person in REM sleep. A rubber ball was strapped into his mouth.

"If he could only escape his jacket," Bester said, "he would know a moment of perfect, absolute pleasure. He would tear out his own eyes, bite off his tongue, render himself by degrees into one of his own victims. It's the only thing he can imagine that might give him peace, allow him to escape from the things he sees—and he can never do it. He'll stay bound for the rest of his life or he'll die. It's that simple."

"It's horrible. And what you did to all of those people . . ."

"Five doctors go duck hunting," Bester said. "A general practitioner, a pediatrician, a psychiatrist, a surgeon, and a pathologist. A bird comes flying over. The GP is the first to see it—he raises his shotgun, but he doesn't shoot. He thinks, 'Maybe it's not really a duck. I should get a second opinion.' By then the bird is long gone. Another bird flies overhead, and this time the pediatrician gets it in his sights. But he thinks, 'I'm not sure if that's a duck—besides, it might have babies.' And so, on flies the bird. Next bird flies over, and this time the psychiatrist sees it first. Being pretty sharp-eyed, he knows for sure it's a duck, but he thinks, '*I* know it's a duck—but does *it* know it's a duck?' and while he's worrying about that, the duck escapes. Now along comes a fourth bird, and this time it's the surgeon's turn. Boom! He shoots immediately. Down comes the bird. The surgeon turns to the pathologist and says, 'Go see if that was a duck, will you?' " He smiled. "I'm the surgeon, Lyta. Sometimes you just have to call one in."

"You'll pardon me if I—if I don't think that's at all funny."

"Was what I did somehow more horrible than what he did? Worse than what he would have done again, if he had escaped, or the courts had released him? Now there's nothing to fear. The second he's unrestrained he'll start killing himself. You don't find it poetic?"

"No."

"I hear you've applied for a transfer to business."

"Yes."

"That might be just as well, if you don't have the stomach for police work."

"Mr. Bester, I just can't believe this is what police work is supposed to consist of."

"Lyta—" He sighed. "One day, sooner or later, you will understand. In a way, I'm sorry for that, because the truth won't set you free. It will circumscribe you. It will make you understand what has to be done, and

that what has to be done isn't necessarily pleasant. I don't enjoy what I do. But I know that it's the right thing."

"You'll pardon me again, Mr. Bester, if I can't take your word for all that."

"Of course. It's been a pleasure working with you, Lyta. I trust we'll meet again."

"No offense, Mr. Bester, but I sincerely hope not."

He smiled indulgently, wondering if he ought to do something about her. There was little chance she could cause him any harm, unless . . .

He rubbed his jaw. What if she worked for Johnston and his cronies? He was more certain than ever that this whole situation had been a trap, set by the director. The assassination attempt had confirmed that, at least to him.

But what if the assassin were merely a feint, a distraction? What if the real attacker was Lyta Alexander, who might now level charges against him? Such charges would—under ordinary circumstances—be buried by the Corps.

Unless the Corps wanted to bury Al Bester instead.

The defiance in Lyta's face had become mingled with uncertainty. "Sir?" she said, questioning. He realized that he had been staring at her, silently, for quite some time.

"Nothing, Lyta," he said softly. "Just wondering if you are a shovel."

"I don't understand."

"No," he said, with some relief, "I really don't think you do. Good day."

He watched her go. He would ask Anne to arrange to have her things searched just in case she had been carrying any recording devices. He still had Anne to back him up.

Unless Anne . . .

No. Paranoia was healthy, but if he went too far in that direction, he would be as mad as the man in the cell, and Johnston would have won.

Let it go this time. Lyta would come around. She wasn't his enemy, she was one of his own, and someday she would realize it.

He peered back at the man in the cell, and he calmed down, like a troubled child recognizing its father.

Bester smiled, and the man started trying to scream around the rubber ball. Bester left him like that. He was humming a phrase from *The Rites of Spring* as he strolled up the corridor. Stravinsky.

6

Bester killed most of his velocity. The Black Omega Starfury retained a bit of spin, but he left it so he could watch stars wheel glacially by. Even though his sub-Doppler was watching for unexpected ships, he disliked the idea of not being able to see all approaches, of blind space at his back.

Besides, he liked the cold beauty of stars. He liked the irony, even, of that characterization, that the very furnaces of creation, in whose life and death all of the elements were born, consumed, reborn, should be, at a distance of poetry and literature, described as cold.

He studied his sub-Doppler radar. The other ship—the one expected—was still decelerating on a plume of newborn helium, but it was a bare exhalation now. Through the view port he could just make out the ship, moving into eclipse behind the asteroid. He saw no others.

He gave it time to reach its destination, then nudged his thrusters to life. His sleek mechanical steed responded, moving now along the curve of the potato-shaped chunk of planet-that-never-was, coasting up the kilometer or so of its length. At the end, a neat hole came into view, no more than thrice the diameter of his Starfury. He maneuvered into the hollow core of the stone.

Fifty years ago, just after the turn of the century, miners had claimed this rock, hollowed it out, refined its metals for Earth's Malthusian hordes. In the twenties, the bottom had dropped out of the domestic metals markets. The miners had cut their losses, broken down their machinery, and pulled out, leaving an empty shell of stone.

Another time, the old mine might have become the basis of a colony—many such hollowed-out asteroids had been sold to idealistic world-founders just a century earlier. But with jumpgate technology and much more hospitable colony worlds awaiting, this rock languished.

Until Bester had found it, on an old claims chart. Now it had uses once again.

He coasted along the axis until he reached the far end, where several

narrow docks waited. The other ship—a battered, unmarked vessel—was already there. He hooked up to a cylinder that connected him to the air lock, making certain that there was pressure on the other side—and that that pressure consisted of an oxygen/helium mix. Then, still in his pressure suit, he moved from the ship into the inner lock. It was a small place, with ladders leading in three directions, each "down." He stepped into one and let the gentle tug of an eighth of one Earth gravity drag him down the rail.

He emerged like a slow-motion fireman into a cramped, unadorned room. The walls had been melted and smoothed. There were already three people in the room, all in shirtsleeves. Two nodded greetings to Bester. The third—a man strapped into a chair with steel bands—merely looked at him with a sort of awful understanding. The only light in the room was a deliberately unpleasant actinic cone directed at the man in the chair.

Bester removed his helmet and, in an unhurried fashion, the rest of his pressure suit. Then he walked over to the prisoner.

"Hello, Mr. Jackson." He sat carefully on a small stool and rubbed his hands together. "I want to explain something to you. Come, look at me. Don't be afraid."

Jackson reluctantly dragged his gaze around to focus on Bester. He was a young man, only twenty-five. He had grey eyes and clean features. He looked a little like Brett had, when he had been that age, a Psi Corps poster boy.

"I don't want to do this," Bester said. "I truly don't. We are both telepaths, you and I. We are both Corps, and the Corps is our mother and our father. You're like my own child, in a deeper sense of the word than any mundane could possibly comprehend."

"The Corps is mother, the Corps is father," Jackson whispered.

"You see? We are the same. Frankly, if you were a mundane, we wouldn't be having this discussion. I would have already started doing unpleasant things to you. But you are one of mine, Timothy—may I call you Timothy? You are one of mine, and I don't want to hurt you. Even though you serve the other side, I still consider you one of mine.

"I don't want to hurt you, but if you make me, I will. There is something happening at Syria Planum. There is something happening in EarthGov. They are linked. Do you understand, Timothy? Something is happening to *my* telepaths, my people, my brothers and sisters and— children, and I don't believe it's anything good."

"Sir, I can't betray the Corps—"

Bester clucked his tongue. "Timothy, you're so young. I know you think you see things clearly now, know where your loyalties lie. I was *born*

in the Corps, raised by the Corps from birth. I've never flinched from serving the Corps, even when great sacrifices were called for." He lifted his clenched hand. "Don't presume to tell *me* what betrays the Corps. Someone is delivering our people into the hands of someone—maybe some*thing* else. There are traitors in Psi Corps, and you have worked for them."

"Sir, the director—"

"Is a mundane, Timothy. He is a creature of the Senate, of wealthy mundanes." He inclined his head. "I don't have a lot of time. I am closely watched, and I will be missed. Timothy, I'm prepared to make another sacrifice today. It will hurt me terribly to harm you. I will carry it as a wound on my heart. But it will be one wound of many, and for the sake of my people, I *will* do it. That's why I risked coming to question you myself—because I cannot, *will* not ask anyone else to take this burden for me. I'm asking you—one last time—to help me."

"Sir—" His voice trembled. "Sir, I'm scared of them."

"Of course."

"They—they found something on Mars. A ship."

"I know about the ship, Timothy. I know one man touched it and died—I know a telepath touched it and went insane. I know that when it was excavated, another ship just like it came and took it away. But whose ship was it, Timothy? What race? And what do they have to do with my people?"

"Sir, I don't know. You have to believe that."

"I can't afford to believe it. You know that."

"They're all tied up with IPX, and EarthGov, like you said. I've seen EarthForce officers, and an aide to Vice President Clark—"

"The aliens," Bester softly reminded him.

"Interplanetary Expeditions tracked their ship out to the rim, a planet called Alpha Omega 3. They plan to send an archaeological team to investigate. That's all I know."

Bester nodded, sadly. "I believe you, son." Then he hit him with a hard scan.

Jackson hadn't lied, but the scan gave him more details. Faces of the IPX men, some of whom he recognized. The aide connected to Clark. More detail to help him flesh out the cabal, but not much more.

No, everything really useful had come from the boy's mouth, sad to say.

He studied the other two people in the room. To one, a tall man built of right angles, he said, "I want him reconstructed. Carefully. He still has two weeks of leave left—implant a nice memory of backpacking in the

Tetons or somewhere. Rebuild his personality as much like the original as possible, but leave me a key to get in, okay? We may need him one day."

"I understand, Mr. Bester."

"I know you do, Mr. Ts'ai. I'll check on him in a few weeks." He put his hand on Ts'ai's shoulder. "Some of what we have to do is hard, but it's better than the alternative. Remember that."

"Of course." Ts'ai looked surprised that Bester had even bothered to say it. Stout fellow, Ts'ai.

"As for you, Ms. Donne—good work."

Donne shifted her competent, muscular physique and nodded briskly. "Thank you, sir."

"Is my—appointment—arranged?"

Something that was almost—but not quite—a smile ghosted Donne's tight lips. "Mr. Bester, I think you will be pleased."

"Good. I'm sure I will. Ms. Donne, another thing. I'd like some improvements in our intelligence inside IPX. And I need to know everything about this mission to the rim. We need someone on that ship."

"I'll see to it," Donne promised. "I'm headed back to Geneva as soon as we're done here."

"I know you will—and we *are* done here. Well. A pleasure seeing the both of you again. Hopefully next time we meet we can do something more pleasant—have dinner, perhaps."

Bester returned to his ship. Once free of the asteroid, he fired the thrusters in a single, brief burst, then waited until he had drifted for almost an hour before cutting in the main engines and pointing the Starfury's nose toward a certain transport that awaited his return.

"Did you have a nice flight?"

Bester looked up from the task of shucking off his pressure suit. He saw an earnest young man with close-cropped, blondish hair.

"Hello, Byron. Yes, very nice actually."

"Any sign of the transport?"

"None at all. It might be that we got a bad steer this time out. I wonder if we shouldn't backtrack to Ceres and start over. I'm not convinced that the captain there was entirely truthful with us."

"Mundanes never are, are they?"

"They can't help it," Bester said. "It's in their nature to fear us. What were you up to while I was out?"

"Reading one of the books you suggested. The one by that Rand person."

"Ah, yes. Did she convert you to objectivism?"

"Not exactly, but I can see what you mean. It is hard to deny that some people count more than others, in the grand scheme of things."

Bester shrugged the rest of the way out of his suit. "You have to put her in context. The discovery of the fact of evolution by Darwin created a new paradigm for thinking about old issues. It was fashionable and convenient to believe that those who were wealthy and successful were so because they were inherently superior." He changed the subject. "I'm starving. Shall we get a bite to eat?"

"Delighted," Byron replied.

A few moments later, over barely identifiable, microwaved lasagna—Bester hoped it was lasagna, in any case—Byron cleared his throat. "Do you think there was anything to it? Social Darwinism?"

"Survival of the fittest? It was a misunderstanding about how evolution worked, really. Looking back on it, it's all pretty silly—mundanes squabbling about who was more evolved. From our point of view, it's sort of like a couple of chimps arguing about which walks most upright. Social Darwinism was a pseudo-scientific rationale for laissez-faire capitalism, class domination, and racism. It was an ideology, not a scientific understanding.

"But there *is* such a thing as evolution, of course. For almost a million years, *Homo sapiens* remained virtually unchanged biologically—culture essentially arrested natural selection. Society protects its weak and stupid, helps them breed. Whatever the social Darwinists of the twentieth century thought of themselves, they were, in fact, the end product of a million years of unnatural and unplanned selection—every bit as much as the factory workers and welfare cheats they lorded themselves over.

"In a million years, the only biological improvement in the Human race has been *us*, Byron." He smiled. "You see, I'm not a social Darwinist—just a Darwinist, plain and simple."

"It seems obvious," Byron said. "That's why normals fear us."

"Imagine what the apes who stayed in trees must have thought of those new creatures who went walking upright across the savannah. There has to be an impulse in a species that understands it's about to be replaced, a last desperate effort to rescue itself, to save its genes from oblivion."

"So why did you suggest I read Rand, if you think so little of the premises of her reasoning?"

"Why, to make you think, Byron. A Psi Cop has to know how to think, how to evaluate, how to judge. I picked you to train because I think you have more potential than I've seen in a long time—you can be a first-rate Psi Cop, if you want. Not a bloodhound—of course, we need

good bloodhounds, don't get me wrong—but you could be a leader. You could go far."

"I—I appreciate the opportunity, sir. I hope I don't let you down."

"It's a pleasure, Byron. I'm sure you'll make me proud. I could wish for a son like you . . ."

He broke off, unsure why he had said that—he said things like that all the time, because making people feel special made them like you, and that made them useful.

Except—he saw what bothered him—he genuinely meant what he had just told the boy. He liked Byron. He enjoyed teaching him, shaping him. It was odd. It was the first such feeling he had experienced in a long time. He really wasn't sure whether he liked it, whether it was appropriate. Perhaps he should pass Byron along to someone else to tutor. Yes, that might be best, all in all. He would have to give it some more thought.

Meanwhile, they did have a rogue to catch, an important date to keep. The diversion to the asteroid had been just that, a diversion so he could conduct business secretly. While most of the transport crew were from his inner circle, others—Byron, for instance—still didn't need to know everything he did.

The man they were tracking was almost certainly headed for Io, in hopes of using the jumpgate there. He had to be stopped, but there was really no hurry. What he didn't know was that there was a tracking beacon on board his stolen vessel. There always had been. Telemetry placed his ship on a trajectory to Jupiter, and their transport could easily catch up.

And now, there was another matter that required his immediate attention. He needed to know everything, and more than everything, about the expedition that was headed toward the rim.

A few minutes in front of his AI terminal got him a screenful of data—Donne, efficient as ever, had already filtered a lot of the information.

The *Icarus*. Ostensibly an IPX ship. He scrolled through the assignments, saw a few familiar names. Chang. Hidalgo—Bester smiled. Hidalgo owed him a few favors.

Another name caught his eye—Sheridan. Anna Sheridan. A relative, perhaps, of the famous war hero?

He would have to check on that, too.

They hadn't assigned a telepath yet—indeed, it would be some weeks before they started actually assembling the crew. Good. That gave him time. He could concentrate on the business at hand, on his coming appointment. All he had to do was plausibly draw this telepath hunt out for another two days, and everything would be in place.

7

Bester shook off the lingering nightmare that clung to his backbrain.

"Very *good*, Byron. That was well done."

"Thank you, sir." He beamed. "Though I suspect you let me win."

"I didn't *let* you win. I offered you an opening, true, but it's an opening that very few would have noticed. I don't give praise unless it's deserved—surely you know that about me by now."

"So they tell me. Can we go 'round again? I'm still having trouble with that middle series of blocks."

"Best rest up. In eight hours we'll catch up with the Blip, and I don't want you all worn out."

"Does that mean I'll be going along?" The eagerness in his voice was palpable.

"Yes, I think you're ready."

"I don't feel ready."

Bester considered for an instant. "There are ways of preparing, other than scan/block drills. How would you like to watch a movie?"

"A movie?"

"An old-style vid."

"Sounds fun, but—"

"There is a point to this, I assure you. It's called *Rashomon* . . ."

As he watched the black-and-white images play across the screen, Bester felt an odd sort of peace. He had wondered, once—when he was the "statue of the day"—how many different roles he would play in life. Now, as his years advanced, he had a sort of answer, but not one he had ever imagined as a boy.

He had been the child, the prodigy of Cadre Prime. He had been the apprentice—had he failed Bey or had Bey failed him? It didn't matter; it had failed. He had been the young lover, another failure. He had been, for a short time, the husband. Yes, he was still married, but he was no longer husband in any real sense, hadn't been for decades. Father? Well,

there was a man who counted him his father, but that was as far as it went.

He wasn't so foolish or self-damaging as to take all of the blame for those failures—Cadre Prime, Bey, Montoya, Alisha—all of them shared the failures, and there had been less visible hands at work in his life as well. Yet still, no matter how he rationalized it, he had passed briefly through roles but never lived them, never owned them, never been anything *Human*. Only the efficient hunter, the cop.

But now, imperceptibly, it seemed, he had grown into another role, one he might at last do well at. He had never quite been child, brother, son, lover, husband, or father. But the young people under his command—well, to put aside false modesty, many of them worshiped him. He had respect, and adulation. He had a chance with them, a chance to create a kind of legacy. When he looked at Byron, he saw him through the same eyes that Bey had seen *him* through, all those years ago.

Perhaps all of the failures, all of the trials, had brought him to this one moment, this one role he would finally fill perfectly—that of mentor.

A risk, perhaps—the risk of failing again—but it seemed worth it. It made him feel paradoxically young.

"Turning, sir," Ysidra Tapia said, from the pilot's station. The ship vibrated subtly, and the view changed. Byron gave a soft gasp of admiration. Besides the three of them, the bridge was empty—it would be some time before a full complement was needed.

"Your first time this close to Jupiter?" Bester asked.

Byron nodded, his features betraying awe. "It's magnificent. What a bloody magnificent planet."

"Yes it is."

"I mean, I've seen vids, and holographs, but still—"

"Wait until you see it from Io," Bester said. "That close, there's nothing *but* Jupiter. You can lose yourself in it, watching a tiny whirl in a storm, and then realize that that little spiral could swallow all of Earth. An eddy so insignificant that if you looked away, you could never find it again. It tends to create a certain—perspective."

Just then, Jupiter was the apparent size of a grapefruit. They were falling toward the king of gods at many klicks per second, but the scale of things dwarfed their speed. They ate up thousands of kilometers without any perceptible change in the gas giant.

Still, you couldn't escape the feeling that once Jupiter had you, it would never let you go. And Jupiter had them. It would take more thrust than was needed to escape the surface of the Earth to climb back even this far out of the hole Jupiter's mass had dug around them.

"You *are* keeping track of our target as you appreciate this grandeur, I hope."

"Oh, yes—I've still got him on the optical telescope. He comes and goes on the other sensors."

"Of course. Using Jupiter's EM as a screen is a game as old as criminals in space."

"It's good we got the optical lock on him before we went too deep into the field."

"Yes. Have you tried to touch him yet?"

"He's too far away, isn't he?"

"You never know, when you have line of sight. It's a funny thing. Give it a try."

Byron nodded. He closed his eyes, relaxed the muscles of his face, then opened them again. He concentrated on the distant dot for a few moments, then, with a soft grunting noise, tightened his lips. Sweat broke out on his brow.

"Easy, Byron," Bester cautioned. "Don't strain yourself. I only said to try. It's always worthwhile to try."

"I'm sorry, sir. I couldn't get anything."

"It's too far, or he's blocking, or both," Bester told him. "Don't worry. We'll get him."

While Jupiter stayed roughly the same apparent size, the dot in the optical scope grew quickly, gaining definition. It was an old ship, a modified asteroid tug more than fifty years old. Bester was surprised it was flying at all. Certainly it had no chance of out-distancing his state-of-the-art craft.

Or of outfighting it. When they were within a hundred klicks, it opened its single weapons port and fired two missiles. After they shot those out of space, it fired on them with a mining laser.

"What now?" asked Tapia, at the weapons console.

"I want him alive, of course," Bester murmured. "See if you can get the idiot to answer another hail. If you can't, try a pinpoint strike at the laser. That hull won't take much of a pounding."

"Right."

The hail failed again, so Bester ended up watching, tight-lipped, as Tapia drew the wicked scalpel of their own laser cannon across the other ship.

"I think that gets it, sir. His hull still looks good."

"Perfect. Well done, Ysidra."

"Thank you, sir."

"Well, Byron, are you ready to fly a Starfury?"

Byron's grin was more eloquent than any other answer he could have given.

Bester watched Byron's Starfury as it grappled the tug and reeled it in.

"Omega 7 to Omega 1. He's still not responding. Could he be dead? Or unconscious?"

Bester considered that. "It's possible," he allowed. "Cover me, now, while I grapple."

A few moments later, the task done, he returned his attention to the ship. A funny feeling swept over him.

"Okay," Byron said, over the headset. "I'm preparing to go EVA, so I can force the hatch."

"Hang on, just a second, Byron." He stared at the battered ship, willing himself to see beyond—wrong approach. He opened his mind, instead, as if listening to a city. As in some of his earliest drills, he started filtering the voices out, one by one.

When he had pared it down to just himself and Byron, he still had no sense that there was anyone on the ship.

Frowning, he called Tapia on a secure channel, so Byron couldn't listen in.

"Sir?"

"Ysidra, who planted the tracking device on this ship?"

"Let me see—that would have been Zee."

"Where did he do it?"

"On Ceres, sir. We guessed that our Blip would come through there, and Zee left this ship where it would be 'available' to him."

"Yes, yes, I remember the plan." Something was wrong. Bester had arranged things very carefully—or so he thought. He'd needed an excuse to visit the asteroid belt, so he could interrogate Jackson, and another excuse to go to Jupiter. He'd set things up so that a certain Blip would find his way to Ceres, steal a ship with a tracking device, and flee toward Io.

A delicate plan, but so far, so good. But what if—

"Find Zee. Check with him. I want to know the serial number and configurations of the ship he wired."

"That might take a few moments."

"We've nothing but time."

Which wasn't true, of course. He had someplace to be in under ten hours, and a narrow window in which to be there. But his instincts—

Well, they wouldn't have stopped him when he was twenty. Maybe it was just old age and paranoia. Of course, for him, the distinction be-

tween paranoia and common sense was rather pointless. But if someone knew what he was up to right now—the wrong someone—that could be very, very bad.

"Sir?" It was Tapia, and she sounded a little funny.

"Yes?"

"Zee's been missing from Ceres base for two days now."

"Ysidra, move the transport away, now, *go.*" He punched over to Byron's frequency. "Byron, cut loose and hit your thrusters."

"What? Sir, what's—"

"Do it!" He cut his own, hit thrusters, and spun around, then engaged all four ion jets at once. With the sudden g-force, directionless space acquired an up-and-down—his back was down, the ship was down, the stars were up, far away.

And so it was below him that a flower of light opened its petals, from below him that a thousand shards of hull metal spattered onto his own hull, into the straining Copeland engines. His own weight seemed to wrap around him like a hand, squeezed impossibly tight, and then mercifully loosened. Direction vanished again, and he was merely tumbling through the void. A band tightened across his chest and eyes, blood thundered in his ears, and he almost lost consciousness. He almost lost his breakfast, too, but he kept it down.

Groggily, still fighting dizziness and double vision, he ran through his systems, looking for something that worked.

The first thing he noticed was that he was about to explode. His instruments—those still functioning—warned him the ion suppression tines on the drives had melted and crumpled in, but the engines were still on.

He cut them, but odds were that wouldn't be good enough.

"Ysidra? Ysidra, are you there?"

Static.

"Byron?"

He should jettison. But if he did that, and both the transport and Byron were disabled . . .

He gritted his teeth, watched the instruments. Things were starting to cool down now, though he wasn't nearly out of the danger zone.

Well. Someone had tried to kill him.

That struck him as funny, and he started to chuckle. He was still chuckling when he heard Byron's voice in his head.

Mr. Bester? Are you okay?

Hello, Byron. Yes. What about you?

I've lost two engines, but I think I'll be fine. Are you—laughing?

Yes.

May I ask why?

The universe is full of irony, Byron. Never forget that. He paused. *I'll explain it to you, someday. Can you see the transport?*

Yes, sir. I've got Ysidra on the com. But we couldn't raise you.

My systems are pretty badly damaged. In fact, now that I know you guys are okay, I'm jettisoning . . .

He paused. How smart was that? What if Ysidra, Byron, the rest—what if they were *in* on it?

Well, then he was doomed. Screw it.

He jettisoned.

Have Ysidra send someone out to reel me in, he 'cast.

They're already on their way. What do you think happened?

Our friend was never on the ship. It was a trap.

The rogues are more vicious than I ever imagined, Byron 'cast, shimming self-righteous indignation.

Bester sighed. For all of his good qualities, Byron was a bit naive. Still, at the moment there was no point in disabusing him of the notion. Besides, there was some very small chance that the attempt *had* been made by the underground. Certainly that's who would officially end up taking the blame.

But Bester—he knew better. That's why he laughed. Synchronicity.

Ganymede was a ruined jade, cracked and spalled white as if the gods had used it in a few too many cosmic games of marbles. Bester liked her blemished beauty. Ganymede was a dark woman with many secrets.

They were dropping toward one of those secrets just now.

"They're asking for clearance, sir."

"Put them on."

A voice came through, edged with the constant crackle that colored all transmissions near Jupiter. The static, however, couldn't hide the crisp Manchester accent.

"I repeat, identify yourselves."

"Mr. Drew, this is Alfred Bester. What seems to be the problem? You've identified my ships, I'm certain, and we sent the security codes."

"But, Mr. Bester, this is highly irregular. I was not informed that you would be arriving."

"My crew and I have been in hot pursuit of a Blip, Mr. Drew. It's been a very hard ride. We in effect lost two Starfuries and our transport is damaged. We need repairs, not to mention hospitality. So I hope you don't mind if we impose on you a bit. We are, after all, family." He forced out a laugh. "Unless you have some sort of standing orders against me in particular . . ."

"Oh, no, Mr. Bester. Of course not. I'm clearing you to land right now. Welcome to Ganymede."

"Thank you," Bester replied.

"A Psi Corps base on Ganymede?" Byron said. "I didn't know."

"It's on a need-to-know basis," Bester said.

". . . and I didn't need to know. Yes, I think I've heard that a few times now, thank you, Mr. Bester."

"There isn't much to it, is there?" Byron noticed, as they shucked off their EVA suits. The chamber that lay beyond the inner lock was cramped and severe, with low ceilings and passageways leading off that were somehow—despite their angularity—more reminiscent of tunnels in an anthill than of Human architecture.

A couple of normals in EarthForce uniforms watched them suspiciously.

A third man—also in uniform but wearing a Psi Corps badge—waited for them to collect themselves, then stepped forward. "It's not a very old base, or a very important one," he said, in the now-familiar accent. "I'm Charles Drew. Welcome to the Icehouse." He chuckled as he said it.

"Thank you," Bester said. "I like what you've done with the place."

"Yes, well, it's spare of necessity. We're a hardened facility—sunk down into the water-ice crust. It requires a certain architectural economy."

"It's a military base, then?" Byron asked.

"You really don't want to know what they do here, Byron," Bester said. "They would have to kill you."

"I thought all the hush-hush stuff went on at Syria Planum."

Drew smiled nervously. "Well, there's hush-hush and then there's hush-hush, if you know what I mean."

"If we keep this up, we'll sound like an ancient locomotive," Bester noted. "*Hush*-hush-hush-hush *hush*-hush-hush-hush . . ."

Drew laughed. It sounded almost genuine. "Indeed," he said. "Would you gentlemen join me for some refreshment?"

"Wonderful," Bester said. "Some hot tea would be very nice."

They traveled up one of the corridors to a small kitchenette, where Drew busied himself making tea. As Bester and Byron seated themselves, another man entered the room from an opposite passage. He was a handsome fellow, dapper in a crisply pressed suit. He had black hair and dark, haunted eyes.

"Well—here's what all the fuss was about," he said, taking in Bester and Byron.

"Not expecting someone else, I hope?" Bester said. "I'm Al Bester. This is my associate, Byron Gordon."

"Actually," the fellow said, "I *was* told we were expecting visitors . . ."

"Mr. Bester and Mr. Gordon are making an emergency stop here," Drew hastily cut in. "They were quite unexpected. Mr. Bester, Mr. Gordon—may I introduce Dr. Morden?"

"Doctor?" Bester said curiously. He shook his head. "My, my—the people you meet at small outposts. M.D. or Ph.D.?"

"Ph.D. In archaeolinguistics."

"*Really?* Fascinating."

"You know the subject?"

"No, but I am nonetheless fascinated." He let that hang for a moment, as Drew set out the tea service.

"This is really very good," Bester said, after a sip.

"Thank you," Drew replied. "We do try to maintain what amenities we can."

"Dr. Morden," Bester said, "dare I ask what brings an archaeolinguist all the way out to Ganymede?"

Morden exchanged glances with Drew, but Bester wasn't entirely certain what was communicated. Morden was a mundane, but Drew, a P10, would notice a scan.

Morden took a seat. "My position is actually with EarthForce, and not with Psi Corps, so I'm unsure of who I can and can't talk to in these situations. On the other hand, I'm happy to say I don't actually know what I'm doing on Ganymede, so I don't actually have to evade your question."

Bester raised his teacup. "Dr. Morden—you will consider it a compliment, I hope, when I tell you that I feel sure that if you *wanted* to evade one of my questions, you could do so."

"Oh, in all humility, I doubt that," Morden replied.

There followed a silence that Bester sensed was uncomfortable to everyone but him. He hoped it was, anyway.

"If I may," Drew asked, politely, a few moments later, "I should like to ask how many of your crew will be coming onto the station."

"Well, there are twelve of us," Bester said. "Will that press you for room? Dr. Morden mentioned some other guests arriving?"

"Within the hour, actually, and I'll have to excuse myself to go greet them momentarily. I can only accommodate three of your party tonight, I'm afraid."

"Can the others come in just to stretch their legs, a few at a time? I

understand you have an exercise room." He set his teacup down. "Anyone I know?"

"Pardon?"

"Your visitors. Anyone I know?"

Drew appeared to dither for a few moments. "It's classified," he said, after a moment.

"Well, how about this—Whoever it is, you mention to them that I'm here. I don't know why, but I have a hunch that they might want to see me."

"Of course. And yes, your people are welcome to come on for a bit of a stretch."

"Something's up, right?" Byron asked, once they had been shown to their room. The quarters were very simple, bunk beds and a desk that folded from the wall.

"What do you mean?"

"I mean—this is a Psi Corps base, right? So why are all of the guards mundanes? And who is that Morden character? And why are they hiding things from *you,* of all people?"

"Well, Byron, don't exaggerate my importance. As for the rest, it's all perfectly natural. Psi Corps and EarthForce are allies. They work on real black-hole stuff here, things critical to Earth Alliance security, so you shouldn't be surprised by their precautions." He followed with a quick 'cast. *Don't ask too many questions, Byron. And don't imagine they can't hear us.*

Byron's chagrined expression made it clear he understood, but to his credit he managed to cover it by nodding. "Yes, that all makes sense, I suppose. I'm just not used to the world of high intrigue. Well. Good night, sir."

"Good night, Byron."

Bester was almost asleep when the door to their quarters opened and the lights came up. Four men in EA uniforms quickly entered the room. All bore PPG rifles.

One—a burly fellow with a broken nose and two chipped front teeth—nudged Bester with his weapon.

"Get up," he snapped. "You're coming with us."

8

He was little Alfie Bester, being escorted by the Grins to an unknown fate. He was Al Bester, going exactly where he wanted to go, keeping an appointment that was decades late. Could he disconnect memory and perception? It didn't seem so. The only context for understanding the present was the past.

And so, for the second time in his life—albeit with almost six decades intervening—he was hauled from his bed in the middle of the night and brought before the director of Psi Corps.

The years had been kind to Director Johnston only in that they had let him live. Some would argue it was no kindness at all.

Whereas Vacit had been wrinkled like antique paper, Johnston had shriveled. His bones seemed to have crumpled inward with the collapse of the skin, like a plastic figure that had gotten too hot. His hair was sparse, wet-looking. He sat behind a desk, but that didn't hide the rest of what Bester knew was there; the chair kept his body functioning and gave him mobility.

Yet his eyes were still alive. They poked from beneath the brows of his time-wrecked face like the points of steel knives. And his hatred was still there, as fresh and pure as the day Bester had first felt it—when he was six.

The director considered him. At each hand stood a black-clad Psi Cop. The EA men went back outside, doubtless to stand guard. They had already searched him, of course.

"Good evening, Director," Bester said. "Or is it good morning?"

The director didn't say anything for a moment. Then he showed his teeth—still perfect, regular, white. It might have been a grin or a snarl.

"Mr. Bester, what are you doing here?"

"Sir, with all due respect, what are *you* doing here? A man your age—you're in no condition to travel."

Johnston's eyes widened fractionally. "I asked you a question."

Bester scrunched his eyebrows thoughtfully. "The question has a

number of answers, Director. It depends upon what you mean, doesn't it? Do you mean in the philosophical sense—why am I here? Why are any of us here? Are we really here at all? I don't know the answer to that. Do you mean, why am I here before you at this instant? That would be because your men took me from my room, strip-searched me, and hauled me in front of you. If you mean, what am I doing in the vicinity, then you certainly have access to the records I've left of my movements over the last month or so. I'm going to guess, Director, that you don't mean any of these things."

"Mr. Bester . . ." The tone carried both weariness and venom.

"No, I'm going to guess you meant, 'Mr. Bester, what are you doing here when you ought to be dead?' "

Johnston had scowled throughout, sometimes looking as though he was about to interrupt. But now he closed his cracked lips. He looked at Bester for a moment, then bobbed his head. "You are a very stupid man, if you figured that out, and still came here. But I don't suppose you knew I was coming here, too, did you? Well. I had hoped to be subtler about all of this, but you may as well disappear on Ganymede as anywhere. We have the facilities for it."

"Good *thinking,* sir," Bester told him.

"You seem to think I won't do it."

"Oh, it's not that," Bester said, hastily. "But I wonder—would you care to explain why?"

"Why? No, I don't care to explain. You don't fit into the modern Corps, that's all. You're an impediment."

"I see. Director, we've never really talked, you and I. I think we should, just for the record."

"I'm tired, Bester. I don't have any more time to waste with you. I'm going to have you broken, and everyone in your crew. Once we have everything you know, we'll find something convenient to do with you. You have a lot of enemies. No one will wonder about you—or mourn you, for that matter." He signed to the two cops.

"Hugin," Bester said, quietly. "Munin." And at the same time he released a string of key glyphs.

The cops stopped in their tracks—in fact, took a step backward.

"What?" The director scowled.

"Hugin and Munin. Thought and memory. The two ravens who perched on the shoulders of the Norse god Odin."

The director noticed that his bodyguards weren't moving. He looked from one to the other. "Hey!" he said.

"Funny god, Odin. One of his attributes was madness. The warriors he loved best, he would drive berserk, make them gnaw their shields.

They were virtually invincible in battle. Unless, of course, Odin wanted them in his own private war party—you see, he knew one day that the gods were going to have a great battle, a battle to the death, and then he would need the best warriors at his side. So if he looked down and saw a truly *great* warrior, he would—arrange—for them to stumble in battle, or for the sun to shine in their eyes at exactly the wrong moment. A god of madness and betrayal. Not, all in all, a nice guy."

"Stein? Dorset?"

"They can't hear you. Or, rather, they do hear you, but they won't respond. They will respond to me, and only me. May I sit down? Thank you." Bester lowered himself into a chair.

"Guards!"

"No, they can't hear you either. Different cause, same effect— they're dead. See, I've been planning this for a very long time. That little attempt to blow me up yesterday really worried me—not because you tried to kill me, you've done that often enough—but because I thought you were onto me. Years and years of planning, shot to hell. But no, fortunately it turned out to be just a coincidence."

"What are you talking about?"

"Director, I've been planning this moment since I was fifteen. Oh, I didn't know it then—I blamed Bey's death on him, on the underground. Well, Bey was weak, in a way—he did have sympathy for the rogues. It's the same sympathy that allowed him to catch them, and maybe it got a little out of hand. But he was no traitor. And then there was Montoya, and Brett—well, I'm not going to go through it all. I understood that you were a danger to the Corps that first day I met you, when I was six. I knew even then that you hated us."

"I'm the director of Psi Corps, you idiot."

"And a fine one you've been. Slowly selling us out to the mundanes, bit by bit. And to someone else, yes? Aren't you curious as to how I knew you would be here, when almost no one else in the universe did?"

"I think you're going to tell me, regardless."

"When the alien ship on Mars woke up and flew off, it had some effect here as well. I'm not sure what, I'll admit, but a flurry of messages concerning Ganymede was an impossible correlation to miss. So I kept my ear to the ground, and here we are. I knew they would send you here."

"Just who exactly do you suppose *they* are, Mr. Bester?"

"I don't know all of the details, of course. I know some of the players. Vice President Clark, for instance, and the upper management of IPX. Certain senators and industrialists. And—I think—whoever built those ships. I freely admit, I have no idea who they are. I don't really

care—you've betrayed the Corps. Beyond that, you could have betrayed all of humanity and it would be secondary as far as I'm concerned. Do you understand what I'm saying?"

The director straightened, an operation that seemed painful and almost non-Euclidean in its geometry. "Do you plan to scan me? Is that what this is all about?"

"Scan you? Maybe. First and foremost, I plan to execute you."

"Of course. But why? That's what I still don't understand. Bester, I'm an old man. I don't have long to live anyway. Surely you don't think that killing me will change anything? There are ten people groomed for my position, and you won't like any of them any more than you like me. We have too much momentum to be deterred in the slightest by the death of a single man. Kill me if you will, but 'they' will still run over you like an insect."

Bester smiled. "God grant me the strength to change the things I can change, the serenity to accept the things I can't, and the wisdom to know the difference."

"What an amazingly sickening platitude."

"Isn't it? It was hanging, in needlepoint, in the home of some rogue sympathizers I found hiding a Blip. They weren't very serene about what I did to them."

"Your point?"

"You and I are very much alike, on one level. Both of us know the truth of our situation. Oh, we talk the talk in public. 'Psi Corps is your friend.' But you and I, we know the truth. Sooner or later—and probably sooner, in the great, grand scheme of things—it's going to come down to your kind or my kind. Humanity simply won't tolerate *Homo superior* in its midst. Mundanes and telepaths are going to stand face-to-face, but only one is going to walk away."

He leaned forward. "I'm here to tell you, Director, it's going to be *us*. Just as, at the end of this day, it's going to be me and not you walking out of this room. Yes, yes—I know it won't change anything. I know you will die soon whether I act or not. But what matters to me, you see— Director—what matters to me is that *I* kill you, that you *know* I killed you. Do you understand? All my life I've lived for the Corps. I've done everything for the Corps. This—this is just for me. I've been working on it for a long time. Hugin and Munin there, for instance. I studied the criteria you use to pick your personal teeps and started conditioning possible candidates twenty years ago. My greatest worry, Director, was that you would drop dead before I was ready."

Johnston was the color of chalk. "They'll know you did it. They'll kill you, too."

"No. They won't. In fact, I'm going to be injured trying to save you. Isn't that nice? And then—we'll see about the rest. I'm patient, as you have seen. I intend to live a lot longer. I will see my people set right again before I die, Director."

"You won't get anything if you scan me."

"C'est la vie."

"I've had a cascade trigger planted in my mind. A deep scan will set if off and wipe pertinent parts of my memory."

"How you must have hated that—letting a dirty telepath into your head."

Johnston laughed harshly. "I did. But it was necessary."

"Let's see." Bester wrenched into his mind. After studying what he found there a moment, he backed out. "Well. The truth. But I expected it, really. No matter, Director—I'll find out what I need to know elsewhere. I didn't have time to really scan you, anyway."

"This whole conversation has been recorded, you know."

"Actually—it hasn't. You forgot to flip the camera on, I'm afraid."

"They'll be able to tell the switch was tampered with."

"I don't think so. Good-bye, Director. Hugin."

The telepath raised her PPG.

"Careful," Bester cautioned.

She fired. Bester stifled a scream as the burst scorched across his thigh. For an instant he felt a surge of wild hope from Johnston, but then the director must have seen it in Bester's eyes.

"Munin," Bester breathed.

The other telepath walked to the far wall and exploded, even as Bester fell forward to the floor.

Shaped charges are wonderful things, Bester thought, as thunder clapped. A brilliant, dazzling heat scorched every inch of him, but he knew it would be no worse than a bad sunburn. The next step was the risky part, the part that worried him ever so slightly.

The wall was gone. Beyond it was the permanent glacial crust of Ganymede, a small fragment of which had been turned liquid by the burst of heat. Small in terms of the total volume of ice on Ganymede, not in terms of the cubic meters the room could contain. Even as Bester made it to his feet and rushed to the door, the first wave hit him at the knees.

It was *cold,* and the air temperature was dropping very quickly. He pressed the door open and fell through, the water surging behind him now up to his waist. He felt his body going into shock, as if he had just jumped into an arctic sea. He heard a sudden hiss-and-shush behind him

and hoped it was what he thought it was, because he couldn't stand up anymore.

He fell into water that was already thinned down to a few inches and lay there, gasping. He turned back toward the blasted room. The shield door had come down.

Icehouse was hardened, but a nuclear strike would melt the water around it, of course. As a precaution, each individual unit of the facility had been built to cut itself free and float. The section the director was in had been cut off from the rest of the facility, though it was still in place.

Back in that room, temperatures must be rapidly approaching Ganymede normal. That was to say, colder than Satan's heart.

"Mr. Bester!"

He tried to turn, but found he was having trouble moving. Someone rolled him over. It was Drew.

"What happened? You're shot!"

Bester managed to gesture toward the shield door. "The director—tried to save—help him"

Inwardly, he grinned like a cat. If he didn't die of pneumonia—and if Ysidra and the others had taken care of the dead guards—everything was going to be just fine.

"Are you sure you're okay, sir?" Byron asked.

"I'm fine. Just a little freezer burn. The PPG blast missed everything important."

"I wish we'd had a chance to scan those rogues."

"Or whoever they were. But they must be long gone by now. They planned their assassination well."

"I'm glad they didn't get you, too."

In that instant, Bester nearly told him. One day, when he was absolutely sure, Byron would be added to the inner circle, and he would probably find out what had really happened here. He might feel foolish—after all, he was the only one on board completely oblivious to the truth.

Still, it was too soon. Byron had all of the makings of one of the elite, but he hadn't yet truly proved where his loyalties were. He hadn't been marked, initiated. These were important things, not to be dismissed lightly.

But today Bester felt good. He felt—well, invincible. Like that first time he had used his powers against a normal, that train cop en route to Paris.

It was a good feeling to have, at his age. A rare one.

He was almost sure of Byron, but he should wait. It was time to test him.

"Thank you, Byron. I'm glad they didn't get me, too."

Donne's hard face on the screen was unreadable, and her voice was nearly as uninflected as ever, but something about her seemed excited.

"Everything went well at Jupiter, sir?"

"Very. We're repaired and resupplied and headed back to the inner system. Something must be happening on your end."

"Yes, sir. We've been keeping tabs, as you said. I'd barely gotten here when there was an—incident."

"Oh?"

"One of the freelance researchers—an Anna Sheridan—was doing some experiments with some sort of organic technology found at an archaeological dig on Theta Omega 2. She had a business teep named Hilliard try to—scan it."

"This doesn't sound good."

"It turned his brains to jelly. Not only that, but every low-level teep within three miles was affected the same way."

"No," Bester said, slowly. "No, that's not good at all. Are there any more of these devices?"

"Yes."

"I'm putting some calls through, right now. I want that technology confiscated, and I want you on this mission to the Rim. Are you game for that?"

"Yes, *sir.*"

"I don't need to tell you how important this is. To all of us."

"No. I appreciate your trust, sir."

"Keep it. Don't let your—personal satisfactions—get in the way of doing your job. But do what you have to. I give you license. We'll fix it later. It's easier to ask forgiveness than permission, after all." He considered. "All in all, it's a good time for this to have happened. The chain of command will have been shaken by events out here in Jupiter space. Their control will be weakened. They won't oppose me in this."

She chopped her chin in a Spartan nod. "Sir."

"I'll talk to you soon, Ms. Donne."

He watched the blank screen for a moment, feeling the ache return to his various body parts.

Well, invincibility only lasted so long. He had had his fun, but the real business was just getting started. These aliens were at the center, he was certain of it.

These new technologies had to be in the hands of the Corps—*his* Corps, not the mundane puppets. *His* Corps.

He had been brooding for about half an hour, watching Jupiter dwindle to something smaller than a nailhead—when he got a call that cheered him up considerably.

"Some weeks, fate loves me," he murmured, and left for the bridge.

"Got him?"

"Yep. Right there."

"All roads lead to Io these days, I guess."

"Yes, sir."

"Okay. We've got all seven Starfuries up and running?"

"Tip-top shape, sir. We got the replacements for the lost ones the day before we shipped out."

"Fine. Let's take them all out."

"They don't appear to have any weapons, sir," Ysidra remarked.

"I want a show of force," Bester said. "We need to remind them who's boss." He turned to face Byron, manning a console a few meters away. "Byron? Ready for another hunt?"

"Always. I hope this one turns out better than the last."

"No doubts this time," Ysidra put in. "We're far enough from Jove for clear readings. Plus surveillance footage of them boarding."

"Still," Bester said, "keep the transport at a decent distance. And we won't have to board, this time. We'll have them send the teeps out in a lifepod."

He felt a stab of pride as the Starfuries took their positions with geometric precision. He had fought long and hard for the Black Omega Squadron. Initially, no one had thought it was a good idea, but he had proven their usefulness often enough that now no one in EarthGov complained—at least not overtly.

After all, they thought they were keeping him distracted, out and away from Earth, from Admin, hunting rogues among the stars.

Hadn't they ever studied history? Didn't they know the lesson of Caesar? It was foolish to put a general out among the barbarians, with an army, and leave him to his own devices. You never knew when he might march back to Rome and take it for himself.

When the time came, he was sure the Black Omega Squadron would follow him. Absolutely sure.

And it was time to make Byron one of them.

He flipped on his com. "Byron, would you do the honors?"

"Of course." Another crackle as he went to a broader band. Bester

followed him. "This is Omega 7 to the captain of the civilian transport. We have you under our guns. Answer or be fired upon."

A brief pause, then a strained female voice. "Omega 7, I copy. This is Captain Freya Grettirsdottir. How can I help you?"

"Captain, don't play coy with me. You have ten rogue telepaths on your transport. You will immediately turn them over to my custody."

Another pause. "Omega 1, we have your assurance—"

"*Now,* Captain."

"Give us five minutes." She sighed. "We'll put them in a lifepod. We're unarmed, Omega 1, and we won't make any trouble."

"That's very wise."

Less than five minutes later, a lifepod broke loose of the transport and drifted toward its Black Omega counterpart.

"Omega 7 to Omega 1. Blips are clear. Capture transport moving into position."

Across the vacuum, Bester could make Byron out, just barely, through the clear canopy.

Well done, Byron.

Thank you, sir. I hope I sounded authoritative enough.

You were perfect.

He linked to the other Black Omegas. "Hold your positions. I want those Blips on the transport and their identities confirmed before we move an inch."

And so they waited a few moments, until the confirmation came from the transport.

"All clear," Byron said. "We can head back now."

"Not yet, Omega 7," Bester said. He put command in his voice. This was hard for some of them, the first time. They needed to be walked through it. Afterward, they always came to understand. Well, almost always.

What was important was that they felt that this time, they didn't have a choice. Afterward, they would always make the right choice—on their own. "We got this batch . . . but there will be others. We need to send a message."

He could feel Byron's confusion, even across the gulf. "All right . . . I'll arrange for them to be escorted to—"

"Negative, Omega 7. Lock all forward weapons on transport. Prepare to fire."

"Sir . . . they're unarmed. . . . We can't just—"

"Prepare to fire, Omega 7." Bester found that he was actually holding his breath. This was taking longer than it should. Had he misjudged the boy? Could he have been that wrong?

"I can't" Byron's voice was thick.

Bester found he was almost shaking. He couldn't fail here, not after his greatest triumph. Byron would not—could not betray him. Not now.

"I gave you an order Byron. Execute the order or face the consequences."

The other Starfuries turned their weapons systems toward Byron. They knew the drill. Leave him no choice. Later he would understand. Later.

He felt a peculiar lightness in his chest. "They're just mundanes, Byron. And it's them or you. You wanted to run with the big boys, now you have to show you're up to it. Are you? Are you up to it, Byron?"

The moment stretched, and stretched. He was going to do it. Byron was going to fail him—which could only mean that he had failed Byron. Failed in his last *Rashomon* role—

And then there was light. It was the most beautiful thing he had seen in a long time. The transport shredded under the impact of Byron's weapons, and the pitiful mindshrieks of the mundanes were swallowed by night.

Thank you, Byron. You didn't fail me. At the last

He didn't 'cast it. What he 'cast was:

Well done, Byron. Now let's go home.

EPILOGUE

"Yes, Kelsey, come in." He stood at the window in his office, watching a sandstorm arrive across the Martian plain. It looked like a dark brick wall, higher than heaven, falling on all of them.

He made sure it was Kelsey, of course, with a probe. There was no need to turn and face her.

"Sorry to disturb you, sir."

"It's okay. You have news?"

"Yes. I sent it to your terminal, but I thought I should come see you in person."

He turned around then. Kelsey was a tall brunette, coldly beautiful. She was young, arrogant, and entirely trustworthy. Beneath her emotionless facade, she was terribly eager to please him, and he knew it.

"Did they find him?"

"No. Not even fragments. Calculating from the last trajectory, it's possible that his ship actually went down on Venus."

"Which is to say, he's dead. Poor Byron. Do we know what happened yet?"

"It's hard to make out. He was fine until the rogue ship started firing. Telemetry doesn't show him being hit, but it does show an explosion in one of his fuel nacelles. The other Starfuries lost communication with him then, and he seems to have spun out of control. They lost him around the planetary horizon. By the time the fight was over and they were able to break free and go looking for him—nothing."

A faint, terrible suspicion touched Bester then, but he forced it down. Byron would never do that to him. It was bad enough that he should die—he would never betray the Corps, never betray Al Bester.

He felt very cold.

"Tell them to keep searching. He may be in a low orbit, without communications. If he's on the surface, we'll never find him."

"Yes, sir."

"Kelsey . . ."

"Sir?"

"What about that batch of transmissions we hijacked from IPX?"

"Nothing. Still no word from the *Icarus*. They've declared her lost, with all hands. They lost the original probe, too."

"So that's Donne, too. Two lost, Kelsey. Such a shame."

"Yes, sir." She couldn't entirely hide how she really felt, however. She was ambitious—she envisioned herself filling the vacuum that Byron had left.

"Thank you, Kelsey. Leave me now."

She did.

He turned back to the sandstorm. It had nearly arrived now. He could see the lower front it was pushing along ahead of itself, like a giant scuffing up dirt with his boots.

The work went on. The work went on.

In the end, perhaps, his mistake was to rely on individuals to provide him any personal sense of worth. It was ironic, really—the first true lesson that the Corps had taught him, only now revealing the depths of its truthfulness. His role wasn't that of child, brother, apprentice, lover, husband, or even mentor. He had never been meant for any of that.

His role was the Corps' role—watcher, protector. Not of the one, but of the many. He *was* the father, the mother, to all of them—the telepaths in Psi Corps and, whether they wanted and appreciated him or not, the telepaths outside of the Corps. Some of them needed a sterner hand than others, it was true . . .

He remembered something Bey had told him.

My father slapped me once. Actually, he slapped me twice—once with the back of his hand, and then, quickly, with his palm. Later, I understood. The first blow was a rejection—he was rejecting the thing I had done, I don't even remember what it was now.

The second blow—with the palm—was to take me back. "I reject you— but I take you back." That was his message.

It was a good lesson. Sometimes there had to be punishment, but there must always be reconciliation in a family. There must always be a gathering back in, a second slap with the palm. Family.

Bester sat back at his desk and looked over his new orders. He couldn't imagine them coming at a worse time. Another one of Department Sigma's messes. Jason Ironheart, one of the subjects for the stable telekinetic project. It seemed that they had been somewhat too successful.

Well, maybe a challenge was what he needed right now. A hunt. Something to keep his mind off of other things.

And he had never been to Babylon 5 before. It ought to be interesting.

He began to look forward to it.

Outside, Mars vanished into rusty opacity, and even through the dense dome, he could hear the shriek of the wind.

FINAL
RECKONING

For Tom Deitz

ACKNOWLEDGMENTS

J. Michael Straczynski and Walter Koenig
Nancy Delia
Min Choi

ACKNOWLEDGMENTS

J. Michael Sieczynski and Walter Roenig

Nanc Della

Min Chon

PROLOGUE

Joseph Begay caught the scent of monster and grinned. He fired his thruster and drifted deeper into shadow. One uneven edge of the asteroid gleamed like a thin seam of silver in the darkest of all mines. The bare suspiration of carbon dioxide he had just released moved him into total eclipse—the silver thread vanished, and the huge rock became a gaping hole in a sky full of stars, the black maw of the underworld. And in that hole was his prey, lurking.

The comlink in his helmet crackled. "Begay. Where are you going?"

He frowned in irritation. The channel was guaranteed secure, but nothing was more guaranteed than silence. And even P12s leaked sometimes when they spoke aloud—vocalizing triggered the part of the brain that 'cast. Only long years of Corps training enabled suppression of that tendency. It was like trying to revolve one's arms in opposite directions—to the thirtieth power.

"I've made him," he replied.

"Herbst and Cortez are already down there."

"Yeah? Have they scented him?"

"No."

"I have."

"Give the position, then, but keep the high ground."

"No way. He's mine."

"Begay—"

He cut the link. The last thing he wanted now was distraction. Sure, he'd get a reprimand later, but it wouldn't go far. He was the best, and after this hunt no one could ever doubt it.

He had come a long way from being that punk in Ganado, nothing better in his future than the leadership of a smalltime gang and an early, violent death. Whatever its faults, he owed the Corps for that. They had plucked him out of that life, given him a chance to do some good.

He drifted down into the shadows and recalled the stories of his Navajo ancestors—the ones his crazy uncle Hatathli had told him when

he was a kid. Those tall tales were starting to make sense, the ones about the Monster Slayer, who had rid the People of their enemies. After years of laughing at them, he finally understood that the finest thing a man could be was a hero, one of the ones who fought the monsters, who made the Human race better.

This was an age of heroes—Sheridan, Delenn, Lyta Alexander . . . He would find his place among them. Today.

There, the scent again.

Space was the perfect hunting ground. Planets were full of voices—thousands, millions—on Earth, billions. Prey could hide in those voices as a rabbit might in dense brush. But space was quiet, simple, with nowhere to hide. He knew all of his fellow hunters with the intimacy of many hunts, and he could tune out their voices until there was only silence and the breath of the hunted.

That breath was near.

He flipped on his night vision, and the asteroid reappeared. It was cold, the backside of this lump of nickel and iron, but the side facing the sun was hotter, and metal was an excellent conductor of heat. The landscape reflected that: the higher elevations were colder than the low. A firefly appeared, too—Herbst or Cortez, probably. Space suits had to shed heat or their occupants would bake alive, and no technology had been invented that could overcome the basic laws of thermodynamics.

So where were the prey and the other hunter? There ought to be three bright dots.

The answer was simple enough. The prey was hiding someplace—they already knew the asteroid was hollow. That might also mean that one of his teammates had found the monster's bolt-hole and was holding out. Everyone wanted to be the hero who caught this fellow.

Well, Joseph didn't need to see him. He *felt* him. The others were P12s, too, but not all P12s were created equal.

The almost inconsequential tug of the planetoid gripped him now, and he let himself drift toward the surface, guided by small bursts from his thruster. He knew what he was looking for, and soon he found it—a regular, circular opening. One of the old mine shafts. He angled toward it.

The tunnel dropped down straight, perpendicular to the surface. He drew his PPG and went in feet first, the weapon aimed between them.

A reddish blob of heat appeared, and again he grinned like a coyote.

But only for a moment. With line of sight it was simple to read a psychic signature. The blob below was Herbst, not their quarry.

With line of sight it was easier to send and receive without leaking, too.

Herbst?

It's me. I thought he was in here, but I lost him.

Are you sure?

Yeah. The shaft goes down another three hundred feet and dead-ends. Nobody there.

Where the hell did he go?

I don't know. It must have been a false trail. I've heard spooky things about this guy. Maybe—Gott! Above you!

Joseph snapped his head up. At the same moment a psychic attack cracked into his shields. Only yards away, a man-shaped blob dropped toward him.

The attack was strong and simple, aimed at paralyzing. Even as he tried to close the contact of his PPG, he found his finger wouldn't move.

He had killed a boy once, before Psi Corps had found him. He didn't remember much about the fight, only that he had been losing until the anger woke in him, a fury so cold and brilliant it made him feel like a giant. When they had pulled him off the older kid, he'd already pulped in his head with a rock. Begay had been twelve, a minor, and so had been remanded to juvenile court. That's when his psi powers were discovered, and that's when the Corps had given him absolution, and a new life.

Ten years ago. He was a new man.

Except for the anger. It came now, a sheer shuddering blast, meeting the dark wind that was slamming into him head-on and pushing it back, back. The monster was terrifically strong, but he didn't have to win the psychic duel, he only had to move his finger. Just a little, a fraction of an inch . . .

The shaft lit with green light, once, twice. In the second blast he saw a nebula of ice crystals, already billowing out from one rupture.

And that hideous monster's mind—went out.

"Ya-heeeeee!" he shouted. "I got the bastard!"

I thought we wanted him alive, Herbst 'cast.

Well, maybe if you'd helped! He had me. In another second he would have been on me, taken my weapon, killed us both.

You didn't give me time!

There wasn't any time. Besides, this saves the trouble of a trial, doesn't it? Swift justice.

He felt Herbst's disapproval. *That's not the way we do things. That's the way* he *did things.*

You were here. You saw I had no choice.

Yeah. He's dead, right?

As dead as lead. We'll take the body back.

He flipped on his headlamp and the sudden illumination made him

blink. His first shot had split the faceplate open, and what he could see through the mirrorlike surface was a real mess. The second shot had taken him in the chest, from which mist still drifted.

Moments later, they were back in open space, navigating toward the distant transport. He noticed Herbst was favoring his left hand. Joseph reactivated his link.

"—Begay, for the last time—"

"Easy, boss. We got him."

There followed a satisfying pause. "Really?"

"Yeah. I had to take him down, but it was him, all right."

"Well—well done. Is that Herbst or Cortez with you?"

"Herbst."

"He was having comlink trouble earlier. Where's Cortez?"

"I don't know. He was on the surface."

"Well, he isn't there now."

"Must have gone around to the sun side."

"He would have reported."

"Maybe not. Or maybe . . ."

He didn't want to say it. Maybe the monster had claimed one last victim.

"We'll find him. Let's get this stiff inside."

"I'm starting the lock cycle now."

By the time they had reached the transport, the outer air lock was open. They drifted in, and Joseph closed the hatch and cycled it. A few moments later the inner door opened and they were surrounded again by friendly, breathable air. Joseph unlatched his helmet. It popped out of its gasket with a sigh.

The corpse floated, ghostlike, its blood now liquid and drifting into tiny beads. Joseph remembered other stories now, of *chindi*—the evil spirits of the departed, which caused illness. Maybe he should arrange to have a ghostway done when he got back home. He didn't exactly believe in that stuff, but he didn't exactly *not* believe it, either.

Still, *chindi* or not, he couldn't resist. While he fumbled at the collar of the monster's suit, he heard the soft hiss of Herbst taking off his helmet.

The PPG had done a lot of damage, frying skin and cartilage, and explosive decompression had done even more. It took him a few seconds to piece together Herbst's features.

"What?" *Chindi!* his mind shrieked.

"Simple, really," a voice said from behind him. "An old trick, transposing. I did it the first time when I was only six, to win a game of cops and blips."

Joseph went for his PPG, but this psi assault was even stronger than the one before. He managed to twist enough that he could see the man standing over him. Then everything froze.

It was the monster, looking much as he did in his photographs, except that his face was composed, serene. His dark eyes were touched, not by anger or madness, but by quiet melancholy. He was holding a PPG.

"I masked the switch with that earlier attack. As I said, simple. And now you've let me on your ship. Thank you."

Joseph felt his hand inching toward his weapon. He could do it again. He could . . .

"I kill you filthy," the monster said, and then chuckled, as if it were a joke instead of nonsense. Then everything flashed green, and something hot stabbed Joseph in the chest, and he tasted fire in his mouth.

Alfred Bester considered the dead man and shot him again, in the head. You could never be too sure. Then he moved quickly to the hallway.

Their teammate Cortez was already dead of a seizure, lying at the bottom of the shaft. According to what he had gleaned from Begay, that left only two, both P12s. He looked back at the corpse and shook his head sadly. Why did they insist on sending these *children* after him? Maybe the other two would present more of a challenge.

But they didn't. Ten minutes later he jettisoned the four bodies into space, disabled the tracking devices on the transport, and sat contemplating where he wanted to go.

Michael Garibaldi woke with a dry mouth, blurred vision, and a serious sense of disorientation. He cracked one eye and saw a blinking red light. He put it together with the insistent *brreeep* that had disturbed his sleep, but couldn't figure out what it meant.

He sat up, and his body protested. It was a sickeningly familiar sensation, one he had hoped and sworn and prayed he would never feel again.

"God, you stupid . . ." He was talking to himself. Not a good sign. He couldn't remember drinking, not even one drink, but that was how it was sometimes, with blackouts.

His heart was pounding. He couldn't do this again. He couldn't.

Then the details of the day before started to return. He remembered a morning full of pushing paper, lunch with that smug CEO from Amtek, then racquetball with the same little smartass—beat him, too. More pushing paper, a call from Lise, who was on Earth for business, a movie with his daughter, another movie without her, then bedtime.

Everything accounted for. No drinks.

The noise hadn't stopped, but at least he realized what it was now. It was his red-line comlink, which meant it was important. The clock on it solemnly and silently informed him that it was 5 A.M. Martian standard time, February 15, 2271.

Like the months on Earth had anything to do with Mars. Wasn't there some legislation in the works to do something about that?

Five o'clock?

He hit the switch. "Yeah. Garibaldi. This better be *so* good—"

"It's about Bester, sir." The voice was Jim Hendershot, his head of very special security.

"Is he close enough for me to shoot?"

"No, sir."

"Call back in five minutes."

If it was about Bester, he needed to be a little more alert than this.

He went to the bathroom, splashed some water on his face, and looked in the mirror. There he saw the same handsome guy who had been looking at him for fifty-odd years. Some grey in the eyebrows and beard, sure. But he didn't look hung over.

Racquetball. That was it, wasn't it? Jeez, was he *that* old, *that* out of shape, that a game of racquetball against some twenty-five-year-old punk left him feeling like he'd been on a two-week bender?

That was almost more depressing than the prospect that he was in the bottom of a bottle again.

Almost.

He got a cup of coffee and settled down in front of the link. Hendershot called back, right on time.

"Tell me you got him," Garibaldi said.

"Sorry, boss."

"He wasn't at his asteroid hidey-hole? I paid damned good money for that information."

"Oh, we think he was there. An EABI transport—Metasensory Division—went out there on your tip. Their last transmission was that they had him. Then nothing. And the transponder in the transport went quiet."

"*No!*" Garibaldi exploded. "Who the hell did they send out there, the three stooges?"

"Sir?"

"Nothing. We should have known better than to trust the Bureau, especially their telepaths. We should have sent our own team. Hell, I should have gone myself."

"We didn't have anyone in the area. By the time we could have got there—"

"Yeah, yeah. I just don't trust them. Half the people in the Metasensory Division were folded in from the old Psi Corps."

"From the side that split against Bester. Nobody wants Bester more than they do."

"Nobody? Nobody? Man, you don't know *me* very well, do you? Hendershot, Bester *trained* most of those guys who are chasing him. He knows everything about them, and I don't doubt he still has men on the inside. I don't doubt it for a second. Old Psi Corps, no Psi Corps, rotten-to-the-Corps—you can't trust telepaths, not when it comes to one of their own." He put his head in his hands and smoothed back hair that wasn't there. It had been receding since he was twenty and he had finally figured, why wait? Beat it to the punch. Now he had almost grown into it.

Yep, he was getting old, like it or not. Which meant Bester was older. The thought that that son of a bitch might die in his sleep was the worst thing he could imagine. He could almost hear the Psi Cop's triumphant, cynical last laugh.

"Listen, Hendershot. I've had it with playing coyote to this guy's roadrunner. I run one of the ten wealthiest corporations on Mars, and I don't ask for much. But—I—want—Bester. Make me happy."

"I understand."

"And next time, I want to *be* there, *capisce*? No more tips to the Psi Corps hunt squads or whatever nicey-nice name they've given them now. Surface cooperation, yeah—they can still be useful. But I want to be two steps ahead of 'em, which oughta put me only two steps behind Bester."

"Yes, sir."

Garibaldi closed the link and stretched. Tortured, feverish muscles complained.

Bester!

The trick was not to be even one step behind your quarry. The trick was to figure out where he was going, and be one step ahead. To do that, you had to know what he wanted.

He stood and went to the window, opened the metal shield so he could see the beautiful, stark landscape of Mars. The sun stood just above the horizon, throwing all of the shadows on the plain toward him.

"What do you want, Bester?" he asked, gazing at the still-dark sky. "What do you want?"

PART 1

Homecoming

PART I.

Homecoming

1

"I want to go home," Bester said. "I'm tired."

He took a sip of the red wine, resisted making a face, and set the crystal flute back on the stand next to his chair. He managed a smile for his host, a narrow-faced woman with ebony skin and a barely managed shock of gunmetal hair. Her eyes widened.

"Mars? Mr. Bester, I don't think—"

"Not Mars. Earth."

"Earth? Even worse. Mr. Bester, you're wanted on every world and station in Human space, and on quite a few beyond. To return to Earth itself would be—"

"Unexpected," Bester finished. "It's how I survive, always doing what no one expects. They've done their best, tried every trick in the book, but I *wrote* the book. Still, I'm sick of all this. I've never been able to stay on a colony world for more than a year or two. How can I? In a population of hundreds or thousands, I tend to stand out. But Earth has billions. It's easier to hide in a crowd."

"Yes, but things are more *lax* in the colonies, too, Mr. Bester. Earth! The risk of getting you there—of forging the necessary papers, of passing you through quarantine—phenomenal!"

"What quarantine? The Drakh plague is gone."

"Oh, indeed. And EarthGov has no intention of letting another one slip through, intentionally or accidentally. Traffic to ancient and little-known worlds has increased tenfold in the wake of the *Excalibur*'s explorations. Public opinion and a lot of scientists claim it's a disaster just waiting to happen."

"Fine. So I'll go through a screening. What of it?"

"They'll discover you're a teep. They'll have your DNA—everything they need to identify you. You think all off-world teeps aren't compared to the tribunal lists?"

"I am confident of your ability to manage it, Sophie."

"Mr. Bester—the risk isn't just to yourself."

"Oh, that I understand, Sophie. If I'm caught, I doubt I can stop them from finding out whatever they want to. I would never turn in an associate, but they have ways. Yes, if I'm caught, I doubt very much that I shall stand trial alone.

"You and I know that everything we did was justified, but in any conflict, the winners have the privilege of writing its history. We did not win, you and I, and history does not look kindly on us."

"Are you threatening me, Mr. Bester? That isn't very gracious, considering all I've done for you. And as *you* know, I am not wanted by the tribunal. Unlike yourself, I didn't commit any acts that can be construed as war crimes."

Bester broadened his smile a bit. "Ah, truth," he said, taking his glass and studying the play of light in the burgundy fluid. "It's all so . . . relative. Once I was a patriot, an example of everything that was good about the Corps. Now they say I am the most terrible criminal who ever lived. And who better than me to tell them who the other criminals were? After all, I was the evil mastermind."

"You wouldn't."

"Sophie, I want to go to Earth. Get me there with a secure identity. Get me through or around this quarantine. I'm asking nicely, right now. But as I said, I'm weary, and cranky, and I'm tired of cheap off-world wine. Once I'm there, I doubt very much that you will see or hear from me ever again. Oh, the occasional postcard, maybe . . ."

He thought she would relent there, but she went for another round. "I've heard you still have the black ships," she said. "The ones EarthGov and the Corps couldn't admit existed. What about them?"

"Your information is a little outdated," Bester countered coldly. Then he softened his voice. "Sophie, you were a good intern. And I was good to *you*, wasn't I? Wasn't I there for you when things got tough at Kerf?"

Her eyes darted about, like those of an animal seeking escape. But there wasn't any, not from him, and she knew it.

"Very well," she said at last. "I'll do what I can."

"I knew you'd see things my way."

"Mr. Bester, you have a way of making certain there's no other way to see them."

He nodded condescendingly. "Another thing," he said as he rose. "I'll need a supply of choline ribosylase—untraceable, of course."

Her face suddenly transfigured, and he felt a hint of pity. "I'm sorry," she said. "I didn't know."

"Save your sympathy for someone who needs it, Sophie," he replied, more brusquely than he intended.

* * *

Not much later he retired to his room, but found that he wasn't tired enough for sleep. He decided to take a walk. After all, he had never been to the Maui colony, and if things went well he would never be back.

He selected a suit of black silk twill and a caudric shirt the same color, fastening the top button with a brass-colored over-cap. He studied himself for a moment in the floor-length mirror. His hair was almost white, as was his beard, though his eyebrows still kept a reddish brown tinge. His face seemed to have more lines each time he looked at it, but all in all he looked pretty good for a man of eighty-two.

Except for his hands, which jarred him every time. Pink, gloveless—naked. He flexed his right hand, the good one. When he was a teenager, he'd had nightmares now and then that he was out in public, without his gloves.

Telepaths didn't wear gloves anymore, so he couldn't either, not without being noticed. It made him feel dirty.

But, he mused, one adapted.

A few moments later he stepped from Sophie Herndon's rambling abode onto a quiet street. A few natives were out walking, too. The air was cool but not cold, very pleasant except for the faint smell of the sea—fishy, but subtly different from any ocean on Earth. Maui was mostly water—from space you couldn't really see anything else. From what he had seen of it, it was rather charming. It had character.

The original settlers had been mostly Polynesian romantics, bent on recapturing a lost past. Of course you couldn't really do that. And children rarely inherited their parents' infatuations, especially when it meant living in grass houses on a planet somewhat chillier, even at the equator, than Earth.

Still, the architecture had certain South Sea touches, and the streetlamps resembled paper lanterns made in fanciful shapes, a legacy of the second wave of mostly Chinese immigrants. The people seemed pleasant enough and minded their business. Not a bad place to settle for a while. Until they found him again.

Maybe Sophie was right. Maybe going to Earth was too dangerous.

The street took him to a dockside stretch, and as he walked up that, he felt the tickle of minds around him. Somewhere near, tentative lovers were embracing. A man on a boat was silently cursing his mangled nets. An old woman was remembering that the nights had been warmer when she was a girl.

He smelled something cooking, and his stomach reminded him he hadn't eaten in a while. The lights of a restaurant appeared ahead, welcoming, and on impulse he entered. Inside, it was warmer, in tempera-

ture and in mood. The walls were of polished, reddish wood—or, no, maybe coral, or whatever passed for it here. Candlelight provided the only illumination.

A girl at the door asked him to remove his shoes and showed him to a long, low table with mats on either side—no chairs. He sat cross-legged, an act his bones protested a bit. There were others farther down the table, who nodded at him as he sat. He nodded back.

The girl brought him a sweet, mildly alcoholic drink that tasted like sake with a green-tea aftertaste. It wasn't bad, so he took a few sips.

"Something to eat?" she asked, in lilting Anglic.

"Please," he replied. "Whatever's good."

She nodded and left, but returned a few moments later with a young man, whom she seated across from him.

He figured it was probably the custom here to seat together strangers who came in alone. But he wanted to be by himself. He smiled at the young fellow, and was just about to say so, when all the hairs on the back of his neck prickled up.

The man was wearing a Psi Corps badge.

No, that wasn't right. It looked like the old badge, but there was no Psi Corps anymore. This badge merely identified a telepath who was working professionally within some other organization.

"I—ah—guess this is how they do it here," the fellow said hesitantly. He couldn't be more than twenty, a square-faced boy with auburn hair and an infectious smile. He was wearing an EarthForce uniform. Bester felt nothing alarming in his surface thoughts. Could this be a coincidence? He didn't really believe it. Carefully, carefully, he tightened his blocks while at the same time extending his senses.

"My name is Derrick Thompson," the fellow offered.

"Nice to meet you," Bester replied. "I'm Fred Tozzer."

"It's good to meet you, Mr. Tozzer. Are you a native?"

Still not even a whiff of deception. It would take more than a P12 to hide that from him. "No, actually," he replied. "I'm a tourist."

"Where from?"

"Oh, Mars originally, but I suppose you could call me a citizen of the galaxy. I've traveled all of my life, and now that I'm retired, I find that I can't break the habit."

"What brought you to Maui?"

"Oh, I heard the fish was good."

Derrick laughed politely.

"And you? I assume you aren't from around here."

"Nope. Earth, Kansas City. You might have guessed from my uni-

form that I'm in EarthForce. I'm stationed here, on the base at Bue Atoll. Right now I'm on leave and thought I'd take in the sights."

"You must be pretty disappointed to be seated with an old man rather than a young girl. And me not even a local."

He shrugged. "I have a girl already, so this'll keep me out of trouble. I—ah—saw you staring at my psi badge. Telepaths don't make you uncomfortable, do they? I won't take offense if you want me to sit elsewhere."

"No, not at all, it's just—well, I'm an old man. I'm not used to seeing that badge on that uniform. And I haven't been back to Earth since before the—crisis, did they call it?"

"Yep. Well, things are different now. Better. Before the crisis there were a lot of things we weren't allowed to do. Be in EarthForce, for instance. Now the world is wide open."

The waitress arrived with their food, one big bowl and two small plates.

"That looks like boiled shrimp," Al said.

"It is. They farm it off the coast."

"I was hoping for something native."

Derrick smiled. "You want a bowl of plankton? The native life is all microscopic. Anything big enough to see came from somewhere else. But you'll find the shrimp has a unique taste, since they feed on the native stuff."

Al tried one. It *was* unique, if not exactly good. A bit sulfury, like the yolk of a boiled egg.

Derrick smiled at his expression. "Takes a little getting used to. How long are you staying?"

"A few days."

"And where next?"

"I'm not really sure. Just playing it by ear."

"Well, that must be the life." He lifted his cup. "To seeing the universe."

Bester raised his cup. They clinked and drank.

As the night wore on, Derrick and Bester talked of the places they had been and the things they had seen. Bester had more stories, of course, and Derrick listened with fascination. Bester kept buying the younger man drinks but sipping his own, so that by the time the place closed, Derrick was more than a little tipsy. They left together, ostensibly to find someplace that was still open.

Derrick stopped outside, stood swaying slightly and looking at the stars. "Not a single famil'r constellation," he murmured. " 'S the way I like it. Like you, huh? I guess we're two of a kind."

"Actually," Bester said, "I wouldn't mind seeing the Big Dipper again. It's been a while."

Derrick didn't seem to notice the remark. They continued up the dockside walk.

"Y'know," Derrick said, "I have to tell you, you seem awfully familiar to me. Like maybe we've met before. What's that called? Déjà you?" He chuckled at his own joke.

"No, it just means you've seen my picture. I'm really Alfred Bester, the notorious war criminal."

Derrick laughed at that, then became serious. "That's not funny, really. Bester is the worst of the worst, everything that was bad about the old Psi Corps—" He stopped, suddenly, eyes widening as he turned to look at Bester.

"Oh, shit! You *are* him."

Bester nodded sadly and struck hard and fast, blowing through the young man's drink-deadened guards as if they weren't there. Derrick collapsed, and Bester dragged his limp form to a nearby bench. A man and woman, walking some thirty feet behind them, stopped.

"Is he okay?"

"He'll be fine. He's had a touch too much to drink."

"Can you manage him?"

Bester smiled. "It's the story of my life. I'm always the baby-sitter. But thanks for your concern."

The two walked on, seemingly satisfied.

When they were gone, Bester went to work, snipping out the parts of Derrick's memory that included him. But he didn't erase them. Instead, he walled them up, buried them. In time, the memories would return— first Bester's face, then their conversation. And in that, as carefully as one might set down a bird's egg in a pile of glass shards, he placed a destination. When he was certain everything was right, he called a cab and had Derrick taken to his hotel.

In a week or so, Derrick would remember he had been attacked, and like a good little soldier he would have himself scanned so his brave new Corps could learn all of the facts. One thing they would learn was that Bester was headed out of Human space altogether, things finally having got too hot for him. It amused him to think of the hunters, certain that in his old age Bester had finally slipped up.

He went back to Sophie's house, pleased with himself. He could still find the opportunity in any situation. And now he was sure—he had what it took. Dangerous or not, he was going home.

2

"Ah—Paris in spring," Bester said to the cab driver. He meant for it to sound cynical, and maybe it did, but to his own surprise, he didn't feel that way. It *was* lovely, the green track along the Champs-Élysées, the blossoms and golden sunlight, and the sky of that peculiar blue that—impossibly—didn't exist anywhere else on Earth, much less on any other planet.

But what made Earth home was its smell. Spaceships and stations, no matter how much they strove to duplicate planetary atmospheres, always smelled like the inside of a can. Planets each had their own peculiar complex of scents—different incidental gases that mixed in different proportions.

Scent was the most primal and least intellectual of the senses, triggering instincts older than the Human race as inexorably as it did childhood memories. A whiff could bring back a buried memory more vividly than could any other sense. That had been a useful thing for him to know, as a Psi Cop.

Yes, Paris smelled like Earth, and it smelled like Paris. Suddenly he was fifteen again, seeing, smelling, *feeling* the city through the astonishment and wonder of the boy he had been, so long ago.

It felt almost like happiness.

The cabbie, however, was unimpeded by such sentiment. He had caught Bester's original intent.

"Ah, yes, the spring. When great flocks of silly birds descend on the city with their cameras and their 'which-way-is-this' and their *'je-ne-comprends-pas.'* My favorite time of year, to be sure."

"I would think it a lucrative time of year."

"Yes, yes. I make lots of money. But when should I spend it? When should I enjoy it? In the dreary months, when no one wants to come here? When I am old enough to retire?"

"Yes, I can see you've drawn a very sorry lot in life," Bester said.

"But at least you have a ready audience to inflict your angst on, whenever you choose."

"You are offended by my opinions? Monsieur, there is quick relief for that. I can put you out here, on this sidewalk—"

"Yes, why don't you do that."

The driver's mouth dropped open for a second. "Monsieur? We are still very far from your hotel."

"I know the city—well enough to know you're taking a somewhat roundabout route. I prefer to walk."

"Very well."

They were only a block or so from the Place de la Concorde. Bester paid the cabbie with his forged chit and got out. The cabbie drove off, complaining loudly to himself about crazy tourists.

Bester took a deep breath. He had only a small shoulder bag that contained his forged documents and a hand computer. His only clothes were a black leather jacket, black gabardine slacks, and a yellowish brown shirt.

He felt—free.

He started walking, back up the Champs-Élysées, toward the Arc de Triomphe. He had made reservations at a hotel, but suddenly he didn't particularly care if he went there or not. It was morning, and the whole day lay before him.

There was a sense he had not indulged in yet, the best of all. He found a bench lightly shaded by trees, then closed his eyes.

And felt the mind of the city. It was in Paris, as a boy, that he had made an important discovery. Each city, he discovered, has its own psionic fingerprint, a combination of thoughts and conversations and interactions of all of its citizens, emerging into something as distinct and complex as a fine vintage of wine.

He recognized it. An odd thing, really—how many people living in the city today had been alive when he was fifteen? Not many. And yet it was the same, as if the city were a Human body, retaining continuity and integrity even though the individual cells that had made it up one year before were mostly dead and replaced.

Oh, it was a bit different, the mind of Paris. Somehow, inexplicably more vital, more alive than ever. Younger.

He started walking again, and vaguely heard someone whistling. He had gone fifteen steps before he realized that the whistling was coming from him.

Now, this is going too far, he thought. *I can't lose all my perspective, not if I want to survive.*

Nonetheless, a few minutes later he was whistling again.

He stopped at a crepe shop and got one of the pancakelike desserts filled with hazelnut paste. He felt very much like a tourist, but he didn't really care. He topped the snack with espresso, and then continued on.

Hemlines were up, he noted—way up. He seemed to remember reading somewhere that that tended to happen after wars and crises, and humanity had certainly had plenty of those lately. Clothing in general was flashier, more colorful than he remembered. The stereotypical Parisian beret, rare when he had last been here, seemed ubiquitous, though he suspected those who were wearing them were mostly tourists, or those pandering to the tourist trade.

He had the same skepticism about the antique feel of the city—that it was tourist-driven. Oh, Earth in general, and Paris in particular, were conservative, in terms of technology. But Paris actually seemed to have stepped backward in time since he had visited it last. One had to concentrate to see what was being hidden—the phones and personal computers woven invisibly into shirt collars, the electronic-ink displays in shop windows that mimicked disposable paper signs, the police hovercraft that looked like groundcars until they almost apologetically took to the sky.

He wondered if the pretense was some gestalt decision on the part of Parisians or more specifically the result of legislation. If the latter, it wouldn't be the first time that well-meaning laws had been passed to make sure Paris remained Paris. As if it could ever be anything else. He imagined the city snickering at such efforts.

He left the broad avenue and wandered deeper into the heart of the city, gradually working uphill toward the Sacré Coeur. By midday he found himself in the Pigalle, which had once been the red-light district and still had something of its old reputation. Here, where few tourists went, was found the real life of the city. He passed a small, run-down café where two grizzled old men were playing checkers. Children, just out of school, playing soccer, reluctantly parted to let the occasional delivery truck through narrow streets—some still cobblestone—bordered by brick buildings pitted by centuries of rain.

The residents of the Pigalle were a genetic cross section of Earth. For centuries, immigrants from every corner of the globe had settled in Paris, and Paris, in her own inexorable way, had made them Parisian. They always seemed in a hurry. They walked with shoulders square, arms close to the body and usually in front of them, their faces masks of neutrality. But just when you were tempted to think of them as automatons, someone would explode in a burst of laughter, or hurl a stream of obscenities at a car that had come too close, or stop to scold a child.

He was starting to think about supper when he turned a corner and was greeted by shouting. A woman stood in front of a small hotel—the

Hotel Marceau. She was petite, perhaps thirty-five, with pale skin and curly brown hair chopped just below her ears. Her stance was defiant, one hand on her hip and the other shaking in front of her as a fist.

Her voice was defiant, too. She apparently didn't go in for the short skirts of the day—she wore denim pants and a T-shirt.

"—not another cent from me, you hear? Five customers you've chased away from me this week. You say I must pay to protect my business. But when I pay, you ruin it anyway."

For all of her defiance, Bester could feel fear beneath the surface. It was no mystery where that came from. She was shouting at five men, most teenagers, but one of them was an older brute who bore a massive scar on one cheek, a crooked nose, and putty-pale skin. He leveled a thick finger at her.

"You *pay* us because I say to. And I'll tell you another thing—I'm used to better treatment than this from my friends. You *are* my friend, aren't you, *cherie*? Because now that I think about it, you haven't been all that friendly to me."

Bester couldn't help it—he uttered a single, dark laugh. He had seen death and deceit on a cosmic scale, waged wars of empire, battled alien races that possessed godlike powers. Watching these stupid normals, fighting over their little scrap of turf, struck him as unutterably ridiculous.

His laugh got their attention.

"What the hell are *you* laughing at?" the big fellow grunted.

Bester shook his head and kept walking. The question wasn't worth answering. If they didn't understand how absurd they were, they wouldn't notice it just because he pointed it out.

"Yeah, that's right, old man," the fellow called. "You just keep on walking. Nothing to see here."

Bester was planning on doing just that. For a few short hours he had forgotten how much he hated normals, but his mood had done an about-face. Now he remembered. The woman was stupid for standing up to men she had no power against, and if they beat her, or raped her, or killed her, it would make no difference to him. Or to the world at large. If she had been a teep, then he might have helped.

Though given what the rogues and the new-and-improved Psi Corps had done to him, he didn't particularly care for his own kind, either. All his life he had worked for his people, his telepaths. He had saved them more times than they knew, yet in the end they had turned against him, pitched in with *normals*.

He was a man without a people, now—orphaned, divorced, exiled.

Maybe that was why he had felt so free. He no longer felt the slightest responsibility to anyone or anything except himself.

And none at all to this stupid woman.

Still, he paused, to see what would happen. It was like watching a train wreck.

The bravos had turned their attention back to her, though one of the younger ones noticed he had stopped, and was glaring at him.

"Be a smart girl, Louise. Pay me my money."

"Or what? Are all of you big brave men going to beat me up? Tear up a few of my rooms? Go ahead, then. I can't stop you. You can take, but I won't *give* you anything anymore."

"That mouth you got ain't doin' you any favors," the man warned. "Best you put it to some better use. I got some ideas about that—"

"When Mars has oceans."

"Ooh!" one of the younger boys said. "She told you, I think."

The big man turned on his smaller companion. "Shut up," he demanded, and then he noticed Bester, still watching. "I thought I told you to keep walking, you old scab."

"The zoo was closed today," Bester replied. "I didn't get to see the ape house, so I'm making do."

The big man blinked as if he didn't understand, then strode menacingly toward Bester. "You ain't from around here, I don't think. 'Cause if you were, you wouldn't still be standing there. And you sure as hell wouldn't be mouthing off to me."

Bester smiled. "Please know, I find you *truly* terrifying. The fact that it only takes five of you to threaten such a dangerous young woman— well, it puts me in awe. I wouldn't dream of crossing you."

The man grabbed him by the collar and lifted, his face reddening. Bester glanced down at the fist knotted in his shirt. "That's expensive material," he said, calmly.

The man pulled back his other fist, and Bester watched it, unblinking. He could kill the fellow, of course, without lifting a finger, but not without arousing suspicion. Still . . .

"Put him down, Jem," a new voice said. "Put him down right now."

Bester couldn't see who was talking. Jem could, however, and his face set in a sort of sullen resignation. He hesitated for a moment, then lowered Bester back to the street.

"There ain't nothin' goin' on here, Lucien," he grunted. "Not a damn thing."

"I'll be the judge of that."

Al turned slightly, so that he could see that the new voice belonged to a policeman, a stocky fellow in his early forties.

"Have you got a complaint?" the policeman asked Bester.

Bester smiled at Jem, then turned back to the policeman. "Yes. This man doesn't smell good at all. Other than that, everything is just fine."

The cop looked him up and down, made a disgusted noise. "Louise?" he asked.

She hesitated for a moment. "No," she said.

"See?" Jem said. "So why don't you go bother someone else?"

"Why don't you?" the policeman said. "Run along."

Jem glared at him, then shrugged. "Come on, boys. We've got business elsewhere, anyhow." He directed a nasty look at Bester. "Nice to meet you, grandpa," he said. "Too bad you're just passing through."

"It is a shame," Bester agreed. "I'll miss your stimulating conversation."

As he watched them leave, he sent out tendrils of psi, just enough to know their signatures, to recognize them in the dark.

The cop, meanwhile, was confronting the woman.

"Louise, I can't do anything for you unless you make an accusation."

"You know I can't do that, Lucien. I have to live here. And suppose you managed to arrest Jem and his bunch and keep them—not that I think you could, but just suppose. Another bunch would just move in, and they would take care of me in advance, so I wouldn't repeat my mistake with them."

"Then pay them what they ask. Otherwise—well—I can't be here twenty-four hours a day."

"I know that, Lucien," she said.

"Though I could be here more than I am," he hinted.

"I know that, too." She sighed. "You know I'm grateful, Lucien, but I'm just not—"

She suddenly noticed that Bester was still there. "What are you waiting for? Do you want some of my money, too?"

"No."

"I don't know who you are, but you shouldn't have gotten involved. They're like sharks, those men. A little blood and then the frenzy. Why you want to commit suicide, I don't know, but go do it someplace else."

Bester shrugged.

"Listen," the cop said to him. "You could help, here. I know Jem was attacking you. Louise is being stubborn, but *you* don't live around here. If you could swear out a complaint, I could get these guys off of the street. I think you were trying to help Louise, but if you really want to help—"

"I had no intention of helping her," Bester said. "I was just walking around, looking for a place to stay. This is a hotel, and I was looking at it. The gentleman in question simply mistook what I was interested in. You

don't really think an old man like me thought he could handle those fellows, do you?"

The cop cocked his head skeptically. "You didn't look too worried to me."

"I don't worry much, anymore. I've discovered that the universe dumps on you when it wants to. Being upset about it doesn't help a bit."

The cop rolled his eyes in disgust, but Louise quirked a reluctant little smile.

"Have it your way, then," the officer said. "Louise, I'll see you later. Alive, I hope."

"Good-bye, Lucien."

Bester took that as his sign to leave as well, but he hadn't turned the corner when Louise's voice floated after him. "It's ten credits a night, or five a day if you plan to stay for more than a week."

He turned, slowly, really looked at the hotel for the first time. It had a small café—just a room with a few tables and chairs, it seemed—and three stories. The building looked nineteenth-century, maybe early twentieth.

"Does that include meals?" he asked.

"Meals are a credit extra, and you can't complain about what I make."

He walked a few steps toward her. He was, after all, feeling tired, and his juvenile buoyancy of an hour earlier had defiantly reversed itself.

The Alfred Bester hunters were combing the universe to find a man who liked the finest things. The apartments he had abandoned were spacious, capaciously furnished with art, provisioned with good wine and brandy. Who would ever think to look for him in a crumbling hotel in the Pigalle?

"May I see the room first?" he asked.

3

Bester passed a forkful of chicken étouffée to his mouth and chewed. He sensed someone watching him, and glanced around.

It was the hotel owner, Louise. "Well?" she asked. "How is it?"

They were alone in the little dining room, though a young couple had been there when he arrived. Business did not seem brisk.

"I can't complain," he replied.

She nodded. "It's one of my better dishes."

"No—I mean I can't complain. You told me so this afternoon."

She folded her arms and looked down at him. "You don't like it?" she asked.

"I certainly didn't say that."

"What's wrong with it?"

He looked up at her with his "thinking cap" face. "Well—I'm not complaining, mind you—but for chicken I might have made the roux a shade or two lighter. And I would have chopped the onions much finer."

"I see."

"But I'm *not* complaining," he said, eating another bite.

She looked at him severely for a second or two. "You didn't tell me how long you're staying," she said at last.

"Oh, at least a week. Maybe more."

"Very well. But if you stay only six days, I will charge you the ten credits a night, you understand?"

"Perfectly," Al replied.

"Well . . . well," she finished, and went back into the kitchen. A second later, she popped back out. "And don't blame me if Jem and his gang come back and give you a beating. You saw what the situation is. You understand?"

"Yes," Bester replied again, wondering when she would leave him alone to finish his meal in peace.

"Good." This time she stayed in the kitchen. He could hear the pots

and pans banging around as she did dishes. Did she really work here all alone?

Outside, the streets faded to purple, and then the lights came on, puddles of yellow in the dark.

What was he doing here? What was he going to do? Given medical technology and his own good health, he could easily live another thirty years—a small lifetime. He had planned to spend those years guiding the Corps toward its destiny, mentoring younger telepaths, righting all of the wrongs that had plagued his kind. He'd had a mission, and certainty, and had never considered retiring.

For the past several years, running had taken the place of his mission, but he could only run so long. If this worked—if he managed to hide here on Earth, indefinitely—he had to find something to do, or he'd go crazy. But what?

His papers said he was a businessman, a midlevel sales manager for an engine coolant manufacturer that had gone belly-up during the Drakh crisis. Pretty obscure, and he had been briefed about his fictional job, but seeking a similar position was out of the question. First, because he didn't want to be a salesman; second, because any check of his references was unacceptably risky.

So what to do?

He picked at the chicken. There was no hurry.

Sometimes Garibaldi thought his desk was too big. Any desk you could play regulation Ping-Pong on had to be too big, right? Especially on Mars, where every inch of space had to be paid for in oxygen, in power to heat it, in the cost of the dome that kept both of those in and the UV rays out. Hell, his desk was bigger than the bedrooms in some low-rent housing.

Like many things, the desk had come with the office, a legacy of the late William Edgars. When Edgars had sat behind the desk, there had been almost nothing on it. It had been a stark reminder that he was a man with so much wealth, he could afford to pay for as much unutilized space as he cared to have.

Garibaldi could afford it, too, but he had grown up on Mars, taking one-minute showers and sleeping almost standing up. It irked him, that desk, but some perversity made him keep it, maybe as a reminder of where his power and wealth had come from, of what it could do to him if he wasn't careful. A bottle wasn't the only thing that could trap a soul. Of course, he had Lise to remind him of those things.

Lise, who had also come with the office.

Nope, he wasn't going there. That way lay, if not madness, at least

stupidity. He'd behaved stupidly enough with Lise to lose five wives, and by some miracle she still loved him. Let *that* rover lie.

The desk. He had spent years filling it up with odds and ends. A bigger workstation, models of starships and motorcycles, a Duck Dodgers helmet, a hologlobe of Mars. So now it was a big desk covered with junk, and whenever anyone he really wanted to talk to came in, he dragged himself out from behind it and sat on the front edge. He didn't like that distance between him and his friends, and he liked it even less between him and his opponents.

He wasn't sure which he was seeing today, but it didn't matter. He sat on the edge of the desk and watched him enter.

The fellow walked in—just a boy in EarthForce uniform, like so many Garibaldi had seen die. Except for the psi patch. That put everything out of kilter. A lot of things didn't work for him: mousse made out of fish, cats on a space station, zero-g synchronized tumbling, pink T-shirts—telepaths in EarthForce.

"Lieutenant Derrick Thompson, sir," the boy said.

"Don't call me sir," Garibaldi said. "This isn't the military, and I'm not in the chain of command."

"What should I call you then?" Thompson asked.

"Oh, Lord Zeus or Mr. Garibaldi will do. Have a seat."

Thompson did, looking distinctly uncomfortable.

"You're wondering why you suddenly find yourself in my office, aren't you?"

"The thought had crossed my mind. If you'll pardon me, Mr. Garibaldi, you say you aren't in the chain of command, but I sort of wonder about that."

Garibaldi smiled tightly. "Let's just say I have a lot of friends—or people who like to think they're my friends—and leave it at that, okay?"

Thompson nodded.

"Let's get something right out in the open, Thompson. I don't trust you. Not that I don't want to—from your record you seem like a good kid, hardworking, disciplined, dedicated. No one you've served under has anything bad to say about you, which is surprising, and no one who has served *under* you has anything bad to say about you either, which is impossible.

"Now, I'm not a trusting sort of guy, though under ordinary circumstances I might turn my back on you now and then, for a second or two. But—I don't trust you. Bester has been in your head, and that makes you a threat. And I think I can say with confidence that EarthForce sees it that way, too. You can stay in fifty years and you'll still be a lieutenant. They'll stick you behind a desk and quietly hope you go away."

Thompson's face went almost the color of his hair, brick red. "You think I don't know that, s—*Mr.* Garibaldi? You think I wanted this to happen to me?"

"I want to know why you didn't recognize Bester. You went to the academy, when you were a kid."

"Mr. Garibaldi, I went in when I manifested, when I was twelve. In those days there wasn't much of a choice. It was only three years later that the crisis changed things. I never met Mr. Bester during that time."

"You never saw a picture of him? You couldn't sense that he was a telepath?"

"Sure, I saw pictures of him—I even thought he was a little familiar looking when I met him. But he had a beard, and he wasn't in uniform, and—I just wasn't expecting to meet a war criminal on leave on Maui. It's a big universe, Mr. Garibaldi, and if you move around in it, you see people you think are other people, you know that. And he didn't *act* like a monster. He was funny. He seemed like a nice guy."

"Until he cored out your mind."

Thompson nodded miserably. "But he didn't do a perfect job. I started remembering, and the second I did, I authorized recovery scans. Those *hurt,* Mr. Garibaldi, especially when someone of Bester's power puts guards in against scans."

"Yeah, I'm sure it did hurt. But see, here's the part I can't figure out, the part maybe you can help me with. Bester is evil. No argument from me there. He's probably one of the five most evil sons of bitches in the last two centuries. He's cold, and manipulative, and he has no more soul than the Great Whoozits gave a piranha. But what he *isn't,* is sloppy. If he thought you were a threat he would have killed you, or burned your brain into a fraggin' pile of slag. He wouldn't have done the half-ass job he did on you unless he had a reason to."

"Maybe he didn't have time. Or maybe he's getting old. There were rumors he was nearly killed during the telepath crisis, that he lost the use of most of his power."

"Yeah? A rumor and two credits will get you a cup of coffee. I don't believe it—I know some of the things he's done since then. And I don't believe he screwed up on you. Now, I know you're awfully concerned about what I *do* think, aren't you?"

"Sure."

"I think that you are, *one*—" he held up his index finger "—a Trojan horse. Everyone thinks you're fine and then one day, blam, you kill Sheridan or somebody."

"Mr. Garibaldi . . ."

"Or, *two*—" he ticked off another finger "—you're a false lead. After all, you had information that pointed toward his destination, right?"

"Yes, sir. Apparently I *did* fight him . . ."

"Uh-huh. Like I said, if he had the slightest worry that you could ever point a finger in his general direction, you'd be taking a dirt nap about now. See, I don't trust you, but I do trust Bester. He thinks things through. So why are you alive and functioning?"

"Are you accusing me of something, Mr. Garibaldi?"

"I dunno. Do you feel accused?"

"If you'll pardon me, Mr. Garibaldi, I don't think you have any damned idea what you're talking about. You don't know what I've gone through, and—"

"Don't I? Bester got in my head, screwed with my mind. Made me betray my best friend, almost ruined my life. After all these years I still don't trust *me*, Lieutenant."

Thompson's mouth dropped open, then closed. "I didn't know," he said.

"I don't advertise it," Garibaldi said. "But maybe you understand, now, why you're in my office."

"No, actually, I don't. You have a grudge against Bester. You think he let me live to deliver a lie, to lay a false trail. You seem pretty convinced of it, and you're even implying I may have cooperated in the whole thing. You seem to have all of the answers, Mr. Garibaldi. So what do you want with me?"

Garibaldi scooted back on the desk and put his hands on his thighs. "Well, I figure it this way. If you're on the up-and-up, you may have it in for Bester almost as much as I do. He messed with your head and ruined the life you'd picked out for yourself. In that case, I can use you.

"You were the last person known to have contact with him, and you're a telepath. You might recognize his psychic imprint or whatever. Did I mention I don't trust telepaths? I don't. Especially not the ones in the Metasensory Division, which you aren't, and that puts you a little ahead in my book. On the other hand, if you are one of Bester's pals, or if he's put some kinda sleeper program in you that the monitors didn't catch, I'd rather have you right here where I can watch you."

"Are you offering me a job, Mr. Garibaldi?"

"You catch on pretty fast, Thompson. I like that. Yeah, I want to offer you a job. And I want my own team to look you over—they won't dissect you or anything, but I want you examined."

Thompson shook his head, slowly. "You're a very confusing man, Mr. Garibaldi."

"I try to keep it that way," Garibaldi replied.

<p style="text-align:center">* * *</p>

Bester watched his enemies gather, and smiled coldly to himself. This was where it ended, this ridiculous war. This was where he paid them back.

"Proud of yourself?"

Bester jerked out his PPG and spun toward the voice.

"Byron! You're—"

"Dead?" The younger man's eyes were contradictions. Sad, compassionate, but at the same time sharp and condemning. Bester hated them.

He noticed, as always, the ghostly flames licking up around his one-time student.

"Truth doesn't die, Bester."

But Bester's pounding heart was calming. "You aren't the truth," he said. "You're just the memory of a ghost, an imprint in my brain."

"Yes. When I died—"

"Killed yourself."

"When I died, you reached out to me, to try to stop me. It was touching, in death, to know how much you cared. And it allowed me to leave you this little gift, this piece of me, like an angel on your shoulder, like the conscience you never had."

"You always were self-important, Byron—but imagining yourself an angel? You started the war, set telepath to fighting telepath. You began the slaughter when you killed yourself, and neatly ducked out of responsibility at the same time. Coward."

"You could have given us what we wanted. Freedom. Our own Homeworld."

"Oh, yes, your little telepath's paradise, your imaginary Nirvana where you would all live in peace and harmony with your chanting and your candles. A place where the mundanes would *never* bother you, never become suspicious or worried about you. Your fantasy was the ultimate capitulation to the normals, Byron, the ultimate act of cowardice. Earth was our birthplace. It was always meant to be ours, one day. The normals have been trying to kill us from the beginning—from the first pogroms when our kind were discovered, to Edgars' scheme a few years ago. Do you think they'd like anything better than to have us all in one place? Do you think they could tolerate the idea of a planet full of telepaths?"

"This is what I think," Byron said. "I think you did such terrible things in your life, in the name of the Corps, that you couldn't see any other way without losing your mind. Now that I'm part of you, that's clearer than ever. What was the girl's name—Montoya? Your first love?"

"Leave her out of this."

"But you loved her. I can see it in you, the space where love was, the fossil of it. And you turned her in."

"She was going rogue. It was my duty. I'm not going to defend myself to you."

Byron laughed. "But I'm *not* me, am I? I'm you, or part of you. You said so yourself." He cocked his head. "Why didn't you ever have me removed? It would have been a simple matter."

"Shut up."

"Maybe you think you need me, since you have no heart of your own. To help you feel the guilt."

"I feel no guilt. I only did what I had to do. You were the one who divided us, who made me—" He broke off.

"Made you kill your own kind? The Corps is mother, the Corps is father. You always thought of us as your children. And yet you slaughtered telepaths, tortured them. You made the reeducation camps into killing fields . . ."

"You did that," Bester said. "Until you, I never understood how diseased the rogues had become. What you were planning would have destroyed us all. What you did accomplish *will* destroy us. It will be a slow death, by degrees. Psi Corps was always meant to be a tool for the normals, allowing them to control us.

"I fought to take that tool and turn it against them, to put the Corps in control of telepaths. I succeeded, finally, and you chose just that moment to make your grand play, your idiotic attempt to create paradise, just like every other self-deluded messiah with a mindless following. You could never see the big picture, the reality, that the normals are always waiting, waiting for us to relax, until our guard is down. They fear us as they fear no alien race, because we are them, only better. The next step in evolution. And you wrecked it all, gave it all back to them. They've won, thanks to you."

"Now who is a self-deluded messiah?"

"Do you know who backed your precious rebels after you died? Who funded them?"

"My love, Lyta."

"Lyta. For all her power, she was as much a fool as you were. A child given too big a gun. No, the man behind the rogues was a mundane— Garibaldi. A teep-hating bigot who got his fortune from another teep-hating bigot. To see us destroy ourselves must have given him terrible pleasure. You asked why I keep this little part of you alive? This is why. So you can see what you have wrought."

"So you can say I told you so."

"Yes."

"Petty."

"It's all that's left me. Everything I've ever worked for lies in ruins. A lifetime of accomplishment swept away. I always believed that if I had nothing else, I had my people, my telepaths. You took even that from me, Byron. Even that."

"So lie down and die, then."

"No. I'm not you. I am not a coward. I live with the consequences of my actions. And I *live.*"

"Well, then, by all means—let's watch this."

"No. This is a dream. I can end it."

"No, you can't. You know that. Not until it's done."

"Let me go, Byron."

"I can be petty, too."

He tried to turn away, but the scene just followed him.

It would have been the masterstroke. It would have ended the rebellion, brought the rogues to their knees. Two hundred of his finest, his most loyal . . .

He could still hear their screams, still feel the terror of their obliteration, the awful snuffing of their lives, their very souls.

"You ran away," Byron said. "You found out, seconds before, and you ran away. You saved your own skin and let your men die."

"They were going to die anyway. There was nothing I could do."

"And you call *me* a coward."

"Shut up."

"Listen to them, Bester."

"Shut up!"

"Listen." Byron's eyes were holes, holes in a skull, and the flames were everywhere. Byron was Satan, surrounded by damned souls.

"Listen!" Byron was Bester, the cold face in the mirror, smiling without humor.

"Shut up!"

Then he awoke, with someone trying to kill him.

4

Old instincts sent his hand darting for a PPG that wasn't there, but even older ones collected a mental assault with lightning speed. Sometimes the space between two breaths meant life and death.

In this case, it was fortunate that between that first waking gasp and the exhalation, he realized he wasn't under attack at all, that it was Louise standing over him, a look of concern fading from her face like Martian frost touched by first light.

"Monsieur Kaufman? Are you okay?"

For an instant he wondered who she was talking to, but then everything snapped into focus. Claude Kaufman. That was the name he had given.

"What are you doing in my room?" he asked.

"First of all, it is *my* room—you merely rent it. In the second place, I heard you in here shouting as if you had seen a Drakh. I thought you were in trouble—now I see it must have merely been a bad dream."

"Yes," Bester confirmed. "A bad dream. I'm sorry, it was just confusing, to wake and find you there, especially after that nightmare."

"You have many nightmares?"

"I have my share."

"My father used to have nightmares," she said. "About the war. The Earth-Minbari War."

"It's not the sort of thing you forget, war," Bester said, dryly.

"No. I suppose it isn't." He noticed lances of pale gold light shining through holes in the curtains, turning dust motes into tiny, furious suns. "What time is it?"

"Almost eleven o'clock."

"I've missed breakfast, then, haven't I?"

Her expression softened a bit. "I think I can find something for you, if you want to come down."

"I will, then. Thank you." He hesitated an instant. "Thank you for your concern."

"It is nothing," she replied. "Imagine the trouble I'd have if someone died in one of my rooms!"

"Ah, yes. Coroner's inquest, what to do with the body, cleaning up the mess. You have a way of making a man feel special, Ms. . . ."

"Bouet," she said, after a second's hesitation. He thought he caught another name, floating on her surface thoughts. Colis? A great deal of pain associated with that name. A name that was also a wound.

Much like his own.

"Where are you going?" Louise asked him after breakfast, as he made his way toward the front door.

"Just walking," he replied. "I haven't been in Paris for a long time. I'd like to see it again."

"How long?"

"More than twenty years."

"Oh. Does it seem to have changed, to you?"

"That's what I want to find out."

She hesitated. "Are you going anywhere in particular?" she asked.

"No. Why—do you need me to pick up something?"

"No, but I was going to the market this morning, and to a shop across town. I could use some help carrying things, if you have nothing better to do."

Bester studied her for a moment. Her face was neutral, but beneath he could sense that she felt sorry for him. She thought he was a lonely old man.

Well, so he was, but the pity galled him. Still, there was also an undercurrent of truth. She wasn't lying, she could use help carrying groceries.

"Who will mind the hotel?"

"Francis—an employee of mine—will be by shortly, if you can wait."

"I'm in no hurry," Bester replied.

As promised, Francis—a gangly, teenaged boy with olive skin and black hair—arrived a few moments later, and Bester and Louise started out. She wore a checked blue-and-black skirt, ankle length, and a navy sweater over a white cotton shirt. He noticed, for the first time, that she was a little shorter than he.

He was at first distracted by the strained silence between them, but as they both became more comfortable with the fact that they weren't going to chat, he relaxed, and was surprised to find that, despite the events of the evening before and the ensuing dream, his sense of vitality had returned.

It didn't come so much from within as from without, from the bus-

tling throngs they moved through. The removal of the Drakh plague had been a global reprieve from the gallows, and like a condemned man suddenly freed, humanity was full of joie de vivre, bursting with a sort of energy that he simply did not remember from his Earth-bound childhood or any subsequent visit.

And Louise was part of it. Oh, she was reserved, cautious, but as they walked along he felt the crackle of joy in her step, the pleasure she took in the air, the feel of the breeze, the scent wafting from a patisserie as they walked by. He tried not to listen, but her voice was as compelling as the city itself, not because it was simple, or pure, but because it was alloyed. It was the joy of someone who had known sorrow, but whose heart still worked.

They walked up the hill to the Sacré Coeur. As they reached the top, he noticed Louise was watching him, an odd expression on her face.

"A bit out of my way," Louise admitted, "but if you'd like to play the tourist . . ." She shrugged. He sensed that she felt she had been rude to him, and wanted to make it up. Pity, again.

"No need for that," Bester said. "We can just walk where you are going."

As they crossed the sightseer-packed square, a man—a street artist—practically leapt in front of him, sketchbook in hand.

"You have an interesting face," he said. "Surely you want a souvenir to remind you of your visit here." He was already sketching, his hand describing a series of arcs with his charcoal.

"Not today," Bester replied, and moved on.

"No, no, wait. You don't know how cheap this will be, practically nothing. And when you see how I have captured you . . ." He stopped, noticed Louise. "Oh, but of course—you would rather have a sketch of the lady?"

"No, of neither," Bester replied, still walking.

The man followed, his hand moving ceaselessly. "You'll thank me when I am done, monsieur, do not doubt it."

Bester wondered if he shouldn't give the fellow a little mental push. A sudden fear, nausea. He decided against it. Telepaths still had to be registered, and the last thing he wanted was to call that sort of attention to himself. He glanced at his naked hands ruefully. There had been a time when the mere sight of him and his gloves would spare him this sort of harassment.

"Look, he isn't going to pay you," Louise told the man. "We aren't tourists, and we know this game."

"Then I will keep it myself," the man said, defiantly.

Bester's heart skipped. He couldn't have *that*. There were plenty of

other street artists on the square, and most of them displayed sample sketches. How many people walked through this square a day? Thousands? And of those thousands, how many *might* recognize Alfred Bester, with or without a beard?

So he was on the point of buying the drawing anyway. Strangely, however, Louise, who was still shooing the man, suddenly fell silent. She took the sketch from the fellow and looked at it for a moment. Then, still without speaking, she reached into a pocket and produced a credit.

"There," she said. "Now go away."

She took the picture and rolled it up. The artist walked off, a bit smugly. "I told you so," he called over his shoulder.

"Why did you do that?" Bester asked, as they continued on.

"I like the picture."

"I don't understand."

"I like to watch the sky," she said. "I like all sorts of skies. Pale, powdery blue, indigo near twilight, or laced up with clouds. But my favorite sky is one with black clouds, when—through the clouds, just for an instant—a crack of gold peeks through."

"I still—" But he got it before she explained. It was much the same thing he had been thinking about her, moments earlier.

"You have seen much, I think, and a little of it made you happy, yes? You are like a dark cloud. But there was an instant, a moment ago, just an instant, when your gold appeared. The first since I met you. And this fellow, this street artist caught it. In that, he showed genius of a sort. Enough to deserve a credit."

"May I see?"

"You may not laugh at me."

"I won't."

She handed him the paper, and he unrolled it. And stared. It wasn't him.

Oh, it looked like him. The man had put the same weary lines in his face, the proportions were right. But the eyes were young, touched by wonder.

It made him feel very peculiar, and a little guilty. What the man had seen on his face was him admiring Louise. It was her, reflected in him.

"What will you do with it?" he asked.

"It's yours," she replied. "You should hang it where your mirror is, to remind yourself you can look like that."

He didn't want it. On the other hand, if she kept it . . . "Thank you," he said.

* * * *

He bought a book.

The shop across town turned out to be a *librairie*, which hadn't interested him at first. But there had been a time when he had loved to read. An old mentor of his, Sandoval Bey, had given him the taste for it, introducing him to classic and contemporary alike. Even after the old man was murdered, Bester had continued to read—a sort of tribute to Bey's memory.

But as he got older, the stories he read tasted more and more like the paper they were printed on. And one day he had stopped. Thinking about it, he couldn't even say when that was. Ten years ago? Twenty?

What were people reading these days?

He looked over the bestsellers. Memoirs were hot, especially those of the *Excalibur* crew and other explorers. One caught his eye in particular: *Freedom of Mind: Memoirs of a Telepath Mystic.*

He picked it up. He bought it.

The next afternoon he sat in a dim café called Le Cheval Heureux, hunched over the last few pages. Little Corinthian columns of cigarette smoke seemed to hold up the low ceiling, and the light from the various table lamps didn't reach far. Despite all of that, it seemed a popular place to read. Seven or eight other people were doing so.

"Insipid," he grunted, closing the book and making a face.

"Indeed?" A gaunt fellow, perhaps thirty, peered at him over old-fashioned wire-framed glasses. These were surely an affectation, given that any defect in eyesight could be corrected by a few seconds of inexpensive outpatient surgery. "I just read that and found it illuminating. How does it seem insipid to you? Or did you mean the coffee?"

"No, I meant the book," Bester replied.

"Well, then?"

"Rather presumptuous, don't you think, demanding an explanation? Perhaps I threaten your opinion, and thus threaten you?"

A hint of curve turned up the man's lips. "Perhaps. Shall I ask more politely? Or are you afraid you can't defend your opinion?"

"It isn't in need of defense." Bester turned away, then turned back. "But if you must know—I found the style gaudy, trite, and simplistic. The philosophy is rehashed twentieth-century quasi-Buddhist sentimentality, which was rehashed even then, with a healthy bit of theft from the Book of G'Quan. The first person, present tense is pretentious, and the stream of consciousness sequences would have made Faulkner reverse his lunch."

"I thought it was poetic and insightful."

"Well," Bester said, "you were wrong. Don't blame me."

The young man stuttered a little, contemptuous laugh. "Would you care to put that in writing?"

"What do you mean?"

"I edit a small literary journal. Paris is full of writers these days, and most think they are quite brilliant. Most aren't. I think some sorting needs to be done, and I need critics to do it."

"But we don't agree about this story."

"Agreement is beside the point. To read, to think, to express what you think—"

"—to sell your opinions to those who can't think for themselves?"

"Yes, *exactly*. Or, in a few cases, to those who will argue against you. Ninety-nine out of a hundred people, had I challenged them on their opinion, would have capitulated or turned away. Why bother, eh? It's only art, not worth arguing about—except that it *is*, because nothing is so pointless as undiscussed, uncriticized art, yes, and so—"

"What does this pay?"

"Oh. The inevitable crass question. It pays ten credits for every hundred words. You are interested, yes?"

Bester, to his own great surprise, heard himself answer, "Yes."

He returned to the hotel. It had rained, so his shoes broke pastel puddles, wet canvases left by the downpour and painted by the sunset. The silver-winged silhouettes of swallows spun in the lambent air, and for an instant he saw, not birds, but Black Omega Starfuries coursing across the universe-devouring face of Jupiter. *His* ships, *his* people, unstoppable. He trembled, with the thought of what he had been. He brought down governments, diverted rivers of destiny to fill new oceans. Without him, the Shadows would have won, destroyed all of humanity.

That never seemed to come up, at the hearing. He had never seen it once in any of the gory stories about him.

Sheridan knew. Sheridan the hero, the one honest man. He knew, but remained oddly silent. Garibaldi knew, too.

Of course Garibaldi wasn't a big-picture sort of man. Garibaldi only cared about Garibaldi—what Garibaldi liked or didn't like. What had given Garibaldi pleasure, what had hurt him. Especially what had hurt him. There was probably a wasp somewhere that had stung Garibaldi when he was five, that his operatives were still trying to track down . . .

His mind was wandering. Where was he? Ah, yes, the next street over.

He had commanded thousands, saved the world, saved his own people—whether they knew it or not, appreciated it or not.

Now he was going to write a column for a third-rate literary review?

Well, *that* certainly wasn't something Alfred Bester would do. Garibaldi and his Psi Corps lapdogs would be a long time searching before they started to check the literary reviews.

He turned the corner and found the street busy, confusingly so. There was a crowd, and police cycles, and a fire truck.

The excitement, the lust of the crowd struck him. They wanted to watch something burn down, to see Human forms come writhing out in flames. Just like the crowd at the hearing, screaming silently for *his* blood—

Wait. That was the Hotel Marceau, Louise's hotel. The place where he was staying.

He began pushing his way through.

The crowd was going to be disappointed. The blaze had been a small one, and it was nearly out. The front window had been shattered, and the small dining room blackened, but otherwise the hotel seemed to have survived.

Louise stood, watching the firemen work, her face blank with shock. As Bester arrived, the cop, Lucien, was talking to her, though she didn't seem to be listening.

"Nobody saw anything," he was saying. "Of course. Louise, you *must*—"

"Leave me alone," she said, distractedly. "Just . . . leave me be."

A swift anger passed across the policeman's face, but then he gave a little Gallic shrug and did what she asked. Bester stood for a moment, wondering if he ought to say anything.

She noticed him. "Monsieur Kaufman," she said, in a small voice, "I withdraw what I said earlier. I won't charge you extra for leaving early."

Bester nodded. He was about to tell her he would have his things out as soon as the fire died down. After all, he was trying to avoid attention, not court it. And there were bound to be reporters.

No. There was already one here, pushing forward, news-taper close behind.

He felt, suddenly, like a trapped animal, his heart picking up several beats per minute. If his face appeared, even on a local newscast . . .

He stepped quickly away, ducking into the crowd. He touched the reporter and found no image of himself in the man's surface thoughts. He hadn't been noticed, and he wouldn't be remembered. The camera, though—had *it* seen him?

If it had, it would probably be edited out.

Get ahold of yourself, Bester, he told himself. *No one noticed you.* But his heart was still beating too fast. How he hated this feeling, this helpless, watched feeling.

That's when he noticed Jem and his buddies, observing it all, wearing wide, bestial grins.

Suddenly his helplessness turned to cold anger—an old, comfortable friend. Here was something he could deal with.

Jem hadn't noticed him. Bester went up an alley, until he could just see the thug, and there he waited.

Soon night fell. Jem and his friends left, but they didn't leave alone. Bester followed them down the narrow streets, his step quiet and purposeful.

This was what he was, a hunter. Bester had been meant to chase prey, not run from predators. In the old days, a rogue knew his days were numbered when Alfred Bester was on his trail. He smiled thinly at the familiar rush.

He followed them to a set of apartments a few blocks away, which they entered, laughing and slapping one another on the back. Bester kept watching, waiting.

Hours passed, and an orange moon rose into the faintly hazy sky. Bester was patient—he knew more about waiting than perhaps anything else. He listened to Paris; he hummed old tunes to himself.

Finally, well after midnight, the gang members began to slip off. He counted them as they went, until he knew Jem was alone. Then he brushed his jacket with his hands, adjusted his collar, and walked up to the building.

It was an old building, but it had a fairly good security system. There were a series of contacts and a small vidscreen. To enter, he would either have to bypass the system, which he hadn't brought the tools to do, or get Jem to buzz him up. He could go back to his room, get the matrix chip that had allowed him to pass Earth security—but no, where was the challenge in that? He could make Jem open the door.

Closing his eyes, he tuned out the mind of Paris, bit by bit, as though through a sieve, running everything through it until finally only a faint something remained. *Very* faint.

Without line of sight, making contact with a normal was almost impossible, even for a P12. But Bester had been at this for a long time and found that the limits of his abilities were extended by his belief in them. He couldn't scan Jem from here, couldn't burst the blood vessels in his apelike brain. But he could touch him, just a little. He could suggest that one of Jem's friends had just buzzed . . .

Jem's mind was already confused. It was a rough sea, queasy to the touch, thickened and slowed by alcohol, salted with drugs of some sort. He was already hearing things that weren't there. If Bester had asked him to make himself more vulnerable, he could not have.

Still, it took fifteen minutes of terrific concentration before he heard the lock click. The outer door opened, revealing two more doors on either side and a stairway going up.

He felt Jem above, and so took the stairs. When he stood in front of what felt like the right door, he knocked softly.

An instant later it opened, and Bester found himself staring down the ugly hole of an automatic pistol.

5

"Well," Jem grunted. He wore a black tank top and sweatpants. "If it ain't my old friend grandpa. Come in. Now." He extended the gun meaningfully, and Bester noticed it was an old Naga 12mm, probably with mercury-filled slugs that would leave an exit wound the size of a softball.

"Don't mind if I do," Bester said, calmly.

Jem watched him with bloodshot, small-pupiled eyes. The apartment was large, and furnished in moderately expensive but poor taste. Gaudy. A poor boy's idea of what having wealth was all about. Bester noticed a bottle of red wine and picked it up.

"Ah, the '67 Château le Ridoux," he said. "Not a bad year—a poor choice with pizza, however." He'd noticed the delivery boy coming in earlier, and the remains of the meal were scattered about on a large wooden table.

"It costs a hundred credits a bottle."

"Oh, well, then it must go with *anything*," Bester replied. He went to the wine rack, selected a glass, and poured himself a bit.

"What the hell do you think you're doing?"

"You know," Bester observed, "you were cheated. This is a cheap côte du rhône, rebottled. I would say you paid ninety-five credits too much."

"You've got about six seconds to live, old man."

"Oh, I don't think so." He took another sip of wine.

With a sort of animal growl, Jem jumped forward, swinging the gun at Bester's face like a club. Bester seized his voluntary nervous system and watched him go down, felt the bright tinkle of pain, like the sound of glass breaking. Only it was Jem's nose that had broken, on the parquet floor. And several of his teeth.

"Yes, please, make yourself comfortable," Bester said. "We have a long night ahead of us. At the end of it you will be dead, but I intend to take my time about it. It's so rare I get to do this, these days." He took

another sip of the wine, rubbed his good hand on his permanently clenched one. "Shall we begin?"

He had frozen Jem's vocal cords, so all the thug could make was a sort of clucking noise. But his brain—ah, that was filled with panic, with a beautiful sort of terror.

Just a bad trip, Jem was telling himself. *Not real . . .*

Bester inserted his thoughts like a scalpel into butter. *No, I'm afraid not. This is more real than you can imagine.*

And with the scalpel he began to cut, to whittle Jem away, piece by piece. He made sure that the thug felt himself die, watched what he had lost slip away. His wide eyes faded and misted, his throat pulsed with the urge to scream, but Bester wouldn't give him that.

And then he was dead, though his body was still working. Everything that had actually been Jem was cut away from him.

Bester took a break, sipping a little more wine while the breathing corpse stared at the ceiling. He moved away, since Jem's bowels and bladder had emptied themselves, opened a window for a bit of fresh air. He stretched, tried to work the crick out of his neck, flipped on the vid to see what, if anything, had been reported about the fire. It got a ten-second spot on the local update. The footage showed the hotel, Louise, the fire trucks, but he didn't see himself.

He went to the kitchen and made some coffee, then returned to where the body lay, specter-eyed. Then, with due consideration, he started putting Jem back together.

It was almost morning when he returned to the hotel. The broken window had been boarded up. He used his key to open the door and was greeted with a pungent, wet, burned smell.

A single lamp was on, on one of the unburnt tables. Louise sat in its light, an empty bottle of wine in front of her. She looked up wearily.

"You've made other arrangements, I take it, and come to get your things?"

"No. I thought I would get some sleep, instead."

She shook her head. "The hotel is closed."

"Why? The damage is only cosmetic."

"There's nothing cosmetic about a firebomb tossed through the window."

"You don't want to close the hotel."

"Who are you to tell me what I want? You know *nothing* of me."

"I know the woman I first saw, defending what was hers. I know she would not give in so easily."

"There's nothing easy about it. About any of it. For five years I've

tried to keep this place going. Five years, watching my savings dwindle. It's enough. I'm finished."

"You don't have the money to clean up a little fire damage?"

"What would be the point? They'll only do it again, or worse—unless I start paying them again, which I also can't afford."

"You might be surprised."

"What do you mean?"

"Just that you might be surprised, that's all. Things happen. Things change."

"Some things don't." She patted her hand slowly on the table. "You know, at first I thought you were hoping for something from me. To share my bed. Is that it? Is that why you persist?"

"No."

"What, then?"

"I need a place to stay, that's all. And I don't like bullies. I don't like being told what to do."

"I suppose you don't. You were in the war, weren't you?"

He froze, uncertain what to say. Which war did she mean? "Yes," he finally settled on.

"I thought so. You have a way about you. I think you have already seen the worst thing you could ever see, and it ate all of the fear in you. And maybe more than your fear." She looked up at him, but he didn't think she was expecting an answer.

"Have you ever been in love, Mr. Kaufman?"

"Yes."

"What happened to her?"

"Nothing I want to talk about."

"I was in love, once. Crazy, stupid in love. Now all I have is a broken-down hotel." She picked at the table. "He left me. See, that is none of your business, but I tell you anyway. I don't know why—the wine, maybe. He left me with my debt, and my empty room, and he left me with no notions of love whatsoever. I no longer believe in it, I think. Is that what happened with you? Did you leave her? Are you hiding from your old life?"

Bester nearly echoed that it wasn't *her* business, but instead, he sighed. "No," he said, remembering Carolyn the last time he had seen her alive and conscious, wired and meshed with Shadow technology. Worse than dead. But he hadn't left her.

"No, I tried everything I could to be with her. I—went to great lengths." He smiled briefly. "It just didn't work out." He remembered what was left of Carolyn, after a rogue terrorist had bombed the facility. Remembered how angry he had been, because he had *promised* her that

he would make things all right. But putting a shattered body back together was quite different from rebuilding a psyche.

Some promises shouldn't be made, because they couldn't be kept. "No," he repeated, softly, "it didn't work out."

Because of Byron. Because of Lyta. And most of all, because of Garibaldi, whose engineers had doubtless built the weapon that had killed his love.

"Yes, well, that's life, isn't it?" she said. "It doesn't work out. We grow old, we die. The universe doesn't care."

"You've had too much wine."

"I haven't had enough. Did you know I wanted to be a painter? I studied at the Paris Académie d'Art. I was very serious about it, but I gave it up. For love. For this." She swept her hands disgustedly around the room.

He sat silent, gripped by the unaccustomed feeling of not knowing what to say.

"You still paint?"

"Hmm. Yes. Walls and doors, mostly. This room most recently. Do you think it needs a new coat of black?" She indicated the film of carbon that coated the once-white walls.

"I think you should go to bed and think more clearly about it later. And I think I should do the same."

"I would prefer to sit here and feel sorry for myself for another day or so. Would you care to sit with me? You seem to feel at least as sorry for yourself as I do."

"What makes you say that?"

"Your every word and expression. The way you study things." She frowned. "Except the other day in the square, when that man drew you. You were different, then. What was different? What occurred to you?"

Again, he tried to think of something to say. Because he knew what the painter had seen in his eyes. He had seen Louise.

"I don't remember," he answered.

She shot him a skeptical glance, but didn't dispute him.

"I got a job," he offered.

"Really."

"Yes. As a literary critic."

"That's a strange job for someone who was in your line of work. Your papers say you were a salesman."

"A boyhood dream. I'm retired, and now it's time to live out my fantasies, I suppose. Live in Paris, write."

"Well, Mr. Kaufman. Welcome to your fantasy." She hesitated. "This writing job. Is it full time?"

"No."

"How would you like free rent for a while?"

"That depends, of course."

"Help me clean up this mess. I'll pay you a day an hour. It's a good deal."

"So you aren't throwing in the towel, after all."

"I suppose not."

He nodded.

She rose, steadying herself with the table. "I suppose I'll catch a few winks."

"Good night—or morning, rather."

"Yes. To you, too. And . . . thank you."

The words surprised him so much he didn't know what to say. That seemed to happen to him a lot, talking to Louise. What had he done to be thanked for? Had he been sympathetic? To a normal?

He went back over the conversation in his head and realized that he had. What had made him do that?

He would think about it later. Destroying and rebuilding Jem had taken a lot out of him. He would be more reasonable after a few hours' rest.

He woke with the remains of a headache, something like a hangover, but otherwise felt pretty well. He got up, splashed cold water on his face, and began to plan his day.

Well, he was a reviewer, now. So he needed something to review. And something to review it on—a desktop AI or something of the sort. His pocket computer could take dictation, but somehow he felt he ought to use an old-fashioned keyboard, if not pen and paper.

Over the years, writers had generally agreed that the disjunction created by the mediation of fingers between thoughts and the written word was necessary. Writing was a different form of communication than speaking, a different way of thinking—a more considered one.

It looked as if the day was going to be a warm one, and all he had was his leather jacket and black pants. Another thing he needed to do something about: he needed to acquire a wardrobe.

Louise was downstairs, already scrubbing the walls.

"Ah. Good morning," she said, taking in his outfit with an up-and-down glance. "I have some work clothes I think will fit you."

"Excuse me?"

"You are going to help me fix all of this, aren't you?"

"I distinctly remember that I did *not* agree to help you," he replied.

"And I distinctly remember you talking me into staying here, which makes you responsible. So. Are you going to help or not?"

He eyed the room distastefully. "I would rather not," he replied.

"Too bad. The clothes are on the counter over there."

"I have things to do."

"You can do them later."

"But . . ." Bester frowned.

Up went the brush, down went the brush. Bester watched the thick paint streak over the grey beneath. At this rate, it would take him all day to paint a single wall.

"You've never painted before," Louise said. It wasn't a question.

"No, as a matter of fact. Am I doing it right?"

"No. You use the brush to do the trim work, then roll the large sections."

"Trim work?"

"Here." She stepped over and took the brush from his hand, then knelt down next to him.

"See? I've put tape on the floor next to the baseboard. Now I paint the baseboard, like so."

Her hair, caught up in a kerchief, smelled clean, and faintly of lavender. Also of paint—she had managed to coat a few hairs with it, despite her headcover.

He realized that it had been a long time since he had been so close to a woman.

He hadn't had much luck with women. As a boy he'd had a crush on a girl—another telepath in his cadre. He had unexpectedly come upon her and another boy, kissing, and had the unpleasant experience of psionically sharing the pleasure they got from one another.

Later, as a cadet, he had truly fallen in love, with fiery Elizabeth Montoya, whose passion for him had nearly swept him away. But she hadn't loved *him* enough—not enough to stay in the Corps with him. She had tried to go Blip, to run away, and he had been forced to turn her in.

He had been so angry at her, for forcing him to do that. Now he felt nothing at all. He couldn't even remember her face.

The Corps had arranged a marriage, of course, a genetic match guaranteed to produce telepathic offspring. There had never been love there, though for a time he had thought there might be at least companionship. Until he had come home to find Alisha in the arms of another man.

He supposed he was married still, and his son—if indeed it was his son, which he much doubted—was a stranger.

No, probably during or after the telepath wars Alisha had sued for a

divorce. Who would want to be married to the terrible criminal, Alfred Bester?

And Carolyn. He had loved her. She had proved to him that his heart wasn't as empty as he had thought. Which in the end only proved he could still be hurt. It wasn't worth the trade.

So why was he noticing the smell of Louise's hair, the way her fingers gripped the brush, the stray, white-coated hairs straggling across her face?

Ah. That would be because he was an idiot. She was less than half his age, still young and beautiful. His body was responding to her, that was all, a last gasp of hormones. Or maybe he liked the fact that she needed him, if only a little. He had once had thousands of people who depended upon him, and he had been without that for years. Empty nest syndrome? It was an elementary fact that you could make more friends by making them feel like you needed them than the other way around.

Yes, simple physiology and psychology. He wasn't really attracted to her. And she *certainly* was not attracted to him. Why was he wasting time with this?

Perhaps because, against his will, he was *painting* for the first time in his life.

There was a knock at the door. Her head jerked up, and her cheek brushed against his. He banged his head into the wall jerking away.

"You!" Louise shouted, her voice trembling with rage and fear.

Jem stood in the doorway.

Louise picked up a piece of charred chair leg from a pile of rubble. "Get out. Get away from here."

Jem's face spasmed with sudden pain. He looked confused. Bester frowned. Maybe he had been more tired than he thought. Maybe . . .

But then Jem cleared his throat. "Look, ah, madame, I'm—I went too far. I'm sorry. This isn't good business, this kind of thing, and I shouldn't have done it."

"What? Don't play with me. I'm sick of you. So help me . . ." She hefted the makeshift weapon.

Jem withdrew a card from his pocket and held it out. "There's eight thousand credits on that. If it doesn't cover the damage and the lost business, I'll transfer more. Okay?"

Louise just stared for a moment, utterly amazed. Then her expression took a turn back toward suspicion. "What are you up to, Jem? Are you going to snatch that away from me, maybe grab my hair, try to give me a good beating? If you do, you'd better kill me."

Jem set the credit chit carefully on the counter. "There it is," he

murmured. "Check it out. It's real." His eyes flickered once to Bester, and his face spasmed again. Then he turned and left.

"What the . . ." She picked up the chit, looked it over, then went behind the check-in desk.

"Eight thousand credits, just like he said." Her tone was so unbelieving, Bester couldn't suppress a small grin.

She noticed it. "Did you—what did you do to him?"

"Me? Nothing."

"Last night, when you were telling me something might come along—you meant this! How did you know?"

"I spoke philosophically," Bester said. "It's just that I've been around long enough to know you can never guess what's really around the next corner."

"No. You knew. How?"

"I promise you, I didn't. Don't you think it more likely that your policeman friend got some of his buddies together, off duty? That they went and, ah, 'talked some sense' into Jem? Or maybe he really had a change of heart."

"No, not Jem. But Lucien—no, I don't believe that either. He's too upright, too respectful of the law."

"He likes you. Maybe this attack was just too much for him."

"Maybe. I don't believe it."

"Yes. He knows you don't like help, like to fend for yourself—"

"Oh, do I?" Her eyes narrowed again, but this time there was something playful about it.

"That's my impression."

"Gathered in only three days?"

"Maybe I'm wrong."

"No, you're right. I usually do. But whoever did whatever they did to Jem—has my thanks." She held his eyes for a moment, then went back to work.

Bester reflected that, if she actually knew the details of what he had done, she would probably take a very different attitude toward it.

Still, it felt good, her thanks.

Physiology and psychology. It was always good to feel needed—even when you didn't want to be.

6

Garibaldi walked carefully around the room, as if his feet were bare and the floor covered in broken glass.

"He was here," he muttered. "I can smell him."

He couldn't, of course, not literally. But sometimes he thought he had developed a sort of sense—not telepathy, of course, but something older, deeper, more primal. Animal, even.

"It's a good bet," Thompson drawled. "This house was registered to one Susan Taroa, but that was just an alias. We traced her back through several other fake names, until we came to Sophie Herndon. She was one of Bester's interns."

"And that's the woman they fished out of the drink a couple of weeks ago?"

"Yes. Someone sunk her in a fishing net. But a ship went down in the same area in a storm, and the search and recovery mission found her. When they did an ID check, irregularities popped up. Sheer luck."

"Not for her."

"No, I guess not."

"I want a full tracing team in here. DNA, everything."

"The local police already did a sweep."

"They didn't know what they were looking for. I want another one."

"Of course."

Garibaldi continued his survey of the monster's lair. The clues Bester had left with Thompson hadn't led anywhere—or more accurately, they'd led everywhere *except* to any trace of Bester. The man was a ghost when he wanted to be. He could screw with people's heads, make them forget, make them remember things that had never happened.

Make them do things they never wanted to do.

Garibaldi had tried following the money. Bester had to have money, to keep moving like this, but even the considerable Edgars resources had failed him. Some banks really were tamperproof, unbribable, beyond his ability to influence, as perverse and unthinkable as that seemed.

So, what was left to follow? A trail of corpses? Bester was usually careful about that, too. Then again, it seemed as though he was starting to slip up. That was a hopeful sign.

"What are you looking for, Mr. Garibaldi?"

"I don't know. Something. Anything. How about you? Can you pick up any—I don't know—psychic signature?"

"No, nothing. Strong telepaths sometimes leave them, it's true, but they don't last long. Hours, maybe a day. There's nothing like that here."

"Damn." He went to the drawers of the polished coral dresser and started opening them. Nothing. Searched under the mattress. Nothing.

He reached to pat under the bed, and his fingers touched something small, cool, smooth.

"What's this?" He got a cloth from his pocket and reached again, came up with a small cylinder.

"This is an ampoule," he grunted. He stood and lifted it toward the light. "Some sort of pharmaceutical."

"That should be right up your alley."

"Or on my gravy train, anyway. Yeah, I've got a guy I want to see this. And Thompson, I don't want you talking to anyone about this—understand? Right now this is just our little secret."

"Got it."

Niles Drennan was a slight, stiff young man, the sort you could never really imagine cutting loose and having fun. Garibaldi didn't like him, but he was one of the best synthesizers in the business.

Technically, his job was to examine the herbal and folk remedies from a thousand worlds and try to isolate their active ingredients. Lately he had worked more on the various biogenic materials turned up in the hunt for a cure for the Drakh plague.

In actual fact, he was a sort of alchemist-inquisitor, someone who could drag the secret out of any compound he was given, no matter how strange or complex. So Garibaldi didn't really care if the guy knew anything about living it up.

"It's choline ribosylase. It controls the production of certain irregular neurotransmitters."

"Which means what? In English? In *plain* English."

"How much do you know about neurons?"

"Sixth-grade stuff."

"Hmm . . . Well, nerves are often compared to wiring, or to some other linear, conductive system. It's a bad analogy, on any number of levels. The nervous system—the brain, the spinal cord, sensory and motor nerves—are all composed of specialized cells called neurons. But

neurons, strictly speaking, don't act as conductors. They act as generators, in a sense, each one producing its own electrical pulses."

"So far I'm with you."

Drennan's face said *I should hope so,* but he held his tongue. "A neuron has a sort of branching tree of dendrites that *almost* connect it to other nerve cells—I'll get to that in a moment. Each one also has a longer appendage called an axon. When an electrical pulse is generated by the neuron, it flows down the axon until it comes to the next neuron—or, rather, to the gap separating it from the next neuron, the synapse."

"And the pulse jumps the gap or not, right?"

"Not exactly. The impulse itself doesn't cross the space. When the impulse reaches the end of the axon, it triggers small packets, telling them to release a combination of neurotransmitters. These are complex chemical compounds that float across the intervening space and tell the neuron next door what to do—whether to generate its own electrical pulse or not. There are upwards of fifty kinds of neurotransmitters in most people. They're triggered by different sorts of impulses, and in turn cause neighboring neurons to react in different ways. When these neurotransmitters malfunction, especially when they are underproduced, they cause neurological problems. Alzheimer's, for instance, involves among other things the underproduction of a neurotransmitter.

"Certain kinds of messages can't be carried from one neuron to another because there is no messenger that will do so. Most psychotropic drugs mimic neurotransmitters in some way, causing neurons to react to stimuli that don't really exist."

"So these are irregular neurotransmitters?"

"There's a long list of them, but I imagine you're interested in the case at hand. There is a rare condition involving a viruslike organism that mimics glial cells—the cells that maintain the biochemical functions of the brain. Imagine them also as the packing pellets that support the fibrous, fragile neurons. Given time, these mutant cells can subvert and replace all of the brain's natural glial cells. What's interesting is that in most cases, this process is harmless, as the invasive cells perfectly mimic those they replace. They have latent genetic machinery that makes them different, but it isn't ever activated. In a minority of cases, however, they stimulate the production of certain neurotransmitters that don't occur naturally in the human body. This scenario is limited to telepathic individuals, and—"

"Hold it right there. Telepaths?"

"Yes."

"Why?"

"We don't know. We still don't know exactly how telepathy works.

Telepaths have quirky glial cells anyway, and we've never quite hammered out the link."

"Okay. So this is a disease, right? A virus?"

"Not exactly a virus, but it's not a bad analogy either."

"Natural?"

"Good question. We don't really think so. The imitative cells are too, um, well-designed, so to speak."

"What does it do, this disease?"

"At first, nothing. There actually seems to be some enhancement of telepathic abilities—or more specifically, of the processing of telepathic information and impulses. It speeds it up. But inevitably, the neurotransmitter starts overproducing, triggering functions without threshold electrical potential—"

"It short-circuits?"

"Put crudely, yes."

"And only telepaths get this. I bet they were all Corps telepaths, weren't they?"

"I can check."

"Yeah. The Corps had dozens of black-box experiments designed to make telepaths stronger, or make them telekinetic. Five will get you ten this was the result of one of them."

"They experimented on themselves?"

"Man, have you been asleep all your life? Those guys in Psi Corps did experiments on people that would have made Josef Mengele lose his lunch. What do you think all of those trials were about a few years ago?"

"I don't pay much attention to the news."

Yeah, I'll bet you don't, Garibaldi thought to himself. Not important.

"Still, I can't imagine *this* guy volunteering to be a guinea pig." He scratched his chin. "Of course, he had enemies in the Corps, or if the insertion was done with a virus, like you said, he may have gotten contaminated accidentally." He smiled suddenly, clapped Drennan on the back, and indicated the choline ribosylase diagram on the notebook. "Doesn't matter. What happens if he doesn't take this?"

"Oh—first euphoria, heightened senses, faster cognition. Like being on a stim. That's followed by hallucinations and seizures, and finally the collapse of the nervous system."

"Any other treatment?"

"Not that I know of. The mutant cells are resistant to gene tampering. You can insert a replacement sequence to try and normalize them, but within weeks they return to the state they started in. We think they somehow code their genetic information in non-DNA form in the neural net itself—another good indication that they are engineered. In fact, in

that way, they resemble the Drakh plague. You can't kill them all and replace them with normal cells, either, because in the meantime the neurons they keep alive, functioning, and supporting would die. Besides, there aren't enough people who have this to make the research worthwhile, and it doesn't seem to be communicable."

"But if the man using this inhibitor takes this medication every—how often?"

"Once a month."

"Once a month, he's okay?"

"Yes. The drug is a hundred percent effective, when used on schedule."

"Yes!" Garibaldi said. "That's great. Thanks, Drennan."

The fellow nodded, but he'd turned away. Apparently the whole conversation had already been forgotten in favor of whatever he was working on.

Garibaldi left the lab whistling.

"One of your own damn bugs bit you, Bester. Serves you right. And now I've found your little trail of breadcrumbs. When I find you, you're gonna wish the wicked witch had just eaten you."

But at that a thought dampened his spirits, if only a little. Bester was sick. What if he couldn't get the treatment? What if he was dying?

No. Nothing could beat him to the punch—nothing. Garibaldi took comfort in knowing something about his enemy, and that included one very important fact: Bester wanted to live. And nobody and nothing got between Bester and what he wanted.

In that one way, he and Bester were alike.

Here was something he could trace, something Bester had to have. At last he had a real lead.

7

"Always dark clothes," Louise said, her voice somehow laughing and complaining at the same time.

"I'm a winter," Bester replied, checking the price tag on a gabardine suit.

"Even in winter it isn't always nighttime. What about this?" She held up a deep burgundy jacket with a flaring collar. Big collars had come back in style while he had been gone, apparently.

"Not me," he replied.

"So you ask me to come shopping with you, and now you disregard all of my advice."

"I didn't ask you to come shopping with me," Bester replied, mildly.

"Well, you should have. You have terrible taste. You dress like a gangster."

"Maybe I am a gangster."

She put her chin between her fingers. "Yes. That would explain why Jem has been so nice to me for the last several weeks. You put the squeeze on him, as they say."

Bester shrugged. "Maybe he was just intimidated by my massive physical presence."

"And your black clothes. Come, just let me select one outfit for you."

He cocked his head and looked over at her. "Okay. On one condition."

"No more painting?"

"That's not it."

"What then?"

"You let me pick one outfit for you. And pay for it."

Her mouth dropped open as she realized that she had been trapped.

"Pick it, yes, though I warn you I won't wear black. Pay for it—I can't."

"Yes you can. You haven't bought anything new since I met you. I insist."

She looked as if she were preparing another objection, but then she arched one eyebrow. "I pick out *any* outfit for you, and you will wear it?"

Uh-oh. "Within reason. And given my conditions."

"Done," she said, grabbed him by the hand, and started pulling.

It was his bad hand, the clenched one. She had never mentioned it, never asked about it, never touched it—until now.

He actually felt a blush coming on. In the Corps, you always wore gloves, except when you were alone—or intimate.

He had a sudden flash of Elizabeth Montoya, the first woman he had slept with. Another telepath. They had just passed a field test, and they were drunk, and they had started kissing. When they got to the hotel room, she had stripped off his gloves and kissed each finger, digging her tongue between them to the soft junctures, sucking insistently on the tips . . .

It was such a powerfully erotic memory that for a moment nothing existed but the remembered sensations and the warmth of Louise's fingers on his crippled hand. It had been that hand, too, that Liz had kissed, long before the accident that had robbed him of its use.

He shook himself out of it, and worried. Had he actually gone into a fugue state? Had he missed a dose of his medication?

No, he had taken his last shot less than two weeks ago. He was fine. It was just the hand. The hand . . .

Normals made fun of it. He had seen vid comedies lampooning telepaths and their "hand fetish." But then, they always made fun of what they didn't understand, and what they could never, never have. They could never know what it meant to feel both sides of pleasure.

Louise wasn't like that. She didn't judge. Sometimes he thought he could tell her who he was, tell her everything, and she would somehow make a place for it.

He didn't think that very often, because he knew it wasn't true. No matter how much better she was than the average normal, no matter how understanding, no one could ever understand him, or the things he had done. No one.

He blinked. They were standing in front of a rack of clothes. Very bright clothes. Shimmering clothes.

"Within reason," he reminded her.

Moments later, he was looking dubiously at himself in the mirror. The slacks were okay—a sort of dark chocolate, some material from Centauri Prime that resembled shantung silk. The jacket—wasn't a jacket. It was a sort of dressing gown, loose, flowing, with wide sleeves, and it hung halfway down his calves. It was a smoky brown, but almost-

paisley curls of subdued gold and rust shimmered and vanished in the light.

"See? Not so bad."

"I—where would I wear this?"

"You're a writer now! It's all the rage. Voltaire had a coat almost exactly like this."

"That was five hundred years ago."

"It's back in style. It's the literati uniform. Surely you've noticed."

In fact, he had. Young men dressed like this in the coffeehouses, and the look had somehow irritated him. It seemed pretentious.

But part of him had to admit that on him, it didn't look half bad.

"Well . . . I suppose I could wear it around the hotel. It looks like something you would wear to breakfast."

"You'll see. It will grow on you."

"Okay," he said. "Okay, you win. And now it's my turn."

Louise went through the women's section rather nonchalantly. "This is nice," she said, fingering a practical denim jumper. "And this," a modest suit. Bester nodded at each. She was trying to fool him into buying her something cheap and practical.

Her thoughts betrayed her, however. He wasn't scanning her, of course, but people leaked feelings, and when she saw the evening gown, he felt a sudden surge of desire from her.

For an evening gown of the times, it was modestly cut, but the fabric was Centauri tersk, a material once reserved only for Centauri women of noble birth. The Centaurum had fallen on hard times, however, and they were, in many ways, a practical people.

Tersk was as thin and iridescent as a film of oil. It was affected by body heat and chemistry, so it never looked the same on any two women.

And it was expensive.

He chose the nicest of the things she pointed to, a navy blue dress.

"Thank you," she told him when they were done. "I can wear it to the opera next week."

"A bargain is a bargain," he replied.

"Do you want to get something to eat? There's a nice bistro around the corner."

"No, I'm afraid I have business to attend to. I'm meeting with my editor in half an hour."

"Very well, then. See you this evening. I'm making the étouffée again—perhaps I can manage to get the roux right, this time."

"Well . . ." he said dubiously, ". . . good luck."

She hit him lightly over the head with her wallet. "That, for you, monsieur connoisseur."

"See you this evening."

Jean-Pierre barked a little laugh. " *'The plot staggers like an epileptic in shock'*? Don't you think that's a bit much?"

"Not at all," Bester replied, sipping his espresso.

"Well, far be it for me to censor my most popular critic."

"Me?"

"Well, you certainly draw the most response from our readers. Half of them think you're a genius, the other half hate you with a raging passion. A good balance for a critic."

"I aim to please."

Jean-Pierre took a drag on his clove cigarette and exhaled grey plumes from his nose, a fragrant Chinese dragon. "This isn't a criticism, just an observation—I've noticed you never review anything favorably. Don't you like anything?"

"Sure I do. *Hymns for the Damned* was one of the best books I've read in ten years."

"But you didn't review *Hymns for the Damned.*"

"Exactly. Why should I review something I liked? What's the use in that?"

"You're an odd man, Kaufman. Are you certain you weren't born in Paris?"

"As certain as I can be of something I don't remember, I suppose."

Jean-Pierre nodded absently and stubbed out his smoke in a small jade ashtray. "I have some good news, of sorts. We're increasing our circulation. The magazine is selling better than we hoped. I have to admit, I am of two minds about it. We've begun to attract attention."

"I'm sure that's what you wanted."

"Yes, but we are beginning to get . . . offers."

"Of what sort?"

"Publishers are asking us to review certain books."

"Ah. And to take a certain stance in those reviews."

"An insidious business, yes? But I started this magazine to tell the truth, not to pander to commercial interests."

"Good for you," Bester said, dryly.

"Still, it might be worth it to—compromise a bit, if it means we can expand our readership."

"Not to me," Bester said. "I like doing this. I don't *have* to do this, and I won't if I can't do it my way."

"Yes, of course, I agree with you completely. Completely. I would

never ask you to give a favorable review to a book you didn't feel deserved it. But if you were to be presented with a book and *liked* it—"

"No. I've just explained that to you. The object of the critique is to improve literature. Nothing was ever improved by applause."

"What do you mean?"

"Fear of failure, fear of criticism, fear of rejection—those are the only things that writers are accountable to. Praise makes people weak. Why improve if you think you are doing things right?"

"You've never heard of positive reinforcement?"

"I've heard of it. I've also heard of unicorns and minotaurs. Do you think any sort of evolution works by positive reinforcement? It is the *eliminative* process of natural selection that makes biological evolution work—positive traits are only positive in the sense that they aren't negative. The same is true in literature. We can cut away the chaff, but we can't improve the quality of genius in good writers simply by feeding their egos. Nothing works like that. It's a simple fact."

"Well. Magazines don't get printed without money. That is another simple fact."

Bester shrugged. "Whether or not the magazine is printed is your problem, not mine."

"You've had other offers?"

"A few. I won't take them unless you force me to."

Jean-Pierre pulled out another cigarette and lit it with a Narn touchwand. "I give up. I suppose a critic must be incorruptible."

Bester smiled. "I'm not incorruptible. I'm so corrupt nothing you can offer me is tempting."

"Well, it works out the same, yes? Very well. There are others who will write the sort of review we need."

"I'll take them to task."

Jean-Pierre frowned. "This is not *your* magazine, Mr. Kaufman. I still decide what gets printed and what doesn't."

"I'm sure you do. And I know you'll make the right decisions." He smiled in such a way as to cast doubt upon that.

He made a stop on the way home. When he arrived, the hotel's little café was full. Business had been good since Jem and his boys had moderated their behavior.

The étouffée *was* better this time, and the wine Louise brought out was almost exquisite. He suspected special treatment—it looked like the house wine on the rest of the tables.

He finished his meal and went to work on his next review, there in the café. There was something about the place, something that felt more

like home than anyplace had since he had fled his apartments on Mars. Perhaps it was the fact that he had helped restore the dining room. The personal investment.

It was late before dinner was done. Louise came out of the kitchen, brushing her hands on her apron.

"May I join you?"

"Of course." He pushed his AI back.

Louise poured herself a glass of red wine and sat down with a sigh. "Ah, it feels good to be off of my feet."

"Long day?"

"A madhouse. All of the rooms are full!"

"Well, that's good, isn't it?"

"Very good." She frowned. "I left your new outfit in your room. I thought you said you would wear it around the hotel."

"Oh, I just went up long enough to get my AI. I'll wear it tomorrow, I promise."

"Well, I'll let it pass this once. Anything interesting happen to you today?"

He told her about the conversation with Jean-Pierre, and she nodded. "I had no notion that you were so idealistic," she said.

"It has nothing to do with idealism," Bester replied. "I don't have it in me to write that sort of thing. It would be like a monkey trying to do ballet, or a horse singing opera."

"Speaking of opera," she said, taking another sip of the wine, "I think I mentioned I'm going next week. I'll wear the dress you bought me. I was wondering if you liked that sort of thing."

"Dresses? They don't look so good on me. My calves are a little thick."

"Opera, you idiot."

"Ah. Unfortunately, I have things to do that night. I can't go."

"Oh."

"But, I did remember you mentioning it. And it occurred to me that the dress I got you today was no good for the opera."

"It's perfect."

Bester shook his head and reached into the sack by his chair. "No," he said. "*This* is perfect." He set the box on the table. Louise looked at it, then back up at him.

"What's this?"

"Open it."

She put her wineglass down and took the wrapping from the box, then removed the lid, then gasped.

"I saw you looking at it," he explained.

It was the gown of Centauri tersk, glimmering faintly in the candle-light.

"Mr. Kaufman, I can't—"

"You can and will. You can't return it—I made certain of that. And I won't."

"But . . . no, it's too extravagant. When will I wear it?"

"At the opera."

"Yes, but I go only once a year!"

"Well, perhaps you should go more often."

She stared at the material, touching it lightly with her fingers, watching it change colors.

"I don't—I . . ." A tear slipped from one of her eyes, a small ruby in firelight.

Bester cleared his throat. "Anyway. I think it's time I turned in. I've had a long day, too."

"No one has ever given me anything like this," she said.

"Well, someone should have," he said, quietly. "Good night."

"Good night, Mr. Kaufman," she said, very softly. "And thank you."

It didn't sound right. It sounded like she was thanking someone else. He suddenly, powerfully wanted to hear her say *his* name. Bester. Al. Alfie . . .

"What's wrong?" she asked.

He smiled. "Nothing. I was just reminded of an—old friend of mine."

"You seemed sad."

"My friend has passed on. He would have liked to have seen you in that dress. It would have made him happy. He liked beauty."

"It will not look as good on me as it looks by itself. It's fantastic."

He hovered for an instant, thinking to correct her, to explain that it was picturing her in it that led him to buy it. He decided against it, and left her there.

It took him a long time to fall asleep.

Once, he had lost his soul—not figuratively, but literally. He had been much younger, and had volunteered to perform deathbed scans. These were often necessary in the case of a victim of a violent crime, who might know the face of his killer, or of a mortally wounded rogue who could reveal where his comrades were hiding out. It was hard and dangerous, following someone into death. Most telepaths could only stand to do it once. A few had done as many as four.

He had done eight.

Eight times, and each time a part of him had died with them. Finally,

when he slipped beyond the final doorway they all passed through, he had looked into his own heart and had seen nothing there. Nothing.

But then, decades later, there had been Carolyn, and now . . .

So he lay there, listening as Louise came up the stairs, as the door to her room closed softly. Lay there wondering; if a man lived long enough, could he grow a new soul?

8

"Michael, what the hell is this?" Lise Hampton-Garibaldi demanded.

"Shhh. I just got her to sleep!"

"Oh." Lise dropped her voice to near inaudibility. "I thought she would be in bed by now."

"I tried to get her to go, but she wanted to see the end of the flick. Not that she made it, anyway. Here, help me put her to bed."

Lise nodded, closed the front door of the apartment carefully.

Mary had fallen asleep with her head in his lap, her mouth slightly open. He eased his arms under her and lifted her off of the couch.

She stirred, and one eye came open. "I wanna watch the rest of the movie," she said, sleepily.

"You did," he said. "You made it, champ. Now me and mom are going to put you in bed."

"Mom?"

"Right here, sweetie." Lise bent and planted a kiss on her four-year-old forehead. "Did you have a good day?"

"Yeah. We played baseball. And then we went for a walk outside."

"Oh, you *did*?" Lise's voice edged back toward the danger zone.

"Heh," Garibaldi said. "Wasn't that going to be our little secret, sport?"

"Oh—yeah."

"C'mon, let's put you to bed." He carried her into the next room, her room, with its Red Sox posters; her mobile of *jeuf,* an airborne sort of lava lamp that was a Minbari thing—a present from Delenn, probably meant for meditation rather than to amuse a child; stuffed animals; model starships; a scattering of clickbricks on the floor. She was already in her pajamas, so he eased her into the bed and under the covers.

"Good night," he said, giving her a kiss on the forehead.

"Tell me a story."

"I need to talk to mom right now."

"Just a short one."

"Ah, well. Okay. Once upon a time, there was this little girl named—umm, Mary. She lived in Olympus Mons, and one day her mom sent her down to the market with three credits to buy some swedish meatballs for dinner—"

"Yuck!"

"And you know, even though swedish meatballs are considered one of the most perfect foods in the known universe, that's exactly what the little girl said. And so while she was going to the swedish-meatball vendor's stall, this weird-looking alien came up to her. He was all covered with black feathers, and had an orange bill—"

"—like Daffy Duck."

"Yeah, a lot like that. Only with big ferlarls."

"What's that?"

"Don't interrupt daddy. And he said, 'Hey kid, I've got something a lot better than swedish meatballs.' And so the little girl said, 'Like what? And I've only got three credits.'

" 'Well, by coincidence, that's exactly what it costs,' the guy said. 'It's a boom-boo seed, from all the way out on the Rim.' And he held out this big, black seed.

" 'What's it do?' she asked.

" 'Well, you just plant it outside, and it'll bring you fame and fortune.' Well, the little girl liked the sound of that, so she paid him the three credits. Her mom was pretty mad when she didn't bring home the meatballs, 'cause that's how moms get when—"

Lise cleared her throat behind him.

"—Of course her dad got mad, too," he added quickly. "Because little girls are supposed to do what their parents say. They sent her to bed without supper, because that's what they did back then. Well, she snuck out the air lock and planted the seed, and the next morning there was this huge plant, a boom-boo, growing so high in the sky it went all the way up to Phobos . . ."

He had barely gotten the little girl to the garden of the giant slothman when Mary's breathing evened out. Once he was sure she was asleep, he stopped, kissed her on the forehead again. Lise bent over and kissed her, too.

"Isn't she beautiful, Lise?" he breathed. "I never imagined . . ."

"Yes. And you're good with her. *I* never imagined."

They stood there, looking silently at their child for a moment, before she tugged on his hand. "C'mon. We need to talk."

"First of all, I thought we agreed on no more trips outside, not till she's older."

"But Lise, she wanted to. She begged all day. And this is Mars—kids need to learn how to handle themselves outside early. What if the dome ruptures?"

"A suit rupture is a thousand times more likely." She made a face. "I know you're right. But it's so dangerous."

"I'm careful. You know I wouldn't ever let anything happen to her." She nodded and reached to squeeze his hand.

"Okay. We'll talk about that later. Right now I want to talk about this." She tapped her notepad, held it up so he could see the display.

"Oh, yeah. I was going to tell you about that."

"It would have been better if you had told me *before*. We're supposed to make decisions like this together."

"Yeah, Lise, I know, but—"

"I mean, I don't get it. There are fewer than two hundred prescriptions written for this stuff. It costs four times as much to produce it as consumers pay for it, even with the subsidy. It lost money for Tao-Johnson—they wouldn't have produced it if it wasn't mandatory, and they hadn't had the bad luck to develop it. Now we own it, so *we* take the loss. Do you know something I don't? Is there about to be an outbreak, or something?"

"No. But believe me, it's worth the investment. To me, it is. And I'm sorry I didn't bring it up with you, because—"

"This has something to do with Bester, doesn't it? A medicine for telepaths. That has Bester written all over it."

"Yep. You got it. That's one of the things I love about you, Lise, always on the ball."

"Never mind the flattery. I'm vaccinated. Explain."

"It's a medicine he needs to live. Only a few people in the whole universe take it—and I still can't find him. Somewhere out there, someone is being supplied with this, but they don't need it. They send it to somebody, and they send it to somebody, who sends it to a Swiss bank, or something. I don't know how he gets it. But it's the only lead I have, and it wasn't taking me anywhere."

"So you bought the monopoly rights to produce it."

"Yes."

"How does that help?"

"I own the supply. I can cut it off."

"Michael! What about the rest of the people who have to have it to live? You wouldn't kill all of them just to get Bester! I know you! I know you're obsessed with this man, but—"

"No, Lise, calm down. I'm not gonna let anyone die. But I can claim that our people have discovered possible side effects and insist that any-

one who uses the stuff submit to an examination before their next dose. Then somebody shows up, we test 'em, find they don't have the disease, and we know he's our link to Bester."

"Michael, I thought this was over. I mean, after the war, and all of the death, the hearings—"

"It's not over until Bester is someplace he can't hurt anyone, ever again. I owe it to Sheridan, to Lyta, to the thousands he destroyed. Have you ever seen footage of the reeducation camps, Lise? Have you? I owe my daughter a world without him in it. And yeah, I owe it to *me.*"

"Michael, I love you. I'm on your side. But Bester's your new bottle, your new addiction. It's not healthy."

"Lise, I've let most of what was bad about my past go. My life is here, now, with you and Mary. Except for this one thing.

"I can't get past him, I can't get around him. Not if he's still out there, still free, laughing at all of us. I can't. The only way out is dead straight *through* him."

She stared at him for a long, hard moment, before her face finally softened. Her shoulders relaxed, and she put her arms around him and leaned into his neck. "I know," she breathed. "Just be careful. I've lost you too many times. I can't bear the thought of losing you again—not to the real Bester, not to your obsession with him. And I don't want you hiding things from me, like you used to try to hide your empties when you'd been on a bender. If you do this, *we* do this. Understand?"

"Aye, aye."

"Fine." She kissed him, first tenderly, then playfully, then with awakening passion. He kissed her back, trying to force the leering face of Bester out of his mind.

9

Bester wiggled his fingers slightly, so that the point of his épée described a small circle. His opponent, a much younger man whose name he had forgotten, rapped at his bell guard. Bester took two quick retreats, then beat sharply and feinted toward the foot. As he had expected, the boy parried instead of retreating. Of course—he was fencing an old man, wasn't he? He was sure to be quicker.

But it's better to be right than quick, Bester mused. In fencing, precision is everything. Bester put the defending blade in a bind and drove the point into the fellow's shoulder. His jacket flashed a bright green.

"Rats!" the fellow shouted. It sounded like American English.

Bester took off his mask. "Nice bout, Mr.—"

"Nary. Thanks."

"I'm guessing you normally fence foil."

"Yeah."

Bester shook his head. "A young man's sport. All of that jumping and lunging." They shook hands.

Bester wiped a little sweat from his brow. When he had been in the Corps, he had followed a fairly strict exercise regime. Sure, a good Psi Cop wasn't often called on to possess physical dexterity, other than marksmanship, but he had learned early that when those times did come, it was usually a matter of life and death. So he had practiced various martial arts, run a few miles every day.

His years in exile had softened him in that way, as they had toughened him in others. It just hadn't seemed worth the trouble. Now, though, he was suddenly conscious of those few extra pounds and wanted the harder muscles of youth back. He had tried his old routine, but found it depressed him. His new life needed a new regimen.

He had fenced in the academy and been quite good. Fencing other telepaths had been useful for developing strategies of mental blocking, sending false signals, and so forth—but after the academy he had thought of it as a sport, with no practical application.

Well, that was his life now—a life without practical application. He wrote literary critiques, he bought young women dresses, he fenced. He was in Paris—why not?

And fencing normals was satisfying. Years as a Psi Cop had taught him to read body and facial language without scanning, but if he really needed to, he could pick up their strategies without them noticing. He didn't feel bad about it—men with long arms didn't feel bad about having more reach, after all. But he was careful. Though he hadn't met any other telepaths who used the salle, you never knew when one might come in. Another P12 might just notice him using his abilities, even at a very low level.

He was done for the day, he decided. He said good-bye to the maître d'armes, a knotty old man named Hibnes, and hit the showers, where he enjoyed the feel of hot water on his abused muscles. They were tightening up, he noticed with pleasure. He was leaner and felt years younger than when he had arrived on Earth. Paris almost seemed to be aging him backward. Yes, it had been right to come here. Perfect. That became more obvious with each passing day.

He took a roundabout way back to the hotel. He never followed the same route twice—having a routine an enemy could pick up on was a bad idea, and some habits shouldn't die. After all, it wasn't paranoia when people really were out to get you. And there was a whole universe of people out to get Alfred Bester, all of whom would give anything to know where he was at the moment.

Today his walk took him through the Bois de Boulogne, finally bringing him to the Metro station at Boulogne–Pont de St.-Cloud. He stood waiting for the train as the platform filled up.

He remembered Louise in the dress, how it clung to her contours. She looked embarrassed, but her surface thoughts told a different story. She *knew* she looked good in it.

That had been last night. He hadn't seen her this morning, and he wondered idly if she had met someone at the opera and gone home with him. Or maybe Lucien, the cop, had finally talked her into going out with him.

He found he didn't like that thought much. Maybe he *should* have gone with her. But he didn't want to be obvious, a pathetic old man chasing a younger woman.

Of course, he *could* just read her mind, find out what she did think of him. But with Louise, that seemed somehow wrong, a violation.

No, he said to himself. *That's not it. You're just afraid of what you'll find. That she likes you and pities you, but has no interest in you as a man.*

He felt a sudden anger. That was the ghost of Byron, taunting in his head. What made him even more angry was that it was probably true.

A train arrived, but it wasn't his. He stood there, frowning, some of his good mood dissipated.

And he caught someone watching him, felt a telepathic touch.

He jerked his head around, and a face jumped out of the crowd. An older face, pale, snub-nosed, weak-chinned. He recognized it in an instant—he had always had a good memory for faces.

A telepath. What was his name? Askern? Ackeron? Ackerman. He had worked at one of the reeducation camps . . .

The fellow looked away. Bester managed a light scan, one he knew would be undetectable to a telepath of Ackerman's feeble abilities. Bester looked familiar to Ackerman, but the fellow hadn't placed him. The beard made a big difference.

Bester started pushing through the crowd, but the man was boarding the train. By the time Bester got there, the doors had shut.

Ackerman hadn't recognized him, he was sure. He hadn't.

He suddenly realized his hands were shaking.

"What's wrong?" Louise asked. "You look like a ghost."

Bester settled wearily into his chair. "Maybe I am," he said, bleakly.

"Well, if you want to talk about something—"

"How was the opera?" he cut in. "It must have been a long one. I never heard you come in."

Her face darkened. "You were here, eh? I thought you had something to do last night. I thought that's why you couldn't come with me."

"I lied. I hate opera."

"You're still lying. I've heard you playing it in your room."

"Louise—"

Her face softened. "I'm sorry," she said, with an odd abruptness. "It's none of my business, and I'm sorry. Just as it's none of your business that I came in late, yes?"

"Yes," Bester replied, nodding, feeling somehow relieved.

She stood for a long moment, unspeaking. It should have been uncomfortable, but it wasn't.

"Will you come with me? I want to show you something."

"Of course." He stood, his legs feeling a little light. His medication was a day late, but it couldn't be that—he still had a week before he would become symptomatic. He wasn't worried about that.

Maybe just old age.

He followed Louise from the café and up a flight of stairs, all the way to the upper loft of the building. Bester had asked about it once, about

why she never rented that space out, but she had tersely changed the subject.

She unlocked the door with one of the old-fashioned keys on her ring, revealing a spacious room with high ceilings and tall panels of windows. Lavish afternoon sunlight draped golden on the polished wooden floors. Other than that, the room was empty, except for an easel with a canvas on it, a wooden paint box and pallet, and a chair.

"This is where I lived with my husband," she explained. "After he left, I couldn't stand to even come up here. I hadn't opened that door in five years. This morning I did."

"You're taking up painting again?"

"Yes."

"Well, I'm glad."

"Are you? Good. Then you shall agree to model for me."

"What? No, I couldn't do that."

"And why not? You've used up the free rent you earned helping me clean and paint. Here's your chance to make a bit more."

"No."

She dropped her bantering mood and laid her fingers on his arm. "Please? I want a chance to capture what that street-scribbler did. I want a chance to paint something difficult, hidden, and true. I think, once, I could have done that. I want to see if I still can."

The sincerity in her voice got to him.

"Very well," he said. "I suppose it can't hurt. But you won't get me out of my clothes, young lady."

"No? Then you will wear the outfit I picked for you, yes?"

He shrugged. "Why not?"

They stood there for a moment, until she said, "Well?"

"Well, what?"

"Go change."

"Don't fidget. There, like that."

"Can I breathe?"

"Breathe, talk, whatever you want, just hold that position, more or less."

"I'll try," he said, dryly. In his peripheral vision, he saw her regard him, then the canvas, then tentatively lift her brush.

"I've never painted portraits before, you know?" she said, after a few moments. "It was considered passé when I was in school. Minbari dialectic perspective was all the rage."

"Minbari what? You're making that up."

"No, sorry to say, I'm not. It was a key philosophy in the nouveau post-ante-postmodern tradition."

"You're making that up, too."

She laughed, a musical trill, the first such laugh he had ever heard from her. A child's laugh.

"Somebody made it up. It wasn't me. I've read your literary columns, you know. Don't play the epistemological innocent with me."

"You read my column?"

"Yes, now and then. You have a most apt way with insults."

"Is that a compliment?"

She chuckled again, this time in her more accustomed, more cynical voice. "What good is a compliment? No one ever gained anything from praise."

"Ah. So you *have* read my column."

"Yes. If you don't mind me saying so, Mr. Kaufman, I don't really approve of it."

"Criticism of criticism? Now you try to improve me?"

"It's easy to take a house apart. It's harder to build one."

"Meaning?"

"Meaning you have a way with language, and you ought to use it in a positive way. Write something of your own."

"So that it, in turn, might be criticized?"

"That's what stops you, then? Fear?"

Bester considered that. "No. To be honest, it actually never occurred to me to write anything."

"You seem like a man with a lot to say. Isn't there anything you want people to understand, something you think the Human race has missed, somehow?"

From the place in his mind where he kept Byron, he heard a sardonic chuckle. *Yes, Mr. Bester. Wouldn't you like to make them understand? Understand why you made me slaughter defenseless mundanes? Why you murdered your own kind? Why the gutters of the reeducation camps ran with tears and blood? Tears and Blood—now there's a title for you.*

"Maybe you're right," Bester said, trying to ignore Byron. "I'll have to think about it."

For whatever reason, his medication hadn't shown up in his secure postbox. The one thing he really needed from what remained of his network, and it hadn't come. It was three days late now. What could have happened? The people involved simply couldn't betray him—he had too much on them, and in some cases, *in* them.

In another week, things would start to get bad. He would start leak-

ing, telepathically. Louise, if no one else, would find out what he was. She might even be able to handle it, but would she be able to handle it when he lost his mind and began the agonizing process of dying? Would she be able to handle having to spoon-feed him like a baby, change his pants?

He wouldn't put her through that, no matter what, not that she would do it anyway. No, he would end up in the hospital, where eventually a routine DNA check would slip past his insiders in the Metasensory Division of the EABI. Then the hunters would come. But of course they wouldn't find much, would they?

It was just a delay, nothing more. The ampoules would arrive tomorrow, and everything would be fine.

When two more days passed with no sign of his medication, he did something he did not want to do. He went to a pay phone and dialed a certain number. That connected him to an AI in Sweden, which in turn uplinked him to Mars, and finally to the off-world colony of Crenshaw's World. Supposedly, at each node there was only a two-percent chance of being traced either way, and through three transfers he should be safe no matter what.

The call took a long time to connect. Finally, someone answered the phone.

"Hello."

He stood stock-still. He didn't answer. He knew the voice well enough, but it wasn't the one he had expected.

"Bester? Is that you? You know who this is, don't you?"

It was Garibaldi.

"I'm coming for you, Bester. I'm coming for you, you son of a bitch."

Bester hung up.

Jem made a stuttering sound when he opened the door to find Bester standing there. It took him several seconds to compose himself enough to invite Bester in.

"I haven't been giving Louise a hard time," he rushed to say. "In fact, I've been keeping trouble away from her and givin' the other hotels in the neighborhood *more* trouble so she'd get more customers. Just like you said."

"I know, Jem, and I'm very pleased. That's not what I came here for."

"No?"

"No. I need some help with something, something right up your alley."

"Oh. Uh—sit down, won'tcha?"

"I don't mind if I do," Bester replied, taking a seat in an overstuffed armchair.

"Mind if I get a drink?"

"Not at all."

"You want one?"

"It's a little early in the day for me."

Jem poured himself a tumbler of scotch, then sat on the couch, rolling the glass between his palms. "What's the deal?" he asked.

"It's pretty simple, really—a little breaking and entering."

"Where, what, and when?" Jem's voice was smoothing out now, growing more confident now that they were talking about something he knew how to deal with.

"A pharmacy downtown, the big one on the Boulevard St.-Germain."

"I know the place. It's pretty tough. During the plague there was a rumor that they had a cure, but only the rich were getting it. After a few break-ins they screwed security down good. What do you need? I can probably get it on the black market."

"Not this. And it's the only place in Paris that has what I want."

There were four people in Paris besides himself who suffered from his condition—he'd checked that before coming. He had even acquired their names and addresses, against just this sort of eventuality. His original contingency plan had been to simply go to their houses and take their doses if he needed them. That was before Garibaldi got involved. The drug was made by a rival company, but Garibaldi must have discovered Bester's condition somehow and tracked down Bester's supplier.

That complicated matters considerably. The number of people who needed the inhibitor were few enough that a man with Garibaldi's resources could have tracked them all down. If one of them turned up dead, or had to apply for another dose, it would attract attention. So far, Garibaldi didn't—couldn't—know where he was. His contact on Crenshaw's World couldn't have given up his location because he didn't know it.

But if he took the serum from one of the other telepaths in Paris, Garibaldi would know where he was, probably within days, certainly in under a month.

Hitting the pharmacy itself was safer, more oblique. Pharmacies got robbed all the time. The trick was simply to make certain no one could tell *why* it had been hit.

"I need you to torch it, too."

"Why?"

"That's on a need-to-know basis, Jem, and you don't need to know. How about it?"

"Sure thing, Mr. Kaufman. I'll do it."

"Actually, *we'll* do it. I need to be there."

Jem absorbed that with clear surprise, but didn't say anything. He took another gulp of his drink and stared down into the amber fluid. "What did you do to me, Mr. Kaufman?" he asked, in a small voice. "I tried . . . I tried to tell my buddies, but I couldn't. Sometimes I try to think about killing you, too—" he winced, suddenly "—but I can't even think about it. And the dreams I have . . . I keep dreaming I'm dead, that I'm just this walking hole in the air.

"I haven't asked please in my whole life. Never, not even to my old man. But I'm asking now. Please. *Je vous en prie.* I'll do whatever you say. Anything. But just—can't you make the dreams stop?"

Bester tilted his head. "You'll do anything I say, no matter what, or it'll get worse, and worse, and worse, until you can't stand to even blink. You know that. I don't have to do anything for your obedience. As far as you are concerned, I am God, the only thing in the universe that really matters."

"Please." He was weeping.

Bester reached over and patted Jem's shoulder. The big man flinched. "I'll consider it, after this job. Consider it, mind you."

"Okay," Jem said, and finished his drink. His eyes didn't seem to hold much hope.

"Now, why don't you be a good little boy and go check out the pharmacy? Everything—floor plan, guards, security equipment. I'll give you two days to get all of that together, then I'll meet you back here and we'll make our plans. Okay?"

"Okay. I'm right on it."

"Good boy. I'll see you in two days."

10

Bester's skin itched, and the light played games with his eyes. He found it more difficult than ever to sit still, and Byron's voice was louder in his head. So were strange voices, floating in from the street like unpleasant and unwanted fumes.

He told himself it would be okay. Tonight he would speak to Jem again, and in a few days he'd have the inhibitor. If not—if not, he would do what he had to. Find one of the other teeps, take their dose, and leave Paris.

The thought of being on the run again, beneath cold and unfamiliar stars, hurt more than he thought it would. For a terrible instant, he actually thought he would weep. He was losing control of his emotions, not a good sign.

"You seem sad today," Louise observed, from her place at the easel.

The sound of her voice soothed him, but it also highlighted his dilemma. Soon he would start leaking, telepathically. Soon she would know what he was, maybe even *who* he was. Would she hate him then? Probably.

Definitely, Byron mocked.

"I'm just feeling sorry for myself. A common failing in the old."

"You aren't *that* old—but I must say, you do seem rather alone in the world, Mr. Kaufman. Don't you have any family, any friends?"

The Corps is mother, the Corps is father. We are the children of the Corps, Byron interjected, in a snide tone.

"Not anymore," Bester said wearily. "What about you? Don't you have family?"

"I had a pretty big family," Louise said. "Three brothers and three sisters. I was the middle child."

"Where is this big family of yours?"

"Well, it's not so big now. Dad suffered a heart attack six years ago. My youngest brother, Pierre, was on the *Victory* when the Drakh took her out. Jean and Francois immigrated to Beta Colony years ago. Mom is

remarried and lives in Melbourne; we talk on the phone but it's been two years since I saw her. One of my sisters, Anne, fought with Sheridan against Clark, and my oldest sister was in Clark's personal guard. They haven't spoken since, and after one attempt at making peace between them, I haven't spoken much to them, either."

"That leaves a sister."

"Ah. I stole her boyfriend and made him my husband."

"Oops."

"Yes. I keep hoping she'll forgive me—you'd think she'd see by now that I did her a favor. But I'm not going to beg."

"I'm sorry to hear all of this."

"Don't be. I still love them, and I think they all still love me. You never really lose family—you just misplace them now and then. But I've learned that it isn't smart to count on them, either. A lot of people from big families never really learn to be independent. I did, and I'm glad. The rest will work out, eventually."

"And now *you* seem sad."

"Sad, yes. Depressed, no. And you dodged my question, I think. About your family."

"I had a big family, too," Bester said, and to his surprise he realized it wasn't exactly a lie. "I had a brother—Brett. We were always rivals, I guess, always trying to one-up each other. In a way, I think I was closest to him, of all my siblings." He watched the clouds in the sky beyond the window. He thought he could see faces in them, Milla, Azmun, and yes, Brett. The kids from his cadre, the ones he had grown up with. What were they, if not siblings?

"Brett's been dead for many years. I still miss him, even though it sometimes feels like he's looking over my shoulder. Our parents—" *The Corps is mother, the Corps is father* "—our parents were tough, but fair. Pretty old school."

He smiled, but behind his eyes a memory flashed so vividly that for a moment he didn't see Louise, or the clouds, or anything else. Instead he saw fire and smoke, a rogue stronghold on Mars almost half a century ago.

The leader of the rebel telepaths was dying at his feet. A man who claimed to have held Bester as a baby, to have known his real parents. Matthew and Fiona Dexter, the kingpins of the underground until they were killed in 2189, the year he had been born.

He shot the rogue for saying that, shot him until the fist holding the gun clenched permanently, into a useless, dead—

"Claude? What is it? What's wrong?"

He blinked. Louise was watching him with a look of concern in her face.

"Nothing. I . . . just a memory."

"Must have been some memory. Are you sure you're okay?"

"I . . . yes. Don't worry about me. You just keep painting."

"I can't. I'm not seeing what I want to—that thing in you I wanted to capture. I think it's never been farther from your face."

"I'm sorry to disappoint you."

"I'm disappointed in myself, not in you. But I'll find it eventually."

"May I see the painting?"

"Not until it's done. Old tradition. Still, we're done for the day, I think."

"Now *I'm* disappointed," he blurted, and was instantly sorry he had done so.

She didn't answer, though he thought he felt a mental blush from her. The air seemed to dance, and not in a good way.

He was getting worse. He had to see Jem.

"I'm not sure we can do it," Jem explained.

"Why?"

"They went the whole nine yards and made it a smart building. Anybody goes in there gets detected by motion, sniffers, and sound. Sends an alarm to the security company and the cops. The response time was only six minutes last time somebody tried to get in, and it could be even quicker.

"The whole thing is run by an AI, so there's no way to fool it. It's wireless and has its own power supply, so there are no lines to cut. Plus, there's a live guard. Even if we get the job done fast enough, it'll take records of us—the damn thing is lousy with eyes and sniffers, and most of 'em are probably hidden."

"I think I can solve that problem," Bester said.

"How?"

"With this." He held out a small black chip, about the size of a book of matches.

"What's that?"

Bester tumbled the object between his fingers. It was one of the things that had gotten him to Earth through the tight security and quarantine. A bit of Shadow technology that Psi Corps had been able to copy and make use of.

"Have you ever read Descartes?"

"Uh, no."

"You should broaden your mind, Jem. It's good for you. He said, 'I think, therefore I am.' "

"Yeah, I've heard that."

"You understand it?"

"I guess so."

"It was part of a larger point Descartes was making. I know I exist, but how do I know anyone or anything else does? Can I really trust the information I receive from my senses? Maybe not. It could all be an illusion, or a delusion. I might be imagining all of it."

"I know the feelin'," Jem said. "What's this got to do with the security system?"

"Just this. The building is an artificial intelligence that examines the information provided by its sensors, decides what it has seen, heard, smelled, and then acts upon that data. *This* device—" he held up the black chip "—can map the AI's system, then impose its own logic. In effect, it will make the AI unable to act upon the data it receives— because the AI won't 'believe' it."

"You're going to screw with the computer's head."

"Exactly."

"I've heard of that kind of thing. Usually it doesn't work—the computer recognizes it as a virus or whatever."

"This isn't a virus. It can perfectly mimic the AI, which won't recognize that any foreign intervention is involved. The internal alarms won't go off, and the 'OK' signals will go out just as before."

"I guess I'll take your word for it."

Bester smiled. "As in so many things, Jem, you don't have a choice."

The street was quiet enough at two in the morning, but Paris was never truly quiet. In the distance, groundcar horns blared, voices rose in protest, anger, and joy, adding to the background noise that was building in his head.

The April rain was a godsend. Oh, it was miserable and cold, winter having its last say, but it drew a beaded curtain across the world. In the rain, people put their heads down and hurried to wherever they were going. People missed things, in the rain.

Bester found that he liked it. Years—maybe decades, now that he thought about it—had passed in his life without him ever feeling a drop on his cheek. The closest thing to rain that Mars ever got was a subtle condensation, a frost. Nothing like this, this smell of wet pavement, of the air itself being washed clean.

Jem seemed less happy. He hunkered against the downpour. He was probably one of those people who tried to calculate whether he would

get wet faster running or walking. As if it mattered, Bester mused. As if a tiny bit more or less wet could make a difference.

A car passed, and the rain became gems, falling in slow motion, white-hot metal, dripping . . .

Get a grip, Bester, he thought. *Just a little longer, and this particular problem will be solved.*

What then? Byron asked. *Will you go somewhere else and pretend not to be a monster?*

"Shut up," he muttered.

"Eh?" Jem asked.

"Nothing."

"Well, we're here. This is the back door I was telling you about."

"Oh." He fumbled the black chip out of his pocket, touched one of the contacts. Almost immediately, a green light flicked on.

"That's got it," Al said. "You can open the door now."

Jem opened his heavy black bag and pulled out a bulkhead drill. He stuck it against the lock and turned it on, pulsing bursts of coherent X rays in rapid cycles.

Rain began to hiss against the door as the metal heated up. A few moments later, Jem pushed it open. It went with a sigh, the loudest sound either of them had made so far.

Al pulled a Colt 9 mm from his coat pocket and made sure the silencer was in place. Not the PPG he was used to, but those were hard to come by on Earth. In space they were great, because the phased helium plasma they fired could wreak terrific havoc on flesh and bone without punching a hole through a bulkhead. But PPGs were expensive, generally limited to security and military personnel, and in the end no better for killing quickly than a slug thrower. Less so, in fact, in many ways.

As they ghosted into the building, Bester concentrated and probed for the guard, but came up with nothing. That was odd. His senses should be heightened by his condition, not dulled.

Maybe that was the problem. The city was practically shouting at him. The gentle murmur and cadence of minds—which had once so intrigued him—had, in the past few days, become a loathsome racket. What was that line from Poe?

"Above all was the sense of hearing acute. I heard all things in the heaven and in the earth. I heard many things in hell. How, then, am I mad?"

Yes, if he didn't get the serum soon, he would end as the protagonist of that story, screaming madly about some imaginary telltale heart . . .

He shook his head to clear it, and scanned again. This was no time for slip-ups.

Still nothing. Maybe the guard had the night off.

Jem could move with admirable grace when he wanted to, like some sort of big cat. And Bester, of course, had the benefit of long years of practice, from that first time he had gone after Blips, on his own, when he was only fifteen. That had been in Paris, too . . .

He caught it, then, the sudden feeling that someone was walking on his grave. And the almost forgotten sensation of brushing across someone's blocks.

Blocks. *Blocks.*

The guard was a telepath. Of course. Telepaths could do almost anything these days, couldn't they? The possibility had never occurred to him.

"Hold it. Hold it right there."

No. It had never occurred to him, and as a consequence, the telepath guard was right behind them.

"Don't make it worse on yourselves. So far it's just breaking and entering, not theft or possession. The police are already on their way. I know one of you is a teep, but don't think you can get away with any funny stuff. I'm a P10, and I'm well-trained for psi combat."

Bester suddenly felt absolutely absurd. Caught napping by a P10.

Kill him, Jem, he sent.

Jem dropped and spun, pulling two pistols, like a cowboy from some ancient vid. Muzzle flashes lit the scene. Bester got a glimpse of the teep ducking behind a row of shelves, letting one round go as he did so.

As Bester jumped up and ran the other way, Jem came back to his feet, firing into the shelving, obviously hoping a blind bullet would punch through and hit his target.

Bester ducked low and scuttled down the row.

He must have been leaking and not known it. The teep had been on to them from the beginning. He had called the cops, which meant they had a few minutes, at best.

Behind him, the firefight continued. The guard's gun wasn't silenced—it cracked, loud and brassy. Jem's weapons were almost inaudible—the thunk and whine of his bullets, whizzing into and through things, had a ghostly quality.

Bester reached the vault. The choline ribosylase would have to be stored there. How many minutes left?

He needed the drill. Jem had it.

Not for the first time he cursed the Corps gene-whizzes, the scientists who had created his damnable condition. They'd been too technology-

happy, in those days. Enhancements—*dust,* for God's sake! Whose bright idea had it been to give *normals* the gift of telepathy?

Not his. He had fought tooth and nail against it, but that was before . . .

Concentrate. Byron was laughing at him. *Ignore it. Concentrate.*

He slipped back though the aisles, searching for the guard, but his pistol had stopped firing. So had Jem's. Was it over? He reached out, felt Jem. The big man was radiating pain. He was probably hit. But the guard . . .

Behind him again.

Bester didn't drop, or roll, or dodge. He just turned around and fired, as thunder exploded a few feet from him. He felt something hot graze his face, but he didn't flinch. Why should he flinch? Who could dodge a bullet? Might as well try to avoid getting wet in the rain.

Then the teep was squirming on the ground. He'd been hit in the chest, probably not a mortal wound. For a moment, Bester felt a sudden pang. This was one of his own, one of his family. A telepath.

Then he remembered Byron, and the war, and the hearing.

He shot the man in the head, twice. The body twitched grotesquely and stopped moving.

Jem was hit. Bester couldn't tell how bad.

"Jesus, it hurts," the big man grunted.

"I know. We'll get it looked at, soon. But first we have to get what we came for. Can you walk?"

"Yeah." He came jerkily to his feet. They found the satchel and went back to the vault. Outside, Bester could hear the weird sound of Parisian police cars, that undulating call that hadn't changed much in centuries.

The vault took a tad longer than the door, and once they were inside, it took Bester a few minutes to locate the serum. Meanwhile, as instructed, Jem stuffed his bag with the drugs that had street value.

"Got it," Bester said. His fingers were shaking. There were four ampoules. He took them and slipped four similar ampoules filled with water in their place. "I'm going now, Jem," he said. "Take care."

"Okay," Jem replied. He sounded unsure, his voice shaking. "What's happening? What am I doing?"

"It's okay, Jem. You'll be okay. And you won't have any more nightmares, just like you asked. Okay?"

"Okay."

Bester left him then, back out the door they had come in. Cars were everywhere. Most were out front—he had seen their lights through the window. But there was one here, in the side alley. Two uniforms held guns pointed at him, shielded by their car.

"Don't move," one of them said.

"I'm unarmed," Bester replied.

"Put your hands where I can see them."

"Okay, okay—just don't shoot." He walked slowly toward the car.

"I said stand there!" the cop commanded.

Bester continued to sidle away from the door.

One of the cops got up and came forward, his gun unwavering. "Down on the ground. Hands behind your head."

"As you say, Officer."

It wasn't a loud explosion—but it was a bright one, and very hot. Six grams of Kerikan X in Jem's bag. The doorway into the building might as well have been a tunnel into the sun. Bester had his eyes closed and was facing the ground, and he still saw the light, felt the heat lick across his back.

The cops weren't so lucky. Still, they would have had a slightly better than even chance of recovering their sight if he hadn't carefully placed a bullet in the brain of each before he walked off into the night.

He wasn't followed—there were no other cops on this side of the building, and the ones out front had their own worries to occupy them.

"No more nightmares, Jem," he murmured, feeling the ampoules in his pocket. "No more."

11

"You're sitting well today, Mr. Kaufman," Louise said.

"Thank you," Bester replied. "I feel better today than I have in a while. I think I had a touch of something."

"I thought so, too. I was starting to get worried about you." She dabbed at her palette, scrunching her face and twisting her nose to one side. Bester found himself watching her, not for the first time.

Yes, he felt a hell of a lot better, as a matter of fact. His symptoms had faded entirely, leaving him only with a slightly jumbled memory of what he and Jem had done, two nights before.

Looking back on it, he was amazed he hadn't been caught, so close had he been to the edge of reality. Still, his instincts had pulled him through, if not his intellect. He knew about trails, had been following them all his life, and so he knew how not to leave them.

There were three possible complications, of course. Someone might have seen him and might be able to describe him. That was the one he was least worried about, given the rain and the general mayhem that had been involved. His second was that when they began to investigate Jem—if they ever managed to figure out who he had been—it could bring inspectors around who might recognize him.

The third—and the one that most worried him—was that Garibaldi would somehow notice the caper. True, when they found what remained of the ampoules where they ought to be, and a drug dealer's body in the shop, they would have no reason at all to check for traces of the serum among the melted glass.

But they *might*.

He really should leave. Leave Paris, leave Earth. The vacation had been fun, but there was no reason to take chances.

"You were out awfully late the other night," Louise said. "Did you have a hot date?"

"You might say that," Bester replied.

"Really? Anyone I know?"

"No, I was kidding. I was just out, walking and thinking. About what you said—about writing a book of some sort."

"Memoirs?"

"No, that would be too close to home. A novel, perhaps. Something that would allow me to approach things more obliquely."

"I think novelists are cowards, sometimes."

"I thought *I* was the literary critic here."

"You are. I would have assumed you thought the same. Novelists put the things they'd like to say themselves in the mouths of fictional characters. It distances them from it. They can always claim it was just the character saying those things, that they were simply portraying an opinion rather than expressing one."

"Sometimes they are."

"Yes. An effective smokescreen, I think, for their real thoughts."

"So you think I should write memoirs."

"I didn't say that. I don't know enough about your life to know if it would be interesting without making things up. But I bet it is." She put down her brush and looked squarely at him. "Who are you, Mr. Kaufman? What are you?"

A little chill walked up his spine. She sounded almost—angry. Where had *that* come from? Had he let something slip, while he was sick? He wished he had a clearer memory of those days.

"I don't understand."

"The other day. After the opera, when you wondered where I had been. You thought I was with someone, didn't you? A man?"

"I didn't give it a thought. Besides, didn't you just ask me something similar?"

"Very good," Louise said. "In the same breath you say 'no I didn't,' but if I *did*—' et cetera. Be honest. You thought I was with someone, and you didn't like it."

He didn't answer that, just tried to look at her as if she had gone crazy.

She shook her head and walked toward him.

"No. You know where I was that night? Walking. Thinking. Trying to make some sort of *sense* out of a man who would give me a dress fit for an empress, then wiggle out of taking me anywhere in it. A stranger who appeared in the worst hour of my life and was *there* for me, like no one else has ever been. And for no good reason. Or no reason he will admit."

"What do you mean?"

"You know what I mean. You either know it or you are stupid. I've thought a lot about this. And these past few days—the whole of last

week—you seemed . . . unguarded somehow. I saw things on your face, obvious things. But they're gone now. Why?"

"I don't have the slightest idea what you're talking about," Bester said, trying to sound irritated, rather than as he felt—at sea, almost panicky.

"Must I be blunt? I think you have fallen in love with me. Have you?"

For a second his head rang as if he'd just fended off an attack by two P12s. And try as he might, he couldn't tear his gaze from the floor, couldn't confront her eyes.

"Yes." He sighed.

She abruptly turned her back to him and paced a few steps. Then she came back, closer and closer, until she stood over him, her arms folded defensively in front of her. He could feel her staring at the top of his head, but he had no sense of what she was thinking at all. None. It was as if he had been given sleepers, as if his psi were turned off.

"You stupid man," she said. Then she took his chin in her fingers and tilted it up. She bent and kissed him, softly, on the lips. She took his head in her hands and kissed him more firmly, but finally, finally he understood what was going on, and his lips remembered what to do.

He got his feet under him, and his arms around her, and he was shocked by the warmth, the solidity of her in his arms. Startled by the shape of her back, by the close scent of her, by how different her face looked, this near his own.

He felt like a comet, a million years in the void beyond Pluto, finally approaching the Sun, ice turning to vapor . . .

Her room was neat, and tidy, and mostly blue, and not something he paid much attention to when they finally reached it. Not when he had her hair, and her sky-bright eyes, and eventually the delicious feel of warm flesh, the tangle and sliding of limb against limb, face against belly, kisses that had long since gone from precious to hungry. He felt like a boy, like a man. He felt nothing at all like any Alfred Bester he had ever known.

He cheated a little—he could feel what she felt, which made him a fast learner. He slightly stimulated certain brain centers at the appropriate time, too—he wanted to give her everything he could. He wished she were a telepath, so she could feel what he did, know what he had just found in his heart. But then she might see how otherwise empty he was, too, and the things he had done, and be afraid.

They didn't speak afterward, either, as night crept into the streets outside, but curled together and fell slowly asleep, as if both understood that words were pointless. He didn't sleep long, though. It had been a

very long time since he had shared a bed, and he wasn't used to it. He watched her face in the pale illumination of the small lamp on the dresser.

He got up quietly, to turn the light off, but paused at the window. He moved the curtain aside and glanced down on the empty street.

In his reflection on the dark glass he saw Byron's face, Byron's sardonic smile.

You don't deserve her. You don't deserve anyone, Byron said.

"Deserving has nothing to do with it," Bester whispered. "I have another chance. A real chance. I've never been happy, never in my life. I've never known how to be."

He closed his eyes. "I don't need you anymore, Byron. You are a part of what I was. You're a part of what I couldn't let go. It's like I fell in a fast-moving river, and for years did nothing more than hang onto the rocks, my arms aching, trying to tear from their sockets. I might have died, holding onto that rock. Instead, I'm going to see where the river goes. I'm turning loose."

That's not you, Byron said. *That's never been you. You have to have control. Always control.*

"Good-bye, Byron."

And Byron was gone, unraveled. His haunting was over.

Then Bester lay against Louise, and she made a happy sound. He fell asleep, and he did not dream.

Garibaldi woke up with the sweats, wondering where he was.

There was a certain kind of dream, the kind when you think you've done something horrible, irrevocable. There were mild versions—the dream that you had an exam coming up for a class you never attended, for instance. There were darker ones, too—the kind where you've committed a terrible crime, which you could try to hide. But not forever, never forever . . .

In his dream, he'd betrayed the best man he had ever known to the worst people he had ever known, on purpose, with malice aforethought.

The thing about dreams like that, usually, was that you could wake up from them and realize that it *had* been a dream. No exam, no manslaughter, no betrayal.

But for Garibaldi, waking only made it worse, because then he remembered it was true. He'd really done it, and no dream could capture the depth of the harm he had wrought.

And while he would never get over the feeling that some of the blame was his to shoulder, he inevitably came back to one fact. Bester had been the cause. It wasn't an excuse, nor the old "devil made me do

it" line, but the literal truth. Garibaldi had been programmed, like some kind of wet-brained robot.

That's the alcoholic in you, he thought. Alcoholics always had excuses explaining why they weren't responsible for what they did. It was one of the things that had caused him to drink, back when he had done so. It gave him a license to screw up.

Well, he'd kicked the bottle. So maybe Lise was right. Maybe Bester *was* his new addiction. Maybe it was time to kick the Bester habit, too.

He lay there for a while, listening to Lise's gentle breathing, trying to shut down his mind, to get some sleep.

After half an hour, he gave up. He went into the next room, switched on his AI, and stared sleepily at the screen. He called up his choline ribosylase hotlist.

No bites. Everyone who had been tested, except the guy on Crenshaw's World, really had the condition, and no one had applied for an extra dose. Nor had any been stolen.

Wait . . . Four people in Paris had put in for prescription refills, only hours ago. What was up with that?

Within moments, he had the story. An attempted robbery had gone bad, a drug-crazed mobster had blown himself up when he got caught.

It didn't look like any of the inhibitor had been taken. There was a rundown of everything his company needed to replace, and all four doses of the stuff were accounted for in the drugstore safe. Destroyed, but accounted for.

Still . . .

He ran down the dead crook's record. Jemelah Perdue, thirty-two years of age, with a police record that accounted for twenty-three of them. No surprises there. No visible ties to Psi Corps.

What about the teeps? He ran them down, too, and they all looked clean, but you could never tell.

He shook his head and looked at the clock. Three in the morning. What the hell was he doing?

Lise *was* right. How many drugstores had been robbed that night? A quick inquiry brought that up, too. Six hundred thirty-three robberies or attempted robberies of drugstores reported. That meant, in all of Human space, there were at least that many again that hadn't been reported yet, or he hadn't gotten the record for.

"Say good night, Mike," he grunted, flipping off the screen.

Garibaldi had a life to live, and Bester had already taken too much of it. No more. The hell with him.

He went to bed.

PART 2

Reckoning

PART 2

Reckoning

1

Paris in summer. For Bester the days were molds filled each morning with golden heat, ordinary and extraordinary intimacies, flowers, and candlelight.

"I've never fallen in love like this," he told Louise one morning, in a little restaurant called Isabelle, tucked in a corner of the new market off the Rue de Martin.

"Like what?" she asked.

"Like this. Quiet evenings, and moonlit walks, and breakfasts in bed."

"No? How did you fall in love before?"

"In the war. On the go. Shells falling all around—that sort of thing. Or earlier, in school, when I wasn't supposed to."

"Ah. Forbidden romances. The sort they write books about. How does this compare?"

He took her hand, marveling, still, that her fingers gripped him back. "It doesn't," he said. "Before, there was always something I wanted more than a relationship. I was in love with my goals, my work. And love, however pleasant, was just . . . in the way.

"It isn't like that now. If I had known you fifty years ago, or even twenty . . ."

"If this were twenty years ago, you would be arrested for pedophilia, at the very least."

"There is that," Bester replied. "I still don't know what you see in an old man like me."

"Age doesn't matter much to me," she said.

"So I see."

"No, I don't think you do. I think it worries you."

He shrugged. "Okay—yes. Maybe not for exactly the reasons that you think. When I was in the military, I held a position of some authority. It attracted young women to me, in search, I think, of the father they had always wanted. One of those psychological things."

"Electra complex. Woman seeks man like her father because she's subconsciously in love with her father and knows she can't have him."

"That's it."

"Would it help if I told you, you are nothing like my father?"

"I'm sure it would."

"You're nothing like my father."

"Well, if you say it, I believe it."

"Credulity. I like that in a man. What else shall I ask you to accept without question?" She paused, as if to think about it, then looked him levelly in the eye. "How about this? You are the very best thing that has happened to me in a very long time. I don't know what brought you to my hotel, but I'm glad it did."

"I wouldn't question that," Bester said, a bit stiffly. "I might doubt it, but I couldn't question it. You make me . . ." He searched, but everything sounded so trite, so awkward. "You make me happier, I think, than I've ever been."

"Well," she said, her eyes flashing, "now that we've got the mutual appreciation out of the way, how shall we spend the rest of our day off?"

"Hmm. What's the one sick, secret thing you've always wanted to do in Paris, the one thing no real Parisian would ever be caught dead doing?"

"Oh, that's easy. The Eiffel Tower."

"The Eiffel Tower it is, then."

"Eh. We have to go disguised as tourists, then."

"Yes, of course. Cameras."

"Shorts and knee socks for you."

"An 'I love Paris' T-shirt for *you*."

"And ugly shoes for the both of us. Fine. A perfect idea. And you have to ask directions."

"But I *know* the way to the Eiffel Tower."

She mussed his hair. "If we are going to play tourist, we have to play it all the way. I don't want anyone recognizing me. Oh, and sunglasses for the both of us, yes? Big ones."

"You look hideous," Louise observed, an hour or so later, when they were dressed much as they had discussed. "The Hawaiian shirt is a particularly awful touch."

"Thank you, my dear. You look my perfect match."

"I say we're ready to go, then. Are you sure you're up to it?"

"From here on out, I speak no French at all," Bester replied.

They pretended to be Ugly Americans and gape-jawed Marsies. They asked for "real" ketchup in restaurants and demanded ice in their

drinks. When they couldn't make themselves understood in English, they spoke English very loudly and very slowly. They were utterly obnoxious, and Bester found he was enjoying himself more than he had in a long, long time.

They took a tour down the Seine, wandered around the Louvre, then went to the top of the Eiffel Tower, where they stood with a mixed group of mostly Japanese and Narn tourists and watched the sun touch the horizon.

"I came up here once, as a little girl," Louise told him. "I haven't been here since. It's a shame, really." She squeezed his hand. "I've had a wonderful day. It's been a long time since I felt like being silly."

"Is that what this is?" Bester replied. "I'm not even sure I know the definition of the word."

"Probably you don't. You take life pretty seriously. Too seriously, I think."

"This was *my* idea."

"I know. But it's funny—I've wanted to do something like this for a long time. It's almost as if you read my mind."

"Hah. I wish I could. I never know what you're thinking." But of course, he had. Why should he feel guilty about that? But he did, somehow. It felt like cheating.

"Oh, I think you do, sometimes." She squeezed his hand again, and they were silent for a few moments.

And in the midst of a glowing, quirky contentment, he felt someone try to scan him.

His smile froze on his face, and he looked around slowly, searching the crowd. After a moment he found him. It was Ackerman, the same fellow he had seen on the train platform.

And Ackerman was thinking *ohmygodohmygodohmygod* . . .

"Louise, dear," Bester said, "I'm getting tired. Would you mind terribly if we got a bite to eat and went home?"

"Home sounds good," she replied. "I can fix us a sandwich."

Bester tried to hide his agitation. Ackerman had recognized him this time, of that he was perfectly certain. As he went by, Bester lifted his surface thoughts. He probed just a little deeper and found an address.

Home sounds good. Louise's thoughts rang in his head, but with a bitter edge. Alfred Bester, it seemed, was never to have a home.

2

"Going somewhere, Justin?" Bester asked softly.

The bent figure froze, stopped shoving things into a suitcase, and straightened slowly.

So it is you, he 'cast.

"Shh. Talk to me, Justin. How long has it been? Seven years?"

The old man turned, slowly, to face him. "About that long. I'm surprised you remember me, Mr. Bester."

"You were a good man. Loyal to the Corps. Believe me, I noticed people like you." He looked back down at the half-packed suitcase. "You look like you're in a hurry. Can I help?"

"You followed me?"

"Yesterday you practically 'cast where you were staying. I didn't think you'd mind an old friend paying you a visit."

"N-no, of course not. Can I—ah—offer you something to drink?"

"Water would be nice," Bester replied. "Just a tall glass of cool water."

"Sure." Ackerman went off to the kitchen. Bester quietly closed the door behind him and went and stood in the window. The hotel overlooked the Bois de Vincennes, a large public park. A group of children in school uniforms were playing soccer on the lawn, supervised by a couple of nuns.

Ackerman returned with the water. "There you go, sir."

"No need for the 'sir' anymore, Justin. I'm a civilian now, just like you. Trying to live a quiet life, just like you."

"Yes, s—Mr. Bester. That's all I want."

"Are you on the run?"

"No, sir. I served two years in prison, and then they let me out on parole. I've been out for almost a year."

"I'm sorry that happened, Justin, but at least it's behind you now, isn't it? I wish I could say the same." He looked up and smiled. "But I imagine they would give me more than two years, don't you?"

"I . . . think so, Mr. Bester," Ackerman said, very carefully. He was still holding the water out. Bester took it and drank a little.

"It was a terrible thing, the war. Not something I ever thought would really happen. I never believed I would see our people divided like that, turning on each other like a pack of starving dogs. And even later, in the hearings—some of my oldest and dearest friends sold me out, testified against me. Made deals to spare themselves. Tell me, you personally oversaw the execution of at least five of our prisoners of war. How did you manage to get only two years?"

"Mr. Bester, please—"

Bester raised an eyebrow. "Come, now. I'm just curious. I'm not accusing you of anything."

"I—I know."

"Relax, Justin. I didn't come here to hurt you. Just to talk. To see what your intentions are."

"What do you mean?"

"A lot of people would like to know what you know at this moment. A lot of people would pay very well for the information only you possess. You've just been released from prison. You must be a little down on your luck. You must be tempted—just a little—to do what so many of my colleagues have already done."

"No," Justin said, emphatically. "I just want to forget it—forget all of it. No offense, Mr. Bester. I always admired you, even when the others started talking against you. I always thought you had it right, about the normals, about the rogues—about all of it. Whatever you may think, I didn't witness against you. Okay, I gave some people up, but not you. You can look at the court records."

"I'm not interested in revenge," Bester told him. "Even if they did coerce you into some sort of betrayal, I wouldn't really blame you. I haven't tried to take revenge against anyone who betrayed me. I understand their choice. I don't agree with it. I think it stinks, really, but I understand it. Let it be on *their* consciences. I'm done with it. What I'm concerned about is the future, not the past."

"Me, too," Ackerman said. "Me, too, Mr. Bester. Like I said, I just want to forget it all—you included. And I want the world to forget me."

"Well, we're the same, then, Justin. So what can we do about it? How can I give myself peace of mind, where you're concerned?"

"I swear to you, Mr. Bester, I won't tell. I won't tell anyone."

"I believe you mean that. But don't they check up on you? Isn't that part of the new process, they monitor your activities to make sure you haven't been 'abusing' your abilities? Make sure you've been good and not evil little telepath boys and girls?"

"Ah—yes."

"And so what if they find me in there, in your head when they start digging? Good intentions or not, the end result might be the same for me."

"They won't. I won't let them."

"Again, I think you believe that. But I can't depend on it. You wouldn't, if you were in my shoes, would you?"

"I guess not."

"See? I knew you were reasonable."

"Please don't hurt me. I'll go someplace no one can find me. I'll—"

"All I want to do," Bester said, "is make a few alterations in your memory. Take *me* out of there. You know my reputation—you know I'm a pro. You won't feel a thing, and you won't miss it when it's gone." He paused. "It's not the *only* solution I can think of, but it's the best one for both of us. Think about yourself. If they found out you have been hiding *me,* just how long do you think your parole would last?"

Ackerman sat down on the stiff-backed chair and put his head in his hands. "I'll do it," he said. "I'll do anything you say. I want to help."

Bester put his hand on Ackerman's shoulders. "You're one of the good ones, Justin. I knew I could count on you. And I appreciate it."

He took his time, carefully cleaning any memory of himself from Ackerman's mind. Then he put the other telepath into a sound sleep and carefully wiped everything that might leave fingerprints or significant traces of DNA. Then he departed, his head pounding from the exertion.

He bought Louise some roses on the way home.

That afternoon, he sat for her again. The painting was nearer completion.

"Are you seeing what you want, now?" he asked, as she dabbed and made little satisfied sounds.

"Yes."

"You knew what it was all along, didn't you? That what you saw in me was me seeing *you.*"

She blushed. "No. Not at first."

"You were so—alive. So vital. It woke me up, made me alive, too."

"I can't believe you were ever otherwise."

"I was. My life has had its disappointments, Louise. I was tired of feeling—feeling anything. Because you can't feel joy without opening to the possibility of pain. It's hard to risk that, when you've had a . . . disappointing life. Wake to your feelings, that is."

She came over and kissed him. "Well, I'm glad you did."

"Can I see it yet?"

"Not quite. There's a little more to do. But soon. And promise me you won't peek while I'm gone."

"Gone? Where are you going?"

"Oh, I thought I told you. I'm going to Melbourne to see my mother, and my sister, Helen. That's the one I stole the husband from. I think it's time I finally set things right between us."

"What brought this on?"

"You. Us. I want to move on with my life, Claude, and I want to do so with you. I've had some disappointments, too, and there are too many things I've left tangled up. I want to unsnarl a few. I think—I think it will be better for us. You deserve someone whole."

"You *are* whole." He wanted to tell her that she didn't *need* her family, not when she had him. That it would only make things harder. One of her sisters had been in Clark's guard. Odds were good that she'd seen Alfred Bester, at least once or twice.

But he couldn't say that to her, because he knew she was right. Reconciling with her sister was best for her, and he wanted what was best for her, even if it opened a little hollow place in him. After all, he was used to hollow places. He could bear it.

"I'd ask you to go with me, but it would just complicate things. I hope you don't mind." She must have seen something in his face, then. "I'm not being presumptuous, am I? I mean, I know we haven't known each other for that long, but I think we're—I mean, I think we have some sort of a future."

A future. Would she follow him from planet to planet, if he had to run again? Could he ask her to?

But that was what he wanted. He wanted it, the brass ring he had never even been able to see before, never imagined existed. The chance to really be happy, before the end.

He deserved it.

He took her hand. "I'm glad for you," he said. "Go see your sister, get this off your chest. And we'll go forward from there."

She kissed him, sweetly, on the lips. "Thank you, Claude. I knew you would understand."

"Well, I must congratulate you, Mr. Kaufman."

Jean-Pierre stood over him, adjusting his fashionably pointless eyeglasses.

"I'm sure you must," Bester replied, sipping his coffee. He hadn't noticed Jean-Pierre enter Le Cheval Heureux. The normally sleepy café was full today, nearly bursting with tourists—an unusual but occasional

event. "But is there any particular compulsion to do so, this time? Or is it just your general admiration for me overflowing?"

"Don't play coy with me. You know *Le Parisien* has started running your column."

"Believe me, Jean-Pierre, my interest in playing coy with you could not be observed even at the quantum scale. I haven't heard anything about this."

"No? Well, it's true." He dropped a paper in front of Bester. "They ran this today."

"This is my review of *Farther Clouds.*"

"Yes, so it is. The one we published only a few days ago."

"I never gave them permission to run that."

"Well, *I* certainly didn't," the younger man said, icily.

Louise had left the day before, and Bester had been feeling more and more uneasy ever since. Now his disquiet took a sharp dig at the inside of his ribs. *Le Parisien* had a circulation of six million, not just in Paris, but in Quebec, Algeria—on Mars.

It could have been worse. They could have run his picture beside the column. Of course, they didn't have one to run . . .

"We'll see about this," he said. "Where are their offices?"

Simon de Grun was a round man made of round parts, and even in an impeccably tailored suit he looked like an overdressed balloon. He smiled at Bester and offered him a black cigarette tipped with gold.

"No, thank you," Bester said. "I would much rather discuss plagiarism."

"Got your attention, didn't it?" de Grun said, lighting his own smoke and taking a satisfied drag. "I've been trying to contact you, you know. Your present publisher wouldn't supply me with an address or a phone number."

"He doesn't have them. I value my privacy."

"But I take it he also did not pass my messages along to you."

"No, I don't believe that he did."

"It's very simple, Mr. Kaufman. I like your column. Paris likes your column." He opened a desk drawer, removed an envelope, and passed it to Bester.

"There's a chit with two thousand credits in there. You'll get one of those each and every time I publish one of your reviews—and I plan to publish one every time you write one. I daresay that's a better deal than you have with that pretentious little rag you've been working for. Not to mention the fact that many of our readers buy their issues on *real* paper.

Think of it, Mr. Kaufman—to see your name in *ink,* like Faulkner or Liu."

Bester stared at the envelope. "You're kidding."

"No, I'm not. You have bite, Mr. Kaufman. You have style, and a vicious streak a mile wide. The response to your first column in our publication was astonishing, even better than I expected."

"I don't know what to say." He felt totally disarmed. As a child, there was nothing he had wanted more or worked harder for than the admiration of his peers. In time, he had gotten beyond that, and the work itself had become more important than the praise. Yet the praise had continued. There was a time when every young Psi Cop wanted nothing more than to *be* Alfred Bester. He had become comfortable with his accomplishment, with excellence.

It was only after the sea of respect he floated on had vanished that he'd understood just how much it had buoyed him up, how much weight it had taken off his feet.

Now, for the first time in years, he felt some of that lightness again. And the funny thing was how wholly unexpected it was. He hadn't sought praise—it had found him of its own accord. Of course, they didn't know who he really was, but that made it all the more delicious.

And dangerous. How could he risk it? He had taken too many risks already.

He was about to push the envelope back toward de Grun when an equally unexpected flash of anger hit him. Why *shouldn't* he do this? Had he become so timid that all he could think of was hiding, making himself smaller and smaller, until he just vanished? That was what his enemies wanted, wasn't it?

"Three thousand," he said.

De Grun didn't blink. "Twenty-five."

"You have a deal," Bester told him. "But only on my terms. I review what I want, the way I want to."

"I can live with that."

"Well, then. Good day, Monsieur de Grun."

"Wait. How can I contact you?"

"Don't worry. I'll contact you. I still value my privacy, all the more if my audience is going to increase."

"We'd like to run a picture of you with your column."

"Out of the question. I'm very shy."

De Grun burbled a laugh. "You don't seem shy to me."

Bester looked him dead level in the eyes. "I'm shy," he repeated. "If you run a picture of me, or even take one, I'll sue you."

"What, are you some sort of war criminal?"

"Yes, of course," Bester said, sarcastically. "I'm the secret leader of the Drakh."

De Grun shrugged jovially. "You could be, for all I care. Fine. No picture. Anything else?"

"Nothing else. You'll have your next review tomorrow."

But he didn't start on the review right away. Instead he went back to his room, and he savored a small glass of Pernod. And for the first time, he started to see a coherent road before him.

From the day he was born, the path stretching in front of him had been as straight and sure as the arrow of entropy. He had never doubted where he was going, though the trail had often been narrow, no more than a tightrope.

Then came the war, the aftermath, and flight. Suddenly there were no roads before him at all—or rather, all rocky paths leading nowhere good. Then Paris, where he discovered that he might do almost anything, be almost anything. Where he first understood the concept of freedom.

But even freedom needed direction, a path, a plan. And here it was forming, from chaos and joy. It was so wonderful, so *delightful*, that he was afraid of thinking about it, of making plans, of stepping out of the moment.

But if he just kept depending on fortune, he was bound to get into trouble. Life had taught him that God *did* play dice with the universe. And any game of dice went, not to the man with the lucky rabbit's foot, but to the man who knew how to toss the dice just so. Or to switch them for the weighted ones in his cuff.

He stared at the blank sheet in front of him, and thought about the book Louise wanted him to write. He thought about the cosmic crap game, and began fooling with titles. *Loading the Dice: A Telepath's Story*. No, that wouldn't do.

He sipped his drink. The dice were already loaded in favor of telepaths, if they knew how to throw. Normals knew that. That's why normals had always tried to keep them out of the game, kill them, lock them away, or tame them as pets. Telepaths were the next step in evolution, as pivotal as that first primate ancestor who had been born with one finger that curled differently, that opposed the others.

That was it. He cleared the screen.

The Third Thumb, he wrote.

It wasn't his story he wanted to tell, but the story of his people. Of all of his people, even those who had betrayed him, and worse, betrayed their own kind.

He would do it. But first, he had something else to do.

* * *

Justin Ackerman looked at him without comprehension for a few seconds, then recognition dawned.

"Mr. Bester?" he asked.

Bester scanned him lightly, nodding in satisfaction. "Well, I did do a good job on you after all. You don't remember me, do you?"

"Yes, sir—of course I do. We worked together in the Brazilian camp."

"Yes, yes, I meant—oh, never mind."

Ackerman glanced around nervously. "Would you, ah, like to come in, sir?" He turned slightly, gesturing into the room, his gaze retreating from Bester.

"No, Justin. But I do need you to come with me."

"Why?"

"You've known me for a long time, Justin. Did you ever question me before? It's important."

"But sir, I was just going to bed. It's late, and I—"

"Please. I'm asking as an old friend, not as an old commander."

Ackerman hesitated for another second. Bester could taste his fear and curiosity.

"Let me get my coat."

The doorman wasn't on duty. Bester had suggested that he take a nap, something he'd been close to doing anyway.

The air was warm as they walked through the midnight city, until finally they came to the quay along the Seine. Far to the left, the Eiffel Tower thrust its ancient silhouette against the city-lit underbellies of the clouds. They looked, Bester thought, like the sulfurous clouds of Herig 3, heavy and poisonous.

"Sit with me here," Bester said, letting himself down onto the quay. It was quiet, far from the heart of the city.

Ackerman did, tentatively. "I can't believe you're on Earth, sir," he ventured. "It's dangerous for you here." He paused, looking at Bester's hands. "Especially if you keep wearing those gloves. We don't wear them anymore."

Bester smiled thinly. "It's dangerous for me everywhere," he said, watching a small boat move almost soundlessly up the black glass surface of the Seine. "I tried almost everywhere. Little colony worlds. Non-Human worlds. I spent almost a year in one of my old asteroid bases, going stir-crazy. They always found me. Maybe they'll find me here, maybe they won't.

"When I decided to come here, I thought Earth was my best chance. I still do. But I'm going to ask you, Justin, do you know of a place?

Somewhere I can go where they will never think to look, where I can live out my life in peace?"

Justin shook his head.

"Think carefully, Justin. This is very important to me."

"No, sir. They want you bad. I can't think of any place."

"Well. I had to try. There was a small chance that you had thought of something I hadn't. And I owed you that chance."

"Mr. Bester, please—" Ackerman started to raise his eyes toward Bester, but his gaze never reached him. Bester had already placed the muzzle of the pistol against Ackerman's head and squeezed off the first round. The weapon sighed, sighed again. Ackerman did, too, as the small-caliber bullets ricocheted around inside his skull, shredding his brain but leaving no exit wounds, no ugly spatters of blood.

Ackerman swayed, then began to slump. Bester caught him and held him upright, then took a plastic bag and a rubber band from his coat pocket, and fastened the bag around Ackerman's head. That would keep what little blood there was from getting on anything.

The plastic sucked up to Ackerman's nostrils, and his chest heaved uselessly for another minute or so. Bester kept himself tightly blocked— he didn't want to feel Ackerman's death. He had done that too often in his life—once he had thought it had cost him his soul.

He had his soul back, and he wasn't about to risk it again, not now.

When he was sure Ackerman was dead, he removed the bag. Then, almost gently, he pushed him into the river. The body sank as the current took him away. He would surface again, of course, but as in any large city on Earth, people were murdered in Paris every day, every night. He would become another statistic, nothing more. There was nothing to connect him to Alfred Bester, much less to Claude Kaufman.

On the way back to his room, he began outlining the first chapter of his book in his head. It helped. By the time he got there, his sadness had faded to melancholy.

3

Bester paused typing in midsentence, a smile creasing his face.

Louise was home. He could feel her blowing through the front door, a zephyr, a breeze with scents of honeysuckle and paint. He closed what he was working on and hurried down the stairs. When he reached the café, Louise was indeed there, just setting down her luggage.

"Claude!" Her smile seemed to explode across her face, and an instant later he had her in his arms. Tensions melted away as he felt the solid warmth of her, doubts eased back into his subconscious. This was worth anything.

She kissed him briefly but warmly on the lips. "Are you ready?" she asked.

"Ready for what?"

"Just hold my hand and tell me you love me."

"I love you. What . . ."

"So *you* must be Claude."

He turned toward the source of the slightly disapproving female voice.

"Yes, this is him," Louise said, brightly. "Claude, meet Major Genevieve Bouet, my sister."

Bester smiled at the tall brunette with all of the false charm he could muster. Louise needn't have bothered giving her rank—it was plain enough on her EarthForce uniform. He saw a bit of Louise in her serious, no-nonsense face, but he would have never guessed they were sisters.

"Enchanté," he murmured, taking her hand. Her grip was firm, and the thoughts that flooded his mind as they touched were ordered and clear. The disapproval was real, but came mostly from concern for Louise—the major didn't want to see her sister hurt again. To his vast relief, he sensed no hint of recognition.

"Likewise," the major said. "I must say, Mr. Kaufman, you have a lot

to live up to. Louise has been rattling on about you like a schoolgirl, something she never does."

"Well, I'll do my best," he replied. "If ever I had expectations worth living up to, Louise would provide them. She didn't tell me your rank. I'm quite impressed."

"You needn't be. The last ten years have taken their toll on officers, and promotions have come cheap."

"From what Louise has told me, I think you're being modest. You were in Clark's personal guard, weren't you?"

She nodded at that, and there was an uncomfortable moment of silence. Bester filled it.

"So when did you two hook up?" he asked Louise. "I thought you were going to see your other sister—the one in Melbourne."

"I did," Louise replied. "That didn't go so well as I hoped—but by good luck Genny was there on leave, and I managed to talk her into a visit. I wanted to show off my new boyfriend."

"Well, I'm hardly a boy, as your sister has noticed."

He was rewarded by a slight feeling of shame from the major.

"I wouldn't care if you were two hundred," she said, "so long as you make my sister happy." That was half a lie, but Bester accepted it in the spirit with which she meant it, nodding graciously.

"We're starving," Louise said. "Why don't you two chat while I fix us something?"

"Nonsense," Bester replied. "I'll cook, you two sit and have a glass of wine. I'm sure the flight must have taken a lot out of you."

"Claude doesn't think much of my cooking," Louise said, playfully. "He doesn't realize it's all a ploy to get him to wait on me hand and foot."

"Well, I do now," Bester said. "But really, I just bought a bottle of chateau neuf. Let me get it. Give you two a chance to compare notes on the boyfriend."

"I won't refuse *that*." The major smiled. Bester grinned back, not at her words, but at the grudging feeling behind them. This was going well.

"Well, no man who can cook like that can be all bad," the major said, laying down her fork next to the remnants of soufflé. "Some of these older models run pretty well, it seems."

"No need to tell me," Louise beamed.

Bester raised his glass. "To family reunions," he said.

"To *some* family reunions," Louise corrected, but she toasted anyway.

"Oh, yes. So things didn't go so well with Helen?"

"She'll come around," Genevieve said. "Helen is good at holding grudges. She puts a lot of energy into it. But it was a good start. At least she spoke."

"At least," Louise allowed. "Of course, she comes by that trait honestly."

A cynical smile flitted across the major's face. "Let's not bore Mr. Kaufman with our family squabbles. At least the two of us are friendly again. Like I said, a good start."

"I'm not in the least bored," Bester said. "I could never be so complacent about something that concerns Louise so much."

The major sighed. "Be careful what you wish," she said. "You might get it. Another glass of wine or two, and we might get into it, and we'll be here all night." Her steely gaze settled on her sister. "For the record, Louise, I think you're right. I've been trying to get in touch with Anne. After all, it's been almost ten years. If EarthForce can be reconciled, the two of us can, too." She turned back to Bester. "The problem, you see, is that our family tends to be a passionate one, often at the expense of common sense." She swirled her wine around. "No, enough. Mr. Kaufman, I understand you were in the military?"

"I was, sort of. Hush-hush stuff. Fortunately, I was a private citizen when Clark took office, so I wasn't involved in the civil conflict. The choice you had to make wasn't one I would have wanted, but I respect it."

The major shrugged. "For me, at the time, there was no choice. It's the job of the senate and the courts—and ultimately the voters—to determine the legitimacy of a president and his decisions. It is emphatically *not* the task of officers in the military to do so. If that precedent held, where would we be? Privately, I question the worthiness of every single instance that puts my soldiers in danger. But publicly, no military can function without an unquestioning chain of command."

She shrugged. "My sister didn't see it that way. I imagine she still doesn't. Looking back on it, in some absolute scheme of things, I believe she was right. But put in the same situation, I would make the same choice. But you know what? One gets older, and as certain parts get stiffer, others loosen up, *n'est-ce pas?* I'm tired of having this between me and Anne."

"To loosening up," Bester said, raising his glass again.

"I'll drink to that," Louise said. And they all did.

"She likes you," Louise told him, that night in bed.

"She's dubious of me," Bester replied. "She thinks I'm a cradle robber."

"She's cautious, that's all. But she's my sister, and she loves me. She wants what's best for me, and anyone around you for half an hour can see that what's best for me is you."

He rolled over so he could see her face. Her eyes glistened faintly in the dim light that filtered in from the street outside. "You make me humble," he said. "You give me memories I've never had and dreams I've never imagined." He paused. "I started writing a book yesterday."

"Really?"

"Yes."

"When can I read it?"

He chuckled. "When can I see the painting?"

"When it's done."

"Well, then you know my answer, too." He felt a prickle of fear. One day she would read the book, and then she would have to know, at the very least, that he was a telepath. She would know that he had been lying to her, in a sense—the lie of omission. But at the moment it was impossible for him to believe she wouldn't understand, wouldn't forgive. He had never in his life been this close to a human being, not even to Carolyn. It was the most frightening and the most wonderful feeling he had ever known.

"How long is she staying, your sister?"

"A few days, maybe a week. You don't mind, do you?"

"No. You need this." That was a lie, too, but not a big one. His fear that the major would recognize him seemed to be groundless. There hadn't even been a hint of it, the whole evening, not even a subconscious reflex. And he had been watching, carefully. This roll of the dice had come out in his favor.

"Thank you, Claude. It's all because of you, you know. You made me understand that it was worth the risk, to love again, to repair fences. You gave me that."

"I understand perfectly," he breathed. "Perfectly."

She kissed him, and kissed him again, and the night dissolved into soft sighs and touches, nothing urgent about it, but sweet, comfortable, happy.

Afterward, drifting to sleep, he thought of Justin, of his body sinking slowly into the river. He thought of what Louise would say, if she knew, and he felt an odd little catch, an explosion of grief so strong it nearly choked him. Faces passed across the darkness behind his eyelids. Byron, Handel, Ferrino, people whose names he couldn't remember.

This was the end of it. This was the end of him. It occurred to him that when Louise had said his name earlier—*Claude*—he hadn't flinched, as he once had. Hadn't wished she could call him Alfred. Alfred Bester

didn't deserve Louise, wasn't worthy of her. But Claude—well, perhaps Claude wasn't either, but he *could* be. If he worked at it, if he always reminded himself he could be better.

I'm sorry, Justin, he thought. *I had to do it, but I'm sorry. You are the last man Alfred Bester will ever kill. Because Alfred Bester is dead.*

"Claude?"

"Yes?"

"Are you crying?"

"I—" He was. He hadn't recognized the sensation, but his face was wet.

"Why?"

"Because I'm happy," he replied. "Because I'm so very happy."

4

"He was dead before he hit the water," the examiner said, adjusting his gloves. "Not a drop of water in his lungs." He touched a contact on the edge of the examining table. A ribbon of blue light appeared on the toes of the naked corpse and moved slowly toward his head. "Let's see what the toxicology shows us," the doctor murmured.

Inspector Girard nodded wearily. He had just pulled four shifts back-to-back, and was having a hard time concentrating on what the examiner was saying. That was bad, but it was better than going home, where his wife would either start screaming at him or just sulk, sullenly, burning him with her eyes. And going to Marie, now, was out of the question.

He was a detective, yes? He should know better. The mistake every criminal made was in thinking that *they* were smarter than every other criminal, that *they* were the ones who wouldn't be caught. He, an inspector with almost twenty years behind him, and he had thought he could keep his affair with Marie a secret?

He supposed he might have, *if Marie hadn't become pregnant,* or if . . .

Bah. No ifs. He had been stupid.

He shook his head, trying to clear the amorphous fish-things trying to obscure his vision.

"Another tourist?"

"I don't think so," the examiner said, prodding the head to one side as the blue strip of light finished its journey. "Lamp, high," he said. Harsh white light suddenly filled the room.

The corpse was an old fellow. Rigor mortis had come and gone, and his blue-tinted face was composed, almost serene. *What did you try to get away with, my friend? What business has this ended for you? Was death a relief, in the end? A well-deserved peace?* He shook his head again when he realized he had missed what the doctor had just said.

"I'm sorry. What?"

"I said it looks pretty professional. Small-caliber slugs, so there are no exit wounds. I think the killer put a bag over his head, too—there is a faint ring of capillary damage around the throat, here." He pointed to what, for Girard, was an invisible line, but if the examiner said it was there, it was. The man was a necromancer, a wizard of the dead, and Girard had come to respect him deeply.

"The muzzle was placed right against the skull, too, so the killer was close."

"Was he bound?"

"No sign of it. No abrasions of any sort on the hands or feet, no odd muscle positions."

Girard had a sudden flash. *Two men talk to one another, like old friends. One casually pulls a pistol, as though he's taking out a cigarette lighter. The other doesn't notice, until the steel touches his head, and now he's puzzled. His puzzlement deepens as he feels a thump, and everything goes strange, as if he is very drunk, and he forgets where he is, what he's doing, and there is another thump, and another* . . .

Girard had these flashes. He had wondered, often, if he might not be some sort of telepath, but all the tests came back negative. No, he was merely damned to have that sort of imagination that put things together without consulting his intellect, a brain that dreamed while it was awake. It made him a good detective, but he didn't like it. Sometimes, when he was wrong, when his flashes proved incorrect, he was actually more relieved than when he was right.

It didn't happen often that he was wrong.

"Have you identified him yet?"

"That's the puzzling part. Considering how professional the execution was, you would think the killer would have tried harder to get rid of the body. Dissolve it in acid, or somesuch. Cut off the fingertips, knock out the teeth."

"The killer was working alone," Girard said. "If this were a syndicate hit of some sort, there would have been no body, as you say. And I'm guessing that not only is this poor fellow's DNA registered someplace, but the killer knew it. So. Since he didn't have the means, or the time, to entirely destroy the body, he did the next best thing. He disposed of it in an entirely conventional way, hoping we wouldn't notice him in the piles of bodies we fish from the river every day."

"Or perhaps it really was just a robbery-murder, by someone with a professional technique."

"Perhaps." He paced around the corpse. His personal troubles began to fade, overwhelmed by the puzzle. "His DNA *was* on file, yes?"

The examiner tapped a small display. "Let's see. Yes, you're right. He—"

"No, don't tell me who he was, yet."

"As you wish, Inspector."

"The killer killed him near the water, so he wouldn't have to carry the body."

"That could be. He soiled himself when he died, but the pattern of absorption by his clothes suggests he was immersed almost immediately."

He tried to picture it another way. A tourist out for a stroll, an out-of-luck, unemployed hitman looking for his next meal. He walks up, asks for a match or something, and when his victim looks down, kisses his head with the end of his pistol.

No. Why the bag? The killer had wanted his victim dead, fast and certainly. And the way the victim was dressed in no way suggested a rich man. This was never a robbery. He couldn't make that scene come alive in his head.

"If his DNA was on file, he was probably either a convicted felon, in the military, or a telepath. Which one?"

"A telepath."

Well, that opened up a lot of possibilities. A hate crime? A lot of people hated telepaths for a lot of reasons. That might explain the execution-style slaying. The killer saw himself as a cleansing force, out to make the world safe for those without unholy powers.

Or it might have been an old grudge, yes? There must be plenty of grudges after the telepath war. Two telepaths, once friends, on opposite sides of the conflict. A pretense of reconciliation—that would explain why the victim wouldn't notice murder coming up to him, didn't even flinch as his bloody-minded companion drew his weapon with cold, certain intent.

Except it couldn't have been *that* cold. There were mistakes here, and a lack of planning that suggested panic . . .

No, wait—where had he gotten panic? A panicked man didn't calmly place a gun against someone's head and pull the trigger, then produce a plastic bag.

Ah, but people didn't always know they were panicking, did they? When Marie told him of her pregnancy, he had believed himself to still be in control. He had fooled himself, suppressed the fear, told himself that all he needed to do was act calmly and everything would be all right.

But there was nothing logical about adultery, about ruining a marriage of thirty years, the humiliation of his own children realizing what he had done to their mother. No, he hadn't acknowledged his panic. He had

swallowed it, and it had poisoned him. It had made him stupid even as he convinced himself he was clever.

The mind worked like that. This wasn't the first time he had seen it.

So what did he have? Someone who wanted to kill a telepath, probably a telepath himself. Someone who thought he was doing the murder for all the right reasons and with all the proper precautions, while at the same time he was frightened at the most fundamental level possible.

Maybe the victim had learned something he shouldn't have, yes? Telepaths had a way of doing that. Maybe the meeting was at the victim's behest, an overture to blackmail. And the killer saw, with terrible lucidity, that the way out of the trap was to destroy the trap itself.

Enough. "Who was he?"

The examiner, who had become busy examining the man's stomach contents, didn't bother looking at the vid display. The faint gleam on the narrow goggles he wore suggested the information was scrolling there. "Justin Ackerman. Born in North America, in Toronto. Sixty-three years of age. He was a telepath, a P7. A war criminal, as a matter of fact. He had just finished serving his sentence and was out on parole. Applied for a work visa two months ago, rented an apartment near the Rue de Paris. He worked part time as a night guard at the club Pugeot."

"Have you informed Psi Corps yet?"

"No, Inspector. But we're supposed to inform them within twenty-four hours."

"We still have ten, then, yes?" He walked toward the door, snagged his jacket from the skeleton-coatrack that held it on an outstretched arm. "Hold off as long as you can. I want to talk to his landlord and his employer, before the EABI shows up and takes this one away from me."

Though why he should care, he couldn't say. Wouldn't he be better off without one more case? But he had a long-standing dislike for the Metasensory Division of the EABI. In the old days when they had been MetaPol, they had swept in like birds of prey, arrogant, dismissive, heavy-handed. He didn't like having them in his city. Oh, they were better on the surface now, but the arrogance remained. And perhaps he was envious of their abilities—sure, they claimed not to use them, but he knew better. Who wouldn't? He had never been able to escape the feeling that it was unfair, cops who could read minds, as often as he wondered if he himself didn't have a touch of their power.

No, this was his city, not theirs. His murder, his murderer.

And, he thought cynically, another thing to keep his mind off how his life was slowly disintegrating around him.

* * *

"He didn't *have* any friends. At least none that I saw."

Margarite de Cheney might have been attractive once, before life had scrubbed her face red and bruised her eyes with disappointments. Girard wondered, looking at her, if she ever felt joy in anything anymore.

He wondered if she could kill. If one's own life was gone, it was easier to take another's, yes?

He wondered wryly if that meant murder was next on his agenda. Would his life be easier if he had killed Marie? No, because he would have been caught. Everyone got caught, sooner or later.

Besides, he did love her, in his way. And the thought of another child, while immensely complicating, was not without appeal.

"No one came or went?"

"You'd have to ask the doorman. I never saw anyone, but then I don't spy on my guests. Is he in some kind of trouble?"

"He's dead."

He watched her reaction—this was the moment when a lot of them blew it. They always imagined they should act surprised, shocked. Real reactions were slower than that. Death was something people spent their whole lives pretending couldn't be real. When confronted with it, there was usually a comprehension gap, a moment searching through the words they had just heard, trying to see if there was some other way to interpret them.

"Dead? You mean . . ."

"Dead," he repeated, disappointed. But then, he hadn't really thought she was guilty. "Murdered."

"Here?" *That* scared her.

"Maybe," he lied. "We found his body in the river, but he could have been killed anywhere. Which is why it's so important that you recall everything you can."

"There are two doormen, one for night, the other for day. I'll give you their names and addresses, but Etienne is here already. You want to talk to him?"

"Of course. But first, I would like to see Mr. Ackerman's room."

"Oh, yes. This way."

They went upstairs to room 12. De Cheney exhaled into the cheap chemical lock and the door sighed open. There wasn't much to the place. A couch and two chairs that looked like they belonged there. Some clothes in the closet, a night guard's uniform and one new suit, undoubtedly the one he had received on release from prison.

The forensic team would be here soon, and he was loath to spend much time inside, for fear of contaminating the place, of erasing the

trace elements and bits of hair, the physical clues that sometimes led nowhere and sometimes everywhere.

He just wanted to see it, to picture where the man had spent his last days. If Justin Ackerman had been killed for being Justin Ackerman, then knowing the victim would help him know the killer. If he had been killed simply because he was in the wrong place at the wrong time, well, it wouldn't help much at all. But it couldn't hurt.

"Was he noisy? Did anyone complain about him?"

"Not that I know of."

"The rooms next to his—are they occupied?"

"That one is. A Mademoiselle Carter." She pointed to the door on the right.

Girard knocked. After a few moments, a young woman answered. She was blond, perhaps twenty years old, a bit disheveled looking, pale but not unattractive.

"*Oui?*" she said. Her accent was terrible. An American.

"Mademoiselle Carter, my name is Raphael Girard," he said in English. "I'm a police inspector. I wonder if I can have a few words with you about your next-door neighbor?"

"Sure." She stood in the door frame and folded her arms, her eyes suddenly lively, interested.

"You've lived here for how long?"

"About a month, since the school year started. I'm studying antiquities at the Sorbonne."

"A graduate student?"

"Yes."

"I've always been fascinated by history. What period do you specialize in?"

"The early Roman period in Gaul, actually."

"Oh. Asterix, eh?"

She smiled, openly and genuinely. "Very good," she said. "I rarely meet anyone who has even heard of Asterix."

"My father was a professor of twentieth-century literature. He was responsible for the reprinting in the sixties."

"Well, thank him for me," she said. "I collected those, as a child." She smiled again. "Now that you've put me at ease, Inspector, what did you want to know about my neighbor? I'm afraid I can't tell you much."

"Well, did he ever have visitors? A girlfriend, anything like that?"

"No, not usually. Though somebody came by a couple of nights ago. I remember noticing it just because he never had visitors. I was studying, and someone knocked on his door. I could hear them talking, but not what they said. I was sort of surprised, y'know?" She scrunched up her

face. "I think they left. I wasn't really paying attention. Something happened to him, didn't it?"

"We found him murdered."

"Oh."

"You don't sound surprised."

"I am—that he was murdered. I think . . . I think I expected him to die, though. When you asked me about him just now, I thought you had found him dead—in there." She gestured toward the room next door.

"Suicide, you mean?"

"Yes."

"Why?"

"He just seemed . . . sad. Worn out, or something. He spoke to me once, in the hall. You know that way that people act, when you speak to them, and you can tell they don't do it very often? The way they want to keep talking, even though all you meant to do was say hello? But I was pretty busy, and I was suddenly anxious. I need this place to study, and if I suddenly had this needy friend next door, always coming over—" She broke off and frowned. "So I sort of ignored him, after that, or just nodded at him and acted like I was in a hurry. I felt guilty about it, and I sort of worried—Well, but when he had a visitor, I remember thinking 'Oh, good, he has a friend.' "

"But you didn't see this friend."

"No. It was a man, though, I'm sure of that, from his voice. They spoke English, I'm pretty sure."

"And this was about what time?"

"Oh, midnight, maybe."

Another flash. *The same two men talk, but Ackerman knows how it's going to end. So there's no surprise when the gun touches his head. He knows running is useless. Maybe he doesn't care. Thump . . .*

Girard blinked rapidly. The girl was looking at him funny. "Does that help?" she asked, her tone suggesting that she was repeating herself.

"Yes. That's very near the time of death."

"Oh, my God. I heard the killer."

"Yes."

"Do you think I—"

"I don't think you are in danger, but you should be careful. Take normal precautions. Don't answer the door unless you know who it is— that sort of thing. Let me give you my card . . ." He produced a slip that had his name and address written on it. "It has my phone code in it, prepaid. All you have to do is swipe it through a payment slot. If you need anything, I'm at your service. And I'll come by to check on you, if you want."

She smiled, timidly. "That would be nice. But that isn't what I was going to say. I was wondering if there might have been anything I could have done, if I might have stopped him."

Ah. Young Americans. They always imagined the world would be a better place if *they,* personally, took an interest in it. "Don't worry about that," he told her. "There was no way for you to know. Besides, if you had tried, I would be asking these questions about you, I fear, and that would be a most unpleasant task. I much prefer having met you this way." He started to say more, but stopped. Was he flirting again? This was how he had met Marie.

"Once more, thank you, and good day," he said, and backed out, quickly.

The doorman didn't remember anyone, and looked uncomfortable about it.

"Well, *someone* came in," Margarite said, a little shrilly. "What do I pay you for?"

"Maybe it was another tenant," Etienne mumbled. "He might have just gone down the hall, for all we know."

"That's true. But let us suppose, for a moment, that you were distracted—" *say, by the inside of your eyelids* "—or were away from your post, maybe in the toilet. Couldn't someone have come in and out without you knowing it?"

"No, Inspector. The door records everyone who goes in and out, anyway. You're welcome to view the record, if you wish."

"Let's see it."

They searched for three hours either side of midnight, but found no trace of anyone other than tenants coming in or out.

"Monsieur Ackerman went out," Girard said. "Of that, there is simply no question. And yet, I do not see him here. How can that be? Is there another way?"

"No."

"A window?"

"The windows are sealed," Margarite said. "The building is environment-controlled, and open windows muck that up."

"We should check them, anyway. What is sealed can be unsealed. What about the recording device? Could it have been tampered with?"

"I don't see how. It's AI-controlled. Nothing I could do to it, if you're implying that," Etienne said, defensively.

"I'm not," Girard replied, suddenly recalling something. Hadn't there been something recently, in another part of town? Yes, an attempted robbery of a pharmacy, and even though one of the perpetrators

had been found dead in the building, he hadn't shown up on the surveillance. The security company in question had claimed that the clumsy recovery techniques used by the police had badly damaged the circuits, but the experts he knew in the department had flatly denied the possibility. Still, nobody could figure out how the device might have been fooled, either. And since a guard and three policemen had died in the incident, there had been considerable effort in that direction.

Wait a minute. Hadn't the guard at the pharmacy been a telepath?

Could telepaths influence AIs? He had never heard of such a thing, but then, if they could do it, it might be a pretty closely guarded secret. Hadn't there been some rumor that telepaths had been able to do something to alien ships, back during the Shadow War?

And a telepath could easily have erased the doorman's memory, or fogged his mind, or whatever. Ackerman could have done it himself, for that matter.

This was getting interesting. Very interesting. Something *was* going on here, something to do with telepaths, he could feel it in his bones. Which meant he had better use the hours remaining to him very wisely, before Metasensory showed up. Otherwise, he might never know what had happened here. When any division of the EABI showed up, cases sometimes just vanished, as if they had never been.

His city. His murder.

5

Girard sipped his vile coffee and glanced through the paper. He flipped to the arts section and read the book review. It was the new reviewer, and Girard enjoyed his acerbic sense of humor.

The plot of the book seems to be revealed only on a need-to-know basis—and apparently the author feels the reader doesn't need to know, he read, and chuckled.

Behind him, Louis Timothee, his deputy assistant, gave a sudden soft exclamation.

"Look at this," Timothee said.

"What is it?"

"Maybe we shouldn't feel so sorry for Ackerman after all. Did you realize that he worked in the Psi Corps reeducation camp at Amiento?"

"Yes."

"Really? I just found that. It was past one of the security curtains . . ."

"Yes, he was acquitted of most charges and served his time, so of course they make it difficult to access that part of his past. It's in keeping with the forgiveness statutes passed after the Civil War. We can get to them, we just have to work bloody hard."

"Acquitted?" Timothee said, incredulously.

Girard turned, and found his assistant staring at an image. It showed a heap of dead bodies. He clicked, and another scene came up—a group of men, women, and children, emaciated but alive, stared blank-eyed at the picture taker.

"He rolled over on some of his superiors, of course. The age-old cry of the footman butcher, you know? 'I was only following orders.' "

"Well, what do we care this son of a bitch is dead, then?"

"We care because it's our job," Girard replied. "Furthermore—listen, give me your best guess. Who killed Ackerman?"

Timothee gestured at the screen. "One of them. Or the brother or sister or son of one of the dead ones. He oversaw the systematic torture,

mutilation, and murder of thousands. Just because he was acquitted doesn't mean he's forgiven. *I* would have tracked him down, if one of mine had been in that camp."

"That's a good guess. Statistically, it makes the most sense. And you're right, in a way. I don't condone vigilantes. We can't. But maybe I wouldn't look far beyond the obvious, if I jumped to the conclusion you have. Maybe I would figure the killer was justified, and let it go at that."

"Damn straight."

"But that's why I keep my conclusions tentative. That's why I formulate alternate hypotheses. And if the one I've come up with is correct, I think you'll agree we should keep this investigation open."

"I don't see any alternative hypothesis."

"Well, you've blinded yourself then—not a good way to start an investigation. It's just like science, you know. You form various hypotheses and then you start testing them, or at least seeing which one best fits the facts you know."

"If you have a better fit for the data, what is it?"

"Maybe not a *better* fit, but I have *another* fit. There is another sort of man who might want to kill Ackerman, a sort with a motive other than revenge."

Timothee paused for a moment.

"Turn off the screen. It's distracting you. All you can think of is what you would do to a man involved in *that*."

Reluctantly, Timothee did so. He continued staring at the blank space where the picture had been.

"Well?" Girard asked, after a few moments.

"Holy shit."

"See?"

"You think it was someone else who *worked* at the camp? One of the war criminals who got away. Fernandez, or Hilo, or—" he paused "—*Bester*."

"Eh. La."

"Holy shit," he repeated. "One of the real mindfraggers, here in Paris? I thought they all were supposed to be off-world."

"Where would *you* hide? On a space station with a few hundred thousand, a colony world with a few million at best, or on Earth, hidden in a crowd of more than ten billion souls?"

Timothee sat open-mouthed for a few heartbeats, then lunged for his computer.

"We can cross-reference," he said, "find out who worked there, who was caught, who is dead, who—"

"—got away," Girard finished for him. "Only one, and you've already said his name."

But Timothee had it, now.

"Bester," he murmured. He might as well have been speaking the name of the Devil. "Alfred Bester. My God, if he's here in Paris—hey!" His screen went blank. He started working furiously to try to get it back.

Alarmed, Girard turned back to his own AI unit and found it similarly blank. It was still working, but when he tried to return to the screen with Bester on it, he got an icon that read "information not found."

"Uh-oh," he murmured.

"What happened?"

"I have no idea," Girard responded. "But I want to find out. We're supposed to have clear access to that database, and no one has the authority to cut us out of it. Not the EABI, nobody. When—"

At that moment, the com on his desk burred for attention. Girard stopped in midsentence, frowning. "Answer," he said.

"Picture?" the wall asked.

"Sure."

The screen came on, revealing a balding man of middle years. There was something very familiar about him, and when he spoke, recognition came. Girard had seen his face half a hundred times on ISN broadcasts.

"Hi," the face said—in English. "My name is Michael Garibaldi. And you would be Inspector Gerard?"

"Girard," Girard corrected.

"Whoops. Well, I guess that high-school French was a total waste, huh? Except there was this pretty blond thing who liked it an awful lot when I called her Ma'moiselle." He smiled. "But that's neither here nor there, is it? Look, it's come to my attention that you've been poking around in the law enforcement database that relates to one Alfred Bester."

"You're spying on me."

"Nooo, I'm spying on Alfred Bester's file. And keeping tabs on who looks at his file. That isn't strictly illegal, either. I checked."

"Yes? Well, neither is my viewing it."

"Of course not. But I think you oughta stop."

"It would seem I have no choice."

"Yeah, well, it looks like—by coincidence—there's been some sort of disruption in the system. Probably turn out to be solar flares, something like that, y'know? In an hour or so, you can probably access it again. That's how long it usually takes to get this sort of thing fixed."

"You sound like an authority on the matter."

"Authority? Me? Nah. Just an interested citizen who's seen his share of equipment breakdowns. Used to happen all the time on the station. All I'm sayin' is, when it comes back on line, I wouldn't look at Bester's file again, unless you want to be hip deep in feds from the EABI on down, that's all. And if you're like most locals I know—myself included, when I was a security officer—you don't want that."

"I'm not a security officer, Mr. Garibaldi. I'm an *agent de la police* of the city of Paris. I *have* to report this matter to the EABI—in a few hours, anyway."

"Maybe so, maybe not," Garibaldi said, though a brief look of approval flashed across his face. "I might be able to help with that, if there's reason. Why did you call up his file?"

"That's really not your business, Mr. Garibaldi."

"Look, I don't like to throw my weight around, but I'm making it my business. I can do it officially, which will make your life very hard—but what do I care? I *hate* Paris. It's not like you'll get a chance to spoil one of my vacations, or something. On the other hand, you and I can come to a friendly understanding, and help each other."

"I don't like being threatened."

"I wouldn't either, if I were in your shoes. But right now your choice is between me and some Metasensory squad from EA—and me. What's it gonna be?"

Girard let out an angry breath and tapped his desk for a few moments. Marsies. Worse than Americans.

"There's been a murder, an ex-convict named Ackerman. Professional job, but under odd circumstances. Ackerman was a telepath—he worked in the reeducation camp near Brasilia. I was just checking to see who his higher-ups might have been."

"Huh. You think someone did a 'see no evil, hear no evil' job on him, then. Bester?"

"A remote possibility."

"This telepath, do you know if he had a prescription for choline ribosylase?"

"I do not."

"Might want to check that—wait, I'll do it." There was a very brief pause, during which Garibaldi looked down at something. "Nope. Oh, well."

"Would that be significant?"

"You know it."

"Why?"

"Aha. Now you're getting interested in what I might have to say,

right? I can be a big help to you, if I want to be. And I'll give you this for free—it's not a bad bet that Bester is in Paris. It's worth checking out."

"I assure you, I'm doing so."

"I believe you, but Bester has slipped through my hands one time too many. This is the first thing like a real lead I've had in a long time. And I'll tell you this, if Bester really is involved, you can't trust Metasensory people from the EA or anywhere else. He still has people inside. If the EABI knows you're looking at this, Bester will know an hour later, and an hour after that he'll be so long-gone, he might as well be a passenger pigeon."

"If he did this, I'm thinking he's gone already."

"Maybe. But maybe not. He may be overconfident. There was another incident, a few weeks ago—"

"The attempted robbery of a pharmacy?"

Garibaldi's eyes widened. "Hey. I'm starting to like you. This could be the beginning of a beautiful friendship. You tell me why you link the two, and I'll share what I've got."

"In that case and in this one, some sort of device was used to override AI security devices. Not much of a link, really."

Then he listened intently as Garibaldi outlined his connection—the drug for a condition only telepaths contracted.

"That's very interesting," he allowed.

"It's more than interesting," Garibaldi said. "I think he was there. I think he's *still* there."

"And I still have to report it to Metasensory."

"No, you don't. I have friends in some pretty high places. Listen, you want this guy, right?"

"Of course."

"So do I. Only thing is, *I* don't care if I get credit for it. I just want to see it happen. I want to be there, if it's possible. So just hold off. You'll get confirmation in an hour or so from EarthGov, guaranteeing that you won't get in trouble for holding out on the psifeds. Some government guys will come in to oversee, but ones I trust, and I promise you they'll just fade away after the collar. It'll be all you, a local bust by the local man."

"And what do you get out of this?"

"Satisfaction. The satisfaction of finally seeing that bastard put where he belongs, in a cave so deep he'll have to look up to see hell. Take everything you've heard about Bester, leave out the stuff that's merely heinous, and raise the rest to the sixth power. Then you've just begun to understand what he's capable of."

"I sense a personal grudge."

"You have a problem with that?"

"Not if you don't. This is my city. If you come here with some idea of taking personal vengeance, I'll lock you up myself—I don't care *who* your friends are. Is that clear?"

"Clear as vacuum. I'm on my way. I'll be there in four days."

"And if I catch him before that?"

"You won't."

"You seem pretty sure of that."

"I am. See ya."

The contact broke.

Girard gave another sigh, but then shrugged his shoulders. One more thing to keep his mind off the unsolvable problems, anyway.

He turned to find Timothee staring with eyes like saucers.

"Do you know who that *was*?"

"Of course."

"He's friends with Sheridan himself."

"So I hear. Things will become very interesting in a few days, if we don't have our man. I intend to prove Mr. Garibaldi wrong. I intend to catch Bester before he arrives. So let's not waste any time. If you were a war criminal and in Paris, where would you hide?"

Timothee snorted. "In the government. Where else?"

For the first time in days, Girard felt a genuine smile crease his face.

Garibaldi made his flight arrangements, then kicked back and gazed at the ceiling.

Lise was going to kill him.

Boy, what a schmo he'd been, convincing himself he didn't give a damn about Bester anymore. Of *course* he did, and anyone in his position would feel the same.

But his was a position that allowed him—no, *obligated* him—to do something about it.

Still, Lise would kill him. Maybe he should come up with a little white lie, in case none of this panned out. Tell her there was some emergency situation he had to attend to, right away. At least that way she wouldn't worry about him.

Probably Bester was gone already, anyway. He was too smart to hang around after a murder. Even the cleanest murder was a mess, right?

But something deeper—that monster-sniffing animal in him—didn't believe it. Something had happened. Something had changed in Bester's pattern. The bastard had some reason for hanging in Paris long after it

wasn't smart to do so. He didn't know what, but he knew it, knew it in his ever-more-creaky bones.

This time Bester wasn't getting away without a fight. This time it was Bester, or him.

And he knew who *he* was betting on.

wasn't up to do so. It didn't know what. But he knew it knew it in his more-creaky bones.

This time it was. wasn't going away without a fight. This time it was beaten or not.

And no, knew who he was betting on.

6

Bester returned from Le Cheval Heureux, mulling over what he was going to do for the next day's column. He found himself in the unfortunate position of having liked the book he had just read. Not just liked a few things about it, but truly enjoyed it from start to finish.

Which, by his own criteria, didn't make it worth reviewing. Oh, he could nitpick about the strand of slightly disingenuous naiveté that ran through the work, except that, in context, it *worked*. He could point out that the demiplot was cribbed from Shakespeare's *Tempest,* except that it had clearly been a deliberate and charming homage, with nods to other liftings from the immortal bard—most amusingly, *Forbidden Planet.*

So what was he to do? He was in a critic's hell. He had no choice but to lie or not do a column, since his deadline was only hours away.

He could tell the truth and say he liked it, but who would want to hear that? His readers would assume he had sold out, was turning into another saccharine-spewing lapdog for the publishing industry.

The thought brought a small grin to his face. Was this the worst of his troubles? It seemed so. Almost a week had passed since he had silenced Justin, and the murder hadn't so much as made the papers. He was back in touch with his contact inside Metasensory, and they had heard nothing. Fortunately, this contact was one he knew he could trust.

Ford is in his tower and all is right with the world, he thought.

Now *there* was a book he hated. Why couldn't he have picked one of the thousands of insipid dystopian allegories that crammed the shelves these days, to read and trash?

He supposed it was because he couldn't bear to read another. Ah, well.

He reached the hotel just in time to almost bump into Lucien d'Alambert. Bester's grin widened as he caught the cop's disgruntled surface thoughts—surely he had come to see Louise, *not* Bester.

Lucien surprised him, however. "Ah, Mr. Kaufman. Just the man I wanted to talk to."

"Good afternoon to you, too, Officer," Bester replied. "I hope you've had a good day."

"Could have been better, could have been worse," Lucien replied.

"Well, that's the best most of us can ask for, I suppose," Bester said, brightly.

"Hmm. That's not what you said about *The Fugitive Paragon.*"

"You read my column?"

"I suppose I do," the officer replied.

"Well, it's always nice to meet a fan."

Lucien quirked his mouth. "I wouldn't exactly call myself a fan. You're much too harsh, in my opinion."

"People are more interested in reading things they disagree with than things they don't, I've found. It's the nature of the beast. But what can I do for you, Officer d'Alambert?"

"You can tell me about Jem."

"Jem. Jem. You mean the street thug I met my first day here?"

"I'm sure you remember him. He was about to *dis*member you?"

"Yes, of course. I never forget a threat. What about him?"

"You may have read that he was killed trying to break into a pharmacy downtown, some weeks ago."

"Louise mentioned it, yes. I can't say I was surprised. Were you?"

"Actually, I was, for a couple of reasons. Jem had his fingers in a lot of things, but he rarely put himself deliberately at risk, especially these last few years. He didn't have to—he had lackeys for that.

"And his lackeys, I think, were genuinely puzzled by the whole business. None of them seems to have been in on the robbery, even though we know a man escaped."

Bester frowned. "Well, that's very interesting, I suppose, if you are a police officer investigating the man—but I'm not. This Jem was a bother to Louise, and I'm just as glad he's gone."

"That's the other thing. He stopped bothering Louise right after you came along."

Bester raised his eyebrows. "Did you know that upward of ninety-nine percent of the people who contract cancer wear shoes?"

"What's that supposed to mean?"

"I mean a simple correlation doesn't show cause and effect. Do you honestly think I had something to do with Jem's change of heart? Louise thought perhaps *you* did something, after the fire. I supposed the same thing, since you were clearly interested in her. In fact, I wonder if that doesn't motivate a lot of things you do."

"I'm not in love with her. I care about her, and I don't want to see her mixed up with the wrong sort of people, that's all."

"Like Jem."

"For one."

"And me, for another? Is there something wrong with me, other than the fact that I'm not *you*?"

The policeman's face clenched. "Look, this has nothing to do with how I do or don't feel about Louise. It's got to do with a police investigation in this neighborhood. In fact, I hate to admit it, but you seem to be good for Louise—*seem* to be. But I'll be frank, Mr. Kaufman—there's something not quite right about you. Your record is clean, too clean, really. And nothing in it explains why a man of your background and means would come here, live in a small hotel, and start writing a newspaper column."

"I thought this wasn't about me?"

"I didn't say that, Mr. Kaufman. I said it wasn't about my feelings toward Louise. You may be right—Jem's peculiar behavior and your arrival might be sheer coincidence, but I only resort to coincidence as a means of explaining something I can't explain in any other way. You can help me eliminate some possibilities by clearing up why you came here and why you stay here."

Bester cocked his head. "I thought you were a street cop, not a detective."

Lucien was silent for a few seconds, then he sighed. "Yes. I am. What I'm doing now is . . . outside the job. There *is* an investigation. A detective downtown, and some feds of some sort. They've gotten interested in Jem all over again. They're searching through his old place, interviewing his cronies. They talked to me, of course, since this neighborhood is my beat. Here's the thing, Mr. Kaufman—I *always* thought you had something to do with what happened to Jem. A friend in the mob, an old black-ops contact, *something*. I didn't care, really. The neighborhood is a lot better off without him, and the investigation didn't get very far when they found out who he was and what sort of fellow he was.

"But now, they're digging deeper. Now, Louise is in love with you—yes, everyone knows that. I don't want to see her hurt, and I don't want her implicated. I'm certain she can't be tied up in this, because I know her, have known her for years. But this detective from downtown, he *doesn't* know her. And when he finds out all of the facts, he's going to be suspicious of you, just as I am. And he's going to be suspicious of Louise because she benefited from it. If you go down for this, Mr. Kaufman, it *will* hurt Louise—"

"But you'll be right there to pick up the pieces, won't you?"

"It will hurt her," Lucien continued, stubbornly, "and she has al-

ready been hurt enough. But worse, she might also end up paying for your crime."

"What crime?" Bester snapped. "This is all in your head."

"Then why won't you answer my questions?"

"Because they're *personal.*"

Lucien said nothing, but looked skeptical.

"Look," Bester said. "You may not understand this, but I'm eighty-two years old. That's a bad age to realize you've been on the wrong track all of your life. How much longer will I live? Ten years? Twenty? Thirty or forty, if I'm lucky. I want to live the life I missed, Officer D'Alambert. I want to laugh, and do work I enjoy, and sit in the sun. I've seen a hundred planets, and I want to forget them all.

"I first came to Paris when I was fifteen. *Fifteen.* Do you remember how much potential you had when you were fifteen? How many things you had in you, how many buds just waiting to bloom if the right kind of rain came along? I fell in love with this city then. What did I do about it? Nothing. I went on to waste everything important that was in me, squander it, sacrifice it to the gods of success, while everyone I loved and cared for died.

"That happens to everyone, I suppose, but most people fill those gaps in their lives, make new friends, take new lovers. I didn't. If I had made a deliberate plan to become a heartsick, lonely old man I couldn't have done it better. Then one day, I saw it. I faced the truth, and I came back here, and I walked until I saw something interesting. Here. I didn't know it, but I fell in love with Louise the instant she spoke to me. How could I know? I had forgotten what love was. I couldn't even conceive of it. Now . . ." He broke off, folding his face into what he was sure was a convincing simulacrum of on-the-verge-of-tears.

He looked back up at the officer, who stood silently. Bester knew why. When Bester met people, he mentally profiled them, sorting clues from surface thoughts, from actions, from the congruence and incongruence of word, thought, and expression. He had chosen his words carefully, almost scientifically. He knew d'Alambert shared many of these feelings, knew the man couldn't help but sympathize. Just then, the officer was seeing himself in forty years or so, lonely, in search of elusive truth, of love.

"Look, I won't say I didn't wish Jem harm," Bester said, softly. "I won't say I'm sorry about what happened to him. But if you don't want Louise hurt, imagine how *I* feel. She's the first human being I've loved since before you were born. That's a special kind of love, Officer d'Alambert, one I sincerely hope you never have the opportunity to ap-

preciate. But if you do, I can only hope it is with someone as precious as Louise."

The two men stood there on the street, facing each other. Then the cop nodded slowly. "I've a suspicious mind," d'Alambert finally said. "I can't help it. And you're right, I did—do—have feelings for Louise. I'm also smart enough to know she won't ever return them." He met Bester's gaze, squarely. "I won't help them, won't point them here, but they'll come. Maybe I believe you—about not having anything to do with Jem. But they'll still come, turning over rocks. When you turn over rocks, you usually find something unpleasant underneath. I hope you're ready for that, and I hope Louise is."

"I've got a clear conscience," Bester replied. "They can ask anything they want."

"I'm relieved to hear it. Well, good day, Mr. Kaufman." He held out his hand.

Bester shook it and smiled. "I hope one day you'll trust me, and be happy for me."

"So do I," the policeman replied. "It would make me a better man."

Bester's breath quickened as he started up the stairs to his room. It had nothing to do with the stairs. For once, he was glad Louise wasn't around. She and her sister had taken a day trip into the country and wouldn't return until late that night.

Why were they investigating again? Could they link him to Jem somehow? What if someone had seen him coming and going from the thug's apartment?

When he got upstairs, he poured half a glass of port to calm his nerves, but he kept hearing Garibaldi's voice, on the phone.

I'm coming for you.

He threw the glass against the wall, suppressing the urge to scream. It shattered, and wine ran down the wall like thin blood.

Oh, wonderful. Louise will notice that.

He went to the bathroom, soaked a rag in cold water, and tried to wipe the wall clean. But of course it wouldn't come clean. The color faded to pink, but anyone walking into the room would still see it, still—

—and now the wallpaper was starting to tear.

What had he done wrong?

But that was a stupid question. He had done everything wrong. Coming to Earth, falling in love—yes, falling in love.

If he had just kept walking, let Jem go on with what he was doing, he wouldn't be in this mess. If he hadn't been playing tourist like some silly boy, he would never have gone to the Eiffel Tower and seen Justin again.

Or even if he had, he would just have mindwiped him and left town, left the damned planet, headed back out where it was safe . . .

His heart was hammering, too hard for an old man. He sat on the bed, put his face into his good hand, ground the balled, white-knuckled hand into his knee.

"Did you do this to me, Byron? Are you still in there? Did you do this to me?"

It made a certain amount of sense. It was as if a part of him had been planning this all along, planning to back himself into a corner, painting big bright arrows on the universe with notes screaming *Look here for Alfred Bester! Look here!*

"Byron?"

But Byron wasn't there, hadn't been there since the night he had let him go.

So the problem was with him, Alfred Bester.

No, the problem was with the world. How could a world—a *race* he had served so well, despite their hatred for him—think of this as just? Part of him must have refused to believe it. Part of him had somehow imagined that it would all go away, if he pretended hard enough.

But they wouldn't go away. They hadn't gone away, leaving his first mentor, Sandoval Bey, in peace. They had killed him, the best man Bester had ever known. And they had killed Brett. Oh, yes, Brett pulled the trigger himself, but there was never any doubt in Bester's mind as to who had really killed him. Or Carolyn—they had gotten her, too. And how many times had they tried to get Alfred Bester?

Well, they wouldn't. If he accomplished nothing else in what remained of his life, it would be denying them all the satisfaction. Garibaldi and his cronies, Metasensory—all of the faces that *they* now wore. He was old, but he was smarter than them, better than them. He always had been.

Maybe he had done all of this just to prove that to himself. Subconsciously he had needed a real challenge. He remembered reading about certain head-hunting tribes who considered it more prestigious to return from war with the head of a woman or a child than with that of another warrior, because that meant that they must have gone into the heart of the enemy's territory, entered the village itself, killed, and escaped carrying the unwieldy trophy.

Was that what he was doing, in essence? Letting them get near enough almost to taste him, then dancing forever out of their reach?

Why was he having to second-guess himself? Was he finally losing his mind?

He realized he was weeping. *Stupid old man. You think you love her, but it's all been a part of your game . . .*

Liar.

For an instant he thought that was Byron again, but it wasn't.

He sat there, taking deep breaths, growing calmer. His mind stopped darting about like a trapped rat, and began to work rationally again.

I'm Alfred Bester. Bester. Alfred Bester. Remember who you are!

They didn't have him yet. This all might still slide right past him. The reinvestigation of Jem might have nothing to do with him after all. Panicking. Yes, that was what he was doing, panicking like some green Blip with a bloodhound squad after him. He could afford to wait a bit. Be careful, but wait. Stay the course, not let on that anything was wrong. He could do that, and watch, and wait.

But he might as well be prepared. When the time came, he might have to go on a minute's notice.

So he thumbed on his pocket tel-phone, dialed a number he had hoped never to dial, and spoke to someone he hoped never to speak to again. He was smooth again, composed. He cajoled, he threatened, and within five minutes, a new identity began taking shape. A new *him,* somewhere safe.

Then he called his contact in EABI Metasensory. She still hadn't heard anything. He still trusted her, too. She couldn't deceive him, in that most precious meaning of the word *couldn't*—the literal one. He told her to take extra care, watch extra hard.

Then he lay on the bed, doing relaxation exercises. When he felt Louise come home, hours later, he put on his best smile and went down to see her, to ask how her day had been, to make small talk.

Rain made Michael Garibaldi nervous, more nervous than the hard, invisible sleet of radiation from a solar flare or the remorseless, terrible arrival of a Martian sandstorm—though intellectually he knew it shouldn't.

But there were just certain things water ought not to do. It ought not to collect in pools miles deep and thousands of miles wide. It ought not to form grinding, juggernaut mountains. And damn it, it ought not to fall out of the sky.

He was explaining this to Derrick Thompson as they made their way down a Parisian street, shoved by crowds of rude people with umbrellas. "I mean, water is dangerous stuff. It corrodes metals. It's a conductor. It carries all sorts of diseases and parasites—"

"Rain doesn't carry disease," Thompson disagreed, reasonably.

"Yeah? I'm not so sure. Every time I get caught in this stuff I come down with a cold."

"I enjoy the rain," Thompson said. "Not so much like this; I enjoy the sound and the smell of a good thunderstorm."

"Oh, yeah, perfect. Uncontrolled gigavolts of electricity jumping down from the sky. Wonderful."

"I've had other Marsies tell me rain was a real revelation when they first felt it—brought them back into contact with their ancient Human roots."

"I don't believe it. They're making it up. The only roots I've ever discovered in the rain are the ones that try to grow out of my toes. And the only thing I want to get in touch with is a healthy—" He stopped short, appalled. He had almost said "shot of scotch." *Damn,* he could almost taste it. "—cup of coffee," he finished.

"Coffee is a tropical plant. Doesn't grow so well without rain," Thompson pointed out.

"Coffee grows in little bags labeled 'coffee,' as far as I'm concerned," Garibaldi said. "Here, this looks like as good a place as any."

They ducked into a café-looking place. It was crowded—some Parisians, at least, shared his feelings about the unnatural thing the sky was doing—but they managed to find a table. He took his duster off and slung it over the back of a rickety wooden chair, brushed droplets from his stubbly scalp, and looked around for service.

"Don't hold your breath," Thompson told him.

"Oh, right. Paris." His face showed what he thought of Parisian service. "So, what do you have to report?"

"Two possible sightings at the airport. One witness gave me permission to scan, and yes, I think it was him."

"Happy birthday to me," Garibaldi said. "What name was he going under?"

"*That* we couldn't recover, but he's probably changed it already anyway. That's his pattern—travel under one name, then trade it once he lands someplace."

"Right. But sometimes people break patterns. He's broken his here, I'm pretty sure. The question is, why?"

"Could he have family here?"

"Family? You know better than that. Bester wasn't just raised by the Corps, they gave *birth* to him. There are absolutely no records linking him to any other human being."

"I noticed that. That's weird, even for the old Psi Corps. Keeping track of genealogies, notably for breeding purposes, was everything, especially back then."

"*Especially* back then?" Garibaldi echoed, suspiciously.

Thompson colored. "Well, uh, of course teep marriages aren't arranged, like they used to be."

"But you guys still like to marry each other."

"Sure. It's hard enough making a marriage work between any two people, but if one's a teep and the other is a mun—uh, *not* a teep, it's even harder."

"Uh-huh. People used to say that about mixed-race marriages."

"They still do, on Earth, some places. You don't think racism is a thing of the past, do you?"

"I don't think we've lost *any* of our old baggage," Garibaldi said, "just put it in prettier bags."

"No offense, but I find it odd to hear you say that, considering your attitude toward teeps."

"What do you mean?"

"You wouldn't marry one, would you?"

"Nope. I wouldn't want a wife who knew my every thought."

"That's not how we operate. One of the first things we learn is to respect the privacy of others."

"Sure. Just like one of the first things I learned was that it's not polite to eavesdrop, but that doesn't mean I didn't catch my parents fighting, sometimes, hear them saying things they never meant me to hear. And I sure as hell knew I shouldn't peep on my buddy Devin's older sister when she was in the shower, but I did that, too." He hunched forward, lacing his fingers together. "When I was first assigned to Babylon 5, I was buddies with a Centauri named Londo—"

"Mollari? *The* Emperor Londo? You were *friends* with him?"

"Things were different then. *He* was different then. In a way, I think I'm still his friend. Anyway, that's beside the point. At the time, the Centaurum was in bad shape. The Narn had just invaded one of their colonies, and some relative of Londo's was there. The telepath on the station, Talia Winters, was probably one of the most scrupulous, law-abiding people I've ever known. Well, until—" he looked down at the table "—nope, that's a different story. Anyway, she just chanced to bump into Londo as he came out of a lift. Damn good thing, as it turned out, because she accidentally picked up on the fact that Londo was on his way to assassinate the Narn ambassador. She told me, and I managed to stop him without any fuss or muss."

"And this wasn't a good thing?"

"Sure it was. But that's not the point. It got me thinking about Talia."

"You had a *thing* for her."

"See? Now *you're* doing it," Garibaldi accused.

"Baloney. I saw it on your face."

"How do you know? How can you tell? Maybe when you *think* you're reading expressions you're really subliminally picking up on my surface thoughts. Maybe you've been associating the two for so long you don't know the difference."

"I doubt that."

"But you don't *know.*" He leaned back again. "She slapped me one time, you know. Talia."

"I bet you deserved it."

"No. I was looking at her—well, never mind what I was looking at. And I was thinking—no, never mind that, too. But she *knew,* even though I was standing so she couldn't see my face. That's not right. It's not what we *think* that's important, it's what we *do.* I'd go crazy if I thought my private thoughts weren't private, and anyone else would, too. As a telepath, you don't have that worry. *You* can sense those things—*you* can block them. I can't. So no, I wouldn't marry a telepath."

"And ninety percent of normals would agree with you. So why this objection to us marrying each other?"

Garibaldi looked at him frankly. "Because it's making us different species. Competing species. And competing species fight. Look, the big fallacy behind racism is the belief that people with different skin colors have different innate abilities, that one is superior to the other. That's not true, but people like to believe it because people generally like to think they're superior. But when one group of people has something that really *does* make them superior, it only gets worse. Pretty soon they get bored with treating their inferiors as equals."

"That's funny," Thompson cut in. He was becoming angry. "Of all of the violence and flat-out pogroms I can think of in the history of telepathy, not *one* has involved telepaths slaughtering normals. But I can think of a damned lot of mass killings of telepaths *by* normals."

"You're forgetting Bester; he and his thugs killed normals aplenty. And that was just the beginning for him, as the hearings proved. If the telepath war hadn't come along—"

"Bester is one man. You can't judge us all by him."

"There'll be more Besters. One day one of them will get the ball rolling."

"Really? More Besters? So why do you care so much about *this* Bester, who happens to be the real, actual Bester?"

Garibaldi grinned. "*The Three Amigos*? I knew I liked you, Thompson. Why *this* Bester? Look, I'm not Sheridan. I'm not out to save the universe or anything. I just call things like I see 'em and do the best I can for me and mine. Bester—you remember that telepath I was talking about? Talia?"

"The one with the nice 'whatever'?"

"Yeah. Nothing ever happened between us, but she was a friend. I thought she was. And yeah, if she had *wanted* something to happen . . . Well, like Londo, I was different then. But the Talia I knew wasn't real.

"Bester and his buddies had reamed her out, built a fake personality, hidden the real, nasty her way down deep. Or maybe it was the other way around. Maybe the woman I liked was the real person, and the buried creation ate her alive. Whatever the case, Talia, as I knew her, died because of Bester. And that was just the start of it. That was before he got inside of *me*. I won't try to pretty this up, because I don't think it needs prettying up. Revenge is a long and honorable tradition, in its own way. Nobody is going to cry over Bester."

"Are you saying—"

"I'm saying, Junior, that when the time comes, don't you be in my line of fire."

Thompson seemed to struggle with that for a moment, then nodded. "I understand."

"Good. I'm glad we're clear on that."

"So what about this war you see coming between telepaths and normals? You don't think separation is the answer, but you can't see your way clear to actually mingling your genes with ours either."

Garibaldi sighed. "I don't know. There was a time—" He remembered Edgars' telepath virus and shuddered internally. "I thought there was an answer. Now I'm just content to hope it happens after my time, and after my daughter's time. Maybe a miracle will happen and we'll all just learn how to get along."

"I think the new laws are a good start to that."

"Maybe. Or maybe they're just window dressing. Time will tell." He looked up. "Where's the damned waiter? I'm all for French atmosphere, but this is ridiculous. Hey, you! *Garçon!*" A narrow face turned toward him, and he belatedly realized that the server was female. Oops. He *was* getting old.

The server came over. "Yes, madame?" she asked, coldly.

"Sorry about that. We'd like some coffee."

"As you wish," she replied. "And you?"

"Just coffee," Thompson said.

"I will do my best to fill such a difficult and complex order," she said, and walked off.

"Anyway," Garibaldi said, rolling his eyes, "we got way off course. The question of the hour is, why has Bester broken his pattern? And why did he break it in Paris?"

"Why not? Who would notice him here? He grew up in Geneva, so he probably speaks French as well as he speaks English, if not better. Most of the landlords in this city won't bother checking into you as long as you pay your rent on time—minding your own business is an art form here. Plenty of places to go, if he has to run. Borders are pretty easy to cross these days, with the exception of those around planets. If he leaves Paris tonight, he could be anywhere on Earth by tomorrow morning."

"I want someone at every airport and train station and especially at the spaceports."

"Fine. So he'll rent a car and drive out. Or take a bicycle. You can't button up Paris with anything short of an army backed by martial law. And seeing as how you're trying not to let the EABI in on this—which I still think is a mistake—you can't muster a fraction of that kind of manpower, even if you have it."

"So we'll have to sniff him out. How close would you have to be to sense him?"

"You're kidding, right? I only met the man once, and anyway, I don't have any training as a tracker. What you need is a Metasensory tracking unit, and you know it."

"He has a man inside. I know he does. The minute Metasensory knows he's here will be sixty seconds before he's gone."

His coffee arrived. He thanked the girl and took a sip. It was good—damn good. Better than what he could usually get on Mars.

His tel-phone trilled. He took it out and opened it up. "Garibaldi," he said.

It was Inspector Girard. "Mr. Garibaldi, I have some good news for you, if you'd like to come hear it."

Garibaldi was more imposing in person than on the vids. Not physically—he was actually smaller than Girard had imagined. But he had an effortless presence, an energy, that made one feel rather—ordinary.

"So what's the big news?" he asked, draping himself onto the chair that Girard kept in his office to make his visitors uncomfortable. Somehow Garibaldi defied the hard wood and sharp angles, made himself look perfectly at ease.

"The thug who was killed in the pharmacy break-in, Jemelah Perdue. One of his neighbors saw a man visit him a few weeks ago. A man fitting Bester's description."

That got his attention. His eyebrows arched, his eyes widened—Girard could almost swear his *ears* pricked up.

"Do tell. This just in?"

Girard bit back a sarcastic comment. He was starting to wonder if having Garibaldi and his goon squad around was any better than having Metasensory straddling him. He settled for an icy "Yes."

"What does that mean?"

"Perdue ran a small-time organization in the Pigalle—drugs, protection rackets, and so forth. He was very, ah, local. Didn't usually do things outside the boundaries of his territory."

"Let me guess. Except for the drugstore heist."

"Exactly."

"So let's assume this witness wasn't high on monkey grass or something, and he really saw Bester. That means maybe the man who got away was Bester himself."

"I wouldn't think so. More likely another of Perdue's people."

"No, it was Bester. You don't know him like I do. Bester isn't a coward. He's a real hands-on kind of guy. I'm betting he got what he came for—the inhibitor—and replaced the ampoules with water or something. I guess it's too late to check that now. But I bet he arranged

for this Perdue fellow to die there, to throw you off the track. *Damn!* I almost dug deeper into that back then. Why didn't I?" He looked back at Girard. "So how did Bester know this man?"

"What do you think I am, the answer wizard from *Science Kingdom*?" Girard asked, irritably. He had had a hard night. Marie had called—called his *house*. He had tried to get rid of her as quickly as possible, but his wife had known, of course. Not that it was a secret anymore, and not that his wife would forgive him any time soon, but he had sworn to her that he wouldn't talk to Marie again. His wife had said nothing after the call, hadn't cried or raged. She just poured herself a glass of vodka and sat there, staring into space.

"He must have been involved with Perdue before," Girard heard himself saying. "They must have had some relationship before the pharmacy job."

"Would that mean Bester was a local? That he lived in the area?"

Flash. Two men confront each other, men from very different worlds. One is at the pinnacle of his short career, the leader of a pack of losers and thugs. The other was once something much, much more. They've met the way Jemelah—no, everyone called him "Jem," yes?—Jem always meets new people. When he threatens to break their arms. He's made a mistake, though, a bad one, and doesn't know it.

The other man is Bester, and he knows Jem has made a mistake. Jem has come to hurt him, or extort from him. Bester can break his mind. But Bester thinks, "This fellow might be of some use, down the road." Then, one day, Garibaldi cuts off Bester's supply of a needed drug, and Bester knows that the day has arrived, that it's time Jem paid in full . . .

"Yes," Girard said. "He might even be a shop owner, or something. Someone Jem tried to extort protection from."

"Jem? You guys on a first-name basis all of a sudden?"

"Perdue. Jem was what the locals called him."

"So this Pigalle, can we seal that off? Quietly?"

"With all of the men and equipment you brought? Maybe so." He made sure his disapproval registered, however.

Garibaldi was more perceptive than he seemed. In fact, Girard was beginning to think that when the man seemed to miss some insinuation, it was deliberate. "You're the one who knows the city. How do you think we ought to proceed?"

"With the local gendarmes, the ones who know the place back and forth. But we can set up a plainclothes perimeter, using some of that spying equipment you brought, establish an HQ in the area."

"My friend Thompson here is a telepath. He might be able to get a read just walking around, or something."

"Better we wait until we have something to read, yes?"

Garibaldi nodded reluctantly. "Yeah."

"Something wrong, Mr. Garibaldi?"

"It just seems like we're so close," he said. "Too close, too easy. Makes me nervous. And Bester as a shop owner? That's ridiculous. I wonder if this is another one of his elaborate false trails?"

"Well, we won't know until we find out, will we?"

"Nope. You can't break eggs without breaking a few eggs. Or something like that."

"Something *like* that, I should hope, since that made no sense at all."

Garibaldi shrugged. "Wait till you meet Bester. His sense of humor will *slay* you."

Girard grinned ruefully. "You Marsies. Sometimes I think everything you say is explained on a need-to-know basis—and I have no need to know."

Garibaldi's face went flat. "Is that a French expression? Where did you hear that?"

Girard was taken aback by the violence of Garibaldi's reaction. "I suppose it's French. It's just a thing some people are saying these days. I think it comes from a popular literary or movie critic or something."

"A movie critic."

"Yes, I think so. Kaufman? Something like that. Why?"

Garibaldi's face relaxed again. "Nothing, I guess. Just nerves. Well. Shall we go catch ourselves a telepath?"

8

They took Louise's sister to the train station the next morning, where the two women hugged and wept a little.

The major spared a hug for him, too. "Take care of my little sister," she whispered into his ear. "She's more fragile than she seems. But I think she's in good hands."

"I would never do anything to hurt her," Bester replied.

She released him from the embrace and stepped back. "You two will come visit me next, of course. Louise, this was too long. Let's not let it happen again, no?"

"No," Louise said.

The depth of what the two women felt for each other was almost more than Bester could take. It made him feel small, and it made the things he *felt* feel small. Fraudulent.

That's not fair, he thought as they walked her up to the platform. *I'm risking my very life for Louise. What could be more real than that?*

When the train left, he felt a sudden terrific urge to be on it.

"Let's take a trip," he told Louise, abruptly.

"What? To where?"

"Anywhere. The south of France. London."

"Oh, Claude, that sounds wonderful. When shall we go?"

"Now. This minute."

"You crazy man! I just got back from a trip."

"So?"

"And I'm not packed."

"I've got plenty of money, and I just got a raise from the paper. We'll buy what we need as we go."

She laughed and kissed him. "You *are* crazy. What a wonderful, romantic notion. But impossible. I was gone for a week, and I've neglected things while Genny was here. I need a few days, at least, to get everything back on track."

"We'll have lost the impulse by then," Bester argued. "When one has a romantic impulse, one must act on it right then."

She frowned prettily. "You *are* serious about this."

"Yes. Absolutely."

She hesitated, and hesitated longer. All he had to do was push her, just a little, just nudge the part of her brain that loved him, loved this idea. And then, and then, he would find some way to explain, some way that would leave her still loving him, and—

—and the moment passed. Her mind settled and set like concrete, so that it would have taken a *real* push to change it. "I'm sorry, love," she said, fondling his hand. "I just can't, right now. I don't want to. I want to sleep in my own bed, with *you* in it. I want to putter around the hotel. Can't we find some way to make that romantic?"

He laughed it off. "Of course," he said. "It was just an idea."

"And a sweet one. A wonderful one. I never knew you could be so spontaneous."

But he understood, suddenly, that one of the reasons she loved him was his normal *lack* of spontaneity. Her husband had been spontaneous, romantic, impulsive.

Those things could turn on you. The same childlike whimsy that could seem so charming when it suggested a sudden trip to Spain was much less charming when it turned into an impulse to go off alone, on foot, unburdened by marriage and commitments.

"I'm usually not," he said, to reassure her. "I think I was just going a little stir-crazy without you around, and then sharing you with your sister. But when we get back, it will be just the two of us, won't it?"

She smiled. "Why don't we just go see how that works out, right now?"

Later that night, when she was asleep, he got up and checked the messages stored in his tel-phone. There was one he was expecting. He keyed it up. It was his government contact.

"Your new papers are on the way. They'll arrive by special courier. Good luck, sir. Some of us are still rooting for you."

He smiled thinly, and without humor, then erased the message. Then he went back to bed.

Garibaldi looked over the rooftops of Paris, restless.

"Somewhere down in there," one of the local policemen told him. "That's the Pigalle."

"Huh." The streets looked like worm trails. He could see this be-

cause they were both on a hill, standing in a room on the top floor of a four-story building.

When you lay in wait for a telepath, it was best to keep out of any possible line of sight, let mindless electronic machines do the watching for you. Garibaldi kept this in mind, even though it was unlikely Bester even knew he was in the city. Banks of screens were reporting, focusing on each person they observed, comparing the images with lightning speed against a fund of possible ways in which Bester might have altered his appearance.

Chemical sniffers were doing their job, as well—everyone in the world had a different chemical composition, so everyone left a signature trail of compounds behind them. Of course, it was a blurry signature, since diet caused it to vary, and air pollution muddied the picture even more. So the sniffers put up a lot of false red flags, most of which could be discounted within seconds by cross-referencing them with the visual images.

Thompson came up, obviously excited. He had just been on the phone with Girard.

"What's the latest?" Garibaldi asked.

"One of the local cops thinks he knows Bester. He's staying at a local hotel."

"Why haven't we grabbed him yet?"

"He was out. The cop didn't say anything to the landlady because apparently she and Bester have some sort of thing going."

"Really. I guess there really *is* someone for everyone. Especially if you're a telepath."

"What?" Thompson's excitement was replaced with equally apparent irritation.

"Hey, don't get touchy. I'm not talking about you, or any normal telepath. I'm talking about *Bester.* This guy doesn't hesitate in the slightest to screw with people's minds to get what he wants. How else would a dried-up bastard like him get a girlfriend? He probably thought it would be good cover."

"Didn't you tell me he had a lover before? One that the Shadows did something to?"

"Yep. She was a Blip, one of his prisoners. *You* figure it out."

"Sir?" That was one of his team.

"Yeah?"

"Possible positive from both chemical and visual sensors."

"Hot damn. Which location?"

"This one, sir."

"You mean right below us?"

"Yes, sir."

Garibaldi was in motion before the affirmative was even out of the man's mouth.

He took the stairs, bounding down four and five at a time. His knees might complain about it later, but for now they were just fine. He felt twenty years younger.

On the street he did a quick right-left-right. "Which one?" he asked to his link.

"The one in the checked shirt, about a hundred meters to your left, now."

Thompson burst from the stairwell behind him, puffing.

"Cover me," Garibaldi commanded. He palmed his PPG and ran up the street. The possible looked right from the back—the right build, right hair color.

A couple stepped from a side street, and he bumped the woman. She shouted in outrage, and the man yelled after him. He didn't even slow. Surely Bester had heard that, and would bolt.

But he hadn't. He was just walking along like nothing happened, and then Garibaldi was on him, swinging him around—

The frightened face confronting him wasn't Bester. Plastic surgery?

No. Bester would be there, in the eyes. It wasn't him. Unless, unless he was playing some sort of fraggin' mind trick.

"Mr. Garibaldi. Stop. Stop it. That's not him."

That was Thompson, tugging at his elbow. Garibaldi suddenly realized he had the PPG pointed in the man's face, and that the man was gibbering in French.

"You sure, Thompson? Could he be screwing with me?"

"No. I'd know. I promise you. Put your gun away."

"Yeah," Garibaldi said. "Yeah. I guess I oughta do that." He released the man, who backed quickly away, shouting. They had drawn a small crowd, now—a disapproving one.

Man. I'm really letting this get to me, he thought. He put the gun back in his pocket. "Sorry, folks, show's over," he said, as jovially as he could manage. "Just a little mistake." He drew a deep breath.

"Are you okay?" Thompson asked.

"Yeah. Damn. Poor guy." From long habit, he scanned the street carefully. Getting shot in the back once in his life was plenty, thank you, and Bester was still out there, wasn't he? It would be just like him to send out someone matching his physical description, to create a distraction. He wished, now, he had questioned the fellow.

He laughed, suddenly. "Now *that's* paranoid," he said.

"What?"

"Hmm? I was just imagining Bester, when he was three, secretly manipulating the genes of some other kids, making Bester-look-alikes and smell-alikes. Planting them all over the world." He broke off again. "It's the waiting. It's getting to me."

A man in a magazine stand shouted something at him, probably for him to get moving. Garibaldi realized that people were still keeping their distance—who wouldn't, after all? He was a crazy man who'd been waving a gun. Crazy men with guns probably weren't good for this guy's business.

"Hey, sorry," he said, producing a few credits. "I'll buy something." Then he remembered Girard's comment from the day before. "Ah, which paper does that movie critic write for?"

The man looked as if he was going to pretend he didn't speak English, but apparently decided an answer might get Garibaldi to go away all the more quickly. "All of them have movie critics."

"You know the one. The 'need-to-know-basis' guy."

"Oh. *Book* critique," he said. *You idiot Marsie/American/non-Frenchman* was only implied, but Garibaldi heard it, nonetheless. "Here." He handed Garibaldi a paper.

He found the column as he was walking back toward the building. No picture. *That* was suspicious.

"It's in French."

"Of course," Thompson said. "You want me to read it to you?"

"You know French?"

"No. But I thought I would offer anyway. Yes, of course I can read French. I'll translate it for you."

Garibaldi handed him the paper. Thompson studied it for a few moments, then cleared his throat and began reading.

"There are moments in literature, rare and wonderful, that stretch us as human beings, push us beyond our ordinary boundaries of thought and experience. *A Gift of Gratitude* is a novel filled with such moments. Unfortunately, the boundaries pushed and the epiphanies experienced by the reader are in no way intended by the author. Anyone who reads often has experienced the banal, the saccharine, the self-indulgently lachrymose, but never to the extent we experience it here. Through these pages we step beyond the ordinary to a sort of über-banality we never could have imagined, in our most sedentary dreams, ever existed." Thompson stopped to chuckle. "Jeez, this guy's a riot."

"That's Bester," Garibaldi said. "Jesus K. Copernicus. That's Bester."

At that moment he noticed someone coming up from the right, fast. He turned, reaching for the PPG.

"Michael Garibaldi? It *is* you."

It was a pretty young woman in a mini-suit. He had never seen her before in his life.

"What?" he said.

"Mr. Garibaldi, could you tell us what the altercation a few moments ago was about? What's a hero of the Interstellar Alliance doing accosting citizens on a Paris street?"

That's when he noticed the newstaper floating over her left shoulder and it all snapped into place.

"Hey, hey, hey! Turn that thing off!"

"If you could just answer a few questions—"

"How do you people *do* this? What, do have some kind of pneumatic tubes under the sidewalk, that just shoot you up wherever there's trouble?"

She motioned, and the red transmission light went out on the taper. "To tell you the truth, Mr. Garibaldi, I've been following you, hoping for an interview. You were spotted at the airport, and I got the assignment. This is better than I hoped for. What's going on here? I thought you had retired from military service, but you're still carrying a PPG."

"Look, you don't know what you're messing with here. You could screw everything up. Just please—hold off, and I'll make sure you're there for the *big* story. And when I say big, I mean Jupiter-sized."

"Ah, well, we were *live*, Mr. Garibaldi. I already got you chasing that man, too. It's been on the air." The red light came back on. "So if you could just answer a few questions—"

"Oh, jeez," Garibaldi muttered. "I'm on vacation. Lemme alone."

She followed him to the building, where he at least had the satisfaction of slamming the door in her face.

A second later, though, he changed his mind. After all, his cover was already blown, wasn't it? If Bester didn't already know he was in town, he'd have to be deaf, dumb, and blind.

It was time for plan B, then.

He went back down the stairs and found her—as he knew he would—still waiting.

9

Bester glanced at the clock and put down his pen. In an hour, the courier would be at the hotel. He should head that way—it wasn't as if he was getting anything done, anyway. All he was really doing, in staring at his notebook and gripping his pen, was avoiding the decision he was going to have to make soon.

Or thought he was. Things had been remarkably quiet since his talk with Lucien. That could be a good sign or a bad sign.

He switched his notebook to newsmode, another thing he had taken to doing every few minutes. So far, it had been an exercise in paranoia, but that didn't mean it wasn't a sensible precaution.

Which point proved itself instantly, because there was Michael Garibaldi's face, not nearly as big as life, but as ugly as always. Bester had set the device to search certain news items first, using keywords like *Bester, Psi Corps, Jemelah, Telepath(s)*—and of course, *Garibaldi.*

He keyed the story on, saw a brief vid of Garibaldi attacking some fellow on the street, a fellow he couldn't help noticing resembled Alfred Bester more than a little bit.

"Oh, no," he said. He recognized the place, too. Not far away. And Garibaldi not only had a PPG but some kind of link on. People didn't just wear links—tel-phones, yes, or collarphones. That was a police link.

I'm coming for you.

Well, so he was. And he was close.

Bester closed his eyes, trying to sort it all out, squeeze down the rising panic and the flood of attendant emotions. It was survival time, now. They must have linked him to Jem, somehow, maybe even to Ackerman's murder. It had just taken longer than he thought it would.

Fine. By now they would be showing his picture to people like Lucien. No—he checked the time on the story he had just seen. Only ten minutes ago. What else was queued up?

Just as he was wondering, his own face appeared in the priority column. An old picture, from back during the hearing. Probably the most

famous picture of him, in full Psi Corps uniform, gloves and all. It seemed like a lifetime ago.

He keyed the story, kept it on mute mode, and watched the words scroll out.

Paris. Police have revealed that Alfred Bester, the fugitive war criminal indicted for numerous crimes against humanity, may be at large in Paris. He is apparently living—and writing—under the name of Claude Kaufman, a name that will be familiar to readers of Le Parisien. *This recent picture was taken in the offices of* Le Parisien *only weeks ago.*

Anyone with any information on the whereabouts of this man is urged to come forward. Michael Garibaldi, CEO of the Edgars-Garibaldi pharmaceutical empire, is offering a one-million-credit reward for information leading directly to his capture. This is in addition to the one million offered by the high crimes tribunal.

Alfred Bester's story is a long and lethal one, and it begins in Geneva—

He switched it off. He knew the popular version of his life well enough.

He had to assume they knew where he lived, or would in a very short time.

On the way out of the café he tossed his credit chit to a beggar who hung out every day on the corner. "Buy yourself a hot meal and some new clothes," he said. He wouldn't be using Kaufman's credit again. If the bum used it, it would at least pull the search in the wrong direction for a few minutes. Minutes and seconds would be crucial now.

Garibaldi thought he had him trapped, but as usual, Garibaldi had made a mistake. He hadn't meant to be noticed by reporters, that much was certain. That's why Bester's face was everywhere, now—though the pieces of the trap weren't all in place, and now Garibaldi would be desperate.

His tel-phone blipped.

"Yes."

"Mr. Bester? This is Sheehan. They're on to you."

"Tell me something I don't know. Is the Bureau involved yet?"

"Yes, sir."

"Are you with them?"

"Yes, sir."

"Have they located my residence?"

"The hotel? Yes."

"Okay. This is what I need you to do."

The Psi Cops had changed their name, the color and cut of their uniforms, and some of their tactics, but they were still unmistakable

when they arrived. They came in a pack, eight of them, dripping arrogance.

"Well," Garibaldi said, as they swept out of the elevator and into the search headquarters. "That took longer than I thought it would."

They didn't waste any time with pleasantries—another thing that reminded him of the bad old days. The leader was a woman, perhaps thirty-five, very professional looking, with closely cropped brown hair. She wore a lieutenant's insignia.

"Michael Garibaldi, you are under arrest," she said. The other teeps were fanning out briskly into the adjoining rooms, except for a hulking fellow who might have been a Viking if he had been born in an earlier era. He was a lieutenant, too, but there was no question which of the two officers was in charge.

"You don't say? What's the charge?"

"Criminal obstruction of an ongoing investigation."

"I think if you'll check out my clearances—"

"Oh, we will. For the moment, however, you may consider yourself my prisoner. If you could hand over any sidearms, please, and your link."

"You're arresting *me*, with Bester out there?"

Her eyes flared. "Did you really expect to capture a telepath of Bester's power and training without *us*? Thanks to you, we almost lost him."

"Almost? You mean—"

"We have confirmed sighting at Gare du Nord. A team of hunters is on it right now."

"Why haven't I heard about this?"

"Just who do you think you are, Mr. Garibaldi? I don't care who you *were*, or who your friends are. At the moment you are a private citizen, with no jurisdiction in this matter whatsoever."

"Funny. You guys didn't take that attitude when I was supplying you with funds and weapons during the war. You seemed to think I had a legitimate interest in these matters then."

She ignored that and turned toward Girard. "I don't know how he managed to bully you into this," she told the Frenchman, "but there will be a full investigation of your department by an independent authority, I can assure you."

"I don't doubt that," Girard replied. He sounded doleful but not exactly repentant.

"As of now, I have EA authorization to take control of this mess. I want all of your men and equipment off the streets, *now*."

"That's insane," Garibaldi snapped. "You don't *have* him, yet."

"We will. I suggest you start being concerned about yourself. Call

your lawyer. Monsieur Girard, I suggest you consult with your depart-
ment. I think you'll find that the order to stand down is already in the
system."

"Look," Garibaldi said, "if you really think I trust you guys—"

"I don't care *what* you think, Mr. Garibaldi, or who you trust. You're
done here. Your link and your gun—this is the last time I'll ask."

"This is a mistake."

The Viking—Garibaldi mentally dubbed him "Thor"—raised his
own weapon.

Garibaldi hesitated for a long moment. Something wasn't right here.

But then he sighed, took out the PPG, unhooked his link, and
handed them over.

"Thank you. Please take a seat, somewhere. I'll want to question you
in a moment."

Bester watched until he was sure all of the men staking out the hotel
were gone, along with their equipment. By that time it was dark, and
keeping to the shadows, he moved quietly into the building, glyphing
himself as a nonpresence.

He was a little worried—he hadn't seen anyone who looked like a
courier. They might have been scared off by the surveillance, or they
might have been captured. Or, if they were smart, they were inside,
registered as a guest.

He had to take the chance that the courier was in there. It would be
too difficult to get replacement papers at this late date.

The front office and café were dark and quiet when he entered, but
he immediately felt Louise's presence, and his guts knotted up. He
wasn't looking forward to this part.

"Claude?" She was sitting in her usual place, a large envelope in
front of her. "Or should I call you Alfred? Or Robert?"

"Louise—" He stopped. The impact of her saying his real name was
almost staggering.

"Were you going to tell me about this? Or were you just going to
leave without saying good-bye?"

"I was going to say good-bye."

"Really? Or were you just coming for these papers?"

"How did you get those?"

"A boy came by with them. The men watching the hotel tried to take
them, but I insisted they were mine. Your courier had a choice of giving
them to me or to the police. He wisely chose to give them to me."

She didn't sound angry. She didn't sound *anything*.

"I know you don't believe me," he said, softly, "but I do love you. I

had hoped this was all behind me. I had hoped to spend the rest of my life here."

"This is why you wanted to leave yesterday. Why didn't you tell me? You know I would have gone."

"You—would have?"

"Of course, you stupid fool." Now she *did* sound angry. "Do you think I didn't suspect something like this? Do you take me for a complete idiot? I don't care what you've done, or who you've been. Whatever you were like then, I know who you are *now*. You're not the same man they're talking about on the vids. You're a good man, a loving man. I—" Her voice caught. "I don't understand all of this. I don't know everything that's happening. But I do know I love you, and I think . . . you need me."

He realized he hadn't moved a muscle. He unfroze and walked slowly over to the table and lowered himself into a chair.

Her eyes were red—she had been crying. He reached out to touch her cheek, and she didn't stop him.

"You don't know what you're saying," he said, softly. "You don't know what it's like to run from world to world, having to leave everything at a moment's notice. I couldn't ask you to do that."

She raised her chin defiantly. "I think you were *going* to. What changed your mind?"

"Reality. It's not make-believe anymore, Louise. This is the real thing. I fought a war. I fought it for good reasons, and I'm not ashamed of anything I did. I wish I had won, but I didn't. Now I'm just a reminder of everything they want to sweep under the rug. They'll hunt me until they catch me, or I die."

"They can hunt us together, then. I want to go with you."

And there it was.

Once he had been briefly stranded in hyperspace, floating in that miasma that the human eye perceived as red but which serious studies proved ought to have no color at all. In hyperspace, telepathic power extended toward the infinite, and he had felt like an expanding star, as if his mind was becoming everything and nothing.

He felt like that now. Of all the reactions he had imagined from Louise, this wasn't one he had dared. And yet here it was, the simple, elegant answer to everything.

"You *do* love me," he sighed, reaching to touch her face again.

"I do," she said, taking his hand. "I want to stay with you, be with you." He gripped her fingers, knew it was the truth.

He also knew it would never work. She loved him, yes. But could he count on her? When it fully sank in that he had really done the things he

was accused of, would she truly understand? How could she? She was a normal. When it really hit her that she would never see her family again—this family that she was rediscovering, her love for them just reawakening—how would she feel then? When she understood that in harboring him, in going with him, she was becoming as much a criminal as he, that her only doorway to a normal life would be his capture and conviction, what would she do?

It might be days, or hours, or months, but she would turn on him. She had to. She was in love with him, but love wasn't rational. And it was fragile, so very fragile.

But if he left her here, they would question her. They would scan her. She knew his new identity, she knew where he was headed.

"Okay," he said, softly. "You can go with me. I love you, Louise." He bent over to kiss her, savoring the feel of her lips, the emotions that spoke through them, the surge of joy and relief. He wasn't going to leave her, not like everyone else . . .

She went rigid, when he started, and then she struggled. "Claude . . . Claude . . . something's wrong—" She didn't know yet that it was him doing it, but then, in an instant, she guessed, and her eyes widened like a child's, full of betrayal and incomprehension. "What are you—*no!*"

But by then he had her paralyzed, her defenseless mind opened like a ledger. *It'll be okay,* he told her, *this is for the best.* He felt sick, though, almost to the point of throwing up. This was *Louise.* Each part of her he cut out was like cutting out a part of himself. But it was too late, now. It had always been too late.

Snip their summer afternoons together, their long walks along the Seine. *Snip* the day playing tourist, their lovemaking, their laughter at an old movie. *Snip* their quiet talks, washing dishes together, arguing playfully about who would cook supper.

It was all going too fast. He didn't have enough time. Soon the ruse his insiders had set up would be at an end, and the hunters would be back here, for him. Garibaldi would be back for him.

He was trying to be careful, but it was hurting her. She moaned almost steadily, and all of the sweet light disappeared from her eyes, leaving only pain, and loss, and still that awful incomprehension. *Why are you doing this to me? I love you!*

Snip him posing for her, the sun shadowing his face. *Snip* their first kiss. *Snip* the comfort of body against body, in the dark of night, when nightmares woke her.

The artist in the square. The fight with Jem. Tasting wine together and complaining about the vintage. Everything. She passed out long before it was done, thin streams of blood leaking from her nose.

He collapsed onto the table, every nerve raw, utterly exhausted. He felt dead. He wanted to be dead.

But Louise would live. There were holes, of course, things torn, but they would heal, and she would have no memory of him. To her, he would never have existed. But she would live, and with help she could be rebuilt into a normal, functioning, *safe* human being.

He staggered to his feet. One more thing.

Going up the stairs took almost all of the energy he had left. The loft was locked, but he had her key. He used it and entered the room where he had fallen in love with her. The easel and the canvas were still there, quiet, awaiting her hand, her presence. He almost saw her there, hair pulled back, paint smudging her face.

For too long he stood, locked in place by emotion. But it was too late. It was done.

He walked across the room, stood where she had stood when she painted, and at last saw it.

It was finished, and it was him. He wobbled slowly to his knees, almost as if praying.

Because it *was* him. All of him.

How had she done it, with nothing more than a brush and paint?

The face that stared back at him was lonely, and hurt. And yes, there was cruelty there, and cold purpose. She had seen that. She had always known. But she had also seen the compassion he hid, the love that came so hard, his deepest desires and most profound wounds, the ones that remained unhealed from his earliest childhood. The boy, the man, the torturer, the killer, the poet, the lover, the hater, the fearful, the hopeful. All there, in loving brush strokes.

She had known everything important about him, and loved him still.

He had known grief before. But he had never known *this*. A sound came up from his throat that he didn't even recognize, a sort of whimper, a tearing.

"What have I done?"

He had been wrong. Louise would have followed him anywhere, and loved him. She would never have betrayed him.

He took the can of turpentine and emptied it over the painting. He struck his lighter to it and stood there, watching the face dissolve in flame, a damned soul burning in hell.

When it was ash, he ground out what remained of the fire, the smoke stinging his eyes. When he was sure it was out, he went downstairs and got his papers.

He checked Louise's pulse. It was weak, but steady.

He wanted to say something. He couldn't. His throat was tight. *I love you,* he 'cast, knowing it would mean nothing.

Papers tucked under one arm, he opened the door, and went out into the night.

10

After an hour, Girard began seriously worrying about what Garibaldi might do. At first he had railed against Sheehan and her people, then he had grown sulkily quiet.

Now his muscles were starting to twitch.

Girard, he was pragmatic. He had seen this coming all along, and it didn't surprise him. What did surprise him was Garibaldi's arrest. The EABI might not like what he had done, but they had to know they wouldn't be able to make any charges stick. The arrest had to be purely for the purpose of annoying Garibaldi.

It was working, maybe too well. Any minute now, the ex–security officer was going to try something rash.

Was that what they wanted? They hadn't cuffed him or anything. No one seemed to be watching him. But they were telepaths, so they knew better than Girard did that Garibaldi was about to explode. Were they giving him an opportunity to hang himself?

He walked over to where Garibaldi sat, fuming.

"They're letting him get away," Garibaldi said, softly. "Intentionally, deliberately."

"They seem to have the matter in hand."

"They're going through the motions, chasing a ghost. Have you been watching them? They *know* they're chasing a ghost. Sheehan does, anyway."

"You think she's the insider?"

"One of them. There may be more. Hell, they may all be Bester's chosen few."

"How can that be? I thought they were all monitored."

Thompson, a few feet away, nodded. "Sure. But that can be pretty pro forma. Besides, it's not impossible to condition yourself to respond the right way—or *be* conditioned, by someone as strong as Bester."

"Or maybe it's rotten right to the top, like it always was."

"I don't believe that," Thompson said. "For one thing, some of these

people are pretty excited about catching Bester—I can feel it. He's the boogie man for the younger generation of teeps."

"You scanned them?"

"They're leaking it. But you're right about Sheehan. She's up to something. She's sweating it, too."

"They're chasing a decoy and they pulled all of our men off the streets. You know what that means."

Girard nodded. "Of course. It means he's still in the Pigalle, tidying things up."

"But not for long." Garibaldi lowered his voice even further. "We have to get out of here."

Girard laughed bitterly. "Mr. Garibaldi, I have exactly two things worthwhile left right now. One is my life, the other is my job. I don't particularly feel like risking either."

"Thompson?"

The younger man hesitated. "What about that call you made to your lawyer? It can't be long before they release you."

"It doesn't have to be long," Garibaldi grunted. "Just long enough for Bester to vanish. Why else would they even arrest me? Why would they keep me here?"

"The inquiry will show what happened," Girard said. "Sheehan and her cronies will be discovered, surely."

"I don't give a damn about that," Garibaldi said. "It has to be now, not later." He cocked his head at Thompson. "You really think the rest of these guys are straight?"

"I'd bet my life on it," Thompson said.

"Glad to hear it," Garibaldi replied.

"What do you—"

"Hey!" Garibaldi yelled. "I want to call my lawyer again. Somebody bring me a phone."

Sheehan turned from her task of "monitoring" the chase to scowl at him.

"Call him, then."

"You took my link. I need it back."

She grinned, not in a nice way. "I'm sorry, you aren't authorized to use a link. Use your phone."

"I don't *have* one. That's why I had a link."

"Too bad."

"Let me use yours."

She looked more annoyed than ever, but then walked briskly over, producing her phone.

As soon as she got close enough, he leapt.

Girard was impressed by the speed of the maneuver, by the way Garibaldi's limbs uncoiled, straightened, snapped out all in the same breath. He was impressed, too, by the speed with which Sheehan understood what was happening and reacted, dodging back while simultaneously chopping a knife-hand at Garibaldi's throat.

Finally, he was impressed at how quickly it was over, with Garibaldi's forearm clenched tightly under Sheehan's chin and her gun in his hand, pressed against the side of her head. Every telepath in the room had produced a weapon as well, and they were all aimed at Garibaldi—for a moment. Then, as if in response to a silent agreement, several of the muzzles slowly moved, to cover Thompson and himself. He raised his arms, slowly.

"Drop it," the Thor look-alike said.

"Hang on. Everybody just calm down. I want to try a little experiment. If it doesn't work out, I'll let her go. If it *does* work out, I'll let her go. But you're going to let me try it, or so help me God I'm going to splatter her brains on that wall over there."

"Let her go," Thor repeated, but none of them moved.

"Thompson, get her phone."

Thompson did so, moving slowly and deliberately so as not to excite anyone.

"What's your encryption key, Sheehan?"

She didn't answer. Two of the telepaths shifted a bit, presumably to get a better shot at Garibaldi.

"Come on. I don't have all day. I say your boss, Sheehan, here, has something to hide. I say she's been making and receiving calls from the man you're supposed to be chasing."

"That's insane," Sheehan managed to gurgle.

"Is it? Do any of you really think your team is chasing the real Bester? Even if you thought that, why would you pull surveillance from the one place you *know* he was? That can't be procedure."

"What are you talking about?" Thor grunted.

"He's trying to—" Sheehan gasped as Garibaldi tightened his grip.

"It's insane? Then you shouldn't mind giving us your encryption keyword. Prove me wrong."

"I don't take orders from you," Sheehan snapped.

"Thompson, scan her—get it from her."

"No." Thompson said it quietly, but firmly.

"What?"

"I may work for you, Garibaldi, but you can't make me do that. It's not legal and it's not right."

"Of all the—"

But Thompson wasn't finished. He looked squarely at Thor and the other telepaths and addressed them. *"You* can do it, though, if you think she's lying. *I* think she is. It comes off her like a stink, even without me scanning her. Whoops—feel that? She just blocked up. Why would she do that?"

Thor raised an eyebrow. "Mr. Garibaldi, let Sheehan go and drop the gun. Then we can talk about this."

"Sorry," Garibaldi said. "No can do. Not until we hear the last few conversations she had."

Thor took a step closer.

"Stop," Garibaldi said.

"No. I won't. And you won't kill her. I can tell you won't."

"She's lying to you. She's working for Bester."

"We'll see about that. After you let her go." The big man took a step closer.

"Don't try anything," Garibaldi warned. "Don't try a damn thing, or—" he broke off, midsentence, his lips quivering.

For a moment, no one moved, and then Girard noticed something that sent cold chills up his spine.

Garibaldi's finger, spasming on the trigger. Not quite hard enough to discharge the weapon.

Thor took four big steps, reached down, and carefully removed the weapon from Garibaldi's fingers. Then he placed the end of his own gun against Garibaldi's head.

"I'm going to let you move again," he said, "and you will remove your arm from around Sheehan's neck."

Garibaldi's hand suddenly clenched, and he let out a tortured gasp. Then, slowly, he raised his arms.

Sheehan wriggled out of his embrace.

"Bjarnesson, give me my sidearm," she snapped.

"Just hold on a minute, Lieutenant," Bjarnesson said. "I'd like to know—"

"Bjarnesson, that's an *order.*"

The big man stared at her, his blue eyes steady. "Lieutenant, for the record, I think it's best that I temporarily relieve you of duty until I can—" His voice suddenly caught, as if there were something in his throat, then he slapped both hands to his head and groaned. The gun in his hand went flying.

So did Sheehan.

She got it and fired from the floor, hitting one of the younger cops— a young Chinese man—an inch to the left of his heart. The return fire

from the remaining four all went wide, and then it got confusing for Girard because he was diving for cover himself.

He had a glimpse of Garibaldi, in motion again, a pantherlike form. Of the muzzle flash from Sheehan's weapon leaping out to meet him halfway.

He heard three, maybe four more shots, and when he got to look again, there was Garibaldi, clutching his shoulder, standing straddled over an unconscious Sheehan. The whole left side of her face was an angry red.

Thor was getting shakily to his feet, blood running out of his nose and from the corners of his eyes.

Garibaldi bent over and very deliberately picked up the PPG.

"Thompson, call an ambulance," he muttered. "And somebody cuff her. Bjarnesson, are you in charge now?"

"I—ah—" He nodded his head. "Yes."

"Get a squad together. We're going hunting."

Thor hesitated for another second, then chopped his head up and down. One of the cops was tending to the wounded one—probably not for long, given the nature of the wound.

"Derben, you and Messer stay with Li. Inform the Bureau of what's happening. The rest of you—you heard Mr. Garibaldi. Get your gear. We have a monster to catch."

The last time Garibaldi had hunted with a telepath, it had been with Bester himself. The two of them had gone after a dust dealer on Babylon 5. Sheridan, never one of Bester's fans, had forced the thenPsi Cop to take the sleeper drug, to temporarily cancel out his powers. Even without them, Bester had proved a hell of a hunter.

After all of it was over, Garibaldi had developed a grudging respect for Bester. He was a vicious, arrogant man, but what he did, he did well, powers or no.

He still respected Bester, the way you might respect a snake. That didn't mean he thought the man ought to go on breathing.

These cops were good at what they did, too. It was spooky, the way they deployed without speaking a word, each scanning a different sector as they made their way quickly up the narrow streets toward the hotel where Bester was supposed to have been staying.

"I've called my men back," Girard said. "You think he's still there?"

"I can smell him," Garibaldi grunted.

"How's your shoulder?" Thompson asked.

"Nothing I can't live with," Garibaldi answered, grimly.

* * *

Bester had only gone a few steps from the hotel when he felt a gun pointed at him.

"Hello, Officer d'Alambert," he said.

"Hold it right there, Mr. Bester." D'Alambert's features appeared as he stepped into the light of a streetlamp.

"I'm unarmed."

"You don't fool me. I know what you are."

"Well, you are either very brave or very stupid. I can switch your brain off like a light."

In point of fact, he couldn't. The effort of wiping Louise, without seriously hurting her, and in such a short time, had taken its toll. He could barely sense the policeman's surface thoughts, much less do anything about them.

"If you've hurt Louise, I don't care what you do to me."

"Ah. I thought you protested too much. You do love her."

"What have you done to her?"

"She's in there." He nodded toward the building. "She's not hurt. And I'm out of her life. You ought to be happy."

"Yes, you are out of her life. I'm taking you out of it."

"You'll have to kill me."

"I'll do it."

Bester cocked his head, aware that his time was running out. It almost seemed as if he could hear the hounds coming, in the distance. "You've never killed anyone before, have you, Lucien?" he said softly. "I envy you."

"Shut up."

"No, I do. There's this moment, when they die, when you know you've taken everything from them, and they know it, too. It's an awful moment. People pretend I have no conscience, because they want to pretend they could never do what I've done. The fact is, their ghosts never leave me. I see their eyes, in the dark. I hear the last, sucking gasps. Every man or woman I've ever killed follows me. It sounds unbearable, doesn't it? But it is bearable—it just takes practice.

"In fact, it only takes one time. The first time you kill, and you watch the lights go out, you understand how terrible it is. But at the same time you know you can do it again. That's the worst thing about it: you can never be clean again, never get the blood off your hands, and so a little more doesn't matter, does it?"

The gun wavered. "You're just trying to fool me."

"Stop you, yes. I don't want to die. But fool you? No. You know what I say is true. And Louise, you know her, too. She still loves me, you know. She wanted to go with me, but I wouldn't let her. But if you shoot

me down, me, a defenseless man, her lover, how will she feel about you? Intellectually she might understand, but in her heart she will never forgive you."

"You bastard."

Bester took a step forward. "I'm leaving. I'm not going to hurt you, Lucien. With me gone, Louise will need every friend she has, and she doesn't have many—you know that. I won't take you away from her, too. So you have a decision to make. I hope for all of our sakes you make the right one."

With that, he very deliberately started walking past the policeman. The gun tracked him, and then he could feel the man's gaze, boring into his back, wavering, wavering.

Gone. A moment later, he heard the door of the hotel open. He started to run.

11

When they reached the hotel, the hunters clumped together and then broke like a rack of billiard balls, some darting up side streets, others covering the windows and roofs around them. Two drew a bead on the door.

"Is he in there?" Garibaldi asked Thompson.

"Somebody is," Thompson replied. "I don't feel Bester, but I don't have line of sight, either, and he would be blocking anyway."

"I'm going in."

He sidled up to the door, and with a quick, explosive motion, kicked it open.

In the murky room beyond, someone moved, and he drew the PPG around. "Hold it!" he shouted. "Whoever you are, hold it!"

"I'm not him," said the figure, hunched in the darkness. He spoke in heavily accented English. A man.

Garibaldi kept the man covered while he fumbled for the light switch.

The light revealed a small café. A middle-aged man in a policeman's uniform knelt beside a woman slumped across a table.

"He did something to her," the policeman explained. "He lied. He said he hadn't hurt her. But I can't get her to wake up."

Garibaldi didn't let his aim waver. Who was to say this wasn't another of Bester's tricks, another of his hollowed-out robots? The moment he turned his back, this guy might gun him down.

"Drop your gun and kick it over here," he commanded. Around him, Thompson, Girard, and Bjarnesson covered the stairs and the various other exits. The policeman complied, putting his pistol on the floor and then giving it a good nudge with his foot.

"Is he here?" Garibaldi demanded, retrieving the weapon.

"No." The cop looked back at the woman. "I've called an ambulance, but . . ."

Bjarnesson holstered his weapon and strode over to the two. He knelt by the woman, took her pulse, then concentrated for a moment.

"I think she'll be okay," he said. "She's been wiped—a very professional job, probably Bester's work."

"No? Really?" Garibaldi asked, voice sopping with sarcasm. Then a bit more thoughtfully, "She must have known something. Can you get anything from her?"

"Not right now. She's in a delicate state."

"Try."

"No!" The policeman was suddenly on his feet, eyes blazing. "She's been through enough. Leave her alone. Leave her alone, or so help me—"

"Don't worry, sir," Bjarnesson soothed, with a glance toward Garibaldi. "I won't touch her. Like I said, she's in a delicate state."

Garibaldi absorbed that silently. Was Bjarnesson telling the truth, or was this just another delaying tactic? Maybe he was one of Bester's, too—just more subtle about it than Sheehan.

"I'm checking the rest of the place out," he said.

He moved from room to room, switching on lights, knocking down doors when no one answered them. Thompson and Girard trailed behind him, calming and questioning the hotel guests as he eliminated hiding places.

The whole time, he felt Bester slipping away. But maybe that's what Bester wanted him to think, as he hid gloating in some little corner of the building. He had to search it.

Behind one door he found the remains of an AI, stinking of ozone, probably from a deliberate overcharge. He searched the room quickly, found a weird dressing-robe sort of thing and a rack of mostly black clothes. And tacked to the wall, next to the mirror in the bathroom, a charcoal drawing. Bester's eyes stared from the sketch, mocking him.

"Damn it!" he snarled. He tore the picture from the wall, then went to flip over the bed, rifle through the dresser drawers. Nothing, of course. The AI might still have some information of use in it, though he doubted it. More frustrated than ever, he continued his search.

When he reached the topmost floor, he smelled smoke, and went more carefully. The door to the loft apartment was cracked; he eased it open and peered cautiously in. After he assured himself no one was inside, he went to look at the smoldering pile on the floor, near an easel. The resiny scent of turpentine tingled along the back of his throat. He stared, puzzled, at the burned painting.

Something about that scene convinced him, though he couldn't say exactly what. Bester wasn't hiding in the hotel—he really was gone.

Garibaldi hurried back down the narrow stairs.

The rest were already gathered in the lobby. "Four of the guests recognized his picture," Thompson informed him, "though none of them have seen him lately. But the cop—" He quickly related d'Alambert's story.

Bjarnesson was talking over a link. He glanced up at Garibaldi. "Trang and Sloan think they've picked up his trail," the agent reported. "They've gone ahead."

Garibaldi remembered the canvas, still smoking. "He can't have too much of a lead," he said. "We've wasted enough time here."

Outside, the ambulance had arrived, and they were loading the unconscious woman into it. D'Alambert, the cop, looked on, wringing his hands.

"You had him, didn't you?" Garibaldi said. "And you let him go."

"I couldn't stop him," the man said, miserably. "I tried."

Garibaldi would have felt sympathy if he'd had time for it. He didn't. The colder the trail got, the harder it would be to follow. Bester might be only a few steps ahead of them, but he had the advantage of knowing where he was going.

"No. I won't get this close and fail," he said, under his breath. "Let's go," he told the telepaths.

"My men have almost all of the streets closed off," Girard informed him, "and we have choppers and hovercraft up, too. We'll get him."

"I'll believe it when it happens," Garibaldi replied.

Bester leaned against a building and drew a deep, calming breath. Panic wasn't going to get him anywhere. Panic triggered reflexes that were too ancient, reflexes that knew nothing of the helicopters he heard buzzing about, of infrared cameras, of telepathic hunters. Panic might have been an asset in the days when it helped a naked monkey-thing scramble up a tree, three steps ahead of a pack of hyenas, but it was no help to a teep in his present position.

He couldn't count on his insiders, anymore. By now they had unmasked themselves, outlasted their usefulness. He was on his own.

He clutched his new identity to his chest. It wasn't that bad. All he had to do was get out of Paris. A small area could be searched intensively, but expand that area to France, to Europe, and beyond, and he would be safe again, for a while.

And he wouldn't repeat the same mistakes again. No, he just needed a little distance, and more importantly, a little time. He was too weak, now. A few hours before he would have been able to penetrate a police

barricade, like the one he saw a few streets ahead, simply by willing it so. Now he would be lucky to fool a single normal.

He still had one advantage. He still had the Shadow chip. He couldn't cloud a man's mind, but he could cloud a machine's.

There was a department store on the next corner, wasn't there? He slipped toward it.

He used the Shadow chip to make the security system stupid, but locks were another matter. Like those of the pharmacy, they were independent mechanisms. He took off his jacket and placed it against a window, which fortunately turned out to be glass. He couldn't hold the jacket up with his crippled hand, so he leaned against it and punched with the other. The window shattered inward without much fuss, and he stepped in. Was there a live guard here? Probably, but he didn't remember. He waited, crouching for a few seconds, straining his worn-out abilities to the maximum.

Yes, there was a guard.

When he had him in line of sight, he jolted the fel-low, which was the best he could do, and followed that with a vicious uppercut. He was physically weakened, too, but achieved the desired result. The man—no, woman—fell sprawling, her shock stick bouncing on the floor. He picked it up and hit her with it, twice. Then searched her. No gun. What kind of guard didn't carry a gun?

The kind that didn't think she needed one, obviously. He shocked her again, then knelt, pinched her nose, and covered her mouth.

"Sorry," he said, "but if I just cuff and gag you, they'll feel you when they come by. Can't have that."

So much for his promise not to kill anyone else. Of course, they would notice the broken window anyway—maybe a little sooner if they felt the guard. But how much time would her death actually buy him?

Swearing, he let her breathe again, took her phone, cuffed her hands behind her and around a column.

He was in the women's lingerie section, so he balled up some panty hose and shoved them in her mouth. Then, still cursing at himself, he made his way toward sporting goods.

He had come shopping here with Louise. It was where he had gotten her the dress.

What would she think, when she looked in her closet? She wouldn't remember getting it, but she would know, by then, who had given it to her. Would she throw it away? Or would she keep it, sensing that there must have been something true between them, something real?

It doesn't matter. Concentrate.

He wove through the darkened racks, trying to think of something

else. He remembered playing cops and blips with the other kids in his cadre, when he was only six or so. He had always wanted to be the cop, the hunter, the good guy, but more often than not they had made him play the Blip, the rogue on the run.

He remembered an argument he had had with one of the boys in the cadre—Brett—when they had played Blips together. Brett had insisted that Blips always acted stupid, always made obvious mistakes. Bester had wanted to play as smart as he could, because he hated being beaten, even if he was supposed to be. He had sacrificed Brett to the others that day, made Brett lose, so he could win. He had been punished for that, for turning against one of his own brothers in the Corps, even in a game.

Now he was the Blip, for real. But no, that wasn't right. He wasn't a Blip—he was the last Psi Cop. It was the world that had gone rogue.

For an instant, he was that six-year-old all over again. It was so real, and so vivid, that the intervening years seemed dreamlike, unreal. As if the thing that connected him to the child wasn't a linkage of years, or the passage of time, or personal evolution, but that single, unchanged desire to win.

In sporting goods he picked up a target pistol, a small-caliber weapon that fired fléchettes. Anything heavier would be locked up someplace, and he didn't have time for that. He also picked up a Bowie knife, night vision goggles, and several motion detectors of the sort that campers used for perimeter alarms. He placed one by the broken window and another near the front door.

Then he slipped out the back door and into an alley. They didn't know how weak he was. They would waste time searching the store for him, assuming he was creating a psychic shadow for himself.

He hurried down the darkened street, feeling a little better with a weapon in his hands. He was also regaining his strength—the background babble of Paris grew clearer with each passing moment. Soon he would be able to face his hunters on a more even footing.

Or so he was thinking when he turned a corner and ran square into one of them. It was a young fellow, scarcely out of training. He was as surprised as Bester—Bester could feel his shock like a grenade going off.

The hunter's weapon was already out, and up. He fired.

He missed.

Something whined by Bester's shoulder as he sidestepped left and fired the fléchette gun once, twice. The boy got off another shot, too, but Bester felt a diffraction of pain. It wasn't from being hit himself, but from the darts punching holes in the hunter. The second one hit bone in the shoulder, and the young man gagged on his own tongue. Bester finished putting him down with the guard's shock stick.

He searched the still body, quickly. Oddly enough, the boy was using some sort of fléchette gun, too, and not much better than his own. He traded shock sticks—his own was nearly out of charge—took the gun, and then quickly scanned the boy.

He had a partner, working around the other side of the building. Bester flattened against the wall and waited.

A moment later the second man came around, warily. Bester hit him in the neck with the fléchette gun he had taken from the first hunter.

The response surprised him. The man roared in pain, but was not otherwise deterred, pulling his gun up to fire. Bester had only one choice—he leapt forward inside the extended arm, swinging the shock stick. The hunter reacted too quickly, however, and they were suddenly grappling.

The hunter struck—not physically, but with all of the power of a young P12.

Long ago, Bester had studied shaman battles.

The human brain had evolved to process data derived from sensory input. The recent mutation that had produced telepathy hadn't changed any of the other hardwiring. Telepathic input was complicated, it circumvented the sensory nerves, went straight to the brain. Still, the brain, being as it was, interpreted psionic attacks as sensory input. The result seemed eerily optical.

In short, a battle of minds was, on the perceptual level, a battle of illusions—like those described in ancient myths and legends. For Bester, there was nothing mystical about the process, but "shaman battle" was as good a name as any.

His enemy launched a multilevel attack, aimed at pain centers, voluntary muscle control, and at the cerebral cortex more generally, triggering some random and some specific neural firings in Bester's brain. Mechanically, that was what happened.

How Bester perceived it, however, was somewhat less clinical.

A cloud of wasps surrounded him, condensing from the air like dew, tickling his naked flesh from head to foot. Their stings dug into him everywhere simultaneously, and he suppressed a shriek. They crawled into his eyes, his nose, his mouth, his ears, and with them brought agony that curled him like a withering leaf.

Bester gathered what strength he had left and wreathed his tortured flesh in flame, searing the insects away. Their charred bodies fell from him by the thousands, and he tasted the stink of them on his tongue. Even before the last of them were gone, biting hard rain and hail drove into him, quenched his fire. Grimly, he clothed himself in heavy combat armor, but he knew that it would last only an instant.

If he kept playing this defensive game he was going to lose.

His enemy's mind was a spinning disk, a buzz saw, then a jagged globe turning several directions at once. Bester engulfed it in viscous fluid, clogged it. The hunter responded almost instantly, crystallizing the fluid and shearing through it, sending sharp fragments flying back at his opponent. But Bester's move hadn't really been an attack—it had been a feint.

Beneath that assault—really a broadscale isolation of neurons—he had slipped in a jolt to the motor nerves. Bester couldn't see how effective it was, but he felt an uncontrolled trembling that he imagined was a point for his side.

But he was still too weak, and the wasps were back, more of them than ever. Repetition was crude—in fact, all of the hunter's attacks relied on sheer brute strength of mind. Unfortunately, it was a strength the fellow had, and which Bester, at the moment, lacked. Sure, in top form he could beat this kid hands down, but—he was losing. His responses were slow, and inadequate.

He twisted the wasps inside out, but they exploded as they did so, turning his once again naked flesh into a sheath of agony. He gritted his teeth and swore, lashing back without finesse, and without much strength, either. Like a man in the last stages of being throttled, slapping weakly at his killer's face.

And then, weirdly, all of his opponent's power went out of him, sucked down some drain Bester could not see. When Bester sparked out his cortex, he was able to raise only the flimsiest of barriers. The man collapsed, spitting up blood.

Bester reeled against that wall as reality snapped up around him again. He hit the man with the shock stick, just to make sure he stayed down.

A nearly blinding light shone in his face, and for an instant he thought he was still in the mental combat zone, that this was all an elaborate ruse setting him up for the real, final blow. Then he understood. He was standing in the street, in the path of a car.

A man stuck his head out of the car. "Hey, old-timer. You okay?"

"They attacked me," Bester groaned, indicating the bodies. "They—" He lifted the gun and pointed it between the man's eyes. "Do exactly what I say, and you will live."

"*Sacré merde!* You are the fellow on the news."

"So pleased you recognized me," Bester said. "Step around and open the passenger door. Around, not through the car." He sidled closer.

The man was probably in his fifties, greying, with a long, solemn face. "No problem," he said. "Just take it easy with the gun, yes?"

"Yes. As long as you follow my instructions."

Obediently, the man went around and carefully keyed open the passenger door. Bester followed him.

"Now, slide through to your side and shut your door."

The man did so, and seconds later they were both in the vehicle.

"Head north," Bester grunted.

"Whatever you say."

They traveled east for a block, then north. Bester clenched and unclenched his good hand. Where to go? There must be barricades everywhere.

He glanced out the window, and with a dull shock realized that they were on the same street as Louise's hotel. In fact, they were passing it.

He threw his blocks up, built a nothingness around himself. The darkness should help protect him from a physical sighting.

There was quite a crowd in front of the hotel, he noticed. Policemen, an ambulance—had he hurt Louise more than he thought? He might have. He might—

"Keep driving," he told the driver. "Do nothing suspicious."

"Stay calm," the fellow said.

Bester saw a familiar face. Garibaldi. Of course.

They cruised on past, unnoticed. Three blocks later, he began to breathe easier.

"Back north," he directed. "Try to get on the Rue de Flandre."

"I passed a roadblock coming in here," the man said. "I'll bet they have things blocked up north, too."

"You'd better hope they don't," Bester told him.

But at least he had broken the trail—that was the important thing. Even if he had to get out of the car soon. And he knew, for the moment, where Garibaldi was, and more or less what he was up against.

The Rue de Flandre *was* blocked off, and so were the next few streets. They weren't substantial blocks—often just one man—but in his state, Bester knew he couldn't risk it.

But what *did* that leave him with?

"What's your name?" Bester asked the driver.

"Paul . . . Paul Guillory."

"Paul, you live around here, don't you? Inside this perimeter they've set up?"

"No. I live across town."

"Don't lie to me. Why else would you come here?"

"I—okay, I'm sorry. Yes, I live just a few blocks away."

"Do you have a wife? Kids? A girlfriend?"

"I have a wife and a little boy. Please don't drag them into this."

"Sorry, Paul, but I'm afraid I have to. Take me there." He prodded Paul with the gun.

"Yes, sir."

"No need to be so formal, Paul. After all, I'm going to be a houseguest. Call me Al."

Garibaldi noticed the funny look on Thompson's face.

"What is it?"

"Just felt somebody walking on my grave."

"What?"

"Bester." He turned his head, slowly. His gaze settled briefly on the taillights of a passing groundcar.

"He's in that car," he whispered.

"You're sure?"

"Yeah. You were right, about me being able to sense him. His tinkering with my brain left a kind of—wound. It just started hurting again. When I look at the car, it hurts even more."

"That would be like Bester," Garibaldi said. "Driving by the scene of the crime, so he could watch us all shaking our heads in confusion. So he could gloat."

"Shall we go after him?"

"On foot?"

Girard spoke up. "I can have a car here in a few moments."

Garibaldi shook his head. "No. No car chase. Look, we know where he is right now, and he thinks he's pulled one over on us. This is the best break we've had." He looked sidewise at Thompson. "You're *sure* it isn't some sort of decoy?"

"Sure as I can be."

"Okay. Girard, can you have that car followed?"

Girard nodded briskly, pulled out his phone, and spat some French into it. Garibaldi recognized the make and model of the car, and the identification number. "It ought to have a transponder," he explained. "Most people have them put in, in case of theft."

He got some sort of answer a few moments later.

"Yes. They have a lock on its signal," he said.

"Good." Garibaldi rubbed his hands together. "Now about that car you said you could get *us* . . ."

12

"Nice place you have here, Paul. Good day, Ms. Guillory."

Guillory's wife was a stout, pleasant-looking woman with very dark hair and very pale skin. She nodded at Bester politely, though clearly she was puzzled.

"Paul should have told me he was bringing company. I just got off work, and picked up some dinner, but I'm afraid there isn't very much. I hope you like Chinese food."

"That sounds wonderful," Bester said.

"Papa!" A boy, perhaps five years old, came scuttling out of an adjoining room and leapt into Paul's arms. Bester strolled over and glanced in the boy's room, as father and son hugged.

"Pierre, this is my friend Al. He's going to be visiting with us tonight, and I want you to be good, yes?"

"Ha!" the mother said. "He's not only good, he's excellent—at getting into trouble. Pierre, tell papa what happened in school today."

"Oh, eh, well nothing really happened, Papa. Nothing, really."

Bester stepped into the boy's room. The floor was strewn with toys, books, coloring books, and random bits of paper. He found a single window, shuttered with venetian blinds. He lifted the blind and peered out. The view was of the second floor of another, very similar apartment building across the street.

"Now, Pierre, either you tell him or I tell him—excuse me? Can I help you?" The woman suddenly noticed what he was doing.

"Sorry," Bester said. "It's just been so long since I've been in a child's room, and I didn't want to interrupt what you all were talking about." He smiled. "It sounded important."

"Well, that's okay, but I would have made Pierre straighten up if I knew you were coming."

"So what did you do at school, Pierre?" Bester asked, reentering the room and squatting next to the boy.

"I, eh, I put some glue in this girl's hair. Jesse."

"Oh, dear. Why did you do that?"

" 'Cause she's dumb." He looked down at his feet. "I dunno."

Bester smiled and mussed Pierre's hair. "Kids," he murmured. He looked up at the mother. "I'm sorry, what was your name?"

"Marie," she answered. "And you were Al?"

"Yes. Marie, I think Paul has something to tell you. Pierre, why don't you show me some of your toys while they talk?"

"Okay."

"What?" Marie asked.

"Do as he says, dear," Paul told her, his voice strained.

Bester followed the little boy back into his room as a hushed conversation followed in the kitchen.

"I think I'm in trouble," the boy confided, shuffling through his things. He extracted a toy Starfury from an agglutinated mass of clothes and crumpled paper. "Here's a toy."

"Yes, it is," Bester said. "I used to fly one of those."

"Nu-uh!"

"Yes, I did."

"In the war?"

"Yes. In several wars, actually."

"No, you didn't."

"Sure I did," Bester replied.

"I want to fly one one day. Do you think I can?"

"Well," Bester replied, "that depends upon your parents. And whether or not you stop putting glue in girls' hair. They frown on that kind of thing in EarthForce." He noticed Paul and Marie were back in the living room. "Oh, hello. Done talking?"

Marie's face was paler even than when he had first seen it. "Pierre—" she said, her voice rattling.

"Why don't you get that Chinese food ready?" Bester said, softly. "I'll be fine with Pierre. Which reminds me, Paul, didn't you have some errands to run?"

"Oh, yes. I clean forgot. I'll, ah, bring back some more food, too."

"Why don't I kick in for that?"

"No need. You're our guest."

"Well, thank you. I must say, you make me feel very welcome."

After Paul left—his reluctance and worry were actually almost painful in Bester's reviving senses—Bester turned back to the boy. "Pierre, let me tell you about flying a Starfury, and you show me the rest of the house, okay?"

It was a small place. The master bedroom had a window with the same view as Pierre's bedroom. The combined kitchen–dining room was

decorated in a cheerful eclecticism, with a vase of tulips, a cheap imitation Aztec wall calendar, a bowl of papier-mâché fruit, and a laughing Buddha carved from Martian hematite. Marie was forking kung-pao chicken and lo mein from cardboard containers onto yellow ceramic plates. She glanced up at Bester, often.

"Go wash your hands, Pierre," she said.

"Oh, yeah!" the boy responded, and ran off to do so. Then he turned, and bouncing on one foot, beckoned to Bester.

"I forgot to show you the best thing!" he said.

With a what-can-you-do? shrug to Marie, Bester followed Pierre into the cramped bathroom.

"See? See?"

What Bester saw at first was that the wallpaper had come off one of the walls and hadn't been replaced. But the boy was gesturing at something more specific—a sort of drawer set into the wall. He pulled it open, revealing a shaft that dropped straight down and then curved off after a few feet.

"What is it?" Bester asked.

"Dad says these apartments are real old, and in the old days they used t'put their garbage down this. He said this must have been part of the kitchen before they made smaller rooms."

"Huh." Bester peered down the shaft. "So that probably goes all the way to the basement somewhere."

"Yeah. I wanted to slide down—"

"Supper!" Marie called from the next room. "Are your hands washed?"

"Better wash them," Bester said.

"What about you?"

"I'm grown up. I don't have to if I don't want."

He went back to the kitchen. "What do you want with us?" Marie whispered.

"I just need a place to rest for a little while," he said. "You'll hardly notice I'm here."

She started to say something, hesitated, started again. "We aren't political here," she said. "I mean, we don't—"

"Don't what? Vote? Why should I care about that?"

"All I mean is, I know they're after you, but it's something political, and we don't care about that. Just don't—don't hurt my son."

"Dear me. Why would I do a thing like that? And to someone showing me such hospitality?"

"I—guess you—wouldn't?"

"Let's say I'd *rather* not, and leave it at that, shall we?" Bester replied.

"See? Clean!" Pierre said, running back in from the bathroom.

"Well," Marie said, composing herself. "Let's eat."

"There he is," Garibaldi grunted. "You guys cover me." He got out of the car and crossed the street to where another man was just leaving his car, the same tan Cortez sedan they had followed to these apartments, then back out to a grocery store and a train station, then back here.

"Hey, buddy. You speak English? Can you help me out with something?"

The fellow looked up warily. "I'm in a hurry," he said, shouldering a backpack.

"Sure, sure. I just need some directions."

"Where are you trying to go?"

"To wherever you've got Alfred Bester stashed. *Shh!*" He made sure the man—Paul Guillory, his registration called him—noticed the PPG.

The man froze. "I don't know what you're talking about. He's that war criminal they're looking for, no?"

"He's that war criminal *we're* looking for, *yes,* and he's up in your apartment."

"No, I don't think so. That's silly."

"Sorry, buddy."

The man heaved a deep sigh, and to Garibaldi's mortification, a tear slipped from one eye. "Monsieur, he has my wife and my little boy up there. He has a gun. He will kill them if anything goes wrong, I am quite certain of it."

"What's this?" Girard asked. "I'm Police Inspector Girard. He has your family as hostages?"

"Yes. He sent me out to get some things. He said if I wasn't back in an hour, he would start to hurt them. It's been almost an hour."

"What did he send you for?"

"Train tickets. Some food. Please, I have to take them to him."

"I'll help with that," Garibaldi offered.

"No!"

"Look, we've already got your place surrounded."

"Don't you hear me? He'll *kill* them."

Garibaldi looked at Girard. "Gas? What? There's gotta be some way to get him out of there."

"Without endangering the family?" Girard replied. "I much doubt

that. Why not wait until he leaves, in the morning? We know what train he's taking, now."

"Just one problem with that. He'll scan Paul here when he gets upstairs and get an instant replay of this whole conversation. Who *knows* what he'll do then?"

"You did it on purpose," Paul said heatedly. "Spoke to me on purpose. To trap me."

Garibaldi shrugged. "It ain't pretty. But look, this guy just mind-fragged his *girlfriend* for Chrissakes. You think he's gonna even blink with you guys? Man, every *second* he's with your family they're in danger. You think he's just gonna walk away from the three of you, especially after he sent you to get train tickets for him? No way. All three of you are dead or as good as dead without us. We're the only thing between you and Bester, and you'd better believe it."

"That's the problem," Paul said. "You *aren't* between us. There is *nothing* between him and my little boy. Nothing."

"Well, then. Let's put our heads together and see what we can come up with, then. And, considering your deadline is almost here, I think it oughta be pretty fast, don't you?"

Bester felt a sudden flash of heat that had nothing to do with the kung pao sitting uneasily in his stomach. It felt more like a hot wind in his skull, followed by a contrasting cold that lingered.

He'd felt it before, just before walking into Lyta's trap. He'd felt it on Mars, seconds before a terrorist bomb had depressurized his office.

There was an old exercise for picturing how gravity worked. You imagine space as a sheet of rubber, extending in all directions. You put a ball bearing on the sheet, and it creates a small dimple. You place a cannonball on the sheet, and it makes a large one. Place the ball bearing near enough to the cannonball, and it rolls down the large dimple to join the cannonball. The lesson is that mass warps space, and that the "attraction" of gravity is merely a by-product of that warping.

Bester had long ago used that same visualization to think about telepathy, with the ball bearings and cannonballs and what-have-you representing minds. A normal made a tiny dimple, a P12 a deep one. But it was more complicated than that. The older a telepath got, the more experience he acquired, and the more he learned from his instincts, the stronger his telepathic gravity became and the more the plane of thought curved around him. The deeper his imprint became, so to speak.

At the same time, he became more and more sensitive to other perturbations on the imaginary rubber sheet. Yes, real telepathy, the transfer of coherent ideas from one mind to another, depended upon

proximity and, ideally, line of sight. But there were older senses that telepathy could engage, senses that worked below the level of rational thought.

He had felt Lyta, that day. Her Vorlon-enhanced abilities had made a huge dent in the fabric of psi-space, and his backbrain had fairly shrieked *Get out!* What he felt now was no less compelling—a bunch of little ball bearings were rolling toward his cannonball, and the deep-warning-system of his brain was yammering for attention. *This* was an instinct he had learned to trust.

Yes, something was wrong.

"You can keep us covered all the way up?"

"Yes," Bjarnesson said, matter-of-factly. "Telepathy works on line of sight, and he won't have that until we open the door. It's easy to disguise the faint impressions he might feel until then."

"So I've heard," Garibaldi answered.

Girard had begun to wonder just what the hell he was supposed to be doing here. His investigation had spiraled completely out of his control. Just like his life. First Garibaldi had horned in, then the EABI, now Garibaldi again.

Looking back on it, it had almost been a relief. When he, Girard, was in charge of things they tended to go wrong, especially lately. When he learned that one of the century's worst war criminals was the object of his pursuit, he had talked himself out of his case. He had been a coward, in that way, ready to let outsiders take the risks, even if it meant they would also get the prize.

Now things had gotten damn muddy, though. Who was in charge? Garibaldi, clearly, mostly by the force of his bullying, but also because he had been *right*. And because Sheehan's betrayal had mired the EABI forces in uncertainty.

Parisian citizens were paying for all of this, though. His citizens. The people Girard was sworn to protect—the people Garibaldi and the rest didn't give a damn about.

He took Garibaldi aside. "I'm going through the door," he said, mildly.

"It's okay, Girard, I've got that covered."

"No, it's not okay," Girard said. "There's a woman and a little boy up there in danger. I will not let you burst in, guns blazing."

"Look—"

"No, *you* look. You aren't an officer of the law, Monsieur Garibaldi. You are just a man with an unhealthy obsession and far too much money,

who thinks he's a cowboy from the American West. We'll do this my way. Period."

"What's your way?"

"I go in with Paul, alone and unarmed. I explain to Bester that he's surrounded—"

"Oh, give me a break," Garibaldi said, rolling his eyes. "He'll just take one of them hostage. Or maybe you."

"He already has them hostage. He won't get far if he tries to leave with them."

"But with the element of surprise—"

"Now you give *me* a break. We haven't surprised this man yet, and despite assurances all around, I'm not confident he *can* be surprised. My way. If he isn't amenable to reason, *then* you can do what you wish."

"This is a bad idea."

"Right now, my men outnumber yours ten to one, even if we include the telepaths, who don't seem to know who they're working for anymore. I can have you arrested again, and I won't make the same mistake they did. I'll have you hauled down to the station and held until this is all over. Understand?"

Garibaldi was a man who was used to getting his way, but that had been a relatively recent development. Deeper than that, beneath the veneer of the rich tycoon, there was a man who had spent most of his life following orders. He nodded reluctantly. "I still think it's a mistake."

"So noted. But that's how we're doing it."

"Your funeral, buddy. And it probably will be."

Girard smiled ruefully. "I just have this image of you and Bester— one man made of matter, the other of antimatter. If I let you rush into that room . . ." He shook his head. "I won't let that happen."

Girard checked to make sure everyone was in place. Snipers in the apartments across the streets, men below the windows, several on the roof. All were told to stay out of line of sight and let their surveillance equipment do the watching for them. Once he felt secure, he waved Paul over.

"I'm going in unarmed, to talk to him. I'll do my best for your family, I swear."

Paul just shook his head. "We should hurry," he said. "I told him I'd be back."

He positioned two teeps and two normals at the base of the stairs, then let Paul lead him to the lift. There were eight of them in all: Paul, Garibaldi, Thompson, Bjarnesson, another teep named Davis, and three special-ops policemen armed for bear.

He tried not to pause when they reached the door and the others took their positions. Then, screwing up his courage, he knocked.

"Who is it?" A woman's voice.

"Police Inspector Girard," he answered, in a loud voice. "I'm unarmed. I'd like to talk to Alfred Bester, please."

A pause of several heartbeats followed before she answered.

"Come in."

13

"The door is locked, madame," Girard said.

"I can't come to the door," the woman replied.

"It's a trap," Garibaldi hissed. "Break it down."

"I would rather use Monsieur Guillory's key."

"Oh. Yeah. Well, if you want to be lazy."

"Don't follow me in," Girard warned. He took the key and opened the door.

Guillory's wife and child sat on the couch, watching them.

"Monsieur Bester, I wish to speak to you," Girard called. He didn't see Bester anywhere. "I am unarmed, but there are armed men in the hall and surrounding the building. I want to come to some accord that will settle this without any more violence."

"He's gone," the woman on the couch said.

"What? Impossible. And if so, why didn't you answer the door?"

"He told us not to."

"But if he isn't here . . ." Girard walked slowly around the living room. Nowhere to hide there. He looked in the kitchen next, checking the cabinets even though he didn't really imagine a grown man could fit into them. He looked in the bedroom, the boy's room, the bathroom. No one there, not even behind the shower curtain.

When he came back into the living room, the two were still sitting there. Garibaldi peeked around from behind the door.

"He doesn't seem to be here," Girard admitted.

"He went down the garbage chute," the boy said.

"What?"

"In the bathroom," the woman said. Paul had called her Marie, yes? It wasn't a name he could hear without experiencing some troubling thoughts just now.

"No way." Garibaldi grunted. "I'm coming in."

"Watch it," Thompson called from out in the hall, "he *might* still be in there. He might just be telling you he's not."

"Can he do that?" Girard asked, incredulous.

"Yes, against normals, certainly."

"Okay. Let's all search, then." He noticed that Marie and the boy were both sitting exactly as they had been, and little spider legs tickled up his back.

"You can get up now," he said.

"No, we can't," Marie said, tears starting in her eyes. "He *told* us not to."

"He compelled them," Bjarnesson said. "Should be easy enough to fix. He couldn't have had much time."

That was too much for Garibaldi. He entered the room, and *he* wasn't unarmed.

"Where's the garbage chute?"

The boy pointed the way with his eyes.

Garibaldi gazed in dismay at the dark shaft.

"Damn it. Where does this go?"

"We don't know," Paul called, from where he knelt with his family, soothing them, telling them that everything would be all right. "The basement, I guess."

"Perimeter reports no one went out the window or exited from the building by the doors," Bjarnesson relayed. He paused. "I think he *is* gone. I don't think he could fool all three of us working together."

Garibaldi looked back down the shaft, speculatively. The inside was filmed with dust, and what looked like fresh scratch marks.

"I'm going in," he muttered.

"I've sent a detail to try and find the basement, so that end is covered," Girard said. "If you want to follow the cobra into its den, more luck to you."

"Just call me Ricky-Ticky," Garibaldi replied.

Bester was smaller than Garibaldi was, that was clear from the start. He'd known that, of course, only it was hard to think of Bester as small, at least until he was confronted with the fact that he, Garibaldi, fit into the shaft like a cork just a micron shy of a perfect fit. There was little he could do other than wriggle and let gravity do the work. As it was, he had to stretch his arms out above him.

It wasn't until he'd managed, catching and bumping, to descend about ten feet that he considered what might happen if Bester was still at the base of this thing. He would be a perfect target, coming out legs first. A sitting duck.

What the hell did that mean, anyway, a "sitting duck"?

He slid down what he estimated to be another ten or fifteen feet.

Then the chute angled sharply. Until that point, he hadn't been able to see how far down it went, but he figured the building was two stories, with a generous basement. So he ought to be about two-thirds of the way down.

Good, because he was getting itchy. The chute was too damned small, and he couldn't *move* . . .

But he had dropped only another five or six feet before his feet came to rest on something solid. He kicked around, and found that the chute simply came to an end. Which was stupid, but . . . come to think of it, he'd never known anyone who lived in a building with a garbage chute. It had never occurred to him it might not be functional. On Mars, you didn't build something unless you were going to use it, and if you decided you weren't going to use it you took it out, to free the space for something else.

Of course, on Mars you weren't dealing with three-hundred-year-old buildings that had been tinkered with incrementally over the years.

"Nice insight, Garibaldi," he muttered to himself. "Now how are you going to get out of here?"

A couple of minutes of frantic wiggling proved to him he wouldn't be able to reverse the process that had brought him down. He couldn't get any leverage with his arms up over his head, and his elbows didn't have room to flex out.

He felt panic rising and batted it down. He didn't like tight places. He *hated* not being able to move his arms and legs, scratch his nose.

"Hey! Get something you can use to pull me out of here," Garibaldi called up. "Hey! Somebody!"

No answer. And he was hit by the sudden, terrible image of Bester, standing among the corpses of Thompson, Girard, and whoever else had remained in the apartment. Bester, grinning as he heard Garibaldi's voice, trying to decide whether to toy with him or cut right to the chase.

He looked up, but all he could see was the smallest sliver of light. Enough of a window for someone to pump a few bullets or PPG blasts down?

Sure.

The light flickered as a shadow crossed it.

"Did you call, Garibaldi?" It was Thompson.

"Yeah. Get me the hell out of here. This doesn't *go* anywhere."

"That means—"

"Yep. It means he's still up there, somewhere."

"Oh, shit. I—" Then Thompson made an odd noise.

"What was that, Thompson?"

Silence. Then a sort of muted chuckle.

"Well. Mr. Garibaldi. We meet again. And under very odd circumstances, I must say. I always knew you were beneath me, but to have it brought home so graphically, well, it's really quite amusing."

"Bester. Damn you, I'll—"

"Sorry. No time for chit-chat. I'll be back in a few minutes, though."

Bester closed the garbage chute and surveyed his handiwork. Thompson was down but still breathing, and would probably continue to. The big telepath wasn't so lucky. He had shot him in the head, first thing, while he was concentrating on taking the inhibitions off Marie and Pierre. Crude and amateurish, but he was a P12 and Bester still wasn't as strong as he ought to be.

Bester had sparked out the police officer and Paul—they would recover any moment now. Only Thompson had given him a minute of real worry. Someone had removed the fail-safe he had planted in the ex–EarthForce officer, so he'd had to clobber him. Fortunately, the teep had been busy talking to Garibaldi.

Garibaldi, who would die next. But first Bester had something else to attend to.

It had all worked out pretty well, really. It had taken him only a few moments to do what was needed to Marie and Pierre—both were pretty weak-minded, and after all, he didn't do much to them. He planted the very strong suggestion that he had gone down the garbage chute, forbade them to remember his real exit, then forbade them to get up and walk around. None of these suggestions bore the force of permanence, though quick had also meant brutal. At the very least the two were going to suffer bad dreams for a few weeks.

What he had actually done, before his pursuers had arrived, was leave the apartment, cross the hall, and knock on a neighboring door. The sleepy tenant who answered had been easy to control, and better yet, single. The door had been shut, his new host down for the count, for about ten seconds when he heard the lift open.

For several long moments he could do nothing but wait, and hope, and make himself appear as an empty place in the universe.

When he heard some of them come tearing back out, and the lift went down, he knew his plan had worked. Yes, part one had gone very well—it was good to know he could still improvise.

Time for part two.

He found a roll of heavy tape in the kitchen and used it to bind up everyone who was still alive. He taped their mouths shut, too—everyone except the cop, Girard. He prodded Girard awake, scanning as he did so.

"What a complicated life you have," he said to Girard, as the cop's

eyes flickered open. "Not one woman, but two. I've never really understood that, myself. I've never been able to be in love with more than one woman at a time. Here you have two, and you may lose them both because of your greed. You should be ashamed of yourself."

"Murderer."

"Ah. You want to change the subject. Good enough, I don't have time to be polite. We're going to use your link to make a call. You're going to tell them that Paul admitted it was all a ruse, that I've been gone for hours, and that I'm on the train to Amsterdam. I'll give you all of the information. Now, before you can object, let me tell you *why* you are going to do this, and why you'll do it just as I say.

"See, I could make you do it, but that would be very painful for you, and more important, fatiguing for me. On the other hand, I can easily slip into your mind, hear your every word before you say it. I'll know if you plan to betray me. If you try that, not only will you not have a chance of succeeding, but I'll kill one of these people and then we'll try again. And again, until you get it right. Do you understand?"

The policeman looked at him with a weary sort of comprehension.

"Yes."

"Good. Here's the information. And make it believable."

Girard performed flawlessly.

"Perfect," Bester told him, patting his head. "You've just saved a few lives." He wrapped a piece of tape around Girard's head. Then, carrying the dead teep's pistol, he went back into the bathroom to kill Garibaldi.

Garibaldi had felt like a sucker plenty of times in his life, but this was going to stand out as the high point—the Olympus Mons of suckerhood—if he managed to survive it.

And Lise wasn't going to like this story, not at all. Best not to tell her. Of course, when it hit the papers—well, that might take a while. If Bester killed everyone who knew he'd come down here, they might just miss the body until the smell started percolating.

That did it. Yep, he was panicking. He always got silly when he panicked.

He strained at the chute again, as if by some miracle the physics of the situation might suddenly change. But the mechanical problem stayed the same. Try as he might, he couldn't climb up.

He might get better purchase if he dropped his PPG, but at the moment that was his one and only chance. Bester might not know he had a gun, and he might get off the first lucky shot.

He doubted that Bester would leave something like that to chance,

though. He'd probably heat up a pan of oil and dump it on him first, something like that.

He rolled his eyes. Perfect. He was thinking of things to help Bester out, just on the off chance Bester hadn't thought of them himself. Could he be scanned from up there? Did a tiny glimpse of him constitute line of sight? Probably.

Even in a straight-up exchange of gunfire, he would lose. PPG shots were globs of superhot phased helium plasma. Once they made contact with any surface they began to lose integrity. With this angle, he might be able to sort of blister his enemy's face. Meanwhile, Bester had a variety of weapons to choose from, including slug throwers, which would work much better in this situation.

He couldn't wait for that. He had to do something. It had already been too long—what, five minutes? Ten? Bester wouldn't hang around much longer.

He couldn't go up. He had tried to flex like Hercules and break the chute with the mighty strength of his limbs—no luck there, not even the slightest reason to hope. He couldn't go down, either.

"Wait a minute," he breathed. Why couldn't he go down? What was he standing on, anyway? Not the foundation—he hadn't dropped far enough for that.

He raised his right heel the full five inches he could manage, and kicked down. Kicked again.

Something gave, slightly.

He kicked with the other foot, then punched down with both feet.

"Making a lot of noise down there, Mr. Garibaldi." Bester's voice sounded as if it were right in his ear, and for an instant he thought it must be telepathy. His skin crawled to think Bester might once again be in his head. But, no, it was just the acoustics of the shaft.

He fired up the chute without looking. Jumped and kicked, fired again. Jumped and kicked.

The air grew warm in the chute, thanks to the dispersing plasma. But something was certainly giving way beneath him.

He fired again, and this time the PPG didn't recharge. He dropped it, and used his arms as best he could to shove down, down, against the weakening floor of the shaft. At least he desperately hoped it was weakening.

Something finally broke beneath his feet, and he fell until his upper body caught in the too-small opening, nearly dislocating his arm. At the same moment, something like an angry hornet stung his ear. He wriggled frantically, his feet kicking free in a large, open space, his upper body still

stuck in the shaft. Then something hammered unbelievably hard into the top of his shoulder, and he was through, falling free.

Then slamming into something that broke with a lot of noise. That part wasn't even so bad; all of the air had been knocked out of him by whatever had hit his shoulder.

He grunted and sat up. He was on the ruins of a coffee table, in the middle of someone's living room. The someones, an elderly couple, gaped at him from a dingy sofa. "Hi. Sorry," he managed.

A dizzying wave of pain hit him as he stood. His left arm hung like a noodle, and he realized that he was bleeding, though not heavily. A bullet had shattered his collarbone, but not penetrated any further into his body. He looked up at the gaping hole in the roof of the apartment, then, thinking better of remaining beneath it, moved aside. With Garibaldi's luck, even a blind ricocheting shot might hit him right between the eyes. Or maybe Bester had grenades, who knew?

Bester. A floor or two above him!

He picked up the drained PPG and popped another charge into it.

The old people were yelling at him, now—in French, naturally.

"Okay, okay. Keep your shirts on. I'm not here to hurt you. And I'm going. If I were you, I'd do the same, at least for the next hour or two."

He didn't wait to see if they understood him or not, but found their front door and left as fast as he could, which, given the fact that the world was doing a slow spin, wasn't too fast.

Back in the hall, he located the stairs and stumbled toward them.

14

Bester left Paul's apartment in a hurry, cursing and wondering exactly where Garibaldi had gone. The ancient shaft must have ended in someone's ceiling, which probably meant he was a floor or two down.

Bester's second shot had drawn a flash of pain, but he couldn't tell how badly he had hurt the ex–security officer. Not badly enough, in all likelihood.

He decided to take the stairs. At least there he could reverse direction quickly, and he wouldn't be trapped in a box. Of course, Garibaldi would be thinking the same thing.

The disadvantage was that he had to pocket his weapon briefly to open the stairwell door, which was precisely when the lift opened.

He spun and reached for his weapon at the same time. Then, to his vague surprise, he saw that it wasn't Garibaldi, but a uniformed young man with a mustache and close-cropped hair, accompanied by a similarly dressed, dark-haired, pretty woman. The man's eyes widened, but he acted quickly, pushing the woman down and firing well before Bester even had his pistol out. Bester heard a dull hiss and something struck him sharply in the chest.

It didn't stop him from returning the fire. His first shot missed, but the second took the fellow in the thigh as he ducked back into the lift. The doors closed again.

Bester took the moment to pocket his weapon and yank the stairwell door open again. Only then did he examine his chest. A small hypo-dart stood out from it. He yanked it out. What was it? A knockout drug?

Bester ran down the stairs, determined to get as far away as possible before the drug took effect. He could only hope that Girard's orders had been taken seriously, that the cordon around the neighborhood at least had some holes in it now.

He was almost to the ground floor when he heard the first-floor door above him open, and then a hoarse, familiar shout.

"Bester!"

He looked up to see a bloody Garibaldi taking aim. He threw himself to the left and fired just as a PPG burst sizzled by. Though his arm was grazed, Garibaldi stood his ground, ignoring Bester's shot, and fired again.

Bester leapt over the rail, dropping five feet. It felt like twenty might have, in his prime. His knees didn't like it at all. Behind him, Garibaldi said something colorfully slanderous about Bester's sex life.

Well, I hit him, at least, Bester thought, as he kicked the door open to the ground floor corridor and made for the outside door. *It should slow him down, and we seem to be even in the arm department.*

No one seemed to notice him as he bolted out onto the street, and he didn't wait around to give any remaining hunters a chance.

He ran, thinking how odd it was that he was running at all. If the dart had contained something to knock him down, it should have done so by now. Could it have been empty, by mistake? He was feeling a little queasy, but that was all.

He turned a corner, changed direction as often as he could.

He needed a goal. Where was he going? For the time being, he would simply settle for getting out of the immediate area. Then he would have a little more opportunity to think.

His lungs started to burn, and between one footfall and the next something turned around in his mind. He was fifteen again, racing through the same darkened city. He had broken the academy rules, set out after a dangerous rogue on his own, and tracked her to Paris. It was the first time he had been in a city other than Geneva, where Teeptown was located, and Paris had come as a revelation.

That was when he learned that the city had its own mind, of sorts, a voice that was really millions of voices. That was where he had met Sandoval Bey, the mentor who had changed his life.

And now, so many years later, he was running through these same streets. And again his lungs were burning. Of course the first time, they had burned because one of them had a hole punched through it, not because of his age. Still, that boy of fifteen would have been caught long before now. What he had lost physically was more than made up for by what he had gained in experience. And Paris still sang to him.

No—it didn't. He realized that what had put him on that train of thought was the itchy feeling that something was missing.

It was. He couldn't *p'hear* anything. *Anything.*

Even at his weariest, he should be getting a background hum. But the silence in his head was as profound as if he were in space, solo, a light-year from any other mind.

The answer came to him like a cold, frozen hand on his chest. He

remembered his psychic duel with the teep, earlier that night, the one he had shot with his partner's hypo-gun, the one whose power had just suddenly drained away. Sleepers. The hypos contained sleepers.

Once before he had taken them, as a condition for conducting an investigation on Babylon 5. It had been unpleasant, but he had dealt with it. This would be much harder to deal with.

He turned another corner. The darkness seemed to be wrapping around him, collapsing of its own dead weight. Dead was a good word— the world felt dead, lifeless around him. And he was alone in that dead world. The first time, he had at least had someone to talk to—Garibaldi, in fact, of all people.

They had actually been a good team. That had been when he first realized how useful Garibaldi could be to him. But now he had no one, just the silence, the claustrophobic, sticky silence. And the terrible knowledge that if death found him now, he might not even feel it coming. He had to remind himself to keep looking back over his shoulder.

How could normals live like this? Why didn't they just shoot themselves, become as dead as the world they inhabited?

Garibaldi's legs buckled as he stepped out onto the sidewalk. The initial shock was wearing off, and his injury was really starting to hurt.

Bester wasn't anywhere in sight. Which way? If he made the right choice now, he stood a chance of catching the bastard. If he chose wrong, it was all over.

Superstition at least as old as ancient Rome won out. He went left, the sinister direction. And as he entered the alley, he caught a glimpse of a Human silhouette against the next, dimly lit street, running, favoring one arm.

Yes. His legs tried to fail him again, but damn that. He remembered the last time he had tried to kill Bester, the sickeningly helpless feeling of wanting to pull the trigger, *trying* to pull the trigger—and being totally unable to do it. There Bester had stood, laughing at him, that stupid smirk on his face, talking to Garibaldi as he might to a little child. He explained that he had "Asimoved" him, put a little subroutine in his head that wouldn't allow him to harm Bester, or permit him to come to harm.

Eventually, Lyta had been the key to his release. They had struck a bargain. He had helped her rogue telepaths, and she had removed the block. Good old Lyta. Good old scary-as-hell-there-at-the-end Lyta. Her death was another thing he owed Bester for. But who was counting?

He was. It was what kept him going, when his body told him to just lie down. For Sheridan, and the torture he had endured. For Talia, dead

even though her heart was probably still beating, somewhere. For himself. For himself.

For himself.

It worked. His arm jangled like a live wire, but he picked up the pace.

Girard rubbed his mouth. The tape *hurt* coming off.

The young man who had untied him didn't look like he was in good shape. He had left a trail of blood on the way in.

"We have to do something about your leg," the young woman with him said. Girard remembered the man—he was EABI. The woman he had never seen before.

The young man sat down heavily. "I won't argue," he grunted.

The tape was still lying where Bester had left it. It would do for the moment, until he could get an ambulance here. "What's your name, son?" he asked.

"Diebold, sir. Benjamin Diebold."

"I think he saved my life," the woman explained. "He pushed me out of the way."

"That was Bester, wasn't it?" Diebold gasped, as Girard cut his trousers away with his pocket knife.

"Yes."

"But we got orders to break the cordon"

"I know. Hold still."

Diebold said something else, but Girard didn't hear. A sudden flash exploded in his head.

Two men, running. Old enemies. Garibaldi chasing Bester. No question what will happen when they meet. There will be no arrest, no capture, no trial, no prison. One of them will die, or both.

"Bester!"

Garibaldi's shout sounded strangely tinny, depthless. Words were the tips of icebergs, and Bester was used to seeing the mountain that lay beneath the waves, the really dangerous mass of emotion and cognition that thrust words up for the ear to hear.

Normals talked and wrote of being able to "hear" anger or desperation in a voice, but like the parable of the blind men describing an elephant, they had no idea what they were talking about.

He didn't care what Garibaldi was thinking, per se—he could guess that well enough. But it would help to know how badly his foe was injured. He *did* seem to be favoring one arm.

Bester stopped, turned, aimed, and squeezed off a shot.

Green fire answered him, but missed by a yard, and he ducked around a corner.

Something cold and wet struck him on the cheek, and he turned the weapon up toward the sky. Another drop of water hit his forehead.

It was raining.

Bester remembered a duel he had read about. A young man had challenged an older. They had started with swords, but when it became clear to the other fellow that the young man was no match for him, he had thrown down his rapier in disgust and suggested something different. So the two got into a carriage, each tying a hand out of the way so that they couldn't use it. Wielding knives in their free hands, they fought while the carriage was driven around and around a park.

Bester seemed to remember both men had died. Probably Garibaldi would be happy with that. Bester was starting to think it would satisfy him, too. After all, how much longer before the other hunters came? The gunfire and smell of blood would bring them running back. With his psi he might have been able to deal with them. Not now.

Fine. If Garibaldi wanted a duel, he would give it to him. If nothing else, Bester would kill the man who had brought him so much misery. He ducked into a recessed doorway and waited.

The rain started as a few isolated drops, but within seconds it was hammering the avenue in undulating sheets. Garibaldi bit back a string of colorful expletives. Telepaths could hear you better when you spoke out loud, right? Or was it just more clearly? Whatever, Bester had more of an advantage than ever. Garibaldi was half-blinded by the rain, and the telepath would be able to *feel* him coming.

He took the next corner a little more cautiously, but he didn't want to slow up too much. Water was running into his eyes. Squinting, he did a slow pan of the street with the PPG, wishing he'd had time to stop and collect some night goggles. But of course, if he had, Bester would be gone.

If he wasn't already. He was nowhere to be seen. Had he had time to make the block? It didn't seem so, but adrenaline, pain, and the weird susurrus of the rain were doing funny things to time.

Prickles crawled across his scalp. He was here someplace, wasn't he? Masking himself, screwing with his mind. An invisible man.

The hand holding the PPG was shaking. It might have been shock from his wound, it might have been that little voice in his head that reminded him that Bester always, always won. *He's smarter than you,* the voice said. *He's always one step ahead.*

Feeling like a blind man surrounded by snipers, he flattened against the wall, his heart hammering.

Bester, blinded by the downpour, didn't notice Garibaldi until he was a few feet away. Tightening his jaw, he stepped out from the door, found his target—a vague man shape in the dark and wet—and pulled the trigger.

Someone stepped quickly from a doorway. Garibaldi didn't think at all. His finger squeezed the contact of the PPG.

The result was spectacular, and not at all what he expected. A green ball of fire seemed to explode in front of him as the rain refracted the coherent plasma into sudden incoherence. Murderous heat singed his eyebrows, and a dragon's tongue licked his hand. He dropped the PPG and hurled himself to the side.

Rain. He *knew* the damn stuff was dangerous. He blinked his eyes, trying to clear them.

A wave of steam and cooling plasma slapped Bester like the palm of a sun god. He lost his weapon in a moment of agony. He might have even blacked out for a second.

When he managed to look up, through the spots in his eyes, he saw Garibaldi rising up between him and the next streetlamp. With an inarticulate cry, Bester scrambled to his feet and launched a punch with his good arm. His face felt scalded. Maybe he was already dying.

The fist connected, but all wrong, and he nearly broke his wrist. Still, Garibaldi grunted and fell back. Bester dropped and swept, and had the almost religious satisfaction of feeling the impact, of seeing Garibaldi leaving the ground, hearing the meaty thud as he struck pavement. He kicked out again, catching Garibaldi in the ribs, and again.

The third kick met only rain. Garibaldi was in motion again, back on his feet, advancing.

They circled each other warily.

"Still a loser, aren't you, Garibaldi?" Bester sneered. "What's the matter, do you need a few snorts of Dutch courage?" He had to keep the ex–security officer off-balance, mentally and emotionally. Garibaldi had a greater reach and was three decades younger than him. "Or are you just too dumb to know when you're outmatched, with or without the booze?"

Garibaldi laughed harshly. "I'm not the one running like a jackrabbit. That would be you."

"I'm not running anymore," Bester returned. "I'll admit I'm in a

hurry, but I figured if you wanted me so bad, I could do a favor for an old friend. Especially one with whom I've been so . . . intimate."

"Don't even try to play that," Garibaldi said. "You're caught. Admit it. I've got you."

"You and what army? Oh yes, you *do* have an army, don't you? You didn't have the guts to come after me on your own. Afraid I'll turn your mind inside-out again?"

"They aren't here now. It's just you and me."

"You know why you hate me so much, Mr. Garibaldi? It's not anything I've done to you, like you pretend. It's because I *know* too much. I'm the only one who knows how dirty you are in there, in your private little hell. I've seen it all, and you can't stand the idea of anyone walking around who has even had a peek at it."

"Shut up."

"I didn't make you anything you weren't. In fact, I had to do remarkably little to turn you against Sheridan. You always resented him. You resent anyone who's stronger than you, with more strength of character than you. Like Sheridan. Like me." Garibaldi *was* favoring his arm—and badly.

"Don't even say your name in the same breath as his."

"You know it's true. Congratulations, by the way—I see you've had my Asimov removed. Lyta? Of course, Lyta. Only she would have been strong enough. Funny, Mr. Garibaldi, how your bigotry takes a backseat when it serves your own interests. Letting another dirty telepath into your mind must have been—"

Garibaldi lunged, and Bester was ready. After all, *he* had been living and fighting with only one arm for almost half a century. Garibaldi, for all of his size and training, was clumsy.

Bester sidestepped, snapped a hard jab into Garibaldi's wounded shoulder. The ex–security chief choked out half a scream, which cut off when Bester snapped a vicious knife-hand into the base of his skull. Garibaldi dropped to the pavement.

"What, did you think this would be easy, Mr. Garibaldi? You have to *work* for revenge. I could tell you things . . ."

Garibaldi was on his hands and knees, coughing. Bester kicked him as hard as he could, angling his toe up to catch the solar plexus.

Garibaldi felt ribs crack and tasted blood in his mouth. Stupid. He'd been stupid. Again.

If you let Bester talk, you lose, he thought grimly. He could feel your fears, play you like a harp, know your every intended move. His words would soften you up, and then he had you.

He felt rather than saw the next kick coming, and he took it, only this time he curled around it, caught the foot. Bester tried to twist away, but Garibaldi held on. Clawing for the rest of the leg. Somewhere, he found a hidden reserve of strength, and yanked.

Bester went down.

They got back to their feet at the same time. This time, Garibaldi didn't let him talk. He lowered his head and charged like a bull, letting his reflexes do the fighting rather than his brain. Bester hammered at his broken shoulder, and he felt the sickening scrape of bone against bone. But he didn't care anymore. Now that he had his hands on the teep, Garibaldi wasn't going to let go.

The wall stopped them both, but Bester took most of the punishment. The telepath's hand came up, clawing at Garibaldi's eyes, but he slammed him into the wall again. Then he unwrapped his arm and dealt Bester an uppercut. Hitting him felt good. He did it again, for good measure, with all of the strength that he could muster.

Bester kicked him in the crotch. It hurt, of course, but he really didn't care what happened to his body anymore. All he could see was Bester's face; all he could hear were his taunts. He got a good handful of hair and cracked Bester's head against the wall again, again, again. The telepath moaned and slid to the ground like a sack of potatoes.

Garibaldi, swaying, stepped back. He walked a few feet to where he had dropped the PPG. The rain had slackened, but he wiped the muzzle thoroughly, and to be sure, he placed it against Bester's head.

The telepath's eyelids flickered open. They had ended their brawl near a streetlamp, so it was light enough to make him out, but his eyes were black, like holes in space. Like Lyta's in all her unholy glory.

"Go ahead," Bester murmured. "It's what you want. But you know I'm right. I know how sick you are inside, and you can't stand that."

"You *are* right," Garibaldi said. "You're always right, aren't you? But you don't know me anymore, not like you think you do. Yeah, maybe on the inside I'm a bastard—we all are, one way or another. Maybe I can't blame it all on you. Maybe I do have to shoulder some of it. I'm willing to try. But you—you were responsible for the death of thousands. Millions, for all I know. And you don't have any remorse at all."

"No," Bester said, quietly. "I don't. There are things in my life I regret, but none of them would mean anything to you. And listen to yourself. All you're doing is trying to work yourself up to killing me, to justify it. Just *do* it, you pitiful gutless coward."

Garibaldi's finger trembled on the contact. "I don't need to justify it," he said, softly. "I can do it because I want to."

He counted five, then squeezed the trigger—or tried to. He found that he couldn't.

"Who has you Asimoved now, Mr. Garibaldi?" Bester asked, mockingly.

Garibaldi didn't let his weapon waver. "You owe me, Bester. You owe it to me to die like the dog you are. No, strike that, I *like* dogs. But as much as you've hurt me, as much as you've wronged me, there are a thousand others who you owe more. I'm not going to deny them, just to satisfy myself. I thought I could, but I can't. Your life belongs to everyone you've screwed, not just to me."

Bester managed a weak laugh. "Nice speech. You *are* a coward."

"Maybe. Maybe I am. But I'd rather be that than what you are. What I would be if I pulled the trigger."

With relief, Girard sagged against the wall and lowered his gun, still not sure what he would have done if Garibaldi had gone through with it.

No, he knew. He wouldn't have stopped Garibaldi, but he would have arrested him, and then turned in his own badge. He was flexible on certain points—cynical, some might say—but down deep, he believed. Believed in the law, believed in *right*.

What he had done to Paulette—yes, Paulette, he could think of her by a name other than "my wife"—hadn't been right. That was the crux of the problem, the thing he had been dancing around. He could pretend that her reaction was extreme, that he was only upset because he'd been caught, that Marie was being a nuisance, that it was the inconvenience of the whole thing that bothered him. But those were lies. He was upset because he was *wrong*, and he had to look it full in the face.

But first things first. He took out his cuffs and went to help Garibaldi.

15

The War Crimes tribunal facilitation committee met today, to discuss the feasibility of acceding to the demand of the French government that the trial of Alfred Bester be conducted in Paris and not in Geneva.

Speaking before the committee, French President Michel Chambert reiterated his claim that since Bester was arrested on French soil he should be tried there. Senator Charles Sheffer of the United States vehemently opposed this position, calling it a "cynical ploy on the part of the French government to exploit what will surely be the trial of the century.

"Bester stands accused, not by France, but by the Human race," Sheffer went on, "and should be tried in EarthDome."

A number of other Earth senators protested as well, but by the end of the day, it was clear that the committee would likely agree to French demands. Dr. Eugenia Mansfield, a professor of law at Harvard, pointed out in testimony to the rules committee that, if denied the larger venue, France could press for trial on local charges, which process might take months—after which every other jurisdiction with some grievance against the infamous telepath could well press to do the same. This could delay the EA War Crimes trial indefinitely, something EarthGov is not likely to permit.

Senator Nakamura seemed to sum up the majority opinion when he said, "After waiting for so long for a final resolution to the telepath crisis, the world is hungry for justice. We should not deny the people that justice simply because France chooses an inappropriate time to assert its sovereignty."

Garibaldi watched the vid images come and go, fiddling with the controls from his hospital bed. He was thankful that, for the most part, the hospital had managed to keep the reporters at bay. Oh, one would appear outside of his window now and then, pleading soundlessly for an interview, but only two had managed to actually get in disguised as doctors. That had been a bit disturbing, since Girard had a couple of uniforms outside, just in case Bester had any vengeful allies left. On the

other hand, letting them through might have suited the Frenchman's idea of a prank.

The result was that there were exactly five shots of him that repeated endlessly on the vids: his attack of the Bester look-alike and subsequent dismissal of the reporter, a brief shot of him being loaded into the ambulance after he collapsed at Girard's feet, and two views of him in the hospital bed, puffy-faced and looking incredibly old. In one he simply scowled and pushed the call button. In the other he made a six-word statement summing up his feelings. They were unfortunate words to become famous for. He wasn't exactly Churchill or Sheridan, he thought wryly.

He had hoped to hear from Sheridan, but the president of the Interstellar Alliance seemed to have dropped out of known space again. He had a way of doing that.

"Well. I'm glad I found you here, and not in the morgue, at least."

Lise stood in the doorway, more beautiful than ever.

"Hi, honey." He tried to look calm.

Her lips compressed, and he prepared for the worst, but after a moment or two, she walked over to his bed and took his hand. "Are you okay?"

"Broken ribs, shattered scapula, ruptured spleen. Bester in custody. Never felt better."

"You left without telling me where you were going. You won't do that again." She didn't qualify it. She didn't even say "or else," but he was left without any doubts.

"I won't do that again," he said, and meant it.

She nodded, then smiled, briefly. "You didn't kill him."

"No. I couldn't."

"The Michael Garibaldi I love wouldn't kill him. I'm glad to know you're the man I thought you were."

"I try to be, Lise. The man you see in me is the best of me. It's just the rest that's a mess."

"Not a mess—just a little untidy."

"Where's Mary?"

"Outside. I wanted to see you first. I wasn't sure how you would be, how I'd react." She brushed his cheek. "Now that this is over—"

"It's not over yet. There's still the trial, and the sentencing, all that good stuff. I want to stay for the trial."

"But for you, it's over," she said, firmly. "And now that it's over there's going to be a hole in your life, Michael. You'll have to be ready to deal with that."

"No hole. Just a wound, finally closing up. I knew that, when I finally had him." He squeezed her hand. "You think I don't have enough?"

"You aren't a quiet man, Michael. You aren't comfortable just with happiness."

He laughed. It hurt. "I bet if I put enough effort into it, I can be," he said. "And believe me, I intend to put a lot of effort into it."

She smiled a little skeptically, then kissed him.

"By the way," she said, when they came up for air. "*You* can explain to our daughter what those words mean. The ones they keep playing on the newscasts."

Bester felt as if he were looking down on the courtroom from a great height, as if the witness stand were Olympus. For weeks, others had sat here, but they had seemed small to him, lost in the crowd of humanity, in the humming of newstapers, there in the almost baroque splendor of the French hall of justice.

Small. Even Garibaldi looked small, perched in that place that demanded the truth. Old enemies and old friends came, spoke, and went. A few struggled, unwilling even now to betray him in an entirely unqualified way. Most of these were already in prison.

Others were glad to proclaim him a monster, to paint him as something more removed from humanity than the Drakh or even the Shadows. He listened to them, watched them shrink into history even as he felt himself grow larger, a towering shadow. People would remember Alfred Bester, yes, but these others were mere footnotes.

It might have been different, he mused, if Sheridan had come. Perhaps Sheridan would have even said something good about him. After all, Sheridan understood, as the rest of these insects did not. Understood about the sacrifices one made for the common good, the stains one would accept on one's own soul when something higher was at stake.

Yes, all of this was inevitable. Oh, his lawyers tried. Hadn't Bester been an appointed official of an organization created and overseen by the EA Senate? Had he really been doing anything more than implementing the policies of Psi Corps, the president, EarthGov itself?

All of that was just marking time. The prosecution was full of answers. Nothing in the Psi Corps charter allowed for the murder of unarmed civilians, the blackmail of EA senators, unauthorized experiments on detainees, torture, distribution of illegal substances. No, Bester had taken matters into his own hands, creating a government within a government, and had gone to war against not only the law, but everything that was right and decent.

Inevitable.

Now he sat in the chair himself, the place of truth. He wore a black suit. He didn't wear his telepath's badge. He smiled when the mouth-piece for the prosecution—a young EA senator named Semparat—stepped onto the floor. Semparat looked . . . small.

"State your name, please, for the record."

"My name is Alfred Bester," he replied. He paused, cocked his head slightly to the side. "Or would it make you feel better if I said my name was Hitler, or Stalin, or Satan?"

"Alfred Bester will do," the senator said, dryly. "I think by the end of this we will see that it will do quite nicely."

"Oh, but you knew that coming in, didn't you?" Bester asked. "You had no need of a trial, did you?"

Semparat frowned, but ignored that last.

"Mr. Bester," he continued, "you have heard all the charges against you before, at your hearing. At that time, you maintained that you were innocent. After all of the witnesses that have come before us, do you still so maintain?"

Bester raised his eyebrows. "Of course I do."

"Really."

"I do."

"You deny, for instance, the murder of forty-three unarmed civilians connected to the telepath Resistance on Mars?"

"I deny their murder, yes."

"You deny the evidence brought before this court that you ordered their executions and killed three yourself."

"I don't deny killing them. I deny the charge that it was murder. And I applaud your semantic games, Senator. What you now call the telepath Resistance was at the time universally recognized as an illegal, subversive organization of terrorists. The normals involved were also terrorists and subversives."

"But they weren't armed, were they? Did they try to resist you?"

"Frankly, I did not care to give them the chance. Their activities had already resulted in the deaths of at least sixty-four of my colleagues. Senator, it was a war. However you look at it, those people fought in that war and they were casualties of it."

"Who declared this war? You?"

Bester raised an eyebrow mildly. "The terrorists declared it when they bombed our facilities on Mars. Everything we did after that was response, kind for kind."

"We've heard evidence that you, Alfred Bester, murdered civilians long before the beginning of the telepath conflict. Are you going to claim that that was war, as well?"

"Of course," Bester said.

"I, for one, am confused by that statement, Mr. Bester, and my guess is that many of this court are equally confused. Would you care to explain?"

"I would be delighted to, Senator," Bester replied.

"Please do so then."

Bester took a sip of the water next to him. "One hundred and fifty-eight years ago, the existence of telepaths was known to almost no one. One hundred and fifty-seven years ago, it became common knowledge thanks to an article in the *New England Journal of Medicine*.

"By the end of that year, eighteen thousand telepaths were dead. No war was declared by any government. They were killed one at a time, they were killed en masse and buried in pits, they were aborted when DNA testing revealed what they were as fetuses."

"Mr. Bester, I'm sure we all know the history."

"Really? Funny, I've never heard a word about it during this trial. You asked me to speak—I'm speaking. Don't I have that right?"

"This isn't a platform for your political views."

Bester laughed, sharply. "It seems to be a platform for *yours*. More than half of the so-called crimes you're accusing me of were committed with the consent of the legitimate government of the time. You represent the new order, so of course you would like nothing better than to discredit the old one, in order to legitimize yourself.

"This entire trial is nothing more than the final step in rewriting the last century-and-a-half of history to suit those of you who are in charge now. And yet you claim that this trial is not a platform for political views? Senator, your hypocrisy and the hypocrisy of this court sickens me. Either afford me my right to speak without interruption, or send me back to my cell. Frankly, I don't care which this kangaroo court sees fit to do. But do one or the other."

That drew a deep murmuring from the audience, and not all of it sounded negative. What he felt was still overwhelmingly hostile, however.

"Very well, Mr. Bester." The senator sighed. "Just get on with it."

"Thank you. As I said, once telepathy was discovered, the murder of telepaths began. It hasn't stopped. I could draw your attention to last month's case in Australia, or the one reported this week in Brazil, but there really is no need for a list of examples, is there? Each of you know it's true. To grow up telepathic is to grow up with the constant menace of death, the vague but real threat of dying at the hands of someone who doesn't even know you, only knows what you *are*, what you represent to

them. *I* grew up with it. The first time I left the academy grounds, to go on a hike with my friends, I was attacked. The *first* time."

He paused. "This undeclared, unrecognized war has been fought for a hundred and fifty-seven years. Its casualties—have always been on *my* side. And when this killing began, what did EarthGov do about it? They built a telepath ghetto called Teeptown, and they gave us badges to mark us, separate us. They gave any normal who wanted to kill a telepath the means to find us and identify us. Then they used telepaths to control telepaths. Why? The implicit threat was always there—ask any telepath old enough to remember. *Either you control yourselves, or we will control you.*

"That was the choice I grew up with. Hunt down and sometimes kill my own kind, with the blessings of EarthGov and every normal citizen who voted for it, or be subjected to the same uncontrolled genocide that was visited on us in the beginning.

"You made that, each and every one of you. Oh, you might try to pawn it off on your ancestors, but you reified it each generation, gave it the nod. I spent the first seventy-two years of my life being told what a *good* little boy I was, how *well* I served humanity by hunting down my people. I have the commendations to prove it, a drawerful.

"Now, suddenly, you've decided that maybe Psi Corps wasn't such a good idea, and you want to sweep it all under the rug. You want to pretend it just went bad, somehow, and that it was *my* fault. You also know that isn't true.

"You blame me for continuing to fight the war that started in 2115? You blame me for defending my people? I suppose you do. Psi Corps was developed to keep telepaths in their place. An act of war, of suppression. You want to know who the real telepathic Resistance was? It was *us*. Protecting ourselves against you. Sure, along the way we protected you, too, whether you knew it or not, and more than you will *ever* know.

"But in the end, all of us inside knew what was coming. That one day some bright boy would hit upon the 'final solution' for the 'telepath problem,' and there we would be, all caged up and ready for the gas. Only we didn't play the game that way.

"Now you're upset. Who can blame you? Hitler would have been upset, too, if the Jews in Warsaw had turned out to be armed to the teeth and ready to fight."

"Oh, come on—"

"No, Senator. *You* come on. You want to pretend a century and a half of continual violence against telepaths never existed? Fine. You want to pretend that Psi Corps wasn't created by the EA Senate? Fine. You want to silence me, lock me away, maybe even kill me? Well and good.

But you know the truth. In your hearts, all of you do. This isn't over. You've divided and conquered, scattered my people. And yet, they still wear the badges, don't they? They still have to report to be examined, don't they? They're still registered at birth, marked more certainly and permanently than anyone who ever wore an armband with a star—because that, at least, you could take off.

"In fact, the *only* thing that has changed is that you've taken away our ability to fight back, when the time comes. And, boys and girls, the time is coming. All of your wishing and hoping and praying won't stop it. The mass of humanity won't tolerate our existence. Tomorrow, in ten years, in fifty—it's coming, and this playacting, my trial, its context will become abundantly clear.

"So, yes, I have killed, like any good warrior. I have fought the good fight, and I lost. I regret nothing. I would change nothing in my power to change, I would—"

His tongue stumbled. As he spoke, he had been sweeping his gaze over the crowd, and from camera to camera. He wanted every single person watching to know he was speaking to *them*, personally. To let them know they *all* shared the blame.

And there, six rows back, toward the center . . .

Louise, staring at him with those eyes he knew so well, a faint wrinkle in that forehead he had kissed. Her hair—he could almost smell it, feel it between his fingers.

I regret nothing. She rebuked him, by her mere presence, made him the liar. For in her eyes, there was nothing about him. No recognition, no love, only faint puzzlement, perhaps a hint of revulsion. Nothing.

If he hadn't cut her up, she would love him still, and her eyes would be an anchor, her words a safe harbor, even in the midst of all of this.

He suddenly felt very old, and very tired, and very, very alone. He *had* killed—the one person in the universe who might have spoken for him. For that, if for no other crime, he deserved whatever came.

"Mr. Bester? Are you through?"

Louise realized he was looking at her, and her brow creased angrily. Even if she didn't remember him, she knew what he had done to her. Even if he could start over, she wouldn't love him again.

"Mr. Bester?"

"I've said everything I'm going to say," he murmured. "You'll do what you want anyway. I'm through. I'm through."

16

In his dreams he heard the singing mind of Paris. Sometimes Geneva, sometimes Rome, or Olympus Mons or Brasilia—but mostly, usually, Paris. In his dreams, he sat watching the sky wrap up in watercolor shrouds as it died for the evening. He sipped coffee and thought about how much of his life lay ahead, how many possibilities.

Or sometimes, in his dream, he sat with Louise, thinking how much of his life was gone, but how good the rest of it would be. And still Paris sang like an immense choir, with Louise the featured soloist, the brightest, loveliest voice among them.

He awoke knowing that it was the city and its sighing mind he had truly loved, and Louise, who represented it, personified it. But both were gone now, forever.

In dreams, in dreams. He preferred them. Awake, the world was dead, a cave of bone.

But wake he must, at times. He rose that morning as he did every morning, splashed water in his face, went to the window, and looked out upon his childhood. Teeptown.

In the distance, he could just make out what had once been the cadre houses. Just below him, clearly visible, was the quad common with its statue of William Karges, which he and his friends had called the "Grabber."

Of course, the Grabber was no longer grabbing. There was nothing left of him but a pedestal and part of one leg. The statue of Karges had been blown up, along with much of the quad, during the wars.

Just as well. Karges had been a secret telepath who had saved President Robinson's life at the cost of his own. When Bester had been little, they had taught him that Psi Corps had been created by Robinson to honor that sacrifice. That wasn't true—the Corps had existed in essence, if not in name, for decades. It had never been one of the lies he liked—it suggested too much that only by sacrifice did telepaths prove they had the right to exist.

So good-bye, Grabber, and good riddance.

They had tried to shut Teeptown down, as they had the Corps, but it hadn't quite worked out. The scores of private academies that had sprung up to instruct young telepaths hadn't worked very well, just as he had predicted they wouldn't. Over the years, he had watched the Psionic Monitoring Commission gradually reimplement almost all of the old Corps institutions, though in darling new baby-doll clothes. Once again Teeptown was a campus, a center of telepath life and activity. Many older teeps never left their quarters there—life among normals had proved too hard, too uncertain.

And so Teeptown remained a ghetto. Again, as he had predicted. It gave him some small comfort, to be right. It gave him little, though, to know that this maximum security facility was his own creation. He had built it to hold telepaths—and so it did. War criminals.

He heard footsteps in the corridor. "Good morning, James," he said.

"Morning Mr. Bester," James said, in his faintly mocking tone. "How're the memoirs coming?"

Bester glanced over at the simple AI on his bed.

"Pretty well," he said.

"I have some news for you."

"Oh?"

"Olean passed last night."

Bester absorbed that silently for a moment. "How did he manage to kill himself?" he said at last.

"It was pretty clever, but I can't tell you, of course. You might imitate him."

"I'm not going to kill myself. I won't give you the satisfaction."

James, the jailer, shook his head. "I get no satisfaction from it. I think you know that."

"The world, then. They'd love it. It's what they want. Life sentence— absurd. I was sentenced to death, death by suicide. I just refuse to carry out the sentence."

James hesitated. "You may be right, there. But you condemned thousands of teeps to the same fate—you made *them* take sleepers."

"I never did that and you know it. I enforced the law, I didn't write it."

"You understand me, then, why I have to give you this." He indicated a small gun-shaped device at his belt.

"Skip it this week. Just once."

"I can't."

"Just once. You know I can't escape. I just want to *feel* again."

"So did Olean, and Brewster, and Tuan."

"Once. One week."

James shook his head. "If it were up to me—"

"It *is* up to you," Bester said, gritting his teeth.

"Be a good boy and take your medicine, Mr. Bester."

And so he did, stood still while the needle pricked his arm and the sleepers went in, as they had for ten years now. He barely felt the stupid feeling spread. He had never had the extreme reaction to the sleepers that some did—the listlessness, the deeply drugged feeling. No, they left his mind pretty much intact, so he could be acutely aware of how crippled he was.

James left, and Bester fought the gloom by working on his memoirs. He was nearly done with them, had been nearly done with them for years. He just kept fiddling. He liked to fiddle with his history—it was the only thing he still had control of, his version of things. Let the historians wrangle endlessly about what was true and what wasn't. *He* knew, and they didn't, and it was the only power he still had.

Well, that and the power of his predictions, of his insights. Those would validate him, one day.

Two days later, a week from Birthday, he got an early present. The vidcom on the ceiling came on, unannounced. It did that rather rarely—he could request programming and sometimes get it, but it usually took awhile. When it came on of its own accord, it usually meant bad news, some new announcement from the prison director.

This time, however, as he watched and listened, a ghost of his old smile returned to his face. The smile broadened when he understood that most everyone else in the world was starting to weep, or denying reality, or cursing softly. They would look back on this day and everyone would remember where they were, what they were doing. Garibaldi, for instance, probably was not taking it well.

Yes, they would all remember where they were when Sheridan died.

Of course, Bester would—how could he forget? *"Let me see,"* he imagined himself telling someone. *"That day I must have been—why, yes, I was in prison . . ."*

Sheridan had been no friend of Bester's and he'd been a hypocrite besides. They said the best revenge was living well; it wasn't. It was *much* simpler than that. It was seeing your enemies die.

Now if he could just outlive Garibaldi, then even *this* life would have a certain sweetness.

He listened intently, in the hopes that Garibaldi had been involved and perhaps had died as well. No such luck. Ah, well, he would settle for Sheridan for the moment.

* * *

They were putting up a new statue where the Grabber had once stood. At first Bester thought they were clearing away the pedestal and its pitiful half-leg altogether, but they were just cleaning it off for a new occupant.

This interested him, as nothing had for some time. He entertained himself by speculating who it might be. Lyta? Byron? More likely Byron—he had been the martyr, the one who had acquired everyone's sympathies. Lyta had led them, too, but she had been frightening even to her allies. Still, it was she who had struck the real blows, wasn't it? Ultimately, Byron had been a coward.

A few days later he awoke to find a crowd gathered, and the statue in place, covered by a tarp. He put his face against the monomolecular glass, his heart working oddly in his chest. *Oh, come now,* he thought to himself, disgustedly. *You don't really care that much.*

But he did, somehow. The symbol that the slowly reforming Corps chose for itself would tell him much about its character, about its leaders. Would they choose the warrior queen, the mystic martyr—or perhaps even himself, a sort of dark reminder of what *not* to become?

He watched the crowd, wishing he could *p'hear* them. He had heard that when a normal lost a sense—vision, for instance—their other senses sharpened, to take up the slack. Not so with telepathy. His other senses were only fading. Not that any normal sense could begin to replace his birthright.

Speeches began, but he couldn't hear them. The crowd applauded—he couldn't hear that, either.

He hit his call button. After a long delay, James answered. "Yeah?"

"I wonder if I could get the audio for the ceremony outside."

"The dedication? Sure. Don't see as how that would hurt anything."

A moment later the sound cut in. The speaker was winding up.

". . . dark days, but they represented hope, created it, held it aloft like a candle. It was their memory that carried us all through to the liberation, their sacrifice that represents the best in us."

Bester nodded sullenly. He thought it had looked like two statues. Byron *and* Lyta, then.

"And so, all of you, it's my great honor to present our ancestors. Not in fact—for their only child, their great hope, vanished or was killed in the vicious raid on their hidden camp. But spiritually, and morally—" The speaker paused.

"Those of us who grew up in the Corps were taught that the Corps was our mother, and our father. But if we must look to a common,

spiritual mother and father, let us look to those who represented freedom, not oppression. Tolerance, not intolerance. Hope of liberty, not the despair of repression.

"My friends, my kith, my kin, I give you Matthew, Fiona, and Stephen Dexter."

The shroud came off. Time slipped for Bester, a weird plummet between heartbeats.

He sat in a tree, at the age of six, watching the stars, searching for the faces of his parents. Sometimes he could see a hint of them, of his mother's eyes, a suggestion of auburn hair, an echo of her voice.

He was older, on Mars. The oldest and most successful of all the rogues, Stephen Walters, lay crushed against a bulkhead, one leg bent under him in a very strange way, one arm missing at the elbow. He still had his mask on, but Bester had the distinct impression the eyes behind it were open.

I know you, Walters psied.

The hairs on the back of Bester's neck stood up. *I was in New Zealand,* Bester replied. *I tracked you here.*

No. Before that. I know you. Oh, God in heaven. It's my fault. Fiona, Matthew, forgive—

It paralyzed Bester. The sense of familiarity was like a drug. It wasn't pleasant, it was horrible, but he needed it somehow. Somehow—somehow it was a piece of him that was missing.

What are you talking about?

I know the feel of you. I saw you born—after all I had done, after all the blood on my hands, but they let me watch you come into the world, and you were so beautiful I cried. You were our hope, our dream—

My name is Alfred Bester.

We called you Stee, so you wouldn't be confused with me. They gave you my name, made me your godfather. Your mother, Fiona, how I loved her. Matthew, I loved him, too, but God— a terrible spasm of pain stopped him then, and almost stopped his heart. Bester felt it tremble. *It was me that lost you,* Walters went on. *I thought I could save them, but they knew they wouldn't make it. All they asked was for me to get you out, keep you free, and I failed them. Failed—*

Matthew and Fiona Dexter were terrorists, Bester replied. *They died when the bomb they were planting in a housing compound went off early. The bomb they set off killed my parents.*

Lies. He was getting weak. *They fed you lies. You are Stephen Kevin Dexter.*

No.

Walters cocked his head wearily, and then he reached up to Bester's

face. With a trembling hand he pulled his breather up and off. In the gloom, his eyes were colorless, but Al knew they were blue. Bright blue, like the sky. A woman with dark red hair and changeable eyes, a black-tressed man, both all smiles. He knew them. Had always known them, but he hadn't seen their faces since the Grins had banished them. They were looking down at a baby in a crib, talking baby talk. And Bester could feel a love so strong—was it love? He had never felt anything just like it, because there was no hint of physical desire, no desperate need, just deep, abiding affection, and hope . . .

He was seeing through Walters' eyes, through the filter of Walters' heart. But then, horribly, another image superimposed itself. The same two people, but looking down at him, and he was the baby in the crib, and behind Mother and Father stood another man, a man with bright blue eyes, as bright as the sun . . .

They loved you. I loved you. I love you still. Psi Corps killed them and they took you away. I tried to find you . . .

Bester wasn't aware of finding the PPG. Suddenly it was there, in his left hand and in front of him. His hand clenched on it, and Walters' face turned bright green, uncomprehending.

Shut up.

His hand clenched again, another viridian flare.

Shut up.

The mind images were dropping away, but not fast enough. He tried to shoot again, but the charge was gone. He tried and tried, squeezing the contact, throttling the lying glyphs in his brain.

Fiona . . . Matthew . . . Walters was still there, pulling the images about him in a blazing cloak. His eyes were still there, too, resigned, full of gentle reprimand. He stood near a gate, the doors of which were just beginning to crack open. *You can't destroy the truth.*

And he was gone, and finally the images shredded, a thousand visions of his parents, dancing, fighting, embracing, holding him . . .

No! He took it all in his fist and he squeezed until it went away.

His fist had never opened again. Never.

He shook his head, becoming aware of his cell again.

There they were below—the man and woman he had never known, save in dreams, and visions, and from the mind of a dying man. Matthew and Fiona Dexter, the mother and father in bronze. And in their arms, the lovingly held bundle—

Of course it was true. Of course he had always known it.

It felt like a cough, at first, so long had it been since he laughed. He hacked up another, and had to sit back on his bunk.

James must have thought he was dying, because he showed up a few minutes later, looking worried. "Bester?"

"It's nothing," Bester managed, waving him away. "Just the universe. Don't believe anyone when they tell you irony is just a literary convention, James. It's a universal constant, like the coefficient of gravity."

"What are you talking about?"

But Bester shook his head. Another thing that only he knew. No one else on Earth or in the stars knew what had happened to that baby, immortalized in bronze. That the symbol of hope for the brave new world was none other than the most hated criminal of the old.

Maybe there *was* hope for them, after all.

Still smiling, he lay down on his bunk, trying to frame what to do about it. Would that go in his memoirs? Maybe, but it might be better, more delicious, to never let them know, to never tell *anyone*.

For now he was tired. He would think about it in the morning. He sighed and closed his eyes, and felt an odd softness in his arm, his left arm. A sort of warmth. And movement, like something unfolding.

And he dreamed—maybe it was dream—that his left hand opened like the petals of a flower, and the fingers wriggled, and he laughed in muted delight.

When James found him the next day, it was the first thing he noticed, the hand. Palm up, fingers only lightly curled, free of the fist that had trapped them for so long.

Bester was free, too, a faint weird smile on his lips, his face looking somehow younger. He really did look like he was just sleeping.

EPILOGUE

Girard wondered again what, exactly, had brought him to the graveyard. It was raining lightly, not a nice day even if you were somewhere pleasant, somewhere that didn't remind you that you were shuffling ever faster toward the off-ramp of the mortal coil.

He looked out over the garden of marble headstones and shrugged. Well, he had been in the neighborhood, and he rarely got to Geneva. That he should be here when his most famous case died—it seemed, somehow, that he was fated to watch them put Bester in the ground. And he didn't like to argue with fate *too* much.

Few others seemed to have felt so compelled. Some thirty people accompanied the body to the graveside, but of those, most were clearly with the press, come for photographic Grendel-heads to assure the world that the monster was dead at last. There were four or five people who might have been family members of Bester's victims, here to find that assurance in person. Another four or five simply looked curious.

The only weeping was from the sky. No one had come to mourn Bester, only to bury him.

There was no graveside service. After the press had been run off, a man in EA uniform checked the coffin. Girard saw him lift the lid, nod, and speak briefly into a recorder. The lid came back down, four men in prison uniforms put the box in the hole, a fifth in an earthmover covered it over, and that was that.

He had half expected that woman to show up—what had her name been? Louise? She had looked Girard up, years later, to ask him what he knew about *her* role in things. He had thought she would eventually talk to Bester himself, but maybe that hadn't been allowed. Surely she knew—his death had made the news everywhere, and even now the sordid details of his life were being rehashed on the networks.

But no. The men did their work in almost eerie silence. No words, gentle or harsh, were spoken. No benediction, no blame. He almost felt as if he should say something himself.

But he didn't. Girard watched until the men left. He wasn't in any hurry. His wife was shopping, and he had nothing to do for several hours. He stayed, thinking that surely, *surely* someone else would come.

He realized he was still waiting for the woman, Louise. After all, it was Bester's love for her that had gotten him caught . . .

Merde, but I'm a romantic! Girard thought. Yet here was the proof, love *could* be destroyed, cut out as if it had never been. And a man really *could* go to his grave ungrieved. It made him feel better about his own life, his own choices. Despite himself, Girard had people who loved him.

As he was finally walking away, some instinct made him look back. He had just passed into a small copse of trees, and a breeze mingled the scent of clay with the green scent of the leaves fluttering wetly around him. Life mingled with death. It was nearly dark, and at first he thought he had turned for nothing, for some ghost in his own brain.

But then his peripheral vision made out a shadow approaching the grave. As Girard watched it move into the open, it became more distinct. A man, not a woman. The man knelt by the fresh earth, staring at it for a long time. Then he lifted something—Girard couldn't make out what— and put it on the grave. He got up and strode away without looking back.

Girard recognized him then, by his walk. Garibaldi.

He almost went after him, to say hello, if nothing else, but somehow felt it would be inappropriate. There had been something solemn, almost sacred about Garibaldi's movements, something inviolable.

Still, when Garibaldi was gone, Girard walked over to see what he had placed on the grave.

When he saw it, he shook his head and chuckled softly. It was a wooden stake, pushed into the yellow clay as far as it would go.

"Amen," Girard whispered. And, "Peace." Then he left the dead where they belonged.

When he reached the street, he flipped his phone open and ordered flowers for his wife. As he walked to the hotel, he began humming to himself. The rain kept up, but it didn't bother him in the slightest. There were worse things in life than a little rain.

ABOUT THE AUTHORS

Born in Meridian, Mississippi, in 1963, **J. GREGORY KEYES** spent his early years roaming the forests of the native state and the red rock cliffs of the Navajo Indian reservation in Arizona. He earned a B.A. in anthropology from Mississippi State University and a master's degree from the University of Georgia, where he did course work for a Ph.D. He and his wife, Nell, live in Seattle, where in addition to full-time writing, he practices ethnic cooking—particularly Central American, Szechuan, Malaysian, and Turkish cuisines. Since moving to the Northwest, he can no longer participate in his favorite sport—*Kapucha Toli,* a Choctaw game involving heavy sticks and few rules—so he has taken up fencing. Greg is the author of *The Waterborn, The Blackgod, Newton's Cannon,* and *Babylon 5: Dark Genesis.*

J. MICHAEL STRACZYNSKI is one of the most prolific and highly regarded writers currently working in the television industry. In 1995, he was selected by *Newsweek* magazine as one of their Fifty for the Future, described as innovators who will shape our lives as we move into the twenty-first century. His work spans every conceivable genre—from historical dramas and adaptations of famous works of literature (*The Strange Case of Dr. Jekyll and Mr. Hyde*) to mystery series (*Murder, She Wrote*), cop shows (*Jake and the Fatman*), anthology series (*The Twilight Zone*), and science fiction (*Babylon 5*). He writes ten hours a day, seven days a week, except for his birthday, New Year's, and Christmas.